PRAISE FOR
RETREAT, HELL!

"Another solid entry . . . Veterans of the series will enjoy finding old comrades caught up in fresh adventures, while new-guy readers can easily enter here and pick up the ongoing story."
—*Publishers Weekly*

"Griffin, who served in Korea, sticks more closely to the action and moves ahead with galvanized self-assurance."
—*Kirkus Reviews*

"The author has a knack for smoothly combining fact with fiction, giving his work a realistic veneer." —*Booklist*

W.E.B. GRIFFIN'S CLASSIC SERIES
THE CORPS
The bestselling saga of the heroes we call Marines . . .

"THE BEST CHRONICLER OF THE U.S. MILITARY EVER TO PUT PEN TO PAPER." —*The Phoenix Gazette*

"GREAT READING. A superb job of mingling fact and fiction . . . [Griffin's] characters come to life."
—*The Sunday Oklahoman*

"THIS MAN HAS REALLY DONE HIS HOMEWORK . . . I confess to impatiently awaiting the appearance of succeeding books in the series." —*The Washington Post*

"ACTION-PACKED . . . DIFFICULT TO PUT DOWN."
—*Marine Corps Gazette*

continued . . .

HONOR BOUND

The high drama and real heroes of World War II . . .

BROTHERHOOD OF WAR

*The series that launched
W.E.B. Griffin's phenomenal career . . .*

"A MAJOR WORK . . . magnificent . . . powerful . . . If books about warriors and the women who love them were given medals for authenticity, insight, and honesty, *Brotherhood of War* would be covered with them."

—William Bradford Huie, author of *The Klansman*
and *The Execution of Private Slovik*

BADGE OF HONOR
Griffin's electrifying epic series of a big-city police force . . .

"DAMN EFFECTIVE . . . He captivates you with characters the way few authors can." —Tom Clancy

"TOUGH, AUTHENTIC . . . POLICE DRAMA AT ITS BEST . . . Readers will feel as if they're part of the investigation, and the true-to-life characters will soon feel like old friends. Excellent reading." —Dale Brown

"COLORFUL . . . GRITTY . . . TENSE."
—*The Philadelphia Inquirer*

"A REAL WINNER." —*New York Daily News*

MEN AT WAR
*The legendary OSS—fighting a silent war of spies
and assassins in the shadows of World War II . . .*

"WRITTEN WITH A SPECIAL FLAIR for the military heart and mind." —*Kansas Daily Courier*

"SHREWD, SHARP, ROUSING ENTERTAINMENT."
—*Kirkus Reviews*

"CAMEOS BY SUCH HISTORICAL FIGURES as William 'Wild Bill' Donovan, Joseph P. Kennedy, Jr., David Niven, and Peter Ustinov lend color . . . suspenseful."
—*Publishers Weekly*

TITLES BY W.E.B. GRIFFIN

THE CORPS

BOOK VIII

IN DANGER'S PATH

W.E.B. GRIFFIN

JOVE BOOKS, NEW YORK

THE BERKLEY PUBLISHING GROUP
Published by the Penguin Group
Penguin Group (USA) LLC
375 Hudson Street, New York, New York 10014

USA • Canada • UK • Ireland • Australia • New Zealand • India • South Africa • China

penguin.com

A Penguin Random House Company

IN DANGER'S PATH

A Jove Book / published by arrangement with the author

For information, address: The Berkley Publishing Group,
a division of Penguin Group (USA) LLC,
375 Hudson Street, New York, New York 10014.

ISBN: 978-0-515-12698-3

PUBLISHING HISTORY
G. P. Putnam's Sons hardcover edition / January 1999
Jove mass-market edition / December 1999

PRINTED IN THE UNITED STATES OF AMERICA

28 27 26 25 24 23 22 21 20

THE CORPS is respectfully dedicated to the memory of
Second Lieutenant Drew James Barrett, III, USMC
Company K, 3rd Battalion, 26th Marines
Born Denver, Colorado, 3 January 1945
Died Quang Nam Province, Republic of Vietnam,
27 February 1969
and
Major Alfred Lee Butler, III, USMC
Headquarters 22nd Marine Amphibious Unit
Born Washington, D.C., 4 September 1950
Died Beirut, Lebanon, 8 February 1984
and to the memory of Donald L. Schomp
A Marine fighter pilot who became a legendary
U.S. Army Master Aviator
RIP 9 April 1989

"Semper Fi!"

PROLOGUE

[ONE]
Shanghai, China
November 1941

Countess Maria Catherine Ludmilla Zhivkov, formerly of St. Petersburg, was united in holy matrimony to Captain Edward J. Banning, USMC, of Charleston, South Carolina, by the Very Reverend James Fitzhugh Ferneyhough, D.D., canon of the cathedral, in a 10:45 A.M. Anglican ceremony on 12 November 1941. It was the first marriage for both.

Throughout the ceremony, the tall, black-haired, blue-eyed bride, age twenty-seven and known as Milla, wondered when and how she would take her life.

She loved Ed Banning madly; that was not the problem. She had felt something special the moment he walked into her small apartment off the Bund. And this spark had almost immediately, almost frighteningly, turned into excitement and desire.

The problem was that they really had no future; and she was fully aware of that. Ed Banning was an officer of the United States Corps of Marines, about to leave Shanghai, almost certainly never to return, and she was an escapee from what was now the Soviet Union. In Imperial Russia, she had been born into a noble family. Now she was a stateless person without a country. Her Nansen passport—issued to stateless Russians who had fled the Revolution and from whom the Communist government had withdrawn citizenship—was a passport in name only. It was not valid for travel to the United States, or, for that matter, for travel anywhere else.

The Japanese army in Shanghai was poised to take over the city. This might happen in the next week or two, or else somewhat later. In any event, it was going to happen, and when it did, she would be at their mercy.

Once American, French, British, German, and Italian troops had been stationed in Shanghai to protect their own nationals—but de facto all westerners, including the "Nansen people"—against Japanese outrages. That protection was in the process of being withdrawn.

At the start of the war in Europe, the Italians, the Germans, and the Japanese had become allies, called the "Axis Powers." Soon afterward, the Italians and Germans left Shanghai; yet even before that, it was clear they were not going to challenge Japanese authority in the city in any way. Meanwhile, following their defeat in Europe, the French had withdrawn their troops from China and had signed a "Treaty of Friendship" with the Japanese that permitted the Japanese to use military air bases and naval facilities in French Indochina. Finally, in August 1940, the British had announced their withdrawal from Shanghai and northern China.

That had left only the Americans in Shanghai.

Now they too were leaving. War between the Japanese and the Americans was inevitable. Until war actually came, the Japanese in Shanghai would probably behave no more badly than they had when the Americans were stationed in the city. They were still paying lip service to the "Bushido Code of the Warrior" and were not entirely deaf to world opinion. But when war came, that would be the end of any pretense. Meaning: every westerner, except Germans, Italians, and the rare citizens of neutral powers, would be at the mercy of the Japanese. It would be rape in every sense, not just the physical rape of women. They'd ravage bank accounts, real estate, everything.

All the property that Ed had turned over to her—the convertible red Pontiac of which he was so fond, the furniture in the apartment, and the paid-three-years-in advance lease on the apartment—would disappear.

And Japanese officers liked white women. If they were now willing to pay a premium for Russian whores, what would happen to her when rape was the norm?

If her future offered nothing but becoming a whore for some Japanese officer, Milla preferred to be dead.

The first time Milla saw Ed Banning, he had a long, green cigar clamped between what she thought of as perfect American teeth. He was in uniform, tall, thin and erect, and just starting to bald; and, she learned a little later, he was thirty-six years old.

Earlier, Banning had telephoned Milla in answer to her advertisement in the *Shanghai Post*: "Wu, Cantonese and Mandarin Conversation offered at reasonable rates by multi-lingual Western Lady." On the telephone, he told her that he was an officer of the 4th Marines. His voice was very nice. Deep, soft, and masculine. "You sound British," he went on to say.

She recognized that as a question and answered it: "Actually, I'm Russian," and added, "Stateless."

She knew that any sort of a relationship between stateless people—sometimes called "Nansen people"—and American diplomatic and military personnel was frowned upon or outright forbidden. It was better to get that out in the open now, she knew, rather than opening up the possibility of an embarrassing scene when they actually met.

To a great many Nansen women, forming a relationship with an American officer—becoming his mistress—was a far better way to earn their living than any of their other options. But Milla wished to make it clear from the beginning that she wanted nothing but a professional, student-teacher relationship. She didn't want to become the girlfriend of an American officer, much less his mistress. She wasn't quite that desperate. She knew it wasn't likely that she could turn her at-home language classes into a real school that would support her. But she had some jewels hidden in her underwear drawer, sewn into her mother's girdle when they fled St. Petersburg. A few of these still remained. When the last of them was gone, then she might have to consider something like that. But not yet, not now.

In fact, her Nansen status did not seem to bother him. Later, when they actually discussed it, he explained to her that he was the intelligence officer for the 4th Marines, and as such judged "other officers' inappropriate relationships." Any relationship he had himself, he said, smiling smugly, was of course appropriate.

Anyhow, when he asked over the phone if he could come right over, he could be there in fifteen minutes, she told him, "yes." Then she stationed herself at her window, curious enough to peek through the curtains, waiting for him to arrive.

He drove up in a bright-red Pontiac convertible, the top down. And a moment later he hired a man on the street to watch his car while he was inside—demonstrating to her that he was not entirely ignorant of Wu, the Chinese language most commonly used in Shanghai.

But that was a minor detail just then. What really hit her the moment she saw him walking across the street to her building was the certainty that he was going to change her life.

And she knew as soon as he saw her that his reaction was similar.

When she opened the door to his knock, he blurted, startled, "My God, you're beautiful!"

"You wish, as I understand it, to improve your conversational Chinese?" she replied coldly.

"Absolutely," he said. "I didn't mean to offend."

Milla ignored that.

"You already speak some Chinese," she said, and without thinking, added: "I saw you speaking to the man about your car."

"What were you doing," Banning asked, chuckling, "peeking out from behind the curtains?"

"I just happened to be looking out the window."

"Of course," he said. "Yeah, I speak some Wu and Mandarin. But I'd like to perfect it."

"Speak only? Or read and write?"

"I read a little, but I have not mastered much writing."

"We could work on that, too, if you like," she said.

Their first session proved that he was serious about perfecting his Chinese. It was also apparent that he was highly intelligent. So when he asked if they could meet twice a week, maybe more often if he could find the time, she readily agreed.

When he came back, he was a perfect gentleman. There was not the slightest hint that he thought she was a Nansen girl looking for an American benefactor.

After their fifth session, very correctly, he asked her if she would have dinner with him. She accepted uneasily. This man was exciting in ways she had never experienced with other men.

Over dinner, she learned a little bit about him. The enormous ring on his finger, for instance, signified graduation from a private military school called The Citadel. His father—who had been an Army officer, a colonel—had also graduated from The Citadel. As had his grandfather, and his great-grandfather. They had all been soldiers; he was the first Marine in the family.

Though she had also come from a military family, she didn't tell him everything there was to say about that. She did tell him that her father had been an officer, but not that he had been a lieutenant general on the General Staff of the Imperial Army, for fear he would not believe her, or else think she was boasting. Neither did she tell him that her father had been a count, and that, on the death of her parents, she had come into possession of the title.

Every other Russian in Shanghai with a Nansen passport claimed he was a Count, or a Grand Duke. So what? That life was gone forever anyway.

All through dinner, Ed Banning behaved with absolute correctness. And when they danced, he carefully avoided all but the most necessary body contact.

At her apartment door, he very properly shook her hand, thanked her for the pleasure of her company, and asked if they could have dinner again sometime soon.

When she went to the window to watch him leave, he was already gone. The depth of her disappointment surprised her.

Twenty minutes later, just as she was about to slip into bed, the telephone rang.

"Milla, this is Ed," he said. His voice sounded strange.

"Is something wrong?"

"Yeah, I'm afraid so."

"What?"

"I probably should have told you this at dinner, but I couldn't work up the courage."

Oh, God, he's going away! Or, just as bad, our perfectly innocent, wholly businesslike relationship has come to the attention of his superiors, and despite his claims to be able to discern inappropriate relationships for himself, he has been told to sever his relationship with me.

"Tell me what?"

"I'm in love with you," Ed Banning said, and the phone went dead.

That's insane, if it's true. If it isn't true, then he wants me for his mistress—the proposition he's been hiding behind his gentlemanly mask. If he really means what he said, about being in love with me . . . that's hopeless. People in love get married . . . unless the people concerned are a Russian refugee with a Nansen passport and an officer in the United States Corps of Marines. For them marriage simply is not possible.

Milla got very little sleep that night, as she ran the possibilities through her head over and over again. None of them was appealing.

What she would do, she finally decided, was speak to him the next day when he showed up for his lesson. She would tell him that under the circumstances it would be better all around if he found someone else to help him perfect his Chinese.

But when he appeared next day at her door, she was suddenly struck dumb. All she could do was smile—carefully not looking at him—and motion him into her living room. Their conversation session was perfectly routine. Afterward, all she could remember was that he was wearing an aftershave lotion that smelled like limes. When the time was up, he stood up and offered her his hand. Touching it made her feel very strange in her middle.

"Thank you," he said.

"Don't be silly," she said.

"And thank you for not being offended by my call last night."

"Were you drinking?" Milla asked.

"Not then, except for the wine we had at dinner. Afterward. Yeah."

He let go of her hand and walked to the door.

Milla suddenly knew what she wanted to do. Had to do. No matter what the ultimate cost.

"Just a minute, please, Ed," Milla said.

"What?"

"It won't take a minute," she said, then walked into her bedroom and closed the door.

And then she stared at the closed door and glanced around the room.

It was, of course, insane.

Her eyes fell on a faded photograph of her father.

"Life is a gamble, Milla," the former Lieutenant General Count Vasily Ivanovich Zhivkov had told her many times. *"Sometimes, if you want something very much, it is necessary to put all your chips on the table, and wait to see where the wheel stops. If you understand that the ball will probably not fall into your hole, you will know, when it does not, that you at least tried. It is better to risk everything and lose than not to take the chance."*

Looking at herself in the faded mirror of her dressing table, she unbuttoned her blouse and shrugged out of it and let it fall to the floor. Then she slipped out of her skirt and underwear and leaned over to pick up her only—and nearly empty—bottle of perfume. She dabbed perfume behind her ears and between her breasts and then—embarrassed, averting her eyes from her reflection—between her legs.

Then she threw the cover off her bed, crawled in, and pulled the sheet up under her chin.

She called his name. She didn't seem to have control

of her voice. She wondered if he had heard her through the closed door.

"What?"

"Would you come in here, please?" she called.

He opened the door, and asked "What?" again when he saw her in the bed.

When she didn't reply, he said her name, "Milla?" and she saw that he was having trouble with his voice, too.

"I have been in love with you from the moment I saw you drive up in your car," she said.

And then she threw the sheet away from her body and held out her arms to him.

"Oh, Jesus H. Christ, Milla!" Ed said softly, and then got in bed with her and put his arms around her.

She had, she knew, just put her last chip on the table.

[TWO]

"I got a cable from my father today," Captain Ed Banning announced a week later.

They were in his apartment. He was on his back, his hands folded under his head. She was on her stomach, her face on his chest, her right leg on top of his. Their coupling had been intense, and he had been sweating. Even though she could smell his underarms, she didn't mind that at all, but worried—because she'd been sweating, too—that her own odor might offend him.

"Is something wrong?"

"No, as a matter of fact, things are looking up."

"I have no idea what you're talking about."

"First things first," he said. "Will you marry me, Maria Catherine Ludmilla Zhivkov? Will you promise to love, cherish, and obey me, in sickness and in health, et cetera, et cetera, so long as we both shall live?"

She felt the tears come.

"Don't do this to me, Ed," she said softly.

"What is that, a no? After I spent all that money—it's twenty-two cents a word—cabling my father about you?"

"You cabled your father about me?"

"Uh-huh."

"What did you tell him?"

"Not much. I told you, it's twenty-two cents a word, but I did tell him that if he wants to be a grandfather, he'd better go see good ol' Uncle Zach and ask him to pass a special law allowing the future mother of his grand-child into the States."

"Ed, I have no idea what you're talking about."

"You haven't answered the question," Ed said. "Let's start with that."

"What question?"

"Will you marry me, Milla? Would you rather I got out of bed and got on my knees?"

"We can't get married; you know that as well as I do."

"Well, for the sake of argument, if you could, would you?"

"Ed, for the love of God, don't start saying things you don't mean, or making promises you won't be able to keep," Milla said. "Please."

"I never do," he said, a little indignantly. "Answer the question."

"Oh, Ed, if it were possible, I would try very hard to be a good wife to you."

"I didn't detect a whole hell of a lot of enthusiasm."

"How can I be enthusiastic about something both of us know will never happen?

"You don't seem to understand, Milla," he said. "I'm trying to tell you that the Marines have landed, and the situation is well in hand."

"Damn you! Stop this. I don't think it's funny. It's cruel. It's perverse!"

"Before I cabled my father," Ed said, "I went down to the legation and asked the consul general some ques-tions." He caught her eye. "He's a nice guy and won't run off at the mouth about that."

"Questions about us?"

"About you," he said. "Your Nansen status. Specifi-cally, I asked him how I can get you into the United States."

"And he told you that that's impossible. I'm surprised

you don't know that. You can't immigrate to the United
States on a Nansen passport."

"Unless you get a special law passed by Congress, is
what he told me."

"What do you mean, a 'special law'?"

"The Congress of the United States in solemn assembly
passes a law stating that so much of the applicable laws
pertaining are waived in the case of Maria Catherine Ludmilla Zhivkov, and the Attorney General is hereby directed to forthwith issue to the said Maria Catherine
Ludmilla Zhivkov an immigration visa."

"That's possible?" she asked incredulously.

"We can't get married here. I'd need permission, and
the Colonel would never grant it. And I can't resign from
the Corps now. Resignations have been suspended for
what they call 'The Emergency.' "

"So what are you talking about?"

"What we have to do is get you to the States," he said.
"Once you're in the States, we can get married. I won't
be the first Marine officer with a foreign-born wife. And
I really want to stay in the Corps."

"You're dreaming the impossible. Didn't your consul
general tell you what we both know? I can't get into the
United States on a Nansen passport."

"That's where good old Uncle Zach comes in with his
special law," Ed said. "My father's cable said that he had
gone to see Uncle Zach, and Uncle Zach came on board."

"Your Uncle Zach has political connections?"

"He's not really my uncle. He and my father were
classmates at The Citadel. But I've known him all of my
life."

"But he has political connections?"

"The Honorable Zachary W. Westminister III has the
honor to be the Representative to the Congress of the
United States from the Third Congressional District of
the great state of South Carolina."

"And he will help?"

"The way my father sounded, it's a done deal. It won't
happen next week, but it can be done."

Oh, Holy Mary, Mother of God, is it possible? Has the

*wheel stopped spinning and the ball really dropped into
my hole?*

Milla started to weep.

He raised his head to look down at her and saw the
tears running down her cheeks.

"Hey," he asked, very tenderly, touching her cheek with
his fingers. "What's that all about?"

"Ed, I want so much to believe, but I'm so afraid."

"I told you, baby, the Marines have landed, and the
situation is well in hand."

"What does that 'Marines have landed' mean?" she
asked, confused.

"It means that between now and the time the next Pan
American Clipper leaves for the States, we have to go to
the legation and get certified true copies made of all your
documents, including your Nansen passport and what they
call a 'narrative of the circumstances' by which you
wound up here. Then we stuff everything in an airmail
envelope and send it off to Uncle Zach. Who will get a
special law passed for us."

"Really, Ed? This can be done?"

"Really, baby. It will be done."

Believe the dream. Why not? A dream is all I have.

She kissed his chest.

"But we don't have to do that right now," Ed said.
"And, anyway, I see that something else has come up
we're going to have to do something about."

"Excuse me?" Milla asked, looking up at him.

He pointed to his midsection.

"Oh," she said.

"Does that suggest anything to you?" he asked.

Milla put her hand on him, rolled over onto her back,
and guided him into her.

[THREE]

They had three months together.

Without telling Ed, Milla went to her Russian Orthodox
priest. Father Boris didn't have a church. He supported

himself exchanging one foreign currency for another. He'd even shaved his beard and wore a suit so that he would look like a respectable businessman. But before the Revolution, he had been a priest at St. Matthew's in St. Petersburg. She didn't remember him there—she had been too young—but he remembered her family, and he had buried both her father and her mother here in Shanghai with the holy rites of the church. Several times, when he looked particularly desperate when she saw him on the street, she had given him a little money, and once, a little drunk on the anniversary of her mother's death, she had gone into the hem of her mother's girdle and taken a stone from it—one of the small rubies—and given it to him "for the poor."

When they met, he called her "Countess"; and when she asked, he heard her confession. She was having carnal relations, she told him. And while she was sorry to sin, she was not ashamed, for she loved the man very much.

Since she was not willing to swear an oath to break off the sinful relationship, Father Boris could not grant her absolution. But she believed him when he told her he was sorry. "Your sin is now between yourself and God," he went on to say, "and you will have to answer to him."

That was all right with Milla. She didn't see how a merciful God could be angry with her for being in love. God had to know that she and Ed would already be married, if that had been possible. And just as soon as it was possible, she would marry him, and be a good and faithful wife to him.

In a sense, they *were* married. She didn't feel like a mistress, even though, after the first week, she slept more in Ed's apartment than her own.

In time, a letter came from the congressman, acknowledging receipt of her documents, and advising Ed that he would move on the special bill as quickly as he could, but that it was going to take time.

A very nice letter also came from Ed's mother. "You must really be a special person," she wrote, "because we had always assumed that Ed was married to the Marine Corps until we got the wire from him announcing your engagement. . . . Meanwhile," the letter continued, "we're anxiously waiting for you to come to the States. When you arrive, why don't you plan on living in our house with us, for the time being at least. There's plenty of room, and I look forward to the company." She signed the letter, "with much love to my new daughter-to-be."

With one exception, she didn't meet any of Ed's fellow Marines. She understood why. Theirs was an inappropriate relationship in the eyes of the United States Corps of Marines.

The one Marine she met, a corporal, was a very strange young man. One morning Ed asked her if she would prepare a little dinner party for this young man. The next day he was returning to the United States.

She was happy to do that. She roasted a chicken, made blini and rice, found some nice wine, and even, since it was a farewell party, a bottle of French champagne.

When Ed introduced the young man to her—his name was McCoy—the one thing Milla most noticed about him was his cold eyes. He also looked as though he didn't approve of the inappropriate relationship. And a few moments later, when Ed told him to relax and take off his uniform tunic, Milla was startled to see that McCoy was wearing a nasty-looking dagger strapped to his left arm, between his hand and his elbow.

She was also surprised that he spoke better Chinese—Wu, Mandarin, and Cantonese—than Ed did, and even knew a few words of Russian.

He didn't stay long after dinner; and when he left, Milla asked Ed if the rules were different in the U.S. Corps of Marines than in Russia. Could officers have friends who were common soldiers?

"The Killer's not a common soldier, honey," Ed said. "Not even a common Marine. And, though he doesn't know it yet, he's going to be an officer. He thinks he's being reassigned. But I've arranged for him to go to Officer Candidate School."

" 'Killer'? What's that mean?"

"He hates to be called that," Ed told her, "but the truth of the matter is that he's killed a lot of people. Around the Fourth Marines, he's something of a legend."

He went on to explain that he had met McCoy when

assigned to defend him against a court-martial double charge of murder. What had actually happened was that four Italian Marines had ambushed McCoy—Ed had had to define the word for her—and he had killed two of them with his knife. "It was self-defense," Ed said. "But I thought he was going to go to prison anyway. It was the word of the two surviving Italians against his, and they said he had attacked them."

"So what happened?"

"Do you know who Captain Bruce Fairbairn is?"

"Yes, of course."

Fairbairn was Chief of the British-run Shanghai Police Department, and one of the best-known westerners in Shanghai.

"Fairbairn came to me—he and McCoy are two peas from the same pod. They're friends, and that knife McCoy carries is the one Fairbairn designed. He gave it to McCoy and taught him how to use it—anyway, Fairbairn came to me and said that if the Marine Corps went forward with the 'ridiculous' court-martial, he had three agents of his Flying Squad prepared to testify under oath that McCoy was the innocent party, they had seen the whole thing."

"Had they?"

"I don't really think so, baby. But Fairbairn didn't think McCoy attacked anybody, and he wasn't going to see him sent to prison for twenty years—or life—so an unpleasant diplomatic incident could be swept under the rug."

"So he was set free," Milla observed. "And now they call him 'Killer.' He has a killer's eyes."

"He's a tough little cookie," Ed said. "But the Italians weren't the only people he had to kill. One time when he was on a supply convoy to Peking, the convoy was ambushed by Chinese 'bandits'—almost certainly in the employ of the Kempeitai, the Japanese Secret Police. Anyhow, McCoy and the sergeant with him, Zimmerman—but mostly McCoy—really did a job on them. After it was over, there were twenty bodies. When that word got out, he became 'Killer' McCoy for all time."

"Incredible!"

"He likes you, Milla," Ed said.

"How can you say that?"

"He talked to you. For the Killer, he talked a lot. And he just doesn't talk to people he doesn't like."

"Are most of your friends like him?"

"I really don't have many friends, Milla," he said after a moment, thoughtfully. "To me a friend is somebody you can trust when the chips are down—do you know that expression, 'when the chips are down'?"

She nodded.

"I trust the Killer. Like I trust you, my love."

[FOUR]

One day, in the middle of the morning, he came to her apartment, unexpected. Milla knew it was over as soon as she looked in Ed's eyes.

"I don't know how to break this to you easy, honey," he said, just looking at her, not even kissing her.

"Tell me."

"The Fourth has been transferred to the Philippines," he said. "I'm on the advance party. I fly out of here the day after tomorrow."

I knew it was too good to be true, too good to last.

"Good God!"

"Which means we don't have much time."

"Two days . . ."

She wrapped her arms around him and fought back the tears.

"I've got to transfer title to all my stuff to you."

"I don't want anything!"

"You're my wife."

"I am not."

"You will be at eleven o'clock tomorrow. Jim Ferney-hough—Father Ferneyhough—at the Anglican Cathedral says he'll marry us, and to hell with getting permission from my colonel or anybody else."

"But you will be in trouble with the Corps of Marines."

"Oh, to hell with that, baby."

[FIVE]

Milla came very close to taking her life the day Ed left Shanghai. When she saw him enter the huge, four-engined Sikorski Pan American Airways "China Clipper," she was absolutely convinced that she would never see him again. And without Ed, she didn't want to live. Not the way things were now in Shanghai, and certainly not in the Shanghai that was soon to be. Even though Ed was an intelligence officer and should know how things really were, she was sure she knew what really was going to happen better than he did.

Because it had a basement garage, and she wouldn't dare leave the red Pontiac on the street in front of her own apartment, Milla drove from the wharf to Ed's apartment—which by now she had begun to think of as their apartment, their home.

Maybe, she thought, *it would be best to take my life in our apartment, where we were so happy.*

The bed was still mussed from their last time together. Wondering why she was doing it, she made it over with fresh sheets.

The towel in the bathroom was still damp from his last shower, and he had forgotten to take a half-empty bottle of his aftershave lotion that smelled of limes.

She went so far as to take out the Colt automatic pistol he had left with her, after teaching her how to load and cock and aim it.

Then she decided she would wait until the 4th Marines actually left Shanghai. The advance party, to which Ed was assigned, would fly to Manila to arrange for the arrival of the regiment, which would be moved by ship.

She did not want Ed to receive news that she was dead. But if she took her life before the regiment left, especially in his apartment, it was possible someone would notify him in Manila.

It would be different after the 4th Marines were gone. No one would then care if a Nansen person shot herself in an apartment once occupied by an officer of the 4th Marines.

[SIX]

Two days before the 4th Marines had finished loading
aboard the USS *President Madison*, the ship sent to transport them to Manila, Milla had a visitor in her apartment.
It was a Marine, a sergeant. He was short, barrel-chested,
round-faced, and stubby-fingered; and her first impression
was that he was stupid and crude. Behind him was a flat-
faced Chinese woman, with a pair of children in tow—
obviously half white—and a third in her arms.

"Mrs. Banning?" he asked.

It was only the second time in her life that she had
been so addressed. The English priest at the cathedral had
been the first. "May I congratulate you, Mrs. Banning, on
your marriage, and offer my best wishes for a long and
happy marriage?" he had said, knowing full well how the
odds were stacked against that.

"I am Mrs. Banning," she said.

It was the first time in her life she had ever said that.
It sounded strange and made her want to cry.

"Sergeant Zimmerman, ma'am," he said. "Fourth Marines. This is my woman, Mae Su, and our kids."

The woman nodded at Milla but did not speak. Milla,
somewhat unkindly, thought they were a well-matched
pair. Mae Su was built like Zimmerman, short, squat, and
muscular, and looked no more intelligent.

"How may I help you, Sergeant?"

"I don't need any help, but Mae Su and the kids are
probably going to need some help. Before he left, Killer
McCoy said I should get the two of youse together. And
before he left, I asked Captain Banning about it, and he
said it was a good idea that the two of youse could probably help each other out."

"Well, if my husband said that, Sergeant, I'll be happy
to do anything I can for you," Milla said, noting what she
had said. It was the first time she had ever used the phrase
"my husband."

*This is insane. I'm insane. I'm in no position to help
anybody. What I need is somebody to help me.*

"Okay," Sergeant Zimmerman said. "The Killer said

you was smart and would know how fucked up things are going to get around here once we get on that fucking ship and sail off."

The Killer said I was smart? Obviously, what has happened here is that Corporal the Killer was boasting to his friend the sergeant that he had met Captain Banning's woman—my God, we weren't married when the Killer went to America; that's all I was to him, his Captain's Nansen person equivalent of this Chinese peasant—and that the two women *should get together.*

So why did this sergeant call me Mrs. Banning? Because Ed told him we were married? I don't think so. He just decided that Captain Banning's Nansen person woman would like to be called Mrs. Banning, it would make her feel less like a mistress, less like one more Nansen person whore.

"Exactly what did you have in mind, Sergeant?" Milla asked.

"Nothing now," he said. "But sure as hell, something will fucking well turn up."

"Would you like to come in? Can I offer you a cup of tea?"

Sergeant Zimmerman spoke to the woman, repeating her offer in what sounded like perfect Mandarin. The woman shook her head, "no."

"We don't have much time," Sergeant Zimmerman said. "We looked for you first over at the Captain's apartment, waited around for you, and then we come here."

"I see."

"What I think would be best would be for youse two to get together once I'm gone."

"Whatever you think is best," Milla had said. She smiled at Zimmerman's woman, who did not smile back.

Sergeant Zimmerman put out his hand.

"Captain Banning told me I would like you," he said, and added, "Would it be okay if I told you I think he's one hell of a fucking officer?"

"Of course."

"And if anybody can get you out of this fucking place, Mrs. Banning, the Captain can. That's the real reason I wanted youse two to meet."

Could that possibly mean that Ed thought this woman, this Chinese peasant, could help me?

Sergeant Zimmerman nodded at her, gestured for his woman to turn, and then walked away from Milla's door.

[SEVEN]

For reasons she didn't quite understand, Milla got all dressed up before driving Ed's red convertible Pontiac to the Yangtze River wharf to watch the 4th Marines sail away from Shanghai aboard the *President Madison*.

She was not, she saw, the only Marine's woman to come to the wharf to watch her man—and her future—sail away. At least twenty Chinese women were there, many of them with children, as well as four white women, two of them with children. She recognized two of them, and presumed all four were Russians. They looked as desperate and pathetic as she felt.

She also saw Sergeant Zimmerman, leaning on the rail of the ship, and his woman and their three children on the wharf.

As the lines tying the ship to the wharf were loosened and picked up, and the *President Madison* began, just perceptibly, to move away, a sudden impulse sent Milla out of the Pontiac, and she found herself walking to Sergeant Zimmerman's woman.

The woman nodded to her but didn't speak.

When Sergeant Zimmerman waved, Milla waved back. His woman—Milla remembered her name now, Mae Su—waved just once, and then just stood there, watching as the distance between the ship and the wharf grew.

"Come with me, I'll drive you home," Milla said.

Mae Su looked at her and nodded her head, just once, but didn't speak.

The current of the Yangtze River finally moved the *President Madison* far enough away from the wharf to allow her engines to be engaged. There was a sudden powerful churning at her stern, under the American flag hanging limp from a pole, and she began to move, ever faster, both farther away from the wharf and down the Yangtze.

Milla and Mae Su watched until it was no longer possible to make out individual Marines on her deck, and then Mae Su looked up at Milla, and they walked to the Pontiac and got in.

The Zimmerman apartment was far larger and better furnished than Milla expected. Did a Marine sergeant make enough money to support something like this, she wondered, or did they have a second source of income?

"You have a very nice apartment," Milla said, as Mae Su changed the diaper of her youngest child.

"Thank you," Mae Su said, and then as if she were reading Milla's mind, went on: "My man is without education and crude, but he is not stupid. We supplied all the houseboys who took care of the Marines in their barracks. And had other enterprises."

Milla nodded politely.

Mae Su thought of something else. "And, after much instruction, he became a very good poker player. There was always a little something extra in the pot after payday."

"Oh, really?" Milla asked, smiling.

"I will really miss all of this," Mae Su said. "We were here five years."

"You're going to leave?"

"Sell everything and leave," Mae Su said. "Before the Japanese really get bad. I have already made some arrangements."

Milla nodded again.

"I went with my man to your apartment because he wanted me to," Mae Su said. "He thought we could help each other. I had the feeling you did not agree."

"How could we help each other?" Milla asked.

"Much would depend on how much money you have, in gold or pounds or dollars—gold would be best—and on how much you could get for Captain Banning's possessions in these circumstances."

The circumstances were, Milla knew, that the only potential purchasers of a westerner's property were Chinese, and the Chinese were fully aware it was a buyer's market.

Ed's things would not bring anything close to what they were worth. Milla seriously doubted she could find a buyer for the Pontiac at all. Who would want to pay good money for an expensive American automobile when it would almost certainly—under one pretense or another—be confiscated by the Japanese?

"Specifically, what do you have in mind?" Milla said.

"At first, I am going to return to my village," Mae Su said. "I have a tractor, a Fordson, and a small caravan large enough for a stove and to sleep in on the road."

Milla could see that in her mind. Tractors pulling rickety four-wheel carts were a common sight outside the city, rolling along at five miles an hour on bare tires mounted on axles from ancient automobiles.

She was also suddenly aware that she was talking to Mae Su as an equal. The woman wasn't nearly as stupid as she looked.

"And then?"

"Then I think I shall do what my man said to do. Go north and then west, and try to make it through Tibet and into India. Or perhaps even further north into Mongolia, and then into India through Kazakhstan."

"Kazakhstan is in Russia," Milla said with a sense of terror.

Her father had refused to return to what had become the Union of Soviet Socialist Republics—for good reason. As a former general in the White Army, he would have been imprisoned, or more likely shot, if he did. His refusal had stripped him and his family of Russian citizenship; and the Russians, like the Americans, did not permit holders of stateless person Nansen passports to cross their border.

"Kazakhstan is Kazakhstan," Mae Su said. "It is possible to get through it to India. Gold opens all borders."

"Why India?"

"My man said for me to find an American consulate, and give them our marriage paper, and the papers he has signed saying he is the father of our children. Maybe they will be able to help us. They would probably help you. You are the wife of an American Marine officer."

Yes, I am, Milla realized, somewhat surprised.

"But I only have enough money for us," Mae Su said. "If you want to come with me, you will not only have to pay your own way, but, if necessary, to share what you have with me."

"I have some money," Milla said, thinking out loud. "All that my husband had here. And a little of my own. And the car, and the furniture in the apartments. I don't think any of that will bring very much."

I sound as if I'm willing to go with this woman, by tractor-drawn cart, to some nameless village in the interior of China, and entrusting her with all I have in the world.

But she sounds so confident, and what other choice do I have, except to stay here and hope the Japanese officer who wants me for his woman will be kind to me? Or to end it all, once and for all?

"If you would like," Mae Su said, "I could deal with the disposition of your property. I know some people. I might be able to get you more for it than you think."

"All right," Milla said. She knew a Chinese could strike a better deal than she could.

"I have two guns," Mae Su went on. "A shotgun and a pistol. My man took them from the Marine armory."

"My husband left a pistol with me."

"And do you know how to use it? If necessary, could you use it?"

Milla nodded. "Yes," she said. "I know how to use it."

"That may be necessary," Mae Su said. "Now, if you will stay here and watch the children, and give me the keys to your apartments, I will see about selling your things."

"All right," Milla said, and added: "Thank you, Mae Su."

Mae Su, for the first time, smiled at her.

Milla wondered if she would ever see Banning again.

I

[ONE]
Apartment 4C
303 DuPont Circle
Washington, D.C.
0905 8 February 1943

Fourteen months later, and half a world away, Major Ed Banning, USMC, opened his eyes, aware of the phone ringing. The next thing he noticed was that he was alone in bed.

As he swung his feet out of bed and reached for the telephone, he read his clock, remembering that Carolyn had told him she absolutely had to go to work, which meant catching the 6:05 Milk Train Special to New York. Which meant she had silently gotten out of bed at five, dressed without waking him, and gone and caught the goddamned train. The kindness was typical of her, and he was grateful for it, but he was sorry he missed her.

He was—especially when she showed him a kindness—

shamed by their relationship. Even though she had known from the beginning about Milla, the truth was that Carolyn was getting the short end of the stick. They could be as "adult" and "sophisticated" as they pretended to be about their relationship, but the cold truth was Carolyn was doing all the giving, and he was doing all the taking, and Carolyn deserved better than that.

"Damn!" he said aloud, as he picked up the telephone. He had the day off—he had worked the Sunday 1600–2400 shift in the cryptographic room, and would not be expected at work again until 0800 tomorrow morning. It would have been nice to spend that time with Carolyn.

"Liberty Four Thirty-four Thirty-three," he said into the telephone.

It was standing operating procedure in the U.S. Marine Corps' Office of Management Analysis to answer telephones—in the office and in quarters—with the number, not the name. That way a dialer of a wrong number would learn only that he had the wrong number, not the identity of the person or office he had called by mistake.

"Sorry to do this to you, Ed," his caller said, without wasting time on a greeting.

He recognized the voice. It was his boss, Colonel F. L. "Fritz" Rickabee, USMC, Deputy Director of the U.S. Marine Corps Office of Management Analysis. After Ed had been evacuated from the Philippines, just before they'd fallen to the Japanese, Banning had been assigned to the little-known unit.

Even its title was purposely obfuscatory—it had nothing to do with either management or analysis. It was a covert intelligence unit that took its orders from, and was answerable only to, Secretary of the Navy Frank Knox.

"Oh, no!" Banning said.

"One of the sailors apparently has a tummy ache," Rickabee said.

"When?"

"Right now," Colonel Rickabee said. "A car's on the way."

"Oh shit!"

" 'Oh, shit'?"

"Aye, aye, sir," Major Banning said.

There was a final grunt from Colonel Rickabee and the line went dead.

Banning marched naked to his bathroom and stepped under the shower. Five minutes later, he stepped out, having made use of time normally wasted standing under the shower by shaving there. He toweled himself quickly and then paused at the washbasin only long enough to splash aftershave cologne on his face. Then he went into his bedroom to dress.

He took a uniform from a closet, still-in-its-fresh-from-the-dry-cleaners-paper-wrapping, ripped off the paper, and laid the uniform on the bed. With a skill born of long practice, he quickly affixed his insignia and ribbons to the tunic. His ribbons indicated, among other things, that he had seen Pacific service, during which he had twice suffered wounds entitling him to the Purple Heart Medal with one oak-leaf cluster.

Next he took a fresh, stiffly starched khaki shirt from a drawer and quickly pinned a gold major's oak leaf in the prescribed position on its collar points. He slipped on the shirt, buttoned it, tied a khaki field scarf in the prescribed manner and place, and put on the rest of his uniform. The last step before buttoning his tunic was to slip a Colt Model 1911A1 .45 ACP pistol into the waistband of his trousers at the small of his back.

The entire process, from the moment the telephone rang until he reached the apartment building's curb where a light green Plymouth sedan was waiting for him, had taken just over eleven minutes.

Though the car had civilian license plates, the driver, a wiry man in his thirties just then leaning on a fender, was a Marine technical sergeant. He was in uniform, which told Banning that when the call from the crypto room came in, no one around the office had been wearing civilian clothing—and there'd been no time to summon somebody in civvies. Standing operating procedure was that the unmarked cars were to be driven by personnel in civilian clothes. The sergeant straightened up, saluted, and then opened the door for him.

"Good morning, sir," he said.

"That's a matter of opinion," Banning said, smiling, as he returned the salute.

"The Colonel indicated you might be pissed, sir," the sergeant said.

"I left that goddamn place nine hours ago," Banning said. "And now another eight hours!"

"War is hell, isn't it, sir?"

"Oh, screw you, Rutterman," Banning said.

Sergeant Rutterman drove Major Banning to the Navy Building, where Banning underwent four separate security screenings before reaching his destination. The first was the more or less *pro forma* examination of his identity card before he could enter the building. The second, which took place on the ground floor, required him to produce a special identity card to gain access to the Secure Area. When this was done, he was permitted to enter the elevator to the second sub-basement. Once he was in the second sub-basement, armed sailors carefully matched a photo on his Cryptographic Area identification card against a five-by-seven card that held an identical photograph. The successful match allowed them to admit him to the area behind locked steel doors. The final security check was administered by a Navy warrant officer and a chief petty officer at a desk before still another heavy, vaultlike door.

Although they both knew Banning by sight, and the warrant officer and Banning had often shared a drink, they subjected him to a detailed examination of the three identity cards and finally challenged him for his password. Only when that was done, and the chief petty officer started to unlock the door's two locks—the door also had a combination lock, like a safe—did the warrant officer speak informally. "I can see how delighted you are to be back."

"Is he in there?" Banning said.

"Oh, he's been in there, Major, waiting for you."

There was no identifying sign on the steel door, and few people even knew of the existence of the "Special Communications Room." Even fewer had any idea of its function.

In one of the best-kept secrets of the war, cryptographers at Pearl Harbor had broken several of the codes used by the Japanese for communications between the Imperial General Staff and the Imperial Japanese Army and Navy, as well as between Japanese diplomatic posts and Tokyo. Most, but not all, of the cryptographers involved in this breakthrough had been Navy personnel. One of the exceptions was an Army Signal Corps officer, a Korean-American named Lieutenant Hon Song Do.

Intercepted and decrypted Japanese messages were classified TOP SECRET—MAGIC. The MAGIC window into the intentions of the enemy gave the upper hierarchy of the United States government a weapon beyond price. And it wasn't a window into the Japanese intentions alone, for some of the intercepted messages reported what the Japanese Embassy in Berlin had been told by the German government. In other words, MAGIC also opened a small window on German intentions as well.

But it was a window that would be rendered useless the moment the Japanese even suspected that their most secret messages were being read and analyzed by the Americans.

The roster of personnel throughout the world who had access to MAGIC material fit with room to spare on two sheets of typewriter paper. It was headed by the name of President Roosevelt, then ranged downward through Admiral William Leahy, the President's Chief of Staff; Admiral Ernest King, Chief of Naval Operations; General George C. Marshall, the Army Chief of Staff; Admiral Chester W. Nimitz, the Navy Commander in Chief, Pacific; General Douglas MacArthur, Supreme Commander, South West Pacific Ocean Area; and Major Edward J. Banning, USMC; then farther downward to the lowest-ranking individual, a Marine Corps Second Lieutenant named George F. Hart.

Almost as soon as the system to encrypt and transmit MAGIC messages had been put in place, the senior officers with access to it—from Roosevelt on down—had realized that MAGIC also gave them a means to communicate with each other rapidly and with the highest possible level of security. The result was that nearly as many "backchannel" messages were sent over the system as there were intercepted Japanese messages.

"Okay, Major," the chief petty officer said to Banning, and swung the vaultlike door open. Banning stepped inside and the chief swung the door closed after him. Banning heard the bolts slip into place.

Inside the room were two desks placed side by side, a safe, and two straight-backed chairs. The MAGIC cryptographic machine was on one of the desks, along with a typewriter and three telephones, one of them red and without a dial.

A Navy lieutenant commander rose from one of the chairs. His uniform bore the silver aiguillettes signifying a Naval aide to the President, and he carried a .45 ACP pistol in a leather holster suspended from a web belt.

"Good morning," Banning said.

He had seen the lieutenant commander a dozen times before and didn't like him.

"It was my understanding that this facility was to be manned twenty-four hours a day," the lieutenant commander snapped.

Banning looked at him carefully. He reminded himself to control his temper.

"Ordinarily, it is," he said. "In this instance, one of your swabbies got sick to his tummy, and the Marines had to fill in for him."

"It is also my understanding that the officer in charge will be armed," the lieutenant commander said.

"I'm armed. Do you want to see it, or will you take my word as a fellow officer of the Naval establishment?"

The lieutenant commander looked for a moment as if he intended to reply to the comment, but then changed his mind.

"Well, let's have it, Commander," Banning said. "Time is fleeting."

The lieutenant commander unlocked the handcuff that attached his briefcase to his wrist. After he had placed the briefcase on the table, he unlocked the briefcase itself.

He took from it a clipboard and a large manila envelope, unmarked except for a piece of paper affixed to it in such a way that no one could open it without tearing the paper. To facilitate that, the paper was perforated in its center.

He handed Banning the envelope. Banning wrote his name on one half of the paper. Then he sealed the envelope, tore it loose, and handed it to the lieutenant commander. The lieutenant commander handed him the clipboard, and Banning signed the form it contained, acknowledging his receipt of the envelope and the time he had accepted it. Then he picked up one of the black telephones, dialed two digits, and ordered, "Open it up, Chief."

They could hear keys in the locks, followed by the faint whisper of the combination lock.

Banning ripped open the manila envelope. It contained another manila envelope, nearly as large. This one was stamped TOP SECRET in red ink four times on each side, and sealed with cellophane tape imprinted TOP SECRET.

He didn't open this envelope until the lieutenant commander had left the room and the chief had closed and locked the door after him again. He had to use a pocketknife to cut through the cellophane tape, very careful not to damage whatever the envelope held. Finally, he held several sheets of paper in his hand. They were typed on White House stationery, and bore the signature of Admiral William Leahy, Chief of Staff to the Commander in Chief.

Each page was stamped, top and bottom:

> TOP SECRET
> COPY 2 OF 2
> SPECIAL CHANNEL TRANSMISSION
> DUPLICATION FORBIDDEN

Banning read the message through, said, "I'll be damned!" and then reached for the telephone and dialed a number from memory.

"Liberty 3-2908," a familiar voice answered.

"Sir, I respectfully suggest you come over here. Right now."

There was a pause, long enough for Banning to consider whether or not Colonel Rickabee was going to accept the suggestion.

"On my way," Colonel Rickabee said finally, and hung up.

Banning laid the message on White House stationery beside the MAGIC encryption device, made the necessary adjustments to the mechanism, and began to type. From the far side of the encryption device, a sheet of teletypewriter paper began to emerge. It was covered with apparently meaningless five-character words, in one block after another. When that process was complete, Banning tore the teletypewriter paper from the device, laid it on top of the original message, threw several switches, and began to type the encoded message back into the machine.

To ensure accuracy, standing operating procedure was to decrypt a Presidential Special Channel after it had been encrypted, so that it could be compared with the original before it was transmitted. It was a time-consuming process, and Banning wasn't quite through when the sounds of keys in the locks and the twirling of the combination device announced the arrival of Colonel Rickabee.

"Almost finished, sir," Banning said.

Rickabee waited more or less patiently for Banning to finish. And then, because it was quicker to do that than for Banning to make the comparison himself, he held the teletypewriter decryption while Banning read the original message aloud.

```
T O P  S E C R E T

THE WHITE HOUSE

WASHINGTON

0900 8 FEBRUARY 1943

VIA SPECIAL CHANNEL

GENERAL DOUGLAS MACARTHUR
```

SUPREME COMMANDER SWPOA

FOLLOWING PERSONAL FROM THE PRESIDENT TO
GENERAL MACARTHUR

MY DEAR DOUGLAS:

I'M SURE THAT YOU WILL AGREE THE
FOLLOWING IS SOMETHING AT LEAST ONE OF US
SHOULD HAVE THOUGHT OF SOME TIME AGO. I
WOULD APPRECIATE YOUR GETTING THIS INTO
FLEMING PICKERING'S HANDS AS SOON AS
POSSIBLE.

ELEANOR JOINS ME IN EXTENDING THE MOST
CORDIAL GREETINGS TO YOU AND JEAN.

AS EVER,

FRANKLIN

END PERSONAL FROM THE PRESIDENT TO
GENERAL MACARTHUR

FOLLOWING PERSONAL FROM THE PRESIDENT TO
BRIG GEN PICKERING

MY DEAR FLEMING:

FIRST LET ME EXPRESS MY GREAT ADMIRATION
FOR THE MANNER IN WHICH YOUR PEOPLE
CONDUCTED THE OPERATION TO ESTABLISH
CONTACT WITH WENDELL FERTIG IN THE
PHILIPPINES AND MY PERSONAL DELIGHT THAT
JIMMY'S COMRADE-IN-ARMS CAPTAIN MCCOY
AND HIS BRAVE TEAM HAVE BEEN SAFELY
EVACUATED. PLEASE RELAY TO EVERYONE
CONCERNED MY VERY BEST WISHES AND
GRATITUDE FOR A JOB WELL DONE.

SECOND, LET ME EXPRESS MY CHAGRIN AT NOT
SEEING THE OBVIOUS SOLUTION TO OUR

PROBLEM VIS A VIS OSS OPERATIONS IN THE
PACIFIC UNTIL, LITERALLY, LAST NIGHT. I
WOULD NOT HAVE DREAMED OF COURSE OF OVER-
RIDING THE WHOLLY UNDERSTANDABLE
CONCERNS OF GENERAL MACARTHUR AND
ADMIRAL NIMITZ THAT HAVING THE OSS
OPERATE IN THEIR AREAS OF COMMAND WOULD
MEAN THE INTRUSION OF STRANGERS WHICH
MIGHT INTERFERE WITH THEIR OPERATIONS.
IN THEIR SHOES, I WOULD HAVE BEEN
SIMILARLY CONCERNED.

WHAT IS NEEDED OF COURSE IS SOMEONE WHO
ENJOYS THE COMPLETE TRUST OF BOTH ADMIRAL
NIMITZ, GENERAL MACARTHUR, AND DIRECTOR
DONOVAN. I HAD FRANKLY DESPAIRED OF
FINDING SUCH A PERSON UNTIL LAST NIGHT
WHEN I WAS STRUCK BY SOMETHING CLOSE TO A
DIVINE REVELATION WHILE HAVING DINNER
WITH OUR GOOD FRIEND SENATOR RICHARDSON
FOWLER AND REALIZED THAT HE . . . YOU
. . . HAD BEEN STANDING IN FRONT OF ALL
OF US ALL THE TIME.

I HAVE TODAY ISSUED AN EXECUTIVE ORDER
APPOINTING YOU DEPUTY DIRECTOR OF THE
OFFICE OF STRATEGIC SERVICES FOR PACIFIC
OPERATIONS. I AM SURE THAT GENERAL
MACARTHUR AND ADMIRAL NIMITZ WILL BE AS
ENTHUSIASTIC ABOUT THIS APPOINTMENT AS
WAS DIRECTOR DONOVAN. I HAVE FURTHER
INSTRUCTED ADMIRAL LEAHY TO TRANSFER ALL
PERSONNEL AND EQUIPMENT OF USMC SPECIAL
DETACHMENT SIXTEEN TO YOU, AND TO ARRANGE
FOR THE TRANSFER OF ANY OTHER PERSONNEL
YOU MAY FEEL ARE NECESSARY.

WHILE YOU WILL BE REPORTING DIRECTLY TO
DIRECTOR DONOVAN, LET ME ASSURE YOU THAT
MY DOOR WILL ALWAYS BE OPEN TO YOU AT ALL
TIMES. I LOOK FORWARD TO DISCUSSING

```
FUTURE OPERATIONS WITH YOU JUST AS SOON
AS YOU FEEL YOU CAN LEAVE BRISBANE.

WITH MY WARMEST REGARDS

FRANKLIN

END PERSONAL MESSAGE FROM THE PRESIDENT
TO BRIG GEN PICKERING

BY DIRECTION OF THE PRESIDENT

LEAHY, ADMIRAL, USN

CHIEF OF STAFF TO THE PRESIDENT

T O P   S E C R E T
```

In what was for him was an extraordinary emotional reaction, Colonel F. L. Rickabee blurted, "I will be damned!"

"Yes, sir," Banning said.

"You better take it to Radio, Ed," Rickabee said. "I'll see that this stuff is shredded and burned."

"Aye, aye, sir," Major Banning said, and reached for the phone to tell the chief to open it up.

[TWO]
Office of the Supreme Commander
Supreme Headquarters
South West Pacific Ocean Area
Brisbane, Australia
1505 8 February 1943

When the Military Police staff sergeant on duty in the corridor saw the Signal Corps officer approaching, he smiled at him and gave him permission to enter the outer office of the Supreme Commander with a wave of his hand.

By and large, the enlisted men of Supreme Headquarters, South West Pacific Ocean Area, liked Major Hon Song Do, Signal Corps, USAR. Not only was he a pleasant officer, who treated the troops like human beings, but he was known to be a thorn in the sides of a number of officers whom the troops by and large did not like.

"How goes it, Sergeant?" Major Hon Song Do greeted him, smiling.

He was carrying a battered, Army issue leather briefcase. It was held to his left wrist with a chain and a pair of handcuffs. The right lower pocket of his tunic sagged with the weight of a .1911A1 Colt automatic pistol.

"Can't complain, sir."

Major Hon was a very large man, heavyset and muscular, with 210 pounds distributed over six feet two inches. His thick Boston accent was a consequence of his before-the-war years at the Massachusetts Institute of Technology, where he had been a professor of theoretical mathematics.

Major Hon pushed open the door to the outer office of the Supreme Commander and walked across the room to a large desk. Behind the desk sat a tall, rather good-looking officer whose collar insignia identified him as a lieutenant colonel serving as aide-de-camp to a full (four-star) general.

"Good afternoon, sir," the Major said. "I have a Special Channel for General MacArthur."

Lieutenant Colonel Sidney Huff raised his eyes briefly from the typewritten document he was working on, then returned his attention to it. His actions were a hairsbreadth away from being insulting.

Finally, he raised his eyes to the Major. "I'll see if the Supreme Commander will see you, Major."

Now that's bullshit, Huff, and you know it. You and I both know that the arrival of a Special Channel gets El Supremo's immediate attention, ahead of anything else.

Except perhaps if he is occupying the throne in the Supreme Crapper when it gets delivered, in which case it will have to wait until he's finished taking his regal dump.

"Thank you, sir."

Major Hon was not sure why Lieutenant Colonel Huff disliked him.

One possibility was that Huff disliked Orientals, and it didn't matter whether an Oriental was the Emperor of Japan or—as he was—a Korean-American born to second-generation American-citizen parents in Hawaii, and a duly commissioned officer and gentleman by Act of Congress.

A second possibility was that it was dislike by association. Major Hon—as were the others associated with MAGIC—was assigned to the Office of Management Analysis, and were not members of MacArthur's staff. Hon's immediate superior officer was Brigadier General Fleming Pickering, USMCR, Director of the Office of Management Analysis, who didn't think much of Colonel Huff, and did not try very hard to conceal his opinion.

A third possibility—and Major Hon was growing more and more convinced this was the real reason—was that he played bridge at least once a week with the Supreme Commander and Mrs. MacArthur, and they both called him by his nickname, "Pluto." This really offended Huff's sense of propriety. A reserve officer—maybe even worse, an academic—who had not been in the Philippines with El Supremo getting close to MacArthur violated all that Huff held dear.

Colonel Huff knocked at the Supreme Commander's closed door, opened it, stepped inside, and closed the door.

A moment later, a sonorous but pleasant voice called cheerfully through the door, "Come on in, Pluto!"

Pluto Hon pushed open the door and stepped inside.

"Good afternoon, sir," he said.

General Douglas MacArthur, wearing his usual washed-thin-and-soft khakis, was at a large, map-covered table. A thick document stamped TOP SECRET that was almost certainly an Operations Order also lay on the table. "Set it on the table, Pluto," MacArthur ordered, pointing at the briefcase with a thin, black, six-inch-long, freshly lit cigar. "I suppose it would be too much to hope that it's good news for a change?"

"At first glance, sir, it strikes me as lousy news," Pluto said.

That earned him a dirty look from Colonel Huff.

Pluto set the briefcase on the table, unlocked a small padlock, removed the padlock, delved inside, and came out with a sealed manila envelope, stamped TOP SECRET in red letters. He handed it to MacArthur, who nodded his thanks, tore it open, took out two sheets of typewriter paper, and read them.

"I see what you mean, Pluto," the Supreme Commander said. "I will, pardon the French, be damned."

"Yes, sir," Pluto replied. "My sentiments exactly." He glanced at Colonel Huff, whose frustrated curiosity was evident on his face.

Another reason good ol' Sid doesn't like me. I get to know a number of things he doesn't get to know. And will not get to know unless El Supremo decides he has a reason to know.

There were only two officers in Supreme Headquarters, SWPOA, authorized access to Special Channel communications: MacArthur and his G-2 (Intelligence Officer) Brigadier General Charles A. Willoughby.

Plus, of course, the people at SWPOA who handled the actual encryption and decryption of Special Channel messages (by means of codes used for no other purpose). There were only three of them: Major Hon Song Do, USAR; First Lieutenant John Marston Moore, USMCR; and Second Lieutenant George F. Hart, USMCR.

Major Hon had been recruited from MIT to apply his knowledge of theoretical mathematics to code breaking. Cryptography and mathematics were not, however, his only talents. He was also a linguist—fluent in Korean, Japanese, and several Chinese languages. And equally important, he was an analyst of intercepted Japanese messages. He had been sent from Hawaii to Australia not only to encrypt and decrypt MAGIC messages to and from MacArthur, but also to lend his knowledge of the Japanese to the analysis of intercepted Japanese messages.

Lieutenant John Marston Moore was primarily an analyst. Because he had lived for years in Japan with his missionary parents, studied at Tokyo University, and was completely fluent in Japanese, he was deeply familiar with Japanese culture, which meant he also knew something about the Japanese mind. On the other hand, though he had learned the mechanics of cryptography, he did not, like Pluto Hon, understand the theories and mathematics behind it.

The third of Pickering's men with authorized access to MAGIC, and thus the Special Channel, was Lieutenant George F. Hart. Hart spoke only English, and had a mechanical knowledge—only—of the MAGIC cryptographic device. Officially General Pickering's aide-de-camp, he was really a former St. Louis police detective who had been recruited from Marine Boot Camp at Parris Island, South Carolina, to serve as Pickering's bodyguard. As Hart thought of it, he had been taught to "operate the machine" because there was just too much work for Pluto and Moore.

Pickering himself, who was Secretary of the Navy Frank Knox's Personal Representative to both SWPOA (MacArthur) and CINCPAC (Nimitz), also had MAGIC clearance.

"Do you suppose, Pluto," MacArthur asked thoughtfully, waving the Special Channel, "that General Pickering had any inkling of this?"

"I don't think so, General," Pluto replied. "I don't think the possibility ever entered his mind."

MacArthur grunted. "No," he said, almost to himself. "Neither do I. One generally knows precisely what Pickering is thinking."

"Yes, sir," Pluto said, chuckling.

Lieutenant Colonel Huff's curiosity was nearly out of control.

MacArthur either saw this and took pity on him, or perhaps simply decided that this was a MAGIC Special Channel message that his aide-de-camp should be familiar with. He handed it to him.

"Take a look at this, Huff," he said.

Huff took the two sheets of teletypewriter paper containing President Roosevelt's Special Channel Personal to General Douglas MacArthur and Brigadier General Fleming Pickering.

Pluto watched Huff's face as he read the message. It was a study of surprise and displeasure.

"Where is General Pickering, Pluto?" MacArthur asked. "Still on Espíritu Santo?"

"So far as I know, sir. I've had no word from him."

"You had best get the President's message to him as soon as possible," MacArthur ordered.

"I've already had Radio do that, sir."

"You didn't think, Major," Huff snapped, "that you should have waited for the Supreme Commander's authority to do so?"

Pluto's temper flared, although it did not show on his face.

"What I thought, Colonel," he said coldly, "was that General MacArthur would expect me to immediately carry out the wishes of the President."

"Absolutely," MacArthur said with a smile.

"I was thinking, sir," Huff explained, somewhat lamely, "that the President's message was classified MAGIC. There's no one on Espíritu Santo cleared for MAGIC."

"No, Colonel," Pluto said, in the manner of a professor explaining something simple to a dense student. "The President's message was classified Top Secret, not Top Secret—MAGIC. The President—or, more likely, Admiral Leahy—chose to transmit it over the Special Channel, probably because that would guarantee the most rapid transmission."

Huff's face tightened.

Whether MacArthur saw this and decided to pour oil on obviously troubled waters, or whether he was simply in a garrulous mood, he decided to change the subject. "The miracle of modern communications," he said. "Did I ever tell you, Pluto, that I am a qualified heliograph operator?"

"No, sir," Pluto said. It took him a long moment to search his brain until he could recall that the heliograph was a Spanish-American War–era method of transmitting Morse code from hilltop to hilltop using tripod-mounted mirrors to reflect the rays of the sun.

"I was seven or eight at the time," MacArthur went on. "A Signal Corps officer on my father's staff was kind enough to take the time to teach me. By the time I was finished, I could transmit twelve words per minute, which was the speed required of enlisted men assigned to such duties."

"I've only seen pictures," Pluto said.

"I believe there's a photo in my album," MacArthur said. "I'll show it to you tonight, Pluto, before we begin our bridge game."

"Thank you, sir," Pluto said.

"About half past seven?" MacArthur asked.

"Whenever it's convenient for you, sir."

"Then seven-thirty," MacArthur said. "Thank you, Pluto."

[THREE]
Espíritu Santo Island
New Hebrides, Southern Pacific Ocean
1620 8 February 1943

At 1130 that morning, Rear Admiral Jerome J. Henton, USN, the commander of US Navy Base (Forward) Espíritu Santo, summoned Captain Howell C. Mitchell, Medical Corps, USN, who commanded the Navy hospital, to his office. Henton told him that he was about to receive six patients, U.S. civilians, four of them female, all in need of urgent medical attention.

"Sir?" Mitchell was confused.

"They were evacuated by submarine from Mindanao, and a Catalina picked them up at sea," Admiral Henton explained.

Mitchell's eyes widened—Mindanao was in the hands of the Japanese—but he said nothing.

"It's part of a hush-hush Marine Corps operation," Henton went on. "And the man running it, Brigadier General Pickering, will probably be on the beach to meet the Cat. A very interesting man. Hell of a poker player. And— forewarned is forearmed, as they say—he has friends in very high places."

"I will treat the gentleman accordingly."

Six patients in need of urgent medical attention translated to three ambulances. Captain Mitchell ordered four ambulances to the beach, plus four doctors, four nurses, and twelve corpsmen.

When he himself arrived at the beach, he found that the ambulances were already lined up in a row, backed up to the beach. He looked around to see if General Pickering had arrived, and decided he hadn't. Neither of the two staff cars on the island used to transport flag and general officers was in sight. Nor did he see any sign of a general officer's aide-de-camp, or of a vehicle adorned with the silver star on a red tag that proclaimed it was carrying a Marine brigadier. The only other vehicles around were a three-quarter ton truck, carrying the ground crew who would guide the Catalina ashore, and a jeep. Both were parked at the far end of the line of ambulances. Only one man was in the jeep. Captain Mitchell decided the man in the jeep was probably a chief petty officer sent to supervise the beaching of the Catalina.

Before he took another look at the lone man in the jeep, Mitchell worked his way to the end of the line of ambulances, chatting for a moment with each of the doctors, nurses, and corpsmen while simultaneously checking to make sure everything was as it should be.

But when he came close enough to see who was in the jeep, he realized he'd guessed wrong. The man sent to supervise the beaching of the Catalina wasn't a chief petty officer. Pinned to the collar points of his somewhat mussed khakis were the silver stars of a brigadier general.

He walked up to the jeep and saluted.

"Good afternoon, General."

The salute was returned.

Mitchell's next thought was that General Pickering had intelligent eyes; but, more than that, he also had that hard to define yet unmistakable aura of command. This man was used to giving orders. And used to having his orders carried out.

"Afternoon, Doctor," General Pickering said, and offered his hand. And then he pointed up at the sky.

Mitchell followed the hand. The Catalina was in the last stages of its amphibious descent. And together they watched as it splashed down and taxied through the water toward the beach.

Pickering got from behind the wheel of the jeep and walked to the edge of the water.

"I'll be damned!" he said, a curious tone in his voice.

"Sir?"

"I just saw one of my men," Pickering replied. "I really didn't think any of them would be on that airplane."

"Killer, General Pickering's on the beach," the tall, solid, not-at-all-bad-looking man peering out the portside bubble of the Catalina announced to the man standing beside him. The man who was standing kept his balance by hanging on to the exposed framing of the Catalina's interior.

The insignia pinned to the khaki fore-and-aft cap stuck through the epaulets of the khaki shirt of the man in the bubble identified him as a Navy lieutenant. His name was Chambers D. Lewis III, and he was aide-de-camp to Rear Admiral Daniel J. Wagam, who was on the staff of Admiral Chester W. Nimitz, Commander in Chief, Pacific.

"Goddamn you, don't call me that," the other replied, and then the even-featured, well-built, fair-skinned young man leaned far enough into the now-water-splattered bubble to confirm Lewis's sighting. He did not look old enough to be entitled to the silver railroad tracks and Marine globe on his fore-and-aft cap that identified him as a captain, USMC. His name was Kenneth R. McCoy, and he had recently passed his twenty-second birthday.

McCoy and the other two Marines in the Catalina, Gunnery Sergeant Zimmerman and Staff Sergeant Koffler, were assigned to the USMC Office of Management Analysis. All four men had just been exfiltrated by submarine from the Japanese occupied Philippine island of Mindanao.

When Mindanao had fallen to the Japanese early in 1942, Lieutenant Colonel Wendell W. Fertig, a reserve officer of the Corps of Engineers, had refused to surrender. Instead, he'd gone into the hills, proclaimed himself to be a brigadier general in command of U.S. forces in the Philippines, and commenced guerrilla activities against the Japanese. When he'd finally managed to establish radio communication with the United States and asked for supplies, there was some question about his bona fides. For one thing, General Douglas MacArthur had firmly stated that guerrilla operations in the Philippines were impossible. For another, Army records showed only a Lieutenant Colonel Fertig, not a brigadier general.

In order to better explain these irregularities, President Roosevelt ordered the mounting of a covert operation. This would infiltrate into Mindanao to determine whether Fertig was actually commanding a bona fide guerrilla organization that could do harm to the Japanese, or a pathetic and deluded poseur who, after somehow eluding the Japanese, now had convinced himself that he was a general. Responsibility for the covert operation had been given to Brigadier General Pickering, who had sent McCoy, Zimmerman, and Koffler into the Philippines. They had infiltrated onto Mindanao on a submarine.

Lieutenant Lewis had been assigned to accompany them on the submarine—carrying with him his admiral's authority—and at the very last minute had decided to stay on Mindanao with McCoy and the others.

"Jesus!" Captain McCoy said, then turned from the bubble to a stocky, barrel-chested, ruddy-faced man who had planted himself precisely on the centerline of the fuselage floor. "That's the general, all right, Ernie. I wonder where the hell we're going now."

Ernest W. Zimmerman, who was twenty-six but looked older, grunted.

The man—the boy—beside Gunny Zimmerman looked very much as if he should be in high school and was, in fact, just a few weeks past his nineteenth birthday. But he was also, in fact, Staff Sergeant Stephen M. Koffler, USMC.

"McCoy," he asked, in a still-boyish voice. "You think maybe the General's got a letter for me?" Mrs. Daphne Koffler, Sergeant Koffler's Australian wife, was in the terminal days of her first pregnancy.

"We're back in the world, asshole," Gunny Zimmerman said. "You better get back in the habit of calling the Killer 'Captain' and 'Sir.' "

"I don't know, Koffler," Captain McCoy said. "I wouldn't get my hopes up."

There was a jolt as one of the lowered wheels encountered the sand of the beach, followed a moment later by a second jolt. The roar of the engines increased as the pilot taxied the Catalina onto the shore.

The port in the fuselage opened and Captain Howell C. Mitchell, MC, USN, stepped through it. He glanced at the four men who were standing, then turned his attention to the patients on litters.

"Doctor, would you rather we got out of the way, or got off?" McCoy asked.

"I think it would be better if you got off," Mitchell said.

"Aye, aye, sir," McCoy said, and, jerked his thumb toward the port in the fuselage, ordering the others to leave the plane.

Doctor Mitchell made the same judgment about the young Marine captain he had made about Brigadier General Pickering. This man was used to giving orders. And having them obeyed.

Koffler went through the port first, followed by Zimmerman, Lewis, and finally McCoy.

When McCoy stepped down from the plane, General Pickering had his arm around Lieutenant Lewis's shoulder and was pumping his hand.

Captain McCoy saluted.

The salute was returned with a casual wave in the direction of General Pickering's forehead, which quickly changed into an arm reaching for McCoy. The General hugged the young captain enthusiastically. To judge by the looks on their faces, few of the medical personnel had ever seen such behavior before on the part of a general. "Goddamn, I'm glad to see you guys," Pickering said, "and I've got something for you, Ken."

Pickering walked quickly to his jeep, opened a battered leather briefcase, and withdrew from it a heavy envelope, large enough to hold several business-size envelopes inside. He walked back to McCoy and handed it to him.

McCoy looked at it.

The return address was "Office of Management Analysis, HQ USMC, Washington, D.C."

It was addressed to General Pickering, at Supreme Headquarters, South West Pacific Ocean Area. And it had two messages stamped in red ink: BY HAND OFFICER COURIER ONLY; and ADDRESSEE ONLY.

McCoy looked at General Pickering. Smiling, Pickering gestured for him to open the envelope. It was not sealed. It contained two smaller envelopes. These bore a printed return address on the back:

> MISS ERNESTINE SAGE
> ROCKY FIELDS FARM
> BERNARDSVILLE, N.J.

Without really realizing what he was doing, Captain McCoy raised one of the envelopes to his nose and sniffed.

Oh, God, I can smell her!

Captain McCoy closed his eyes, which had suddenly watered. When he opened them, he saw Staff Sergeant Koffler looking at him as if someone had stolen his little rubber ducky.

If there had been a letter from Daphne for him, McCoy thought, *the general would already have given it to him.*

With a massive effort, Captain McCoy managed to push down the lump in his throat. "Thank you, sir," he said. "I'll read these later. General, what's the word on Mrs. Koffler?"

"She's fine, Koffler," General Pickering said, looking at him. "I told Pluto to bring her to meet the plane tomorrow. And he has had standing orders to let me know immediately if the baby decides to arrive."

Koffler nodded but didn't seem to be able to speak.

It got worse.

A Corpsman chief came up and tugged on McCoy's sleeve.

McCoy gave him a look that would have withered a lesser man.

"Captain, one of the ladies wants to talk to you," the Corpsman chief said.

"Very well," McCoy said, sounding crisply nautical, and followed the chief to a stretcher being carried by two Corpsmen.

It held a skeletal, silver-haired woman. Her eyes were

sunken and her skin translucent, so that her veins showed blue. A bony hand rose from beneath the Navy blanket and reached out toward McCoy. It took him a moment to realize she wanted him to lean over so her bony hand could touch him. "God bless, thank you, God bless," the woman said faintly. "Thank you. God bless you."

McCoy gently touched the hand on his face, and then it was beyond his ability to maintain the dignity expected of a Marine officer.

His eyes closed, and tears ran down his cheeks. His chest heaved and hurt as he tried and failed to control his sobs.

Next he became aware of an arm around his shoulder. He opened his eyes.

"I just happen to have a couple of bottles of Famous Grouse in my hut," General Pickering said. "I don't suppose you'd really be interested, would you?"

"Shit!" McCoy said.

He looked around. The ambulances were moving off the beach.

He remembered what he had just said.

"Sorry, sir."

"Let's go have a drink. Several drinks," General Pickering said, and gently pushed McCoy in the direction of his jeep.

[FOUR]
Flag Officers' Quarters #4
U.S. Navy Base (Forward) Espíritu Santo
New Hebrides, Southern Pacific Ocean
2245 8 February 1943

Brigadier General Fleming Pickering, USMCR, knocked at the door of one of the three small bedrooms in the Quonset hut he had been assigned.

"Yeah, come in," Captain Kenneth R. McCoy called, and Pickering pushed the door open.

McCoy was lying on the steel cot in his underwear, propped up against the wall with a pillow. He had a thin black cigar in his mouth, and there was a bottle of Famous Grouse scotch whisky on the small bedside table beside him.

He was reading Ernie Sage's letters.

The instant McCoy saw Pickering, he started to jump to his feet.

"Stay where you are, Ken," Pickering said quickly.

McCoy nevertheless rose to his feet.

"Do you have another glass?" Pickering asked.

"Yes, sir," McCoy said, stuffed Ernie Sage's letters under his pillow, then walked to a chest of drawers and picked up a glass.

"I was in before," Pickering said. "You were out." It was a question.

"I was checking on Koffler and the gunny," McCoy said, handing the glass to Pickering.

"And?" Pickering asked, as he walked to the bedside table and poured an inch and a half of Famous Grouse into the glass.

"The gunny's playing poker with some chiefs," McCoy said, and smiled. "Who were in the process of learning that all Marines aren't as dumb as they think we are."

"Zimmerman's a good poker player?" Pickering asked.

"There was a lot of poker playing in Shanghai in the old days," McCoy said. "The second time Zimmerman lost his pay, Mae Su—his wife, I guess you should call her—taught him how to play. The Chinese are great poker players."

"Yes, I know," Pickering said. "It was an expensive lesson for me to learn when I was a young man."

They smiled at each other.

"Ah, the good old days!" Pickering said, then asked: "What did Ernie have to say?"

"She was a little pissed with me. Just before we went into Mindanao, I wrote her that if anything happened, she could do a lot worse than marrying Pick." He met Pickering's eyes as he said this.

Captain McCoy and First Lieutenant Malcolm S. "Pick" Pickering, USMCR, General Pickering's only son, had met and become friends at Officer Candidate School.

"She's in love with you, Ken, not Pick. She told me. And you know that."

"Yeah," McCoy said. "She said that, too."

"That's all she said? There were two letters."

"She said there's going to be female Marines, and she's thinking of joining up." The look on his face made his opinion of females in the Marine Corps very evident.

"I gather you don't approve?" Pickering asked dryly.

"Jesus! *Women* Marines?"

Pickering chuckled, then changed the subject. "I need to know what you really think of General Fertig," he said. "Just between us."

"Interesting guy," McCoy said, admiringly. "Knows what he's doing. Knows the Filipinos."

"Is he going to be able to do some damage to the Japanese?"

"If we get him the supplies he needs, he'll cause them a lot of grief."

"In other words, you would say that he is in full possession of his mental faculties? Not suffering from the stress of what happened to him in the Philippines? Or delusions of grandeur?"

"He's a lot saner than a lot of people I know," McCoy said. "Putting on that general's star was really smart. Nobody, Filipino or American, would have put themselves under the command of a reserve lieutenant colonel."

"That's how you really feel?"

McCoy nodded.

"Then that's what I want you to tell El Supremo," Pickering said, matter-of-factly, "and the President."

"Sir?" McCoy asked.

"That's what I want you to tell General MacArthur and President Roosevelt."

"Sir . . ."

When we're alone, sometimes, Pickering thought, *he deals with me like a man who's a friend. But the moment he's not sure of himself, hears something he doesn't like, he crawls behind that shield of military courtesy, that protective womb of superior and subordinate, and starts calling me "Sir."*

"You remember Weston?" Pickering asked. "The guerrilla officer you sent out? The guy with the beard?"

"I only saw him for a few minutes on the beach."

"Well, in case you don't know, he was a Marine pilot who got caught in the Philippines, escaped from Luzon, and went to Mindanao. He was Fertig's intelligence officer."

"Fertig was sore as hell when he heard I'd ordered him out."

"I can understand why. But it was the right thing to do," Pickering said. "Anyway, I ran him past MacArthur and Willoughby. Still wearing his beard, by the way. I thought he made a good impression, and said some good things about Fertig and his operation, but I'm a little worried that by now El Supremo and Willoughby have managed to convince themselves that, fine young officer or not, all he is is a junior officer whose judgments can't really be trusted."

"Sir, I'm a junior officer."

"Who is going to brief the Secretary of the Navy and the President of the United States. I think it's important that El Supremo know what you're going to tell them. It may change his thinking about the impossibility of guerrilla activity in the Philippines, and about General Fertig."

"Sir, I don't suppose there's any way . . ."

"You can get out of it? No. Ken. It's important. You have to do it."

"Aye, aye, sir," McCoy said.

"There's something else, Ken," Pickering said, and reached into the pocket of his khaki shirt. "This is why Admiral Henton sent his aide to take me away from our welcome-home dinner."

He handed McCoy several sheets of paper stamped TOP SECRET.

McCoy carefully read the Personal From The Commander in Chief.

"Jesus H. Christ!" McCoy said.

"Welcome to the OSS, Captain McCoy," Pickering said. He saw on McCoy's face that McCoy didn't like that at all. "I'm sorry, Ken," Pickering said sincerely. "I don't know what I'm supposed to do now, but whatever it is, I'm going to need you to help me do it."

McCoy met his eyes for a long moment.

"Am I allowed to ask questions?"

"I'll answer any question I can."

"What happens to that Gobi Desert operation? Are you still going to be responsible for that?"

Before being ordered into the Philippines, McCoy had been in the first stages of planning an operation in which he would somehow—probably by parachute—be infiltrated into the Gobi Desert to see if he could establish contact with some Americans thought to be there.

Christ, I'd almost forgotten about that. But he didn't. I pulled him off of that to send him into the Philippines. And all the time he was there, he was wondering, "What next? The Gobi Desert?"

"I don't know, Ken," Pickering said. "I don't want you to get your hopes up about not having to be in on that, but that's a Management Analysis operation. We don't work for Management Analysis anymore. And I really don't think you can consider the Gobi Desert as being in the Pacific."

McCoy, still meeting his eyes, thought that over for a moment without expression.

"Aye, aye, sir," he said finally.

That means, of course, that he thinks I'm wrong.

II

[ONE]
Office of the Deputy Director
The Office of Strategic Services
National Institutes of Health Building
Washington, D.C.
1745, 8 February 1943

"And how did you find the Pentagon?" The DDA (Deputy Director for Administration) of the OSS inquired of the DDO (Deputy Director for Operations) when the DDO walked into his office, dropped a heavy briefcase on the floor, and slumped into a green leather armchair.

"It's not hard to find, Charley. You just drive across the Potomac and there it is. Great big sonofabitch!"

"I really can do without the humor," the DDA said, "if that was supposed to be humor."

"You're in a bad mood. Heard from Wild Bill, have we?"

Colonel William J. Donovan, known, though not to his

face, as "Wild Bill," was Director of the Office of Strategic Services.

"Not a word, as a matter of fact," the DDA said, visibly not amused. "What did the Joint Chiefs give you?"

The DDO reached over and picked up the briefcase, then let it fall heavily to the carpet. "I've got a briefcase full of crap from the Joint Chiefs," he said. Then he reached into one of the pockets in his vest and came out with the key to the briefcase, which he tossed to the DDA.

By accident or intention, the toss required the DDA to lunge for the key. When he caught it, he gave the DDO a look he hoped would adequately display his displeasure.

The ten Deputy Directors of the Office of Strategic Services, known informally as the "Disciples" (because there were supposed to be twelve), had been recruited from the upper echelons of business, science, and academia. Before the War, the DDO had been the managing director of the second-largest investment banking concern in the United States and—not unreasonably—considered himself a peer rather than a subordinate of the DDA, who had been a senior vice president of the General Motors Corporation. In short, the DDO did not much like being treated like an underling.

"There was one thing, Charley, that you might want to pass on to Wild Bill if you talk to him before I do."

"And that is?"

"What do you know about the Gobi Desert operation?" the Deputy Director for Operations asked.

"So far as I know, the OSS doesn't have a Gobi Desert operation."

"We do now," the DDO said.

"I really have no idea what you're talking about. I can tell you this, however, Director Donovan has never discussed anything like that with me. What about the Gobi Desert?"

"It's in China. Or, actually, Mongolia," the Deputy Director for Operations said.

"Really?" the DDA replied sarcastically.

"Yeah. It borders on Russia. It's about a thousand miles long, and from three hundred to six hundred miles wide. I looked it up in the *Encyclopaedia Britannica* before I came in here. Or before I went to Wild Bill's office to report to him and heard he was out of town."

"I presume that you eventually will get to the point," the DDA said, and then his curiosity got the best of him. "This Mongolian desert was presumably a subject of discussion at the meeting of the Joint Chiefs of Staff? Specifically, some sort of an operation there?"

"Oh, yes. We hardly talked about anything else. The discussion was yet another fascinating display of interservice rivalry and noncooperation."

"And you *are* going to tell me why the Gobi Desert is important to the war effort? And how this affects the OSS?"

"So far as the Army Air Corps is concerned, it is of great importance because of their plans to bomb the Japanese home islands. Once they get the B-29 operational, of course, and once they've found someplace to base them. To conduct long range bombing operations, they need weather information."

The Boeing B-29 "Superfortress" (first flown in 1942) was a high-altitude bomber powered by four 2,200–hp Wright R-3350 radial engines. It had a takeoff weight of 70 tons; a range of 4,100 miles at 340 mph; was capable of carrying 10 tons of bombs; and was armed with ten .50-caliber machine guns.

"What's that got to do with the Gobi Desert? More important, what's that got to do with us?"

"The weather data has to come from that part of the world. It has something to do with cold air masses moving down from the Arctic Circle across Russia, Mongolia, China, Korea, the Yellow Sea, the Sea of Japan, the Japanese islands, and into the Pacific."

"Why?"

"I have no idea, except that was the one thing on which the Air Corps and the Navy could reach agreement today. I would suspect that it is necessary for both short- and long-range planning."

"Why is the Navy concerned?"

"They need the information for the same reasons the Air Corps does, and they insist they need it now and can't wait for the Air Corps."

"Wait for the Air Corps to do what?"

"Army Air Corps planning has always counted on co-operation from our Russian allies. Even before we got into the war—which frankly surprised me—the Air Corps was thinking about the need for a weather station in that area, first choice Russia. As soon as we got in the war, they formed a weather station unit and asked for permission to send it to Russia. They are still waiting."

He saw that he now had the DDA's attention.

"Representations," the DDO went on, "as they say, have been made at the highest diplomatic levels, but so far problems of an unspecified nature have kept Uncle Joe Stalin from granting the necessary permission."

"God!"

"The Navy, which is always interested in weather information, was informed that just as soon as the Air Corps weather station was up and running, they would be provided with any information it produced, and they should not trouble themselves worrying about it."

The DDO pushed himself out of the green leather armchair and walked to a credenza.

"Thank you, Charley, I *will* have a cup of coffee," he said, and poured himself a cup from a stainless-steel thermos.

"Okay. Where was I?" he asked, rhetorically, as he slumped back into the armchair. "Right. The Navy, in effect, was told to butt out, the Air Corps had the situation in hand. The Navy, however, apparently did not share the Air Corps' faith in our Russian allies' willingness to fully cooperate with us in every possible way. But what to do?"

"What, indeed?" the DDA asked impatiently.

The DDO saw that he had succeeded in annoying the DDA and was pleased. "Furthermore," he went on, "the Navy has a card in the hole—if not an ace, then say a jack, or maybe even a queen—which, from their perspective, entitles them to preeminence vis-à-vis weather stations in the Gobi Desert."

"Which is?"

"It has come to the attention of Naval Intelligence . . ."

"Naval Intelligence, overt?" the DDA broke in. "Or that

Office of Management Analysis covert intelligence outfit
Frank Knox operates?"

"Secretary of the Navy Knox was represented at the
meeting by his Administrative Officer—he does for Knox
what you do for Wild Bill—Captain David W. Haughton,
USN."

As intended, this statement annoyed the DDA, who
thought of himself as Chief of Staff to Director Donovan.

"I know who Haughton is," the DDA said, somewhat
snappishly. "Knox wasn't there?"

"No," the DDO said. "Maybe he was off somewhere
with Wild Bill."

"If that were the case, I would certainly have been advised."

"Yes, I'm sure you would," the DDO said sarcastically.
"And, before today, I never heard Haughton admit he has
even heard of the USMC Office of Management Analysis,
much less that Knox has anything to do with it."

"Today he did?"

"Today he not only did, but announced that for some
time the Office of Management Analysis has been planning an operation to set up a weather station in the Gobi
Desert."

"Director Donovan is right," the DDA said, somewhat
righteously, "Management Analysis should have been
brought into the OSS at the beginning! They're a loose
cannon running around on the deck. They have no authority to do anything like that!"

"What Captain Haughton said," the DDO went on, "is
that Naval Intelligence—not further defined—has learned
that a number of members of the Marine Guard at the
Peking legation—and some other U.S. military personnel—have not all entered Japanese captivity, as previously
believed. Some of them instead headed for the hills, the
hills of Mongolia, accompanied by a number of retired
Marines and soldiers and sailors."

"Retired Marines and soldiers and sailors?" the DDA
asked, incredulous.

"A total of sixty-seven Americans, Navy, Marine
Corps, and Army, plus a not-specified number of wives

and children," the DDO finished, ignoring the interruption.

"*Retired* Marines and sailors?" the Deputy Director repeated. "And wives and children?"

"Remember the halcyon days of gunboat diplomacy? The Yangtze River patrol? The Japanese strafing of the *Panay*?"

On 12 December 1937, Japanese bombers had attacked and severely damaged the U.S. Yangtze River gunboat *Panay* near Nanking. A number of American sailors had been killed.

"Yes, as a matter of fact, I do."

"I'd really forgotten about it, at least about the Yangtze River patrol," the DDO confessed. "But Captain Haughton delivered an illuminating lecture on the subject of the American military in China."

"Can you please get to the point?"

"Bear with me, Charley," the DDO said. "I really didn't come in here to waste your valuable time."

They locked eyes for a moment, and then the DDO went on: "Anyway, Haughton said that many of these guys—the enlisted men of the Fourth Marines, the Army's Fifteenth Infantry, and the Yangtze River patrol— just stayed in China. *Retired there*. Once there, they got time and a half toward their retirement."

"What?"

"They got six weeks' credit toward retirement for every month they served in China. Which meant they could retire after about twenty years of service as if they had served thirty years. And a good many of them acquired wives after they'd been there for a while."

"*Chinese* wives?" the Deputy Director asked, his tone making it clear that he found the idea distasteful.

"Mostly Chinese, but according to Captain Haughton, a number of these chaps married White Russians. After the Bolshevik takeover in Russia, thousands of Russians fled into Shanghai, Peking, et cetera. Many of them had been aristocrats. Anyway, after fifteen, twenty years in China, these people had acquired wives and children. And their pension checks would go much further in China than in the States. So they didn't come home. Some of them, according to Haughton, opened bars and restaurants. Some went into the countryside and bought farms. Anyway, they stayed. And rather than let themselves be imprisoned—or shot—by the Japanese, they took off. Presumably, they are hoping that they can get out through Russia. And the safest route to Russia is through the Gobi Desert."

"Fascinating. But I still don't see what all this has to do with the OSS."

"If I may continue, Charley," the DDO said. "There has been some radio communication with these people. Erratic. They apparently don't have very good equipment."

"So they can't furnish the weather data?"

"They need meteorological equipment and better radios. Plus, of course, meteorologists to operate it. Which the Navy proposes to send in to them."

"How do they propose to do that?"

"Haughton was a little vague about that."

The DDA snorted.

"The Navy came to the meeting hoping to convince Admiral Leahy that since the Air Corps has been unable to get a weather station operating in the Soviet Union, and since the data generated in the Gobi Desert would be more useful anyway, and since they have these military retirees already in the Gobi Desert—"

"With whom they are not in communication," the DDA interrupted.

"—they be given the weather station mission," the DDO finished.

"And the Navy, not surprisingly, got their way, right? And we have been directed to cooperate with them?"

"Not exactly. 'Cooperate' isn't the precise word. I don't know whether Leahy didn't want to slap the Air Corps down, or appear to be too partial to the Navy, but the Solomon-like decision of the Joint Chiefs of Staff is that the OSS will determine, as a high-priority mission, whether or not the 'assets' presently in the Gobi Desert can be reinforced so that they can operate a weather station, and if so, to do so."

"Which means that we are expected to establish communication with these people—who may or may not exist?"

"Not only establish *reliable* communication with them, but, if feasible, use them in setting up a secret weather station."

"God!" the DDA said.

"Leahy threw a bone to the Air Corps. They can still send their weather team into Russia as soon as they get permission from Uncle Joe. In other words, if and when."

"The Navy is really not capable of taking on something like this," the DDA said thoughtfully. "The Gobi Desert is some distance from the nearest ocean."

"The Marine Corps is part of the Navy," the DDO said. "The Marine Corps could be given the mission. But that would annoy the Army Air Corps. If we do it . . ."

"I take your point," the DDA said. "On the subject of the Marine Corps, you are aware that General Pickering is now the OSS Deputy Director for Pacific Operations?"

"Yes, I am."

The DDO knew General Fleming Pickering, USMCR, only by reputation. And he also knew that Pickering had been named OSS Deputy Director for Pacific Operations by the President of the United States, who had not consulted OSS Director Donovan before making the appointment.

"Since when is Mongolia considered in the 'Pacific,' Charley?" the DDO asked.

"I think Director Donovan will determine that it falls in General Pickering's area of responsibility," the DDA said.

It took the DDO a moment to figure that out, but then it made sense. Or, rather, he saw what good ol' Charley had in mind: While the DDA hoped, of course, that General Pickering would quickly accomplish the task of establishing contact with a group of former enlisted men and their Chinese wives roaming somewhere in the Gobi Desert, it was possible that he would fail. That would, of course, disappoint Director Donovan. On the other hand, Director Donovan had not appointed General Pickering to run OSS Operations in the Pacific; consequently, he could not be held responsible for his failure.

The DDO knew that if Director Donovan had been consulted vis-à-vis General Pickering's appointment, he would have strongly advised against it. Director Donovan was not an admirer of General Pickering, for a number of reasons he had shared with the DDO immediately after learning of the presidential appointment. The DDO had decided that that conversation had been private and so had not shared it with good ol' Charley. But now it seemed obvious to him that Donovan had also complained to good ol' Charley.

"Presumably, there is written notification of this assignment of mission in the briefcase?" the DDA asked.

"Duly initialed by all parties concerned."

"I'll bring it to the Director's attention as soon as I see him."

"If you see him before I do, Charley, ask him to give me a ring, will you?"

"In connection with the Gobi Desert operation?"

The DDO pushed himself out of the green leather armchair.

"Actually no," he said. "Something else. Thanks for the coffee, Charley."

He was pleased with himself. He had nothing really important for Donovan, nothing that couldn't wait. But the DDA didn't know this; and, with a little bit of luck, he'd worry all afternoon about what the DDO was going to discuss with the Director.

[TWO]
Paotow-Zi, China
8 February 1943

Milla, Mae Su, and the children left Shanghai on November 30, three days after the 4th Marines sailed away aboard the *President Madison*. It took them six weeks to travel to Mae Su's home village in the tractor-drawn cart. Milla dressed as a Chinese. At night, they stopped by the side of the road. And when they passed through a village, she hid herself in the cart, sometimes for five or six hours.

Mae Su dealt with the curious who came to see what they could sell to—or steal from—the travelers. Several times, it was necessary for her to brush aside the flap of her loose, thigh-length blouse to make the curious aware of the Mauser Broomhandle machine pistol hanging there, but there was no serious trouble.

By the end of the third week on the road, Milla knew she was pregnant.

She prayed that wasn't so—not in this worst of all possible times to bear a child. Into what horrible kind of world would she be bringing it?

And worse, it would not have a father. Not now, certainly, with Ed in the Philippines, and probably—facing reality—not ever. Even on the back roads they were traveling over, they heard stories that the Japanese had attacked the American Navy base in Hawaii, and that America and Japan were at war. Ed would certainly be in that war. Facing reality, he would probably die in it.

That left the entire responsibility for rearing a child on her shoulders. Facing reality, that meant finding enough food for it to eat, a place for it to live, and medicine for it when it became ill.

Facing reality, she was not equipped to do any of those things. If she was arrested—facing reality, a real possibility—her possessions would be searched and the gemstones in her mother's girdle, her only means of buying food and shelter for herself and an infant, would be seized.

God did not answer her prayers. She was pregnant.

Suicide was no longer a possibility. Suicide was a sin, but she had been willing to endure whatever punishment God gave her for doing it to herself. But now suicide would mean killing the life in her womb, and she could think of no greater sin. She had no option but to bear the child and do whatever she could to keep both of them alive.

Finally, she told Mae Su, very much afraid that Mae Su would decide the only way to keep herself and her own children alive would be to abandon the Nansen stateless person and her unborn child.

"It will make things more difficult," Mae Su responded. "There is a midwife in my village, but she will expect to be paid not to report another birth to the authorities. We are going to have to be very careful with our money."

Mae Su then matter-of-factly laid out what they could expect once they reached Paotow-Zi, a small farming village of less than a thousand people. She had relatives there, but her parents were both dead. The head of her family, who was also the presiding elder of the village, was her uncle, her father's brother.

"He is of the old school," Mae Su said. "He has difficulty understanding the justice of a woman—particularly a woman who has borne a foreigner's children—having a larger house, and more land, and of course more money, than he does, the head of the family and the village. Ernie, my man, told him he would kill him if he tried to take our property. But now he will naturally start to wonder whether or not Ernie will ever come back.

"That means practically that he can only be trusted not to report your presence in Paotow-Zi—or, for that matter, my presence, and my half barbarian children—only as long as that poses little risk to him . . . and only as long as we make regular gifts to him.

"If the authorities discover that we are in the village, he will do nothing to protect me, my children, or you. He will tell the truth, that Ernie threatened him. Other people besides my family heard what Ernie said to him about stealing from me."

From what Mae Su had told her, Milla expected the uncle to be a village elder, old, dignified, with maybe even a wispy beard. But when they finally reached Paotow-Zi, Gang-Cho turned out to be clean-shaven, muscular, and tall, certainly not yet forty, who was the head of the family simply because he was of the generation of Mae Su's parents. One of Mae Su's brothers actually turned out to be older than he was.

When they met, Gang-Cho was courteous to them. But he looked at Milla the way a man looks at a woman he wants.

Almost immediately Mae Su began to make regular trips with one or more of her brothers to Baotou, a city of half a million people thirty miles away. They traveled in Mae Su's cart, but now it was drawn by a small horse rather than the tractor. The tractor was placed on blocks and hidden behind a wall in Mae Su's house. The horse really only had to work going in one direction, for the entire party was able to float back from Baotou to Paotow-Zi aboard a raft powered by the current of the Huang-He (Yellow) River.

The purpose of Mae Su's trips was twofold. First—publicly—to sell sausage and chickens, and once in a while ducks and pigs, in the Baotou marketplace. Secondly—very privately—to sell a few of Milla's precious stones to make a present of gold to Gang-Cho, in exchange for his silence. Mae Su hoped he believed the gold came out of the profits from her businesses; she didn't want him aware that she and Milla both had gold and gemstones.

On 9 August 1942, six months after her arrival in Paotow-Zi, Milla was delivered of a healthy boy by the village midwife. She decided to name the baby Edward Edwardovich, in the Russian custom. Though she worried she would not have enough milk to nurse the infant, she had more than enough. And Edward Edwardovich quickly proved to be a healthy child, and a happy one.

Obviously, Milla thought, *because he does not yet understand the terrible situation, in a terrible world, that his mother has brought him into.*

Before long, Mae Su turned over half the work of the sausage making business to Milla. Mae Su handled the pig farm part of it, including the slaughter of the animals, then delivered the meat and the spices to Milla so she could prepare the mixture.

The large sausage grinder and stuffer had the legend "Thos. Graves Co. Boston Mass. USA" cast into the side of its mouth. The meat had to be run through the machine twice, first to grind it, and then to stuff it into the intestines after it had been seasoned and blended.

Since there was no refrigeration in Paotow-Zi, most of the sausage was smoked to preserve it. The fire beneath the clay smokehouse had to be fed with wood gathered in the countryside and tended every four hours, around the clock, seven days a week. The smokehouse, including the wood gathering and tending the fire, also became Milla's responsibility.

Milla also cared for the chicken hutch. She gathered eggs and slaughtered the chickens, and sometimes ducks. Some went to their table; most were smoked for sale in Baotou.

The business grew, largely because Milla's work making and smoking the sausage left Mae Su more time for the Baotou market or else buying and selling livestock. One by one, Mae Su's sister, her two sisters-in-law, and a niece were also put to work in the sausage factory. They were well paid.

Gang-Cho, meanwhile, said nothing, although Milla sensed that Mae Su's success made him uncomfortable. To make his discomfort more bearable, the size of their gifts to him increased; and he expected—and received— gifts from the women Mae Su and Milla had put to work.

With Mae Su making regular and frequent trips to market, their product line expanded. It soon included fresh sausage, which commanded a higher price than the smoked, as well as smoked pork loins and hams and smoked duck. Milla prepared the fresh sausage, in a frenzy of activity, the day and night before Mae Su left on a trip.

In December 1942, Mae Su returned from Baotou with news for Milla. "One of your people is in Baotou," she said, "recently arrived from Shanghai."

"An American?"

"A Russian. A Nansen person."

"What is he doing there?"

"He gambles and he makes business," Mae Su said, "from what I hear."

The next time Mae Su went to Baotou, she—very reluctantly—carried a message from Milla for the Russian Nansen person gambling businessman.

The message was simple. Just "Ludmilla Zhivkov. St. Petersburg," written in the Cyrillic alphabet on a small piece of paper. Nothing that would really identify her, nothing that the gambling businessman could turn over to the authorities to curry favor. Even if there was a reply, she told Mae Su—meaning it—she would think long and hard before actually meeting this person. If he in fact existed.

When Mae Su and the cart and the pony came again floating on a tiny raft down the Yellow River three days later, she brought a reply.

Praise God for His mercy in Preserving you.

If you tell this woman to tell me where you are, I will come pray with you.

God bless you, my child.

✝ *Father Boris*

Three weeks later, in the first week of January 1943, when Edward Edwardovich was now five months old, Father Boris walked up the steep path from the Yellow River. He did not look much like a Russian Orthodox priest. Most of his face was hidden by a conical straw hat; and he now had a full, yellow-white beard, which hung below the top buttons of his ankle-length black cotton garment, the dress of the successful elderly. He wore sandals and carried a heavy staff. And he was accompanied by four Chinese, each almost as large as he was, each carrying a similar staff.

When he saw her with Edward Edwardovich in her arms, his face reflected both pleasure and great sadness.

The first thing Milla said to him, defiantly, was, "I am married. In the eyes of God, I am married. This is my son."

"He is a beautiful baby. God loves him."

"He is not christened."

"I will take him into the arms of Holy Mother Church."

"And will you now grant me absolution?"

"Are you sorry for your carnal life? Will you abstain in the future?"

"I am married," she said.

"How can that be?"

"I tell you, I am married."

"By whom, my child, were you married?"

"By an Englishman, an English priest. In the Anglican cathedral in Shanghai."

His face beamed.

"The Anglican apostolic succession is valid," Father Boris said. "I am happy for you, my child."

"I don't know what you're talking about."

"Their priests, Anglican priests, like those of Holy Mother Church and the Roman Church, can trace their ordination in an unbroken line back to the Holy Apostles. If an Anglican priest gave you the sacrament of marriage, it is as valid as if I did."

Milla began to weep.

Father Boris raised his hand and made the sign of the cross. "In the name of the Father, the Son, and the Holy Ghost, I grant you absolution. Go and sin no more, my child." He held out his hand, and she kissed his ring. "And we will take the child into Holy Mother Church," he said, adding, "after we have something to eat."

After Father Boris had time to think it over, while devouring an entire duck, and a huge plate of rice and peppers, the christening of the baby initially had seemed to pose problems he had not originally thought of. "I don't know where we are going to find a second male godparent," he said. "We are surrounded by heathens, of course, and we need Christians. Two Christian males, because the baby is a boy, and one Christian female. In extraordinary circumstances like these, you may serve as the child's godmother."

"And you will be his godfather, Father Boris?" Milla asked, pleased by the notion.

"That is impossible," he said, suggesting disapproval of her lack of canonical knowledge. "Lee Tsing is a Christian," he went on, indicating the larger of the four men he had with him, "but we need two males."

"My children are Christian," Mae Su announced. It was the first word she had spoken.

Mae Su had watched the initial encounter between Father Boris and Milla with mingled suspicion and curiosity.

Father Boris looked at her. "How is that? You were educated by missionaries?"

"My man is a Catholic. He took them to a Catholic priest."

Later that afternoon, Father Boris invited Gang-Cho, both as Mae Su's uncle, and as the presiding elder of the village, to the christening of Edward Edwardovich Banning. He placed him in a position of honor beside the blue porcelain vessel he had put to God's use as the baptismal font, and then very respectfully explained to Gang-Cho that the baby was now under the protection of God and Holy Mother Church. It was instantly clear to Milla that Mae Su's uncle understood this to mean, in a temporal sense, that the child was now under the protection of the four large Chinese men who accompanied Father Boris, at least two of whom—including Edward Edwardovich's new godfather, Lee Tsing—were carrying Mauser Broomhandle 9 mm machine pistols under their long black robes.

After his first visit, Father Boris visited Milla at Paotow-Zi regularly, at intervals of two or three weeks. On his second, and subsequent visits, he brought Mae Su's uncle a bottle of the very best rice wine, as a gesture of respect between Wise Elders, always thanking him profusely for using his wisdom and influence to protect Milla and Mae Su and their children. Before long, Father Boris became known in the village as the Wise Foreigner.

And he brought news of the war.

Most of that was not good, at least at first. But Father Boris thought Milla especially should have the knowledge.

The Japanese struck the American Pacific Fleet at Pearl Harbor on December 7, 1941, and sank most of America's battleships; they took the British Colony at Hong Kong on Christmas Eve; Singapore surrendered; they invaded the Philippine Islands; and after a long battle, the Americans there had surrendered. The Japanese were all over the Pacific. They were on New Guinea, off the Australian continent, and for a while it looked as if they would invade Australia itself.

Meanwhile, the Japanese behavior in Shanghai was even worse than anyone expected. They had all been wise to leave Shanghai when they did, Father Boris explained to Milla.

The news was not all bad. The Japanese were a long way from winning the war. There was even a story that American bombing airplanes had struck Tokyo itself, and in August 1942—the month Edward Edwardovich was born—American Marines had invaded an island called Guadalcanal in the Solomon Islands. The Japanese had promised to throw them back into the sea within days, but as there had been no announcement, Father Boris assumed that the Americans were still on Guadalcanal.

Milla had never heard of Guadalcanal, had no idea where it was, and it didn't matter anyway. Ed's—and Ernie Zimmerman's—4th Marines had been sent to the Philippines, and the Philippines had surrendered. The best outcome for either of them was maybe they had managed to avoid being killed in the battles and were now prisoners. Which, in itself, was a false hope, considering how much the Japanese hated Americans, and how they treated prisoners.

She had to accept the fact that Ed was probably dead. What she had to do now was survive the war, pray the Americans and the English would somehow win, and then somehow establish contact with Ed's mother and father, in Charlestown, South Carolina, USA, so that Edward Edwardovich could be taken to them and enjoy his heritage.

Once she accepted that hope and that responsibility, things somehow didn't seem so terrible. She and Edward Edwardovich were safe in Paotow-Zi. There were more than enough precious stones still sewn into the seams of her mother's girdle to last four, five years, maybe longer— as long as Mae Su's uncle's demands remained more or less "reasonable."

Meanwhile, Father Boris was now handling the sale of the stones, and she had also made frequent "investments in business deals" with him. Milla wasn't sure whether there were really business deals, or whether he had run low on the cash he used to gamble. But most of Father Boris's deals had turned a profit. In fact, half a dozen times Mae Su had returned from Baotou with the stones Milla had given her to sell.

And she stayed busy in Paotow-Zi. There was Edward Edwardovich to care for, of course, which took more and more of her time as she got older.

Milla was tired when she went to sleep. She went to bed early and rose early.

It was not really a suitable life for the Countess Maria Catherine Ludmilla Zhivkov, she often told herself, or for Mrs. Edward J. Banning, wife of an officer of the U.S. Corps of Marines, but it was infinitely better than the life she would have had if Ed had not introduced her to Corporal McCoy, and if Corporal McCoy had not told Mae Su's Ernie about her. Without them, she would now be either a Japanese officer's mistress or a whore in a Japanese Army comfort station.

Now she had hope, if not for herself, then for Edward Edwardovich. All she had to do was be patient, and pray for God's protection until the war was over.

Zi-Ko, as the former Countess Maria Catherine Ludmilla Zhivkov was known in Paotow-Zi, was supervising the making of sausage when Song, the elder of Mae Su's boys, came into the kitchen and told her the Wise Foreigner was coming.

Milla was pleased. Paotow-Zi had few visitors. While this was desirable—or rather, the absence of visits by the authorities was desirable—Milla sometimes felt very alone.

The Wise Foreigner was an especially welcome visitor.

Milla picked Edward Edwardovich up from the floor, where he was happily rubbing pork fat on his face, wiped him as clean as she could, sniffed to make sure he didn't need a fresh nappy, and carried him out of the smokehouse to greet Father Boris at the head of the path leading up from the Yellow River. (The Chinese baby-diapering technique was to allow the baby to go around naked, letting things fall where they might. Her refusal to follow it, as far as the other women in Paotow-Zi were concerned, was another proof that foreigners were indeed strange.)

Father Boris was accompanied by only Lee Tsing and one other of his usual Chinese escorts. He had referred to them, jokingly, as his altar boys.

She made a bobbing bow and kissed his ring, then

waited until she and Edward Edwardovich had received
his blessing before she spoke. "I didn't expect to see you
so soon again," she said. "You'll have to take potluck."

Usually, she had a good idea when he was coming, and
was thus able to prepare something like an elegant meal.
He was especially fond of her chicken and chicken liver
dumplings.

"We have to talk, my child," he said.

It must be important, Milla thought. *Usually there is
nothing but Holy Mother Church more important to him
than eating.*

And then the truth of that set in. Something was wrong.

Gang-Cho appeared in order to receive his expected gift
between wise elders. Lee Tsing opened his sheepskin coat
and took a bottle of rice wine from a purse hanging across
his chest. Milla saw his Mauser machine pistol under the
coat.

Mae Su's uncle repaid the gift with a live chicken. Father Boris took it and handed it to Lee Tsing.

"I must discuss, Wise Brother, some personal matters
with my daughter," Father Boris said.

Gang-Cho didn't seem to mind.

Milla led Father Boris into the kitchen. They could talk
in Russian, which the women making sausage did not understand.

Mae Su followed them into the kitchen.

"Is this personal?" she asked in Wu.

Milla looked at Father Boris.

"Of course not," he said. "And it concerns you, Mae
Su, and your children. But . . ."

Taking his meaning—that her in-laws would hear what
he had to say if they spoke Wu—the three of them left
the kitchen and stood at the edge of the cliff overlooking
the Yellow River.

"The Japanese Kempeitai are rounding up all white
people in Baotou," Father Boris began. "It is no longer
safe for me there. Sow Key and Yon Fu have already 'left
my service.' "

Milla recognized the names of the two missing "altar
boys."

"I will very much miss you, Father," Milla thought out loud.

"It will come to the attention of the Kempeitai that the Nansen person businessman whom they cannot locate employed Sow Key and Yon Fu," Father Boris said. "And they will look for them. Or they will go to the Kempeitai by themselves. Or the Kempeitai will inevitably learn there is a white woman—"

"And a Chinese woman with half-white children," Mae Su interrupted, "living in Paotow-Zi."

"Yes," Father Boris said.

"But where will we go?" Milla asked, sick to her stomach.

"India," Father Boris said.

"India?" Milla parroted.

"India will now permit holders of Nansen passports to enter," Father Boris said.

Milla remembered Mae Su talking about India before they had left Shanghai.

"Through Kazakhstan?" Mae Su asked.

"Yes," Father Boris replied, obviously surprised that Mae Su even knew the route to India.

"If you know the Kempeitai are in Baotou," Mae Su said, "it will only be a matter of time before my uncle learns. If he doesn't already know. We will have to leave as soon as possible."

"Immediately," Father Boris said. "I have arranged for two horses and a cart. They're twenty kilometers downstream."

"We will take chickens and sausage and a pig with us," Mae Su said. "And tell my brother we are going to Baotou."

"That probably would be best. But what do we do about Milla? How do we get her out of the village?"

"Tonight when it is dark, she will get in the cart. With Edwardovich and my children. We will leave at first light. It will be several hours before he learns we are all gone."

"I will get him drunk tonight," Father Boris said, practically.

"Yes," Mae Su agreed.

Father Boris looked at Milla with sympathy. "We are

in the hands of God, my child," he said. "After we have something to eat, we will pray for His protection."

Milla nodded.

"There is one other thing," Father Boris said. "I don't know if it is true or not, but from merchants who have come to Baotou from the Gobi Desert, I have heard that Americans are there. . . ."

"Americans?" Milla asked incredulously.

"If there are, and I don't really know, perhaps they are trying to reach India, too. In numbers, sometimes, there is strength. And if there are Americans, and if we can cross the desert, it would help to be with Americans when we reach the Kazakhstan border."

Milla thought they had as much chance to find Americans in the Gobi Desert as to be taken bodily into heaven to serve as handmaiden to the Mother of God.

What were Americans doing in the *Gobi Desert?*

[THREE]
Supreme Headquarters
South West Pacific Ocean Area
Brisbane, Australia
0915 10 February 1943

Second Lieutenant George Hart, USMCR, pushed open the door to the office of Lieutenant Colonel Sidney Huff and held it open until Brigadier General Fleming Pickering, USMCR, followed by Lieutenant Chambers D. Lewis III, USN, and Captain Kenneth R. McCoy, USMCR, had marched in. Everyone was far more formally dressed than they had been on Espíritu Santo. The Marines were in greens, with Sam Browne belts. The breast of Pickering's superbly tailored Marine tunic was adorned with ribbons attesting to his valor in two world wars. The breast of McCoy's equally finely tailored tunic and Hart's off-the-officer's-clothing-store-rack tunic were bare. Hart, however had the golden cords of an aide-de-camp hanging from his epaulet. Lewis was in high-collared whites, and also had the golden cords of an aide-de-camp hanging from his shoulder.

Captain McCoy's fine tailoring was something of an accident. Officer Candidate McCoy had ordered his officer's uniforms from the same place that Officer Candidate Pickering had ordered his, and at his suggestion, the Custom Department of Brooks Brothers in New York City. Officer Candidate McCoy had no idea at the time what the uniforms would cost, though he had been assured that Brooks Brothers would happily extend him credit.

Lieutenant Colonel Sidney Huff rose to his feet behind his desk.

"Good afternoon, sir," he said.

"How are you, Sid?" General Pickering replied, offering him his hand.

Huff took the hand, then nodded at the junior officers. "I'll tell the Supreme Commander you're here, General," Huff said. "I'm not sure the Supreme Commander is expecting these gentlemen. . . ."

If that was a question, Pickering ignored it. "Thank you, Sid," he replied.

Huff walked to the door to the inner office and opened it. "General Pickering is here, General," he announced.

"Send him in," MacArthur replied cheerfully.

"The Supreme Commander will see you, General," Lieutenant Colonel Huff announced formally.

"Thank you," Pickering replied with what could have been a smile of amused contempt. He had heard MacArthur's voice as clearly as Huff had. Pickering made a quick gesture telling the others to stand fast, then walked through the door and past Huff. He stopped halfway to MacArthur's desk and saluted.

There was a question about whether the salute was actually proper, under the circumstances. Navy protocol decreed that salutes were not exchanged indoors unless under arms. But Douglas MacArthur was a soldier, and Army protocol stated that juniors saluted seniors. Fleming Pickering had enormous respect for Douglas MacArthur. For that reason he decided that saluting MacArthur was the proper thing to do.

MacArthur returned the salute with a casual gesture in the general vicinity of his forehead, then came smiling from behind his desk with his hand extended.

"My dear Fleming," he said, "I was wondering when I was going to see you."

MacArthur's use of Pickering's first name was yet one more of the many reasons Colonel Sid Huff did not like General Fleming Pickering. It indicated Pickering's special position in the pecking order surrounding the Supreme Commander.

In the vast majority of instances, when MacArthur addressed one of his officers directly, it was by rank. A privileged few close to the throne were addressed by their last names. And on some rare occasions, a very, very few officers—for example, Generals Sutherland and Willoughby, and Lieutenant Colonel Sidney Huff, all of whom had escaped with MacArthur from the Philippines—would be honored to be addressed by the Supreme Commander by their Christian names.

General MacArthur rarely addressed General Pickering by anything but his first name.

"Thank you for receiving me on such short notice, sir," Pickering said.

"Nonsense, Fleming," MacArthur said with a wave of his hand. "You know my door is always open to you." Then a smile crossed his face. "I mean, after all, Fleming, once the camel's nose is inside the tent, there's not much sense in closing the flap, is there?"

Pickering was surprised to see that MacArthur was responding to his appointment as Deputy Director of the Office of Strategic Services for Pacific Operations as something like a harmless joke. He had imagined that MacArthur would be as furious and frustrated as he himself was.

"General," Pickering said, "before we get into that, I thought you might wish to talk to the officers who went onto Mindanao to meet with General Fertig. They're outside."

"And then we can discuss this new development?" MacArthur asked, smiling.

"Yes, sir. Whenever you wish to, of course."

"Perhaps you're right, Fleming. It probably would be best if we discussed the OSS privately, unofficially, between friends. Are you free for cocktails and dinner tomorrow? Unfortunately, Mrs. MacArthur and I are dining with the Prime Minister tonight. Can't get out of it."

"Yes, sir."

"Then that's the way we'll talk about it," MacArthur said. He turned to Colonel Huff. "Sid, would you ask General Pickering's officers to come in, please? And then telephone Mrs. MacArthur and tell her General Pickering will be joining us for cocktails and dinner tomorrow?"

Captain Kenneth R. McCoy, USMCR, and Lieutenant Chambers D. Lewis III, USN, marched into the Supreme Commander's office and came to attention before his desk. They did not salute. They were officers of the Naval Service.

"Stand at ease, please, gentlemen," MacArthur said.

"General, Captain McCoy and Lieutenant Lewis," Pickering said.

MacArthur offered both officers his hand, then took a closer look at Lewis.

"Haven't I previously had the pleasure, Lieutenant?"

"I'm flattered the Supreme Commander remembers," Lewis said.

"And where was that?" MacArthur asked.

"Corregidor, sir," Lewis said. "I was aboard the *Remora*."

MacArthur's suddenly increased interest in Lieutenant Lewis was visible on his face.

"Frankly, I had been searching my memory to recall the name of your admiral," he said, gesturing toward Lewis's aide-de-camp's cord. "But now I remember! Of course. It really is good to see you again, Lieutenant."

He turned to Pickering.

"The submarine service did not share the belief of the rest of the Navy, Fleming, that it was too hazardous to attempt breaking through the Japanese fleet to reach us."

"Yes, sir, I know," Pickering said.

"They came, again and again," MacArthur continued emotionally. "Until the very end. They couldn't bring us much, but at least they tried!" He returned his attention to Lewis. "You made more than one voyage to Corregidor, didn't you, Mr. Lewis?"

"Three trips, sir."

"And, more recently, if I correctly understand the situation, you left your sinecure as aide-de-camp to . . . ?"

"Admiral Wagam, General," Pickering furnished.

". . . Admiral Wagam," MacArthur went on, "to undertake the infiltration of Mindanao, a mission posing great hazards! Your courage is inspirational!"

Lewis, visibly embarrassed, did not reply for a moment, but then blurted: "Sir, that was my first rubber-boat mission. It was Captain McCoy's third!"

MacArthur looked at McCoy. "Is that so?"

"McCoy was on the Makin Island raid," Pickering replied, "with the President's son. And then he went onto Buka to replace our Coastwatcher team there."

MacArthur looked at Pickering. "Presumably, Fleming, recommendations for decorations for these two fine young officers are making their way through the bureaucracy?"

"There really hasn't been time for that yet, sir," Pickering replied.

"I was thinking that I would be honored to decorate them myself," MacArthur said thoughtfully, and then announced, "And by God, I will!" He looked at Colonel Huff. "Sid, go down the hall to G-1"—the General Staff section that dealt with personnel—"and get a couple of Silver Star medals," he ordered. "Silver Stars would be appropriate, don't you agree, Fleming?"

"Yes, sir. I think they would be. But General, there were two enlisted men on McCoy's team."

"Silver Stars for the officers, Bronze Stars for the men," MacArthur decreed. "General Pickering can prepare the citations later."

"Yes, sir," Huff said, and left the room.

III

[ONE]
Quarters of the Supreme Commander
Supreme Headquarters
South West Pacific Ocean Area
Brisbane, Australia
1815 11 February 1943

Jeanne (Mrs. Douglas) MacArthur offered Brigadier General Fleming Pickering her cheek to kiss. "I'm delighted to see you back, Fleming," she said.

"Thank you."

"And I would offer my congratulations on your new appointment, but I'm not sure that's the thing to do."

My God, Pickering thought, *she knows all about it. That message from the President was classified Top Secret, and wife to El Supremo or not, she had no right to know what it said.*

I wonder what else she knows?

Dumb question. She knows whatever El Supremo feels

like telling her, which probably means she knows more Top Secret material than most of the officers around here.

"Darling," MacArthur said, "would you please ask Manuel to bring us two stiff drinks of Fleming's excellent Famous Grouse scotch?"

Master Sergeant Manuel Donat, late of the Philippine Scouts, was MacArthur's orderly. Pickering had provided the MacArthurs with several cases of Famous Grouse whisky from the stores of a P&FE freighter that had called at Brisbane. Fleming Pickering was Chairman of the Board of Pacific & Far East Shipping.

"Then congratulations *are* in order?" she asked.

"What we're celebrating is the safe return of two of Fleming's officers from their mission to see this Fertig fellow. I had the privilege of decorating both of them."

So she knows about that, too. Why am I surprised?

"Curiosity overwhelms me," she said. "I hope Charley was wrong."

Charley was Brigadier General Charles A. Willoughby, MacArthur's intelligence officer. Though Pickering thought that Willoughby was actually bright, he had also concluded that his closeness to MacArthur was based more than anything else on his absolute loyalty to, and awe of, the Supreme Commander.

"Charley was wrong about what?" Pickering asked.

"He said the poor fellow was . . . that the stress had been too much for him."

"Jeanne, according to my people, General Fertig is perfectly sane, and, if we can get supplies to him, is going to cause the Japanese a good deal of trouble."

"Would you ask Manuel to bring us the drinks, Jeanne, please?" MacArthur said.

Obviously, El Supremo wants the subject changed, Pickering thought, but as soon as his wife had left the room, MacArthur proved him wrong.

"And that, presumably, is what your officers are going to tell the people in Washington?" MacArthur asked. "That this Fertig fellow knows what he's doing?"

"Yes, sir."

MacArthur raised his expressive eyebrows and shook his head.

Pickering thought it over for half a second and decided he was obliged to make the Supreme Commander even unhappier.

"Fertig made quite an impression on both McCoy and Lewis, General. What Lewis thinks, of course, he will report to Admiral Wagam, and more than likely to Admiral Nimitz. And just before I went back to Espíritu Santo, there was a Special Channel message from Colonel Fritz Rickabee, suggesting I prepare McCoy to brief the President just about as soon as he gets off the plane in Washington."

"Who is Rickabee? How would he know what the President wants? For that matter, why would Franklin Roosevelt want to hear what a captain thinks?"

"Rickabee is my deputy—*was* my deputy—before this OSS thing came up. I don't know this, but I suspect the President told Frank Knox that he wants to talk to Mc-Coy."

"Why would he want to do that?"

"McCoy is held in high regard by Jimmy Roosevelt; they were both on the Makin raid."

MacArthur snorted.

"And Frank Knox told his assistant, Captain Houghton, who told Colonel Rickabee," Pickering finished his thought.

MacArthur considered that for a moment. "Don't misunderstand me, Fleming," he said. "I admire this Fertig fellow. And I will move heaven and hell and whatever else has to be moved to see that he gets the supplies he needs."

Sergeant Donat, in a crisp white jacket, arrived with a tray holding glasses, ice, and a bottle of Famous Grouse.

"Good to see you again, General," he said.

"Thank you, Manuel," Pickering said.

Donat poured two stiff drinks, then looked at Mrs. MacArthur, who smiled and shook her head, "no."

"A toast, I would suggest, is in order," MacArthur said. "To your brave young officers, Fleming."

"And the enlisted men they had with them," Pickering responded. "Better yet, to all the brave men who are carrying on your fight in the Philippines."

MacArthur considered that, then sipped his drink. "So what are you going to do now, Fleming?" he asked.

"Now that my nose is under your tent flap?"

MacArthur smiled and nodded.

"I'm going to meet with Colonel Waterson first thing in the morning," Pickering said.

Colonel John J. Waterson was OSS Brisbane Station Chief, which is to say head of the Office of Strategic Services detachment assigned to Supreme Headquarters, South West Pacific Ocean Area.

"In your new role as Deputy Director for Pacific Operations of the OSS?"

"Yes, sir."

"You have not previously met the gentleman?"

Pickering shook his head, "no."

"Coast Artillery Corps. Class of '22 at West Point," MacArthur recited. "Resigned in 1934, with twelve years of service, after failure of selection for promotion to captain. Commissioned as major artillery, reserve, in 1939. Called to active service October 1940. Instructor—mathematics—at the Artillery School, Fort Bliss. Detailed to the OSS January 1942. Promotions to lieutenant colonel and colonel came shortly after he joined the OSS. In his civilian career, Colonel Waterson was a vice president of Malloy Manufacturing Company—they make hubcaps for automobiles—which is owned by his wife's family."

It was not a very impressive recitation of military credentials, and both men knew it.

MacArthur, looking very pleased with himself, smiled at Pickering.

"You know more about him than I do," Pickering confessed.

"I thought that might be the case," MacArthur said.

"What was that? 'Know your enemy'?" Pickering asked.

"Your phrase, Fleming, not mine," MacArthur said, smiling. "And I certainly don't think of *you* as the enemy."

"Thank you."

"Unfortunately, I was never able to find time to receive

Colonel Waterson," MacArthur said, obviously pleased, "and now it won't be necessary, will it?"

Pickering suddenly understood why Douglas MacArthur was pleased that the President had appointed him OSS Deputy Director for Pacific Operations.

He thinks I'm going to get Roosevelt and Donovan off his back.

And in his shoes, I would think the same thing. He knows he's right about the OSS; and he knows I think he's right, and I can plead his case in Washington better even than he can.

Just before Pickering left Washington for his current Pacific trip, the President of the United States had personally given him a subsidiary mission: to convince General Douglas MacArthur to find time in his busy schedule to receive Colonel Waterson.

OSS Director William Donovan had complained to Roosevelt that following a very brief meeting with General Charles A. Willoughby, MacArthur's G-2, shortly after his arrival in Brisbane seven weeks before, Waterson had been waiting in vain for the meeting with MacArthur Willoughby had promised to arrange "just as soon as the Supreme Commander can find time in his schedule."

When Pickering had raised the subject to MacArthur soon after his arrival in Brisbane, he was told that MacArthur had decided that the OSS was going to be more trouble than it was worth. Receiving Colonel Waterson would therefore be tantamount to letting the nose of an unwelcome camel into his tent. MacArthur had no intention of doing that.

Pickering thought MacArthur was right. The OSS probably would be more trouble than it would be worth in the kind of war MacArthur was fighting. The situation here was completely different from Europe and Africa, where the OSS had proven very valuable.

It was a relatively simple matter to infiltrate OSS Jedburgh teams into France and other German-occupied areas of the European landmass by parachute or even by small fishing boats setting out from England. Once inside enemy-held territory, agents who spoke the language and were equipped with forged identification papers could relatively easily vanish into the local society, aided by in-place resistance movements. Once in place, OSS agents in Europe could go about their business of blowing up railroad bridges and harbor facilities, of gathering intelligence, and of arranging for resistance groups to be armed and equipped with communications equipment.

None of the conditions that made the OSS valuable in Europe prevailed in the Pacific. For one thing, there was no contiguous landmass. The war in the Pacific was already becoming known as "island hopping." Hundreds—often thousands—of miles separated Allied bases from Japanese-occupied islands.

Simply infiltrating OSS teams onto a Japanese-held Pacific island would pose enormous—probably insurmountable—logistical problems.

And, with the exception of a few Americans and Filipinos who had refused to surrender when the Philippine Islands had fallen to the Japanese, there was no organized resistance in Japanese-occupied territory anywhere in the Pacific. In other words, there would be no friendly faces greeting OSS agents when they landed.

Furthermore, no matter how well he might speak Japanese, no matter how high the quality of his forged identification papers, a Caucasian agent stood virtually no chance of passing himself off as a Japanese soldier, or making himself invisible in a society whose brown-skinned citizens often wore loincloths, filed their teeth, and spoke unusual languages.

And finally, on the Pacific Islands where MacArthur intended to fight, there were very few railroad or highway bridges or industrial complexes to blow up, and really very little intelligence to gather.

Aware that his thinking was probably colored by his personal feelings toward OSS Director Colonel "Wild Bill" Donovan, Pickering thought the very idea of setting the OSS up in the South West Pacific Ocean Area probably had more to do with Donovan playing Washington politics than anything else.

Pickering had little use for Donovan, a law school classmate of President Roosevelt who had been a highly successful Wall Street lawyer before Roosevelt had appointed him to lead the OSS.

Lawyer Donovan had once been engaged by Chairman of the Board (of the Pacific & Far East Shipping Corporation) Pickering to represent P&FE in a maritime legal dispute. Pickering had liked neither the quality of the legal services rendered—the suit had been decided against them—nor the size of the bill rendered, and had called Donovan on the telephone and bluntly told him so.

William Donovan was not used to people talking to him the way Pickering did; and he was Irish. He was still angry two weeks later when he ran into Pickering in the lobby of the Century Club in New York City. There was some disagreement about who uttered the first unkind remark, but it was universally agreed that only the intervention of friends—strong friends—of both gentlemen had prevented adding to the many Century Club legends a fistfight in the main lobby between two of its most prominent members.

The enmity between the two men had continued after Donovan became Roosevelt's intelligence chief as head of the newly created Office of Strategic Services and Pickering had performed various intelligence services—separate from the OSS—for Navy Secretary Frank Knox, leading to his appointment as head of the highly secret Office of Management Analysis. The new marriage—at Roosevelt's direction—between Pickering and the OSS was likely to become a marriage made in hell from the point of view of everyone except the President.

Brigadier General Fleming Pickering looked at General Douglas A. MacArthur, shrugged, shook his head, took a healthy swallow of his Famous Grouse, and then shook his head again.

"Yes, Fleming?" MacArthur asked. "What is it you are having such a hard time saying?"

"I was wondering how a simple sailor like myself ever wound up between a rock named MacArthur and a hard place named Roosevelt," Pickering said.

"All I ask of you, Fleming, with every confidence in the world that you are incapable of doing anything else, is to tell the President the truth. I don't think the OSS can play a valuable role here—I wish that it were otherwise—and neither do you."

Pickering didn't reply.

"Elsewhere in Asia," MacArthur went on, "India, China, Indochina, Burma, the OSS may prove, under your leadership, to be very useful."

Christ, I didn't even think of those parts of the world! Are they considered within the area of responsibility of— what the hell is my title?—"OSS Deputy Director for Pacific Operations"?

"I hadn't even thought about China, or India," Pickering thought aloud. "I can't believe that Roosevelt would give me the responsibility for intelligence and covert operations in those areas."

That's not true. I did think about that when McCoy asked me if he could expect to be sent into the Gobi Desert. And I told him I didn't think so. And I told him that because the Gobi Desert doesn't sound like the Pacific to me.

And now MacArthur is telling me that I'm wrong.

"If I were in his shoes," MacArthur said, "I would."

"It borders on the absurd," Pickering said.

"Absurd? No. Imaginative? Yes. I guess you're just going to have to ask the President for clarification of your role."

"Yeah," Pickering said thoughtfully.

"When are you going to Washington, Fleming?"

"As soon as I can," Pickering thought aloud. "The day after tomorrow, if I can get things here organized by then."

"Please be good enough to personally pass to the President and Mrs. Roosevelt the best regards of Jeanne and myself," MacArthur said. "Now, with that out of the way, would you like another drink before I speak to Manuel about dinner?"

"I would very much like another drink, please, General," Pickering said, and raised the glass in his hand to his mouth and drained it.

[TWO]
Water Lily Cottage
Brisbane, Australia
0815 12 February 1943

Second Lieutenant George F. Hart, USMCR, knocked at
the door to Brigadier General Fleming Pickering's room.
"General, Colonel Waterson is here."

Using the first joint of his thumb as a gauge, Pickering
was in the act of pinning his brigadier general's stars to
the collar points of a tropical worsted shirt.

"Offer the Colonel a cup of coffee—for that matter,
breakfast—and tell him I'll be right out," Pickering called.

Pickering had specified the time he expected Colonel
Waterson to arrive at Water Lily Cottage: 0830. Waterson
was fifteen minutes early.

*What the hell, if I was meeting my new boss, I would
err on the side of being too early myself.*

*But does he know that I'm his boss? Or does he think
I summoned him over here to tell him he's finally going
to get the audience with El Supremo that Willoughby
promised him?*

He pushed the pins on the underside of the star through
the cloth of the right collar point, then compared that with
the star on the left collar point. It was close enough. He
picked up his fruit salad—an impressive display of colored ribbons, all mounted together, representing his decorations and services in two world wars—and started to
pin the device to the shirt. And then changed his mind.

While he certainly wasn't ashamed of his decorations,
wearing some of them sometimes made him uncomfortable—especially the Silver Star Admiral Nimitz had given
him for taking the con of the destroyer USS *Gregory*
when her captain had been killed and he himself painfully
wounded; he thought that was worth no more than a Purple Heart. He was proud of his Navy Cross. He had been
too young and stupid to think about what he was doing
at the time, but the bottom line, looking back, was that
he had behaved in Belleau Wood the way Marines are

supposed to behave and the Navy Cross proved it.

To judge by the curriculum vitae MacArthur had provided, Colonel Waterson was not going to have many ribbons pinned to his chest; and Pickering decided that he was not going to make him uncomfortable by using his own ribbons to rub it in that Waterson had never heard a shot fired in anger. It was going to be bad enough as it was. MacArthur had made it quite clear that he still had no intention of permitting the OSS to operate in the South West Pacific. There was only one role he saw for Waterson, and he probably wasn't going to like it. Nor would Donovan when he heard about it.

Pickering put the shirt on, tucked it in his trousers, zipped up his fly, checked in the mirror to see that the button line on his shirt was aligned with his belt buckle and the trousers fly, shifted the belt buckle until it was in alignment, and then walked out of his bedroom.

Waterson, a chubby forty-odd year old who brushed his hair straight back, was sitting on one of the upholstered rattan couches in the living room. He was in civilian clothing—which surprised Pickering—a well-tailored, single-breasted, tropical worsted suit, a white button-down collar shirt, a finely printed silk necktie, and well-polished wing-tip shoes. When he saw Pickering, he stood up.

He looks more like a business executive than an Army colonel, Pickering thought.

But, of course, that's what he really is. El Supremo told me he had been vice president of some company—Malloy Manufacturing. He's no more a bona fide colonel than I am a bona fide brigadier general.

"Good morning, Colonel," Pickering said, offering his hand. "I'm Fleming Pickering."

"Good morning, sir."

"Have you had your breakfast?"

"I had some coffee, sir."

"Well, I'm about to have my breakfast," Pickering said. "You can either have some with me, or you can have a cup of coffee and watch me eat."

"That's very kind of you, sir."

"George," Pickering ordered. "Round up Pluto and ask him to come to the dining room. I want you there, too."

Pickering gestured for Waterson to precede him into the dining room.

"I have—this sounds like a line from a B movie—no secrets from either Hart or Major Hon," Pickering said. "Not only because they have to know everything that's going on, but also because they generally know things before I do. They both have MAGIC clearances. Pluto—Major Hon—knew about this latest development before I did, because he decrypted the message when it came in. You are familiar with this latest development?"

"I received a radio message from Colonel Donovan, sir," Waterson said, "telling me that OSS Station Brisbane is now under your command."

"Have a seat, Colonel," Pickering said, as he sat down himself.

Pluto came into the room, trailed by George Hart. Pickering introduced Pluto.

"Let's go over our problems," Pickering said. "Problem One is that General MacArthur doesn't want the OSS here at all."

"But, General . . ." Waterson began.

Pickering held up his hand to shut him up.

"Problem Two is MAGIC," he went on, "which breaks down into three subproblems: the analysis part of MAGIC; MAGIC clearances; and people to assist Pluto in the encryption/decryption."

"General," Waterson said, "you're going a little fast for me."

"Let's talk about MAGIC," Pickering said. "How much do you know about that, Colonel?"

"I know it exists," Waterson said.

"That's all? I'm disappointed."

"I probably know more than I should, General," Waterson said.

Pickering made a "give it to me" gesture with both hands.

"We've broken the Japanese codes," Waterson said.

"*Some* of them," Pickering corrected him. "Enough to be of enormous value. And obviously, it's the most important secret of the war."

"Obviously," Waterson agreed.

"People with a MAGIC clearance cannot be placed in any situation where there is any chance at all they will be captured," Pickering went on. "Right now we have three people here, Pluto, Hart, and Lieutenant Johnny Moore, who have MAGIC clearance. Hart will be leaving with me. And two people are not enough to handle the traffic, particularly since the big brass have learned that the Special Channel is the best way to get a message through securely and in the shortest possible time."

"Is that why Director Donovan has had trouble gaining access to the Special Channel?"

"Donovan is on the MAGIC list, but General MacArthur decides who is to be given access to the Special Channel to SWPOA. I presume he decided the OSS didn't need it. But that's something else that's been changed. I have MAGIC access, and I have every intention of using it—when necessary—to communicate with you."

"Does that mean I'm to be given MAGIC access?"

"I don't think so. For one thing, it would cause trouble with MacArthur. In SWPOA, only he and Willoughby have MAGIC clearances. If I suddenly arranged for the Brisbane Station Chief to be placed on the list, MacArthur would think I had betrayed him. I don't want to do that."

"Sir, I don't quite know quite what . . ."

"What I want from you are the names of two of your officers—now two of our officers—who (a) can be trusted with MAGIC information; and (b) are junior to Pluto. I don't want anybody trying to tell Pluto how to do his job. Bear in mind that once they get MAGIC clearance, they will no longer be available to do anything operational."

"Let me think about that, sir," Waterson said. "About the names, I mean."

"Pluto will have the right of rejection," Pickering said. "And then, once these men—one at a time—are taught how to encrypt and decrypt MAGIC, Pluto will see that you have access to it."

Waterson thought this over a moment, then said, "That will work."

"Pluto and Moore are also analysts," Pickering continued. "It would be nice if the people you select could be helpful in that area as well."

"I think I have the guy," Waterson said. "Let me think about it."

Good. He's cautious.

"It would also be nice if he were a bridge player," Pluto said. "A *good* bridge player."

"You're a bridge player, Major? So am I."

"So is El Supremo," Pickering said. "Pluto, see if you can subtly let it drop to El Supremo that Colonel Waterson plays bridge."

"Anything to get the camel's nose further into the tent?"

"Precisely," Pickering said with a smile. He looked at Waterson again. "I want to make sure you understand the command structure," he said. "I have just decided to name Major Hon and Lieutenant Moore to my personal staff. Appointments two and three."

"Who's one?" Pluto asked.

"McCoy," Pickering said, and met Waterson's eyes. "That way, if Director Donovan tells you to simply order either of them to do something, your reply is that you can't do that, General Pickering made it quite clear that they are not subordinate to you."

Waterson nodded. "Sir? May I speak freely? Before these gentlemen?"

"Of course."

"Question. I'm aware, of course, of the . . . relationship . . . between Director Donovan and yourself."

"I thought you might be," Pickering replied.

"The question: What are the chances of a truce?"

"I've been wondering the same thing," Pickering said. "Frankly, I don't have high hopes. If the . . . relationship . . . between myself and Donovan is awkward for you, Colonel, feel free to ask Donovan to reassign you."

"Oh, I don't think I'd want to do that, General. From everything I've heard, I think I'm going to enjoy working for you."

"Four," Pickering said.

"Sir?" Pluto and Colonel Waterson asked in chorus.

"Appointment Four. I need Banning. Fritz Rickabee won't like it, but whatever I wind up doing, I'm going to need Ed Banning to help me do it."

"Yeah," Pluto agreed thoughtfully.

That was not the proper military response, Pickering thought, *but it means, Thank God, that Pluto agrees with me.*

"General, I'm getting the idea you're going home soon?" Waterson asked.

"Tomorrow," Pickering said. "I've got some good-byes to say here, and then I'm going to Washington."

Where, unless I'm mistaken, Pickering thought, *I am going to get assigned one hellishly impossible project in the deserts of Mongolia.*

IV

[ONE]
Aboard Transcontinental & Western Airlines
Flight 303
Above Philadelphia, Pennsylvania
1530 16 February 1943

Fleming Pickering was not the only one traveling to the United States just then.

"And there it is, the City of Brotherly Love," the pilot of the DC-3 announced to the two other pilots in the cockpit, gesturing out the windshield at the city below.

The two other pilots chuckled dutifully.

The pilot picked up his microphone, checked to see that the proper frequency was set, and called the Philadelphia Tower.

"Philadelphia, TWA 303, ten miles north at 3500. Request landing instructions."

"TWA 303, Philadelphia. You are cleared as number two to an Eastern DC-3 now on final to runway one-seven. The altimeter is two-niner-eight, winds are negligible."

"Three-oh-three understands number two to one-seven after the Eastern DC-3 on final. I have him in sight."

"Affirmative, 303."

"You want to sit it down, Charley?" the pilot asked of the copilot.

"Thank you very much," the copilot said.

With an exaggerated gesture, the pilot took his hands from the wheel.

"You've got it," he said.

The copilot retarded the throttles and began a shallow descent.

"TWA 303, Philadelphia," the radio went off again.

"Three-oh-three, go ahead."

"Three-oh-three, be advised you will be met by a Navy ambulance and a medical team. You are requested to off-load the Navy patient before, repeat, before, you off-load your passengers."

"Oh, shit!" Captain James B. Weston, USMCR, said, shaking his head. He was riding on the jump seat between and just behind the pilot and copilot.

The pilot looked at Jim Weston curiously, then reached for the microphone again. "Philadelphia, TWA 303. We will off-load the Navy patient first," he said. Then he turned and looked at Weston again. "Do you know what's that about?"

"I'll bet that ambulance is for me," he said.

"Something wrong with you?" the pilot asked with concern.

"Not a goddamn thing, but I am having trouble convincing the goddamn Navy about that," Weston said, adding, "It's a long story."

The pilot did not press for an explanation. He had earned his own wings as a Naval Aviator at Pensacola, and had tried to get back in the Navy after Pearl Harbor. They told him he was (a) too old and (b) there was a shortage of airline pilots because all the younger ones were going back into the service. Logic told him the Navy had been right, but he still felt a little guilty to be flying an airliner between St. Louis and Philadelphia instead of a Navy plane in the Pacific.

Especially when he saw a kid like this one, who didn't look old enough to be a captain, and wearing not only wings but ribbons representing the Silver Star, Purple Heart, and Pacific service.

For that reason, he had asked him if he would like to fly up front when he saw him get aboard. For the same reason, if the kid didn't want to talk about why the Navy had sent an ambulance to meet him, he wasn't going to embarrass him by asking.

"You ever fly one of these?" the pilot asked, indicating the DC-3.

"Some," Weston said. "I'm rated—I *was* rated—in it, but most of my multiengine time is in Catalinas."

"You fly Catalinas?"

"Past tense," Weston said. "I'm a fighter pilot."

"I'm jealous," the pilot confessed.

"The Corsair is one hell of an airplane," Weston said.

The pilot looked at the window and picked up his microphone.

"Philadelphia, TWA 303 turning on final."

"Three-oh-three, take taxiway twenty-seven right. The Navy ambulance will meet you at gate eleven."

"Understand twenty-seven right, gate eleven," the pilot said, and then turned his attention to see how well his copilot was going to handle the landing.

The ambulance was a civilian vehicle, a Packard painted white with US NAVY lettered on its doors, rather than the GI ambulance that he was used to, which was built on the frame of a Dodge three-quarter-ton truck, the sides and roof decorated with large red crosses. The medical crew consisted of two Corpsmen, in hospital whites, and a very well-assembled nurse in a crisp white uniform. She wore a stiffly starched white cap, perched precariously, and very attractively, atop her short blond hair. Her face was very serious. She looked to be in her very early twenties.

Because I am a Marine officer and a gentleman by act of Congress, with certain standards to maintain, I would not kick that out of bed.

The Corpsmen were equipped for any eventuality. They had a wheelchair, and also a chrome stretcher on wheels that sat on the ground beside the open rear door of the ambulance. As soon as the pilot had shut down the left engine, a curt nod from the nurse directed the Corpsmen toward the airplane. She walked in front of them.

The pilot turned to Weston, putting out his hand.

"Good luck," he said.

"Thank you," Jim replied, "and thanks for letting me ride up front."

"My pleasure," the pilot said.

"Mine, too," the copilot chimed in and offered his hand.

Weston rose from the jump seat and fastened it in the up position, then left the cockpit and started down the aisle. When he turned after taking his small canvas bag from the rack over his seat, he saw that the nurse was already in the plane.

She looked at him curiously as he walked down the aisle.

"And good afternoon to you, Lieutenant," Jim said with a smile.

"Are you my patient?" she asked, as if surprised that he could make it down the aisle by himself.

"I don't think so," he said.

"I'm looking for a Marine captain named Weston," she said.

"Then this is your lucky day," Jim said. "And perhaps mine, too. Captain James B. Weston at your service, ma'am. I didn't catch the name?"

"If you'll come with me, please, Captain," she said.

"That's a funny name for a pretty girl," he said.

She colored, gave him a dirty look, then turned around and got off the airplane. He went down the stairs quickly after her.

The fatter of the two Corpsmen pushed the wheelchair toward him.

"Is someone ill?" Weston asked innocently.

"Please get in the chair, Captain," the nurse said.

"Thank you ever so much, Lieutenant, but I don't need a wheelchair."

"It's procedure," she said. "Please get in the chair."

"Something wrong with your hearing, Lieutenant? Is that ambulance our transportation?"

"If you'll please get in the back, Captain."

He walked to the rear of the ambulance and looked inside.

"There're no seats in there," he said reasonably. "Where am I supposed to sit? On the floor?"

"You're supposed to lie down on the stretcher," she said.

"Again, thank you but no thank you," he said. "I'll just ride in front, if that would be all right."

"I would appreciate it if you wouldn't give me any trouble," she said.

"Captain," the fatter Corpsman said, "Sir, you've got to ride in the back."

"Butt out!" Weston said coldly, tossed his small bag in the back of the ambulance, and then walked to the front and got in.

The nurse and the corpsmen had a discussion, following which the fatter Corpsman got behind the wheel and the nurse slipped in beside Weston.

"Perhaps there's been some sort of mix-up," the nurse said. "The officer we were supposed to meet was just rescued from the Philippines."

"Oddly enough, I was in the Philippines until a couple of months ago," Weston said. "Until Christmas Eve, as a matter of fact."

"You were hospitalized ... in the Pacific ... until now?"

"I haven't been hospitalized at all," he said. "Do I look like I need hospitalization? In your professional judgment, I mean?"

"Let's go, Nevin," she ordered.

"Yes, ma'am," the chubby Corpsman started the engine.

"I suppose this really isn't any of my business, Lieutenant, but is there anyone in your life, in a romantic sense, at the moment? What I'm leading up to is wondering if you're free for dinner?"

"You're going to be in a hospital bed when I have my dinner," she said. "But thank you just the same."

"Well, we could have dinner there, I suppose," Weston said reasonably. "I really hate to eat alone."

"You understand that I'm going to have to report your conduct?" she said.

"I wouldn't have it any other way," he said.

"Please sit in the wheelchair," she said when they had pulled up to the Admissions entrance to one of the buildings in the hospital complex on South Broad Street.

"I thought we already had this discussion," he said.

"You have to!"

"Where do I report in, Lieutenant?"

"Nevin," she ordered, "go find a couple of psychiatric Corpsmen."

"Yes, ma'am," the chubby Corpsman said, and hurried into the building.

What are they going to do? Wrap the nutty escapee from the Philippines in a straitjacket and drag me inside to a padded cell?

The two muscular Corpsmen who appeared moments later—almost running—did not have a straitjacket with them.

They don't need one. I have seen smaller gorillas.

"Would you please escort this patient to Five-B, please?" the nurse said.

"Yes, ma'am," one of them said. "You want to get in the wheelchair, please, Captain?"

"No," Weston said evenly.

"Why not?"

"I don't need a wheelchair; I don't like wheelchairs."

The Corpsman looked at him intently for a long moment. "Yes, sir. Will you come this way, please, Captain?"

"Certainly," Weston said. He turned to the nurse. "The memory of our meeting, Lieutenant, will remain with me always."

She ignored him. "I'll call Commander Kister and alert him that you're coming," she said to the Corpsmen, and walked quickly into the building.

"What's Five-B?" Weston asked the larger gorilla. "Or is that a military secret?"

"It's preliminary evaluation, Captain," the Corpsmen answered. "Nothing to worry about. They'll keep you there for a couple of days, and then you'll get transferred to one of the other wards for treatment."

The entrance to Ward Five-B was barred. A Corpsman as large as the two who had escorted him there unlocked and pulled open a barred door.

"Put him in Four," he ordered.

Four was a small room furnished with a small desk and two chairs. The window was covered with a steel mesh.

Weston looked out the window—it opened on an interior courtyard—and then tried the door. He was not surprised to learn he was locked in. He walked back to the window and half-sat on the windowsill. He took a long, thin, green cigar from a breast pocket on his tunic, looked at it, decided he really didn't want a smoke right now, and returned the cigar to the pocket.

Five minutes later, the door opened and a chubby, red-headed man in a white smock walked in, carrying a manila folder.

"I'm Dr. Kister," he announced.

Weston touched his index finger to his temple in a mocking salute.

Dr. Kister sat down at the desk and laid the manila folder on it. "You gave Lieutenant Hardison a hard time," Kister said.

"That's the nurse?"

Kister nodded. "Nice girl," he said.

"Nice-looking, too."

"Then why did you give her a hard time?"

"I *didn't* give her a hard time. I *did* tell her I didn't need her wheelchair, and that I had no intention of lying on a stretcher in the back of her ambulance."

"That's standard procedure. She was just obeying orders."

"Never let common sense get in the way of standard procedure and obeying orders, right?"

"You want to tell me why you're so pissed off, Captain?" Dr. Kister asked.

"Are you really interested, Doctor?" Weston asked. "Or . . . ?"

"Will you settle for 'curious'? I *am* curious."

Weston looked at him for a moment, shrugged, reached into the lower right outer pocket of his tunic, and with some difficulty pulled out a large manila envelope, folded in half. He unfolded it, opened it, rummaged through it, found what he was looking for, and handed it to Dr. Kister.

It was a long sheet of yellow paper, a carbon copy of a Teletype message. Kister took it and read it. As he did, his eyebrows went up.

```
HQ USMC
1705 08 FEB 43
PRIORITY


COMMANDING OFFICER
MAG-21
EWA MCAS OAHU TERRITORY OF HAWAII

1. DEPUTY CHIEF OF STAFF FOR PERSONNEL
USMC HAS INFORMED THE UNDERSIGNED:

A. NO EXCEPTION TO STANDING OPERATING
PROCEDURE REGARDING MISSING OR CAPTURED
PERSONNEL RETURNING TO USMC CONTROL WILL
BE GRANTED IN CASE OF CAPTAIN JAMES B.
WESTON, USMCR, USMC SPECIAL DETACHMENT
16, CURRENTLY ON TEMPORARY DUTY VMF 229,
MAG 21, EWA MCAS.


B. IN VIEW STRONG OBJECTIONS VOICED BY US
NAVY BUREAU OF AERONAUTICS TO COMMANDANT
USMC CONCERNING RETURN TO FLIGHT STATUS
OF OFFICER WHO HAS BEEN OFF FLIGHT STATUS
FOR TWELVE OR MORE MONTHS WITHOUT
SUCCESSFUL COMPLETION OF PRESCRIBED
BUAIR RETRAINING PROGRAM CAPTAIN
WESTON'S TRANSITION TRAINING INTO F4U-1
AIRCRAFT AND HIS FLIGHT STATUS WILL BE
```

TERMINATED IMMEDIATELY UPON RECEIPT OF
THIS MESSAGE.

2. YOU WILL IMMEDIATELY ISSUE ORDERS
DIRECTING CAPTAIN WESTON TO PROCEED BY
FIRST AVAILABLE AIR TRANSPORTATION TO US
NAVY HOSPITAL, PHILADELPHIA, PENNA.,
REPORTING ON ARRIVAL THEREAT TO
COMMANDING OFFICER, TO UNDERGO PHYSICAL
AND PYSCHOLOGICAL EVALUATION PRESCRIBED
FOR PERSONNEL RETURNING TO USMC CONTROL
AFTER ESCAPE FROM ENEMY CONTROLLED
TERRITORY.

3. FOR YOUR INFORMATION, PRESUMING
CAPTAIN WESTON'S PHYSICAL AND
PSYCHOLOGICAL CONDITION IS JUDGED TO BE
SUCH THAT HE CAN RETURN TO ACTIVE DUTY, HE
WILL BE ORDERED TO THE GREENBRIER HOTEL,
WEST VIRGINIA, FOR THIRTY DAYS
RECUPERATIVE LEAVE, NOT CHARGEABLE AS
ORDINARY LEAVE. HE WILL THEN BE SENT TO US
NAVY AIR STATION, PENSACOLA, FLORIDA, TO
UNDERGO PRESCRIBED BUAIR PILOT
RETRAINING PROGRAM. IF SUCH COURSE OF
INSTRUCTION IS SUCCESSFULLY COMPLETED,
IT IS CONTEMPLATED THAT CAPTAIN WESTON
WILL BE ASSIGNED TO VMF-262, US NAVAL AIR
STATION, MEMPHIS, TENN., FOR TRANSITION
TRAINING INTO F4U-1 AIRCRAFT.

4. NO REQUESTS FOR RECONSIDERATION OF
ABOVE OR COMMENTS CONCERNING THESE
DECISIONS ARE DESIRED.

D.G. MCINERNEY
BRIG GEN USMC
DIRECTOR USMC AVIATION

Doctor Kister looked at Weston. "Very interesting," he
said.

Weston went into the envelope again and came out with a long form, which he handed to Kister. "That's a flight physical," Weston said.

"Would you believe I've seen one before?" Kister asked, and read it carefully. Then he looked at Weston. "How'd you get this?"

"I went to the Navy Hospital in Pearl Harbor. They examined me for several hours and decided I could see lightning and hear thunder well enough to be allowed to fly."

"According to this, aside from being a few pounds underweight, you're in excellent health."

"As, indeed, I am," Weston said. "So what the hell am I doing in a psycho ward?"

"Interesting question," Kister said. "This is dated five weeks ago. Have you been flying?"

"Yes, I have. And four hours after I passed my rating check ride in a Corsair, I got orders to come here."

"Anybody who has been a prisoner of war and escapes gets sent here," Kister said, "to determine what kind of shape he's in. You were a POW, right?"

"No."

"Your paperwork," Kister said, tapping the manila folder he had brought with him, "says you escaped from the Philippines."

"I was *ordered out* of the Philippines. You asked if I had been a POW."

"What were you doing in the Philippines?"

"Would you believe it if I told you I was G-2 of U.S. forces in the Philippines?"

Kister examined him carefully and, Weston thought, with disbelief.

"With overwhelming immodesty," Weston said, "I have a Silver Star to prove it. It was personally pinned to my breast by General Douglas MacArthur."

Kister opened Weston's records jacket and went through it carefully. "Your Silver Star somehow didn't get into your records," Kister said. "And you're not wearing it."

Weston reached into his manila envelope again, came out with a four-by-five-inch glossy photograph, and handed it to Dr. Kister. "I have six more copies of that, eight-by-tens, in my luggage, wherever the hell my luggage might be."

Kister examined the photograph. It showed the Supreme Commander, South West Pacific Ocean Areas, in the act of pinning the Silver Star to Weston's tunic. Weston was wearing a full beard.

"I'll be damned," Kister said. "Nice beard."

"Thank you," Weston said.

"Who's the Marine general?" Kister asked.

"His name is Pickering."

"Maybe he's the guy who can straighten this out," Dr. Kister said. "I don't think I'd have much luck getting General MacArthur on the telephone."

Weston chuckled.

"What I don't understand is how you went back to flying," Kister said. "You want to tell me about that?"

"I got as far as Hawaii when I was given the choice of a thirty-day leave in the States or getting checked out in the Corsair," Weston said. "I chose the Corsair."

"You didn't want to come home on leave? Why?"

"I don't have much of a family here," Weston said. "Weighed in the balance, an aunt I hardly know and haven't seen in years came up short when the alternative was getting back to flying fighters."

"And then, it would seem reasonable to assume, the bureaucracy caught up with you, and you're back in the Escaped POW Pipeline."

"So it would seem," Weston said. "If I told you I'm mightily pissed off, would that certify me as a loony?"

"No. But getting off on the wrong foot with Lieutenant Hardison does."

Weston smiled.

"So now you're going to call in the corpsmen with the straitjacket?"

"No. It's too late to do anything about this today. So what I suggest is that we get you a bed for the night. Could I give you an off-the-ward pass to visit the O Club for dinner and a couple of drinks with reasonable assurance that you would behave yourself?"

"In other words, you want my word as an officer and

a gentleman that if I encounter Lieutenant Hardison, I will not drag her off into the bushes and ravish her?"

"Her or any other female you encounter, including those who imply they would like to be dragged into the bushes."

"I do solemnly swear," Weston said, and held up his right hand with the three center fingers extended. "Boy Scout's Honor."

"I'll take the chance," Dr. Kister said. "One thing. Go easy on the booze. I'm going to schedule you for a physical first thing in the morning, and I don't want your blood test coming back reading 'mostly alcohol.' "

"Why another physical?"

"It will allow the physicians, nurses, and Corpsmen involved to feel they are making a contribution to the war effort, okay? And as sure as Christ made little apples, when we start looking into this, the first question somebody is going to ask is, 'How do we know that Hawaiian physical isn't somebody else's?' "

"Okay. Easy on the booze," Weston said. "Thank you, Doctor."

"Welcome home, Captain Weston," Dr. Kister said, and offered Weston his hand.

[TWO]

"I will be damned," Lieutenant (j.g.) Janice Hardison, NNC, exclaimed as she was driving her 1937 Ford Business Coupe northward on South Broad Street approximately one hour later. The insufferably arrogant patient who had given her all the trouble earlier, and who should by now be mildly sedated, dressed in a bathrobe, and either asleep in his bed or listening to the radio in the dayroom of Ward Five-B, was instead marching purposefully down the sidewalk six blocks from the hospital compound in full uniform. He was carrying a brown paper bag.

She made the next left turn and headed back to the hospital. She would tell the Shore Patrolman on duty at the gate. A Shore Patrol detail would be instantly dispatched, and he would be returned to the hospital, in handcuffs if necessary.

Janice had a change of heart before she reached the hospital. She admitted to herself that she was being controlled by her personal emotions and was therefore responding to the situation in a nonprofessional manner.

Marines were, almost by definition, arrogant. But in the arrogance department this one stood head and shoulders over any other Marine she had ever met. She could not recall anyone ever in her entire life having made her so angry in so short a time as had this blond-haired, blue-eyed gyrene sonofabitch. And while it probably would be good for his character, long term, to be subjected to the humiliation of being hauled back to the hospital in handcuffs, she had, as a practitioner of the healing arts, to consider the short term.

God only knew what horrors he had experienced in a POW camp. The proof of that seemed to be that he denied having been a POW. The memories were simply too horrible for him to accept. That veneer of arrogance was paper-thin, concealing all the effects of severe psychological trauma. She could not, as a nurse, add humiliation to the other psychological burdens he was already carrying.

She turned the Ford coupe around and turned onto South Broad Street again.

Before she saw him, she had just about convinced herself that she would not be able to find him.

She pulled to the curb, leaned across the seat, and opened the door. "Weston!" she called.

He looked at her and smiled, pretending to be really glad to see her.

"I'll be damned," he said. "Is this how you spend your off-duty hours, cruising the streets and picking up Marines?"

"Please get in the car, Captain," Janice said.

He walked to the car and squatted on the sidewalk so that their faces were on a level.

"Does this mean you've changed your mind and we're on for dinner?"

"Please get in the car," she said. "I'll take you back to

the hospital. With a little luck, the Shore Patrol won't ask for your pass, and we will just forget this ever happened."

"Actually, I have other plans," he said. "Made, of course, after you so cruelly rejected me. Her name is Caroline, and she is at this moment anxiously awaiting my appearance."

He's lying, she thought. *He made that up. There is absolutely no way, in the short time he's been here, that he could have made a date.*

"But thank you just the same," Jim Weston went on. "You may consider yourself forgiven for your outrageous behavior at the airport."

"*My* outrageous behavior?" Janice asked incredulously.

"Yes," he said. "We'll just pretend *that* never happened, and perhaps I can even fit you into my schedule later in the week. But right now, I'm running a little late, so you'll have to excuse me." He stood up and resumed walking up South Broad Street.

She leaned over and with difficulty reached across for the open door and closed it. When she looked out the windshield, she saw him trying and failing to flag down a taxicab.

Where the hell is he going? If I don't get him back to the hospital, he's headed for real trouble.

She put the Ford in gear and went after him. "Get in, and I'll give you a ride," she called to him when she pulled to the curb again.

"If I get in your car, Florence Nightingale, you'll try to drive me back to the hospital. I can see it in your eyes."

"I'll take you wherever you want to go," she said.

"Girl Scout's Honor? I don't have much faith in that officer and gentleman—gentle*lady*?—word-of-honor business."

"Where are you really going?"

"Will you really take me there?"

"Yes, I will. I said I would, and I will."

He opened the car door and slipped in beside her.

"Where to?" Janice asked.

What he's going to do now is make another pitch to take me to dinner, and I'll turn him down again and take him back to the hospital.

Oh, what the hell, I have to eat. Having dinner with him will calm him down—stroke that enormous ego—and then it will be easier to get him back to the hospital.

She could smell his aftershave lotion.

He handed her a slip of paper on which was written: "Caroline. 98 Stevens Ave., Jenkintown, PA 19046."

I'll be damned. He really has a woman waiting for him. A tramp, more than likely. Maybe even a lady of the evening, who does that sort of thing for money.

And I have agreed to take him to meet her.

"Do you know where that is?" Weston asked.

"The other side of Philadelphia," she said, "past the other end of Broad Street."

"If that's out of your way, Florence," he said, "then just drop me where I can catch a cab."

"My name is Janice," she corrected him. "And I said I'd take you and I will," she added firmly.

"Thank you," he said.

Fifteen minutes later, as they headed up North Broad Street, she asked two questions: "What's in the paper bag?"

"A pineapple."

"A *pineapple*?"

"*Ananas comosus*," he clarified. "One eats them. You don't know what a pineapple is?"

Janice fell silent for ninety seconds, then asked about the second thing that had piqued her curiosity. "How did you get out? If you don't mind my asking?"

"I climbed the fence," he replied matter-of-factly.

"But there's barbed wire on top of the fence," she replied, "and a walking patrol."

"I noticed," he said.

"And how did you plan to get back in?"

"You must be reading my mind," he said. "I don't suppose you could stick around awhile? What I have to do won't take long, and you could drive me back."

"What I have to do won't take long"?

"On the way we could have dinner," he added.

Janice did not reply.

*　　*　　*

Ninety-Eight Stevens Avenue in Jenkintown turned out to be a large, brick colonial house set two hundred feet back from the road on a large, tree-studded lot. A Mercury station wagon was parked on the drive.

Janice parked behind the station wagon.

"Are you going to wait for me, Florence?" Weston asked.

"I told you my name was Janice," she snapped.

He snapped his fingers, indicating that he now remembered.

"So you did," he said. "Well, *Janice*, are you going to wait for me, or are you going to just leave me here to face the dangers of suburban Philadelphia all by myself?"

"What are you going to do in there?"

"God only knows what time will bring," he said solemnly. He stepped out of the car and walked toward the house.

When he was halfway to the door, she got out and followed him.

As he walked up the shallow flight of stairs, the door opened. A tall, good-looking blonde smiled at Weston. *An older woman*, Janice thought. *She must be at least thirty.*

"You have to be Jim," the woman said.

"And you have to be Caroline," Weston said. "Have a pineapple, Caroline." He handed her the brown paper bag. She opened it and smiled. "Picked by the skipper himself," Weston added.

"And I have never seen a more beautiful pineapple," she said.

"As splendid an example of *Ananas comosus* as Charley could find," Weston said. "It must have taken him as much as ten, fifteen seconds to pick this one."

She laughed.

"Come on in, quickly," she said. "Our air raid warden takes his duties seriously."

She looked at Janice curiously and smiled.

They stepped into the foyer, and Caroline closed the door.

"If I knew you were with your girl, I wouldn't have told you to come right out," Caroline said.

"She's more like my keeper than my girl," Weston said.

"But I'm working on it. Caroline, Janice. Janice, Caroline."

"Your keeper?"

"She's a nurse in the psychiatric ward of the hospital," Weston said.

"Charley wrote about that. The letter came this morning," Caroline said. "That's outrageous!"

"Pay attention, Florence," Weston said.

"Janice, damn it!" Janice blurted.

"Hello, Janice," Caroline said. "I'm Caroline McNamara."

"How do you do? I'm Janice Hardison."

"It was very nice of you to bring Jim out here," Caroline said.

"Nothing is too good for us lunatics, right, Janice?"

"Will you shut up?" Janice snapped.

"We've only known each other four hours, and we're having our first lovers' quarrel," Weston said.

"We are not lovers!"

"I'm working on that," Weston said. "I'm certainly willing to give it a shot."

Caroline laughed. "Why do I suspect Jim is your first Marine Aviator?" she asked.

"He's not my first anything," Janice said.

"They take a little getting used to," Caroline said. "But once you acquire the taste, you won't be satisfied with anything less."

"Pay attention to the lady, Janice," Weston said.

"If you don't shut up . . ."

"You'll hold your breath until you turn blue?"

Caroline laughed.

And Janice realized she was smiling. "You *are* crazy, you know that?"

Oh, my God! I can't believe I said that! What's the matter with me?

"No, Florence Nightingale, Dr. Kister and I are in agreement that I am not crazy."

"Who's Dr. Kister?" Caroline asked.

"Navy psychiatrist."

"Wait until Dr. Kister hears that you went AWOL. Climbed over the fence."

"You're going to tell him?"

"You went AWOL?" Caroline asked.

"Perhaps, *technically*," Weston said. "But if it gets down to a court-martial, my defense is going to be that I was simply carrying out a legal order."

"What legal order?" Janice asked.

"From my last commanding officer, Captain Charles M. Galloway," Weston said. " *'The first thing you do when you get to Philadelphia, Weston, is take this pineapple to Caroline.'* "

Caroline chuckled.

"What he did—he didn't have a pass, of course. They never give off-base passes when a patient is in Five-B . . ." Janice said.

"Five-B is the loony bin, Caroline," Weston clarified.

"What he did was climb the barbed-wire fence," Janice went on, wondering why it was important to her to explain herself to Caroline. "I found him brazenly walking up South Broad Street—"

"And you brought him here," Caroline interrupted. "That was a very nice, a very kind thing for you to do, Janice. Thank you."

"Yes, it was," Weston said. "Thank you, Janice."

Janice was not quite sure if he was making fun of her or not.

"Now the problem is getting him back on the base," Janice said.

"Is that going to be a problem?" Caroline asked.

"No," Weston said immediately.

"Yes, it is," Janice insisted.

"Changing the subject," Weston said. "At the risk of sounding forward, Mrs. McNamara, Captain Galloway suggested that you might offer me a small libation, presuming I delivered the *Ananas comosus* while it was still suitable for human consumption."

"Oh, God! Where's my manners? Keeping you standing here in the foyer! Come in the living room, please."

He called her "Mrs. McNamara." So where's Mr. *McNamara?*

Weston misread the look in Janice's eyes. "Not to worry, Janice, I gave Dr. Kister my word that I would go easy on the booze. That was after he told me he scheduled a physical for me in the morning."

"Good," she said, a trifle self-righteously.

"To completely put your mind at rest, Janice, I also gave the good doctor my word as an officer and a gentleman—or was it as a Boy Scout? It *was* as a Boy Scout, now that I think about it, which means that I was really serious—that I would not drag you into the bushes."

"What?" Janice asked incredulously.

"So you can stop looking at me as if you think I have that in mind."

"That thought would never occur to a Marine officer, right?" Caroline said. "Particularly a Marine fighter pilot?"

"Perish the thought," Weston said piously.

They were now in a well-furnished living room, standing before a sideboard turned into a bar.

"What would you like, Jim?" Caroline asked.

"I'd like one of each," Weston said. "But I'll settle for a small scotch."

"Janice?"

"Nothing, thank you."

"Oh, come on," Weston said. "Try to remember you're an officer of the Naval establishment."

"If she doesn't want anything, don't push her," Caroline said, coming to her aid.

"I'll have a light scotch, please," Janice said.

"And afterward, I've got some steaks warming up in the kitchen."

"Warming up?" Janice asked.

"One of the many things that Charley taught me is that meat tastes much better if you get it to room temperature before you cook it."

"You have a lovely home, Mrs. McNamara," Janice said politely.

"My husband, thank God, had the morals of an alley cat," Caroline said.

"Excuse me?" Janice asked.

"If he had obeyed that promise he made to keep himself only to me until death did us part, I would still be married to him, I would still be supporting him, I wouldn't have gotten this house as part of the divorce settlement, and I wouldn't have met Charley," Caroline said.

"I'll drink to that," Weston said.

Janice looked at him and could not keep herself from smiling.

[THREE]

"The first reasonably deserted place I see," Lieutenant (j.g.) Hardison said to Captain Weston, "I'm going to stop so you can climb in the trunk."

"You're not serious."

"I'm perfectly serious," she said. "You're AWOL, goddamn it!"

"I like it when you talk dirty," he said.

"That's profane, not obscene."

"Say something obscene."

"I will not," she said, shaking her head.

"Just drop me a couple of blocks away, and I'll go back over the fence."

"This would be easier."

"Your trunk is probably greasy, and I will ruin my nearly brand-new uniform."

"You would probably tear your nearly brand-new uniform going back over the barbed wire," she said. "And my trunk is spotless!"

"I am putty in your hands," he said. "Now that I've considered that a dry cleaning job is much cheaper than a new pair of pants, anyway."

Her trunk was clean, but it was small. Weston had to lie on his back, with his knees pulled up. Janice was just about to close the trunk lid on him when he motioned for her to come close. Then he grabbed her and kissed her on the forehead. "Nighty night, Mommy," he said.

"You are insane," she said, and slammed the trunk shut.

When she opened the trunk in the parking lot behind the Female Officers' Quarters, he had trouble climbing out. "God," he said seriously. "That brought back a lot of memories. The last gate I sneaked through was guarded by Japanese soldiers."

"Really?"

"Actually no," he said. "But now that I know you're impressed with heroic efforts, I'll try to invent some more."

"You're really terrible. I believed you."

"It was a joke," he said.

"I don't think I like your sense of humor," Janice said.

That's not true. He's really a funny guy.

"What did you think of Caroline?"

"I like her," she said.

"She liked you. And I like you. That leaves the question, do you like me?"

"I don't think so," she said.

That's not true, either. I really like him.

"I suppose that means a goodnight kiss is out of the question?"

"Yes, it does," she said firmly.

But then she looked into his eyes, and she kissed him.

"Jesus H. Christ!" he said. "That was not what I expected."

"What did you expect?"

"Not that," he said. "When do you want to get married?"

"Good night, Captain Weston," Janice said. "Sleep well."

"After that? Don't be absurd."

"That was nothing special."

"When can I expect special?"

"Never," she said. "Go to bed."

She marched toward the door of the Female Officers' Quarters. When she had pulled it open, she turned and looked back at the parking lot.

He was still standing where she had left him, looking at her.

She looked at him for a long moment before she went into the building.

V

[ONE]
The White House
Washington, D.C.
1420 17 February 1943

"Jim was right about you, Captain," the President of the
United States said, gesturing toward a tall, slender, bald
man in the uniform of a Marine major. "You are a remarkable young man, a fine Marine."

"Hear, hear," Senator Richardson K. Fowler (R.-Cal.)
said. Fowler, sometimes described by President Roosevelt
as "the chief of my more or less loyal opposition" and
Brigadier General Fleming Pickering, USMCR, had been
close friends for thirty years.

"He was a Raider, Dad," Major James Roosevelt said.
"What did you expect?"

"Well, in that case, I presume, as one Raider to another,
you will make sure that Captain McCoy is well taken care
of tonight? And that, by order of the Commander in Chief,
he gets some well-deserved time off?"

"With pleasure," Major Roosevelt said.

The President had a tangential thought. Looking first at Senator Fowler and Navy Secretary Frank Knox, and then at McCoy, he asked: "Tell me, Captain, how do you feel about your assignment to the OSS?"

"I'm a Marine, sir," McCoy said.

"Does that mean you'd really prefer to go back to the Raiders?"

"Sir, I would like to go back to the Raiders, but what I meant was I'm a Marine officer, and I do what I'm ordered to do."

"I wish there was some way I could make that splendid attitude contagious around here," the President said. He leaned forward in his wheelchair and offered McCoy his hand. "Thank you very much, Captain," he said, "not only for the briefing, but also for what you and the others did when you went into the Philippines to hook up with this Fertig chap."

"He told you, Dad," the President's son said. "He's a Marine officer. He does what he's told to do. 'Get in the rubber boat and start paddling.' Right, Killer?"

"Yes, sir," McCoy said.

" 'Killer'?" the President quoted. "I think I'd like to hear about that."

"No, you wouldn't," Major Roosevelt said.

But the President was already turning his attention to the Secretary of the Navy. "I'd like a few minutes of your time, Frank, please," he said.

"Of course, Mr. President," the Secretary of the Navy replied.

McCoy sensed that he was being dismissed. Confirmation came a second later as Major Roosevelt touched his arm and nodded toward the door of the upstairs sitting room. He saluted and marched out of the room. Major Roosevelt and Senator Fowler followed him.

As they entered the corridor, a Secret Service man closed the door after them.

"Good job, McCoy," Major Roosevelt said. "You really impressed the Old Man."

McCoy blurted what he was thinking, "It wasn't as bad as I thought it was going to be."

Senator Fowler chuckled. "Jimmy's father can charm the socks off you, if he's so inclined," he said. "You have to remember to ask for your shoes back. I didn't say that, Jimmy."

Major Roosevelt laughed. "I won't tell him what you said, and I won't tell you what he says about you."

"Fair enough," Fowler said.

"Okay," Roosevelt said. "Now we have to find a place where the Killer can rest his weary head."

"I thought you weren't supposed to call him that," Fowler said.

"Those rules don't apply to Raiders," Roosevelt replied. "So what's your pleasure, Killer? I'm sure we can put you up here, but I'll tell you I don't stay here myself unless I'm forced to. And there aren't very many nubile young things prowling these historic corridors."

"Ken's taken care of," Fowler said.

"Oh, really?"

"Across the street," Fowler said, "in General Pickering's apartment."

"Well, I can't top that offer," Roosevelt said. "But what about money? Have you been paid lately?"

"I'm all right for money," McCoy said. "I drew a partial pay at Pearl Harbor."

"Anything? Incidentally, my father meant it when he said to take some time off. Take at least two weeks off, and tell anybody who asks that it's administrative leave, not chargeable as ordinary leave. By direction of the President."

"Can I get away with that?"

"Yes, you can," Roosevelt said firmly. "The least I can do is get you a car to drive across the street."

"I've got my car, but thank you just the same," Fowler said.

Roosevelt put out his hand to McCoy. "It was good to see you, Ken. And when you see Zimmerman, tell him I sent my best regards. He's still in Australia?"

"With this OSS business, there's no telling," McCoy said. "It was good to see you again, too, Major."

"I'll walk you downstairs," Roosevelt said, putting an arm around his shoulders.

[TWO]
The Marquis de Lafayette Suite
The Foster Lafayette hotel
Washington, D.C.
1445 17 February 1943

A soft chime sounded, announcing that someone was in the sixth-floor corridor seeking entrance. The three men in the sitting room of the six-room suite looked at the door. Major Edward J. Banning put his drink on the coffee table in front of the red leather armchair where he was sitting, walked to the door, and opened it. He was in uniform, but had removed his tunic, pulled his field scarf loose, and turned up the cuffs of his shirt.

"Good afternoon, Senator," Banning said politely, and smiled at Captain McCoy.

"Hello, Banning," Senator Fowler said. "I return this young man to your capable custody."

"He looks to me as if he could use a drink," Banning said.

"We both could," Fowler said, and stepped into the room.

The other two men rose to their feet. One of them, Captain Edward Sessions, USMC, was a tall, lithely muscular, well-set-up Marine captain in his late twenties. He, too, had removed his uniform tunic. A ring on his finger identified him as a graduate of the U.S. Naval Academy. An intelligence officer assigned to the Office of Management Analysis, he had met McCoy during a covert operation staged by Banning in China before the war.

The other was a tall, slight, pale-skinned, unhealthy-looking man, wearing glasses and an ill-fitting gray suit.

"Good afternoon, Senator," Colonel F. L. Rickabee, USMC, said.

"Good to see you, Colonel," Fowler said. "And to quickly put your mind at rest, Ken did himself proud."

"I expected nothing less," Rickabee said, "but I think we can give him a drink nevertheless."

"I'll even make them," Captain Sessions said. "What's your pleasure, gentlemen?"

"I don't know about Ken," Fowler said. "But I think I will dip once again into General Pickering's bottomless well of Famous Grouse."

"Ken?" Sessions asked.

McCoy nodded.

Sessions walked to a rolling cart on which sat a dozen or so bottles of whisky, glasses, a soda siphon, and the other paraphernalia of a bar.

"It went well?" Colonel Rickabee asked as he sat down again.

"I bear orders from the Commander in Chief," Fowler said. "This 'remarkable young man, this fine Marine' is to get 'some well-deserved time off.' "

"Consider it done, Senator," Colonel Rickabee said.

"I told you you'd live through it, Ken," Major Banning said.

McCoy looked at him. "Specs was there," McCoy said. "That helped a lot."

"Specs?" Banning asked.

"Major Roosevelt," McCoy said. "He was the only guy on the Makin Raid who wore glasses. We called him 'Specs' behind his back."

Sessions handed McCoy a squat glass dark with whisky.

"You hungry, Ken?"

McCoy nodded. "Yeah, a little."

"You didn't have any lunch," Sessions said.

"Get on the horn, Sessions," Colonel Rickabee ordered, "and order up a steak for this 'remarkable young man, this fine Marine.' "

"Aye, aye, sir," Sessions said.

"A large steak, Ed," Major Banning said, "big enough for two people, and a dozen oysters on the half shell."

"I don't know about the oysters," McCoy said.

"Don't let those brand-new railroad tracks go to your head, Captain McCoy," Colonel Rickabee said. "When a superior officer tells you to eat oysters, it's because he thinks you need oysters. What you say is, 'Aye, aye, sir. Thank you, sir,' and eat them."

For some reason, Colonel Rickabee, Major Banning,

and Captain Sessions looked very pleased with themselves.

Sessions called room service and ordered a very large steak and a dozen oysters, the larger the better. Then he turned to Colonel Rickabee. "Can I fix you another drink, Colonel?"

"No. No, thank you. We're going back to the office. I think this remarkable young man, this fine Marine, needs some time to himself."

"Yes, sir."

"I've got to go back to work, too," Senator Fowler said. "Ken, do I have to tell you if I can be of any help, in any way, all you have to do is call?"

"Thank you, sir," McCoy said.

"Duty calls, gentlemen," Rickabee said, stood up, and gestured for them to precede him out of the apartment.

"If you get bored later on, Ken," Captain Sessions said, "call me at the apartment after seventeen thirty."

"Why should he get bored?" Major Banning said. "He's a remarkable young man, a fine Marine. That means he should be able to find something to do to keep himself from getting bored."

"I don't want to see your smiling face for at least two weeks, Captain McCoy. Consider that an order," Colonel Rickabee said.

"Aye, aye, sir," McCoy said.

"On the other hand, let us know where we can get in touch with you," Rickabee said.

"Aye, aye, sir."

In a moment, McCoy was alone. He took off his tunic, tossed it on the couch, pulled down his tie, and carried his drink over to the windows overlooking Pennsylvania Avenue and the White House.

Jesus H. Christ! I really was in that building, with the President of the United States.

You're a long goddamned way from the machine-gun section of Baker Company, 4th Marines, in Shanghai, Corporal McCoy.

He slowly sipped his drink.

When the chime sounded, he was in the process of making himself another.

He opened the door and the floor-service waiter wheeled in a cart loaded with silver lidded dishes, cutlery, a vase holding a single rose, and a towel-wrapped bottle in a silver wine cooler.

"May I open the champagne for you, sir?"

"No. No, thank you."

I don't want any champagne. I don't even like champagne.

"Is there anything else you require, sir?"

"No, thank you. This is fine."

"Yes, sir. Thank you very much, sir."

The waiter left.

No check was presented. There was a standing rule in the Foster Lafayette Hotel from Mr. Foster himself. No check would ever be presented to anyone staying in the Marquis de Lafayette suite as a guest of Brigadier General Fleming Pickering, USMCR. Foster's only child, his daughter Patricia, was married to Pickering.

McCoy lifted the lids on the plates. The steak was enormous. And so were the dozen oysters on their bed of ice under another lid. He dropped the lid over the oysters back in place, sat down on the couch, and reached for the telephone on the coffee table. "Person-to-person to Miss Ernestine Sage," he ordered. "Try her first at J. Walter Thompson, the advertising agency, in New York City. I don't know the number. If she's not there, try Gramercy 5-4777. If there's no answer there, try the Sage residence in Bernardsville, New Jersey. I don't know that number either."

He put the telephone in its cradle, leaned back against the cushions of the couch, and closed his eyes.

He opened them quickly and sat up when he heard the sound of a door being opened.

A young woman was walking across the sitting room toward him. She had jet-black hair, worn in a pageboy, and she was wearing a black negligee that was almost invisible in the light coming through the windows behind her.

She picked up the telephone. "You can cancel that call to Miss Sage, please, operator," she said.

She looked down at McCoy. "Well, now I know," she said.

"You know what?"

"That I *am* more important to you than eating a steak."

His face contorted. His chest shook. He began to sob.

"Oh, baby," Ernie Sage said, and went to the couch and put her arms around him.

He tried to sit up. "I'm sorry, honey! I'm . . ."

"Shut up!" she said, then held his face against her breast and ran her hands through his hair, until, after a moment, he stopped crying.

"I wonder if they'll work," Ernie said.

"What?"

"The oysters. There's a dozen of them."

"I wondered what those bastards were up to with that oyster business," he said.

"Those bastards called me the minute they heard you were in California—which is more than you did. And they called me again when they knew when you were due in Washington. If it wasn't for those bastards, you'd still be trying to talk to me on the telephone.

"Okay. Sorry. Are you really starved? Or would a couple of oysters hold you for a while?"

"Oh, God, Ernie, I love you."

"If that's the case, what are we doing here in the living room, with all your clothes on?"

He stood up and looked down at her, then leaned over and picked her up and carried her toward the bedroom. Halfway to the door she kissed him, which caused him to lose his sense of direction, and he collided with the door frame.

But he quickly made the necessary course corrections, passed through the door to the bedroom, and kicked the door shut behind them.

[THREE]
Officers' Club
U.S. Navy Hospital
Philadelphia, Pennsylvania
1745 17 February 1943

"Hi," Captain James B. Weston, USMC, said to Lieutenant (j.g.) Janice Hardison, NNC, when she slipped onto the barstool beside him.

"Hi."

"May I say that you do more for that uniform than any other member of the Naval Officer Corps I have ever met?"

Janice blushed and was furious with herself.

"I hope you're hungry," he said. "I didn't get any breakfast, as you know, and what they offered for lunch was unfit for human consumption."

"I have something to tell you about me," she said.

Oh, shit. What? You've got a boyfriend? Hell, yes, you've got a boyfriend! Someone as good-looking as you are, in the midst of all these nice young men, is not going to be alone for long.

"I'm all ears."

"I want you to promise, first, that you won't make some smart-aleck reply."

He held up his fingers in the manner of Boy Scouts vowing the truthfulness of what they are about to say. "Boy Scout's Honor," he said.

"I'm a virgin," Janice said.

Just in time, he stopped himself from saying what immediately came to his mind: *No problem. We can fix that tonight.*

"If that was intended to surprise me, it didn't."

"And I intend to stay that way," she said. "So maybe you may want to change your mind about . . ."

"What I am offering, Lieutenant Hardison, is a lobster dinner."

"You know what I mean," she said. "I just wanted to have things clear between us."

"They are crystal clear," he said. "Now, would you like a drink?"

"Yes, please," she said. "A weak scotch."

He signaled the bartender and ordered her drink.

When it was delivered, she took a quick, small sip, put the glass on the bar, looked at him, found him looking at her, and quickly dropped her eyes to her glass.

"How do you like it?" Weston asked.

"Excuse me?"

"Boiled? Broiled? Thermidor?"

"I don't know," she confessed. "I've never had lobster before."

What does that make you, a lobster virgin?

"Really?"

"Kansas—Wichita—is a long way from the ocean," Janice said.

"It's even farther from Scotland," he said.

"My father's a doctor," she said. "He taught me to drink scotch."

And how to keep it till marriage, right?

"What kind of a doctor?"

"A psychiatrist," she said.

"And that's why you became a psychiatric nurse?"

"I was in a test program at the University . . . of Kansas, at the Medical School. The university offers a four-year course in nursing. You need an undergraduate degree to get into medical school. They wondered how well a B.S.N. would do in medical school—hopefully better than the usual B.S. or B.A."

"B.S.N.? Bachelor of Science, Nursing?"

"Right. So I was one of the guinea pigs."

"How does one get to be a guinea pig?"

"It helps if your father is a professor of medicine," she said.

"So why aren't you in medical school?"

"Well, the war came along, the Navy came around recruiting nurses, and Daddy said I should take it. Daddy said I could get more clinical experience as a nurse in the service than I would get as a psychiatric resident."

Daddy said? Daddy said, "Daughter Darling, go in the

Navy, drink scotch, and hang on to your pearl of great price until you get married"?

Well, what the hell is wrong with that?

"What about you?" Janice asked.

"University of Iowa," he said. "I was raised in Des Moines. Offered a chance for flight school, joined the Corps, and here I am."

"Your parents?"

"My mother died when I was a kid, and my father—he was in the insurance business—died when I was in college."

"Brothers and sisters?"

"Neither. Just an aunt."

"I have two brothers," she said. "Both doctors. One surgeon and one proctologist. My mother was a nurse before she married my father."

"What's a proctologist?"

"It deals with the lower intestines," she said after a brief hesitation.

His face lit up. "I know what it means!" he remembered.

"I thought you might," she said, and smiled at him.

Goddamn, she's really sweet.

Well, why not? Good solid family. Daddy's a doctor, Mommy's a nurse, she was baby sister to two brothers. Either of whom would probably cheerfully break both my legs if I changed her virginal status. Or pull my tonsils through the terminus of my lower intestines with surgical forceps.

"We ate lobster in Iowa," Weston said. "God only knows how it got there, but there it was."

"I'm sure we had them in Kansas, too," she said, loyally. "My family just never ate them."

"Charley Galloway told me to go where we're going tonight," Weston said. "Caroline took him there. Place called Bookbinder's."

"I've been there," she said, "a couple of times. I've gone as far as clam chowder and broiled flounder, but so far I haven't had the courage for lobster or oysters. Raw oysters."

"'I'd stay away from raw oysters if I were you," Weston said without thinking first.

Janice blushed.

Oh, shit. You and your big mouth. She's heard what oysters are supposed to do to you.

And she blushed. She's a nurse, she's heard everything, seen everything, and it hasn't touched her, otherwise she wouldn't be blushing.

"Yes, thank you, Captain Weston," Commander Jerome J. Kister, MC, USNR, said, as he took the barstool beside Janice Hardison, "I will permit you to buy me a drink. I spent most of the afternoon on the telephone about you."

"Do I have to buy you the drink before you tell me what happened?"

"Jim!" Janice said.

"Yes, you do," Kister said, "and let me say how delighted I am that you two have reached some sort of armistice."

"It was love at first sight," Weston said. "But she's having trouble adjusting to that."

"Oh, Jim!" Janice said.

"You mean all you wanted was a lobster?"

"I'm still not sure I want a lobster," she said.

"The Junior Assistant Deputy Surgeon General of the United States Navy," Kister said, hoping to turn their attention away from each other to him. When he had their attention, he went on, "Or was it the Deputy Assistant Junior Surgeon General?"

"You tell me," Weston said. "I'm all ears."

"Whatever his title," Kister said, "he's now the guy who makes decisions in cases like yours. He's a captain." He paused. "I suspect the sonofabitch was an obstetrician in civilian life," he sighed, "and I'd be very surprised to learn he's ever been afloat in anything larger than a canoe. Be that as it may, the Captain is *absolutely* unwilling to accept my professional opinion that you are no crazier than any other Marine. . . ."

"Oh, shit!" Weston said bitterly, and then, remembering the company, quickly added, "Sorry, Janice."

"He said that he was surprised that someone of my

experience would risk his reputation by making a snap judgment."

"So what happens now?" Jim asked, quietly furious.

"That was the bad news," Kister said. "Or almost all of it. I told you they—they being this obstetrician drunk with his own power—would challenge the physical you had at Pearl Harbor."

"And he did."

"And he did. But the good news is that he did agree to accept the opinion of the medical staff here vis à vis your general physical condition."

"I don't understand," Weston said.

"Presuming nothing bad shows up on your lab work— your blood, urine, that sort of thing, and I don't think it will—on the physical you took this morning, I can certify you as physically fit to enter upon your convalescent leave and get orders cut for you to go to the Greenbrier. You can be out of here in a couple of days, in other words."

The downside to that is that if I'm out of here, I will also be away from Janice.

"Explain that 'orders cut to go to the Greenbrier' to me."

"The Greenbrier is a luxury resort hotel in White Sulphur Springs, West Virginia, which you could not possibly afford under normal circumstances. In the abnormal circumstances existing today, however, you can, because it's free. The government has taken the place over, thrown out the undeserving rich, and made it available for the rest and rehabilitation of returned heroes such as yourself."

"And if I don't want to go to this luxury hotel in the wilds of West Virginia?"

"You don't seem to understand. You *will* be placed on orders. You *will*, on temporary *duty* for a period of thirty days, proceed to the Greenbrier Hotel. You *will* rest and recuperate, and incidentally be psychologically evaluated."

"By who? I thought you were the head doctor."

"By a fellow practitioner of the Freudian medical arts. Who enjoys, I think I should warn you, his reputation as one mean sonofabitch. Excuse me, Janice."

"In other words, this luxury hotel is a funny farm?"

"No. But the Navy wants to make absolutely sure that you are in possession of your faculties before you are turned loose on the public. They don't, for example, want you to slit the throat of your friendly neighborhood policeman because you think he is a Japanese soldier."

"Jim," Janice said, "some of the men who have gone through what you have gone through are really disturbed."

He looked at her, and found her compassion-filled eyes both disconcerting and pleasing.

That is not a professional, be-nice-to-the-loony look. I think she really likes me.

By "really disturbed" Janice means loony-tune time. I suppose that explains the ambulance and the two Corpsmen at the airport, and those two gorillas who took me to Ward Five-B.

"I'm not disturbed," he said.

"No," Dr. Kister said, "you're not. But the obstetrician in the Navy Department doesn't want to take any chances. From his point of view, he's just taking a routine precaution. And he has the authority."

"Damn!"

"So you will undergo at least four sessions of counseling and evaluation at the Greenbrier over a thirty-day period. Then you will return here, and presuming you can convince Dr. Bolemann that you pose no threat to the cop on the beat, or anyone else, I will be able to certify you as both physically and psychologically fit for flight status. Then you will go to Pensacola, Florida, where, according to General McInerney, you will be taught to fly all over again."

"Jesus."

"And I also have for you some advice from General McInerney—actually, it's more in the way of an order. You will do what you're told and keep your mouth shut. Are there any questions, Captain?"

"No, sir," Weston said. "Thanks, Doc."

"Nothing to thank me for," Commander Kister said. "I would have done whatever was necessary to get you out of my smooth-running hospital, and get you away from my nurses."

Janice chuckled.

"Can I drive to this place? Or is Janice going to take me there, strapped down to a stretcher in the back of an ambulance?"

"You could, if you had a car," Commander Kister said. "You don't, do you?"

"I was thinking of buying one," Weston said.

"I can see some problems with that," Kister said. "For one thing, have you got a driver's license?"

"I think mine has probably expired," Weston said.

"I'll bet it has," Kister said, chuckling. "Don't tell me you've been carrying it around all this time? In the steaming jungles of Mindanao?"

"No," Weston said, chuckling. "I'm going to have to get one."

"I could take you for your test," Janice said. "They give the test in Fairmount Park."

"Next problem, Doctor?" Weston asked, smiling at her.

"There's gasoline and tire rationing," Kister said. "The war, you know."

"I can deal with that," Weston said.

"And there is a nationwide thirty-five-mph speed limit," Kister said.

"Now, there's a problem," Weston said.

"Why the hell do you want a car?" Kister asked.

"So I can drive from this luxury funny farm you're sending me—"

"*I'm* not sending you," Kister interrupted. "A *grateful nation* is sending you. So far as I'm concerned, I'd put you to work. You've had a whole year off, lying around a tropical paradise, eating pineapples."

"And other interesting tropical fruit. Not much meat, but all the pineapples I could eat."

"Really?" Janice asked.

"This time, really really," he said. "We operated around the Dole pineapple plantations."

"It obviously didn't hurt you any," Kister said. "Maybe you should consider becoming a vegetarian."

"While I was munching on my pineapple, I used to have a dream. There I was, riding down the highway in my convertible Buick, with a pretty girl smiling at me.

The girl, if you must know, looked much like this fine young Naval officer."

"In the unlikely event that you're serious, you could probably get a deal on a Buick convertible."

"Is that so?"

"They guzzle gas. Gas is rationed. And this is the middle of the winter. No one in his right mind wants a gas-guzzling Buick convertible in the middle of the winter."

"You've convinced me," Weston said. "A Buick convertible it is."

"We're back to 'why do you need a car?' "

"So I can drive up here on weekends and see Janice," Weston said.

Kister's eyes swiveled back and forth between them.

Janice blushed.

"I think the time has come for me to fold my tent and silently steal away," Commander Kister said.

"Oh, doctor, don't go, please," Janice said.

"Okay," Kister said. "The three of us can go out and have a lobster."

He waited, with a straight face, until he saw the anguished looks on their faces. Then he chuckled, slapped Weston on the back, and walked out of the bar.

[FOUR]
The Marquis de Lafayette Suite
The Foster Lafayette Hotel
Washington, D.C.
1900 17 February 1943

Captain Kenneth R. McCoy, USMCR, was dozing when the telephone rang. He was almost instantly awake, but for a moment didn't know where he was. A moment later he did realize where he was, and also realized that Ernie wasn't in the bed with him. As he sat up and swung his feet out of the bed, he reached for the bedside telephone. The bathroom door was open, he noticed then, and Ernie was standing in it, naked except for a towel wrapped around her waist. She had another towel in her hand. As he watched, she resumed drying her hair with it.

"I was wondering if you were going to answer that," she said.

My God, she's beautiful!

"I must have dropped off," he said, and picked up the telephone.

"Lieutenant McCoy," he said.

"That's *Captain* McCoy, I think. Why don't you write that on the back of your hand?" Captain Edward Sessions, USMC, said.

"I guess I'm not used to being a captain," McCoy said. "What's up, Ed?"

Ernie was now leaning on the door, listening to the conversation. Dressed as she was, wearing nothing but the towel around her waist, and with most of her left leg peeking out through the flap in the towel, she was incredibly erotic. Even if she didn't mean to be.

Or is she doing that because she knows damned well how it will excite me?

"I've been appointed officer-in-charge of getting you off on your presidentially directed administrative leave," Sessions said.

"Which means what?"

"I've got your orders, new ID card, new credentials, et cetera, et cetera."

"You've been busy."

"And money. Another partial pay."

"And you want me to come over there?"

"No. I'll come there if you want. But what Jeanne wants is for you and Ernie to come over here. To the apartment, I mean. For dinner."

"What is it?" Ernie asked.

"Jeanne wants us to come for dinner," McCoy said.

"Great! I want to see the baby. Tell him yes."

"Unless, of course, we'd be interrupting something important," Sessions said. "I would understand that."

"Screw you," McCoy said.

"Jeanne wants to show Ernie the baby," Sessions said. "What time?"

"How soon could you come? We could have a couple of drinks."

"How soon could you be ready?" McCoy asked Ernie.

"Just as soon as I put some clothes on."

"Ernie says just as soon as she can get dressed," McCoy said.

"Damn you!" Ernie said. "You didn't have to say that!"

"Give me the address, again," McCoy said, and reached for the pencil and notepad beside the telephone.

Ernie removed the towel from around her waist, balled it up, and threw it at him. She waited long enough for him to dodge the towel and then turned back into the bathroom and closed the door after her. But not before offering him a good look at her fanny and hips.

And she did that on purpose, too!

What I really want to do is go in there after her, pick her up, and carry her back in here.

He thought about that for a moment, then stood up, walked to the bathroom and pulled open the door, and scooped her off her feet.

"What took you so long?" Ernie laughed. "I was beginning to wonder if you'd lost interest."

[FIVE]

There are two things wrong with babies, Captain McCoy thought, as he watched Ernie making cooing noises to the Sessionses' infant. *One, they make me uncomfortable. Second, sure as Christ made little apples, it will start Ernie off again, wanting one of her own. Our own. Damn!*

"Cute kid," he said to Captain Sessions.

"You ought to have one of your own," Sessions said.

Thanks a lot, pal.

"Listen to the man, Ken," Ernie said.

I'd like to break his fucking arm!

"You said you have a new ID for me?" McCoy said.

"Yeah, come on in the study. I've got a briefcase full of stuff for you," Sessions said.

"Oh, you're so *precious!*" Ernie said to Edward F. Sessions, Jr.

Ed Sessions stopped in his living room long enough to

make drinks for both of them, then led McCoy into his study, which was slightly larger than a closet, and motioned McCoy into its one upholstered chair.

He picked a briefcase up from the floor, set it on his small desk, and began taking things from it. "You really should, you know," he said, looking at McCoy.

"I really should what?"

"Marry her. Have a baby. That's what's it's all about, Ken."

"Oh, for Christ's sake! What do you think my chances are of coming through this war alive, in one piece? The one thing I don't want for Ernie is to be a widow with a baby. Or a loyal wife taking care of a one-legged, or vegetable, war veteran for the rest of her life."

"You've got to take the chance, Ken."

"Can we change the subject, please, before I punch you out?"

"That would be assault upon a superior officer, punishable by death, or such lesser punishment as a court-martial may decree," Sessions said solemnly. "Besides, I'm larger, stronger, and smarter than you are, capable, in other words, of whipping *your* ass. You should take that into consideration."

"Can we get on with this?" McCoy said, with a glance in the direction of the briefcase.

"Okay. Except that I have to say that with the exception, of course, of Jeanne, they don't come any better than the one you walked in here with just now."

"Yeah, I know. That's *why* I can't marry her. What's all that stuff?"

Sessions flipped him a plastic card.

"New identity card, to reflect the new railroad tracks on your shoulders. Incidentally, congratulations, Captain McCoy."

"Sometimes I wonder if the Corps knew what it was doing," McCoy said. "I don't think I'm qualified to be a captain."

"That's horseshit. You're better qualified to be a captain than ninety percent of the people walking around with captain's bars."

"Captains command companies. Do you really think I'm qualified to command a company?"

"Maybe the advanced officer course would do you some good," Sessions said after a moment, and very seriously. "But you already have a more important qualification they can't teach you at Quantico."

"Oh, yeah? What?"

"You know how to give orders," Sessions said. "When you tell people to do something, they just do it, and think about whether it's smart later. Most people, most captains, including me, don't have that ability."

McCoy met his eyes for a moment. "What other goodies have you got for me?" he asked.

Sessions handed him a stack of mimeographed orders. "That's your leave orders. Fifteen days. Administrative leave. It doesn't get charged against your accrued leave. DP."

"DP? What's that?"

"Direction of the President. Your pal Major Roosevelt called the Colonel and said his father ordered that personally."

"He's not my pal. I was a second lieutenant on the Makin raid. Specs was the skipper, and a captain."

"Tell *him* that. *He* thinks he's a pal of yours."

"Anything else?"

"Gasoline ration coupons, two hundred gallons' worth."

"My car's up on blocks at Ernie's parents' place in New Jersey."

"Take it off the blocks. Or aren't you planning to spend your leave with her?"

"What I meant was that it probably doesn't have plates on it."

"If I were Ernie, I would have paid for plates. That would get her gasoline coupons for her own car."

"And I'm sure my driver's license has expired."

"It's good for the duration plus six months," Sessions said. "Is there some reason you don't want to drive your car?"

"No, of course not," McCoy said. "You know, aside from my uniforms, things like that, that car is the only thing I own. I bought it when I came back from China. It's a 1939 LaSalle convertible. Silver."

"Really?"

"I paid five hundred twenty-five dollars for it," McCoy said. "It was the first decent car I ever owned, and I didn't want to sell it when I went overseas, and Ernie said I could leave it at the farm, so I did."

"So now you have a car. Enjoy it."

"Yeah," McCoy said thoughtfully. "I'll ask Ernie how much trouble it would be to get it off the blocks."

Sessions tossed him a small leather folder.

"New credentials. That was the Colonel's idea. He said the photograph on your old ones made you look like a high school cheerleader."

McCoy opened the folder. It contained a badge and a card sealed in plastic identifying McCoy, Kenneth R., as a Special Agent of the Office of Naval Intelligence.

"I'll have to have the old one back," Sessions said.

"I don't have them."

"Ken, they're not supposed to leave your person," Sessions said.

"I didn't think I'd need them in the Philippines, so I left them in the safe in Water Lily Cottage in Brisbane. And forgot about them."

"The Colonel will be thrilled to hear that," Sessions said.

"I don't think it makes any difference," McCoy said. "Maybe you better keep these."

"Meaning what?"

"After he showed me that Special Channel from the President, the first thing General Pickering said was 'welcome to the OSS, Captain McCoy.' I don't think I belong to Colonel Rickabee anymore."

"Did the General say anything about taking Management Analysis into the OSS lock, stock, and barrel?"

"No," McCoy said. "I don't think that's going to happen, though. I think he would have said something."

"Rickabee's worried about that," Sessions said. "The guy who runs the OSS has been trying to get us all along. Or shut us down."

"I don't think that will happen."

"I hope you're right, Ken. God knows, I don't . . ."

". . . want to go in the OSS?" McCoy finished. "Well, maybe *you'll* get lucky."

"What have you got against the OSS?" Sessions said.

"The only nice thing I can think of about being in the OSS is that probably, now, I won't get parachuted into the Gobi Desert . . . which is what you bastards had in mind for me."

"The last scuttlebutt I heard about that was that the Army Air Corps got to Admiral Leahy, and he told the Navy, which means Management Analysis, to butt out. The Air Corps's going to set up a weather station in Russia."

"Good luck to them!" McCoy said.

"Pickering didn't tell you what you'll be doing?"

"I don't think he knows. I don't think he knows what *he'll* be doing."

Sessions grunted but said nothing. He went back into the briefcase and came out with a stuffed business-size envelope.

"And this little jewel contains your partial pay. One thousand bucks."

"I drew a partial in Pearl Harbor," McCoy said. "But as you pointed out, I will be spending some time with Ernie, which means I'm going to need this. Thank you."

"That's about it," Sessions said. "I think you better keep those credentials."

"Whatever you say."

"How do you feel about lying to me?"

"Not good. About what?"

"You could tell me you destroyed your credentials before going into the Philippines. Or while you were there. And then I'll send a Special Channel to Pluto, and tell him to go in the safe, find your credentials, and burn them. It would keep you out of hot water with the Colonel."

"What's he going to do? Send me to the OSS?"

Sessions chuckled, then detected an odd tone in the way McCoy was looking at him.

"What, Ken?"

"You've been in Washington too long, Ed. You're learning to lie like the rest of the bastards around here."

"I was just trying to be helpful," Sessions said.

"Yeah, I know you were," McCoy said. He held up his nearly empty glass. "You got any more of this stuff?"

"Absolutely," Sessions said, and went to fix fresh drinks.

VI

[ONE]
Muku-Muku
Oahu, Territory of Hawaii
1345 17 February 1943

When Second Lieutenant George F. Hart, USMCR, saw
Brigadier General Fleming Pickering, USMCR, walk onto
the patio at Muku-Muku wearing a terry-cloth bathrobe,
he quickly slid out of the inner tube he had been floating
in, swam to the side of the pool, and hoisted himself out.
He almost lost his borrowed, too-large swimming trunks
in the process.

"You manage to get some sleep, sir?" he asked, as he
pulled the trunks up.

"Not a goddamn wink, thank you just the same," Pickering said. "Every time I closed my eyes, there was Wild
Bill Donovan leering at me from the fires of hell."

Hart chuckled. "Now what, sir?"

"You get on the horn, George, call the flag secretary at
CINCPAC and ask if Admiral Nimitz can give me ten or

fifteen minutes to make my manners. And then we'll have some lunch. Or did you eat?"

"I thought I'd wait for you, sir."

"Did you check on our flight?"

"Yes, sir, it's laid on for 1945."

"You better tell the flag secretary that time," Pickering said.

"Aye, aye, sir."

Pickering nodded, slipped out of the terry-cloth robe, and took a running dive into the pool. He swam the length of the large pool in a smooth breaststroke, turned, swam back, and repeated the process. He hauled himself out of the pool, put the terry-cloth robe back on, and looked at Hart, who pointed at the telephone.

"I'm waiting for it to . . ." Hart began. The telephone rang. Hart picked it up. "General Pickering's quarters, Lieutenant Hart speaking, sir." He listened a moment. "I'm sure the General will find that convenient, sir. Thank you very much." He replaced the telephone in its cradle.

"What time will he see me, George?"

" 'If General Pickering does not find this inconvenient, CINCPAC and Admiral Wagam will call on him at 1600,' " Hart quoted.

"You made it clear, I hope, George, that I wanted to go into Pearl Harbor?"

"Yes, sir. The flag secretary told me he would speak with Admiral Nimitz and see what could be arranged. And call me back. He just did."

"I wonder what they want?"

"They probably want an excuse to get out of CINCPAC for an hour or so," Hart said.

Pickering walked to the wall beside the glass doors leading into the house and pushed a button mounted on it.

Denny Williamson appeared almost immediately. "Ready for a little lunch, Captain?" he asked.

"Denny, I done told you two times already," Hart said, smiling. "I ain't gonna tell you no more. It's *General* Pickering."

"Maybe to you, young man," the elderly black man said. "Not to me."

"Admirals Nimitz and Wagam will be here at four, Denny," Pickering said. "I don't know how long they'll stay, but be prepared for a light supper. Hart and I have to be at Pearl Harbor by quarter to seven."

"What you should do, you know, is not be at Pearl Harbor tonight, and not tomorrow night, either. You need a couple of days off," Denny said.

"You sound like my wife."

"I got my orders from Mrs. Pickering. You show up here, I'm supposed to keep you for a couple of days."

"I really wish I could stay a couple of days, Denny."

"We'll lose the whole war if you do, right?"

"Absolutely," Pickering said. "Could you broil a piece of fish for lunch, Denny? Maybe with a salad?"

"Yes, sir, Captain. Anything special for you, young man?"

"That sounds good to me, Denny."

[TWO]

Admirals Nimitz and Wagam arrived in separate cars at almost precisely four P.M. Nimitz was riding in a black 1939 Cadillac sedan, from the front fender of which flew a blue flag with four stars. Wagam was in a Navy, gray Plymouth, which carried a blue plate with two stars where a license plate would normally go.

A portly captain Pickering did not recognize was in the Cadillac with Nimitz. Lieutenant Chambers D. Lewis III, whom Pickering and Hart had last seen in Brisbane, was in the backseat of the Plymouth with Wagam.

Pickering, who had been waiting on the mansion's wide verandah, walked down the shallow flight of stairs in time to meet Nimitz's Cadillac when it stopped. Nimitz stepped out, Pickering saluted, and Nimitz returned it, then offered his hand.

"Thank you for finding time for me, Admiral," Pickering said.

"I'm a little embarrassed about inviting myself out here, Fleming," Nimitz said, "but I've learned that the only way to keep people from interrupting a conversation is not to let them know where I am."

"You're always welcome here, sir," Pickering said.

"I don't think you know Groscher, do you, Fleming?" Nimitz said, indicating the captain.

I know that name from somewhere, Pickering thought, *but I have never seen this fellow before.*

"How do you do, General?" Captain Groscher said.

By then Admiral Wagam and Lieutenant Lewis were out of their car.

"Good to see you again, Admiral," Pickering said, offering his hand, and smiled at Lewis. "Back on the gossip-and-canapé circuit, I see, Chambers."

"No thanks to you, Fleming," Wagam said, smiling. "He quickly let me know he'd rather have stayed on Mindanao."

"Come on in the house, and we'll see if Denny can't find us something to drink," Pickering said.

"I was hoping you might have something like that in mind," Nimitz said.

They walked through the house to the patio in the rear, where Denny had set up a bar.

Nimitz accepted a Famous Grouse with a little water and no ice, stirred it, and took a sip. Then he looked at Pickering and smiled. "How is Mrs. Pickering?" he asked politely. "Well, I trust?"

"She's doing such a hell of a job running Pacific and Far East, I may not be able to get my job back when the war's over. I tried to call her when I got here."

Patricia Pickering had taken over the management of the Pacific & Far East Shipping Corporation when her husband entered the service. In her husband's judgment— quickly proven—she was the best-qualified person to do so.

"And couldn't get through? I know what the commercial phone service is these days. I think we could bend the rules a little and give you a couple of minutes on one of my lines."

"That's very kind of you, sir," Pickering said. "But P & FE has a dedicated line from the Honolulu office to

San Francisco. The switchboard patched me through on it from here."

"And she was delighted to hear you're coming home?"

"They weren't sure whether she's in Boston or Savannah, but they promised to do their best to get the word to her."

Nimitz chuckled. "Remember that song from the First War, Fleming? 'How are you going to keep them down on the farm, after they've seen Paree'?"

"Sure."

"How are we going to get our ladies back in the kitchen after they've proved they can do anything we do at least as well as we can?"

"It may take whips and chains," Pickering said.

"You've heard there are now lady Marines?" Nimitz asked.

Pickering nodded.

"And how do you feel about that?"

"I decline to answer the question on the grounds that it may incriminate me," Pickering replied.

Nimitz chuckled, and then something in his manner told Pickering the small-talk period was over. "Following the hoary tradition that the best way to know what a junior officer is really thinking is to make him speak first, Fleming, what's on your mind?" Nimitz asked.

"Sir, I wanted to pay my respects," Pickering said. "And to thank you for providing the *Sunfish*."

The submarine *Sunfish* had carried McCoy and his team into Mindanao, and then it had brought him and the others out.

"Thank you for understanding why I didn't want to give you the *Narwhal*," Nimitz said. "I was under orders to give you anything you thought you needed."

"The *Sunfish* worked out well, Admiral," Pickering said.

"I had the idea you might have wanted to talk about your new appointment," Nimitz said.

"I'd hoped we could talk about that, too, sir," Pickering said.

"Good, because that's the reason I wanted to see you. I have an ax to grind, Fleming."

"Sir?"

"What time's your flight to San Diego?"

"Nineteen forty-five, sir," Pickering said.

"Chambers," Nimitz ordered, "get on the horn to Flight Operations at Pearl, and tell them . . . No. Just get me the duty officer at Flight Operations."

Lieutenant Lewis walked to the telephone, dialed a number from memory, then carried the telephone to Nimitz.

"Commander, this is Admiral Nimitz," CINCPAC announced. "General Pickering and his aide may be a little late arriving at Pearl Harbor. Make sure the *Coronado* flight scheduled for nineteen forty-five doesn't leave without them."

He handed the telephone back to Lieutenant Lewis.

"Doing that is probably spinning wheels; but I like to err on the side of caution," Nimitz said. He turned to the portly captain. "Okay, Groscher, here's your chance to make your pitch to the OSS's Director of Pacific Operations."

"Yes, sir," Captain Groscher said. "General, I'm sure that you're aware that timely weather information is of great value to the Navy."

"You can skip that, Groscher. General Pickering has spent as much time on the bridge of a ship as I have," Nimitz interrupted. "He knows how important weather forecasting is."

"Yes, sir," Groscher said, flushing. It took him a moment to collect his thoughts, and then he decided his duty required him to disagree with the Commander in Chief, Pacific. "Admiral, with respect, I'd be more comfortable if I took General Pickering through this step by step."

Nimitz looked at him coldly for a moment.

"Fleming, intelligence officers are like lawyers," he said finally. "You either take their advice or you get yourself another one. Go ahead, Groscher."

Intelligence officer? Pickering wondered. *I thought he was Nimitz's aide.*

"General," Groscher began again, "the movement of arctic air masses across Russia through Mongolia and China into the Pacific . . ."

My God, he's talking about that Gobi Desert weather station operation. I thought I was through with that!

That quick suspicion proved correct. For nearly ten minutes, Captain Groscher, speaking entirely from memory, explained in great detail why the Navy was now handicapped, and would be even more handicapped in the future, by a lack of accurate and timely weather information from the area around the Russia-Mongolia border. Throughout the briefing, Pickering was impressed with Admiral Nimitz's detailed knowledge of the situation. The pertinent questions CINCPAC asked indicated how important Nimitz considered the establishment of a weather-transmitting radio station.

Groscher introduced a number of factors Pickering had previously either not known or not given much thought to. The strength and direction of winds aloft was enormously important to Naval Aviation operations at sea now, and would become more important when—as seemed very likely—the time came for the Navy to strike the enemy home islands from carriers. And even more important when the Army Air Corps began strategic bombing of the Japanese home islands with heavy bombers, including the new B-29.

It had never occurred to Pickering, either, that weather information was a critical factor in the direction of fire from the enormous naval cannon on battleships and cruisers.

Groscher also spoke of geopolitical considerations. Pickering remembered hearing—but not particularly caring—that the Japanese had taken the last emperor of China from his palace in Tientsin (where, stripped of power, he had been in something like house arrest) to Manchuria. There they had installed him as Emperor of Manchuko. Manchuko (formerly Manchuria) was the first nation to join with the Japanese in their Greater Asian Co-Prosperity Sphere. The Emperor of Manchuko, Captain Groscher related, had invited his new Japanese allies to station troops in his domain, and they had done so, which meant that the United States could not use Manchuko/Manchuria—which would have been ideal for the purpose—as a base for a weather station.

That left either the Soviet Union or the Gobi Desert within Mongolia as the only place where such a weather station could be—*had* to be—established. So far as Captain Groscher was concerned, the chances were nonexistent that the Soviet Union would permit the establishment of a weather station/radio station on their territory.

Pickering learned for the first time that the Soviet Union was holding close to one hundred American airmen (and no one knew how many British or other allied airmen) who for one reason or another had landed on Soviet territory. Predictably, the Soviets denied this, even when presented with names, ranks, serial numbers, aircraft tail numbers, and in some cases photographs of the downed airmen in Russia.

"By a process of elimination," Captain Groscher said, "that leaves the Gobi Desert."

Pickering next learned that the Gobi Desert was not, as he had previously pictured in his mind's eye, a vast area of shifting sands. Actually it had very little sand. The terrain was rock, most of it flat. It was possible, he learned, to drive an ordinary automobile for hundreds of miles in any direction without difficulty. Presuming, of course, one had fuel.

As it had been for a thousand years, the area was regularly traversed east to west, and north to south, by camel caravans. The first contact with the handful of Americans who were wandering around in the vast rocky Gobi Desert had been messages sent out on several camel caravans that had reached India.

There had been three messages, Groscher reported. Each had said about the same thing: There were retired U.S. military personnel in the desert. They were trying to reach Allied lines. They had a shortwave receiver and would monitor a frequency in the twenty-meter band at 1200 Greenwich time whenever possible.

Each message was signed differently, Groscher went on. With the rank and initials (not the full name) of individuals who had retired from the Yangtze River patrol, the 15th U.S. Army Infantry Regiment, and the 4th Marines.

"From the available records," Groscher said, "we determined that indeed there was a Chief Motor Machinist's Mate Frederick C. Brewer—corresponding with the initials FCB on one message—who retired from the Yangtze River patrol. And a Staff Sergeant Willis T. Cawber, Jr.—corresponding with the initials WTCJr on another—who retired from the 17th Infantry. And there was a Sergeant James R. Sweatley—corresponding with the initials on the third message—who was assigned to the Marine detachment in Peking, and was presumed to have become a Japanese POW."

"When contact was first established with Fertig in the Philippines," Pickering observed, "there was some question whether it might be a Japanese trick."

"Our gut feeling has been that's not the case here," Groscher replied. "Meanwhile, we were investigating ways to get radio transmitters in to these people, when they suddenly came on the air themselves. Their radio equipment is almost certainly cobbled together from whatever they could lay their hands on, is not very good when it works, and doesn't work very often. But it does give us a communications link with them."

"The transmitter Fertig used to first establish contact with the outside was built by a Filipino sergeant with parts from the sound apparatus of a movie projector," Pickering said.

"The one in the Gobi was probably built by some retired electrician's mate," Groscher said. "Most of these people are probably Yangtze River patrol sailors."

"Why do you say that?" Nimitz asked, as Pickering opened his mouth to ask the same thing.

"Sir, the records indicate that there are far more retired Yangtze sailors in China than Marines, by a factor of five; and by a factor of seven, more river patrol retirees than soldiers."

"Is that somehow significant?" Pickering asked.

"Sailors rarely have—what shall I say?—'the live off the land skills,' or the ability to function as infantry that Marines and soldiers may be presumed to have," Groscher said. "Consequently, when we have to ask the question 'what shape are these people in?' we are forced to operate on the least pleasant likelihood. That is to say, these people are probably more on the order of a group of nomads than anything resembling a military force of any description, especially considering that they are accompanied by women and children."

"A point which the Army Air Corps has made, time and again, to the Joint Chiefs of Staff," Nimitz said. "And, I'm afraid, with justification."

"I've been around the fringes of this, Admiral," Pickering said. "But until now I didn't know what it was really all about."

"Politics are at play, of course," Nimitz interrupted him. "The State Department doesn't want to do or say anything that might annoy our Russian allies, which means we can forget about sending anyone into Mongolia through the Soviet Union. The Army Air Corps are convinced that they should be in charge of this, but they don't really have any sense of urgency. B-29s are not going to bomb the Japanese home islands this year, and probably not until late in 1944. The Navy needs a weather station *now*."

Nimitz, Pickering thought, probably figures that I will now have Donovan's ear, and will be able to plead his case to him. That's why he brought Groscher here.

The problem is that my support of a project like this— my advocacy of any project, for that matter—would be the kiss of death for it in Donovan's eyes.

"Sir," Pickering said. "I'm probably missing something here. But what has this got to do with me?"

"I had a Special Channel from Admiral Leahy two days ago," Nimitz said. "It was the decision of the Joint Chiefs of Staff that the responsibility for determining whether or not the Americans in the Gobi Desert can be used to set up a weather station and get it running will be given to the OSS."

"Admiral, I'm sure that the OSS will do whatever it can."

"Yesterday I sent Admiral Leahy a special channel message expressing my belief that you were the obvious choice within the OSS to assume this responsibility, and asked him to exert his influence to see that you are so assigned."

"I wish I shared your confidence in me," Pickering said. "And I am sure Mr. Donovan doesn't."

"I ask very few favors of Admiral Leahy," Nimitz said. "He generally gives me what I ask for. And so far as Mr. Donovan is concerned, I wouldn't be at all surprised if Admiral Leahy brought the matter up with the President before he discussed your participation in it with Mr. Donovan. And the President, to my knowledge, has never refused Admiral Leahy anything he's asked for."

"I'm back to repeating I wish I shared your confidence in me," Pickering said.

"It should go without saying that CINCPAC will support you in any way we can," Nimitz said. "Groscher has a MAGIC clearance, so you can communicate with him using the Special Channel. And Admiral Wagam will coordinate things, and advise me of any problems."

"Yes, sir," Pickering said. "Sir, may I ask a question?"

"Of course."

"For the sake of argument, suppose that I can—the OSS can—establish contact with these people. Then what? According to Captain Groscher, the odds are that they're nothing more than—what did you say, Groscher?—nomads."

Nimitz acted as if the question—or perhaps Pickering's naïveté—surprised him.

"Fleming, the situation is very much like what you just did with this Fertig fellow on Mindanao. Once you have sent people in to meet with these people and established reliable two-way radio communication with them, we will have a force—a *Naval force*—in position. Then the Navy can reinforce that force. I'm sure that I will be able to convince Admiral Leahy that reinforcing a force in being is a far more sound proposition than waiting for our Russian allies to permit the Air Corps to establish a weather station on their territory."

"Yes, sir," Pickering said.

VII

[ONE]
Carlucci's Bar & Grill
South Fourth Street
Philadelphia, Pennsylvania
1615 18 February 1943

"Why are we stopping here?" Janice asked dubiously.

Carlucci's Bar & Grill did not look like the sort of place one took young ladies for a romantic cocktail and supper.

"I have to go in here for a minute," Weston said. "Would you like to wait in the car?"

Just over two hours previously, when Captain James B. Weston, USMCR, had taken possession of it, the interior of the 1941 dark green Buick Roadmaster convertible had reeked of tanned leather. It now smelled of whatever perfume Lieutenant (j.g.) Janice Hardison, NNC, had dabbed behind her ears—or in more intimate places—just before meeting him outside the gate of the Philadelphia U.S. Navy Hospital.

It was a significant improvement, although, pre-Janice, Weston had always had a soft place in his heart for the smell of leather in a convertible.

"You're going in there?" Janice asked. "Why?"

"It affects our future life together," he said. "Beyond that, I'd rather not say. And I don't think you would want to know."

"Jim, what are you up to?" she asked, half annoyed, half plaintive.

"It won't take me long," he said, and stepped out of the car.

"Wait a minute," she said. "You're not leaving me here alone."

Carlucci's Bar & Grill smelled primarily of beer and cigarette and cigar smoke, although there was a more subtle odor both Janice and Jim associated with Italian restaurants. Most of the seats at the long bar were occupied by large males, who looked as if they worked in the Naval shipyard, Janice thought, or possibly as stevedores on the Philadelphia waterfront. They found seats near the far end of the bar.

A very large, swarthy bartender who needed a shave put both hands on the bar and leaned toward them to inquire, "What'll it be?"

"Scotch, twice," Weston said. "One light, one heavy."

The drinks were served. Weston laid currency on the bar.

"Anything else I can do for you, pal?"

"I was hoping I could talk to Mario," Weston said.

"You're a friend of Dominic's, right?"

"Right. You're Mario?"

The two men shook hands.

Mario turned to the cash register behind him, opened it, lifted an interior drawer, took an envelope from it, and handed it to Weston, who glanced quickly at what it contained, then put it into an inner pocket of his tunic.

"And you got something for me, right?" Mario asked.

Weston took a thick wad of bills from his pocket, peeled money from it, and laid it on the bar.

Mario picked the money up and put it in his trousers pocket.

"I can take care of your other problem, too, if you want," Mario said.

"The sooner the better," Jim said.

"Right now soon enough?"

"How long would that take?"

"Not longer than it would take you to have some pasta," Mario said, nodding at four tables just beyond the extreme end of the bar. "If you don't gulp it down."

"How do you feel about pasta, Janice?" Jim Weston inquired.

"We also got sausage, pepper, and onions," Mario suggested helpfully.

"Fine!" Janice said, without much conviction.

Weston reached into his pocket and handed Mario the keys to the Buick. Mario walked down the bar, spoke softly to an equally large man sipping a beer, and handed him the keys. The man walked out of the bar.

Mario returned to Janice and Jim.

"If you don't like pasta," he said to Janice, "the sausage and peppers is really nice."

"Thank you," Janice said.

"Are you going to tell me what's going on?" Janice asked, almost whispered, after their order had been taken by a very large middle-aged woman in a big white apron. "What's in that envelope that man gave you? Where is the other man going with your car?"

"You are an officer and gentlelady of the Naval Service," Jim said. "You don't want to know. Besides, haven't you seen the poster? 'Loose Lips Sink Ships!'?"

"Jim, I want to know!" Janice said, in such a manner that Jim understood she really wanted to know.

He handed her the envelope. She looked into it, then quickly handed it back.

She looked at him, shaking her head in disbelief.

"That's dishonest!" she said. "I can't believe you did that!"

"It's *not* dishonest," he said. "Dishonesty, by definition, means telling people lies. He had something I wanted, and I paid him what he wanted for it. Where's the dishonesty?"

"It's . . . it's unpatriotic!"

"There's a war on, right?"

"Yes, there is, and the armed forces need every gallon of gasoline they can get, and here you are—"

"The armed forces get all the gasoline they need," Weston said. "The shortage is of rubber. The thinking is that the less people drive, the less they will wear out their tires. I can understand that."

"But you're going to drive. . . . My God, I don't know how many gasoline ration coupons were in that envelope!"

"There's supposed to be enough to buy a thousand gallons of gas," Jim said. "I didn't count them. Mario, I thought, has an honest face."

"But you're going to wear out your tires. Doesn't that bother you?"

"I'm going to contribute my already worn-out tires—the ones that came with the car—to the very next rubber-salvage campaign I come across. Unless, of course, Mario's friend takes care of that for me."

She looked at him for just a moment until she took his meaning.

"Is that where he went with your car? To put new tires on it?"

"God, I hope they're new. But anything would be better than the tires that came with it. I'd never have made it out of Philadelphia on those tires, much less to the wilds of West Virginia. Much less back here to see you."

"You're absolutely incredible!"

"Thank you!"

"I meant to say 'shameless,' " Janice said.

"Shamelessly in love with you," he said. "What would you have preferred? That I die of a broken heart in Sulfuric Acid Springs, West Virginia?"

"White Sulphur Springs," she corrected him.

"Because, because of a few lousy gallons of gasoline, and four tires, I was separated from her whom I love beyond measure?"

"Will you please knock off that 'you love me' business?" Janice said, but Jim didn't think she really meant it. He thought he saw that in her eyes.

[TWO]
The 21 Club
21 West Fifty-second Street
New York City, New York
1745 18 February 1943

Ernest Sage was sitting at the extreme end of the bar, his back against the wall, sipping his second martini. He was a superbly tailored, slightly built, and very intense man, a month shy of his fiftieth birthday, and wore his black hair slicked straight back with generous applications of Smootheee, one of the 213 personal products of American Personal Pharmaceuticals, the company whose board he chaired. He was, as well, its chief executive officer.

When his only child, Ernestine, and her gentleman friend, Captain Kenneth R. McCoy, USMCR, entered the room, he fixed a not entirely genuine smile on his face and raised his right arm to attract their attention. His daughter smiled warmly and genuinely when she saw him. As always, this warmed him.

Captain McCoy's smile was as strained as Ernest Sage's.

"Hiya, Daddy," Ernestine said, and kissed him.

"Hello, Princess," he said, and hugged her.

Oh, Princess, why did you have to get yourself involved with this character?

"Hello, Ken," he said, offering his hand. "It's good to see you. Welcome home."

"Thank you, sir."

"Charley, see what the Lieutenant will have," Sage said to the bartender.

"It's *Captain*, Daddy," Ernie said. "*One* silver bar, first lieutenant. *Two* silver bars, captain."

Oh shit. I knew that. Every time I get around him, I make an ass of myself.

"Well, then, I guess congratulations are in order."

"They certainly are," Ernie said. "And notice the new fruit salad," Ernie said, pointing at McCoy's ribbon-bedecked tunic. "That's the Silver Star, the third-highest decoration for valor."

"Oh, Christ, Ernie," McCoy said.

"He got it from General MacArthur personally," Ernie went on, undaunted.

"Scotch," McCoy, now very uncomfortable, said to the bartender. "Famous Grouse if you have it. A double."

"Ernie, you're embarrassing Captain McCoy," her father said.

"You can call him 'Ken,' Daddy. We're lovers."

"Jesus, Ernie!" McCoy protested.

Ernest Sage pretended he had not heard his daughter. "You got to meet General MacArthur, did you, Ken?"

"And yesterday he briefed President Roosevelt," Ernie said. "In the White House."

"Did he really?" Sage asked, and then curiosity got the best of him. "I'm not sure what that means, 'briefed.' "

"It's sort of a report, sir."

"A report on what?"

McCoy hesitated before answering. The operation had been classified Top Secret, but that was no longer the case. After McCoy's briefing, the President had ordered Navy Secretary Knox to put out a press release: "It will do great things for morale, Frank," President Roosevelt had said, "for the public to learn that these brave men refused to surrender and are carrying on the fight against the Japanese in the Philippines."

"There's a guerrilla force operating in the Philippines," McCoy said.

"A gorilla force?" Sage asked, dubiously.

Ernie laughed at him. She started pounding her chest with balled fists.

"Hundreds of King Kong's cousins," she said, "beating their chests. And looking for Japanese to rip apart. *Guerrillas*, Daddy. Probably from the French *guerre*, meaning 'war.' "

Ernest Sage saw that *Captain* McCoy was smiling, approvingly and fondly, at his only child. "I hadn't heard that," Ernest Sage said.

"It was classified until yesterday," McCoy said.

"And how did you come to know about these *guerrillas*, Ken?"

"He went into the Philippines and made contact with them," Ernie said.

"That's enough, Ernie," McCoy said flatly. "Put a lid on it."

Ernie looked stricken. She did not like McCoy's disapproval.

"Am I asking questions I shouldn't be asking?" Ernest Sage said.

"Sir, I really don't know how much of this is still classified," McCoy said.

The waiter delivered McCoy's double Famous Grouse and stood poised over it with a small silver water pitcher in one hand and a soda siphon bottle in the other.

McCoy held up his hand to signify he wanted neither, then picked up the glass and took a sip.

"What can I get you, Miss Sage?" the bartender asked.

"I'll just help myself to his. He had several . . . too many . . . on the train on the way up here."

McCoy overrode this decision by signaling the bartender to give her her own drink. She did not press the issue.

"Daddy, to change the subject, what about Ken's car?"

At last, a safe subject.

"I called the man at the Cadillac place in Summit," Sage said. "He's sending a mechanic out to the farm. You should have it tomorrow morning sometime."

"I was hoping we could have it today," Ernie said.

"Princess, it's too late for you two to drive anywhere today," Sage said. "This way, we can go out to the farm, have a nice dinner—your mother is making a welcome-home dinner for Ken, turkey—get a good night's sleep. . . ."

"Ken's only got fifteen days, Daddy!"

"It's all right," McCoy said. "Thank you, Mr. Sage."

Sage nodded his acceptance of the thanks and went on: "And I have gasoline ration coupons—don't ask me where I got them—for a hundred gallons of gas."

"You bought them on the black market," Ernie said. "To replace the ration coupons—*Ken's* ration coupons—you 'borrowed' from me." Ernest Sage raised his eyebrows.

"I wasn't going to renew the license plates, honey," Ernie went on. "But Daddy talked me into it. He said we could use the gasoline ration coupons."

Here I stand with a man who just got a medal from General MacArthur, and my daughter takes pains to let him know I'm supporting the war effort by using his gasoline ration.

"I've got coupons for two hundred gallons," McCoy said. "Ed Sessions gave them to me when he gave me my leave orders."

"We'll take his—actually, they're yours—anyhow," Ernie said.

McCoy said nothing.

The guest room given to Captain Kenneth R. McCoy was on the ground floor of the left wing of the Sage house. The bedroom of the daughter of his hosts was on the second floor of the right wing. There was no way her parents could have separated them farther, Captain Mc-Coy realized, unless they had put him in the stable.

On one hand, McCoy was well aware that if he himself had been in the shoes of Mr. and Mrs. Ernest Sage, he would have put this guy who'd caught their daughter's attention in the stable, hoping that with a little bit of luck, one of the horses would go nuts and trample him to death.

On the other hand, the prospect of sleeping without Ernie was unpleasant. They were going to have only fifteen days. If that much. He would not have been at all surprised if something came up . . . "Sorry, get here as soon as you can."

Shit, I didn't call in.

He picked up the telephone, gave the operator the number of the Office of Management Analysis duty officer, assured her the call was necessary, and waited for her to put it through.

Major Banning answered the phone by giving the number.

"McCoy, sir. I'm at Ernie's father's place."

"I thought you might be. I have the number. Having fun?"

"Whoopee!"

"The Boss is back, Ken. He called a while back from Los Angeles. He said to pass 'well done' to you for the presidential briefing. I guess Senator Fowler gave him a report."

"What happens now?"

"You take your leave, Captain McCoy. You *will* have a good time. That's an order. But check in, Ken, please."

"Aye, aye, sir."

Captain McCoy was shortly afterward informed by the Sage butler that Mr. Sage was in the study and wondered if Captain McCoy might wish to join him for a drink.

They were joined in the study by Miss and Mrs. Sage, and dinner followed shortly thereafter. It was roast turkey stuffed with oysters and chestnuts.

"A belated Christmas dinner, Ken," Elaine Sage said. She was a striking, silver-haired woman in her late forties. Ken often imagined Ernie looking like that when she was forty-something.

"That's very kind. Thank you."

"I don't suppose you had a Christmas dinner, did you?"

"The Armed Forces go to great lengths to provide a turkey dinner with all the trimmings to the boys, wherever they are," Ernest Sage said. "Isn't that so, Ken?"

"Yes, sir."

"Where were you on Christmas, Ken?" Ernie asked.

I was marching through the jungles of Mindanao, hoping I could find Fertig before the Japs did. Or before they found me.

"Actually, I did have Christmas dinner," he said, "on a Navy ship."

Two days early. Nice gesture from the Sunfish's *skipper.*

"You see?" Ernest Sage said triumphantly.

"It wasn't as good as this," Ken said.

"Have another glass of wine, Ken," Ernest Sage said.

Following dinner, there was coffee and brandy in the study, and then Miss Sage announced she was tired and was going to go to bed.

Captain McCoy and Ernest Sage shared another cognac, and then they, too, went to their respective bedrooms.

Captain McCoy was more than a little surprised to find that his bed already had an occupant.

"Jesus, Ernie," he said. "They'll know."

"No," she said. "They are determined not to know. Come to bed, baby."

[THREE]
The Greenbrier Hotel
White Sulphur Springs, West Virginia
1825 22 February 1943

On the nearly ten-hour drive from Philadelphia, Captain James B. Weston came to two philosophical conclusions.

The first: there were concrete benefits attached to being a Marine Aviator and certified hero. That proposition had three proofs. The first came in Mercersburg, Pennsylvania, where he had been pulled to the side of the road by a highly indignant Pennsylvania state trooper.

"I've been chasing you for five miles," the trooper had begun the conversation. "Do you know how fast you were going?"

"No, sir."

"Seventy, seventy-five. The wartime speed limit is thirty-five, for Christ's sake."

"I didn't realize I was going that fast."

"Well, goddamn it, you were!"

"Yes, sir. I'm sure you're right."

"I'll need to see some identification, and your orders," the state trooper said, and added, "There's been people wearing uniforms who ain't even in the armed forces."

The trooper's tone of voice suggested he suspected—and indeed hoped—he now had such a person in custody.

"Just got out of the hospital, did you, Captain?" the trooper asked when he handed Jim's identity card and orders back to him.

"Yes, sir."

"Going home, are you?"

"Actually, sir, I'm going to the Greenbrier Hotel."

"I saw that on the orders," the trooper said. "I'd have

thought they'd have shut that place down for the duration."

"No, sir, the government's taken it over."

"What for?"

"It's where they send people when they come back
from overseas," Jim said.

"You just came back from overseas?"

"Yes, sir."

"And you're just out of the hospital. How the hell am
I going to give someone like you a ticket?"

Weston did not reply.

"If I let you go, will you promise to slow it down a
little?"

"Yes, sir."

"I don't think any cop would give someone like you—
especially in a car like this, with good rubber—a ticket
for going fifty or fifty-five. But *seventy-five!*"

"Yes, sir."

"Drive careful, Captain. Now that you're home safe,
you really ought to take care of yourself."

"Yes, sir. Thank you."

The state trooper saluted. Weston crisply returned it.

He had a similar conversation with a deputy sheriff near
Romney, West Virginia, who had clocked him at sixty-
five. The deputy sheriff confided in Weston that he was
thinking of enlisting in the Marine Corps himself. Weston
told him he felt sure the Marines could put a man with
his training to good use. And promised to hold it down.

The third proof came when he filled the Buick's tank
in Frost, West Virginia, about fifty miles shy of White
Sulphur Springs. The service station attendant refused to
accept gasoline ration coupons for the transaction.

"They give us an allowance for spillage and evapora-
tion," the man confided. "More than what we actually
spill, or what evaporates . . . we call it 'overage.' I generally save my overage for when some serviceman like
you comes in."

"That's very kind of you," Jim said, meaning: "I'll use
the gasoline to go see my girl."

"Anytime you come through here . . ."

"That's really very nice of you. I'll take you up on it."

The second philosophical conclusion Captain Weston reached while driving to the Greenbrier Hotel was that he was in love with Janice Hardison.

And from the way she had kissed him that morning when he left her, there was reason to suspect she didn't regard him as the ugly frog, either.

God, she is sweet!

A Navy petty officer of some rating Weston didn't recognize sat behind the desk in the Greenbrier lobby.

Probably desk clerk's mate, second class.

"Yes, sir?"

"Do I report in here? Or check in here?" Weston asked.

The petty officer was not amused.

"You got orders, Captain? Or dependents?"

Weston handed over his orders.

"You're to report to Commander Bolemann," the petty officer said. "Up the stairs, take the right corridor, sign over the door says 'Commander Bolemann.' "

The name rang a bell. Dr. Kister had told him about Bolemann in the Officers' Club bar, with Janice.

And Kister also said Bolemann enjoys his reputation as one mean sonofabitch.

"Wonderful!"

Commander Bolemann wasn't in his office. A pharmacist's mate first class told Weston that "the doctor's in the dining room" and that he was sure he would like Weston to go there.

"You'll have no trouble finding him, Captain. Chubby fellow with a cane."

Weston had no trouble finding Commander Bolemann. The Commander with the Medical Corps insignia on his sleeves was sitting alone at a table by the door to the bar. For him, chubby was an understatement. And the cane was equally easy to spot. The handle was brass, cast in the shape of a naked lady.

Commander Bolemann spoke first.

"You must be Weston," he said as Jim approached the table.

"Yes, sir."

"Kister said I should look for a guy who looks like a

recruiting poster," Bolemann said. "Are you a drinking man, Weston?"

"I have been known to take a wee nip from time to time, sir."

"What I had in mind was a martini," Bolemann said, pointed to a chair, and added: "Sit."

"Thank you, sir."

A waiter appeared.

"Two martinis," Bolemann ordered. "Give the check to this gentleman."

Weston chuckled. There was a row of ribbons on Bolemann's jacket, among them the Silver Star. He wondered how the doctor had come by that.

"Ordinarily, I give Naval Aviators a wide berth. They're dangerous," Bolemann said.

"Yes, sir?"

"The reason I am not standing at the bar in there," Bolemann said, jerking his thumb over his shoulder in the direction of the bar, "is a Naval Aviator."

"How is that, sir?"

"First this idiot proved that he shouldn't have been allowed to fly airplanes in the first place by running his Wildcat into the island on the Enterprise. Then he just sat there, wondering what to do next. When I went up on the wing root to suggest he exit the airplane, its fuel tanks chose that moment to explode. I spent a year learning to walk with a stiff leg, most of it where you just came from."

"I saw the . . . cane," Weston replied, deciding just in time that Bolemann would prefer that to a reference to his Silver Star.

"I need that to beat off all the women with uncontrollable urges for my body," Bolemann said. "Anyway, when I was in Philadelphia, I got to be pals with Kister. I started out as one of his lunatics, of course, but finally he recognized me as a fellow psychiatrist. When they finally turned me loose, they sent me here. Any other questions?"

"No, sir."

"And Kister told me all about you, and I mean all about you, including the unwarranted—or did he say 'unwanted'?—attention you have been paying his favorite nurse, so we won't have to waste any time on that. Unless you *want* to tell me about your heroic service in the Philippines?"

"We ate a lot of pineapples," Weston said. "That what you have in mind?"

"Ah, here's the booze," Bolemann said as the waiter approached the table.

After the waiter had left their drinks on the table, Bolemann lifted his glass. "Welcome to the Greenbrier, Weston."

"Thank you, sir."

They touched glasses and Weston took a sip. Almost immediately, he could feel the alcohol. "Very nice," he said.

"What did you drink in the Philippines?"

"We made our own beer. It was pretty bad, but not as bad as the rum we made."

"And did all the pineapples, the bad beer, and the even worse rum cause you to have nightmares, then or since you came home?"

Weston suddenly understood that the question was not idle or bantering.

"No," he said seriously. "Over there, I used to dream about food. But no nightmares. There or here."

"They're nothing to be embarrassed about," Bolemann said. "I've been blown off the wing root of that goddamned Wildcat at least a hundred times, sometimes twice a night."

"Nothing like that, sir," Weston said.

Bolemann looked at him intently for a long moment.

"While you are here, you will be counseled, once a week," he said. "You just had Counseling Session Number One. Your other duties will consist of eating and availing yourself of healthy recreational activities. These run the gamut from A to B, but do not include trying to make out with either the waitresses or the wives of your fellow returned heroes. The food is free. So are the golf, swimming, hiking, et cetera. The booze you have to pay for yourself."

"What's the pass system?"

"Where do you want to go?" Bolemann asked, and

then, before Weston had time to reply, went on: "You've
got it bad for Kister's nurse, do you?"

"That sums it up nicely, sir."

"We can probably work something out," Commander
Bolemann said, and raised his martini glass again. "To
love, Captain Weston."

"I'll drink to that," Jim Weston said.

[FOUR]
The Foster Lafayette Hotel
Washington, D.C.
1945 24 February 1943

In Washington, Senator Richardson K. Fowler (R.-Cal.)
made his residence in a six-room corner suite on the
eighth floor of the Foster Lafayette Hotel, half of whose
windows offered an unimpeded view of the White House
across Pennsylvania Avenue.

Living in the Foster Lafayette provided benefits he
wasn't aware of before he moved in. Twenty-four-hour-
a-day room service, for one thing. Sneaking people into
the suite for confidential chats, for another.

Thus, when the Foster Lafayette's doorman alerted
Fred, Fowler's butler, that the Director of the Office of
Strategic Services had arrived downstairs, Fred had the
door to Senator Fowler's apartment open when Donovan
stepped off the elevator.

Fred had also been instructed by Senator Fowler to
serve the liquor at a glacially slow pace.

"Good evening, Mr. Donovan," Fred said. "Won't you
please come in, sir? The Senator and the General are in
the library." He took Donovan's hat and topcoat and,
carrying them in his arm, led Donovan to the library.

Both Senator Fowler and General Pickering stood up
when Fred opened the door. Pickering was in civilian
clothing, an impeccably tailored double-breasted pin-
striped suit.

"Hello, Bill," Fowler said, approaching him with his
hand extended.

"Senator," Donovan said, and looked at Pickering. "General," he said.

Well, so much for my not embarrassing Colonel Wild Bill by not rubbing my general's stars in his face.

"Good to see you, Bill," Pickering said, and walked to him to shake hands.

"What can I fix you, Bill?" Fowler asked.

"A glass of sparkling water, with a little lime, if you have it, please," Donovan said.

Is that because he doesn't want a drink, or to set the stage for our sober confrontation?

"Coming right up, sir," Fred said.

"We are at the bottomless well of Flem's supply of Famous Grouse," Fowler said. "He made sure the liquor stocks were sent ashore before he turned his passenger ships over to the Navy."

"I can also make you a deal on the silver from the first-class dining rooms," Pickering said.

Donovan laughed dutifully.

"You kept the merchant ships, didn't you?" Donovan said. "What was that all about? Not that it's any of my business."

"There will always be a need for merchantmen," Pickering said. "But when I came back from Hawaii, right after Pearl Harbor, we made port in Seattle, and I had a chance to see all the B-17s lined up at the Boeing plant. They can fly to Hawaii in hours. It seemed to me that after the war, people are not going to be willing to spend weeks on a ship—no matter how comfortable—when they can get where they have to go in hours."

"In other words, buy Boeing stock?"

"I have. And Lockheed, after I saw drawings of a four-engine transport Howard Hughes wants to make that will carry fifty people across oceans at three hundred miles an hour."

"And what do you think of his wooden airplane? That will carry two hundred and fifty people? Or is it three fifty? Or so he says."

"I heard about that," Pickering said. "I haven't seen it, but my gut reaction would be to bet on Howard Hughes. I would be surprised if it doesn't work as promised. But to answer your question, I was delighted to sell the government my passenger ships. I kept the merchantmen because I thought P & FE could operate them more efficiently than the Navy could."

"And you're probably right," Donovan said, then switched over to the real point of the meeting. "I have something to say to you, Pickering. And not because of the circumstances. I was wrong when I didn't offer you an assistant directorship when you came to see me."

"We were not mutual admirers," Pickering said. "If the shoe had been on my foot—"

"The matter is now out of our hands, isn't it?" Donovan said.

"It would seem that way," Pickering said.

"Is this the appropriate time for me to say 'welcome'? Or maybe, if an old soldier can get away with saying this, 'welcome aboard'?"

"Thank you very much, sir," Pickering said, and offered his hand again.

"You see?" Fowler said. "It's like going to the dentist. Once you sit down in the chair and open your mouth, it's not nearly as bad as you imagined."

"Jesus, Dick!" Pickering said, but smiled.

"How's your health?" Donovan asked.

"Fine," Pickering said. "I was pretty tired when I got off the airplane in San Diego, but then I spent four days at home, lifting nothing heavier than a fork."

"You're ready to go to work?"

"Yes," Pickering said simply.

"Good. There are things for you to do," Donovan said. "But before I get into that, let me give you the lay of the land."

Pickering nodded.

"Am I supposed to be privy to any of this?" Senator Fowler asked.

"Legally, no," Donovan said. "But on the other hand . . ."

"I'm a United States senator?"

"You were there, Dick, having dinner with the President, when he had—what was it he said? his 'divine revelation'—about naming Pickering OSS Deputy Director for Pacific Operations. I don't think that was a coincidence; he wanted you involved. It's difficult knowing what Roosevelt is really thinking about anything, but maybe he's hoping that if—when—Pickering becomes unhappy with something at the OSS, he'd rather have him talk it over with you before he takes it to him. I think it would be valuable if you heard this."

He calls Fowler "Dick" and me "Pickering." Did that just happen? Or is it to remind me that he's the boss?

Fowler nodded.

"Let's clear the air about that," Pickering said to Donovan. "I take my orders from you. If I decide that I cannot in good conscience obey my orders, I will tell you why, and resign."

Donovan looked into Pickering's eyes. "Fair enough," he said. "Then my orders to you are this: If you find yourself thinking of resignation, talk it over with the Senator before you come to me."

"Yes, sir," Pickering said.

"And I will ask you, Senator, not to share anything with your colleagues."

"Of course, not," Fowler said.

"There is an organizational chart at the OSS," Donovan said. "And like most organizational charts, it's primarily eyewash. The basic setup is this: the Deputy Director, Administration, functions as my chief of staff. If you don't like what you hear from him, come to me."

Pickering nodded.

"There is a Deputy Director, Operations, and Deputy Directors, European, Western Hemisphere, and now Pacific . . . you. While you and the other area Deputy Directors are not subordinate to the Deputy Director, Administration, when he speaks, he's almost always speaking for me."

Pickering nodded again. "Okay," he said.

"Come by the office tomorrow. I'll introduce you to everybody."

"Fine. What time?"

"Nine?"

"Fine."

"How much do you know about the people—the Americans—who are supposed to be in the Gobi Desert?"

"One of Admiral Nimitz's intelligence officers briefed me in Pearl Harbor. . . ."

"Nimitz had you briefed on the Gobi Desert operation?" Donovan asked.

To judge by his eyes, Pickering decided, *he doesn't like that.*

"Yes, he did," Pickering replied evenly.

"Did he give any reason for bringing you in on that problem?"

My conversation with Admiral Nimitz was obviously confidential. So what do I do? Break that confidence? Or start off my armistice with Donovan by lying to him?

If I did that, he would sooner or later find out anyway.

And by now he probably has heard what Nimitz asked Admiral Leahy to do.

"He told me that he had recommended to Admiral Leahy that the OSS be given the responsibility for establishing contact with the people in the Gobi, and that it was his recommendation that I be given responsibility for the operation."

Donovan looked at Pickering for a long moment without speaking.

The sonofabitch is trying to make up his mind whether I'm lying or telling the truth!

"The Joint Chiefs," Donovan said finally, "which of course means Admiral Leahy, gave the OSS the mission of establishing contact with these people. Nothing was said about you."

"Then you didn't know about Admiral Nimitz's recommendation?" Pickering asked, surprised.

"No, but I did know that Nimitz is one of your admirers, and that he knew all about your Philippine operation—and, of course, your appointment to the OSS—so I was a little surprised that your name didn't come up in Phase One."

"Phase One?" Pickering asked, not understanding.

"Phase One was a little preliminary work in the OSS, pending my return to Washington. My Deputy Director, Administration, had a memo waiting for me recommending that you be given the operation, giving as his reasons your successful Philippine operation and your position as Deputy Director, Pacific."

"One doesn't ordinarily consider the Gobi Desert to be in the Pacific," Pickering said.

Donovan didn't respond to the comment.

"My Deputy Director, Operations, sent me a memo stating that should your name come up in connection with the Gobi operation, he wanted to go on record early on as being opposed to it. He offered three reasons: First, the point you just made—one doesn't think of the Gobi as being in the Pacific. Second, it would be unfair to you, inasmuch as you have little knowledge of the OSS. And finally, in his view, applying your knowledge of the Pacific Ocean and of shipping generally could be put to more important use in the OSS than running what will be a commando/parachutist covert operation."

"You understand, Bill . . ."

Donovan held up his hand to cut him off.

"Phase Two occurred last night, across the street," Donovan said, gesturing through the window toward the White House. "Where I was honored to break bread with the Commander in Chief and his Chief of Staff. Shortly before the apple cobbler, Roosevelt looked at me, and said—in words to this effect, 'In addition to other things he might be doing for you, Admiral Leahy thinks that Fleming Pickering should command the operation to get a radio station operating in the Gobi Desert. Do you have any problem with that?' Or, as I said, words to that effect."

"And what did you reply to the Commander in Chief?" Senator Fowler asked, chuckling.

"I said the idea had already been proposed to me by one of my deputy directors, and I was delighted General Pickering's appointment would please Admiral Leahy."

"Franklin does that so well." Fowler chuckled. "Makes a suggestion that is impossible to refuse."

"You didn't say what you had decided to do before the President made his 'suggestion,' " Pickering said.

"No. I guess I didn't," Donovan said. "Water under the dam anyway, wouldn't you say?"

"Yes, I suppose so," Pickering said.

"Tell me about your briefing from Admiral Nimitz," Donovan said.

"His intelligence officer, or at least one of them—"

"Groscher? Captain Groscher?" Donovan interrupted.

"Yeah."

"Groscher knows as much about the Americans in the Gobi as anybody," Donovan said. "What did he have to say?"

"Nothing I would suppose that you don't know. Much of it was new to me. There doesn't seem to be any question about whether the weather station is needed, just who will get it up and running."

"And now we know, don't we?"

"It's none of my business, but I think Nimitz and Leahy are right. Flem has a way of getting things done," Senator Fowler said.

Pickering had the feeling Donovan could have happily done without Fowler's comment.

"We'll talk about this tomorrow at the office," he said.

"Okay," Pickering said.

"The President gave you authority to bring anybody you want along with you, in addition to your people already in Australia. Have you given that any thought?"

"Yes."

"I'd like to have the Office of Management Analysis," Donovan said. "Lock, stock, and barrel. Have you considered that?"

"Frank Knox would not stand still for that," Senator Fowler said, thinking out loud.

"The President gives the orders," Donovan said. "Except, of course, to senators."

It didn't take long before we came to serious disagreement, did it? Pickering thought. *Well, to hell with being polite. Get it on the table.*

"I think that Management Analysis should stay right where it is," Pickering said.

"Is that so?" Donovan said coldly. "Why?"

"It's up and running," Pickering said. "I don't want to see it swallowed by the OSS bureaucracy."

"You're now part of that OSS bureaucracy, General," Donovan said, his face whitening.

"I am going to ask Colonel Rickabee if he will give me a couple of people over there," Pickering said. "And there are several other people I'd like to have. But I oppose taking the Office of Management Analysis away from Frank Knox."

It was obvious that Donovan didn't like the response, but he didn't press it.

If I had any tact, and the brains to use it, I would have used words like "think," "suggest," et cetera. Fuck it. Let Donovan know what I think.

"Why don't we reschedule your arrival at the office until, say, half past twelve tomorrow?" Donovan said. "That would give you time to ask Rickabee who he's willing to give you."

"Fine," Pickering said.

"We'll have to do some schedule shuffling to move them through the Country Club," Donovan said. "We'll need your list as soon as possible. This Gobi operation is on the front burner."

"Excuse me?" Pickering asked, confused.

"The OSS training base. Before the war, it was the Congressional Country Club. Everybody who comes into the OSS has to go through it. With very rare exceptions, like you."

My God, McCoy comes home from his third rubber-boat trip onto hostile shores and Donovan wants to send him to basic training?

Senator Fowler saw the look on Pickering's face. "Are you two about ready to eat?" he asked quickly.

This is not the time, Pickering decided, *to debate the wisdom of sending McCoy and Jake to—what did he call it?—the "Country Club."*

"Anytime, Dick," Pickering said.

"Actually, I was hoping the subject of eating would come up soon," Donovan said. "I've got a couple of more stops to make tonight."

"And I have a telephone call to make," Fowler said. "Our mutual friend across the street is staying close to the telephone, waiting for my report on how this went."

"I was right, then?" Donovan chuckled. "You're to be the referee?"

"What he did, Bill, was wave his cigarette holder at me, and smile that smile of his, and ask me—since he and I have a civilized gentleman's armistice—if he was being unreasonable in expecting you two to do the same."

"I knew it," Donovan said.

"I will now be able to happily tell him that you two have kissed and made up."

"Good God!" Pickering said.

VIII

[ONE]
The Foster Lafayette Hotel
Washington, D.C.
0805 25 February 1943

Brigadier General Fleming Pickering, USMCR, the Washington *Star* in hand, was sitting in the marble walled bathroom of his apartment, waiting for his bowels to move, when the telephone rang. He dropped the *Star* onto the floor and gazed, with a sense of moral triumph, at the telephone mounted on the wall.

Men of less imagination and determination, he thought, in a similar circumstance, would be nonplussed. They would be forced to decide between hastily abandoning their attempt to vacate their bowels, or just letting the damned telephone ring.

They would not have installed a phone in the john, as *he* had, over Patricia's firm objections. For reasons he did not pretend to understand, Patricia thought using a telephone in the bathroom was tantamount to using the facilities with the door wide open.

The telephone, which was mounted on the wall beside the water closet, was equipped with a red light, a green light, and a switch. The green light indicated the incoming call was from the hotel switchboard; the red that it was coming in over the private, unlisted line.

The red light was blinking.

With a little bit of luck, that will be my bride, and I can open the conversation by asking her if she can guess where I am.

He flipped the switch to the private line and picked up the receiver.

"Good morning!" he cried cheerfully.

"General Pickering, please," a male voice he didn't recognize replied.

Who the hell is this? Not ten people have this number.

"Who is this?"

"Am I speaking with General Pickering?"

It's that goddamned Wild Bill Donovan, that's who it is! A little demonstration of his ability to do things like get unlisted telephone numbers. And that he's too important to dial the number himself and has some flunky to do it for him.

And, if he senses this has annoyed me, he will have accomplished his purpose.

"This is General Pickering," he said as charmingly as he could manage under the circumstances.

"One moment, please, General," Donovan's flunky said.

"Certainly," General Pickering said graciously.

And before that sonofabitch comes on the line, he'll keep me waiting as long—

"I didn't get you out of bed, I hope, Fleming?"

This voice Pickering recognized, and it wasn't that of Wild Bill Donovan.

"No, Mr. President, I've been up for some time. Good morning, Mr. President."

"I just called to tell you how delighted I was to hear from Dick Fowler that you and Bill Donovan have established an amicable relationship."

"We had a very pleasant dinner, Mr. President."

"So Dick told me. There's one other thing, Fleming. I

meant it when I said that my door will always be open to you, if you have something you wish to share with me."

"That's very kind of you, Mr. President."

"Bill and I have been friends for years," President Roosevelt said. "And I therefore know better than most people how obdurate he can be."

"I defer, of course, to your greater knowledge, Mr. President."

Roosevelt laughed. "As soon as it can be arranged, you'll have to come for dinner."

"I know how you busy you are, Mr. President."

"Never too busy for you, Fleming," Roosevelt said, and the line went dead.

Pickering put the handset back in its cradle.

What the hell was that all about?

You know what the hell that was all about.

Roosevelt being Machiavellian again.

During dinner the night before, Donovan had spoken, with barely concealed anger, of his relationship with FBI Director J. Edgar Hoover. It wasn't that he disliked Hoover—he had been instrumental in having Hoover named head of the FBI—but that Roosevelt refused to clear up a jurisdictional dispute between the FBI and the OSS.

The FBI was charged with intelligence and counterespionage in the Western Hemisphere. The OSS was charged with the same thing worldwide, with the exception of the United States. So far as Donovan was concerned, that meant exactly what it said. So far as Hoover was concerned, the FBI was in charge of espionage and counterespionage everywhere in the Western Hemisphere, which meant that the OSS was marching on the FBI's turf when it operated anywhere in Canada, Central America, or South America.

"Franklin just wants you and Edgar to compete, Bill," Senator Fowler had said, "to see who gets the gold star to take home for Mommy."

"It's not funny, Dick," Donovan had said.

"I know. What it is, is Franklin Rooseveltian," Fowler had said. "And only God can change that."

And now Roosevelt's consciously setting up the same kind of competition between Donovan and me.

Pickering looked at his watch, then at the telephone again.

What I am about to do is absolutely childish.

But on the other hand, one does not have this sort of splendid opportunity every day.

He picked up the telephone, dialed O for operator, asked for long distance, and when the long-distance operator came on the line, gave her a number in San Francisco.

"Is this call essential, sir?" the operator asked.

"Operator, the entire outcome of the war depends on this call getting through."

"You don't have to be sarcastic, sir."

The number in San Francisco rang four times before an operator came on. She sounded as if she might have been asleep at her post.

"Pacific and Far East Shipping."

"This is Fleming Pickering," he announced.

"Good morning, Commodore," the operator said, now fully awake.

"I'd like to leave a message for my wife when she comes to work this morning," he said.

"Of course, Commodore."

"You have a pencil?"

"Yes, sir."

"The message is, 'Guess where I was at eight oh five this morning when the President of the United States called. Love, Flem.' Got that?"

"Yes, sir. Commodore, you don't want to tell her where?"

"She'll know, thank you just the same," Pickering said, and hung up.

As he did that, he noticed, a little surprised and confused, that the green light was illuminated, indicating an incoming call from the hotel switchboard. He shrugged, flipped the switch, and said, "Hello?"

"I hope I didn't wake you," Senator Richardson K. Fowler said, his tone suggesting he didn't mean that at all.

"You mean you've been waiting for me to answer?"

"Only for the last twenty or thirty minutes," Fowler said.

"Actually I was on the phone, having a little chat with the President," Pickering said.

Fowler groaned.

"And how may I help you, Senator?"

"No good deed goes unpunished," Fowler said. "I was about to ask you to breakfast."

"Give me five minutes, Dick," Pickering said.

"Anything special?"

"Something simple. How about a breakfast steak, and a couple of eggs, sunny-side up?"

"Five minutes, Flem," Fowler said, and hung up.

Pickering, tieless and in his shirtsleeves, arrived at Fowler's down-the-corridor door just as the floor waiter was rolling in a food cart.

"That wasn't five minutes, Flem," Fowler greeted him. "I have a full day ahead of me."

"More than you know," Pickering said, as he followed Fowler into his dining room. The table was set for three.

"Good morning, Commodore," Fred said.

"Call me General today, Fred," Pickering said, touching his shoulder. "I have been up most of the night thinking General-type thoughts."

"I need some of that coffee," Fowler said, snatching a silver coffeepot from the floor waiter's cart. He sat down at the table and poured himself a cup. Then he remembered Pickering's recent words.

" 'More than I know'? What's that supposed to mean?"

"Put a little something in your stomach," Pickering said. "It'll put you in a better mood."

"Just put the plates on the table please," Fowler said to the floor waiter, "and then, thank you, that'll be all. I have a terrible suspicion that the breakfast-table conversation will concern topics that nice people shouldn't have to hear."

Pickering waited until the waiter transferred the plates, uncovered them, and left. Fred saw him through the door, locked it, and then sat down at the table with Pickering and Fowler.

"I thought you would be beside yourself with curiosity about my conversation," he began.

"Your conversation with who?"

"Take a wild guess. He smiles a lot—lots of teeth—and smokes his cigarettes in a long ivory holder."

Fowler shook his head.

"And what did our beloved leader have to say?" Fowler asked, and then, before Pickering could begin to answer, added: "Flem, who called who?"

"He called me," Pickering said. "On my unlisted line."

"He *is* the President. What did he have to say?"

"Because he and Colonel Donovan are old friends, he told me, he knows better than most people how obdurate . . . I love that word; I thought I knew what it meant, but when we hung up, to be sure, I looked it up in the dictionary—"

"Hardened in wrongdoing," Fowler said.

"Or wickedness," Pickering said. "According to Mr. Webster, 'wrongdoing *or wickedness*.' I told you I looked it up."

"*And*, Flem?" Fowler said, smiling.

"And because he knows how *obdurate* the good Colonel can be, his door is always open to me."

"That's nice," Fowler said. "You remember our conversation last night about J. Edgar Hoover?"

"How could I forget?" Pickering said.

"Interesting," Fowler said, and stared at his breakfast steak with disdain. "I don't know why I ordered this. If I eat this, I'll fall asleep before lunch."

"I will, of course, take the President at his word, and go knocking at his door. Today, if I have to. Unless you can fix it so that I won't have to."

"What are you talking about?"

"You remember what Donovan said last night? 'I'd like to have the Office of Management Analysis. Lock, stock, and barrel'?"

"And I remember that you told him no."

"And I remember he took my 'no' too easily, as if he expected that reaction and was going to ignore it."

"Yeah," Fowler said, remembering. "Frank Knox wouldn't at all like losing Management Analysis," he added. "He is very fond of his private, personal OSS."

"Which performs a number of valuable functions, and which should not be swallowed up by the OSS."

"I agree," Fowler said.

"I suspect that Donovan has tried to get it before, failed, and sees a new opportunity. He can tell the President I want it. Or, more likely, that he naturally presumed I would want to bring it into the OSS with me. Since the President has told me I can have anybody I want, he will see nothing wrong with this, and will tell Admiral Leahy to take care of it. Once it's in the OSS, he takes it away from me."

"You don't trust Donovan, do you?"

"He's a lawyer, Dick, of course I don't trust him."

"So am I a lawyer," Fowler said, not amused.

"Yeah, but Donovan is a *Democratic* lawyer."

"That's a little better," Fowler said.

Fred chuckled.

"So what do you propose to do? Or propose that I do for you?" Fowler asked.

"Get to Frank Knox, immediately, this morning, and tell him I'll make a deal with him. If he's willing to go along, I'll go to the President with him and tell him I think Management Analysis should remain under Knox. If we both go to the President and tell him no, I think we can prevail over Bill Donovan, done deal or not."

"You understand how quickly Roosevelt's open door is going to slam in your face if you go over Donovan's head your first day on the job?"

"I couldn't do it alone, and I don't think Frank Knox could," Pickering said. "We'll have to do it together. I'll worry about the door slamming in my face later."

"You said 'deal,' " Fowler said. "What kind of a deal? Frank Knox is not well-known for making deals. What do you want from Knox?"

"I want Fritz Rickabee promoted to brigadier general," Pickering said. "And Ed Banning promoted to lieutenant colonel. Incidentally, I've decided I need Banning more than Rickabee does."

"Why is this important to you?" Fowler asked.

"Fritz needs a star to run Management Analysis. If I

have to point this out, he is far more entitled to a star than I am. And when I have to ask him for help, I would like him, frankly, to remember where his star came from."

Fowler grunted.

"And Banning?"

"Several reasons. Some practical, some political. Banning knows China. He was an intelligence officer there for years. God, he had to leave his wife behind him in Shanghai—"

"I didn't know that," Fowler interrupted. "She's a prisoner?"

"Nobody knows."

Fowler shook his head.

"Anyway, I need Banning's brains and expertise. He has a MAGIC clearance, which will be useful."

"Why should he be promoted? That might be difficult. The Marine Corps likes to decide who gets promoted, and when."

"First of all, he's deserving of promotion," Pickering said. "Secondly, I suspect there are a lot of majors in the OSS—the guy Donovan sent to replace Killer McCoy in the Philippines was a major—and I want my deputy to outrank them. As far as that goes, I'm bringing Jake Dillon into the OSS, and I think it's a good idea for him to be calling Ed Banning 'sir' and 'Colonel.' "

"Dillon?" Fowler asked doubtfully. "Your movie press agent friend?"

"Not only is Jake an old China Marine, but he did a hell of a job for me on several occasions," Pickering said, "and he's loyal to me."

Fowler shrugged.

"Don't tell me it can't be done, Dick," Pickering said.

"It can be done. I think Frank Knox will go along with you. And the price will be antagonizing both Donovan and the entire OSS—and the Marine Corps."

"I would worry a hell of a lot more about that if Archer Vandegrift wasn't going to become Commandant of the Marine Corps."

Fowler grunted again.

"But speaking of the Marine Corps: Do you still have 'U.S. Senator' license plates on your car?"

"Yeah, why?"

"I want to borrow your car this morning. I'm going to Eighth and I to see Jack Stecker, and—"

"You would like the word to rapidly spread that Jack Stecker has a friend who is a friend of a senator."

"I'm just trying to save cab fare," Pickering said.

"Why do you want to see Jack?"

"As soon as Vandegrift becomes Commandant, he's going to hear a litany of complaints about the OSS, and probably me, personally, especially about the promotions. So when he asks Jack, 'Just what the hell is your friend Pickering up to?' I want Jack to be in a position to tell him."

"You're going to tell him everything?"

"Everything I decide he has a need to know; as a practical matter, that means just about everything. Why Rickabee and Banning got promoted; all about this Gobi Desert business; everything."

Fowler grunted.

"I strongly suspect," Pickering went on, "that Vandegrift will make his manners to Admiral Nimitz in Pearl Harbor on his way home. And that Nimitz will explain to him the significance of the Gobi operation—and, more important, that he wanted me to run it. If I'm right, Vandegrift's blessing on the operation will grease a lot of skids. What I'm really trying to do is eliminate friction between the Corps and the OSS."

Fowler met Pickering's eyes for a long moment.

"Maybe you're learning how the game is played, Flem," he said, and turned to Fred: "See if you can get Secretary Knox on the phone, please, Fred. I'll speak with Captain Haughton if I have to, but tell him it's important that I speak to Knox personally."

"Thank you, Dick," Pickering said.

Senator Fowler shrugged. "The reason I keep getting reelected is that I have become known for my service to my constituents," he said, straight-faced.

When he heard the door to his apartment open, General Pickering was examining the insignia and decorations on his tunic. He was doing that with great care; this morning he really wanted to look like a Marine general about to go on parade.

"In here, Fred," he called out. "I'll be with you in a minute."

"It's me, General," Second Lieutenant George F. Hart, USMCR, replied.

What the hell is he doing here? He's supposed to be visiting his family in St. Louis.

Pickering turned to his bedroom door and waited for Hart to appear.

"Good morning, sir."

"Where the hell were you when I needed you, George?" Pickering asked, gesturing toward the tunic laid out on his bed.

Hart walked to the bed and carefully examined the placement of the insignia and decorations.

"Shipshape, sir," he said, picked up the tunic, and held it out for Pickering.

"I didn't expect you so soon. You understand that?" Pickering asked as he slipped his arms into the sleeves.

"Well, I could say duty called, but the truth is my girl is in New York, and Washington is closer to New York than St. Louis."

"Well, then why aren't you in New York?"

"I thought maybe you might need me," Hart said.

"This morning, I do," Pickering said. "And then you can go to New York."

"What's happening this morning?"

"We're going to see Colonel Stecker at Eighth and I," Pickering said, "and I really want to look like a general. And you can't look like a general, can you, without an aide-de-camp hovering around you?"

"Who are we trying to impress?" Hart asked, smiling.

"Every feather merchant at Eighth and I," Pickering said. At that moment a thought occurred to him. He went to his briefcase and removed a legal pad. He handed it to Hart. "That's a list of the people we're taking into the OSS. I made it up last night. Have I left anybody off?"

Hart studied the list. "Two questions," he said.

"Shoot."

"The sergeant—maybe I should say the lieutenant—

who was with Weston in the Philippines. Everly. *Percy L. Everly?*"

"Why him?"

"Killer McCoy told me he told him he was going to try to get him out of the Philippines."

"He should be brought out," Pickering thought out loud. "Weston told me about him."

"The Killer must think he's okay. They were in the Fourth Marines in Shanghai. Anyway, just a question."

"McCoy didn't say anything to me about getting him out."

"Once you told him he was going to have to brief the President, the Killer wasn't really himself."

Pickering chuckled.

"He did that very well, by the way," Pickering said. "The President told Admiral Leahy to radio both Mac-Arthur and Nimitz that support of U.S. forces in the Philippines is to be considered essential. Okay. Add his name to the list. If we get him out—*when* we get him out—he finds out he's in the OSS."

"Yes, sir."

"You said you had two questions, George?"

"I noticed Lieutenant Easterbrook's name on the list," Hart said evenly.

Second Lieutenant Robert F. Easterbrook, USMCR (who was known to his friends as "the Easterbunny"), had been a combat correspondent on Guadalcanal. After a Marine who had won the Medal of Honor on Bloody Ridge described him as "the bravest man on Bloody Ridge," he had been directly commissioned as an officer. Easterbrook was nineteen years old.

Making him an officer looked good in the newspapers, but Pickering, who knew and admired Easterbrook, thought making him an officer just about headed the list of stupid acts perpetrated by the feather merchants at Eighth and I.

When he heard the Marine Corps was about to send the boy back to the Pacific in command of a team of combat correspondents—an act that would almost certainly get him, and the men under him, killed—he had decided that Lieutenant Easterbrook could make a far greater contribution to the war effort in the OSS.

It was a moment before Pickering replied.

"We're going to make history, George, and I have decided that we need someone with us to photograph it all for posterity."

"Yes, sir." Hart chuckled.

"If anybody at Eighth and I, or at the OSS, asks you what you know about Easterbrook, you know nothing."

"Yes, sir. Off the record, sir?

"Yeah, sure."

"I approve, and so will Pick when he hears," Hart said. "He was really worried about the Easterbunny going back over there and getting himself killed trying to prove he's really a Marine officer."

The door opened again; this time it was Fred. "Anytime you're ready, General," he called.

"We're ready now," Pickering said.

[TWO]
Headquarters, United States Marine Corps
Eighth and I Streets, N.W.
Washington, D.C.
0955 25 February 1943

The Marine guards at the gate of the compound were armed with pistols suspended from web belts. They were also wearing steel helmets, the new style. Pickering thought of this as "German style," as opposed to the old style, which General Pickering had worn both in France and on Guadalcanal and thought of as "Limey style."

He also thought that wearing helmets here was a little absurd. Their primary purpose was to protect the skull from artillery and mortar shrapnel, or from pieces of exploded antiaircraft shells falling back to earth. And none of that was liable to happen right now in the District of Columbia.

Fowler's 1942 Packard 280 limousine had a license plate: U.S. SENATE 12. The Marine sergeant who approached it was already prepared to be very polite to the august personage the vehicle was carrying.

His determination to be very polite increased by at least fifty percent when he saw the passenger was a Marine brigadier general. He saluted crisply. "Good morning, sir!" he barked. "How may the sergeant assist the General, Sir?"

Pickering returned the salute.

"Good morning, Sergeant. I'm here to see Colonel Jack (NMI) Stecker."

When Colonel Jack (NMI) Stecker, USMC, was a young sergeant in France in World War I, he had won the Medal of Honor. Sergeant Fleming Pickering and Corporal D. G. McInerney had been with him in the action.

"Yes, sir. May the sergeant trouble the General, Sir, for his identification? Regulations, sir."

It is, I suppose, possible that the Axis Powers would, for some nefarious purpose, attempt to gain entrance to Headquarters, USMC, by sending in the agent wearing a Marine brigadier's uniform and in a car they stole from a senator.

"Certainly," Pickering said, removing his wallet and nudging George Hart with his elbow to do the same thing.

The sergeant examined both ID cards carefully.

"Thank you, sir," the sergeant said, handing them back. "One moment, sir, and I'll try to locate Colonel—Stecker, you said?—for you."

"Stecker," Pickering confirmed. "Thank you, Sergeant."

The sergeant walked quickly to the guard shack and consulted a mimeographed list mounted on a clipboard. After a moment, it was evident from his face that he couldn't find what he expected to find.

He checked again, carefully, and then, looking worried, returned to the rear window of Fowler's long black Packard limousine.

"Sir, the sergeant probably misunderstood the General, Sir. The name of the colonel the General wishes to see is?"

"Stecker, Sergeant. Colonel Jack (NMI) Stecker," Pickering said.

"Sir, I couldn't find a Colonel Stecker on my list, sir."

"I know he's here, Sergeant," Pickering said. "Why

don't you call the Office of the Commandant and ask the sergeant major?"

"Aye aye, sir," the sergeant said, and trotted quickly back to the guard shack.

A minute later, he was back. "Sir, if the General will be good enough to wait, the Office of the Commandant is sending someone down, sir, to take you to Colonel Stecker."

"Thank you very much, Sergeant," Pickering said.

Three minutes later a very natty Marine major walked up to the limousine and saluted.

He's a chair-warmer, Pickering decided, somewhat unkindly, and not only because none of the ribbons on the major's chest indicated he had seen foreign service.

"Good morning, sir," the Major said, saluting. "I'm Major Robinson, sir, of the Commandant's staff."

"Good morning, Major," Pickering said. "Do you know where I can find Colonel Stecker?"

"Yes, sir. The Colonel is also on the Commandant's staff. Specifically, he's a Special Assistant to the Commandant, sir. If I may get in the General's car, sir, I will show you where you can park, and then I'll take you to Colonel Stecker."

"Special Assistant" to the Commandant? That means they don't know what the hell to do with him.

"Thank you very much," Pickering said.

After the major had slipped in the front seat next to Fred, they drove into the compound, and he showed Fred where to park behind a redbrick building.

They stepped out of the car.

"I don't believe I've had the privilege of previously meeting the General, sir," Major Robinson said.

"No, I don't believe we've met," Pickering said. "My name is Pickering, and this is my aide, Lieutenant Hart."

Major Robinson shook Pickering's offered hand and nodded at Hart.

"Right this way, sir," Major Robinson said. "Colonel Stecker's office is in the basement."

In the basement, and it's probably a broom closet. That will change when General Vandegrift gets back.

Colonel Jack (NMI) Stecker's office was a little larger

than a broom closet, but not much. There was room for a desk and two chairs and not much else. Stecker was a tall, muscular, tanned man in his early forties. When he saw Pickering, he looked up in surprise. The four rows of ribbons on his tunic were not topped by the white-starred blue ribbon indicating he had been awarded the Medal of Honor.

He's not embarrassed by it. He just doesn't want to hide behind it.

"General Pickering to see you, Colonel," Major Robinson announced.

"Good morning, General," Stecker said.

"Good morning, Colonel Stecker," Pickering said, and turned to Major Robinson. "Thank you, Major. That will be all."

"Sir, the Commandant is not aboard at the moment," Robinson said. "But the chief of staff . . ."

"Please present my compliments to the chief of staff, Major, and tell him I will not waste his valuable time by making my manners. I have no business with him; I'm here to see Colonel Stecker."

"Aye, aye, sir."

"Close the door after the major, will you, please, George?"

"Aye, aye, sir."

Pickering waited until the door was closed, and then smiled at Stecker.

"Hello, you ugly old bastard," he said. "How the hell are you?"

"What the hell are you up to?"

"Well, I heard they'd put you in a broom closet in the basement, and I came to cheer you up."

"They don't know what the hell to do with me," Stecker said.

"Nobody's even suspected that you're going to be the éminence grise behind the incoming commandant?"

"The only one who knows who his replacement will be is the Commandant, and he told me he wants to keep it that way."

"But you are looking forward to the day when General

Vandegrift shows up and rescues you from the basement?"

"I'm looking forward to the day when I can make a contribution," Stecker said.

"Well, I have a few little things you can do for me," Pickering said.

"Hello, George," Stecker said, offering his hand to Hart. "I wasn't trying to ignore you. But the last person I expected to see down here this morning is your boss."

"Good to see you again, sir."

"You're aware, of course, that you are looking at the new Deputy Director, Pacific, of the Office of Strategic Services?" Pickering asked.

"I saw it in the *Washington Post*. What's that all about?"

"According to the Special Channel I got from the President—I got it on Espíritu Santo, a couple of hours after McCoy and the others flew in from Mindanao—the idea of giving me the job came, as a divine revelation, while he was having dinner with Dick Fowler. He said he needed somebody who enjoyed the trust of El Supremo and Admiral Nimitz, and lo and behold, there I was."

"Sounds like you were sandbagged. Everybody was sandbagged."

"Oddly enough, both MacArthur and Nimitz seemed pleased. I stopped to pay my manners to Nimitz at Pearl on the way home, and he told me he'd already arranged—through Admiral Leahy—my first OSS assignment. That's where you come in, old buddy."

"I don't think I'm going to like this."

"I want someone with the ear of the Commandant—by that I mean General Vandegrift, when he takes over—who knows what we're doing, so that when we ask the Corps for something, we have a friend in the right place."

"Flem, not only don't I know what you're going to be doing, but I very seriously doubt that I am cleared to know," Stecker said.

"I thought about that," Pickering said seriously. "And I decided that the authority that came with my appointment includes the authority to decide the need-to-know of anybody I decide needs to know."

Stecker shook his head. "It doesn't work that way, Flem," he said.

"In your case, *Colonel Stecker*," Pickering went on. "You are not, repeat not, authorized to bring anyone but General Vandegrift in on anything you hear from me."

Stecker threw his hands helplessly in the air.

"Did you understand that, Jack?" Pickering said, now obviously very serious.

"Understood, sir," Stecker said after a moment.

"Okay. The mission that Nimitz, who has more confidence in me than I have, arranged for Leahy to get me is to (a) find a group of Americans, mostly retired Marines, soldiers, and Yangtze River patrol sailors, who are wandering around somewhere in the Gobi Desert; and then (b) somehow use them to set up a weather station, which means also a radio station. The Air Corps is going to need it whenever they get their new B-29 superbomber operational, and the Navy wants it now."

He watched Stecker carefully for his reaction. It wasn't what he expected.

"That seems right down McCoy's alley," Stecker said. "And Banning's."

"You don't seem surprised," Pickering said, thinking out loud.

"There's been a need for a weather station in that area for years. As a matter of fact, I think Banning tried to get permission to reconnoiter the Gobi in . . . 1939, 1940."

"And?"

"The Navy was all for it. The State Department said no, it would antagonize the Japanese. So I don't think it happened. If Banning did something on his own . . ."

"Speaking of Banning," Pickering said. "He's on a list of people, Marines, I'm taking into the OSS with me."

"The way that works, Flem, is that you *request* that the Corps detail to you people you want. Then, considering the needs of the Corps, the *Corps* decides whether or not you can have them."

"The President says I can have anybody I want. I think I can take him at his word. I expect resentment, and foot-dragging. What I want from you is to reduce the foot-dragging."

"I don't have any influence around here," Stecker said.

"Right now, Jack, the subject of conversation in the Commandant's office is what does the Brigadier General want with Colonel Stecker? The Brigadier General who arrived in Senator's Fowler's car and works for Secretary of the Navy Frank Knox. You're wrong. You have influence around here, negative influence. None of these chair warmers will dare to cross you."

Stecker's face showed that he didn't like to hear that.

"I don't like it any more than you do, Jack," Pickering said, "but as Fowler told me this morning, I'm learning the rules of the game as it's played around here."

Stecker shrugged and exhaled audibly.

"Okay. Give me your list of people," he said. "At least it will give me something to do besides read the newspapers."

"Give Colonel Stecker the list, George," Pickering said. "I'm going from here to see Fritz Rickabee. Then we're all going to have lunch at the Army-Navy Club. Any reason we can't pick you up here at quarter to twelve?"

"Oh, Flem, I don't know."

"Rickabee won't like it any more than you do," Pickering said. "Think of it as your sacrifice of the day to the war effort."

"What?"

"If any of the Marine brass missed hearing about your influential visitor here, they'll see us all at the Army-Navy Club."

"I should have shot you when I had the chance," Stecker said.

"Quarter to twelve, Colonel. Thank you for your valuable time. I know how busy you are."

Stecker shook his head in resignation.

[THREE]
Office of the Director
The Office of Strategic Services
Washington, D.C.
1425 25 February 1943

The guard who brought them from the lobby was armed, and he had a badge on the chest of his blue, police-type uniform. Pickering—who was idly curious about him, and the OSS security system generally—wasn't sure if he was some sort of a cop, a member of a separate OSS security force, or maybe hired from one of the commercial security outfits like Brink's, or more likely Pinkerton. Pinkerton's Washington/governmental activities went back to the Civil War when they'd worked for Abraham Lincoln.

Whoever was providing security was doing a good job. When he and George Hart arrived in the lobby and announced he had an appointment with Mr. Donovan, it was first determined that he did in fact have an appointment. Then permission to admit Second Lieutenant George Hart had to be obtained, since his name was not on the list of expected visitors. Next, they were asked to provide identification. Once that was carefully examined and accepted, they were asked to sign two forms on clipboards. The first acknowledged their receipt of yellow-bordered badges reading "VISITOR 5th Floor Only." One of the guards—this one wearing a gold badge and a lieutenant's bar—alligator-clipped these to the flap of the right chest pocket of their tunics. The second listed their names, the date and time, the person they wished to see, and the purpose of the visit.

After a moment's thought, Pickering wrote "W. Donovan" and "social call" in the appropriate blocks.

They were then turned over to a guard, who led them to the bank of elevators, rode with them to the fifth floor, then led them down a corridor to a door with an "Office of the Director" sign hanging over it. He pushed open the door, stepped inside, then held the door for Pickering and Hart and said, "General Pickering, to see the Director."

A plump, gray-haired, middle-aged woman moved her

lips in a pro forma welcoming smile, then pushed a lever on her intercom box. "General Pickering is here," she announced.

Pickering noticed that she wore an identification badge with her photograph on it; it had diagonal blue lines running through it.

"Send him in," a metallic voice responded.

"Through the door, please, General."

Pickering pushed the door open and walked through, thinking he was about to face the lion in his den.

He found himself instead looking at a tall man in a well-cut suit. A bronze plate on his desk identified him as the Deputy Director (Administration). The identification badge pinned to his jacket pocket showed his photograph and had diagonal red lines running through it.

"I'm Fleming Pickering."

"The Director was expecting you at twelve-thirty, General."

"Yes, I know," Pickering said. "I was delayed."

"The Director doesn't like to be kept waiting."

"Does anyone?" Pickering asked.

Well, I'm off on the wrong foot with this character, aren't I? Well, screw him. I am not going to start off on the right foot, if that means I have to set the precedent of explaining my actions to this guy. Or did he really expect me to apologize to him?

After looking at Pickering long enough to understand Pickering was not going to offer an explanation for being late, the Deputy Director (Administration) picked up a red, dial-less telephone on his desk.

"General Pickering is here, sir," he announced. After a brief pause while Donovan replied, he added, "Yes, sir," and hung up.

He stood up and gestured to an unmarked door. "This way, please, General. If you wish, your aide may wait here."

"George goes everywhere I go," Pickering said. "Come with me, George."

"Aye, aye, sir."

Colonel Donovan was not alone in his office. Another well-tailored man in his fifties was with him, sitting slumped, his legs extended, his feet crossed, in one of two green leather armchairs arranged to face Donovan's desk. He rose to his feet when Pickering and Hart entered the room and looked at Pickering carefully.

"Hello, Bill," Pickering said. "Sorry to be late."

"First things first," Donovan said, coming from behind his desk to offer Pickering his hand. Then he introduced the new Deputy Director (Pacific) to the Deputy Director (Operations). The two men shook hands.

The reaction of both men to each other was almost identical: *I think I'm going to like this guy.*

Once he had learned that Pickering was joining the OSS, the DDO had taken the trouble to make discreet inquiries about him. They had many mutual acquaintances, and even a few mutual friends, and they all reported essentially the same things about him and about his wife: that Fleming Pickering had done a better job running P&FE than his father, even from the beginning (he had taken over at twenty-six). In this he'd received no little help from his wife. The proof of Patricia Fleming's ability came when she stepped into her husband's shoes after he went to work for Frank Knox.

From the moment he took over, Pickering had preached efficiency (which usually meant the fast turnaround of ships) and had spent a lot of money (quickly recovered) to acquire the most up-to-date technologies and have these installed in P&FE's major terminals throughout the Pacific.

His other crusade was to break the long-standing tradition that the officers of a particular ship "owned it." That is, they stayed with a particular vessel for years. When it was out of service for any reason, so were they, meanwhile continuing to draw their union-guaranteed pay. Under Fleming Pickering, P&FE's officers (and many seamen, just about all of whom expected one day to be a P&FE officer) were expected to sail whichever ship needed their services, whenever those services were needed.

It was an obvious tribute to Pickering's leadership skills that he was able to carry that off, in the face of strong opposition from the Masters & Mates Union, the Maritime

Engineer's Union, and the International Brotherhood of Seafarers.

Despite the sometimes strong pressure from these unions, his officers and sailors trusted him. They knew him well and that he had sailed with them, in every position from Seaman Apprentice to Master Mariner, Any Tonnage, Any Ocean. But, the DDO decided, after sixty seconds of examining Pickering face to face, they trusted him even more because he was that rare man whose character shows on his face and in his eyes, and whom people immediately trust.

Many sources had also pointed out to the DDO that Pickering's success with P&FE had not contributed much to his modesty. He was strong-willed, opinionated, and did not suffer fools.

It was therefore not surprising that Donovan and Pickering had clashed. They were two of a kind. Strong, very successful men who were used to giving—but not taking—orders, and who did not like to have their decisions questioned. He wondered what would happen now that they were in the same ring.

"I'm sure the delay was outside your control, Fleming," Donovan said, and then indicated the empty green leather-upholstered armchair. "Sit down. Coffee?"

"No, thank you," Pickering said, and sat down.

"It was a presidential summons," he went on. "Roosevelt wanted to know what I thought about Frank Knox's objections to taking the Office of Management Analysis into the OSS."

"Oh, really?" Donovan asked. His face whitened.

"I told George to call and tell you we would be late," Pickering said. "I didn't know the protocol of talking about the President's plans on the telephone, so I decided to be careful and explain why we were late when we finally got here."

I think Wild Bill is about to erupt, the DDO decided. *He and Charley thought that was a done deal.*

"And you told the President that you didn't think bringing Management Analysis in here was a very good idea? Is that about it?"

"Actually, I told him it would be a very bad idea," Pickering said evenly.

"Certainly, General, you were aware that the Director thought it was a very good idea?" the Deputy Director (Administration) asked.

"The President didn't ask me that," Pickering explained, as if to a small child. "He asked me what I thought."

The DDO suddenly had a fit of coughing. The look the Deputy Director (Administration) gave him was not one of sympathy.

"I'm sure you considered that the assets of Management Analysis might have been very useful to you in Operation Gobi," Donovan said.

"Frank Knox made a point of telling the President—and me—that the assets of Management Analysis would be available to the OSS for the weather station operation," Pickering said. "And, as I told you over dinner, I am bringing some people from Management Analysis and elsewhere into the OSS. George has a list of their names."

"Give it to Charley," Donovan ordered. "I presume they're Marines?"

"Uh-huh."

"Charley deals with the Marine Corps in personnel matters," Donovan said.

"I wish I'd known that," Pickering said. "It would have saved me a trip to Eighth and I this morning. They have the list George has. And I don't anticipate any trouble having the people I want transferred over here."

"There's only so many training spaces available at the Country Club. Squeezing them in is going to cause some problems," Donovan said thoughtfully. "Nothing that can't be sorted out, but it will be a problem."

I was again wrong about Wild Bill, the DDO decided. Wild Bill did not blow his cork. And I really shouldn't be surprised. He knows when erupting will be advantageous and when it won't.

If Charley came in here with high hopes—and I'm damned sure he did—that General Fleming Pickering was going to come in here and be immediately and firmly put in his place, he's going to be very disappointed.

"Did I detect at Dick Fowler's dinner," Donovan went on, "some question about your people going through the Country Club training program?"

"Yes, as a matter of fact, I'm glad you brought that up," Pickering said. "In the case of two of my officers it seems to me that it would be a waste of time and money. Particularly since, as you said, there's a shortage of training spaces."

"And why would that be, General?" the DDA asked smoothly.

Be careful here, Pickering, the Country Club is Wild Bill's pride and joy. He really thinks it turns nice boys from the better families into the sort of cold-blooded killers the OSS needs.

"Major Ed Banning—he's about to be a lieutenant colonel—and George here have MAGIC clearances. They cannot go operational, so why train them?"

"The Lieutenant has a MAGIC clearance?" the DDA blurted.

In OSS headquarters, only Director Donovan and the DDA had MAGIC clearances. The DDA considered it an indication of his importance . . . and had successfully argued to Director Donovan that the DDO didn't need it, both because Donovan could make him privy to any MAGIC material he needed to know, and because having it would restrict his movements.

"Yes, he does," Pickering said. "I didn't see how he could work efficiently for me without one."

Why do I suspect, Charley, that you are now really unhappy about how this meeting is going?

"That makes sense," Donovan agreed. "That was all there was to your objections about sending your people through training?"

"There was a little more," Pickering said. "I was thinking that some of the men I'm bringing in with me would make excellent instructors at the training school; they don't really need basic training."

"You don't think your men could learn anything at the training school?" the DDA asked.

"Most of the people I'm bringing in with me, including George here, have at least one behind-the-lines operation behind them. Several of them two, and in one case, three," Pickering said. "But, obviously, everybody can always learn something. I have no objection to them learning as much as they can, time and the Gobi operation permitting."

"You can work that out with Charley," Donovan said. "That, and the other administrative details."

"I'm afraid to ask what they are," Pickering said.

"Pay, service records—we keep all service records here—that sort of thing, plus of course deciding who gets which badges," Donovan said, pointing at the "VISITOR 5th Floor Only" badge hanging from Pickering's tunic pocket.

"These are known as 'the barber's pole special,' " the DDO said, tapping his own red-striped identification badge, fully aware that what he was about to say would further add to Charley's unhappiness. "With one of them you have access to any OSS facility anywhere at any time. You'll need one of these, of course, and the lieutenant will, and your deputy—Colonel Banning, you said?"

Pickering nodded.

"But probably all of your people won't need that kind of unlimited access. Just tell Charley who you think should have what."

"We try to limit the Any Area Any Time badges to those who really have a need for them," the DDA said.

Pickering was obviously thinking that over. Finally he looked at Donovan.

"I'm thinking, Bill, that if getting this operation off the ground as quickly as possible is as important as Admiral Leahy thinks it is, it might save time to give all of my people one of these—what did you call them, 'barber's pole specials'? That way, if it becomes necessary to take one of my people to some area, we wouldn't have to run to Charley and get him the proper badge."

"We have never issued anyone at the Country Club a badge giving them access to this building, much less Any Area Any Time," the DDA said.

"Nevertheless, Charley," Donovan said. "General Pickering's point is well taken. Give all of his people Any Area Any Time access."

Charley, this is just not your day, is it? the DDO thought.

"General," the DDO said, "when you're finished here with Bill, perhaps we could get together for a little while and try to figure out where we go from here."

"Certainly," Pickering said. "Thank you."

"You can have him right now," Donovan said. "Unless you have something else, Fleming?"

"No, sir. I can't think of anything."

"When you two have something on paper about where you want to go on this operation, and how you want to get there, let me see it," Donovan ordered.

"Yes, sir," Pickering said, and pushed himself out of the green leather-upholstered armchair.

IX

[ONE]
The Peabody Hotel
Memphis, Tennessee
1655 28 February 1943

First Lieutenant Malcolm S. Pickering, USMCR, was out
of uniform: It was expressly forbidden for officers to appear in public places wearing flight gear, a regulation that
both the Shore Patrol and the Army's Military Police (in
a spirit of interservice cooperation) enforced with what
Pick thought was uncalled-for zealousness.

He had given this regulation—and the zeal with which
it was enforced—some thought before deciding to hell
with it, and leaving Memphis Naval Air Station attired in
a gabardine Suit, Flyers, Temperate Climate and a fur-
collared horsehide Jacket, Flyers, Intermediate, Type G1.

After the fourth time he was written up—three times
by the Shore Patrol and once by MPs—for being similarly
attired in public places, his squadron commander, Captain

Billy Dunn—he had been Dunn's wingman on Guadalcanal—was really getting pissed about wasting his time
answering "reply by endorsement hereto" correspondence
stating that he had counseled and reprimanded the of-
fending officer and was considering other disciplinary action.

But he had told Elizabeth-Sue Megham, a statuesque
Memphis belle with long blond hair, that he would meet
her in the Peabody Bar at 5:30, and he didn't want to be
late. Since he was sure that Elizabeth-Sue would not wait
for him, he took the chance.

On a scale of one to ten—ten being a sure thing—
Elizabeth-Sue was a nine. He had met her the previous
Friday evening at a service club dance on the Air Station.
She had been one of four Memphis matrons chaperoning
a busload of Nice Young Memphis Girls making their
contribution to the war effort by going out to the air sta-
tion on Friday nights to dance with white hats and enlisted
Marines.

Billy Dunn had assigned him to perform roughly similar duties, with orders to make damned sure none of the
enlisted men of VMF-262 consumed intoxicants, behaved
in an unsuitable manner, or tried to drag one of the Nice
Young Memphis Girls off into the bushes, even, Billy had
emphasized, if the Nice Young Girl was suffering from
raving carnal lust.

Although it was not officially stated, Pick was well
aware that his assignment to this duty was punishment for
his last encounter with the Shore Patrol while wearing
flight clothing. The correspondence from the Naval District had landed on Billy Dunn's desk while Pick had been
in California, and Billy had been waiting for him on the
flight line when he'd landed the Corsair.

Greatly pissed was a massive understatement.

It wasn't that he was chasing married women, Pick told
himself. He had danced with Mrs. Quincy T. Megham,
Jr., as the polite thing to do to his civilian counterpart.
And of course they had talked. He let her know, for instance, how much the men enjoyed the dances—even
though he knew the statement was far from true: ninety
percent of the men who showed up did it only because

they couldn't get a pass, or because they were broke. He also told her that chaperoning the dances was a fine thing and that the Marine Corps was really grateful.

"Oh, I like to do it," Elizabeth-Sue said. "My husband is out of town frequently these days. When he is, I'm bored and always looking for a little activity."

She doesn't mean that the way it sounds, Pick decided just then. *Not only is she a respectable Memphis belle, but we haven't known each other five minutes.*

"I'll bet you get bored out here, too, don't you?" Elizabeth-Sue asked. "All alone in your room?"

"Oh, yes," he said.

"I've heard that Bachelor Officers' Quarters are—what is it they say, 'out of limits'?—for lady guests. Is that true?"

"Off-limits," he corrected her automatically, his mind on other things, specifically that Elizabeth-Sue was pressing her abdomen against his in a manner he didn't think was accidental. "Yes, they are."

"Then you must get lonely in there, all alone by yourself."

"Actually, I don't live in the BOQ."

"You're married?"

The pressure of her abdomen against his disappeared.

"No. I live in the Peabody in Memphis," he said. "And I'm not married."

The pressure of her abdomen against his reappeared.

If she keeps that up, I'm going to get a hard-on.

She did, and he did.

The pressure of her abdomen against his remained constant.

Elizabeth-Sue volunteered further information about herself: for example, that her husband, Quincy, Junior, as he was known, was considerably older than she was, was deeply involved with administering War Bond sales in Tennessee, and had to be out of town a good deal. He was, in fact, out of town for the next week.

At that point, Elizabeth-Sue discreetly inquired if living in the Peabody was comfortable, and did he share his accommodations with anyone?

He lied to her in that instance, not to deceive her, but

because it was easier to say he was all alone than to explain that he and Captain William Charles Dunn, USMCR, of the Point Clear, Alabama, Dunns, shared the Jefferson Davis Suite in the Peabody—actually two three-room suites sharing a common sitting room. It was understood between the two men that neither entered the quarters of the other without first telephoning to make sure a visit would not interrupt anything, or embarrass the participants.

"Perhaps we could have a drink sometime," Pick said.

"Memphis is a small town, really," Elizabeth-Sue said. "Everyone knows everyone. If anyone saw us together, there would be talk."

"Well, maybe if we just happened to bump into each other somewhere, say the bar at the Peabody, we could go somewhere where no one would see us."

"You really are a wicked man, aren't you?" Elizabeth-Sue said, clearly aware that the somewhere where no one would see them was his room.

Lieutenant Pickering pulled his Cadillac convertible up to the front door of the Peabody Hotel. After checking up and down the street to make sure no Shore Patrolmen or Military Policemen were in sight, got out quickly and tossed the keys to the bellman on duty. "I won't be needing it tonight, I hope," he said to the bellman. He entered the building and headed for the bank of elevators. Then stopped in disbelief.

Sitting on a leather couch facing the passage between the elevators and the shallow pool in the center of the lobby was a fellow Marine officer and a lady, both of whom he was acquainted with. The Marine officer was in impeccable uniform.

He slid onto the couch beside the Marine officer.

"What the hell are you doing here?" Lieutenant Pickering asked.

"If she's not pulling my chain," Captain Kenneth R. McCoy, USMCR, announced, "I am about to see a flock of ducks march off the elevator, pass right by here, and then paddle around that pool." He described the path with a pointed finger.

"Truth is stranger than fiction," Pick said. "The duck

march is one of Memphis's best-known cultural attractions." He consulted his pilot's chronograph and added: "And if they're on time, and they usually are, that will take place in ninety seconds."

The two men looked at each for a moment.

"God, I'm glad to see you," Pick said.

"Me, too, buddy," Ken McCoy replied.

"Who's the broad?" Pick asked.

"Screw you, Pick," Miss Ernestine Sage said.

"When did you get here? How did you get here?" Pick asked.

"Nine o'clock this morning," McCoy said. "We came on the train. I wanted to drive, but Ernie said she was afraid of the weather."

This was not quite the truth. She had actually said that she would like to get a compartment on the train. She had always had a fantasy about making love in a bunk on a train, with the rails making that clickety-click sound beneath them.

Booking a compartment on the Cotton Blossom hadn't been easy, but Captain McCoy had been highly motivated. In the event, in his view, the trip had been worth all the effort.

"Why didn't you come out to the air station? Or at least call? What did you do all day?"

Miss Sage looked at Captain McCoy as if she feared he would tell Lieutenant Pickering how they had spent most of the day.

"We walked down to the river and watched it roll by," McCoy said. "I called out there, and Billy Dunn said you were really tied up and could we wait until you got off duty? If he told you we were here, he would probably have to court-martial you, because you could be counted upon to desert your post."

"He really takes being a captain a little too seriously," Pick said.

"According to him, you don't take being a lieutenant seriously enough," McCoy said, and then he said, "Well, I will be damned!"

A line of ducks, a dozen of them, shepherded by a

bellman, emerged from an elevator and marched quacking through the lobby into the shallow pool.

"Aren't they *adorable*?" Miss Sage inquired.

"Lieutenant, may I please see your ID card?" a boat-swain's mate second class, USN, with an SP brassard on his sleeve inquired.

"Oh, Jesus, Boats!" Lieutenant Pickering said. "Not again? What were you doing, waiting for me?"

"We just happened to see you get out of your car, sir," the SP said. "Can I have your ID card, please?"

McCoy saw there were two SPs. The second, a seaman first class, was standing a few feet away, his hands folded behind his back.

"Can I see you a minute, Boats?" McCoy said, standing up.

"Sir, this is no concern of yours," the SP said.

"That wasn't a suggestion, Boats," McCoy said, and held up a leather folder before the SP's face, just long enough for him to take a quick look at it.

"Aye, aye, sir," the Shore Patrolman said.

He followed McCoy across the lobby, where McCoy stopped behind a massive pole.

"Sir, could I see your credentials again, please?" the SP said.

McCoy handed him the leather folder again. The SP examined it carefully, looked hard at McCoy, then handed it back.

"You don't see very many of those, sir," he said.

"I suppose not," McCoy replied.

I never thought about that. I wonder how many Special Agents—real Special Agents—of the Office of Naval Intelligence there are, running around?

"How can I help you, Captain?"

"You're interfering with my business with that officer. Can I ask you to just walk away, or are we going to have to get your duty officer over here? Having to do that would annoy me." ·

"No, sir. Those credentials are enough for me."

"Thank you," McCoy said.

"Captain, it may not be my place . . ."

"What's on your mind, Boats?"

"Off the record, sir?"

McCoy nodded.

"That lieutenant . . . Sir, he's an ace from Guadalcanal. And he's a really nice guy. Let me put it this way. Half the time I see him out of uniform, I don't. You know what I mean?"

McCoy nodded.

"But the white hats and the enlisted Marines see him running around out of uniform, and they think they can get it away with it, too. And when I have to write them up, their asses are really in a crack."

"I take your point, Boats," McCoy said.

"I don't know what your business is with him, sir, and I'm not asking. But I really hope he's not in bad trouble."

"Nothing he can't fix by trying to straighten up and fly right," McCoy said.

"Yes, sir," the SP said. "Thank you, sir."

"Thank you, Boats," McCoy said.

The SP motioned to the other one, pointing to the door to the street, and walked away. McCoy returned to Ernie and Pick.

"Come on," he said.

"What did you show that SP?" Pick asked.

"Let's get out of the damned lobby," McCoy repeated. It was not a suggestion.

"You fixed that somehow, didn't you?" Pick said, as he stood up and walked toward the elevator. "How?"

"Didn't you see him wave his magic wand at the SP?" Ernie said. "Absolutely no compartments on a train without a priority? He waves his magic wand, people appear and hand him a priority. The Shore Patrol is about to haul you away, he waves his magic wand. The Shore Patrol goes away."

Pick looked confused.

"However you did that, thanks, Killer," Pick said.

"Jesus Christ!" McCoy said. "I should have let him write you up!"

"That would have really got my ass in a crack with Billy," Pick said.

"Yeah, he told me. Actually, he's pretty disgusted with you. You never learn."

When the elevator stopped, Pick led them down the corridor to the door of the Jefferson Davis suite.

"Is it safe for a nice girl like me to go in there?" Ernie asked.

"My quarters are popularly known as either the Monk's Cell or Celibate City, if that's what you mean."

Ernie snorted. McCoy, shaking his head, chuckled.

"If you hold me in such contempt, why did you try to talk me into marrying your girlfriend if you got yourself blown away?" Pick asked.

"He probably thought I could reform you," Ernie said. She looked around the sitting room. "Surprise, surprise, no naked ladies."

"They're probably hiding in a closet," McCoy said.

"I was about to offer you champagne, but if the two of you . . ."

"I'll pass on the champagne."

"I won't," Ernie said.

"I also just happen to have in my cell, through the door over there, a full case of Famous Grouse, recently flown in in my Corsair from San Francisco, California, in anticipation of the honor of your visit."

He led the way to the sitting room of his half of the suite.

"You didn't know we were coming," Ernie said.

"Both Mother and my father—separately—suggested it was a real possibility," Pick said. "I really hope it wasn't so that we could have a man-to-man, or girl-to-man, chat. I get enough of those from Billy."

"You said something about champagne?" Ernie said.

"You take care of the glasses," Pick said, pointing to a bar in the corner of the room, "and I will extricate the bubbly from the refrigerator."

McCoy went to the bar, found the still-sealed case of scotch behind it, and started to open it.

"Wouldn't you really rather have champagne?" Ernie asked.

"No," McCoy said simply, and removed a bottle of Famous Grouse from the case.

Pick returned with a bottle of Mumm's champagne and started unwrapping the wire cork-guard.

"Mumm's, huh?" Ernie said.

"Actually, I prefer Moët and Chandon," he said. "But it's hard to come by. There's a war on, you may have heard. You found the Grouse, I see, Ken."

"You keep fucking up, Pick," McCoy said, "they're going to send you back to VMF-229."

"There's a lady present, Captain," Pick said. "Please remember that you, too, are supposed to be a Marine officer and gentleman."

"What does that mean?" Ernie asked. "Pick was in VMF-229."

"It's now where they send Marine pilots—fuckup Marine pilots—nobody else wants," Pick explained. "Pilots that nobody else in the Corps but Charley Galloway can handle." He paused. "Would you believe I applied for transfer to VMF-229? Billy turned it down."

"Billy needs you to train his pilots," McCoy said. "*Your* pilots. You're the squadron exec, for Christ's sake!"

"An amazing thing happens when they pin captain's bars on some people, Ernie," Pick said. "They start to think of themselves as generals-in-training." He turned to McCoy. "Just for the record, *Captain*, I have never failed to be at the proper place at the appointed time. I *am* training my pilots."

"Billy said that, too," McCoy said. "But you won't be around to do that for your squadron if your MAG commander gets tired of hearing officially about your social life—and I mean the speeding tickets and the drunk driving, not only this out-of-uniform crap—and gets tired of Billy covering for you."

"I told you, I applied for transfer to VMF-229. And Billy turned me down."

"And now you're trying to force them to send you anyway, right?" McCoy asked. "Why? Because that's easier than going to Pensacola and finding out once and for all?"

"What the hell are you talking about? Finding out what once and for all?"

"You know what I'm talking about. *Who* I'm talking about."

Pick looked accusingly at Ernie.

"He already knew about her," she said. "But we compared notes, okay?"

"Et tu, Brutus?" Pick asked sarcastically.

"If you want to get pissed at somebody, get pissed at Dick Stecker," McCoy said. "He said when he asked—"

"Where did you see Dick?" Pickering interrupted.

Lieutenant Richard Stecker, USMC, the son of Colonel Jack (NMI) Stecker, had gone through flight school at Pensacola with Pickering. He had been severely injured landing his shot-up Wildcat on Guadalcanal's Henderson Field.

"Ernie and I went to see him in Philadelphia when we passed through. That's where they send banged-up aviators, you know."

"I went to see him . . ."

". . . a month ago," McCoy finished. "He told me. He also told me to tell you he is now walking with a cane only."

"When I saw him, he was on one of those things . . . parallel bars set just high enough for your hands. Having a hell of a time. Jesus!"

"He wants to go back to flying," McCoy said. "Anyway, he told me *he* was worried about *you*. Ol' Hot Shot himself. He told me that you told him that Good Ol' Whatsername . . ."

"Martha," Ernie furnished. "Martha Sayre Culhane."

"Thank you *very* much, former friend," Pick said.

"Who, when the dashing Marine Aviator told her 'I love you,' said, 'Thank you just the same, but I am not at all interested.' "

"Don't push me, Ken," Pick said.

"Breaking your heart."

"Honey," Ernie said to McCoy. "It's not funny."

"And causing you to turn to whisky and wild, wild women to forget. Which also caused you to change from being a pretty good Marine officer to a fuckup . . ."

"*Fuck you*, Ken."

". . . about to have your ass shipped to the fuckup squadron. How do you think your father's going to like that?"

"This is my business, not my father's, not yours. Is the

lecture about over, Captain, sir? Frankly, I'm getting a little bored with it."

"Jesus Christ, if this woman is so important to you, why the hell are you quitting? Give it another shot!"

Pick shrugged, but didn't respond directly to the question.

"I asked if the lecture was about over?" Pick said.

"Not quite. Almost."

"Then pray continue."

"And what makes you think Charley Galloway would put up with your hotshot, 'I'm a Guadalcanal ace, the rules don't apply to me,' bullshit?" McCoy said, half sadly, half angrily.

"Ken!" Ernie said warningly.

"I went out to Ewa with Galloway to see Big Steve," McCoy went on. "When Charley walked into a hangar, one of his lieutenants called, 'Skipper on the deck!' and everybody popped to. Including Big Steve. For Christ's sake, Pick, grow up! Charley wouldn't put up with half of the bullshit you're giving Billy."

The doorbell rang just as Pick opened his mouth to reply.

With a little bit of luck, that will be one of Pick's naked ladies, Ernie thought. *Arriving just in the nick of time to keep this from really getting out of hand.*

Pick went to the door and opened it.

Mrs. Quincy T. (Elizabeth-Sue) Megham, Jr., stood there, wearing a perky little hat with a veil, a silver fox cape, and a look that was a mixture of surprise, disappointment, and discomfiture.

"Oh, I hope I'm not interrupting anything!" she said. "I just took the chance . . ."

"Fortunately, you are," Ernie said, and walked quickly to the door. "Hi, I'm Ernie Sage. You got here just in time to help me drink some champagne. These two are on the hard stuff."

"Oh, I wouldn't want to intrude!"

"Not at all," Ernie said, as she grabbed her arm and dragged her into the room. "I'm really glad to see you." She propelled her to the bar and poured a glass of champagne for her. "I'm the closest thing Pick has to a sister,"

Ernie went on. "A *big* sister. And Captain McCoy is Pick's best friend, although Pick sometimes forgets that."

"How do you do?" Elizabeth-Sue said, directing the greeting mostly to McCoy.

McCoy inclined his head and said, "Ma'am."

"You're stationed at the air station, Captain McCoy?"

"You can call him 'Killer,' " Ernie said. "*All* of his friends do."

"Oh, Christ!" Pick said, and laughed.

McCoy shook his head in disbelief, but he seemed more amused than angry.

" *'Killer'*?" Elizabeth-Sue asked incredulously.

"As in 'Lady-killer,' " Ernie explained.

"Oh, really?" Elizabeth-Sue asked.

Pick started to giggle. It had a contagious reaction on McCoy.

"He really is," Pick said. "They both are. My best friends in all the world."

"Then you're not out at the air station, Captain Mc-Coy?" Elizabeth-Sue asked.

"No, ma'am. We're just passing through."

Elizabeth-Sue's relief at hearing that was evident on her face.

"Lieutenant Pickering—Pick—and I are involved in the Friday dance program for the enlisted people at the air station," Elizabeth-Sue said.

"Oh, come on," Ernie said. "I told you we're best friends."

"I don't know what you mean," Elizabeth-Sue said.

"I mean I'll give you five-to-one odds that I'm not the only female in this room sleeping with a Marine she's not married to," Ernie said.

Elizabeth-Sue's mouth dropped open and she looked at Ernie in utter disbelief.

"Jesus H. Christ!" Pick said.

"So why don't we stop pretending," Ernie went on, "and, for example, decide where we can all have a nice dinner where no one who knows you or Pick will see you? After you and I finish the champagne, I mean."

"I just can't believe I'm hearing this!" Elizabeth-Sue said.

"As a general rule of thumb, Elizabeth-Sue," Pick said, "you can believe anything Ernie says."

"You can believe this, Elizabeth-Sue," Ernie said. "Captain McCoy and I are just as concerned as you are about you and Pick not getting caught. Maybe more than you are."

"I never, in my entire life—"

"Yes, or no, Elizabeth-Sue?" Pick interrupted her.

Elizabeth-Sue looked at him for a long moment before replying, "Honey, I just can't think of any place, except one across the river."

"We could eat here," Ernie said. "It would be safer, and I really don't feel like going out anywhere."

"Maybe that would be better," Elizabeth-Sue said.

She drained her glass and extended it to Ernie for a refill. "May I ask you a question?" she asked.

"Ask away."

"What do you do?"

"When I'm not in my camp follower role, you mean?"

Elizabeth-Sue flinched a little at that, but nodded.

"She's the creative director, reporting directly to the account executive for the American Personal Pharmaceuticals account at BBD&O," Pick announced, sounding very much like a prideful brother.

Elizabeth-Sue confessed she really didn't know what that meant.

"It means she takes home probably twice as much money every month as Lady-killer McCoy and I do together."

"That's enough about me, thank you very much," Ernie said. "Get on the phone and order us some hors d'oeuvres."

"Yes, ma'am," Pick said, and went to the telephone.

"How long are you going to be in Memphis?" Elizabeth-Sue asked.

"Just as soon as Ken can get us a compartment on a train to Florida—and he's very good at that sort of thing—we're going to Palm Beach for a little sun. With a little bit of luck, maybe tomorrow."

[TWO]
Temporary Building T-2032
The Mall
Washington, D.C.
0805 3 March 1943

A painfully sunburned Captain Kenneth R. McCoy, USMCR, walked down the sidewalk between the rows of temporary buildings until he came to T-2032, then approached the door and rang the bell. A face appeared at a small window in the door, and a moment later there was a buzzing noise as the solenoid-operated lock functioned. He pushed open the door and stepped inside.

The "temporary" buildings on The Mall, built during World War I, had been designed to last no more than five years. Despite a quarter century's painting and patching to keep them functional, they showed their age. Floors sagged, roofs leaked, and keeping windows and doors operational required a small army of maintenance people.

The sign, painted Marine Corps Green, hung from a small pole on the tiny lawn before Temporary Building T-2032. It read, "USMC Office of Management Analysis." From the street Temporary Building T-2032, a two-story frame building with a shingle roof, looked no different than Building T-2034, "USMC Office of Dependent Affairs," to its right, or Building T-2030, "USMC Office of Procurement Contract Management," to its left.

Inside T-2032, there were considerable differences from the other buildings. Just beyond the ground-floor entrance was a counter behind which sat two Marine noncoms armed with pistols and World War I trench guns— Winchester Model 12 12–gauge pump-action shotguns, with six-round magazines and twenty-inch barrels with bayonet fixtures. They controlled access to the rest of the building. This was through a door covered (as was the wall itself) with pierced steel planking normally used to pave temporary aircraft runways.

"You look like you been out in the sun, Captain Mc-
Coy," Technical Sergeant Harry Rutterman said.

"Oh, you are an observant sonofabitch, aren't you,
Harry?" McCoy said, and touched his shoulder in a gesture of affection between old friends.

And then he reached for his ONI credentials. No one
was passed through the steel planking until the security
provisions had been complied with. There were no special
credentials for personnel assigned to the Office of Management Analysis; if there were, McCoy knew, people
would wonder exactly what Management Analysis did
that required special identification. The less people wondered about Management Analysis, the better. ONI credentials served just fine; everybody knew about ONI; and
no one asked questions of people with ONI credentials.

Rutterman checked the credentials and handed them
back with a smile.

"And who is being honored with the pleasure of your
visit?"

"Got a little last night, Harry, did you? You're in a very
good mood."

Rutterman laughed.

"Major Banning get in yet?" McCoy said.

"He don't work here no more," Rutterman said. "Captain Sessions is here."

"Sessions, then," McCoy said.

Rutterman picked up a telephone and dialed two digits.
"Captain McCoy to see you, sir," he said, listened a moment, and then hung up. "Pass, friend," he said to McCoy,
indicating the door covered with pierced steel planking.

As he reached it and tugged on it, there was another
solenoid buzz, and the door opened. McCoy passed
through it and then up a narrow flight of stairs. Captain
Ed Sessions was waiting for him at the top.

"Don't tell me, let me guess," he said. "You've been
in Florida."

"It's not funny," McCoy said.

"Come with me, Captain, the General wishes the pleasure of your company."

"He's here?" McCoy asked, surprised. General Pickering normally spent very little time in Building T-2032.

Sessions didn't reply. He led McCoy three quarters of the way down a narrow corridor, then knocked at a door before opening it.

"Captain McCoy to see you, General," he said, and motioned McCoy through.

"Christ," Brigadier General F. L. Rickabee greeted him, "what did you do, fall asleep on Palm Beach?"

"Yes, sir," McCoy said. "Good morning, sir. Good morning, *General*."

"Ah, you noticed! I was hoping you might."

"Congratulations, Sir. Well deserved."

"I'm not sure about that. There has been a promotion frenzy around here. I got caught up in it."

"Sir?"

"A silver leaf now adorns Ed Banning's collar points, and sometime this week even Sessions is going to have go buy major's leaves."

"That's about time, too," McCoy said to Sessions, then turned to General Rickabee. "Sergeant Rutterman said Major—Lieutenant Colonel—Banning doesn't work here anymore?"

"I would say Rutterman talks too much," Rickabee said coldly.

"Sir, he wasn't running off at the mouth. I told him I wanted to see Major Banning, and he said, 'Sorry, he doesn't work here anymore.' "

Rickabee seemed only partially satisfied.

"Sir," Captain Sessions said, "not only is he a good Marine, but Rutterman knows McCoy."

"I like that," Rickabee said. "Loyalty is a desirable characteristic of a Marine officer. But—correct me if I'm wrong—what Rutterman was *supposed* to say was, 'Sorry, sir. I don't know the name.' "

"Yes, sir," Sessions said.

"Let it pass, Ed," Rickabee said. "Rutterman *is* a good man."

"Aye, aye, sir."

"Well, now that security has been breached, and the cat, so to speak, is out of the bag, I might as well confirm that Lieutenant Colonel Banning is now assigned to the OSS. And so, Captain McCoy, are you."

"Yes, sir. General Pickering told me that was going to happen."

"Your records have already been sent over there. You know where it is, the National Institutes of Health Building?"

"Yes, sir."

"Maybe when this goddamn war is over I can get you back, McCoy. This is where you belong, and you've always done a good job for me."

"Thank you, sir."

"Send him over there in a car, Ed," Rickabee ordered. "Don't let the doorknob hit you in the ass on your way out, McCoy."

"Sir, I've got the ONI credentials," McCoy said. It was a question.

Rickabee thought that over a moment.

"Banning sold me on the idea of letting him keep his. Said we'll be working together, and they might come in handy. Same logic applies to you. Keep them. I'll deal with ONI if necessary."

"Aye, aye, sir."

Rickabee came from behind his desk and gave McCoy his hand.

"Good luck, McCoy," he said. "Keep your eyes open and your mouth shut."

[THREE]
The Office of the Deputy Director
(Administration)
The Office of Strategic Services
The National Institutes of Health Building
Washington, D.C.
0955 3 March 1943

"The Deputy Director will see you now, Captain," the DDA's secretary said, and motioned him toward a closed door.

McCoy, who had been cooling his heels for the better part of an hour, rose up from the couch and walked to the door. He hesitated, then knocked. There was no answer. McCoy looked over his shoulder at the secretary, who gestured for him to go in. He opened the door and stepped inside.

The well-dressed man behind the desk did not look up from his papers on his desk. After a moment, McCoy closed the door behind him and then stood near it in a position very close to Parade Rest.

Finally the man looked up at him, and after a moment McCoy understood he was expected to speak first. "Good morning, my name is McCoy," he said.

"Good morning. Captain Kenneth R. McCoy, is that right?"

"Yes, sir."

"I'm the OSS Deputy Director for Administration," the man said. "I've just been going over your records, Captain."

"Yes, sir."

"They're a . . . bit unusual," the DDA said. "If I'm reading them correctly, your formal education ended with high school, is that correct?"

"Yes, sir."

"And after service as an enlisted man—in China?"

"Yes, sir."

"You went through the Marine Corps Officer Candidate School at Quantico, and were commissioned second lieutenant?"

"Yes, sir."

"I had been under the impression that a college degree was a prerequisite for going to Officer Candidate School."

"I wouldn't know about that, sir."

"You have to understand, Captain, that you don't quite measure up to what we expect—in terms of education—of applicants for the OSS."

McCoy did not reply.

"On the other hand, your records indicate that you speak Chinese. Does that mean you can only speak—carry on a conversation? Or does that mean you can read and write Chinese?"

"I read and write Wu, Mandarin, and Cantonese," McCoy said.

"And Japanese?" the DDA asked dubiously after having another look at McCoy's service record.

"Not as well as I read and write the Chinese languages," McCoy said.

"And German and French?"

"And a little Italian and Spanish," McCoy said.

"Well, I'm sure you do," the DDA said, "but we'll run you through our Languages Division to see just how well you speak so many languages. Perhaps what the Marine Corps considers fluency . . . You understand?"

McCoy nodded.

"Let me be very frank," the DDA said. "We're going to send you through our training program. It's conducted at a base we operate in Virginia. And I'm frankly wondering if you might have some difficulty with the academic aspects of the course."

McCoy said nothing.

"Well, I suppose the way to handle this is, as I said, to run you through our Languages Division, have you tested, and then send you to the base."

The door to the DDA's office opened and the secretary walked in. "Sorry to interrupt, sir," she said, "but I thought you should know Colonel Banning is outside."

"Tell the Colonel I'm tied up," the DDA said, somewhat impatiently, "and that I will see him as soon as I can."

"Sir, I couldn't help but overhear. Colonel Banning is telephoning a General Rickabee."

"And?" the DDA interrupted impatiently.

"He's trying to locate Captain McCoy."

The DDA thought that over a moment. "Ask Colonel Banning to step in, will you, please?"

Banning came through the door a moment later. "What a pleasant surprise, Captain McCoy," he said. "I was just asking General Rickabee when we might expect to see your smiling face. Also, if I may say so, *really* sunburned?"

"Good morning, sir."

"I'll take the Captain off your hands, sir," Banning said to the DDA.

"I beg your pardon, Colonel?"

"I said I'll take Captain McCoy off your hands, sir."

"Colonel, Captain McCoy is about to go to the Languages Division to determine the exact level of his languages proficiency. That will probably take up most of the morning. After that, he will be transported to the training base."

"Sir, I don't think that's what General Pickering has in mind for Captain McCoy."

"Colonel, why don't you ask General Pickering to discuss that with me?"

"Yes, sir, I'll do that," Banning said, and walked out of the office.

"I gather you and Colonel Banning are acquainted?" the DDA asked.

"Yes, sir."

"Unfortunately, he hasn't been here long enough to understand our system of operation."

McCoy didn't reply.

"Now, where were we?" the DDA said. "Oh, yes. I'll telephone the Languages Division." He reached for one of the telephones on his desk.

His office door opened again.

"I'll take Captain McCoy off your hands, Charley," the Deputy Director (Operations) said.

"I just told Colonel Bann—"

"I just saw him in the hall; he told me," the DDO interrupted.

"—that it was my intention to have Captain McCoy's extraordinary facility with languages tested, and then to send him to the training base."

"Charley, you were there when General Pickering told Wild Bill that one of the officers he was bringing in with him had already done three successful behind-the-lines operations. He was speaking of Captain McCoy. And Pickering wasn't counting what McCoy did for Banning in China before the war. I've just made the decision that it would be a waste of time and money either to test his language skills—I'll take Colonel Banning's word about that—or to send him to the Country Club. Do we understand each other?"

"I'll have to discuss the matter with Director Donovan."

"And at the same meeting, it was decided that all of General Pickering's people will be issued barber's pole badges. Why don't we give McCoy's to him while he's here, and save him time?"

The DDA looked at the DDO for fifteen seconds, then picked up his telephone. "Mrs. Rogers, would you please pull Captain McCoy's Any Area Any Time identification badge from the safe and have him sign for it as he leaves? And then come in here, please. I need to dictate a memorandum for the record."

"You want to come with me, please, Captain?" the DDO asked.

McCoy followed him out of the office.

The DDO watched as Mrs. Rogers made McCoy sign for the identification badge, politely told her, "Thank you very much, Mrs. Rogers," and then led McCoy out of the outer officer into the corridor.

Banning, who had been leaning against the corridor wall, stood erect.

The DDO put his hand out to McCoy. "Welcome aboard, McCoy," he said. "I'm out of time right now—Banning will explain—but we'll find time for a chat as soon as possible. In the meantime, are you familiar with that great truth about any bureaucracy?"

"Sir?"

" 'In any bureaucracy, one may expect to find, near the top, a certain percentage of assholes,' " the DDO said. "You might want to write that down." Then he turned to Lieutenant Colonel Banning: "He's all yours, Ed."

He touched McCoy's shoulder and walked away.

"You owe him," Banning said. "If I hadn't bumped into him in the hall, you would have been doing push-ups and knee bends at the Country Club by the time I found General Pickering."

"Who is he?"

"The number-two guy around here, the Deputy Director (Operations), he's on our side. I'm not sure about the other clown. Come on. I'll show you the White Room, and put you to work."

*   *   *

In order for McCoy to gain entrance to the White Room, it was necessary for one of the two armed guards on duty outside the unmarked door to compare his face with the photo on the identification badge, and then to check a typewritten list under a TOP SECRET cover sheet to make sure his name was on it. He then nodded to the other security officer, who unlocked the door to the room.

The room was windowless, illuminated with concealed lighting. Thick carpets covered the floor and sound-absorbing material was on the walls. A lectern and a projection screen were at one end of the room, a motion picture and slide projector at the other. The large central conference table showed signs of use; it was littered with paper, some of it crumpled, dirty coffee cups, and empty Coke bottles.

The door was closed, and immediately a whirring noise came from the film and slide projectors. The projectors were automatically shut off when the door was opened, McCoy realized. A moment later, a map flashed onto the screen.

Shit, that's the goddamned Gobi Desert! I thought that operation was canceled, or at least on hold!

Well, what the hell did I expect?

"We've been in here for the best part of two days," Banning said. "Without accomplishing very much. You are hereby appointed, *vice* Lieutenant Colonel Banning, cleaning officer."

"Which means?"

"You will pick up every scrap of paper and put it in a burn bag. You will then telephone Classified Files—the number's on the phone—and they will come and collect everything—maps, slides, notes, and the burn bag, or bags—and haul it off. Then you will go outside and sign a certificate stating that the White Room is clean—meaning of classified material; somebody will come and deal with the Coke bottles and coffee cups—and it is available for use by others."

"Aye, aye, sir."

"Let me give you a quick run-through of where we are on Operation Gobi—which frankly is nowhere. And then you can perform your cleaning officer duties and go home. Where is home, by the way?"

"I'm at the Lafayette," Ken said.

"If you're uncomfortable in the General's apartment, you can bunk with me for a couple of days until we can find you something."

"I'm not in General Pickering's apartment," McCoy said. "I'm in the American Personal Pharmaceuticals suite."

"Ernie's with you?"

McCoy nodded.

"Then you go home to Ernie and tell her to do something about your sunburn. You really look awful."

"I feel awful."

Banning walked to one end of the room and stood in front of the map projected on the screen. "What is needed, Ken, is a weather station in this area," he gestured at the map, "to give what Colonel Hazeltine describes as reports of atmospheric fronts and conditions there.

"Now, we have reason to believe that a few Americans are already in the neighborhood, some former Marine guards at the Peking legation, the rest retired Marines, soldiers, and Yangtze River patrol sailors. And their wives and children." He paused. "At any point, Ken, ask questions."

"Aye, aye, sir," McCoy said. He slipped into one of the upholstered chairs and reached for a coffee pitcher.

"Communication with them is spotty at best, and we don't know where they are, and we can't ask them, because they have no cryptographic capability. And, to repeat, the communications are lousy.

"Ideally, we would make up a meteorological team—that's a minimum of four men, and about a ton of equipment, much of it expendable: weather balloons, for example, which will be consumed at the rate of two or three a day, and have to be resupplied, if we ever get that far—and send it in by airplane. Since no airplane has the range to make it back and forth from one of our bases, even if it wasn't intercepted, that means it would be a one-way mission.

"But since we don't know where our people are, or

where the Japanese are, it doesn't make any sense to send in a team on an expendable airplane. Or should I say an expendable team on an expendable airplane? We need knowledge of the terrain, and the disposition of Japanese forces. We have neither."

"Zimmerman spent four months in the Gobi Desert," McCoy said.

"What?" Banning asked in disbelief.

"When he first went to the Fourth Marines, 1938, somewhere around then, there was a bunch of people from the *National Geographic* magazine who went up there. The Fourth Marines provided the truck drivers. Zimmerman was one of them."

"You sure about that, Ken?" Pickering asked.

"Yes, sir. He told me about it. There's hardly any sand, he told me, it's mostly flat and rocky." He hesitated. "I think he went back up there after the explorers left."

"Why do you say that?"

"Out of school?"

"Sure."

"I think he was involved in smuggling," McCoy said.

"Smuggling what? And from where to where?"

"Jade and fancy vases out of China into India, and gold back from India. Or stuff from Russia, through some other country inside Russia."

"Kazakhstan?"

"I think so."

"You're telling me Zimmerman was on a caravan smuggling things into India and the Soviet Union?"

"No, sir. Zimmerman was bankrolling the smugglers—actually his woman was, with Zimmerman's money. He—or Mae Su—bought the jade and the vases et cetera, in China, and then sent them out on caravans. The caravan guys got a percentage of what they sold it for."

"How did he know he would ever see the caravan people again?" Banning asked incredulously.

"Sometimes . . . when *everybody's* making money, people are honest," McCoy said. "And Zimmerman's not the sort of guy anyone wants to cross," he added matter-of-factly.

"In other words, you believe this story?"

McCoy nodded.

"This wasn't big-time stuff. Nothing more than a couple of hundred dollars at a time," McCoy said. "But he and Mae Su have a pretty good-size farm in her village. I went up there a couple of times. They even have a little sausage factory. And they lived good in Shanghai—a lot better than he could live on a corporal's pay. He told me he was saving money for when he retired."

"But you're sure he's been in contact with smugglers?"

McCoy nodded. "And then they would buy the stuff—mostly icons. You know what they are? Sort of folding pictures of saints painted on wood?"

"I know what they are," Banning said.

"They would bring the icons smuggled out of Russia, bring them to Shanghai, and sell them to the antique dealers."

"I don't suppose you were involved in this?" Banning said.

"I thought about it, but I didn't like the odds," McCoy replied.

"This Chinese wife of his," Banning asked, thinking out loud. "Where do you think she is?"

"Well, maybe . . . no, probably, she's playing it safe in the village," McCoy said. "It's called Paotow-Zi, on the Yellow River twenty, thirty miles from the nearest city. Baotou."

"Show me on the map," Banning ordered, went to the table and flipped through a half-dozen large maps until he found what he was looking for, then pulled it from the others and laid it on top.

McCoy found what he was looking for quickly, and held his finger on it for Banning to see. Banning took a compass and made some quick measurements.

"It's a long way from there to the Gobi Desert," he said.

McCoy didn't argue.

"You said Zimmerman's Chinese wife is 'probably' playing it safe in this village. Was there anything significant in that?"

McCoy looked uncomfortable.

"What, Ken?" Banning pursued.

"She may be in the middle of the Gobi Desert with some caravan," he said.

"Doing what?"

"Trying to make it to India. Or, for that matter, into Russia."

"Into Russia? Why the hell would she want to go into Russia? Or India?"

"That's what Zimmerman told her to do, get into India, go to the first American consulate she can find. Have the consul send word to Zimmerman's mother that she and the kids are in India. And then try to get them to the States."

"That seems like a pretty forlorn hope," Banning said. "The American Consul is not liable to pay a lot of attention to a Chinese woman with some half-breed children who says she's married to an American."

"They're married. Some Catholic priest married them. There's a wedding certificate, and Zimmerman went to the consulate and made some sort of statement that the kids are his."

"I don't think that will work, Ken. You have to admire him—both of them—for trying."

"I don't think it will work, either. But strange things happen."

"What did you say about Russia?" Banning asked. "You said something about them trying to get into Russia."

McCoy looked even more uncomfortable.

"Let's have it, McCoy," Banning said very softly.

"I asked Mae Su to try to take care of Milla if anything happened," McCoy said, meeting Banning's eyes.

"You never said anything about that to me."

"I didn't want you to get your hopes up. If I were Mae Su, I would be trying to cover my ass, and protecting the kids, and wouldn't want to have to worry about taking care of a white woman with a Nansen passport."

"And since she's a typical Chinese, she said 'yes, of course, certainly' and then forgot about it?"

"She said she would think about it," McCoy said. "Mae Su's all right."

"You don't really think they're together?"

"I don't know. I've thought about it. On one hand, Mae Su wants to protect her kids, and will let nothing get in the way of that. On the other hand, when I asked her, you weren't married to Milla. I didn't know about that until you told me. But Zimmerman knew, and I'm sure he told Mae Su. A woman married to an American, an American officer, is not the same thing as a stateless woman. Mae Su may have decided that Milla might be useful. Any consulate would do more for a white woman married to an American officer than he would for a Chinese married to a corporal. Mae Su would know that. She's the brains in that family."

"Jesus Christ!" Banning said.

"Did Milla have any money?"

"Not much," Banning said. "All I could lay my hands on on short notice. Whatever she could get for my stuff, which probably was damned little. And she had some money of her own—damned little, I'm sure."

McCoy didn't reply.

"Jesus Christ, Ken, why didn't you tell me any of this before?"

"I didn't think there was anything you could do if you knew," McCoy said. "I didn't want to open the wound."

"Because you don't think that they'll . . ."

"The odds aren't very good," McCoy said.

"There's nothing wrong with betting on a long shot if it's the only bet open," Banning said.

McCoy shrugged what could have been agreement.

"The one thing we'd agreed on in here after two days is that we need to talk to someone who knows more about the Gobi Desert than what he's read in the *National Geographic*," Banning said.

McCoy chuckled.

"So where is Gunny Zimmerman?"

"On his way here," McCoy said. "Which means he's either still in Brisbane, or in Pearl Harbor, or maybe San Diego. Zimmerman and Koffler—and Mrs. Koffler—are coming on the same orders. They're entitled to thirty-day leaves. There's some kind of a rest hotel somewhere . . ."

"The Greenbrier Hotel in West Virginia," Banning furnished.

"I guess the idea was they could hold each other's hands. But I don't think that will last after they get off the first plane. Zimmerman will 'get lost,' and the Kofflers will go on without him. And I don't think that Zimmerman is interested in going to a rest hotel someplace. So he's probably at Pearl, 'Diego . . . anywhere . . . and will check in at Management Analysis when his leave is up. Maybe even before."

"We need him here, and now," Banning said, "which means we're going to have to find him. I'll go see General Rickabee and see what he can do."

McCoy nodded.

"I need a big favor from you, Ken," Banning said.

"Yes, sir."

"When you brief the team tomorrow morning, and you will, I want you to leave Milla and the possibility that she might be with Zimmerman's wife out."

"Okay. But why?"

"Because if either the DDO or General Pickering hears that my wife is involved in this, they'll take me off this operation. It would be too much of an emotional involvement for me to function rationally. You understand?"

"If I can get to Zimmerman first," McCoy said. "I'll tell him to leave Milla out."

"I'll do my damnedest to arrange that," Banning said.

"Ed, don't get your hopes up," McCoy said.

That's the first time since I first laid eyes on him that he's ever called me by my first name, Banning thought.

"I won't. I understand the odds."

McCoy nodded.

But what if he's wrong? What if the long shot comes in? What if Milla is alive? What do I tell Carolyn?

"I'm going over to T-2032," Banning said. "We really need Zimmerman. Can you handle the cleaning by yourself?"

"Yes, sir."

"Then go home and ask Ernie to do something for that sunburn. We can't afford to have you in the hospital."

"Aye, aye, sir."

X

[ONE]
USMC Transient Barracks
U.S. Naval Station
San Diego, California
0720 4 March 1943

Staff Sergeant Karl Krantz had been a clerk for the Delaware & Lackawanna Railroad before a surge of patriotism sent him to the Marine Recruiting Office on December 9, 1941. After graduating from Parris Island, he had been a clerk in the Marine Corps.

That hadn't kept him from being wounded on Guadalcanal; but it had kept him from carrying a rifle on the line. Having seen what happened on the line to people who carried rifles, he was now profoundly grateful for that.

He had been wounded by bomb shrapnel during a Japanese raid on Henderson Field. A half-inch chunk of jagged shrapnel had struck him in the left buttock—which was not nearly as funny as it sounds. In due course, Corporal Krantz was sent to the Navy Hospital at Pearl Harbor. And on discharge from the hospital, he had been declared "limited duty." He could walk, but not very far, and it hurt when he did.

After three months as a clerk at Pearl Harbor—long enough to make sergeant—they sent him home, thus allowing some fully fit sergeant clerk to be sent to the war zone. Back in the States, he had been assigned to San Diego, doing much the same thing he had done for the Delaware & Lackawanna—except here it was people getting on and off ships and airplanes, as well as trains.

He thought of himself as sort of an expediter. He was good at it and took his responsibilities seriously, and this had gotten him another stripe.

Which explained his presence at the office at 0720 on a Sunday morning. The man with the duty—Corporal Vito Martino, who had also been in the wrong place at the wrong time on the 'Canal, and who now had a wired-together jaw that gave him a perpetual leer—did not, in Staff Sergeant Krantz's opinion, have either the dedication or the brains to be relied upon. Sergeant Krantz was not surprised to find Corporal Martino sound asleep on a cot behind the ENLISTED TRANSIENTS REPORT HERE counter. That in itself did not bother him—there was nothing wrong with crapping out if nothing was coming in or going out. What bothered him was that Martino had slept through breakfast. He would, in other words, really rather crap out than eat.

Sergeant Krantz woke Corporal Martino up by kicking the legs of the cot. Corporal Martino opened his eyes, then pushed himself up on the cot, supporting himself with his elbows.

"Hey, Sarge, what's up?"

"That was what I intended to ask you. Anything happen?"

"The 2100 Coronado from Pearl was damned near two hours late. They was getting real worried. But it got here, and I was up to damned near midnight working it."

"Any problems?"

"No. Usual thing. Some brass, some guys who got hit.

Customs caught two guys trying to smuggle in Nambu pistols. The usual shit," Corporal Martino said, and then remembered something. "There was a gunny on it, mean-looking fucker, with some really strange orders."

"What do you mean, 'really strange orders'?"

"They're over there, in the Incoming Enlisted box," Corporal Martino said, pointing.

Staff Sergeant Krantz went to the counter and found the orders Martino considered damned strange.

Headquarters
U.S.M.C. Special Detachment 16
FPO, San Francisco, Cal.

10 February 1943

Subject: Detachment of
Gunnery Sergeant Ernest W. Zimmerman, 56230, USMC.
Staff Sergeant Stephen M. Koffler, 166705, USMC

Previous verbal orders CINCPAC detaching Gunnery Sergeant Ernest W. Zimmerman from temporary duty with 2nd Raider Bn, USMC, and VMF-229 are confirmed and made a matter of record.

Verbal orders of Supreme Commander SWPOA awarding Gunnery Sergeant Zimmerman and Staff Sergeant Koffler the Bronze Star Medal for "Conspicuous valor and intrepidity in the face of the enemy in an extremely hazardous classified operation" are confirmed and made a matter of record. The citations will be forwarded to Hq, USMC when available.

Gunnery Sergeant Ernest W. Zimmerman is detached USMC SpecDet16, FPO, San Francisco, Cal. effective 10 Feb 1943 and attached USMC Office of Management Analysis, Washington, DC, for further reassignment.

Gunnery Sergeant Ernest W. Zimmerman will proceed from present station to USMC Office of Management Analysis, Washington, DC, by first available US Government or commercial air transportation. Priority AA1 is authorized. Under the provisions of USMC PersReg 42-101 "Recuperative Leave for Personnel Returning to USMC Control After POW Status or Other Service Behind Enemy Lines" 30 days Delay En Route Leave Not Chargeable As Ordinary Leave is authorized.

Inasmuch as the exigencies of the Naval Service have caused Gunnery Sergeant Zimmerman's service and pay records to become unavailable, Gunnery Sergeant Zimmerman is authorized to draw a partial pay of no more than ninety-percent (90%) of the anticipated pay of a Gunnery Sergeant with eight (8) years service each month until his records can be located or reconstructed.

Staff Sergeant Stephen M. Koffler is detached USMC SpecDet16, FPO, San Francisco, Cal. Effective 10 Feb 1943 and attached USMC Schools, Quantico, Va., for enrollment in Officer Candidate School.

Staff Sergeant Stephen M. Koffler will proceed from present station to USMC Schools, Quantico, Va., by first available US Government or commercial air transportation. Mrs. Daphne F. Koffler (Dependent Wife) is authorized to accompany Staff Sergeant Koffler. Travel will be arranged so that Staff Sergeant and Mrs. Koffler will not be separated during travel. Priority AAA1 is authorized. Under the provisions of USMC PersReg 42-101 "Recuperative Leave for Personnel Returning to USMC Control After POW Status or Other Service Behind Enemy Lines" 30 days Delay En Route Leave Not Chargeable As Ordinary Leave is authorized.

Authority:

Letter, Office of the Secretary of the Navy, Subject, "Establishment of U.S. Marine Corps Special Detachment 16." 8 Apr 1942.

Verbal Order, BrigGen F. Pickering, USMCR 10 Feb 1943.

BY DIRECTION OF COLONEL WATERSON:

Official:
John Marston Moore
1st Lt John Marston Moore, USMCR
Adjutant

Staff Sergeant Krantz had seen the orders before. Five days earlier Staff Sergeant Koffler and his wife had passed through San Diego. Koffler looked as if he had left boot camp about that long ago, and his wife was an Aussie girl who looked as if she was going to be a mother in the *next* five days.

And now the gunny on the same orders had apparently shown up.

"You should have called me, Martino," Sergeant Krantz said.

"It was midnight, Sergeant," Martino said. "I figured you'd be in the sack."

"Anytime you get something out of the ordinary like this, you call me. Understand?"

"You got it, Sarge."

"You got him into the hospital okay?" Krantz asked.

"Hospital? No. He said he was going into 'Diego and see if he could find a poker game."

"What?"

"I told him to check back at 0900 Monday, by then his tickets would probably be ready, and he could draw a partial pay, and I asked him if he wanted a ride to the Staff NCO quarters. And he said no, he was going to catch the bus, go into 'Diego, and see if he could find a poker game."

"Jesus Christ, I don't believe you," Krantz said. "Didn't you read the goddamned orders? This guy is either an escaped POW—which seems likely, since he doesn't have his service records—or he was doing something behind the enemy's lines."

"So?"

Krantz walked to the wall of the office, took down a clipboard, and threw it to Corporal Martino. "You are supposed to read the goddamned thing every day. If you ever did, you would know people like that get special treatment. First, they go to the hospital, then they go to some rest hotel in West Virginia. *Jesus*, Martino!"

Staff Sergeant Krantz picked up the telephone and dialed a number from memory. "Sir, sorry to bother you at this hour, and on Sunday, but we have a little problem down here. I think you had better come down here, sir."

Captain Roger Marshutz, an enormous man with a temper to match, arrived at the office ten minutes later. After hearing what had happened, he delivered a verbal chastisement to Corporal Martino that Martino would remember for a long time.

Then he set about solving the problem. He personally visited both the officer of the guard and the Shore Patrol Detachment duty officer and explained the predicament.

Both officers were sympathetic and promised to do their very best to locate gunny Sergeant Zimmerman. He was not, of course, to be arrested. You don't arrest somebody who just got out of a POW camp, or wherever the hell he had been, and throw him in the back of a jeep. Whoever found him was to politely inform Gunnery Sergeant Zimmerman that a little problem had come up, and would he please come with them and help them to straighten it out?

Captain Marshutz waited around the office until 1330, in the vain hope that Gunnery Sergeant Zimmerman would be located and delivered to him. Then he went to his quarters, with orders to summon him immediately when anything came up.

Staff Sergeant Krantz waited around the office until 1630, in the same vain hope. Then he went to his quarters. Before he left, he informed Corporal Martino that he didn't give a good goddamn that he had previously promised Corporal Martino the day off, he would stay there for fucking ever, if necessary, until Gunnery Zimmerman was located.

Both Captain Marshutz and Staff Sergeant Krantz were back at the office at 0730 Monday morning. With a little bit of luck, they told themselves, Gunnery Sergeant Zimmerman, in compliance with that idiot Martino's instructions, just might show up at 0900 to pick up his tickets and partial pay.

Oh nine hundred came and passed. And so did 0930 and 1000. At 1025, just as Captain Marshutz was about to pick up the telephone and inform Lieutenant Colonel Oswald that they were having a little problem, and he thought he had better discuss it personally with the Colonel, Gunnery Sergeant Zimmerman walked into the office, looked at Staff Sergeant Krantz, burped, and announced he had been told that by now he could pick up his tickets and draw a partial pay.

"Your name is Zimmerman, Gunny?" Captain Marshutz asked.

"Yes, sir."

"Would you mind telling me where you've been?"

"No, sir."

"You don't want to tell me?"

"Sir, the Captain asked if I would mind telling him."

"So tell me."

"Sir, I went downtown for a while, sir, and then I tried to get a hotel, but they wanted two dollars and fifty cents, so I told myself fuck that, sir, and come back out here and got a bunk in the transient Staff NCO quarters."

"You've been in the Staff NCO quarters all this time?"

"Yes, sir. I told that fucking feather merchant in charge of quarters to wake me up so's I could be here at 0900, and the fucker didn't do it. If the Captain is pissed because I'm late, I respectfully ask the Captain to get that little shit in here and ask *him* didn't I tell him to wake me up so's I could be here on time."

"I'll take your word for it, Gunny," Captain Marshutz said. "But there is a little problem."

"Yes, sir?"

"There's a special program for men like yourself, recently escaped POW's . . ."

"Begging the Captain's pardon, sir. I was never no POW."

"But you were behind the enemy's lines?"

"Yes, sir. Twice. First, on the 'Canal, with the Second Raiders, and the last time we was on Mindanao."

"In the Philippines?"

"Yes, sir."

"So you escaped from the Philippines?"

"Begging the Captain's pardon, sir. Not escaped. They sent us in on a submarine, and then they sent the submarine back and it brung us out. What was the name of that fucking pigboat? The *Sunfish*. That's what it was, the *Sunfish*."

"Well, welcome home, Gunny."

"Thank you, sir."

"As I was saying before, Gunny, there's a special program for men like yourself. . . ."

"Yes, sir."

"First, we run you through the hospital, to make sure you're shipshape, physically, and then you go to a hotel in West Virginia—all expenses paid, of course—for a month."

"No, sir."

" 'No, sir'?"

"Sir, begging the Captain's pardon, the General told me the first thing I do is go to Washington and check in with Major Banning."

"Well, perhaps 'the General' wasn't aware of this program, Gunny. It's relatively recent."

"With all respect, sir, 'An order received will be obeyed unless countermanded by an officer of senior grade.' The General told me to go to Washington and check in with Major Banning. Them's my orders, sir. With all respect, sir."

Christ, he memorized that.

"Sir, I got Major Banning's number, if the Captain would like to check with him," Gunny Zimmerman offered.

"Perhaps that would be a good idea," Captain Marshutz said.

"Sir, Liberty Three, twenty-nine zero eight," Zimmerman said. "That's in Washington, D.C."

He memorized that, too.

A minute later, Staff Sergeant Krantz handed Captain Marshutz the telephone. "It's ringing, sir," he said.

The telephone was answered on the second ring.

"Liberty 3-2908."

"With whom am I speaking, please?"

"Will you tell me who you wish to speak to, please?"

"Major Banning," Captain Marshutz said, a hint of exasperation in his voice. He added "please" as a late-coming afterthought.

"Sir, there is no one of that name at this number."

"Gunny, they say they don't have a Major Banning."

"Bullshit!" Gunny Zimmerman said. "I never forget no numbers. With respect, sir, you got the right number?"

"What is it again, Gunny?"

"Sir, Liberty Three, twenty-nine zero eight," Zimmerman said.

"Is this Liberty 3-2908?"

"Yes, it is. Who's calling, please?"

"There is no Major Banning at this number?"

"That is correct."

Captain Marshutz looked at Zimmerman and shook his head.

"Sir, tell them the call is from me," Zimmerman said.

"Would Major Banning be there if he knew it was Gunnery Sergeant Zimmerman calling?" Captain Marshutz asked very politely, which was his manner when his temper was on the verge of eruption.

"Are you Gunnery Sergeant Zimmerman?"

"Sir, if that don't work, ask for Captain McCoy," Zimmerman said.

"Have you a Captain McCoy?" Marshutz asked.

"Captain *Kenneth R.* McCoy," Zimmerman amplified.

"Captain *Kenneth R.* McCoy," Marshutz parroted.

"Gunnery Sergeant Zimmerman is calling for either Major Banning or Captain McCoy. Is that correct?"

"That is absolutely correct."

"Hold on, please."

There was the sound of another telephone ringing, just once, and then another voice came on the line.

"Yes?"

"With whom am I speaking, please?" Captain Marshutz asked politely.

"Whom do you wish to speak to?"

"Either a Major Banning or a Captain McCoy."

"With regard to what? Who are you, please?"

"My name is Captain Roger Marshutz, USMC," Marshutz said, as he sensed his temper going from simmer to boil. "I'm calling with regard to a goddamned gunnery sergeant named Zimmerman. Does that satisfy your goddamned curiosity?"

"It helps a great deal, as a matter of fact. I'm always happy to chat on the telephone with a fellow Marine, even one who uses language unbecoming an officer and a gentleman. But, pray tell me, how can I help you, Captain?"

"With whom am I speaking?"

"My name is Rickabee, Captain. Brigadier General Rickabee, USMC."

Oh, shit!

"Sir, I was asked to call this number, by Gunnery Sergeant Zimmerman, Ernest W. . . . ."

"Is there some sort of problem with the gunny? Where are you?"

"Marine Barracks, San Diego, sir."

"And he's there, with you?"

"Yes, sir."

"Put him on the phone, please. I want his side of the story first."

"Aye, aye, sir."

Marshutz handed the phone to Zimmerman. "General Rickabee wishes to speak to you."

"I'll be goddamned! General!" Zimmerman said to himself, then spoke into the telephone. "Sir, the General told me to call Major Banning if I ran into trouble. Sorry to bother *you*, sir."

"What sort of trouble are you in, Gunny?"

"Sir, they want to put me in the fucking hospital and then send me to some fucking hotel someplace. I told them I couldn't do that."

"Welcome home, Zimmerman. When did you get in?"

"Sir, about 2300 Saturday."

"Put the Captain back on, will you, please?"

"Aye, aye, sir."

Zimmerman handed the telephone back to Captain Marshutz.

"Yes, sir, General?"

"It is my desire, Captain, that you (a) have Gunnery Sergeant Zimmerman on the next available airplane to Washington; (b) telephone the number he gave you after he has actually taken off, prepared to give me his ETA in Washington."

"Aye, aye, sir."

"As far as this rest hotel business is concerned, Gunny Zimmerman considers himself to be taking a rest whenever no one is actually shooting at him. He's one hell of Marine, and we'll take care of entertaining him here."

"Yes, sir."

The line went dead.

Marshutz looked at Zimmerman. "Curiosity overwhelms me, Gunny," he said. "Just who is General Rickabee?"

"Sir, with respect, I don't think the Captain has the fucking need to know."

"You're probably fucking right," Captain Marshutz said, and turned to Staff Sergeant Krantz. "Karl, get the gunny on the next flight out of here. I don't care who gets bumped to get him a seat."

"Aye, aye, sir."

"And the minute he's airborne, call that number he gave . . ."

"Sir, Liberty Three, twenty-nine zero eight," Zimmerman said.

". . . and give them the ETA."

[TWO]
Main Gate
U.S. Naval Air Station
Pensacola, Florida
1215 6 March 1943

The galling thing about this chickenshit little sonofabitch, Captain James B. Weston, USMCR, thought as he sat fuming in the Buick waiting for the duty officer to show up after he was summoned by the main gate guard, *is that he's a Marine, not a sailor. You'd think a Marine would cut a fellow Marine a little slack.*

The whole trip had not gone well, beginning with the reason he was making it in the first place: Lieutenant (j.g.) Janice Hardison, NC, USNR, had told him, firmly, that she had the duty, midnight to eight, Friday *and* Saturday, and that he should not come up to Philadelphia because there wouldn't be time for them to do anything if he did.

So he had driven *down*, leaving the Greenbrier as early as he could on Friday afternoon, and driving through the night. During the journey, he had been stopped twice for speeding. One of these, early that morning in Georgia, had seen him forking over fifty-five dollars to a justice of the peace roused from his bed by the deputy sheriff who had arrested him.

He had arrived in Pensacola a few minutes before

seven, and had decided the smart thing to do would be to
get a room at the San Carlos Hotel before driving out to
the air station. There would, of course, be a telephone in
the room, over which he could conveniently contact Major
Avery R. Williamson, USMCR.

He had to practically beg the manager to give him a
room, and the only thing left was a two-room suite at
$32.50 a night, a luxury he needed like a hole in the head.
And then, a little later when he got on the telephone, the
air station operator refused to put him through to Major
Williamson's quarters, saying that he would have to telephone Major Williamson's office, which, since it was Saturday, *might* be open after 0800.

So then he stretched out on the bed to wait for 0800,
and wakened at 1200, whereupon he had called again,
requested Major Williamson's office number, and listened
as the number rang and rang and rang and no one answered.

The thing to do, obviously, was go out to the goddamned air station and run down Major Williamson by whatever means proved to be necessary. Seeing Major
Williamson was important.

He got as far as the main gate, expecting to get waved
through after a crisp salute from the guard. But instead he
was waved to a halt by a five-foot-two, 120-pound Marine
PFC, who asked him what his business was at the Pensacola Naval Air Station.

"I'm just visiting," Weston had told him.

The PFC had then asked him for his identification card
and his pass, or orders.

He had only his ID card.

Weston more or less patiently explained that he was on
temporary duty at the Greenbrier Hotel, which was serving as a rest and recuperation facility for personnel returning from overseas, and didn't have a pass because it
was the policy at the Greenbrier that passes were not
needed to leave the place on weekends.

Clearly convinced that he had at the minimum appre-
hended an AWOL officer, and perhaps even a Japanese
spy intent upon infiltrating the air base to blow up the
aircraft on the flight lines, the Marine PFC showed Wes-

ton where he should park the car until the duty officer arrived. Then he stood in the door of the guard shack, his eyes never leaving Weston for more than five seconds. Should Weston attempt to drive off, he was obviously prepared to take any necessary action, like shooting him with his .45.

The duty officer, a lieutenant (j.g.) who was *not* wearing the golden wings of a Naval Aviator, appeared ten minutes later. He eyed Weston warily, while Weston repeated his tale about being at the Greenbrier, and not needing a pass because no passes were required.

"Sir, it's my understanding that the Greenbrier Hotel has been taken over as sort of a hospital for personnel who have escaped, or have otherwise been returned from POW status."

"That's correct."

"You were a POW?" the j.g. asked.

"Yes," Weston said, deciding that this was not the time to tell the truth, the whole truth, and nothing else. "Lieutenant, if you don't believe me, you can call the Greenbrier. I'm sure they will tell you I am who I'm telling you I am."

And if he calls the Greenbrier, and I can't get Commander Bolemann on the line, he is going to be told that while I am who I say I am, the No Pass Required rule is for the "Local Area Only" and does not include Pensacola, Florida.

"Sir, what are you doing at Pensacola?"

"I'm carrying a message to Major Avery R. Williamson," Weston replied, "from a mutual friend."

The way things are going, he'll ask to see the message, and I will really be fucked up. Colonel Dawkins said I was to personally give it to Major Williamson and to make sure nobody else sees it. So I will obey the Colonel, which means I will have to tell this clown, "Ooops, I seem to have misplaced the message."

```
                        MAG-21, Ewa
                     FPO San Francisco
                          13 Feb 43
```

Major Avery R. Williamson
Pensacola NAS, Florida

Dear Dick:

  The day before yesterday, I gave the
bearer of this note, Captain Jim Weston,
his F4U check ride. Since Charley
Galloway trained him, I was not surprised
that he passed it 4.0.

  For unbelievably idiotic reasons,
however, he will soon be sent to P'Cola to
learn how to fly all over again. He will
tell you the details of this moronic
behavior in high places.

  Moreover, he's a friend of Charley's,
Big Steve's, and mine. Do what you can for
him as a favor to all of us.

Always,

Dawk

Clyde W. Dawkins, LtCol, USMC

  "I saw Major Williamson half an hour ago at the Yacht
Club," the j.g. said, displaying a nearly miraculous change
of attitude. "I was sanding my bottom."

  Captain Weston had an instant mental image of the j.g.
sanding his bottom, before he realized he was talking
about the bottom of a boat. The smile that came to his
face, however, was misinterpreted by the j.g. as a gesture
of friendship between fellow sailors. He smiled warmly
back.

"I'd say go down there," he said. "But I think he's probably gone by now."

"I've been trying to get his phone number."

"Marine!" the j.g. ordered, "bring the base phone book over here!"

The PFC delivered the phone book. Major Williamson's name was not listed. The j.g. examined the cover of the phone book.

"This is outdated!" he said.

"Sorry, sir," the PFC said.

"I think the smartest thing for you to do, sir," the j.g. said, "is go to the Main Officer's Club. You know where that is?"

"I trained here," Weston said.

"They'll have the latest phone book," the j.g. said.

"Thank you," Weston said.

"I'm really sorry you were inconvenienced here, Captain. But sometimes—no offense intended—Marines sometimes get carried away."

"No offense taken," Weston said. "I presume I'm free to go?"

"Yes, sir," the j.g. said. "Of course. Welcome home, sir."

The Main Officer's Club was a rambling white stucco building that he remembered as stifling in the summer, but that now had air-conditioning. Weston found it without trouble. The cocktail lounge he also found without trouble. There he decided what he needed before lunch was at least two drinks.

He was about to order the second double scotch when it occurred to him that he might not make the proper impression on Major Avery Williamson if he appeared in a cloud of scotch fumes.

"Where can I find a phone book?" he asked.

"There's a phone booth in the lobby, sir."

Weston paid for the drink and went to the lobby. There was indeed a phone book, and it listed the quarters telephone number for Williamson, A. R., Maj. USMC. Weston wrote it down, then waited for the occupant of the phone booth to finish. She was a slightly portly matron in a floppy hat whose husband, Weston decided, was probably at least a lieutenant commander.

"Sir," a crisp naval voice said in his ear. Weston turned to see a full lieutenant wearing the insignia of an aide-de-camp.

Now what?

"Sir, is your name Weston?"

Weston nodded.

"Sir, the Admiral's compliments. Sir, the Admiral would be grateful for a few words with you."

What admiral? Weston wondered.

"That would be my great pleasure, Lieutenant," Weston said.

The lieutenant marched across the lobby and into the dining room, then led him to a corner table where a vice admiral, a rear admiral, a Navy captain, and a Marine colonel were sitting. Weston recognized the vice admiral.

"Good afternoon, sir," he said.

"Jim, a little eagerness is a good thing," Vice Admiral Richard B. Sayre said, rising to his feet and putting out his hand. "But you're not due here for a month."

"Sir?"

"But we'll talk about that later. I'm really glad to see you. Until General McInerney called, I thought you'd been lost in the Philippines."

Brigadier General D. G. McInerney was the Deputy Director of Marine Corps Aviation.

"I managed to get out, sir," Weston said.

"So I understand. General McInerney and I had a long talk about that, and about Ewa, and about our mutual friend, Colonel Dawkins. He led me to believe you wouldn't be coming here for a month."

"I'm just passing through, sir. On a weekend pass."

"Well, I know that Mrs. Sayre and Martha would be very disappointed to miss you. Could you find time to call?"

"At your convenience, sir," Weston said, then asked, "Martha's here?"

"Yes, she is," Admiral Sayre said simply.

"And where's Greg?"

Jesus, with a little bit of luck, Greg might be here, too, if Martha is.

Admiral Sayre looked at him sharply.

And then the look softened.

"Of course, you were trapped in the Philippines, there was no way you could know. Greg was shot down at Wake Island, Jim. Right at the beginning."

"Oh, *shit!*" Weston blurted bitterly. "I'm so sorry to hear that!"

"Captain Weston, gentlemen," Admiral Sayre said, retaining control of his voice with great effort, "and my late son-in-law Lieutenant Gregory Culhane, USMC, Class of '38, got their wings here together. Jim was Greg's best man when he and my daughter Martha were married."

"And this is the first you'd heard of Lieutenant Culhane's loss, Captain?" the Marine Colonel asked.

"Yes, sir."

"You were obviously pretty busy in the Pacific yourself," the Colonel said, pointing at Weston's fruit salad.

"Jim refused to surrender," Admiral Sayre said. "He made his way from Corregidor to Mindanao, where he was G-2 of the guerrilla organization operating there, until they brought him out by submarine."

Jesus, how did he know about that?

What did he say about General McInerney calling him?

"Really?" the Marine Colonel said, impressed.

"Well, now he's back to flying," Admiral Sayre said, meeting Weston's eyes as he spoke. "Or soon will be. What Mac McInerney and I are trying to do is get him back in a fighter cockpit as quickly as possible."

I'll be damned! McInerney didn't just give up, and give in to those bastards in Washington.

"I'd like to talk to you about that, Jim," Admiral Sayre went on. "If you would have the time while you're here."

"I'm going to have to leave here early tomorrow morning, sir."

Local Area Only authority to leave the grounds of the Greenbrier on the verbal orders of the commanding officer expired at midnight on Sunday.

"We don't want you hungover when you begin your happy rest-and-recuperation program on Monday morning," Commander Bolemann had explained.

"Well, I suggest that you go over to the house and see Mrs. Sayre and Martha now—Jerry, call up and tell them he's coming."

"Aye, aye, sir," the Admiral's aide said.

"And as soon as I'm through here, I'll come home, and we can have a chat. There's someone I want you to meet."

"Aye, aye, sir," Weston said.

"Jerry, run down Major Williamson, and ask him if he could come by my quarters at, say, 1530."

"Aye, aye, sir."

"I'm really glad to see you, Jim," Admiral Sayre said, offering Weston his hand again.

Weston sensed he had been dismissed.

Mrs. Jean Sayre, a tall, slim, gray-haired woman with gentle and perceptive eyes, came out the front door of Quarters Number One as Jim Weston drove the Buick into the driveway.

"Oh, Jim," she said when he stepped out of the car, "when I heard you escaped from the Philippines, I was afraid you'd look like death warmed over! You look wonderful!"

She hugged him. He felt his eyes start to water and closed them. When he opened them he saw Martha, standing in the door. She was tall and slim, and looked very much like her mother. She was deeply tanned and her sun-bleached blond hair hung down to her shoulders.

What is she now, twenty-three, twenty-four? And a goddamn widow! Goddamn it! Did they have a kid?

She came halfway down the walk to him as he walked toward the door.

"Well, look what floated in with the tide," she said.

"Don't I get a hug?" he asked.

She hugged him. He was uncomfortable when he felt the pressure of her breasts against his abdomen, and quickly broke away.

"Mother said I wasn't to ask you how you were, or comment on your appearance," Martha said. "So I won't."

"I'm fine, thank you for asking."

"You look good," she said. "God, Jimmy, I'm glad to see you."

"I didn't know about Greg, until just now," he said. "Jesus Christ, I'm sorry."

"Let's go in the house," Mrs. Sayre said, coming up behind them. "There's no champagne, but I think we should have a drink."

A dark-skinned man in a crisply starched white cotton jacket stood just inside the door.

Christ, he's a Filipino messman. We let them join the Navy, but only as messmen. They're our Little Brown Brothers, not good enough to serve as real sailors.

"Good morning, sir," he said.

"Buenos días," Weston said.

"Pedro, would you roll the bar onto the patio?" Mrs. Sayre asked. "Despite the hour, we are going to have a drink. Possibly two. You remember Captain Weston, don't you? He's a dear friend of the family."

"Yes, ma'am," the messman said.

Does that mean he remembers me? I don't remember him.

"That being the case," Martha said, as they walked through the house and onto the patio, "dear friend of the family, why didn't you call and tell us you were coming? For that matter, why didn't you call and just tell us you were alive?"

He met her eyes, and noticed how blue they were.

"I don't know, Martha," he said. "The last couple of weeks have been really hectic."

They sat down on upholstered white metal lawn furniture. The way she was sitting—innocently, of course—Weston could see a long way up her cotton skirt. She was not wearing hose, and he remembered Janice telling him that silk stockings were almost impossible to find.

Pedro wheeled a bar loaded with whisky bottles onto the patio, then stood, obviously waiting for orders.

"What would you like, Jim?" Mrs. Sayre asked.

Among the nearly dozen bottles on the bar, there was a bottle of good scotch, scotch too good to be diluted with water. Without thinking about it, Weston asked, in Spanish, for "some of the good stuff, a double, please, ice but no water."

"That's new," Martha said. "When did you learn to speak Spanish?"

"Ninety percent of U.S. forces in the Philippines are Filipinos," Weston said, as much to the messman as Martha. "You either learn to speak Spanish, or you don't get much done."

"Permission to speak, sir?" the messman asked.

"Of course," Weston said.

"Sir, there was a story in the newspaper. It said there were guerrilla forces operating on my home island of Mindanao."

"Yes, there are," Weston said.

"Sir, and you were there?"

Weston nodded.

"Just a minute, Pedro," Jean Sayre said. "Make the drinks. I'll have whatever Captain Weston is having."

"Good scotch, ice, double, no water, ma'am."

Weston felt anger well up within him.

"With a little water. Fix a single for Miss Martha."

"Yes, ma'am."

Weston was surprised at his fury at her treatment of the Filipino.

"Then make yourself whatever you want, pull up a chair and sit down with us. Captain Weston's going to start at the beginning and tell us everything."

"Yes, ma'am," the messman said. "Thank you."

Christ, I should have known better. She's what an officer's lady is supposed to be.

He sensed Martha's eyes on him, and knew somehow that she had seen his reaction.

"Pedro's been taking care of us for a long time," Martha said. "He was Daddy's steward on the *Lexington*. When Daddy made rear admiral and came ashore, Pedro came with him. You don't remember him?"

"I thought you looked familiar, Pedro," Weston said.

That's bullshit. If he was here the last time I was here, he was simply part of the furnishings. I was as bad then about our Little Brown Brothers as I thought Mrs. Sayre was now.

Pedro made the drinks, handed them around, then took a Coca-Cola for himself and pulled up a chair.

"The last we heard, Jim, you'd been sent to a Navy Catalina Squadron at Pearl.... Wait a minute. What should we drink to?"

"Greg," he blurted without thinking.

"Greg," Mrs. Sayre said softly, raising her glass.

Martha, looking at Jim, raised her glass but didn't speak.

"You were at Pearl, Jim?" Mrs. Sayre said. "How did you get to the Philippines?"

"I flew a Catalina into Cavite on December eight," Weston began, and related, over the next hour, his experiences in the Philippines. He left out, of course, the less pleasant aspects. But he did tell them, in some detail, about Sergeant Percy L. Everly, USMC—now First Lieutenant Percy Everly, U.S. Army Reserve—and about how Brigadier General Wendell W. Fertig came to be a brigadier general.

"That was very clever of him," Mrs. Sayre said, "wouldn't you say so, Pedro? No one would pay much attention to a reserve lieutenant colonel, would they?"

"I am afraid not," Pedro said. "He apparently knows Filipinos."

"And admires them," Weston said, hoping it would please the messman. His face showed it did.

"I wonder if I could not be useful there," Pedro wondered out loud. "I have sixteen years in the Navy and Mindanao is my home."

"The problem we had with Filipinos when I left, Pedro," Weston said, "was not finding recruits, but sending them away because we didn't have arms for them."

That, too, pleased Pedro, and that pleased Weston.

"And taking care of the Admiral is important, Pedro," Mrs. Sayre said. "I don't know what he would do without you. And he, too, would rather be over there than here."

The door chimes went off.

"That's probably Daddy," Martha said. "He doesn't know how to open a door by himself. I'll go, Pedro."

Without meaning to, Weston got another look up her dress as she lifted herself out of the chair.

It was not Admiral Sayre, it was a Marine major, short, lean, and suntanned, in a blond crew cut. "Afternoon, Mrs. Sayre," he said. "The Admiral asked me to call at 1530."

When Weston politely rose to his feet, he felt a little dizzy. As long as he'd been talking, he managed to remember, Pedro had quietly freshened up his glass whenever it had dropped below half empty.

Christ, I'm half in the bag!

And then he remembered that Pedro had freshened up Martha's drink several times, too. He looked at her. Her face seemed a little flushed.

Mrs. Sayre glanced at her wristwatch.

"Well, if he said half past three, he'll be here at half past three," she said. "Major Williamson, this is a dear friend of the family—"

"So dear that he didn't even call up to tell us he was alive," Martha said.

Jesus, is she plastered, too?

Martha's mother ignored the interruption, and went on: "—Captain Jim Weston."

"How do you do, sir?"

"Weston," Major Williamson said, with no cordiality whatsoever.

I think he senses I have been at the sauce in the middle of the afternoon.

"Can Pedro fix you something, Major?" Mrs. Sayre asked.

Major Williamson gave it perceptible thought before replying, "A light scotch, Mrs. Sayre, would be very nice."

"Captain Weston was my late husband's best man when we were married. He's been telling us of his experiences as a guerrilla in the Philippines," Martha said.

"You were a guerrilla in the Philippines, Captain?" Williamson said, looking at him dubiously.

"Yes, sir."

The door chimes went off again as Major Williamson opened his mouth to press for details.

"That has to be Daddy," Martha said. "I'll go."

Weston got another look up her dress at her spectacular legs as she left her chair again.

You got the look up her dress, because you knew she would probably, and certainly innocently, expose herself that way again when she got out of her chair. Which proves you are a despicable sonofabitch—she's your buddy's widow, for Christ's sake—or drunk. Or both.

What you came here to do was get Colonel Dawkins's letter into Major Williamson's hand, not make an ass of yourself, not be a despicable bastard. And only a despicable bastard would think . . . Jesus, I'd like to run my hands . . .

"Sir," Weston heard himself blurting, "I believe we have some mutual friends."

"Is that so?"

After some difficulty finding it, Weston took Colonel Dawkins's letter from an inside pocket and thrust it at Major Williamson.

"What's this?" Williamson said.

"I believe it will be self-explanatory, sir," Weston said.

Williamson took the letter, unfolded it, and looked at Weston.

"I'll be damned," he said, his tone indicating that he was truly surprised to learn that they did have mutual friends.

Admiral Sayre marched into the room, trailed by his aide.

"Dick," he said, touching Williamson's shoulder, "I really appreciate your coming here on Saturday afternoon."

"No problem at all, sir."

"I won't have the time—as I had hoped to—to talk to you about Weston. But I just got the word that Admiral Wheeler is due in here in about thirty minutes—God only knows what he wants—and I will, of course, have to meet his plane. But at least you got to meet Weston. It's a long story, but he comes highly recommended by General McInerney, and we're going to have to do what we can for him."

"Aye, aye, sir."

"Just as soon as I can find a minute, I'll bring you up to speed on this."

"Yes, sir."

"And I really appreciate your coming here on a Saturday afternoon. Pedro got you a drink, at least?"

"Yes, sir," Williamson said, holding it up.

"And as far as you're concerned, Jim," Admiral Sayre said, "unless you're really in love with listening to a battleship admiral insist that the sole function of aviation is to serve as the eyes of the fleet, you'd better get out of here right now."

"Aye, aye, sir."

"We'll make it up to you when you come here," Admiral Sayre said. "Finish your drink, of course."

"Thank you very much for your hospitality, sir," Weston said.

"Don't be silly."

"Wait until I get my purse, Jim," Martha said. "I'm going with you."

"What?" her father asked, surprised.

"Daddy, I already know that the sole function of aviation is to serve as the eyes of the fleet. I really don't want to hear it again."

"Well, you're imposing on Jim, don't you think? He may have other things on his mind."

"Am I, Jim?" Martha asked, meeting his eyes. "Or can you put up with me for a couple of hours."

"I'd welcome the company," Weston said.

"You see, Daddy?" Martha said, and walked off the patio.

Admiral Sayre waited until she was out of earshot.

"I don't know how tough it will be for you, but I think Martha needs to talk over what happened to Greg with you. She knows how close you and Greg were."

"Yes, sir."

"If you have the time, Jim," Mrs. Sayre said, "I'd appreciate it if . . . what? Take her to dinner or something. She needs to get out of the house, be with someone her own age."

"I'd be happy to, if she'd want to go."

"Thank you, Jim," the Admiral announced, and, trailed by his aide and his wife, marched off his patio.

"Weston," Major Williamson waved Colonel Dawkins's letter in his hand, "do you think this is what the Admiral wishes to discuss with me about you?"

"Yes, sir, I think that's probably it."

"Very interesting. Good afternoon, Captain Weston."

Jim was left alone on the patio. Martha returned several minutes later, finished her drink, and then took his arm and led him back through the house to the driveway.

He was very conscious of the pressure of her breasts against his arm.

From this point on, black coffee, no booze, and absolutely no physical contact.

"I like your car," she said. "Does the roof go down?"

"Yes."

"Put it down, then."

"Yes, ma'am."

[THREE]
Zeke's Shrimp & Oyster House
Alabama Point, Alabama
1815 6 March 1943

The restaurant hadn't changed much from the last time Weston had been here.

And that, he was acutely aware, had been in the company of Second Lieutenant Gregory J. Culhane, USMC (USNA '38); his fiancée, Miss Martha Sayre; and a tall redhead named . . . what the hell was her name?

It was a rickety building on a pier just inside the inlet to the Gulf of Mexico. Shrimp boats were tied up to the pier. The tables were rough planking picnic tables, and waitresses carried plates to them stacked high with steaming shrimp. You made your own sauce in paper cups from bowls of ketchup, horseradish, Worcestershire, and Tabasco, peeled and ate the shrimp with your fingers, and wiped your hands on paper towels. Rolls of towels sat among the bowls of ketchup and other condiments.

There was a jukebox and a piano, and a small plywood dance floor. The patrons were almost entirely young Navy and Marine pilots, and a scattering of aviation cadets who got off-base passes on weekends during the last month of their training. Some of their girls were almost as good-looking as Martha.

"The last time I was here, I was with you and Greg," Jim said.

"I remember," she said.

They found places at a picnic table occupied by two Marine lieutenants—both aviators—and their girls. When the waitress appeared, she asked, "Shrimp and a pitcher of beer?" in a tone suggesting she would be surprised by a "no."

"I'd really like a cup of coffee," Jim said.

"I'll have a scotch," Martha said. "And the shrimp, and the beer."

When she saw the look he gave her, she smiled and said, "Why, Captain Weston. I seem to recall that it was from you I learned 'you can't fly on one wing.' "

"I didn't say a word," he said.

"You wanted to," she said, then turned to the Marines and their girls. "Captain Weston is just back from the Pacific. The first thing he did when he got off the plane was to call me—we're very dear friends—to report that contrary to published reports, he was not only alive but back and on his way to see me."

"Welcome home, sir," one of the lieutenants said.

"You were reported KIA, sir?"

"It was a mistake," Weston said.

"Christ, that must have been tough on your family."

"As well as his very dear friends," Martha said.

"If I'm out of line asking this, shut me up, but what did they do, sir, when they found out they made a mistake? Apologize? What?"

"You must have been in the Corps long enough to know that the Corps never makes a mistake, haven't you?" Weston said.

There was the expected dutiful laughter.

"But I am so glad to see you that I forgive you," Martha said, and kissed him. Not on the mouth, but on his forehead. When she pulled his head down, he found his face against her breasts.

Oh, Jesus Christ! Just as soon as we eat the shrimp, and she drinks as little of the beer as I can arrange, I'm

*getting her out of here. We'll ride around with the roof
down. Maybe that will sober her up.*

*Only a three-star no-good sonofabitch with bells would
take advantage of a girl like Martha when she was in her
cups. And the reason she's drinking is that she's a widow,
your best friend's widow.*

"Here," one of the lieutenants said, handing Martha a
paper cup full of beer. "Until your pitcher gets here."

"Thank you very much," Martha said. "And yes, I
would."

"Yes, you would what?"

"Like to dance. My very dear friend here is a lousy
dancer."

"I'm a good dancer," he blurted.

"Okay, then you dance with me," she said, and stood
up and held arms out to him.

*The last thing in the world I want to do is put my arms
around her.*

He stood up, and she gave him her hand and led him
to the dance floor. He carefully avoided any body contact
beyond the absolutely necessary.

"I get the feeling, very dear friend, from your rigid
body and the worried look on your face, that you think I
am misbehaving."

"I think you've had a little too much to drink," Jim
said. "So have I."

"In which case, I will ease up," she said. "The last thing
I want to do is embarrass you."

"I didn't say you were embarrassing me."

"You didn't have to. I know what you're thinking. I
could always tell."

Christ, I hope not.

He saw over her shoulder that the waitress had delivered their shrimp and drinks—two scotches, no coffee—
and a pitcher of beer.

"We have our shrimp," he said.

"Damn," she said, but she turned out of his arms, and,
hanging on to his hand, led them back to the table.

He was surprised—and greatly relieved—that she
didn't touch the scotch, and drank only a little of the beer
from the pitcher. He was also surprised that they were

able to eat all of the steaming pile of boiled shrimp. And then he remembered he hadn't had any lunch.

Which is why I felt the booze, and allowed myself to forget that a decent human being doesn't look up the dress of a friend, who incidentally happens to be the widow of my best friend.

Or completely forgets Janice!

Jesus, what about Janice? What the hell would I have done about Janice if something had happened?

"I hate to rain on this parade," Martha announced, as she daintily wiped her fingers and mouth with a paper towel. "But I have had a very busy day, and tomorrow is going to be busier. And if we're going to have a nightcap at the San Carlos, we're going to have to leave this charming company now."

"We could pass on the nightcap at the San Carlos," Weston said.

"I wouldn't think of it," Martha said, as she rose to her feet.

The men shook hands, and one of the lieutenants repeated, "Welcome home, sir."

In the car, Weston repeated, "We could pass on the nightcap at the San Carlos's bar."

"There's something I want to show you there," she said. "And didn't you notice that I was a good girl and didn't even touch my scotch? I'm entitled to a nightcap."

It was too cold now to have the roof of the Buick convertible down, or even to have the windows open. In a matter of minutes, as they headed down the two-lane macadam road back to Pensacola, Martha's perfume overwhelmed the smell of the red leather seats.

[FOUR]
The Cocktail Lounge
The San Carlos Hotel
2030 6 March 1943

The bar was crowded with Navy and Marine Aviators and their women, but it was captains and majors, an older, more senior crowd, than the aviation cadets and lieutenants in Zeke's.

After a minute their eyes had adjusted to the darkness, and Jim Weston saw an empty banquette. He took Martha's arm and led her to it.

"You forgot, huh?" Martha asked, as she slid onto the seat.

"Forgot what?"

"That you weren't going to touch me."

"Oh, Jesus, Martha!"

"Your intentions, I know, are very honorable," she said.

A waitress took their order. Martha ordered a scotch, and after a moment's hesitation, Weston said to make it two.

"You said you wanted to show me something?"

"I do. But first, something's been bothering me."

"What?"

"How come you were reported KIA?"

"How did you hear that I was?"

"Daddy told me you had been reported KIA on Luzon on April 3, 1942. He'd seen some kind of a report."

"You're sure of the date?"

"I'm sure of the date. It was another of the red-letter days in my life."

"That figures, then," Weston said, as much to himself as to Martha.

"What figures?"

"On April first, I deserted," he said. "I remember the date clearly, because it was April Fools' Day, and that seemed somehow appropriate."

"You *deserted*?"

He nodded. "I deserted. Probably in the face of the enemy. I didn't mention that while reciting my inspiring tale of heroism to your mother."

"I don't understand, Jim."

The waitress delivered the drinks before he could reply. He raised his to Martha.

"Thank you for a very interesting afternoon," he said.

"Interesting?" she asked.

"How about delightful?"

"You don't mean that either," Martha said, taking a sip of her drink.

"What do you mean by that?"

"I told you, I can always tell what you're thinking. Mostly you've been uncomfortable."

"What gives you that idea?"

"We're back to 'I can read your mind'," she said. "Finish the story."

"Okay. I was on Corregidor. That's the fortress in Manila Bay. . . ."

"I know."

"Luzon was about to fall. Corregidor was going to fall. I decided I didn't want to become a prisoner. I had some idea I could get out of the Philippines and make myself useful as a pilot. So I just took off. Deserted."

"Just like that? You just walked away?"

"No. It was a little more complicated. I worked for a major named Paulsen. He knew what I was thinking. So he sent me—and Sergeant Everly—to Luzon, ostensibly looking for generator parts. But he knew we wouldn't be coming back. We didn't. We used the money we were supposed to buy generator parts with to buy a boat, and headed for Mindanao."

"It didn't bother you that whoever needed the parts wasn't going to get them?"

"There were no parts to be bought, and Paulsen knew that when he gave me the money to buy them. But there's an interesting question. What if I had stumbled on some parts? Would I have gone back to the Rock?"

"Would you have?"

"I don't know. Moot point. There were no parts. I went to Mindanao."

"Which constituted desertion."

"Right. Major Paulsen stayed, of course, knowing he was either going to get killed when the Japs took Corregidor, or become a prisoner. As a good Marine officer, he couldn't bring himself to desert. But without actually coming out and saying I should, he helped me to desert. Interesting question of morality."

"In other words, he was like Greg, and you were like . . . you?"

"What do you mean by that?"

"For Greg, everything was black or white. You're

smarter. You understand that everything is really one shade or another of gray."

That sounded like a shot at Greg. Did she mean that, or is that the booze talking?

"Yeah, I suppose so. I can now rationalize, of course, that I was of more value as a guerrilla on Mindanao than I would have been as a prisoner, and now I'm going back to flying. But every once in a while I look myself in the mirror, and there's the guy who deserted his post in the face of the enemy. Another interesting question of morality."

"What's this got to do with you being reported KIA?"

"I think Paulsen must have reported me KIA, two days after I didn't come back."

"Why?"

"There's a couple of possibilities. He had to say something when I didn't come back. Desertion was becoming a real problem. We got lectures about our duty as Marine officers: 'Marine officers don't desert; Marine officers man their posts until properly relieved.' "

"Which you decided didn't apply to you?"

"Sticking around waiting to get killed or become a prisoner when there were other options didn't make much sense to me," Weston said.

"In other words, sometimes what people expect you to do—the conventional morality—doesn't make any sense?" Martha asked, and added: "I've come to the same conclusion myself."

Now, what the hell does she mean by that?

"So, what I think happened was that Paulsen reported me KIA," he said. "He had to report something. If he reported me AWOL, they would have put my name on the list of probable deserters, and the MPs would have been looking for me."

"So you did what you thought was the right thing for you to do, right? And to hell with what other people thought you should do?"

"Yeah, I guess you could put it that way," he said.

"I'm really glad you did, Jimmy," she said, grasping his hand. "You're here. You're alive."

He exhaled audibly.

Martha drained her drink and stood up. "I have to go to the ladies' room," she said. "Order me another drink?"

"Don't you think we'd better call it a night?"

She looked at her watch.

"It is getting late," she said. "Pay the bill. Meet me in the corridor."

He nodded, watched her walk out of the cocktail lounge, and looked around for their waitress.

He was waiting for her in the corridor, beside the elevator, when she came out of the ladies' room.

She walked past him to the elevator.

"Good. It's here," she said. "Come on."

"Where are we going?"

"I told you I had something to show you. I don't want to show it to you in the corridor."

He stepped onto the elevator. She pushed the DOOR CLOSE and STOP buttons.

"Somebody's going to want to use the elevator," he said.

"This won't take long," Martha said. She reached for his hand and put something in it, then leaned against the wall of the elevator, smiling at him.

He looked down at his hand. At first he thought the small, foil-wrapped package was a piece of candy. Then he recognized it for what it was really was. "What am I supposed to do with this?" he asked.

"I think you know what it's for," she said.

"Martha, that wouldn't make any sense at all."

"Don't be a hypocrite, Jimmy," she said. "You want to as much as I do. You've been looking up my dress all afternoon."

"I'm sorry you saw that," he said.

"You shouldn't be."

He looked at her.

"I'm not going to beg you, you sonofabitch!" she said.

She turned from him to the row of elevator buttons.

"Which one do I push?" she said. "Your call."

He didn't reply until she turned to look at him over her shoulder. He saw tears forming in her eyes.

"Six," he said.

She pushed the button, the elevator started to move, and then she was in his arms.

"That's the second time I bought one of those things from the machine in the ladies' room," Martha said.

They were lying in bed, on their backs, staring up at the ceiling.

"What?" he asked.

"Consumed with guilt, are we?" Martha said, and then went on. "I always wondered why they had a condom machine in the ladies' room. To protect the ladies? Or the men?"

"Jesus, Martha!"

"The first time I bought one, he was willing, but when I went to his room, I wasn't. Actually, it was the penthouse, here in the San Carlos. He was a very rich, and very nice, really, young Marine Aviator, and he told me he was in love with me. Maybe if he hadn't said that, I would have gone through with it. Anyway, I didn't. You're the first man since Greg, if you've been wondering. And since he was the first, you're number two."

"Oh, Christ, Martha!"

"I've had a number of offers, of course," she said. "But aside from . . . the very nice, very rich young aviator . . . I never really wanted to. And I didn't go through with that. Until today, when I saw you get out of the car, I had just about convinced myself that whatever I was, I was not the Merry Widow of fame and legend. You know what that means, really, in German?"

"What?"

"The title of that operetta, *Die Lustige Witwe*? Popularly known as *The Merry Widow*? Lustige means 'lusty.' Full of lust."

"Oh, for Christ sake!"

"But when I saw you get out of your car, I realized I was wrong. I was suddenly very *lustige* indeed."

"Martha, for Christ's sake!"

"And now that you know, are you really disgusted with me, or do you think, as a kindness, you could force yourself to put your arms around me? Right now, I feel very lonely."

He reached for her and wrapped his arms around her and comforted her as she sobbed against his chest.

"I thought I was going to die when Greg got killed. I did, inside. And then I started having fantasies about you. Jim would come home. Jim would comfort me."

"Jesus!"

"Today wasn't the first time I've caught you looking up my dress," she said, her sobs turning into giggles. "Thought I didn't notice? I noticed!"

"You're really something, Martha."

"And then *you* were KIA, you bastard!" she said. "And I really died inside all over again. And then you came back from the dead, and *didn't* call, and I understood that I'd been a little crazy, thinking that you felt anything for me—or I felt anything for you. And then, you bastard, you show up without warning at the house, and started looking at me like that."

"You mean looking up your dress?"

"That too," she said. "But I meant the look in your eyes when you saw me. You know the first thing I thought when I saw you?"

"I'm afraid to ask."

"Actually, the second thing. The *second* thing I thought was that I was really glad I hadn't gone to bed with . . . the nice young man."

"What was the first thing?"

"You'll never know. You can probably guess, but I'll never tell you."

"And what are you thinking now?"

"I'm thinking you don't seem very enthusiastic. Anyway, it's time for you to take me home, or Daddy will get suspicious."

"I didn't expect this, Martha," he said. "I'm trying to sort it out."

"You've got to learn to take a chance," she said. "Go for broke. Hope for the best. Like I did when I bought two of those things in the ladies' room."

He didn't reply.

She pushed herself up and looked down at him.

"I'm getting the feeling I'm making you uncomfortable," Martha said. "If I am, for God's sake, don't try to be a gentleman."

He touched her nipple with his finger.

"Only *two?* You should have bought three, four, half a dozen."

She moved her body so that he could get his mouth on her nipple.

"Is that what you were thinking? Is that what you wanted to do?" she asked.

"Oh, God, yes," he said.

"I told you I always know what you're thinking," Martha said, as she pressed her breast against his face. "Oh, God, Jimmy, I'm so glad you're back!"

XI

[ONE]
The Greenbrier Hotel
White Sulphur Springs, West Virginia
0440 8 March 1943

Under the military administration of the Greenbrier Hotel, the desk clerk was called the charge of quarters. Whatever he was called, he was the same petty officer second who had the duty when Weston reported in, and he was asleep in an armchair behind the desk when Weston walked up to ask for his key.

Weston took a certain cruel pleasure in ringing the bell on the desk with sufficient energy to bring the charge of quarters to sudden wakefulness.

Jim Weston was not in a very good mood. He had driven straight through from Pensacola, stopping only for gas and a couple of really terrible hamburgers. During that time, he'd had plenty of time to consider what an unprincipled miserable sonofabitch he was, first for what he had done to Martha, and second for what that meant with regard to his relationship to Janice.

"Sorry to wake you," Weston said with monumental insincerity.

The charge of quarters looked at his watch.

"You just got back in time to keep the shit from hitting the fan, Captain, " he said.

"And what does that mean?"

"Commander Bolemann told me to call him if you wasn't back at 0500. If you wasn't, he was going to call the state police. It's 0441."

He picked up the telephone on the desk and gave the operator who answered a number. "Sir, Ulrich at the front desk? Captain Weston just came in, sir." There was a pause, then Ulrich added: "Aye, aye, sir."

He hung up and turned to Weston. "You're to go to the Commander's quarters, Captain," he said. "Two-oh-one. Take the corridor to the right at the head of the stairs."

Weston was halfway to the wide staircase when Ulrich called his name. He turned and saw that Ulrich was holding out his key and a stack of small yellow sheets of paper. To discourage guests from taking them out of the hotel, the keys were attached to enormous, heavy brass plates.

He turned, walked back to the desk, and took them.

There were eight small yellow sheets of paper, each a message for Captain Weston, each with a date-and-time stamp.

Lieutenant (j.g.) Hardison asks that you call her, Female Officers' Quarters, USN Hospital, Phila.

That one was date-and-time stamped 1540 5Mar43. Ten minutes after he had made his surreptitious early exit from the Greenbrier. He wondered why she didn't give a number, then remembered there was some sort of dedicated line between USNH Philadelphia and the Greenbrier. Commander Bolemann had told him that he could use it if he wanted to.

> Lieutenant (j.g.) Hardison asks that you call her, Ward
> G-4,
> USN Hospital, Phila.

That one was date-and-time stamped 0039 6Mar43. Janice apparently tried to call him again as soon as she went off duty, in her sweet, naively trusting belief that at midnight he would certainly be in bed. *Alone* in bed. There were five more messages, indicating that Janice tried and failed to contact him five more times—one of which coincided with a time when he was engaged in carnal union with Mrs. Gregory F. Culhane in the San Carlos Hotel, Pensacola, Florida. The eighth message had originated within the Greenbrier Hotel:

> *Whenever* you float in, please call upon me in my quarters.
> Bolemann, Cmdr, MC USN.

The date-and-time stamp on that one indicated it had been left for him at just about the time he was leaving Pensacola.

Weston jammed the messages in his pocket and started up the wide staircase to the second floor of the Greenbrier.

"There may be joy in heaven when the prodigal returns," Commander Bolemann, attired in a bathrobe, greeted him at the door of his suite, "but what *I* want to know, you bastard, is where the *hell* have you been?"

"I was in Pensacola, sir."

"Pensacola?"

"Yes, sir."

"Am I correct in presuming, Captain Weston, that you didn't ask my permission to leave the local area to go to Pensacola fucking Florida because you knew goddamned well I would have said 'no, no, *absolutely fucking no*'?"

"Yes, sir."

"What the hell were you doing in Pensacola?"

"I had a letter from my MAG commander at Ewa to a friend of his there."

"They have this thing called the U.S. mail," Bolemann

said. "You give them three cents, and they will deliver letters just about anywhere."

"Yes, sir."

"Well, I should not be surprised," Bolemann said. "One must expect that someone who has not only suffered the severe emotional trauma that you have sustained over a prolonged period, but is trying so hard to conceal its effects, will suffer some sort of dementia."

"No excuse, sir. But I'm not crazy."

"That's not my diagnosis. That's Lieutenant Hardison's diagnosis."

"She called you?"

"Oh, yes. Several times. She has visions of you wandering around in the hills of West Virginia, suffering from amnesia, or perhaps reliving your terrible experiences in the Philippines. For reasons that baffle me, she seems terribly—and I must say most unprofessionally—concerned with your well-being."

"Oh, God!"

"Call her," Bolemann said.

"Sir?"

Bolemann turned and made a "follow me" gesture to Weston. He sat down in an armchair—actually more or less crashed into it—and reached for the telephone on the table beside it.

"Commander Bolemann," he said. "Get me Lieutenant Hardison at the Female Officers' Quarters, Naval Hospital, Philadelphia."

Then he handed the handset to Captain Weston.

"Female Officers' Quarters."

"Lieutenant Hardison, please."

"Jim, where have you been? I've been out of my mind worrying about you!"

"Hi," he said.

"Are you all right?"

"I'm fine, Janice, how about you?"

"Where were you?"

"Wheeling," he said. Wheeling was the only town in West Virginia he could call to mind. He thought about Charlestown, but on second thought decided that was in South Carolina.

"Wheeling?"

"Wheeling, West Virginia."

Dear God, let Wheeling be in West Virginia.

"What were you doing there?"

"Well, I wanted to get out of here for a little while, and then I had a little car trouble, so I took a hotel room."

"Honey, I was so worried!"

"Honey"? Christ, she called me "honey."

"I'm fine, honey."

"I even called Dr. Bolemann," Janice said.

"I know," he said.

"Can you get away next weekend?" Janice asked. "I want to see you so badly."

"Just a moment," Jim said, and covered the microphone with his hand. "She wants to know if I can get away next weekend."

Bolemann looked at him thoughtfully. "You really wouldn't want to hear my initial reaction to that," he said, and motioned for Weston to give him the telephone.

"This is Dr. Bolemann, Janice," he said. "I really don't think I could authorize Jim to drive all that way and back over the weekend. But I think there is a Greyhound bus he could take. If there is, could you meet him at the bus station?"

Janice apparently expressed her willingness to do that.

"Very well, then, we'll check into it and Jim will call you. Here he is."

"Hi!"

"I'll meet you at the bus station," Janice said. "I'll get a forty-eight-hour pass."

"Fine."

"Jim, I think I love you, too," Janice said, and the phone went dead.

Weston put the phone in its cradle.

"You're a lousy liar," Dr. Bolemann said. "If she wasn't in love with you, you'd never have gotten away with that car-trouble-in-Wheeling bullshit. I would be very distressed if you were just fucking around with that girl. She's as nice as they come."

"I love her," Weston said.

Bolemann nodded. "What are you plans for 0800?" he asked.

"I plan to be sound asleep," Weston said. "I drove straight through from Pensacola."

"Tell me, which do you like better, tennis or volleyball?"

"Sir?"

"You heard me. Answer the question."

"Tennis, I suppose, sir."

"Splendid. At 0755, Captain Weston, you will be at the volleyball courts, suitably attired to participate. You will *enthusiastically* participate until the noon hour, or until your ass is really dragging, whichever comes last. Do I make myself clear?"

"Aye, aye, sir."

"Be there, Captain Weston," Commander Bolemann said, and pointed to the door.

[TWO]
The White Room
The Office of Strategic Services
The National Institutes of Health Building
Washington, D.C.
0930 8 March 1943

Gunnery Sergeant Ernest W. Zimmerman, USMC, looked distinctly uncomfortable as he followed Lieutenant Colonel Edward J. Banning, USMC, and Captain Kenneth R. McCoy, USMCR, down the fifth-floor corridor to the White Room. Like many enlisted men of the regular, prewar Marine Corps, he devoutly believed that the route to happiness in the Corps was to stay as far away as possible from officers you don't *really* know. He had been told who was going to be at the briefing, and he didn't hardly know any of the fuckers.

Colonel Banning and McCoy were, of course, not threatening. He had worked for then Captain Banning in the 4th Marines in Shanghai where Banning had been the 4th Marine's G-2. He liked and trusted Banning.

He also liked and trusted Captain McCoy, of course, but McCoy wasn't a *real* officer. The Corps had hung officer's insignia on McCoy because of the war, but that was just temporary. Just as soon as the war was over and things got back to normal, the Killer would go back to the ranks. Probably as a staff sergeant. Maybe, if he got lucky, they'd make him a technical sergeant. He himself would be perfectly happy, when the war was over and things went back to normal, if he got to keep staff sergeant's stripes. That way, with a little bit of luck, he could make technical sergeant himself before he retired.

The Corps really went ape-shit in war time. They'd even pinned a lieutenant's bar on that kid, the Easterbunny. He was living in the hotel, too, running around all dressed up in an officer's uniform, Sam Browne belt and lieutenant's bars and all. There was nothing *wrong* with the Easterbunny. The gutsy little shit had proved he had the balls of a gorilla—and earned that 2nd Raider Battalion patch—on Bloody Ridge, trying to carry his officer down that fucking hill with every fucking Jap this side of Tokyo shooting at him. But that didn't make *him* no *officer*.

And they were even going to make a temporary officer out of Koffler, when he finished officer school at Quantico. Koffler was a good kid, a good Marine—he'd probably make a good corporal. But an *officer?* No *fucking* way!

And the officers he was going to have to face today were all going to be *real* officers . . . *real senior* officers. And the only way to get along with real senior officers was to stay as fucking far away from them as you could get.

Gunnery Sergeant Zimmerman was splendidly turned out in a brand-new, freshly tailored-to-fit uniform. Colonel Jack (NMI) Stecker had shown up at the hotel with a supply sergeant from Eighth & I in tow. The supply sergeant had measured Zimmerman, and then written down all his qualifications and decorations, and then come back no more than four hours later with two complete sets of greens with everything all sewn or pinned on. Stripes, 2nd Raider Battalion shoulder patch, fruit salad, marksmanship badges, hash marks, everything.

While he was examining himself in the mirror, Zimmerman had had to admit that he looked pretty fucking sharp and shipshape.

He also thought that the red-striped badge with his picture on it that McCoy had pinned to the pocket of his new tunic made him look like a fucking dummy in a clothing-store window.

Two guys in cop-type uniforms at a little counter went through some bullshit about comparing his face and signature on some cards they had in a file with his picture and signature on the badge. As they did that, Zimmerman wondered where the hell they had got his signature from. And then one of the cops unlocked the door and motioned them inside.

"Sorry to be late, gentlemen," Banning said. "Would you believe a flat tire?"

"Colonel," Brigadier General Fleming Pickering said, standing up. "I never look a gift horse in the mouth." He turned to look at the others sitting around the table:

The Deputy Director (Operations) of the Office of Strategic Services; Brigadier General F. L. Rickabee, USMC; Captain David W. Haughton, USN; Colonel Jack (NMI) Stecker, USMCR; Major Jake Dillon, USMCR; 2nd Lieutenant George F. Hart, USMCR; and an Army Air Corps officer, whose identification badge identified him as Lt. Col. H. J. Hazeltine USAAC. Rickabee, Stecker, and Haughton were wearing VISITOR 5th Floor Only badges; the others had red-striped any area any time badges.

This told Pickering that Colonel Hazeltine was assigned to the OSS, and not as an Air Corps representative to the meeting.

Pickering went to Zimmerman and shook his hand, then put his arm around his shoulder.

"Gentlemen, there has been a good deal in the newspapers of late about 'old-breed Marines.' Here's one in the flesh, Gunnery Sergeant Zimmerman, whom I'm proud to say I know and consider my friend."

Zimmerman looked very uncomfortable.

"I think everybody knows everybody else, except . . . Ken, do you know the OSS's weather expert, Colonel Hazeltine?"

"No, sir."

Hazeltine stood up and walked to McCoy and gave him his hand.

"I've heard a lot about you, Captain," he said.

"How do you do, sir?"

Hazeltine turned to Zimmerman.

"And you, too, Sergeant," he said.

"Yes, sir," Zimmerman said.

Hazeltine restrained a smile. Pickering had warned everyone that all they were going to hear from Gunny Zimmerman was "Yes, sir," "No, sir," or "Aye aye, sir," unless it was pried—or dynamited—out of him.

"How do you want to handle this, Ed?" Pickering asked.

"Sir, I thought I would sort of conduct the briefing myself, with the understanding that Captain McCoy and Gunny Zimmerman will interrupt me if I leave anything out, or if—when—I get something wrong."

"Sounds fine. Have at it."

"Jake, I need the number-three China map on the screen," Banning said.

Jake Dillon had once been a sergeant in the 4th Marines in Shanghai. To the surprise of many people—including himself—he'd been directly commissioned as a major, USMCR. At that time, he was Vice President, Public Relations, of Metro-Magnum Motion Picture Studios. It had been the belief of certain senior officers within the Marine Corps that he would be of great value performing similar duties for the Marine Corps.

In that capacity, he had led a team of still and motion picture cameramen onto the beach during the invasion of Guadalcanal. But then he had been pressed into service by General Pickering—they were friends before the war—when Pickering was staging a covert operation on the Japanese-occupied island of Buka. He proved as adept at covert operations as at placing the names of motion picture stars onto the front pages of newspapers. To the great annoyance of the Marine Corps publicity people Pickering had again pressed him into service, this time permanently, by having him transferred to the OSS shortly after Pickering's presidential appointment.

"Aye, aye, sir," Dillon said, and went to the slide projector. In a moment a map of the northern area of China, from Peking (Beijing) north across Mongolia (including the Gobi Desert) to the Russian border, and west to the borders of Kazakhstan and Kyr.

"Captain McCoy, Gunny Zimmerman, and I," Banning began, "have spent most of the past two days discussing this area, with emphasis on the Gobi Desert, which is where Howard thinks we need a weather station."

"Right in the middle of it would be nice, Ed," Colonel H. J. Hazeltine said.

"Gunny Zimmerman is personally familiar with the area," Banning said. "Which means we can send the *National Geographic* magazines back to the library."

There were appreciative chuckles.

"How well do you know the area, Sergeant?" the Deputy Director (Operations) asked.

There was a silence.

"Sir, Zimmerman has made two trips across the desert with camel caravans," McCoy answered for him. "One to the Russian border, and one to the Indian border."

"Yes, sir," Zimmerman confirmed.

"How did that come to be, Sergeant?" the DDO asked.

"Sir, Gunny Zimmerman operated what you might call an import-export business," Banning answered for Zimmerman.

The DDO looked at Zimmerman, who nodded his head.

"The details of which are not, in my judgment, important to us here," Banning went on. Zimmerman looked relieved. "What is important is that Zimmerman is familiar with the workings of the cross-border import-export business and, probably more important, is personally acquainted with a number of people in the business."

Banning waited for that to sink in, then added: "And so is his wife. Who, Zimmerman believes, may be in a small village, Paotow-Zi, which is twenty or thirty miles downriver from Baotou."

He indicated the position on the map.

"I don't know if I should ask you, Ed, or Zimmerman, but why does he think his wife is in this village?" Rickabee asked.

"Sir," McCoy said, "Zimmerman owns a farm there,

and a sausage factory. When we pulled out of Shanghai, he told her to go there."

" 'Pulled out of Shanghai'?" the DDO asked. "What do you mean by that, Captain?"

"When the Fourth Marines were sent to the Philippines, sir," McCoy said.

"Did you know about Zimmerman's wife, Ed?" Rickabee asked.

"No, sir."

"Pity. She might have been useful."

"Zimmerman told his wife," Banning said, "to try to make it into India when she thought it would be safe. She would then find an American consulate, or legation—some American agency—and give them the name of Zimmerman's mother here. The idea was to get Mrs. Zimmerman and their children to the United States."

"That hasn't happened, I gather," the DDO said. "I mean, there has been no word from Mrs. Zimmerman?"

"No, sir," Banning said.

"Does that mean we can presume she's still in this village? Paotow-Zi, you said?"

"No, sir."

"Fritz—excuse me, *General*—have you any assets in that area? Can we find out?" Haughton asked.

"You can call me Fritz in here, David," Rickabee said. "We're among friends. But don't forget to kiss my stars when you leave the room." He waited for the chuckles to die down, then went on: "Simple answer is 'yes.' It would mean diverting them from other things . . . for what, ten days, two weeks? It would probably be three weeks before we had an answer. How important is finding out?"

"Let's come back to that in a minute," Pickering said.

"Aye, aye, sir," Rickabee said. "But, Gunny, as soon as possible, go to Management Analysis and tell Captain Sessions everything you can about your wife and children and this village."

"Aye, aye, sir," Zimmerman said.

"I told Ed that, as I see it, our first priority is to establish contact with the people in the Gobi Desert," General Pickering went on. "And to see what ideas Zimmerman had about how to do that."

"McCoy," Banning said.

"Sir," McCoy began, "Zimmerman feels—with a lot of ifs, and a lot of money—that it may be possible to get radios into the people in the Gobi Desert."

"Money's not a problem," the DDO said. "What are the other ifs?"

"The first is a question, sir," McCoy said. "What kind of radios do we send them? They'd have to be transported by camel. Weight would be a problem. We'd have to talk to some expert in Navy Communications—maybe, better, the Army's Signal Corps . . ."

"Collins Radio," Captain Haughton said. "In Cedar Rapids, Iowa."

"What about Collins Radio?" Pickering asked.

"You remember when Admiral Byrd went to the Antarctic a couple of years before the war?"

Grunts indicated everyone remembered Admiral Byrd's Antarctic expedition. Some of them were dubious: *What the hell does Admiral Byrd and the Antarctic have to do with this?*

"Well, the Navy couldn't maintain radio communication with him. The communications experts were very embarrassed. But a radio amateur, a chap named Collins, in Cedar Rapids, Iowa, *could* talk to Byrd. And did. Just about all the time. That was even more embarrassing. But the point of this is that after this happened, the Navy has spent a lot of money with Collins. He's become the expert in difficult radio communications."

"Wouldn't his equipment be heavy-duty stuff?" Colonel Jack (NMI) Stecker asked. "We're talking about moving this stuff on camels."

"We won't know what he's got, will we, until we ask him?" Pickering said. "Specifically, until Banning asks him." He looked at Banning and added, "As soon as possible."

"Aye, aye, sir," Banning said.

"Jumping way ahead," Colonel Hazeltine said. "Presuming we establish contact with these people and provide them with the necessary meteorological equipment, could we move their expendables in to them by camel caravan?"

"I don't think we'd better count on that," Pickering

said. "But let's get back to Zimmerman's plan to get the first radio in to these people?"

"*Radios*, sir," McCoy said. "Zimmerman thinks the way to do this is to join up with caravans about to go back into Mongolia. Three, four different caravans, maybe as many as six. When they bring back evidence that they delivered the radios to Americans in the Gobi, we give them money—which means gold—enough to make them hungry for more."

"But . . . I see what you mean, Captain, by 'a lot of ifs' . . . but if we get the radios to these people, wouldn't they get on the air to us?" the DDO asked. "We would know if they had them. We'd be talking to them."

"Yes, sir. But Zimmerman said if we pay them anyway, they would be available to carry other stuff in. I don't know what the Colonel meant by 'expendables' . . ."

"Balloons, for example. To check the winds aloft," Colonel Hazeltine explained.

"Okay," Pickering said.

"Then there's the problem of cryptography," Haughton said. "We don't dare send in a code book."

"Sir, we figure the simple substitution code we used for Buka and Mindanao will work just fine here."

"I don't understand what you're talking about," the DDO said.

"Sir," McCoy said, "we worked out a system to establish as secure as possible communication with a Coast-watcher team on Buka. And we used the same system to communicate with General Fertig on Mindanao. It worked twice, and there's no reason it wouldn't work here."

"*How* does it work?" the DDO asked.

"Sir, it's a simple substitution code, using personal data of people we both know and the Japanese have no way of knowing—their mother's maiden name, the name of somebody, or something."

"Any simple substitution code is easy to crack," the DDO said.

"Yes, sir," McCoy agreed. "But it enables us to establish initial contact. It would be enough for them to tell us where they are, and for us to tell them when the weather team is coming in."

"Zimmerman," Pickering asked, "you think we can get radios into these people?"

"Yes, sir."

"Where would you meet them?"

"Let me have China number two on the screen, Jake, please," Banning said.

A moment later, a map of northern China appeared on the screen.

"Somewhere in here, sir," Banning said, pointing to the map. "In the Gobi itself, on one of the caravan routes operating out of Ulaanbaatar."

"That's assuming the caravans are still operating," the DDO asked. "In wartime?"

"Yes, sir," Banning said. "These caravans have been operating for centuries. A little thing like World War Two isn't going to stop them."

There were chuckles.

"A main caravan route runs between Ulaanbaatar, in the Gobi, toward India. We believe the Americans will try to make it into India," Banning said.

"Why not just head for Chungking?" the DDO asked.

Chungking was then the seat of the Chinese Nationalist government. Generalissimo Chiang Kai-shek, the head of the Nationalist government since 1928 and the leader of the Nationalist Chinese during World War II, had retreated before the Japanese to Chungking, where they operated from bomb-shelter caves.

"They wouldn't be sure our Chinese would be there by the time they got there," McCoy said. "And that's bandit country."

"Bandit country?" the DDO asked.

"Warlords, sometimes aligned with Chiang Kai-shek, sometimes with the Communists, and always ready to steal whatever they can from anybody. They don't operate in the Gobi because there's not much to steal there, and also because they use the caravans to smuggle things into Russia and India."

"According to Zimmerman," Banning went on, pointing to the map as he spoke, "Ulaanbaatar is *the* marketplace, the transshipment point, so to speak, for caravans moving all over that area. Into the interior of China, to India, and, for that matter, into Russia."

"Have you been there, Sergeant?" the Deputy Director (Operations) asked.

"Yes, sir."

"I think we're at the point where we can come up with some sort of plan," Pickering said, "and start putting it into execution . . . even though whatever we start will almost certainly have to be changed. I hate that, but I don't think we have any choice."

There were no objections.

"Okay, Ed, tell us what you and McCoy are thinking," Pickering said.

"Given that the priority, sir, is establishing reliable communications with the people in the Gobi," Banning replied, "I think we should get Zimmerman and radios to China—into Ulaanbaatar, if that can be done—as quickly as possible."

"Zimmerman, radios, and gold," McCoy said. "Any radios we can put our hands on right now. With hand-cranked generators. We can get better radios into the Gobi on the airplane. Airplanes. What we have to do is set up communication with those people."

"Fritz," Pickering asked, "did you ever send anybody with a MAGIC clearance to Chiang Kai-shek?"

"What's that all about?" the DDO asked. "What about Chiang Kai-shek and MAGIC?"

"I had dinner with the President, Frank Knox, and Admiral Leahy just before I went back to the Pacific . . . When the hell was that?"

"Fourteen October 1942," General Rickabee furnished from memory.

". . . where I learned that the President had decided to bring Mountbatten and Chiang Kai-shek in on MAGIC. Over the objections of Knox and Leahy."

Admiral Lord Louis Mountbatten, the great-grandson of Queen Victoria, commanded Allied operations in China, Burma, and India.

"Why?" the DDO asked incredulously. "That strikes me as a hell of a good way to compromise MAGIC."

"Which, I think, is why Leahy and Knox objected,"

Pickering said. "But the point is that he told me to find people with a MAGIC clearance we could send to India and China. This, of course, took place before the President decided to send me over here?"

"The answer to your question, General," Rickabee said, "is that I had just about decided to send Colonel Banning to Chungking. This, of course, was before *you* decided to send him over *here*."

"Do I detect a needle in there somewhere, General?"

"*No*, sir," Rickabee answered with monumental insincerity.

"Chungking is where we want to send Colonel Banning now, right? And Sergeant Zimmerman," the DDO said, then added: "And presumably Captain McCoy?"

"That makes sense, Ken," Pickering said, looking at McCoy.

"Aye, aye, sir," McCoy said.

"If we send Banning to Chungking—Chiang Kai-shek—now," Pickering said, "that would mean we would have a MAGIC communications team we control. And it would give us Special Channel communications."

"Yeah," the DDO said, and then asked, "Does the President want Chiang Kai-shek to have unlimited access to MAGIC material?"

"I don't know about the President, but I don't think Frank Knox and Admiral Leahy do," Pickering said. "Which means we would have in Banning someone who could immediately give to Chiang Kai-shek MAGIC material which would be of interest to him. And not—"

"I take your point, General," the DDO said.

"What about the cryptographers?" Banning asked. "I'm sure the British would be delighted to have some of their men trained—"

"But if we have our own men, that wouldn't be necessary, would it?" Pickering interrupted. "The question is, do we have anyone?"

"Me, sir," 2nd Lieutenant Hart said. It was the first time he had opened his mouth.

"Yeah," Pickering said thoughtfully.

"No," Rickabee said. "You need Hart."

"McCoy?" the DDO asked. "Or do you plan to use him operationally?"

"I don't think Ken should have a MAGIC clearance," Pickering said.

Which is one way of telling me I'm going into the god-damned Gobi Desert, McCoy thought.

"Hart," McCoy asked, "how long did it take them to teach you to operate the machine?"

"Four, five days, before they'd let me at it by myself," Hart said.

"The Easterbunny," McCoy said, looking at Pickering.

" 'The *Easterbunny*'?" the DDO asked.

"Second Lieutenant Robert F. Easterbrook," Pickering said. "One of the officers I brought with me." He turned to McCoy. "Yeah," he said. "Where is he?"

"I sent him over to the Smithsonian," McCoy said. "To improve his mind."

"Where's he staying?"

"With me, sir. He and Zimmerman."

"That must be cozy," Pickering said, smiling.

"I can give you Sergeant Rutterman," Rickabee said. "He told me he's going stir-crazy in Washington, and I told him the first thing that came along . . ."

"Could he teach Easterbrook what he has to know?" Pickering asked.

"Yes, sir."

"That would give us two. We need three, at least," Pickering said.

"General," Hart asked, "do you think Colonel Waterson has had time to select and train two of his officers? I'm thinking of Moore, sir. That would also give Colonel Banning an analyst."

"Fritz, you're right," Pickering said. "I really can't do without Hart." He turned to Hart. "As soon as we're finished here, George, Special Channel Colonel Waterson and tell him that as soon as he has two people up and running with MAGIC, he should be prepared to send Lieutenant Moore to . . . Where do I tell him to send him?"

"We've got a couple of days to determine that," Rickabee said.

"You know what to say to Waterson, George," Pickering said.

"Aye, aye, sir."

"Is there a MAGIC machine at this country club I keep hearing so much about?" Pickering asked.

"There is, for training purposes, but I don't think it's connected with the network. Or, for that matter, has current codes," the DDO replied.

"All you need is the machine, sir," Hart said, "to teach someone how to use it."

"We're going to need a staging area and quarters," Pickering said. "And despite the patriotic generosity of American Personal Pharmaceuticals in offering their quarters, I think maybe we better move to the Country Club."

"No problem," the DDO said. "And I'm not even going to ask what American Personal Pharmaceuticals has to do with anything."

Banning and Rickabee chuckled.

"I'll call out there and tell them to give you whatever you need," the DDO went on. "What do you think that will be?"

"Quarters for Lieutenant Easterbrook and Sergeants Zimmerman and Rutterman," Pickering said. "On-call quarters for Banning, McCoy, and Jake. A place to store the radios and whatever else we're going to send to China. On that subject, Jake, I don't think Banning will have the time to go to Collins Radio. You can do that, after you and McCoy lay your hands on what is immediately available."

"Aye, aye, sir," Dillon said.

"I think the thing for us to do," Pickering said, "is to chew over what we've decided. We've made a lot of decisions here today, and we're going to have to change some of them, I'm sure. I think we should get together again tomorrow. Or the day after tomorrow. I presume we can find a secure room out there?"

"Absolutely," the DDO said. "The day after tomorrow. Better yet, Wednesday afternoon. Say about five?"

"Wednesday at five it is," Pickering said, getting to his feet. "Unless someone has anything else?"

"Sir?" McCoy said.

"Okay, Ken, what?"

"Sir, Zimmerman thinks it would be safe for him to accompany one of the caravans to Ulaanbaatar."

"How would he pass himself off as a Chinese, or a Mongolian?" the DDO asked.

"He wouldn't, sir. He said there are a lot of Russians and some Germans and some other people in the area. Stateless persons. Some with Nansen passports, some without. He thinks he could do it if he grew a beard and had a Nansen passport."

"That could be arranged," the DDO said thoughtfully. "I presume Sergeant Zimmerman speaks Russian?"

"No, sir, German."

"You do, too, don't you, Ken?" Pickering asked.

"Not as fluently as the gunny, sir."

Was that modesty speaking? Or was I trying to get out of going into Mongolia with a Nansen passport?

"I think it would be a mistake to send someone in this early in the game," the DDO said. "But down the pike, it might be necessary and valuable. I'll check into the passports. Do you and Sergeant Zimmerman have civilian clothing, Captain?"

"I have a few things," McCoy said. "I'm sure Zimmerman doesn't."

"No, sir," Zimmerman said.

"I think we should put that on our things to do list, too," the DDO said. "Civilian clothing suitable for here. I'll ask our specialists about clothing for northern China, but I suspect you could probably buy that easier there."

"Why civilian clothing?" Pickering asked.

"You heard what he said. Nansen passports and beards. Don't you think that Captain McCoy and Sergeant Zimmerman would attract attention in uniform as they were growing beards?"

Well, that was decided in a goddamn hurry, wasn't it? McCoy asked himself. *If Zimmerman playing camel driver is a good idea, sending me with him is an even better idea.*

"I'll want to think a long time about sending either of them into China with a camel caravan," Pickering said. "In civilian clothing, they could be shot as spies."

"Yes, they could," the DDO said matter-of-factly. "That's the rules of the game we play here."

The implication, McCoy thought, *is that he's surprised and disappointed that General Pickering would say something dumb like that. And it was dumb.*

Pickering's temper flared.

"I'm sure that both Captain McCoy and Gunny Zimmerman are well aware of the rules," he said icily. "But I think you had better clearly understand that before I ask—operative word 'ask'—them, or anyone else, to risk getting shot as a spy, I intend to be convinced that it is absolutely necessary. I don't think this is a game."

The two men locked eyes for a moment, then the DDO walked over to Gunny Zimmerman and offered him his hand.

"Thank you, Sergeant," he said. "For the first time since I heard about this operation, I don't feel we're just spinning our wheels."

"Yes, sir," Zimmerman said.

The DDO then turned to McCoy and opened his mouth as if to speak. But instead he changed his mind and walked out of the room.

[THREE]
Office of the Assistant Chief of Staff G-1
Headquarters, United States Marine Corps
Eighth and I Streets, NW
Washington, D.C.
0905 9 March 1943

Technical Sergeant K. L. Carruthers, Chief Clerk of the Enlisted Personnel Division, entered the office of Lieutenant Colonel Richard B. Warren, USMCR, Deputy Assistant G-1 for Enlisted Personnel, and announced that Brigadier General Pickering wished to see him.

"Who is he?" Colonel Warren thought aloud, and quickly checked into the telephone book of Headquarters, USMC, looking for the name. He didn't find it, which told him that General Pickering was not assigned to Headquarters, USMC.

When Colonel Warren glanced quizzically up at Sergeant Carruthers, the sergeant raised his hands in a gesture indicating he had no idea either.

"Colonel Jack (NMI) Stecker is with him," Sergeant Carruthers offered. "And another brigadier general named Rickabee."

Colonel Warren had heard that name, but he could not recall in what connection. Colonel Jack (NMI) Stecker was an old friend. They had both been sergeant majors in the prewar Corps.

"Ask them to come in, please," Colonel Warren said, and stood up behind his desk.

The ribbons on the chests of General Pickering and Colonel Stecker showed that they had both been around the Corps a long time, and had been in harm's way more than once. Colonel Warren noticed, however, that Jack Stecker was not wearing the blue-starred ribbon of the Medal of Honor. He wondered why he had never heard of General Pickering.

The other general did not have many ribbons. Colonel Warren decided he was probably another administrative officer of some kind. He looked like an administrative type. And he was carrying a battered briefcase.

"Good morning, gentlemen," Colonel Warren said. "How can I be of service?"

"How are you, Dick?" Stecker said, offering his hand.

"Long time no see," Warren said.

After introducing the others, Jack (NMI) Stecker said, "You're going to love this, Dick."

General Rickabee opened the briefcase and came out with a service record jacket. He handed it to Colonel Warren.

"Those are the records of Technical Sergeant Harry Rutterman," General Rickabee said.

"Yes, sir," Colonel Warren said.

"We want to have him promoted to master gunner," Rickabee said.

"I don't think I quite understand, sir," Warren said. "Has the sergeant been recommended for promotion? I've got to tell you, the promotion board has been rejecting just about all recommendations for people who aren't master sergeants."

"Well, I really don't care about any promotion board," General Pickering said. "We need to pin master gunner's bars on Sergeant Rutterman right away."

"Sir, I'm afraid I don't understand."

"Where Rutterman is going, he can perform his duties better if he has a bar on his collar," Pickering said. "This has to do with the efficiency of the mission. Not that Rutterman isn't fully qualified to be a master gunner."

"May I ask what that mission is, sir? What this man will be doing?"

"No. You don't have the need to know, Colonel," Rickabee said.

"Sir, without some sort of special justification, I don't think that it's going to be possible to promote Sergeant Rutterman," Warren said uncomfortably, looking at Stecker, who seemed to be amused by the exchange.

"There's always a waiver," Rickabee said. "What we need from you, Colonel, is to tell us who can grant a waiver in this case."

"Sir, a request for a waiver of this type has to go up through channels. I'll have to check. But, unless I'm mistaken, it has to be approved by the post commander where the sergeant is stationed, and then by both the G-1 and the deputy commandant."

"How about the Secretary of the Navy?" General Pickering asked. "Could he grant such a waiver?"

The Secretary of the Navy? Personally? What the hell is going on here?

"That would be very unusual, sir, for the Secretary of the Navy to become personally involved in something like this."

"If the Administrative Assistant to the Secretary of the Navy told you it was the Secretary's desire to promote Sergeant Rutterman, would that do it?" General Rickabee asked.

"Yes, sir, of course."

"May I use your telephone, Colonel?" Rickabee asked.

"Of course, sir."

Rickabee dialed a number from memory.

"David, Fritz," he said. "We're at Eighth and I. I'm going to put you on the line with Colonel Warren. He's the enlisted personnel guy in G-1, and he needs the Secretary's authority to promote Rutterman."

He handed the telephone to Colonel Warren.

"Captain David Haughton, USN, is Administrative Assistant to the Secretary of the Navy," Rickabee said.

Colonel Warren took the telephone.

He said "Yes, sir" five times; "I understand, sir" twice; and then "Glad to be of service, sir" once.

[FOUR]
Office of the Deputy Director, USMC Aviation
Building F
Anacostia Naval Air Station
Washington, D.C.
1115 9 March 1943

"General," Brigadier General D. G. McInerney's aide-de-camp announced, "there is a General Pickering and a Colonel Stecker to see you, sir."

"Tony, that's *the* General Pickering and *the* Colonel Stecker," McInerney said. " 'A' suggests there's more than one of each, and that's just not the case."

"Yes, sir."

"Send them in, and then lock up the silver. I don't think they're here just to say hello."

"Aye, aye, sir," the aide said.

He turned and opened the door.

"Gentlemen, General McInerney will see you."

They walked into the office.

"To what do I owe the honor of such distinguished visitors to my humble abode?" McInerney greeted them, coming from around his desk.

"You want the truth, Mac?" Pickering asked, as their handshake turned into a hug.

"If possible, that would be very nice," McInerney said, as he gave Stecker an affectionate hug.

"We want to pick your brains," Pickering said, "and eventually steal things."

"Tony, am I flying today?" McInerney asked.

"No, sir."

"In that case, a little nip is called for. Bring in the cheap stuff."

"Aye, aye, sir."

First Lieutenant Anthony I. Sylvester had not been General McInerney's aide for long. He was still on limited duty following hospitalization for injuries to his neck suffered in a bad arrested landing. But he had been around long enough to know that these two officers were somehow special to McInerney. He had never heard of General Pickering, but wondered if Colonel Stecker could be the near-legendary Colonel Jack (NMI) Stecker.

A moment later, Sylvester returned to McInerney's office with two bottles, one of scotch, the other of bourbon, the best available in the lower filing case in the office.

"I said the cheap stuff, Tony," McInerney said. "I had the great misfortune to serve with these two in what used to be called The Great War—I was one of Sergeant Stecker's corporals, believe it or not. They wouldn't know good booze if they were drowning in it."

My God, that is Colonel Jack (NMI) Stecker!

"And even then, Lieutenant," Pickering said, "he was known for his peculiar sense of humor. That liquor will do very nicely, thank you."

"Aye, aye, sir." .

"Lieutenant Sylvester—Tony—just came to me from Philadelphia," McInerney said. "And to answer your question, yes, he knows Dick. I asked him, and he confirmed what I'd heard, Dick's doing all right."

"You're Lieutenant Stecker's father, sir?" Lieutenant Sylvester asked.

Stecker nodded.

"We had therapy together," Sylvester said.

"They do amazing things at Philadelphia," Stecker said. "For a while . . ." He decided not to pursue that thought. "But now," he continued, "thank God, Dick's walking around with only a cane."

"He told me he'd been pretty badly banged up," Sylvester said.

"Young Stecker and young Pickering were in VMF-229

on the 'Canal," McInerney said. "So this is sort of a family gathering. With that in mind, Flem, should I tell Tony to pour himself a drink? Or is this visit official?"

Pickering looked uncomfortable. "I'd rather you decide later, Mac, how much Lieutenant Sylvester should know about what we're going to talk about," he said finally.

"Okay, Tony. Out. Bar the door. Nobody but the Commandant."

"Aye, aye, sir," Lieutenant Sylvester said, and left the office.

"What the hell is going on?" McInerney asked.

"What I said. I need to pick your brains."

"About what?"

"What follows is Top Secret," Pickering said.

McInerney nodded. "Understood."

"We're going to set up a weather station in the Gobi Desert," Pickering said.

"Who is 'we'?"

"The OSS," Pickering said.

"I saw that in the paper—I mean, you going over there. You, too, Jack?"

"Jack is my liaison to the Corps," Pickering said. "Unofficially."

"When is Vandegrift going to take over? Any word on that?"

"He wants to stay with the First Marine Division until he gets it back in shape. Whenever he decides it is, he'll take over," Stecker said.

"So you're going to have to wait awhile for your star?"

"If that ever happens," Stecker said.

"It'll happen. Vandegrift told me it would," McInerney said firmly, then looked at Pickering. "Okay, tell me about your Gobi Desert weather station. I heard the Army Air Corps was going to set one up in Russia. Same idea?"

"The Russians won't let the Air Corps in. Nimitz and Leahy want a weather station as soon as possible. Leahy gave the mission to the OSS, and Nimitz got Leahy to 'suggest' that I be given the job."

"Which means Leahy and Nimitz think you're the guy who can do it," McInerney said. "Proving once again that

I was wrong when I told you you couldn't do the Corps any good."

"You told me that because you believed it, Mac," Pickering said. "And that's why I'm here. I want you to tell me what you believe, not what you think I'd like to hear."

"Okay. I don't think you can do it. That blunt enough? The Gobi Desert is in the middle of nowhere, a long way from anything we control. How the hell are you going to put people in there? On camels?"

Stecker chuckled. "That's one of the options, Mac, but what Flem wants to ask you about is airplanes."

"I don't need a map and a compass to measure the distance. I can tell you the Gobi Desert is beyond the range of any airplane in the inventory—Marine, Navy, or Air Corps. You didn't know that?"

"When you speak of range, you're talking round trips, right?" Pickering asked.

McInerney thought that over for a minute.

"A one-way mission, huh? Who are you going to find to fly it? More important, where will it go?"

"There's reliable information that a group of Americans is somewhere in the Gobi Desert, some of them Marines from the Legation Guard at Peking who didn't surrender. Most of these people are supposed to be retired from the Fourth Marines, the Yangtze River patrol, and the Fifteenth Infantry."

"You're in contact with them?"

"Not reliably. We're working on that."

"We're going to send decent radios to them, Mac," Stecker said. "On camels."

McInerney's eyebrows rose in either surprise or disbelief.

"We also have somebody who's been all over the Gobi desert," Pickering said. "A gunnery sergeant who used to be in the Fourth in Shanghai. He tells us that a good deal of the Gobi Desert is not sand but flat rock. In other words, an airplane could land there."

"Erring on the side of caution, how about 'crashland'?" McInerney said sarcastically.

"Okay. Crash-land," Pickering said. "As long as it delivers the weather station equipment in workable condition, we can write off the airplane."

"If it gets that far, and I have serious doubts that it will, this weather station would be secret, right?"

"It would be better if it were," Pickering said.

"If you sent an airplane on a one-way mission, the wreckage would stick out like a sore thumb in the desert," McInerney said.

"Yeah, I guess it would," Pickering said. "Let's fly an airplane there first, and then worry about concealing the wreckage. What should we use for an airplane?"

"That would depend on where the airplane is going to fly *from*," McInerney said. "You have two choices. Russia, and you say that's out of the question. Or India."

"Tell me about India," Pickering said.

"The Air Corps is flying Curtiss C-46s from Sadiya—something like that, anyway. God, I'm not sure what I'm talking about."

McInerney picked up his telephone. "Tony, bring me maps of India and China," he said, hung up, and then went on: "They call it 'Flying the Hump.' Meaning they have to climb to sixteen thousand feet to fly over it, most of the way on oxygen. They fly supplies over the Himalayas into Kunming, China."

"Kunming is in the south of China," Stecker said. "The Gobi Desert is in the north, the far north."

"I'll have to check the map, but I'm thinking, Jack, that the distances are about the same. A C-46 would have the range, especially if it wasn't planning to make a round trip."

"Correct me if I'm wrong," Pickering said. "But wouldn't you say that even if the Japanese can't shoot these planes down—"

"They shoot them down," McInerney interrupted.

"—they keep track of them. Either themselves, or with informants, spies, on the ground?"

"Sure."

"And wouldn't they notice if one of these C-46s routinely flying to Kunming suddenly went in the other direction?"

"Probably. But it wouldn't be the first aircraft to get lost out there. A friend of mine told me the pilots call it 'the Aluminum Trail,' because you can navigate by the wrecks of planes that have gone down."

"But wouldn't you say they would go looking for an airplane, the wreckage of an airplane, that didn't head for Kunming?"

"Flem, you're going to have to get used to the idea that you don't have many options," McInerney said.

Lieutenant Sylvester appeared with four maps packed in cardboard tubes.

McInerney came from behind his desk, pulled the rolled-up maps from the tubes, and spread them out on the floor. He and Stecker dropped to their knees. Pickering stood behind them.

"Here it is," McInerney said, pointing. "I was right. Sadiya, in the Brahmaputra Valley. From there over the mountains to Kunming." He traced the route with his fingers, and then, using his little finger and thumb as a compass, compared the distance between Sadiya and Kunming and Sadiya and the center of the Gobi Desert.

"Like I thought," he said, "about the same distance. Five hundred miles, maybe five-fifty. A C-46 could make it, one-way, without any trouble."

"Does the Corps have any C-46s?" Pickering asked.

"The Corps has a few, reluctantly contributed by the Air Corps, and none of which I—speaking for the Corps—am willing to give to the OSS for a one-way mission."

Pickering did not reply directly. "What about the R4D?" he asked.

"It has the range, but getting it over the mountains? Risky—damned risky—at best."

"And you can't fly an R4-D through the mountains, or around them?"

McInerney shook his head. "You have to have the altitude to get over them. The R4-D just doesn't have it. There's always exceptions to everything, of course. But so far as I'm concerned, you'd better forget about using an R4-D."

Pickering dropped to his knees and put his finger on the map.

"That, General," McInerney said, "is the Yellow Sea."

"Yeah, General, I know," Pickering said. "I used to be a sailor."

"What are you thinking, Flem?"

"Catalina," Pickering said. "Maybe two Catalinas. From fifty miles offshore, they would have more than enough range."

"Not by the time they reached a position fifty miles off the coast. Not from any base where they are now operating."

"They would if they met a submarine and took on fuel from it," Pickering said.

"A rendezvous at sea?" McInerney said, doubtfully but thoughtfully. "I don't know, Flem."

"The Catalina has a range of twenty-three hundred miles," Pickering said. "It cruises at a hundred sixty knots, or thereabouts. And it can carry two tons of bombs."

"It carries the bombs under its wings," McInerney said.

"But it can lift that much weight, right? Two tons is a lot of meteorological equipment."

"I thought you came here for my expert advice about airplanes."

"We did. And you came up with the same arguments against using India as a base for C-46s that Jack and I did. You ever hear the true test of an intelligent man is how much he agrees with you?"

"I'm not agreeing with you. I am having unpleasant mental images of what would happen if you could talk the Navy into giving you a submarine·or a Catalina."

"What kind of unpleasant images?"

"First of all, the Navy is not going to be thrilled about putting several thousand gallons of avgas in one of their boats," McInerney said. "Avgas tends to explode. And then how would you get it into the tanks of the Catalina? I have visions of white hats trying—and failing—to get drums of gas over the side of a sub into a rubber boat. And then how would you get it from the rubber boat into the Catalina? The fuel receptacles are on the upper surface of a Catalina's wings. You plan to stand up in a rubber boat on the high seas and manhandle a fifty-five-gallon drum of avgas up onto the wing of a Catalina?"

"There has to be a way to do it," Stecker said.

"Jesus, Jack!"

"We got avgas onto Guadalcanal by tossing fifty-five-gallon drums of avgas over the side of those old four-stacker War One destroyers and letting the tide float it ashore."

"So?"

"Barrels of avgas float," Pickering said. "That might be useful."

"Flem, I can think of a hundred reasons this won't work!"

"That's why Jack and I came to see you, Mac," Pickering said. "We figured you could come up with everything that could go wrong. And then the solutions to fix the problems."

"You're presuming the Navy is going to give you a submarine, and Catalinas."

"Or, if we decided we need it, an old four-stacker destroyer or two. And, for that matter, one or more of the Marine Corps' precious C-46s. Whatever we need, Mac."

"What makes you believe that?"

"Because Admiral Leahy has ordered Admiral Nimitz to give us whatever we think we need, and Admiral Nimitz really wants this weather station."

"You know, I was really happy when you two walked in here," McInerney said. "I should have known better."

"Can we buy you lunch, General?" Pickering asked.

"You have ruined my appetite for at least the next three days," McInerney said. "I'm going to have to think long and hard about this, Flem."

"Does that mean you don't want to have lunch with us?" Pickering asked.

"*Eat* with you? I would be happier if I never saw either of you again," McInerney said. "How much time do I have?"

"Would yesterday morning be too soon?"

"Get the hell out of here," McInerney said. "Call me tomorrow afternoon."

"No, we'll come see you," Pickering said. "I don't want to talk about this on the telephone."

McInerney nodded, then thought of something else: "Who's going to fly this airplane?"

"Jack and I were really thinking we need two Catalinas."

"Who's going to fly the *two* Catalinas?"

"We thought you might be helpful there, too, General," Pickering said, and then turned serious. "I want Marine Corps pilots. I want to keep it in the family, so to speak."

"But you're not in the family anymore, are you?" McInerney said, and immediately added, "Sorry, that slipped out. I shouldn't have said that."

"What about 'once a Marine, always a Marine'?" Pickering said. "You ever hear that?"

"I said I was sorry. I am."

"Both of you, knock it off," Stecker said.

They looked at Stecker, and then at each other.

"Okay," McInerney said. "I'll even have lunch with you and your ugly jarhead friend. If he buys."

"That's better," Stecker said.

"Give me a minute to lay some errands on Tony," McInerney said. "And then I'll be with you. You've got a car?"

"We have Senator Fowler's car," Stecker said.

"Bring it around. This won't take me a minute."

He walked with them into his outer office, then waited for them to leave before speaking with his aide.

"I'm going to lunch with them," he said. "By the time I get back, whenever that is, I want the three most experienced Catalina pilots on the base sitting here waiting for me. And I also want, waiting for me on my desk, the draft of a teletype to be sent to every stateside air station soliciting twin-engine—preferably Catalina—qualified volunteers for a mission outside the United States involving great personal risk."

"Aye, aye, sir."

McInerney saw the look in his eyes.

"Yeah, Tony, I am going to explain this to you. After lunch."

"Yes, sir."

XII

[ONE]
Batten, Barton, Durstine & Osborne, Advertising
698 Madison Avenue
New York City, New York
1145 9 March 1943

"There's a *Colonel* Banning on the line for you, Miss Sage," Darlene, the secretary, announced. Ernie shared Darlene with H. Oswald Tinner, the account executive for the American Personal Pharmaceuticals account. Then curiosity got the better of her: "Was he promoted?"

"Yes, Darlene, he was," Ernie Sage replied, forcing herself to smile, as she punched the button for the internal line on her telephone.

When Ed Banning called, she always answered the telephone expecting the worst. Even when it was good news, it generally took her several minutes to calm down.

"Hello, Ed," she said.

"Ernie, as a favor to me, when you see Ken will you do something about his clothing?"

"Excuse me?"

"You'll know what I mean when you see him," Banning said.

"I'll see him late this afternoon," she said. "I'm going to try to catch the 2:40 Congressional Limited. What about his clothes?"

"He's on his way to New York," Banning said. "*We're* on our way to New York. I'm calling from the station. And I have to go, or I'll miss the train. Maybe we'll see you tonight. Do something, please, about his clothes. He'll pay attention to you."

The line went dead, as the red light indicating a call on her private line lit up, and the bell began to ring. She pushed the red light.

"Hello?"

"Baby, I'm on my way to New York," Captain Kenneth R. McCoy announced. "I'm at Union Station."

Well, thank God. That means I won't have to catch the Congressional Limited again.

"Can you spend the night?"

"Yeah. Where should I meet you?"

She thought that over quickly. *If he's catching the train now, that's three hours and something. Call it three and a half. That means he would get into Pennsylvania Station at 3:15. Twenty minutes to catch a cab and come here. Say quarter to four.*

"Come to the office, baby," she said.

"To the office?"

From the tone of his voice, he didn't like that.

"I can't get out of here any earlier," she said. "Come here."

"Jesus, Ernie!" he started to protest. "Christ, I have to go."

"Six ninety-eight Madison, twenty-second floor," she said.

There was no reply.

And then she saw the green light flashing, indicating an incoming call on the interior line. She punched the button.

"Ernestine Sage."

"Your private line was busy," Mr. Ernest Sage announced somewhat indignantly, as if he considered that a personal affront.

"Hi, Daddy! I'm fine. How are you?"

"Since you have a lamentable tendency to miss appointments, I thought it would be a good idea to remind you that we have one this afternoon."

Oh, shit!

"I said I would meet you if I could, Daddy," she said. "That's not quite the same thing as an appointment."

"I gather you cannot? Aren't you getting a little tired of commuting to Washington daily?"

"I consider it my contribution to the war effort," she said, and was immediately sorry. "And I didn't say I wasn't going to meet you. I said we didn't have an appointment."

"Well, may I infer from that that you will meet me?" he asked. He sounded pleased.

"Ken and I will meet you," Ernie said.

"Splendid," he said, considerably less pleased. "Jack and Charley's at five-thirty?"

"We'd better make it six, or even six-thirty," Ernie said. "Ken's coming up by train, and you never know if they're going to be on time."

"Six, then," he said, and hung up.

At half past three, Miss Ernestine Sage was notified by the BBD&O receptionist that a Mr. McCoy was in the lobby.

"Mr. McCoy"? Doesn't she recognize a Marine officer when she sees one?

BBD&O protocol dictated that when an executive-level employee had a visitor, the employee was to dispatch a secretary or other clerical employee from his or her office to the reception desk on the twentieth floor, to escort the visitor to the executive-level employee's office.

Miss Sage was well aware of this protocol, but decided to hell with it.

"I'll be right down," she said, and hung up.

After a quick glance at her watch and her desk, she decided that doing any more work today was a lost cause, grabbed her hat and coat, and left the office.

"See you in the morning," she said to Darlene.

"If someone calls?"

"Tell them I'll be in in the morning," Ernie said, and went to the fire-exit stairwell. That was the quickest way down to the twentieth floor.

As soon as she pushed open the fire-exit stairwell door and entered the reception area, she saw Captain McCoy. What she saw immediately explained why the receptionist mistook him for a civilian and why Ed Banning asked her to do something about his clothes.

I love him anyway, Ernie thought. *But my God! Where did he get those clothes? He looks like a coal miner all dressed up for a night out on payday.*

McCoy was wearing a two-tone sport jacket with a plaid body and blue sleeves. It had four pockets, with flaps, made of the same material as the sleeves. The open collar of a yellow shirt was neatly folded over the collar of the jacket. He had on a pair of light brown trousers, and was wearing his Marine Corps uniform shoes.

Ernie kissed him on the lips, not the cheek, which obviously made him uncomfortable.

"What are you doing dressed like that?" she asked.

"You don't like it, huh? Neither did Banning. I could see it on his face."

"I meant, baby, what are you doing in civilian clothing?"

"It's sort of a long story," he said. "Can we get out of here? I want to go to Brooks Brothers before they close."

"You mean the clothing store?" she asked.

"Yeah. Sure. The clothing store."

"You're going to buy some other clothes?"

"With you and Banning looking at me like I escaped from the circus, yes, I'm going to buy some other clothes."

"Well, Brooks Brothers has nice things," Ernie said. "That's a good idea."

But, unless they're having a fire sale, nothing a Marine captain can afford. Doesn't he know that?

As if he had been reading her mind, he answered the question. "I finally paid off what I owed for my uniforms," he said. "So I suppose my credit is good. And

I've got a two-hundred-fifty-dollar civilian clothes allowance check."

"You bought your uniforms at Brooks Brothers?" Ernie asked, as she led him onto the elevator.

"When Pick and I were about to graduate from OCS, he said the best place for us to buy officer's uniforms was Brooks Brothers," McCoy said. "He didn't mention what they were going to charge for them."

"Oh," Ernie said.

Damn Pick! He should have known Ken couldn't afford Brooks Brothers!

"Anyway, I thought that since I don't know diddly-shit—Sorry, that slipped out . . ."

Ernie made a gesture meaning she wasn't offended by the vulgarity.

". . . about civvies, Brooks Brothers was the place to go for them."

"Good idea."

"Can you go with me?" he asked, almost shyly.

My God, he wants me to help him!

"Of course."

"I thought you would know the right thing to buy."

"We'll find something," Ernie said. "Are you going to tell me why you need civilian clothing?"

"Well, I'm going to grow a beard," he said. "I am ordered to grow a beard, and a Marine officer with a beard would make people ask questions."

"I don't suppose you're going to tell me why you've been ordered to grow a beard?"

"I can't, honey," McCoy said.

What the hell does that mean? Where are they going to send him now where he needs to have a beard? And/or wear civilian clothing? What's he going to be doing? When is he going?

I knew damned well when Darlene said Banning was on the phone that it was going to be bad news.

"The first thing you're going to need is shoes," Ernie said when they had pushed through the revolving door into Brooks Brothers.

"I suppose," he said, looking down at his feet.

"Go in there and ask them to show you some loafers," she said. "I'm going to the ladies' room. I'll meet you there."

He nodded and headed toward the footwear department. She couldn't help but notice the look of amusement, surprise, and contempt one of the salesmen gave him as he walked past. Then she went looking for another salesman.

"I'd like to see the manager," she told him.

"Perhaps I can help you, miss," the salesman said.

"If I thought so, I wouldn't have asked for the manager," Ernie snapped at him, and was immediately sorry.

He didn't look down his nose at Ken. The sonofabitch by the tie counter did.

"May I help you, madam?" a middle-aged man asked a moment later.

"You're in charge?"

"Yes, I am."

"I'm not sure if I have an account here or not. I know my father does."

"Perhaps you have a family account."

"My father's name is Ernest Sage. It's probably billed to him at American Personal Pharmaceuticals."

"I know your father," he said, now smiling warmly. "I've known him for years. How may I assist you? It is Miss Sage?"

"I'm Ernestine Sage," she acknowledged.

"I'm very pleased to meet you, Miss Sage."

"Thank you," Ernie said. "I'm here with a gentleman friend. He needs some clothing, and he needs it right now. Which means you're going to have to put him at the head of the alteration line."

"That may be difficult."

"But not impossible, right?"

"We do try to take the best possible care of our good customers," he said.

"By ten minutes to six, we'll need a sport coat and a pair of trousers altered."

"I think we can handle that."

"And by noon tomorrow, he will also need two business suits, probably two more jackets, and two or three pair of pants."

"That may be difficult," he said.

"We're back to 'difficult but not impossible,' right?" The manager smiled at her.

Ernestine Sage did not look at all like her father, but she was obviously a chip off the old block.

"We will accommodate the gentleman, Miss Sage," he said.

"Now we come to payment," Ernie said. "My gentleman friend has an account here, and will sign for whatever he buys. But I don't want him to pay for what he buys, or to know, right now, that he won't be paying for it. It's sort of a surprise present."

"I understand. And should I bill Mr. Sage?"

"No. I'm going to pay for this. You can either open an account for me—you can check my credit with Bergdorf Goodman, or the Park Avenue and Fifty-seventh Street branch of First National Bank—or I'll send a check down here by messenger."

"So far as I am concerned, Miss Sage, you have just opened an account with us. And checking your credit won't be necessary. I happen to know you're employed."

"How do you know that?" Ernie asked, surprised.

"Your father told me you're the creative director for APP at BBD&O. He's very proud of you."

"I'll be damned," Ernie said.

"Shall we go see what we can do for your gentleman friend?" the manager said.

When they arrived at the footwear department, they found Ken dubiously examining the loafers on his feet. The manager could not quite conceal his surprise when he saw how Ken was dressed.

"I'm going to need some real shoes, too, right, Ernie?" McCoy said.

"Oh, I don't think so, sir," the manager said. "Slip-ons like those are now considered appropriate for wear with just about anything."

McCoy looked at Ernie, who nodded in agreement.

"Okay," McCoy said. "I'll take these."

"One in oxblood," Ernie said. "And one in black."

McCoy considered that a moment, then shrugged.

"What the hell," he said. "Why not?"

[TWO]

S E C R E T
HQ USMC
1705 09 MAR 43
PRIORITY

COMMANDING OFFICERS
ALL USMC AIR BASES AND STATIONS IN
CONTINENTAL US AND TERRITORY OF HAWAII
ALL MAG IN CONTINENTAL US AND TERRITORY
OF HAWAII
ALL SEPARATE USMC AVIATION SQUADRONS AND
MARINE AVIATION COMPLEMENTS IN
CONTINENTAL US AND TERRITORY OF HAWAII

SUBJECT: SOLICITATION OF VOLUNTEERS FOR
HAZARDOUS DUTY

1. YOU WILL IMMEDIATELY DETERMINE WHICH
MARINE AVIATORS UNDER YOUR COMMAND ARE,
OR HAVE BEEN, RATED AS COMMAND PILOTS OF
PBY5, PBY5A AND R4-D AIRCRAFT.

2. YOU WILL IMMEDIATELY PERSONALLY
INTERVIEW EACH SUCH MARINE AVIATOR AND
AFFORD HIM THE OPPORTUNITY TO VOLUNTEER
FOR A CLASSIFIED MISSION INVOLVING GREAT
PERSONAL RISK IN A COMBAT AREA LASTING
APPROXIMATELY NINETY DAYS.

3. THE NAMES OF VOLUNTEERS WILL BE
TRANSMITTED WITHIN SEVENTY-TWO (72)
HOURS OF RECEIPT OF THIS MESSAGE BY THE
MOST EXPEDITIOUS MEANS AVAILABLE
CLASSIFIED SECRET TO HEADQUARTERS USMC,
ATTENTION BRIG GEN D.G. MCINERNEY USMC.

4. THE NAMES OF MARINE AVIATORS WHO ARE
QUALIFIED AS IN PARA 1 ABOVE, AND REPEAT

AND WHO HAVE 1,000 HOURS OR MORE OR WHO
HAVE BEEN RATED IN PBY5, PBY-5A AND R4-D
AIRCRAFT OR A COMBINATION THEREOF AND WHO
DID NOT REPEAT NOT ELECT TO VOLUNTEER FOR
THE MISSION DESCRIBED IN PARA 2 ABOVE
WILL SIMILARLY BE TRANSMITTED WITHIN
SEVENTY-TWO (72) HOURS OF RECEIPT OF THIS
MESSAGE BY MOST EXPEDITIOUS MEANS
AVAILABLE

CLASSIFIED SECRET TO HEADQUARTERS USMC
ATTENTION BRIG GEN D.G. MCINERNEY USMC.

BY DIRECTION OF THE COMMANDANT:

D.G. MCINERNEY BRIG GEN USMC

S E C R E T

[THREE]
The 21 Club
21 West Fifty-second Street
New York City, New York
1930 9 March 1943

"There they are," Mrs. Carolyn Spencer Howell said,
pointing across the crowded room, and then asking softly,
"What's wrong with the way he's dressed? He looks fine
to me."

Colonel Banning saw that Captain McCoy was now
attired in a muted blue-gray herringbone jacket; a white
button-down-collar shirt; and a regimentally striped necktie. The legs he had stretched out beside his table were
covered with gray flannel trousers. He was wearing oxblood loafers and gray stockings.

Ernie did a good job—and damned quickly, Banning
thought. *If it wasn't for that GI haircut, he'd look like he
belongs in here.*

"That's not the same guy I rode up here with on the train," Banning said. "That's Ernie's father with them, probably. Her secretary said she was going to meet him here."

At that moment, Ernie spotted them and waved them over.

"We'll be joining Miss Sage," Carolyn said to the head-waiter, who followed the nod of her head, spotted the Sages, and then unfastened the red velvet-covered chain and passed them into the dining room.

From the look on his face when they approached the table, Ernest Sage liked the looks of Carolyn Howell.

Well, why not? Banning thought. *Carolyn's tall, graceful, willowy, chic, and damned good-looking. Just because you become a father doesn't mean you can no longer appreciate women.*

Ernie gave her cheek to Carolyn to be kissed.

They're two of a kind, really, Banning thought somewhat unkindly. *Two very nice young women sleeping with Marines they aren't married to and don't give much of a damn who knows it.*

"I hope we're not intruding," Banning said.

"Not at all," Ernest Sage said, snapped his fingers to attract a waiter's attention, and signaled for him to bring two chairs to the table.

"Mr. Sage, this is Colonel Banning and Mrs. Howell," McCoy said.

"How do you do?" Sage said.

He picked up on that "Mrs. *Howell,*" Banning thought. Confirmation came when Ernie's father's eyes dropped to Carolyn's hand, looking for a wedding ring. There was none.

Would I put a wedding ring on that finger if there wasn't already a Mrs. Edward J. Banning? Of course I would. Do I regret marrying Milla? I do not. So what does that make me, a would-be bigamist? Or just a no-good sonofabitch for getting involved with Carolyn, getting her involved with me?

"You look very elegant tonight, Ken," Carolyn said. "How's your face?"

"Excuse me?"

"Ed told me about the rash," Carolyn said. "I hope I didn't embarrass you?"

"No," McCoy answered after a pause that wasn't quite awkward. "Of course not. The medics said as long as I don't shave, it will clear up."

Ernest Sage looked carefully at McCoy's face. He could see nothing remotely resembling a rash.

I wonder what that's all about? Ernest Sage wondered. *That rash on his face is obviously hogwash. He had to think quick when she asked him about it; he didn't know what she was talking about.*

But she's right. He does look good in civilian clothes. Why the hell couldn't Ernie fall in love with some nice young man who is 4-F and doesn't have to concoct stories about why he's wearing civilian clothing.

"I called your office," Banning said to Ernie. "Your secretary told me she thought you were coming here."

"Darlene talks too much," Ernie replied, and then: "Oh, hell, I didn't mean that the way it sounded. I'm glad to see you."

"And I'm very happy to meet you, Colonel," Ernest Sage said. "I understand you're Ken's commanding officer?"

"In a manner of speaking, sir," Banning said.

"He and Ken are old friends, Daddy," Ernie said. "They were in Shanghai together."

We weren't exactly friends in Shanghai, Banning thought. *The Corps frowns on captains getting friendly with corporals. But we're friends now, and obviously McCoy thought of himself as my friend when he was Corporal McCoy in Shanghai. Otherwise he wouldn't have leaned on Zimmerman and his Chinese woman to help Milla. Zimmerman didn't do that out of the goodness of his heart.*

"We're working together on a project, Mr. Sage," Banning said. "Since I'm senior to Ken, that makes me sort of his commanding officer."

"For General Pickering, right?" Ernest Sage said. "Now of the OSS, whatever the hell that is."

"Yes, sir," Banning said.

"What kind of a project? Or is that an impolite question?"

"Well, tomorrow morning Ken and I are going to Fort Monmouth to look at some new shortwave radios," Banning said. Fort Monmouth, New Jersey, was the "Home of the Army Signal Corps"; the U.S. Army Signal Corps Laboratories were located on the base.

"Really? What kind of radios?"

"Daddy, stop!" Ernie said firmly. "You're putting him on the spot."

"I'm sorry, Colonel," Ernest Sage said. "I didn't mean to."

"We're really not supposed to talk about what we're doing," Banning said. "I personally don't think this place is crawling with Japanese spies—or any other kind—but orders are orders."

"I'm not asking when he would be going, or where," Sage pursued, "but is whatever you're doing going to take Ken away anytime soon?"

Banning looked at McCoy, who shrugged, and then at Carolyn.

"I'm afraid so," Banning said. "Both of us."

Banning saw the pained look in Carolyn's eyes, but saw, too, that she wasn't surprised.

"And for how long?" Ernie asked brightly.

"We don't know that, Ernie," Banning said.

"In other words, for a long time," she said bitterly. "My God, he just got back!"

"There's a whole division of Marines in Australia, Ernie," McCoy said, "who went over there a year ago, took Guadalcanal, and are now training to take some other island. They haven't been back home since they left, and they have no idea when they will get back."

"That's supposed to make me feel better?" she challenged. "It doesn't."

"We have tonight," Carolyn said. "Let's be grateful for what we have."

"Live today, for tomorrow they die, right?" Ernie said.

"Knock it off, Ernie," McCoy said.

She looked at him, then at Carolyn.

"I'm sorry. I shouldn't have said that," she said.

"Let's talk about where we're going to have dinner," Carolyn said.

[FOUR]
**Apartment 7B
705 Park Avenue
New York City, New York
2305 9 March 1943**

Carolyn Spencer Howell, fresh from the shower and wearing a pink negligee, stood in the door of her bathroom and brushed her hair, waiting for Lieutenant Colonel Ed Banning to notice her.

He was sitting in his pajamas, propped up in the bed, reading the *Daily News*. A bottle of Rémy Martin cognac and two balloon glasses sat on the bedside table.

After she had had time to consider once again that he was a really handsome man, and that she loved him very much, he sensed her eyes on him and let the *Daily News* drop onto his lap.

"I have a profound philosophical insight to share with you," she said.

"And what would that profound philosophical insight be?"

"I hate this goddamned war, and by extension, the goddamned United States Marine Corps, and the goddamned OSS."

"Did this great truth suddenly appear to you, or did something trigger it?"

"Ken," she said.

"I don't think Ken can be blamed for the war, the Marine Corps, or the OSS," Banning said.

"He looked so nice in Jack and Charley's," Carolyn said. "*They* looked so nice."

"Jack and Charley's?" Banning asked, confused.

"Jack and Charley Kriendler own the 21 Club," she said.

"I didn't know that," Banning said. "I'm just a simple Marine from South Carolina. But yeah, the Killer looked fine. Thanks to Ernie. I didn't know he even knew what Brooks Brothers was."

"You know what I thought? In Jack and Charley's 21 Club?" she asked.

"I think you're about to tell me."

"There we were, the nice young man and the nice young woman, in love, and the slightly older female and her gentleman friend, all dressed up—ignoring for the moment your goddamned uniform—and wouldn't it be nice if we could all go home to our respective apartments after agreeing to have the same kind of a night out, say, next week? Or maybe decide to go to the shore for the weekend."

Banning didn't reply.

"Instead of pretending that everything was hunky-dory," Carolyn went on, "and that the two of you are not going God only knows where, and God only knows when, to do God only knows what, except that either or both or you are liable to be killed doing it."

"To coin a phrase," Banning said, "there's a war on, you may have heard."

"I think I did hear something about that," she said.

"I don't know what you want me to say, sweetheart," he said.

"I don't expect you to say anything," Carolyn said. "I just wanted you to know how I feel."

"I wish things were different," Banning said, and then added: "As soon as we finish what we have to do here— which will probably take a couple of weeks—I'm going to Chungking, China, where I will assume the duties of staff officer on the staff of the U.S. Mission to General-issimo Chiang Kai-shek."

"You're serious?" she asked, but it was more of a statement.

Banning nodded.

"Ken, too?"

"Ken, too."

"Why do I suspect—feminine intuition?—that that's not the truth, the whole truth, and nothing but the truth? I like Ken, you know that, but I can't see him passing a tray of canapés around. Or you either, for that matter."

"It's all I can tell you," Banning said. "I probably—probably hell—*shouldn't* have told you that much. What I did tell you was the truth."

Carolyn went off at a tangent: "What's going to happen to them, after the war?"

"I suppose they'll get married and live more or less happily ever after."

"They're from different worlds," Carolyn said.

"How about 'love conquers all'?"

"You think that will apply to you and me, after the war?"

"I have a wife, Carolyn," Banning said.

"Maybe the Mormons have the right idea. I'd be willing to share you, if that was the only alternative to not having you at all."

He shrugged helplessly but didn't reply.

"You think she's still alive?"

He raised his hands in a gesture of helplessness. "I don't know," he said.

"And if she is still alive, will she be the same woman you married? I suppose what I'm asking is will you still be in love with her?"

" 'In sickness and in health,' " he quoted, " 'until death doth you part.' "

"You left out 'forsaking all others,' " Carolyn said, a little too brightly.

He didn't like what he heard in her voice.

"Would you rather I left, Carolyn?" Banning asked. "Maybe that would be the best—"

"It's midnight," she said practically, interrupting him. "Where would you go? You'd never find a hotel room this time of night. And besides, I meant what I said about maybe the Mormons have the right idea."

"You're getting the short end of this stick," he said.

"I know," she said. "But I knew that when we started, didn't I?"

"If you want me to say I feel guilty as hell . . ."

"I know that," Carolyn said. "If you didn't feel guilty, I don't think I'd love you. Or at least love you as much." She turned and went back into the bathroom.

Banning stared at the bathroom door for a moment,

then angrily picked up the newspaper and threw it across the room.

[FIVE]
Office of the Commander in Chief, Pacific
U.S. Navy Base
Pearl Harbor, Territory of Hawaii
1405 11 March 1943

Commander J. Howard Young, USN, Flag Secretary to Admiral Chester W. Nimitz, stood in CINCPAC's door and waited until the Admiral noticed him. "Admiral Wagam is here, Admiral," he said. "With his aide."

Nimitz's face grew pensive: *Lewis knows more about submarines*, he was thinking, *has more nuts-and-bolts knowledge, than Dan Wagam or I do.* In a moment he replied, "Ask them both to come in."

Rear Admiral (Upper Half) Daniel J. Wagam, USN, and his aide-de-camp, Lieutenant Chambers D. Lewis III, USN, marched into the room, stopped, and stood at attention.

"At ease, gentlemen," Nimitz replied. "Good afternoon."

"Good afternoon, Admiral," the two replied in unison.

"Sit down," Nimitz said, gesturing to a pair of upholstered chairs facing his desk. "I'm about to have some coffee. Would you like some?"

Moments later, when they all had coffee, he said, "We have heard from General Pickering."

He opened the center drawer of his desk, took out a large manila envelope stamped TOP SECRET and handed it to Wagam.

"Three possibilities, Dan," Nimitz said with a smile. "The General either has a limited knowledge of correct military form, or none, or he *does*, and doesn't give a damn."

"I see what you mean, sir," Admiral Wagam said, chuckling.

Lewis had to wait to satisfy his own curiosity about

that until Admiral Wagam had finished reading the communication. Then Nimitz said, "I think Lewis better have a look at that, too."

Brigadier General Pickering's proposed Operations Plan was in the form of a personal letter to Admiral Nimitz:

```
T O P   S E C R E T

OFFICE OF STRATEGIC SERVICES
WASHINGTON

0905 GREENWICH 11 MARCH 1943

VIA SPECIAL CHANNEL
DUPLICATION FORBIDDEN

CINCPAC HAWAII
EYES ONLY ADMIRAL CHESTER W. NIMITZ

FOLLOWING PERSONAL FROM DDPACIFIC TO
ADMIRAL NIMITZ

DEAR ADMIRAL NIMITZ:

GETTING WHAT SOMEBODY DECIDED TO CALL
'OPERATION GOBI' UNDERWAY HAS TAKEN
LONGER THAN I HOPED IT WOULD, BUT WE ARE
FINALLY AT A POINT WHERE I CAN BRING YOU
UP TO DATE, AND EXPLAIN THE PROBLEMS WE
ARE HAVING.

WE TURNED UP AN EX-4TH MARINES GUNNERY
SERGEANT WHO BEFORE THE WAR APPARENTLY
AUGMENTED HIS INCOME SMUGGLING GOLD AND
ART WORK INTO AND OUT OF INDIA AND THE
SOVIET UNION USING CAMEL CARAVANS. WE ARE
ABOUT TO SEND HIM TO CHINA WHERE HE
THINKS, AND I BELIEVE, HE CAN USE HIS
FORMER BUSINESS ASSOCIATES TO GET DECENT
```

RADIOS INTO THE HANDS OF THE AMERICANS
NOW IN THE GOBI DESERT.

LT COLONEL ED BANNING, ALSO EX 4TH
MARINES, WHO I BROUGHT INTO THE OSS WITH
ME, TELEPHONED ME AN HOUR OR SO AGO FROM
FORT MONMOUTH TO TELL ME HE HAS HALF A
DOZEN CAMEL TRANSPORTABLE RADIOS.
BANNING, WHO HAS SPECIAL COMMUNICATIONS
SKILLS, IF YOU TAKE MY MEANING, WILL
SHORTLY DEPART FOR CHUNGKING TO TAKE UP
DUTY AS A STAFF OFFICER ON THE STAFF OF
THE US MILITARY MISSION TO CHIANG KAI-
SHEK. AND WILL OVERSEE THE RADIO DELIVERY
FROM THERE. ONCE HE IS PHYSICALLY PRESENT
IN CHUNGKING, WE WILL HAVE SPECIAL
CHANNEL CAPABILITY.

THESE RADIOS WILL NOT, REPEAT NOT, BE OF
MUCH USE BEYOND GIVING US MORE OR LESS
RELIABLE COMMUNICATION WITH THE PEOPLE
IN THE DESERT, AND, OF COURSE, TO GIVE US
A POSITIVE POSITION FOR THEM.

ONCE WE LOCATE THESE PEOPLE AND ESTABLISH
COMMUNICATIONS WITH THEM, WE COME TO THE
NEXT PROBLEM, WHICH IS HOW TO SEND THE
NECESSARY METEOROLOGICAL EQUIPMENT, AND
THE PEOPLE TO OPERATE IT IN THERE.

AFTER CONSULATION WITH GENERAL MAC
MCINERNEY I HAVE DECIDED THE BEST, AS A
MATTER OF FACT ONLY, WAY TO DO THIS IS BY
SPECIALLY EQUIPPED AIRCRAFT,
SPECIFICALLY AMPHIBIOUS CATALINAS. THEY
ARE THE ONLY AIRCRAFT WITH BOTH THE RANGE
AND WEIGHT CARRYING CAPABILITY WE HAVE TO
HAVE. FOR A NUMBER OF REASONS, USE OF
LARGER NAVY AND AIR CORPS AIRCRAFT HAS
BEEN DECIDED AGAINST.

THE IDEA IS TO REFUEL THE CATALINAS BY HAVING THEM RENDEZVOUS AT SEA WITH A SUBMARINE IN THE YELLOW SEA, A HUNDRED MILES OR SO NORTHEAST OF TIENTSIN.

THERE ARE SOME OBVIOUS PROBLEMS WITH THIS, INCLUDING THE HAZARDS OF TRANSPORTING AVIATION FUEL ABOARD A SUB, GETTING THE FUEL OFF THE SUBMARINE AND INTO THE AIRCRAFT ON THE HIGH SEAS, AND OF COURSE MAKING SURE THE SUBMARINE WILL BE WHERE IT IS SUPPOSED TO BE WHEN THE CATALINAS GET THERE.

ANOTHER OF THE PROBLEMS IS THAT NOT ONLY WILL THE AIRCRAFT ALMOST CERTAINLY BE UNABLE TO FLY OUT OF THE GOBI, BUT THEY ARE SOMEHOW GOING TO HAVE TO BE CONCEALED FROM AERIAL AND OTHER OBSERVATION ONCE THEY GET THERE.

MCINERNEY FEELS THAT FAIRING OVER THE FUSELAGE BUBBLES AND THE FORWARD GUN TURRET WILL APPRECIABLY INCREASE BOTH RANGE AND SPEED, THE FORMER POSSIBLY, JUST POSSIBLY, TO THE POINT WHERE BY DRAINING FUEL FROM ONE OF THE CATALINAS INTO THE OTHER, ONE OF THE AIRCRAFT MIGHT BE ABLE TO FLY OUT, EITHER BACK TO THE YELLOW SEA OR POSSIBLY INTO CHINA.

THE COLLINS RADIO COMPANY OF CEDAR RAPIDS IOWA IS DEVELOPING, OR PERHAPS MORE ACCURATELY, MODIFYING, ON AN EMERGENCY PRIORITY BASIS, THE MORE POWERFUL RADIO TRANSMITTERS WHICH WILL BE REQUIRED FOR THE WEATHER STATION ITSELF. THE METEOROLOGICAL EQUIPMENT IS AT HAND. WE ARE IN THE PROCESS OF RECRUITING VOLUNTEER WEATHER PEOPLE, AND MCINERNEY HAS PUT OUT A CALL FOR CATALINA OR OTHER

MULTIENGINE PILOTS WITH LONG DISTANCE
NAVIGATION EXPERIENCE.

SO WHAT I NEED RIGHT NOW IS TWO AMPHIBIOUS
CATALINAS, WHICH WILL HAVE TO HAVE THE
NECESSARY MODIFICATIONS MADE TO THEM,
THE FAIRING OVER OF THE BUBBLES, AND THE
INSTALLATION OF AUXILIARY FUEL TANKS.
PLUS OF COURSE A SUBMARINE SPECIALLY
EQUIPPED TO HANDLE THE REFUELING ON THE
HIGH SEAS.

I AM OF COURSE WIDE OPEN TO SUGGESTIONS OF
ANY KIND.

WITH BEST PERSONAL REGARDS, I AM,
RESPECTFULLY,

FLEMING PICKERING, BRIG GEN USMCR

END PERSONAL MESSAGE FROM DDPACIFIC TO
ADMIRAL NIMITZ

T O P S E C R E T

"Just a few minor problems," Wagam said. "Like transporting several thousand gallons of avgas on a submarine;
making a rendezvous at sea without any navigation aids
to speak of, and then refueling a Catalina on the high seas
in winter."

"*Two* Catalinas," Nimitz corrected him. "But you know
what really bothers me about the way Pickering has set
this whole thing up?"

"No, sir."

"Nothing will work unless we can establish communication with the people who are *supposed* to be wandering
around in the Gobi Desert. It all hinges on this gunnery
sergeant both finding them and then smuggling radios into
them on camelback. We won't need a submarine or two
Catalinas if he can't do that."

"Yes, sir," Wagam said. "My orders, sir?"

"Give him whatever he thinks he wants, Dan. I don't think we have any choice."

"Aye, aye, sir."

"Lewis, you have any thoughts about avgas on a submarine?" CINCPAC asked.

"No, sir. Not a one. But submariners are resourceful, Admiral. We'll work out some way to do this."

[SIX]
Female Officers' Quarters
U.S. Navy Hospital
Philadelphia, Pennsylvania
2025 12 March 1943

Just as Captain James B. Weston, USMC was about to step up into the hotel bus that would carry him to the Trailways bus terminal in White Sulphur Springs, Commander T. L. Bolemann, MC, USN, walked onto the wide outside stairway of the Greenbrier, called Weston's name, and tossed him the keys to the Buick. "If it doesn't shame you to drive that gas-guzzling automobile of yours, on black-market gasoline and wasting precious rubber that is desperately needed in the war effort, I won't stop you. Never let it be said about Ted Bolemann that he erected roadblocks in the path of true love."

"Thank you," Jim said.

"Try to stay on the black stuff between the trees," Bolemann said. "And if you want my advice, stop lying to that nice young woman. Love is only partially blind."

"I'll keep that in mind," Jim replied, as he started for the hotel garage.

I don't want to lie to her, certainly. But I don't think I should give her a full accounting of what happened in Pensacola.

What happened in Pensacola isn't going to happen again. We were both carried away by the emotion of the moment; we were both suffering from that well-known service-connected malady known as enforced celibacy;

and Martha Sayre Culhane—probably because of the emotion—had much more to drink than she could handle.

Plus, of course, I am an unprincipled no-good sonofabitch.

When Jim stopped in Wilmington, Delaware, for gasoline, he telephoned Janice to tell her she didn't have to meet him at the bus station.

"Commander Bolemann called and said you were driving. Where are you?"

Her voice, he thought, sounded a little cold and distant.

"I'm in Wilmington," he said. "I should be there in about an hour."

"I'll wait for you at the FOQ," she said. "Drive carefully."

He was now sure that her voice had sounded cold and distant.

Is there some sort of female intuition that tells them when their—what am I, "boyfriend"?—has been unfaithful?

Or did she sense that I was lying to her about where I spent last weekend? Bolemann said I was a lousy liar and that love is only partially blind.

He was driving around in the FOQ parking lot looking for a place to park when Lieutenant (j.g.) Janice Hardison, NC, USNR, appeared, in her blues, with her uniform cap perched attractively on top of her upswept hair.

She was carrying a leather valise.

That's it. That's the reason she sounded cold and distant on the phone. She has changed her mind about this weekend. She's going someplace, and she wanted to tell me in person and not on the telephone.

Jim stopped the Buick and leaned across the seat to push the door open.

"Hi," Janice said, pulled the seat forward, and put her valise in the backseat.

"Hi," Jim said.

This was obviously not the time or place to try for a kiss.

She opened her purse, found what she was looking for, and handed it to him.

"What's this?"

"Ration coupons for twenty gallons of gas," she said. "They're mine, I've been saving them up."

"I don't need them," he said. "But thank you just the same."

"I don't feel right using black-market gasoline," Janice said.

Well, if you feel that way, why don't we swap the wheels and tires off your Ford? That way we wouldn't be riding on black-market tires, either, thereby ensuring that if we lose the war, nobody can point an accusing finger at you.

What are you making fun of her for? She's right, and you're wrong. Among other reasons, because she is a highly principled woman, and you know what you are.

"Whatever you say, Janice," he said, taking the coupons.

Her perfume had now begun to fill the car.

"I have a seventy-two-hour pass," Janice said. "And I thought it would be nice to get out of Philadelphia."

"Good idea."

"I went to the chaplain—he's a friend of mine . . ."

Of course he is.

". . . and he arranged for rooms for us at the Chalfont-Haddon Hall, in Atlantic City—there's some sort of a program, a tie-in with the hospital. I hope that's all right with you."

Rooms, plural. Of course. You don't go to the chaplain and ask him to help you find a room where you and the boyfriend can carry on carnally over the weekend.

"That's fine with me," Weston said.

"The rooms and the food come with a twenty-percent discount, but not the liquor."

Of course. What self-respecting chaplain would be pushing discounted booze?

"Well, then, we'll have to go easy on the booze," Jim said.

"Have you been drinking a lot, Jim?"

"Oh, I have a drink from time to time with Dr. Bolemann." *No more than three or four beers at lunch, followed, at the cocktail hour, by as many martinis, to give us courage to face the really bad wine they offer in the dining room?*

There you go, you're lying to her!

"He's a really nice man," Janice said. "My father told me he knows him. I'm glad you've become friends." She went into her purse again and this time came out with a road map. "I marked the route," she said. "I think the best way is to go into Philadelphia and take the Tacony-Palmyra bridge."

"I'm Lieutenant Hardison," Janice said to the desk clerk. "And this is Captain Weston. I believe Chaplain Nesbitt made reservations for us?"

The desk clerk checked. "Yes, ma'am," he said. "Two rooms at the Chaplain's Program discount." The desk clerk examined Weston carefully.

And I know what you're thinking, buddy. "What's a nice girl like this one, a personal friend of the chaplain, doing with a guy like you?"

"What time does the dining room close?" Janice asked.

"You don't have much time before food service stops," the desk clerk said. "But there will be dancing until two A.M."

"Well, then," Janice said. "Why don't we eat now, while we still can? Could you have our luggage taken to our rooms?"

"Yes, ma'am," the desk clerk said, and handed them each a key.

"There's a Roman Catholic mass at six-thirty every morning," the desk clerk said, and pointed to a sign announcing religious services. "And a Protestant nondenominational service at nine-thirty on Sunday morning."

"Thank you," Janice said. "We'll try to make the Sunday-morning service."

"And I'm required to remind you not to open your window curtains or blinds at night," the desk clerk said. "At least not while you're burning lights in your room."

"What?" Weston asked.

"Submarines, sir," the desk clerk said. "German submarines. They use lights ashore to locate ships."

"Oh, of course," Weston said.

* * *

They each had a cocktail before dinner, Janice a gin fizz, and Jim a bourbon on the rocks, there being no scotch. And with their "Shore Dinner," they shared a bottle of New York State sparkling wine—made by the "champagne process," according to the label.

Janice's first lobster had been with him at Bookbinder's in Philadelphia. This was her second. She really liked them, now that she'd found the courage to try one.

The band began to play while they were still eating; after their dessert, they danced. Jim very carefully maintained as much distance between their bodies as he could manage.

"I would really like to walk on the beach," Janice said. "Could we do that before we go to bed?"

Our separate beds, of course.

"If there are no lights," he said, practically, "how are we going to see?"

"By moonlight. It's a full moon."

They walked perhaps half a mile down the wide boardwalk, and then Janice stepped over a chain barring access to stairs leading to the beach and motioned for him to follow her.

"The sign says, 'Access to the beach is forbidden during hours of darkness,'" Weston quoted.

"Oh, who'll know?" she said. "And we're in uniform."

He followed her onto the beach.

She caught his hand.

"That's also against regulations," she said. "They call it PDA."

"They call what 'PDA'?"

"It stands for 'public display of affection,'" she said. "'Officers will not show a PDA.' Should we stop?"

"Hell, no."

"I wasn't sure how you were going to answer that," Janice said.

"Excuse me?"

"You've been," she paused, considering her next words, "cool and distant, I guess—since I got in the car."

"I thought the same thing about you," he said.

"I thought maybe I scared you off when I told you I loved you," Janice said.

"As I recall it—and the words are burned forever in my memory—you said, quote, I think I love you, unquote. I was afraid you'd had time to think it over and changed your mind."

"I have had time to think it over, and when I saw you in the parking lot, I knew I could drop the 'I think.' "

"Jesus, Janice!"

He stopped and looked at her.

"Good evening, sir!" a male voice said, adding, "Ma'am."

Weston turned and found himself looking at a Coast Guardsman. He was wearing a pea coat, puttees, and a web cartridge belt. A Springfield rifle was slung over his shoulder, and he was leading a very large German shepherd on a leash.

The Coast Guardsman saluted. Weston returned it in a reflex action, and saw, out of the corner of his eye, Janice doing the same thing.

She's adorable when she does that! And there's something somehow erotic about it, too!

"Sir, you're not supposed to be on the beach during hours of darkness," the Coast Guardsman said.

What is this guy supposed to be doing? Repelling a landing party from a German submarine? Or is seeing him marching up and down with his rifle and killer dog supposed to remind people there's a war on?

Janice dropped to her knees, made kissing sounds, and reached out to the dog, who was sitting on his haunches.

"Watch the goddamned dog, Janice!"

"Don't be silly, he's sweet!"

The killer dog nuzzled Janice's neck and sent sand flying with his tail.

"He's not as ferocious as he looks," the Coast Guardsman said.

"Either that, or he's a very good judge of character," Weston said, and then added: "Actually we have two very good reasons for being on the beach. One, I wanted to make sure for myself that no one has stolen the ocean, and two, this officer and I are trying very hard not to be seen engaged in a PDA."

"PDA?"

"Public display of affection. The punishment for which, I'm told, is death by firing squad."

The Coast Guardsman chuckled. "The thing is, Captain, the Chief rides along the beach in a jeep. If he sees you . . ."

"I'll sic the killer dog on him," Weston said.

The Coast Guardsman laughed.

"No, you won't," Janice said, standing up and brushing the sand off her uniform skirt. "We'll get off the beach. It's time we went to bed, anyhow."

"Yes, ma'am," the Coast Guardsman said, winking at Weston.

I wish what you are thinking was true, but what the lady meant to say was, "It's time we went to our separate beds."

"I'll see you to your room," Jim said, as they waited for the elevator.

"All right," she said. She took her key from her purse, looked at it, and announced, "I'm on eight."

He checked his key.

"So am I," he said.

"Eight oh eight," Janice said.

"Eight ten," he replied.

Adjacent rooms? Probably not. Eight oh nine is probably next to eight oh eight, and eight ten is across the corridor.

But close! Is that an omen?

No. It means that the hotel reserves a block of rooms for the chaplain's healthy and wholesome Weekend in Atlantic City program.

She stopped before the door to 808 and handed him the key. He put it in the lock and she raised her face to be kissed. He kissed her, gently, on the lips.

What that instant hard-on proves is that you are an oversexed sonofabitch, nothing more. She wasn't promising more than you got, and you really should be ashamed of yourself.

Considering how you spent last Saturday night, how could you even think of making love to this virgin?

"Call me when you wake up," Jim said. "And we'll have breakfast."

Janice nodded, touched his cheek, and slipped into her room.

He stared at the closed door for a moment, forced from his mind a very clear mental image of Lieutenant (j.g.) Janice Hardison, NC, USNR, taking off her uniform, then went searching, across the hall, for Room 810.

It wasn't across the hall, it was adjacent to 808, where, at that very moment, Janice was probably unbuttoning her crisp white shirt and getting ready for bed.

He stepped into his room, found his bag, and took from it a bottle of scotch whisky from the Greenbrier's liquor store, with every intention of taking at least one very stiff drink.

But when he poured it, he changed his mind.

Obviously, the last thing in the world you need is a drink. One drink will lead to another, and the next thing you know, you will be knocking at the connecting door to Janice's room and making a four-star ass of yourself.

You don't need a drink, you need a cold shower. A long, ice-cold shower.

A long ice-cold shower gave him goose bumps and the shivers but did little to erase from his mind the image of Janice taking off her uniform. He put on a terry-cloth bathrobe he found hanging on the bathroom door, went into the bedroom, and decided he really did need a drink, for medicinal purposes.

As he felt the scotch warming his body, there was a knock at the door. He opened it and looked out, but there was no one in the corridor.

Jesus Christ, that's Janice knocking at the connecting door!

He went to it.

"Jim?"

"Yes."

Who the hell did she expect?

"Open the door."

He unlocked the door.

She was wearing a terry-cloth bathrobe identical to his.

He had a very clear mental image of her just before she slipped into it.

"Turn off the lights," she said.

"What?"

"You heard what he said, about turning the lights off before you open the curtains."

"Right," Jim said, and went around the room, turning off the lights. When he had finished, he couldn't see his hand in front of his face, but then there was the sound of curtains being opened. And in a moment, his eyes adjusted to the light.

Janice was standing by the window.

He went and stood behind her.

She smelled now of soap, not perfume. Her hair was still wet.

He put his hand on her shoulder. He could feel the warmth of her body even through the thick robe.

"How beautiful," Janice said, and leaned back against him.

He looked out the window. The sky was clear and the moon was full. He could see people walking on the boardwalk, and the surf crashing onto the beach.

"Yeah," he said.

Her hand came up and caught his.

"Do you love me?"

"Oh, God, yes!"

She pushed herself erect and turned around and stood on her tiptoes to raise her face to his. He kissed her and wrapped his arms around her.

He thought for a moment, terrified, that he had gone too far with the kiss, with holding her so tight, for she struggled to free herself. He let her go.

And then he saw what she was doing. She was shrugging out of the terry-cloth robe. She had been wearing nothing under it.

"Don't say anything," Janice said. "Just take me to bed."

XIII

[ONE]
The Joint Chiefs of Staff
The Pentagon
Washington, D.C.
0805 15 March 1943

As Chief, Communications & Communications Security, Office of the Joint Chiefs of Staff, Colonel H. (Hulit) A. (Augustus) Albright, Signal Corps (Detail, General Staff Corps), U.S. Army, had the day-to-day responsibility for the operation and the security of the Special Channel over which MAGIC intelligence data was transmitted—a responsibility he had held virtually from the beginning of the Special Channel.

His immediate superior was Major General Charles M. Adamson, USA, the Secretary of the Joint Chiefs of Staff. The title "Secretary" was somewhat misleading. In almost any other military organization, General Adamson would have been known as Chief of Staff. But someone had apparently decided that a Chief of Staff of the Joint Chiefs of Staff was going to be more than a little confusing, and his position was defined as "Secretary."

General Adamson customarily signed interoffice memoranda and other material with his initials, CMA. Early on, Colonel Albright concluded that these letters actually stood for "Covering My Ass." General Adamson's interoffice memoranda were quite skillfully written to ensure that if anything went wrong, the blame could be laid on any shoulders but his own.

Colonel Albright, a short, barrel-chested man, had been commissioned from the ranks. Specifically, he had served as an enlisted man in the Signal Corps, rising in two years to corporal. He had also sufficiently impressed several senior officers there with his unusual intelligence and character that they had encouraged him to study for and take the competitive examination for entrance to West Point, with the result that he was offered an appointment to the United States Military Academy.

He graduated from the USMA seventh in a class of 240, earning the right to choose his branch of service. Against the advice of his classmate, Cadet Charles M. Adamson, who reminded him that very, very few Signal Corps officers ever rose to be generals, he chose the Signal Corps.

Four years at the U.S. Military Academy in the company of Cadet Adamson had convinced Cadet Albright that Adamson was a pompous horse's ass who had arrived at the visionary conclusion that the key to a successful military career was never to make a decision of any kind without first finding someone to lay the blame onto if anything went wrong.

When the two met at a West Point class reunion in 1939, Albright was forced to admit that Adamson had indeed found a faster route to military advancement than he had. By dint of hard work (he'd taken a master's degree and then earned a Ph.D. in electrical engineering from MIT, among other things), Albright had earned the reputation of being one of the Army's most knowledgeable officers in radio communication, with a sideline specialty in cryptography. He had risen to major. Adamson, meanwhile, had spent the ensuing years shooting and polishing artillery pieces and making the right kind of friends. He was a full colonel.

At the reunion, Adamson somewhat grandly announced to Albright that if he was given command of a division—an outcome as inevitable as the rising of the sun, he seemed to think—he would see what he could do about having Albright assigned as his signal officer.

This was not at all a pleasant prospect for Major Albright. Having all his teeth extracted without novocaine seemed on the whole more desirable than serving under his old classmate. But he smiled and said nothing.

They next met several years later, at Fort Monmouth, New Jersey. Albright was by then a lieutenant colonel, and Adamson was a major general and the Secretary of the Joint Chiefs of Staff. "This means," he explained to his old friend, "that I'm finally in a position to do something for you."

"I truly appreciate the offer," Albright replied, "but I'd like to think I'm really making a genuine contribution to the war effort doing what I've been doing." At that time, he was involved in developing a more efficient and reliable Radio Ranging and Direction system, called "Radar," as well as doing some work he considered important in the area of cryptography.

"Odd that you should mention that, Augie," General Adamson said. "Cryptography's more or less what I came to see you about."

Lieutenant Colonel H. (Hulit) A. (Augustus) Albright preferred to be informally addressed as "Hugh"; he despised "Augie."

"Yes, sir?"

"What I'm about to tell you, Augie, is Top Secret, and not to leave this room," General Adamson said.

"Yes, sir?"

"Navy cryptographers at Pearl Harbor have managed to break some of the most secret Japanese codes," General Adamson announced.

That was not news to Colonel Albright. Not only had he learned from peers in the Navy Department that they were working hard on that problem, but he had arranged for a Korean-American mathematics professor named Hon

Song Do, whom he had known at MIT, to be commissioned into the Signal Corps and assigned to the Pearl Harbor code-breaking operation. He hadn't actually been *told*, in so many words, that the codes had been broken, but he *knew*.

"Yes, sir?"

"Now, I have been charged by Admiral Leahy with setting up an absolutely secure transmission channel for the transmission of this data between Pearl Harbor, Washington, and General MacArthur's headquarters in Australia. And I think, Augie, that you're just the man to handle it."

Oh, shit! I don't want to be a crypto officer. I'm over-qualified to be a crypto officer, and too senior. That's a job for a captain, not a light colonel. What this sonofabitch is trying to do is cover his ass. Again.

"In this connection," Adamson went on pontifically, "intelligence has managed to lay their hands on a German cryptographic device. To our good fortune, the Germans believe the device has been destroyed rather than compromised. . . ."

This caught Lieutenant Colonel Albright's attention. He had heard some interesting things about the German device. For starters, it was such a clever design that decrypting material first encrypted on it was virtually impossible without using a device like it and a matching signal-operating instruction. And, if Adamson knew what he was talking about, and the Germans did not suspect that the device had fallen into the hands of the Allies, it was a major intelligence/cryptographic coup, with enormous implications.

"Yes, sir?"

"The question has been raised: Could we—that is to say, could *you* duplicate this device, if you had your hands on it. It would be used solely for the transmission of the intelligence data, code-named MAGIC, which has been generated in Hawaii."

"They call that reverse engineering, sir," Albright replied. "Yes, sir. If I can get my hands on one, I can duplicate it."

Before going on, General Adamson stared at Lieutenant

Colonel Albright a long moment—obviously weighing whether or not to believe him.

"I'll have to get the go-ahead from Admiral Leahy, of course, Augie, but what I'm thinking is that we should fly you to London, so that you could physically bring this device back to the United States. A destroyer has been made available for this purpose; flying it here is considered too risky."

Maybe, with a little bit of luck, I can do everything he wants, and stay here, and not find myself working for the sonofabitch.

Three days later, Lieutenant Colonel Albright was on his way to England to bring the device to the United States. By the time the destroyer with the device aboard tied up at the Brooklyn Navy Yard, Adamson had arranged for Albright's transfer to the Office of the Joint Chiefs of Staff, as Chief, Communications & Communications Security. He had additionally and not without difficulty, he said, arranged his promotion to full colonel and detail to the General Staff Corps. "Don't make me regret it, Augie," he told him.

Within a month, Colonel Albright learned that he owed his promotion to the suggestion of the chief signal officer, not General Adamson, and that his detail to the General Staff Corps had been directed by Admiral Leahy himself, as a cover for his secret communications role. No one would pay much attention to one more GSC colonel on the Joint Chiefs; but people might wonder what a full bird colonel of the Signal Corps was actually doing.

In three closely guarded rooms at the Army's Signal Laboratories at Fort Monmouth, Albright immediately set up "the factory." There the first machine was carefully reverse-engineered, and the devices based on it—naturally called MAGIC devices, after the code name of the intelligence data itself—were put into production. The first two of these were installed in Washington and Pearl Harbor. The third went to Brisbane, Australia, for MacArthur's use, where it was placed in the care of Lieutenant Hon Song Do, Signal Corps, USAR. In time, the "factory" was capable of manufacturing two of the devices each month.

During the initial setup of the "Special Channel," Major

General Charles M. Adamson, USA, predictably proved to be a royal pain in the ass; but that was the price Albright knew he had to pay for being involved with an operation as important as MAGIC . . . an importance confirmed to Colonel Albright on more than one occasion by Admiral Leahy himself. Leahy privately told Albright that the MAGIC information transmitted over the Special Channel was one of the United States' two most important secret operations, the other being the Manhattan Project under Brigadier General Leslie Groves, USA. Under Groves, a team of physicists and mathematicians was engaged in developing a bomb that would release the energy Einstein theorized was contained in all matter. One such bomb, Admiral Leahy told Albright, would have an explosive force equivalent to that of twenty thousand tons of trinitrotoluene, better known as TNT.

It was now clear to Albright that he'd been wrong to worry about becoming an overqualified crypto officer, a colonel doing a captain's job. In fact, he sometimes wondered if he was qualified to protect the MAGIC secret from compromise. The basic problem, as he saw it, was not technical or mechanical, but human. The MAGIC devices worked flawlessly. The problem was that more and more people were being added to the loop.

The Special Channel was originally intended to provide an absolutely secure transmission channel for MAGIC between the headquarters of Admiral Chester W. Nimitz, Commander in Chief, Pacific, in Hawaii; General Douglas MacArthur, Supreme Commander, South West Pacific Ocean Area, in Brisbane, Australia; and President Franklin Delano Roosevelt, Commander in Chief of the Armed Forces of the United States in Washington.

On the surface, one might imagine that no more than half a dozen people would be involved. Such thinking proved to be overoptimistic. For starters, people had to actually operate the devices. That is, somebody had to actually push the typewriter-like keys that would encrypt or decrypt MAGIC material. Originally, the cryptographers at Pearl Harbor did this. But it didn't take their superiors long to realize that their time could be better spent decrypting intercepted Japanese communications than doing work clerk-typists could do just as well. So a few cryptographers who had been handling routine cryptographic material had to be granted MAGIC clearances, and their names were added to the very short list of people, headed by the President, authorized to know that MAGIC existed.

In time other names were added to the MAGIC list, starting with the Secretaries of the Navy (Frank Knox) and the Army (Henry Stimson). The Director of the Office of Strategic Services (William Donovan) obviously had the Need To Know what the Japanese were up to, and he had gone on the list, as had the Chief of Naval Operations, the Chief of Staff, U.S. Army, the Commandant of the Marine Corps, and the Chief of the USMC Office of Management Analysis. In Brisbane, MacArthur decided that his Chief of Intelligence, Brigadier General Willoughby, had to be on the list, and he was added. Navy Secretary Frank Knox, meanwhile, sent a personal representative to the Pacific, a commissioned civilian named Fleming Pickering. Since he did not wish the Navy brass to know what Pickering was reporting to him, Knox gave him a MAGIC clearance so that his reports could be transmitted over the Special Channel. And Army Secretary Stimson had recently convinced the President that General Dwight D. Eisenhower, soon to command the Allied Invasion of the European Landmass, needed access to MAGIC material; and a MAGIC device had been authorized for his headquarters in England and flown to London. Eisenhower had immediately obtained permission for his Chief of Staff, General Walter Bedell Smith, to be added to the MAGIC list.

The brass had quickly learned that the Special Channel provided them with an absolutely secure means of communicating with each other on matters having nothing to do with MAGIC material. And it had the added bonus of being far speedier than standard Army or Navy communications. Sixty percent of total Special Channel traffic now had nothing to do with MAGIC.

As Special Channel users proliferated, Albright grew increasingly worried that the necessary close control of the Special Channel would be lost. Brass worldwide would inevitably become aware of its existence, and come up with arguments why they, too, should be authorized access to MAGIC material and the Special Channel. Experience had taught him that the more people with access to a secret, the greater its chances of being compromised.

But once Eisenhower and Bedell Smith were included on the MAGIC list, Admiral Leahy had drawn the line and refused all further requests for MAGIC access. After that, few other MAGIC devices were actually needed. The ones operating in CINCPAC headquarters in Hawaii, Supreme Headquarters, Southwest Pacific Ocean Area in Brisbane, and in the Navy Communications facility in Washington all had backup devices in case of equipment failure. So did the one recently sent to London. There were also four other devices. Two of these were under constant evaluation at the Signal Laboratories, and two were used for training, one at a secret Signal facility on a farm in Virginia, and the other now at the OSS training base in Maryland.

With the drying up of demand, Albright had been able to shut down the production line at the Factory at Fort Monmouth. He had six MAGIC devices "on the shelf" (actually, in a bank-type vault in the Pentagon), and that was going to be enough.

Or so he thought until the President overrode Admiral Leahy: Generalissimmo Chiang Kai-shek, the Nationalist Chinese leader, and Admiral Lord Louis Mountbatten, the Allied Commander for China, Burma, and India, were to be brought into the MAGIC loop. That meant that a MAGIC device, with a necessary backup, had to be transported to them and set in operation.

Giving a device to the Chinese and the Brits, in Colonel Albright's view, was tantamount to taking out a full-page advertisement in the *Washington Star* to announce to the world that some of the most secret Japanese messages were being read in Washington, Pearl Harbor, and Brisbane. But he was fully aware that it wasn't his responsibility to decide who received a MAGIC device, it was the President's. His responsibility was limited to making sure that the devices reached Chungking and New Delhi, and were set up and put into operation without problems.

The immediate priority was to get devices to Chungking—under, of course, the close supervision of Major General Charles M. Adamson, USA, Secretary to the Joint Chiefs of Staff.

Colonel Albright was not at all surprised to pick up his telephone and hear ol' Cover My Ass Adamson's familiar voice on the line.

"Can you step in here a minute, Augie? I think we need to talk about China Clipper."

"Be right there, sir."

"Bring the China Clipper Opplan with you, please, Augie."

"Yes, sir."

Two minutes later, Colonel Albright walked into General Adamson's office and saluted. "Good morning, sir," he said.

"Help yourself to some coffee," the General said, holding up his own mug to show that he already had his, "and then tell me how it's going."

Colonel Albright laid Opplan China Clipper on General Adamson's desk, then helped himself to a cup of coffee.

"Where would you like me to start, General?"

"At the beginning. I want every *t* crossed, and every *i* dotted."

"Opplan China Clipper is sort of a carbon copy of Opplan London Fog," Albright began, "suitably modified."

Adamson nodded. London Fog, the plan to transport two of the MAGIC devices to London, had gone off without any problems.

"I had people come up from Monmouth," Colonel Albright went on. "They checked out two of the devices in the vault. When they were finished, I checked them out personally. They are now in crates marked "Personnel Records, Not To Be Opened Without The Specific Written Permission of the Adjutant General.""

"And the thermite grenades?"

"They will be put in place once the crates are loaded aboard the C-46 at Newark Airport. Same system that we used to send the devices to London, except that the airplane will be a C-46 instead of a B-17."

"By whom?"

"I offered General Pickering four CIC agents to handle

that." The Counterintelligence Corps. "They'd go all the way to Chungking with the devices. Though Pickering initially seemed willing to go along with that, Colonel Banning thought that would unnecessarily complicate things, and Pickering went along with him."

"Colonel Banning's giving you trouble?"

"I didn't mean to imply that, sir."

Albright really liked Ed Banning. For one thing, he was a professional, just as Albright was. For another, he had checked Banning out when his name had been ordered onto the MAGIC list. According to Fritz Rickabee, Banning was as good as they came, and Hon Song Do in Australia had said the same thing.

He had been happy to be of service to Banning when Rickabee had called to tell him that Banning was going to Monmouth to find suitable shortwave radios for his current operation and to ask if he had anyone there who could help Banning with that. He himself had arranged to be at Monmouth when Banning got there.

"That's what it sounds like, Augie," General Adamson said. "What does Banning have against CIC agents?"

"Sir, Colonel Banning made the point that you don't have to be a CIC agent to pull the pin on a thermite grenade, and I couldn't argue with that."

"I want CIC agents to put the devices aboard the airplane at Newark," General Adamson said. "Pickering can sign for them there."

"General Pickering's not going with the devices," Albright said. "He's going the long way around, via Pearl Harbor and Brisbane."

"He tell you why?"

Albright shook his head, "no."

"Who will sign for the devices?"

"Colonel Banning, sir. And he will have responsibility for them in Chungking."

"Then *Banning* can sign for the devices *after* the CIC puts them on the airplane."

"Yes, sir."

"Your Opplan, Augie . . ." General Adamson opened the Opplan and found the applicable paragraph before proceeding. ". . . says that the devices, when not in a secure vault, will never be out of the sight of at least one person with a MAGIC clearance. Colonel Banning apparently enjoys the confidence of General Pickering, but what about these other two? Lieutenant Easterbrook and Master Gunner Rutterman?"

Meaning, of course, that you have learned that you don't want to fuck with Pickering. You may outrank him, but the President doesn't call you by your first name.

"I'm sure they also enjoy General Pickering's confidence, sir."

"That's not what I mean, Augie. For one thing, I happen to know that until very recently, Rutterman was an enlisted man who guarded the door at Colonel Rickabee's place of business."

"He comes highly recommended by General Rickabee, sir, and he's been an alternate MAGIC cryptographer for some time."

General Adamson grunted. "I happened to be out at the OSS training with the OSS Deputy Director for Administration, Augie, and he pointed out Lieutenant Easterbrook to me."

"Yes, sir."

"You've seen him, of course?"

"Yes, sir."

"Then wouldn't you agree that he's about nineteen years old, and looks like he belongs in high school?"

"Yes, sir, he looks very young. But on the other hand, he won the Silver Star on Bloody Ridge on Guadalcanal with the Second Raider Battalion."

"That sort of service really doesn't have much relevance, wouldn't you say, Augie, with protection of a MAGIC device?"

"I suppose not, sir. But may I point out, sir, there is nothing we can do about it?"

"I'd really like to know where the hell Pickering got Lieutenant Easterbrook," General Adamson said. "Presumably, he has been satisfactorily trained in MAGIC device operation?"

"I checked him out myself, sir."

And he's a nice, really bright, kid. Unfortunately, ol' Cover My Ass is right. He is just a kid.

"Colonel Banning told me, sir, that General Pickering is flying another man, Lieutenant Moore, John M., who is a MAGIC cryptographer slash analyst, from Australia to Chungking. I am not concerned, sir, about operation of the Special Channel once it's in place."

"The operative words in that sentence, Augie, are 'once it's in place.' Our responsibility, your responsibility, is transporting the MAGIC devices to Chungking."

"Yes, sir."

General Adamson checked the Opplan again.

"Frankly, I'm concerned about these two," he said, pointing to a list of names. "Captain McCoy, Kenneth R., and Gunnery Sergeant Zimmerman, Ernest W. What do we know about them?"

"They both enjoy the confidence of General Pickering and Colonel Banning, sir, and neither of them has a MAGIC clearance."

"The Deputy Director tells me that McCoy was commissioned from the ranks, where he was known as 'Killer McCoy' for his proclivity for stabbing people in drunken brawls. And the sergeant has a room-temperature IQ."

He also speaks four or five languages, including two kinds of Chinese and Russian, but I don't think you want to hear about that.

"They're an interesting pair, sir," Albright said.

"In other words, you would judge that, if necessary, either of them could pull the pin on a thermite grenade?"

And if it was a dud, Gunnery Sergeant Zimmerman could chew both devices up and spit out tacks.

"Yes, sir," Albright said.

General Adamson paused thoughtfully before asking, "What are you going to tell them about the 'personnel records' crates?"

"Nothing, sir, of course."

"You don't think they'll be curious?"

Frankly, I would be surprised if McCoy doesn't have a damned good idea of what's in them. He's very tight with Banning, and he's a very bright young fellow.

"No, sir."

"You don't think Colonel Banning has told them?" General Adamson asked. "Or perhaps even General Pickering?"

"I think that is highly unlikely, sir."

"I have a reason for asking this question, Augie," General Adamson said. "So let me paraphrase. You think it over before answering. If it should come to pass that Captain McCoy or Sergeant Zimmerman were to fall into the hands of the enemy, do you think either of them knows, or has guessed, enough about MAGIC to compromise it?"

"I don't know, sir," Albright said. "But I think it's highly unlikely."

That's not true. McCoy probably knows damned well what's in those crates, and if he does, Zimmerman probably does, too. But what he's after from me is some reason he can get either McCoy or Zimmerman kicked off this operation. I don't know what that's all about, but I'll have no part of it.

Am I endangering MAGIC because of my contempt for this man? I hope not. I don't think so. What I do know is if I could have anybody I wanted to guard the devices, I'd pick this Marine mustang captain and his "room-temperature-IQ" sergeant.

General Adamson grunted, and thought the matter over for a full thirty seconds before going on: "I'm sure Pickering and Banning have asked themselves the same question," he said, "and decided that they don't know enough about MAGIC to pose a risk to it in case of capture. But I don't want you, Augie, to even hint about what those crates contain."

"No, sir," Colonel Albright replied, very formally. "Is there any reason, in the General's opinion, why I should know why the General raised that question?"

General Adamson thought the question over before deciding to tell him, finally concluding that he might as well, because he was going to find out anyway. Albright spent a good deal of time in the Navy Communications facility where the MAGIC device was in operation. No one there would—or should—question his right to read anything being encrypted or decrypted, including Special Channel material that would be coming to and from General Pickering. Albright might not have paid attention to it before, but now that he was curious about this whole business, he would be looking for something, and would find it.

"As you know, I've become rather friendly with the Deputy Director for Administration at the OSS," General Adamson said.

Colonel Albright had first met the OSS Deputy Director (Administration)—whom he had immediately disliked—when he had been ordered to make MAGIC material available to OSS Director Donovan. He had dealt with him again—and learned to like him even less—when he had been ordered to provide a MAGIC device, for training purposes, to the OSS training.camp in Maryland.

The MAGIC device at the Congressional Country Club had nothing to do with MAGIC material being exchanged between Hawaii, Brisbane, and Washington. It was instead shown to OSS agents who were to be sent into Europe. If they came across such a device, they all had orders to make every effort to steal it. The order had come from Admiral Leahy, but it had originated with Albright, who thought it entirely likely the Germans had come up with improvements to their devices that he wanted to know about.

That figures, Colonel Albright thought. *You're two of a kind. Two asshole paper pushers, highly skilled in protecting your own asses.*

"You know what I'm talking about, Augie. He hears things, and passes them on to me, and I hear things. . . ."

"Yes, sir."

"This is one of those times when it is easier to go along than to say no, according to my friend. Admiral Leahy didn't want to say no to Admiral Nimitz; the President didn't want to say no to Admiral Leahy; and OSS Director Donovan, of course, couldn't say no to either the President or Admiral Leahy."

"No about what, sir?"

"General Pickering has been charged with setting up a Navy weather station in the Gobi Desert."

I suppose it's dishonest of me not to tell him that Banning told me all about Operation Gobi when he went to Monmouth to pick radios for the operation.

But then, Banning wasn't simply running off at the

mouth. He needed my help to get radios and decided (a) that if Fritz Rickabee trusts me, he could trust me; and (b) authority or not, I had a bona fide Need To Know. I'm not going to get him in trouble because of that.

"In the Gobi Desert?"

"From what I've heard about this operation, it's really out of left field. Your two Marines are going to try to make their way to the Gobi Desert . . . masquerading as members of a camel caravan! The idea is to establish contact with a group of Americans supposedly wandering around in there, to be followed by the flying in of a weather station."

"That sounds like a tough operation, sir."

"My friend tells me his personal assessment of the chances of success range from one in a thousand to none."

"It sounds pretty—"

"It sounds suicidal to me," General Adamson said. "Not to mention the waste of assets that could better be expended elsewhere. General Pickering's reason for taking the long way around to Chungking is to stop off at Pearl Harbor to discuss getting a submarine for Operation Gobi. The submarine is to rendezvous in the Yellow Sea a hundred miles off the China coast with a couple of Catalinas. After being refueled by the submarine, the airplanes will then fly across China and land in the Gobi Desert. They will not fly out again, of course. The distances are too great."

"It does sound more than a little risky, sir."

"Risky's not the word for it. Insanity would be more accurate."

"Yes, sir."

"So it behooves you and me, Augie, in case Operation Gobi is not successful, to make sure no one can point a finger at us and say that *we* somehow dropped the ball."

You don't give a damn about McCoy and Zimmerman, or the people who will fly the airplanes on a one-way mission, or the sailors trying to refuel airplanes on the high seas in the middle of winter. All you're worried about is covering your own ass.

"Yes, sir."

"Every *t* crossed, Augie, a dot over every *i*."

"Yes, sir."

General Adamson dropped his eyes to Opplan China Clipper.

"Your Opplan states that the devices will be guarded by individuals who have qualified within the last six months with the weapon with which they will be armed. I presume you checked that?"

"No, sir."

"Why not?"

"That paragraph came from London Fog. I found out that two of the CIC agents we used there were ex-cops who had gone directly into the CIC. I learned too late to do anything about it that neither of them had ever fired a Thompson submachine gun."

"What's that got to do with this?"

"All of these people, including Colonel Banning, are (a) Marines and (b) have seen combat at least once. They know all about weapons."

"Indulge me, Augie. When you go out there today, make sure they qualify with whatever weapons they are going to have with them."

"Yes, sir."

"You have another copy of this?" General Adamson asked, tapping Opplan China Clipper with his fingers.

"Yes, sir."

"Leave this one with me, then, please, Augie. I'll take a close look at it, and if I come up with something, I'll give you a ring out there."

"Yes, sir."

[TWO]
The Congressional Country Club
Bethesda, Maryland
0905 15 March 1943

Captain Kenneth R. McCoy was wearing a white button-down-collar shirt, no necktie, a gray V-necked woolen sweater, gray flannel slacks, and a week's growth of beard when he opened the door of his room and found Harry

W. Rutterman, USMC—closely shaven, and immaculately attired in a new uniform—standing in the corridor.

"Hey, Harry," McCoy said. "Come on in. What's up?"

"Banning just called. He's on his way out here with Colonel Albright, and he told me to make sure everybody was in the billiards room at ten. Where's the gunny?"

"In the armory," McCoy replied. "Banning say what's going on?"

"No," Rutterman said simply. He looked around the room and asked: "What the hell are you doing?"

The sitting room of the two room suite was furnished with a library table and a desk. Both were covered with books and maps.

"You mean you can't tell?" McCoy said. "I'm studying for sophomore geography. What do you want to know about Mongolia?" He leaned over the library table and read, " 'The average elevation is fifty-one hundred feet.' How about that? You want to know what goes on there? 'They'—they being the Khalkha Mongols, who speak a language called Khalkha Mongolian—'spend their time grazing sheep, goats, cattle, horses, yaks'—what the hell a yak is, I have no idea—'and of course, camels.' "

"Fascinating!" Rutterman said. "Can I have some of that coffee?"

"Help yourself," McCoy said. "How's the Easterbunny doing?"

"Doing what?"

"Learning how to operate that machine I'm not supposed to know about. How's he doing?"

"Come on, McCoy, you know I can't talk about that."

"Okay. Sorry. Changing the subject: The only camel I have ever seen up close was in a circus in Philadelphia when I was a kid. The sonofabitch looked me right in the eye and spit in my face."

"No shit?" Rutterman chuckled.

"Would I lie to you, Harry?"

"Yes, you would, McCoy," Rutterman said, and held up a coffee cup. "You want some of this?"

"Please," McCoy said. "I shit you not, Harry. That goddamned animal leaned down to me—I thought he wanted me to pet him, or rub his ears—and when he was about five feet away, he hit me with a goober that was probably a quart."

Rutterman laughed. "What did you do?"

"What do you mean, what did I do? Nothing. I was twelve years old. What the hell could I do? But I'll tell you this, I have never smoked Camel cigarettes."

Rutterman chuckled, then asked, "What's Zimmerman doing in the armory?"

"He went nosing around and found they've got all sorts of weapons. He found some Chinese copies of Mauser Broomhandle machine pistols—they fire that Luger nine-millimeter Parabellum cartridge—and he's working them over to make sure they shoot."

"What's that all about?"

"Zimmerman says that's what the camel drivers carry, and he wants to look like a camel driver."

At ten minutes to ten, Gunnery Sergeant Ernest W. Zimmerman, USMC, walked into the billiards room of the Congressional Country Club. He was wearing a brown sport coat, brown gabardine trousers, and a yellow shirt with a polka dot (white on blue) necktie. He smelled of bore cleaner and Hoppe's #9. "I was going to test-fire them Broomhandles," he announced somewhat indignantly.

"It will have to wait. Banning said he wanted everybody here at ten."

"What's up?"

McCoy shrugged, indicating he didn't have any idea. He looked at his watch, then went to one of the tables and started folding the oilcloth that covered it.

Zimmerman examined a rack of cues mounted on the wall, rejecting three of them before finding one that matched his standards. Then he walked to the table.

"There's no fucking holes!" he announced, surprised and annoyed.

"They call this 'billiards,' " McCoy said.

"How the fuck do you play it?"

"I have no idea," McCoy confessed. "I think you have to hit three cushions and then another ball."

"Fuck that," Zimmerman said. "I'll play you close-to-the cushion for a nickel a shot."

"A quarter," McCoy countered.

"You ain't that good, Killer."

Why is Ernie the only man in the world who doesn't piss me off when he calls me "Killer"? Maybe because he was there and knows I only did what I had to do? Or is it because he is such a simple sonofabitch that I hate to jump on him?

"Knowing you're playing for a quarter, are going to *lose* a *whole quarter*, will make you so nervous a six-year-old could beat you."

"Fuck you, Killer," Zimmerman said. "Get yourself a fucking cue stick."

Ten minutes later, McCoy blew the shot he was making when Zimmerman suddenly barked, "Ten-hut!"

As he came to attention, he saw that Colonel Edward Banning, USMC, and Colonel H. A. Albright, USA, had entered the billiards room.

"Stand at ease," Banning said. "Go on with your game. The others will be here in a minute."

"Yes, sir," McCoy said, and then, turning to Zimmerman, said in Wu, "Ernie, try to remember you don't call 'attention' when you're in civvies, will you?"

"Sorry," Zimmerman said in Wu, sounding as if he meant it. Then he asked, "What's that fat doggie colonel got to do with us? That's the third time I've seen him with Banning."

"I think he's in charge of getting us to China," McCoy replied. "He must be all right. Banning seems to like him. My shot, right?"

"Your shot, my ass, Killer! You blew your fucking shot!"

"Only because you shouted 'attention' in my ear when Banning and the doggie colonel came in here," McCoy replied.

Colonel H. A. Albright had learned to speak Wu (and some Cantonese and Mandarin) during a three-year tour with the 15th Infantry in China. Even though he understood what Zimmerman had said about him, he was not really offended. Neither Zimmerman nor McCoy had any reason to suspect that he spoke Wu; very few Americans did, even those soldiers, Marines, and sailors who had spent long years in China.

Their ability to speak Chinese probably explained why they were being sent into Japanese-occupied Mongolia. That and the fact that they had both worked for Banning in Shanghai before the war. He wondered if they knew—or, for that matter, if Banning knew—what the Deputy Director (Administration) of the OSS thought of their chances of getting back alive.

Five minutes later, Second Lieutenant Robert F. Easterbrook and Master Gunner Harry Rutterman entered the room. *Rutterman looks old enough to be Easterbrook's father, Banning thought.*

"Sorry to be late, sir," Easterbrook said to Banning. "I was in the commo section."

"Problem with the radios?" Banning asked.

"No, sir. We were testing the packaging."

"How?"

Easterbrook looked uncomfortable.

" *'How'*?" Banning repeated.

"Actually, sir, we disassembled one of them—took the tubes out, like that—packed everything in the bags with foam rubber, and then I stood on a table and dropped all the bags onto the floor a half-dozen times. Then we put the radio back together to see if it would still work."

"Did it?"

"Yes, sir."

"At the Signal Corps Laboratories at Fort Monmouth, Lieutenant," Colonel Albright said, "we call the 'drop it on the floor and see if we can bust it' testing technique, 'simulated extensive field use testing.' It's really the only way to do it."

"Yes, sir," the Easterbunny said.

Christ, he actually blushed!

"That's why I was late, sir," the Easterbunny blurted. "I just had to see if it would work when I put it back together."

"No problem, you're here," Banning said. "Harry, you want to check the doors, please?"

Rutterman locked the door he had just passed through, then checked the other two doors to make sure they were locked, and finally drew blinds across the windows, after making sure the windows themselves were closed.

"This won't take long," Banning began. "Making reference to Section Two, Paragraph Five(a) of Opplan China Clipper, you may consider that as of this moment, you are alerted for overseas movement. You will depart the United States by military aircraft from Newark, New Jersey, sometime in the morning of 17 March—that's Wednesday—for service in the China-Burma-India theatre of operations."

Colonel Albright heard Gunnery Sergeant Zimmerman mutter, in Wu, " 'China Clipper'? What the fuck is that?"

"Having been so alerted," Banning went on, "you are advised that under the Articles for the Governance of the Naval Service, any failure to appear at the proper place at the proper time in the properly appointed uniform until you have physically departed the Continental Limits of the United States will be regarded not as Absence Without Leave, but as Absence Without Leave With the Intent to Avoid Overseas and/or Hazardous Service, and will make you subject to the more severe penalties for that offense as a court-martial may prescribe."

Colonel Albright heard Gunnery Sergeant Zimmerman mutter in Wu, "What the fuck is that all about?" to which Captain McCoy hissed, in muttered Wu, "Put a fucking cork in it, Ernie!"

"Colonel Albright is in charge of the movement, which he will now explain to you, following which we will all go to the firing range and qualify with the weapons with which we will be armed."

"What the fuck is that all about?" Captain McCoy asked in English.

"Did you say something, Captain McCoy?" Lieutenant Colonel Banning asked.

"Sir, did the Captain correctly understand the Colonel to say, sir, that we are going to the range to qualify with the weapons with which we will be armed?"

"You heard me correctly, Captain McCoy," Banning said. "Do you have any problem with that, Captain?"

"No, sir."

"Splendid! And to answer your first question, Captain McCoy, 'what the fuck is that all about?'—or words to that effect—we are going to do so because Colonel Albright here is under orders to ensure that every *t* in Operation China Clipper is crossed correctly and every last *i* has a dot in the proper place. Have you any further questions, Captain McCoy?"

"No, sir."

"And you, Gunnery Sergeant Zimmerman? Do you have any questions?"

Zimmerman popped to rigid attention. "Sir, begging the Colonel's pardon, sir. What the fuck is Operation China Clipper?"

"You've never heard of China Clipper, Sergeant?" Colonel Albright asked.

"No, sir. Not one fucking word."

"Well, sit back down, Sergeant, and I'll tell you all about it," Colonel Albright said.

The firing range of the OSS training facility was not much of a firing range by USMC standards: A U-shaped berm, no more than twenty feet high and perhaps a hundred feet long, had been built of sandbags on what had been the practice driving range before the OSS took over the Country Club. At the open end of the U were six firing positions. There were no pits. Target frames had been made from two-by-fours and plywood. Two were in position, and another four were lying on the ground. The "feet" of the erect frames sat in sections of pipe buried upright in the ground. Life-size silhouette targets had apparently been obtained from the FBI, for they showed a likeness of John Dillinger, the bank robber, clutching a .45 and glowering menacingly. These had been stapled to the plywood of the two target frames in use. Three-foot-long pieces of two-by-fours laid on the ground showed where the shooter was to stand.

The sandbags in the berm behind the targets showed evidence of the projectiles that had been fired downrange. McCoy noticed a lot of holes in sandbags not directly behind the targets.

Three men were waiting for them, standing by a rough table on which was placed two Mauser Broomhandle pistols, two Thompson submachine guns, and a rack holding five 1911A1 Colt .45 pistols with dowels in their barrels. Two of the men were in U.S. Army fatigues and the third was wearing an Army olive-drab woolen uniform.

He's probably the instructor, McCoy decided, *and the other two are on labor detail.*

The man in ODs—on which McCoy now saw silver first lieutenant's bars and the crossed sabers of cavalry— saw them coming, called attention, and saluted Colonel Albright. "Good morning, sir," he said.

"Good morning," Albright said. "These are the weapons they'll be taking with them?"

"Yes, sir. And they've been checked over by both Gunny Zimmerman and myself."

One of the GIs in Army fatigues handed the lieutenant a clipboard. "These are the hand receipts for the weapons, sir," he said. "I'll need to have them signed."

One by one, Banning and the others signed the hand receipts for the weapons. Banning signed for a 1911A1 .45–caliber pistol only; McCoy and Zimmerman both for a pistol and a Mauser machine pistol; and Easterbrook and Rutterman both for a pistol and a Thompson submachine gun.

Both Colonel Albright and Captain McCoy had private thoughts, which they did not express, about the Thompsons: Albright wondered, if it came down to it, how effectively Lieutenant Easterbrook could use his Thompson. Controlling their recoil was difficult even for a muscular man, and Easterbrook was anything but muscular.

McCoy, who had seen Easterbrook running around on Guadalcanal with a Thompson, was not concerned about his skill with the weapon, but with the weapon itself. These were civilian versions of the submachine gun, which he supposed the OSS had gotten from the FBI, like the John Dillinger silhouette targets. They had fifty-round "drum" magazines. In McCoy's opinion, the drum magazines were unreliable.

"How would you like us to do this, sir?" Lieutenant Colonel Banning asked of Colonel A. H. Albright.

"I don't think we have to bother about the pistols," Albright said, and then changed his mind. He didn't want to have to lie to General Adamson unless he really had to. "But on the other hand, to go by the book, maybe we should. How about a magazine from each weapon at a silhouette? Five out of seven shots from a .45 anywhere in the torso will qualify. And how about one in three shots from the automatic weapons? Say seventeen out of fifty from the Thompsons? How many shots are there in the Mausers?"

"Twenty, sir," Gunnery Sergeant Zimmerman said.

"How about seven shots anywhere in the torso from the Mausers, then?"

"That sounds reasonable," Banning said. He turned to McCoy. "Captain, you are the range officer. I will relieve you after I have fired."

"Aye, aye, sir," McCoy said.

Banning proceeded to the wooden table, examined the pistols until he found the serial number of the one he had signed for, stuck it in his belt, and then charged a magazine from a box of cartridges. "Gunny, would you charge the magazines of the automatic weapons, please?" he said.

"Aye, aye, sir," Zimmerman said, then went to the wooden table and started loading cartridges into a Thompson fifty-round drum.

Banning walked up to the piece of two-by-four marking the firing line, turned, and looked at McCoy.

"The flag is up," McCoy ordered. "With one seven-round magazine, lock and load."

Banning slipped the magazine into the pistol and worked the action.

"The flag is waving," McCoy said. "Commence firing!"

Everybody but Captain McCoy and Gunny Zimmerman put their fingers in their ears. Colonel Albright looked closely at Zimmerman and saw that he had inserted fired 9mm cartridges in his ears as protection against the noise, then saw that McCoy had done the same thing.

Banning raised the pistol and began to fire. The shots were evenly spaced. When the magazine was empty, he raised the pistol's muzzle.

"Cease fire," McCoy ordered. "Clear your piece and step back from the firing line."

Banning turned and walked to the wooden table and laid his pistol on it. Then he followed Colonel Albright to the silhouette target. All seven shots were in John Dillinger's torso.

"I suppose this makes you an expert," Colonel Albright said.

"Colonel, you ain't seen nothing yet," Banning said, then turned and raised his voice. "Can I have some target patches, please?"

One of the soldiers trotted out with a roll of black paper adhesive-gummed patches, and covered the holes in Banning's target.

With Colonel Banning serving as range officer, Lieutenant Easterbrook and Master Gunner Rutterman fired next. First they fired their pistols, both of them scattering all seven shots across the torso area of the targets.

When the holes had been patched, they fired the Thompson submachine guns. Colonel Albright was relieved to see that Easterbrook was familiar enough with the weapon not to lose control of it. He emptied the fifty-round magazine in two- and three-shot bursts. But he was actually surprised when he walked forward to count and patch the holes: Easterbrook had put forty-six of his fifty shots into John Dillinger, including three high (into the head) and five low (two in the crotch and three in the upper leg). Master Gunner Rutterman managed to get only forty-two of his fifty shots into Dillinger, but all but three high and one low were in the torso.

I will report that splendid marksmanship to General Adamson with more than a little pleasure.

"*Actually sir, when they fired, Lieutenant Easterbrook, the officer who looks so young? He actually shot a little better with the Thompson than Master Gunner Rutterman did.*"

Captain McCoy and Gunny Zimmerman fired last. Both put all seven shots from their pistols into John Dillinger's torso, and when the holes had been patched, went to the wooden table and attached the removable stocks to the Broomhandle Mausers, then loaded the pistols.

Colonel Albright heard Captain McCoy quietly issue an order, in Wu, to Gunny Zimmerman: "Shoot him in the head, Ernie."

They stepped to the firing line, and Banning went through his range officer's routine. Zimmerman finished firing a second or two before McCoy did.

McCoy checked to see that his Mauser was no longer loaded, then handed the weapon to Zimmerman. Then he walked to the targets, followed by Banning and Albright.

"It would appear that Gunny Zimmerman shot a little high, Colonel," Banning said. "Most of his rounds seem to have struck John Dillinger in the face."

He then began to count the holes out loud. There were nineteen. A twentieth hole was a quarter of an inch away from John Dillinger's ear.

"I wonder why he missed?" Captain McCoy asked innocently. "Usually he's a pretty good shot."

"You have made your point, Captain," Colonel Albright said, smiling at him.

Banning walked to McCoy's target. The .45 in John Dillinger's hand was no longer visible. Nor was the hand itself. McCoy's twenty shots had obliterated them. There was just one hole in the target, no larger than two balled fists held together.

"Colonel," Banning said, "in the Marine Corps, that's what we call 'a nice little group.' "

"I'm suitably impressed," Albright confessed.

"And does that mean we have crossed all your *t*s and dotted all your *i*s?"

"Yes, I think we can say that," Albright said.

"If you're going back into Washington, Colonel, I think Captain McCoy would like a ride into Union Station."

"You're not going?" McCoy asked evenly.

"He's not going where?" Albright blurted. He had naturally presumed that no one would leave the Country Club until, per Paragraph 12(d)(2) of Opplan China Clipper, the two station wagons departed at 0515 hours on Wednesday to drive everybody and their luggage and equipment to Newark Airport.

"I've decided the best thing for me to do, Ken, is stick around here."

"Where are you going, McCoy?"

"I've decided, Colonel, there being no reason that Captain McCoy has to be here, that he can have a pass until 0900 Wednesday morning, when he will report to base operations at Newark airport. He's going to be in New York City, and I know where to reach him, if necessary."

There is no reason General Adamson has to know that, Colonel Albright decided.

"You want me to call somebody for you?" McCoy asked, and Albright understood that the conversation was now not between colonel and captain but between close friends.

"I don't think that would be a good idea, Ken," Banning said, confirming this. "I may call her from here, but I think everything that has to be said has been said."

McCoy nodded.

XIV

"Just so we understand each other," Miss Ernestine Sage said, as the silver 1939 LaSalle convertible splashed through the slush of a now mostly melted early-morning snowstorm, "You are *not* just going to get out of the car at the gate and wave goodbye to me. I'm going to see you take off."

"I'm not sure I can get you inside, Ernie," McCoy said.

"Wave your goddamned magic wand," she said. "Either that, or I'll throw an hysterical fit at the gate."

"I'll try," he said.

They had spent the night at Rocky Fields Farm. Though he had gone there more than a little reluctantly, Ernie had announced that if they spent the night at her apartment in New York City alone, she would go crazy. And in fact it had turned out better than he thought it would. Ernie's father and mother had not only been very nice, but he finally accepted that they were sorry to see him go. Maybe only because that was going to make Ernie unhappy, but so what?

Her mother had tears in her eyes when they loaded his suitcase—one of two farewell gifts from Ernie: a folding canvas Val-Pak and a leather toilet kit, the nicest he had ever seen, from Abercrombie & Fitch—into the LaSalle; and she had sounded as if she really meant it when she told him to hurry back and to take care of himself.

Her father had been uncomfortable, but McCoy understood that. Ernie hadn't made it easy for him when she ended the evening by announcing, "Ken and I are going to bed now." No father wants to hear his only daughter announce that she's about to do what married people do with a man she is not married to.

But her father was already up the next morning when they went into the kitchen. He made steak and eggs for the both of them, then walked with Ken to the barn to get the LaSalle.

"Honey," McCoy said, as he slowed to stop at the gate, "why don't you drive this thing while I'm away?"

"Because it's a gas guzzler," she said.

"So what?"

An Army military policeman stepped out of his guard shack and looked very suspiciously at the civilian-who-*really*-needed-a-shave.

"This is a restricted area, sir," he said.

"Magic wand time," Ernie said softly.

McCoy produced his Office of Naval Intelligence credentials. They produced the expected result.

"And the lady, sir?"

"She's with me. Where do I find base operations?"

"I'll have to get you a sign for the car, sir," the MP said. "And I'll get you a map."

"See, I told you it would work," Ernie said as the MP stepped back into the guard shack. "Why can't you wave it around, say the magic words, and stay home for a while?"

He didn't reply.

After a moment, she said, "Sorry, honey," and took his hand.

"It's okay," McCoy said.

"You want me to call Carolyn?"

"And say what? I think you better stay out of that, honey."

"She loves him, Ken. I know what she's thinking."

"She knew he was married when they started," he said. "That something like this was likely to happen."

"You think Ed's wife is alive?"

"I think he has to find out, one way or the other."

"That's not what I asked."

"No, I don't," he said, then corrected himself. "I don't know. I think if she was going to get out, through India, it would have happened by now."

"So you think she's dead?"

She's either dead, or sleeping with some Japanese officer, or officers, to stay alive.

"I can't root for Carolyn, Ernie. I like Milla."

"I wasn't rooting for Carolyn," Ernie replied. *Yes, I was. I like Carolyn, and I don't know Ed Banning's Russian refugee wife.*

"Is there somebody you left over there I don't know about?" Ernie was horrified to hear herself blurt.

"No," he said, suddenly very angry, and then went on. "Actually, I have two Chinese wives, one in Shanghai and one in Peking. And seven kids, or is it eight? It's hard for me to keep track."

The MP returned from his guard shack with the Official Visitor sign for the car and a mimeographed map of the airfield with the base operations building circled, just as the lady with the ONI agent called him, "You bastard!"

When they saw the LaSalle convertible pull into a visitor's parking slot, Colonel H. A. Albright, USA, and Lieutenant Colonel Edward Banning, USMC, were inside the base operations building, looking out the glass door. Banning was wearing a web belt with a holster .45 hanging from it.

"They were good cars," Colonel Albright said. "I always wondered why they stopped making them."

"That's McCoy's," Banning said, and wondered aloud, "How did he get it onto the field?"

"There's someone with him," Albright said, and added accusingly, "a woman."

"Well, you know what they say about Marines, Colonel," Banning said. "A girl in every port."

After McCoy took his Val-Pak from the backseat of the car, he and Ernie walked up to the building.

"Well, McCoy's here," Banning said, and then asked, in thick innocence, "I wonder whatever can have happened to the personnel records crates?"

"They'll be here," Albright announced firmly. He checked his watch. "It's not 0900 yet."

"Good morning, Captain McCoy," Banning said. "And, Ernie, what a pleasant surprise, and I mean surprise, it is to see you here."

"Hello, Ed," Ernie said.

She's not amused. And not only because Ken is going away again. She's annoyed with me. In her shoes, I would be, too. She and Carolyn are friends.

"Colonel Albright, may I present Miss Ernestine Sage?" Banning said. "She and Captain McCoy are . . . what should I say?"

"Try 'lovers,' " Ernie said. "How do you do, Colonel?"

"How do you do, Miss Sage? Colonel Banning and I were just wondering how you managed to get on the base."

"I gave Captain McCoy the choice: he could either get me in to watch his plane take off, or I would throw a fit at the gate," she said.

Albright laughed politely. *I like this young woman. Very starchy. And a beautiful girl. And obviously in love with McCoy.*

"How, Ken?" Banning asked.

McCoy shrugged and tapped his jacket pocket. Banning understood he had used his ONI credentials.

"And have you given any thought to how she's going to get off the base?" Banning asked.

"Miss Sage can leave with me," Albright heard himself saying. "No problem."

"Thank you, sir," McCoy said.

Banning touched Albright's arm and nodded toward the glass doors.

A small convoy, consisting of a Chevrolet sedan, a Ford panel truck, and a second Chevrolet sedan, was approaching the base operations building. The three vehicles stopped and a man in civilian clothing stepped out of the first car, trying with little success to conceal a Thompson submachine gun by holding it vertically against his body.

Albright turned to Ernie.

"I'll meet you here, Miss Sage, in just a few minutes," he said, and walked out of the building.

Banning went to a door off the base operations foyer, opened it, and motioned to the people inside to come out. Then he walked back to where Ken and Ernie were standing.

"Five minutes, Ken," he said. "It's the only C-46 in the second line of airplanes. You can't miss it."

"Aye, aye, sir," McCoy said. "Thank you."

"Ernie, when you see Carolyn, tell her . . ."

"What, Ed?"

"That I'm sorry, I guess," he said. "Tell her I never wanted to hurt her."

"Yeah," Ernie said. "I know."

Banning walked out of the building.

Three men came out of the small room into the foyer. Two of them were Marines—a baby-faced lieutenant and an older man. Ernie had never seen either of them before. They were wearing belts with pistols hanging from them, and had Thompson submachine guns cradled in their arms.

"Good morning, sir," they greeted McCoy.

The third man, who was bearded like Ken and wearing civilian clothing, looked vaguely familiar. He had two identical canvas weekend bags, one of which he handed to McCoy.

"You remember Gunny Zimmerman, Ernie?" McCoy asked.

"Oh, yes," she lied, and smiled, and then did remember. She had met him one time in New York, in Pennsylvania Station.

"Ma'am," Zimmerman said, and picked up McCoy's

Val-Pak before following the others out of the building.

Ernie saw that the back of the panel truck had been opened. Everyone put their luggage in the back, then got into the Chevrolet sedans. The little convoy drove away.

Ernie looked into McCoy's eyes.

"Damn," she said.

"Damn," he agreed.

"They don't give you a gun?" she asked. It was all she could think of that was safe to say.

He raised the canvas weekend bag. "There's a machine pistol in here," he said.

"I should have guessed," Ernie said, and then she said what she was thinking. "Goddamn you, Ken, when you come back, you're going to marry me and we're going to make babies."

"If I come back—"

"Don't use that goddamned word, 'if'!"

"Let me finish."

"Finish."

"If I come back, we'll get married," McCoy said.

She threw herself into his arms and stayed there, even though, the way he was holding her and his bag, the barrel of his machine pistol was painfully jabbing into her upper leg.

And then he broke away.

"Jesus Christ, I love you!" he announced, his voice breaking toward the end, and then he walked out of the building.

In a moment, she followed him, and watched as he made his way to a very large twin-engine transport plane with AIR TRANSPORT COMMAND painted along its fuselage. One of its engines was already running. Colonel Albright stood at the ladder leading down from the door in the fuselage. He shook McCoy's hand, and then McCoy climbed the ladder. As soon as he was inside, the door closed. The plane immediately began to move, taxiing with just one engine.

Albright walked to her, and they stood in front of the base operations building while the C-46 taxied to the end of the runway, then roared down it, lifting off and heading for the skyscrapers of Manhattan, just visible on the horizon.

"I understand your Captain McCoy is a very capable officer, Miss Sage," Albright said.

"There has been a change in our status, Colonel," Ernie said. "Three minutes ago, it went from 'lovers' to 'affianced.' "

"Then let me offer my best wishes."

"Thank you," Ernie said.

[TWO]
The Greenbrier Hotel
White Sulphur Springs, West Virginia
1645 18 March 1943

"Ah, there you are, James," Commander T. L. Bolemann, MC, USN, said to Captain James B. Weston, USMC, as Weston slid into a chair at his table. "I was afraid I was either going to have to send out the bloodhounds or pay for my own drinks."

"I was playing pool," Weston said. "And winning. Never give a sucker an even break, as some wise man once said."

"This will serve as your final psychological counseling session," Dr. Bolemann said, "so be advised that I am watching you professionally."

A waiter appeared and delivered two martinis. Weston signed the chit, then picked up his glass. "To your very good health, Commander," he said.

"And to yours, my dear Captain Weston," Bolemann said, and took a very appreciative swallow. "Tell me, James, have you plans for the weekend?"

"I'm not going to Philadelphia, if that's what you were thinking. Janice has duty. And anyway, I'll be in Philadelphia on Wednesday."

"Good, then I won't have to tell you to forget going to Philadelphia, or whatever else you had planned to fritter away your time."

"What I am going to do is spend the weekend here,

watching the clock tick as it counts down on my time in your little rest home," Weston said.

"Tomorrow, at zero nine hundred hours," Bolemann said, "you will be at the Charleston Municipal Airport, to which destination I have been charged by the management to deliver you sober, shaved, shined, and in the properly appointed uniform."

"What the hell are you talking about?"

"You will there be met by a Navy aircraft flying what was described to me as the Pensacola–Norfolk–Washington round-robin. I wonder where the hell that term came from?"

"I don't know where it came from and I have no idea what you're talking about."

"You will be transported on silver wings to the U.S. Naval Air Station, Pensacola. From there you will be transported back to Charleston on Monday next, presumably on a similar pair of round-robin wings, with your estimated time of arrival here fifteen thirty hours."

"Are you going to tell me what this is all about?"

"The flag officer commanding said Pensacola Naval Air Station, one Rear Admiral Sayre, spoke with our beloved commander, Captain Horace J. Johnson, early this afternoon. The Admiral requested, your schedule here and physical condition permitting, that you be allowed to visit the said Naval Air Station, Pensacola, round-robin transportation to be furnished, over the weekend. Our beloved skipper, who has never been known in thirty years of Naval service, most of it on shore behind a desk, to ever have said no to an admiral, was pleased to grant the Admiral's request."

"I'll be damned!" Jim said.

"What's this all about?" Bolemann asked.

"I can only guess," Jim said.

He had a sudden chilling thought. *Jesus, is Martha behind this? That seems unlikely. But on the other hand, what happened in the San Carlos was important to her. It was not a casual roll in the hay. She told me that she had fantasies, after Greg got killed, about me coming home to comfort her, and that she "died all over again" when she heard I was KIA.*

And she is, after all, Daddy's Darling Daughter.

"Daddy, Jim is bored out of his mind at that hotel in West Virginia. Is there any way we could get him here for the weekend?"

"Guess away. Curiosity consumes me," Bolemann said.

"When I was down there before, he . . ."

"I gather you are personally acquainted with the Admiral?"

"When his daughter got married, I was the groom's best man," Weston said. "And General McInerney called him about this idiotic pilot retraining. Anyway, he was going to talk to me about what's going to happen when I get to Pensacola when some admiral showed up . . ."

"It's amazing, isn't it, how these admirals tend to fuck up the best-laid plans of mice and men? Even those of other admirals?"

". . . and he couldn't do it. Either he wants to do it this weekend, or he wants my advice on how to teach people how to fly."

So instead of getting to talk to the Admiral, I took his daughter out, and then to bed, which is probably number one on the List of 100 Really Dumb Things I Have Done Since Turning Twelve.

Jesus, does Admiral Sayre see me as a suitable replacement husband for Greg Culhane?

Oh, my God! Why couldn't you keep your pecker in your pants?

"Sounds logical," Bolemann said.

"That's all I can think of," Weston said.

He finished his martini and looked around for the waiter to order another.

[THREE]
Municipal Airport
Charleston, West Virginia
0855 19 March 1943

Weston was surprised to see a Consolidated Catalina PBY-5A turning on final to land at Charleston. It was a

Navy airplane, and therefore very likely the one Admiral Sayre had ordered to pick him up at Charleston. But he would have expected that a Douglas R4D—a transport, not a long-range reconnaissance aircraft—would be used for Pensacola–Norfolk–Washington round-robin administrative flights.

Whoever was flying it, Weston judged professionally, knew what he was doing. The landing was a greaser.

The last Catalina he himself had been in was the one he'd flown from Pearl Harbor to Cavite in December 1941, shortly before he had been "without prejudice" taken off flight status and transferred to the 4th Marines. Then he saw that PENSACOLA NAS was painted on the vertical stabilizer, leaving little question that it was "his" airplane.

And then came another surprise. When the plane taxied up to the passenger terminal, he recognized the pilot, Major Avery R. Williamson, USMC.

The last time I saw him, I smelled of booze.

When Major Williamson climbed out of the Catalina, he was saluted with parade-ground crispness by Captain Weston.

"Good morning, sir," Weston said.

Major Williamson's salute was far less crisp.

"I think I should tell you, Captain," he said, "that I had planned to spend the day—after rising at a reasonable hour, say 0900—afloat on beautiful Pensacola Bay, alone with the sea, the sky, and my wife, who I see damned little of these days."

"Yes, sir."

"Instead of flying—since 0500—that ugly airplane at a hundred and fifty knots to Asshole, West Virginia, if you take my meaning."

This is not an unscheduled stop on a round-robin; Williamson was sent here especially to pick me up.

"Yes, sir."

"But on the other hand, Captain, when a lowly major is asked by a rear admiral—one of the good rear admirals—if he is willing to render a service, what is one to do?"

"Sir, I had nothing to do with this," Weston said.

"Yeah, I know, Weston," Williamson said. "And I owe Charley Galloway a couple of big ones. So we will make the most of this unfortunate situation. After I visit the gentlemen's rest facility, you will buy me a cup of coffee and tell me how much you know about PBY-5A aircraft."

"Yes, sir."

"It was put to me—not in so many words, of course—that the Admiral would not be displeased if you acquired some bootleg time at the controls of that ugly beast."

"I've got about twelve hundred hours in one, sir," Weston said.

"In the left seat?" Williamson asked dubiously. The pilot sat in the left cockpit seat, the copilot in the right.

"Most of it, sir," Weston answered. "I was rated as an instructor pilot in it, sir."

"I didn't know that," Williamson said. "Where are your flight records?"

"They went up in smoke on December seventh, sir."

"If I were you, Weston, and you still want to fly fighters, I'd keep the twelve hundred hours and IP rating in the Catalina to myself. They just put out a high-priority call for experienced Cat drivers for some classified mission, and most of us are scurrying for cover."

"Thank you, sir," Weston said. "I want to fly the Corsair."

"Don't go so far as dumping the bird on our way back to Pensacola, but on the other hand, don't mention to anyone that you've got IP status and that much time in one."

"What kind of a classified mission?" Weston asked in simple curiosity.

"They didn't say, and I didn't ask," Williamson said.

The copilot, a Navy lieutenant, and the crew chief, a chief aviation mechanic, climbed out of the Catalina. Weston recognized the copilot. He was Admiral Sayre's aide-de-camp.

Weston wondered how the two of them had planned to spend Saturday before Admiral Sayre "asked" them to fly up to Asshole, West Virginia, in the Catalina.

"While it is true, of course, that any landing you can walk away from is a good landing," Major Williamson said, as

Weston applied the brakes and prepared to turn off the runway at Pensacola, "that wasn't too bad, Captain Weston."

It was the eighth landing he had made in the Cat between Charleston and Pensacola. The others were touch-and-goes at an Army Air Corps training base near Midland City, Alabama, a little over one hundred miles from Pensacola.

"Thank you, sir."

"So far as I'm concerned, you've just passed your flight check for recertification as pilot-in-command of, and instructor pilot for, PBY-5A aircraft."

"Thank you, sir."

"Unfortunately for you, I'm going to have to make a record of that. I'll try to see if I can't get Flight Records to lose it for a while—there's a Marine sergeant who works there who owes me a couple of favors—at least until after General McInerney finds the eight unfortunate volunteers he's looking for."

"Thank you," Weston said, meaning it.

Admiral Sayre's aide drove him to Quarters Number One.

Mrs. Sayre and Martha—who was wearing white shorts and a T-shirt—came out to the drive to welcome him. Very warmly.

He was very careful to kiss Martha with slightly less passion and intimacy than he kissed Mrs. Sayre.

"You got here just in time," Mrs. Sayre said. "We're having a few people over for shrimp and hamburgers, and when we heard you had to make a precautionary stop at Midland City, I was afraid we were going to have to drive up there to get you."

"Major Williamson let me shoot some touch-and-goes," Jim said.

"That's what Daddy said they were probably doing when he told you not to worry," Martha said, and turned to smile dazzlingly at Weston. "How did you do?"

"Okay, I guess," Jim said. "Everybody was able to walk away from the airplane."

Martha and Mrs. Sayre laughed dutifully.

"Major and Mrs. Williamson will be here," Mrs. Sayre

said. "Together with some other people the Admiral wants you to meet before you actually report for duty."

"That's very kind of you," Jim said.

"Don't be silly. You're like family."

"Like family" is one step shy of "family," he thought, *which I strongly suspect is next on everybody's agenda. I have been adjudged to be a suitable replacement for Greg Culhane.*

Why am I surprised?

Admiral and Mrs. Sayre are intelligent, perceptive people, and if Martha is telling the truth that until me she hasn't been interested in any man since Greg got killed—and I think she is—they've seen this and have naturally been concerned about it.

And here comes Greg's best friend, back from the dead, delivered right into their laps, and Martha comes back from the dead herself.

How the hell am I going to get out of this?

The first step on what may turn out to be a very long journey is to keep my hands off her, and my pecker firmly tucked in my pocket.

"Martha will show you your room, and then come out on the patio," Mrs. Sayre said. "Where you can admiringly watch the Admiral make his world-famous grilled shrimp."

"Even funnier than that," Martha said, "is watching people pretend to like them."

"You should be ashamed of yourself!" Mrs. Sayre said.

Martha led him inside and to one of the bedrooms. "Remember this?" she asked.

He shook his head, "no."

"This is the room where Daddy puts people he likes," she said. "It has its own bath." She walked to the bathroom door and opened it. "Everybody else gets a guest room with the bathroom down the hall."

"I'm flattered," he said.

"Are you going to kiss me, or what?" Martha asked. "I thought Mother made it perfectly clear we were to have a minute or two alone."

"Of course," he said.

*I will kiss her as a friend. No passion whatever. Maybe
I can send her a subtle message.*

That noble intention lasted until he felt the pressure of
her breasts against his abdomen and her tongue against
his lips.

The next thing he knew, she was pushing him away.
They were both breathing heavily. Martha leaned against
the wall and pulled her brassiere back in position over her
breasts.

"For a moment, I was afraid you weren't glad to see
me," she said.

"Don't be silly!"

"I don't know what we're going to do," Martha said.
"But I'll think of something. Now go wash the lipstick
off your face."

"Yes, ma'am," he said.

"And as much as I hate to say this, I think it would be
a good idea if you closed your fly."

[FOUR]
United States Submarine *Sunfish*
159° 33" East Longitude 25° 42° North Latitude
Pacific Ocean
0705 20 March 1943

There were four officers in the tiny wardroom of the *Sunfish* when the chief of the boat, Chief Boatswain's Mate
Patrick J. Buchanan, pushed the curtain aside and word-
lessly, with raised eyebrows, asked permission to enter.

"Come on in, Chief," said Lieutenant Commander Warren T. Houser, USN, the *Sunfish*'s skipper. Houser was a
stocky man in his late thirties who wore his blond hair in
a crewcut.

Buchanan, a wiry thirty-seven-year-old with twenty
years in the Navy, fifteen of them in the Silent Service,
nodded at the other officers and slid into an empty chair
at the tiny table.

Lieutenant Amos P. Youngman, USNR, the executive
officer of the *Sunfish*, pushed a silver coffeepot and a

heavy china mug across the table to him. He was tall,
thin, balding, and wore glasses, which gave him an intel-
lectual look.

Before helping himself to coffee, Chief Buchanan made
three gestures toward the skipper with his right hand. He
balled his fist with the index finger extended upward.
Then he turned his balled fist downward and described a
circle. Finally, he balled his fist with the thumb extended
upward.

Houser correctly interpreted the gestures to mean that
the *Sunfish* was on position, making wide circles on battery power a hundred feet below the surface of the Pacific
Ocean, and that everything was hunky-dory.

Commander Buchanan returned the thumbs-up gesture.

"You may be wondering why I have asked you in for
this little chat, Chief," Houser said.

Buchanan smiled at the one officer who was not a submariner. His name was Major Homer C. "Jake" Dillon,
USMCR.

"I'm afraid to ask," he said. "Where is the Marine
Corps taking us this time?"

The *Sunfish*'s last three combat patrols had all been to
Mindanao. They had gone like clockwork, but Chief
Buchanan was a devout believer in odds. The more times
you did anything, the greater the odds that something
would go seriously wrong.

"All we're going to do is run around in a circle," Major
Dillon said. "We should be back at Pearl Harbor before
it gets dark."

"As I recall, the Marines are pretty good at running
around in circles," Chief Buchanan said.

This prompted another hand gesture, this one from Major Dillon. He held his balled fist upward with the center
finger extended.

Captain Houser chuckled.

"In ten minutes, Chief," he said, sliding a sheet of typewriter paper stamped TOP SECRET across the table to
Buchanan, "at 0715, we're going to take the boat to periscope depth. Then, presuming we don't find ourselves in
the middle of a Japanese fleet, we are going to surface
and Sparks will transmit the following identifier—Code

Group One—on that frequency, for a period of five minutes. He will simultaneously monitor the specified frequency, listening for the phrase specified. If within five minutes he receives the phrase specified, he will transmit what is described on that as 'Code Group Two.' "

Chief Buchanan took the sheet of typewriter paper and read it carefully before looking at the skipper for further orders.

"Copy the data," Captain Houser ordered. "That Top Secret goes right back in the safe."

"Aye, aye, sir," Buchanan said, took a small, wire-spiral notebook and pencil from the pocket of his khaki shirt, and wrote down the radio frequencies and code groups.

"I think, Major Dillon," Captain Houser said, "that your obscene gesture to Chief Buchanan has so intimidated him—he is, of course, such a gentle person—that he's not even going to ask what this is all about."

"The hell I'm not," Buchanan said.

"With a little bit of luck, Chief," the third submariner in the wardroom said, "a Catalina somewhere within a hundred miles of our position will be able to get a radio fix on us, and there will be a rendezvous at sea."

The third submariner was Lieutenant Chambers D. Lewis III, USN, a tall, good-looking member of the Naval Academy's class of 1940, and now aide-de-camp to Rear Admiral Daniel J. Wagam, one of the more powerful members of the staff of Admiral Chester W. Nimitz, Commander in Chief, Pacific. Lewis was on Chief Buchanan's very short list of very good officers. Before he had become Admiral Wagam's aide, he had served aboard the submarine *Remora*. Among other hairy patrols, *Remora* had three times run the Japanese blockade of the Philippines to Corregidor, taking in desperately needed medicine and evacuating the Philippine gold reserves as well as nurses and blinded soldiers and Marines. He had also been on the *Sunfish* on her first trip to Mindanao, had gone ashore with the Marines, and stayed with them until evacuated later by the *Sunfish*.

"We're practicing personnel movement?" Buchanan asked, sounding a little surprised.

The *Sunfish* had twice met with seaplanes on the high sea, transferring to them people evacuated from the Philippines.

"That, too," Lieutenant Lewis said, waited for that to sink in, and then went on. "Following is Top Secret, Chief, to be shared with no one without my, or Major Dillon's, specific permission in each case."

Buchanan nodded his understanding, but Chambers waited for him to say, after a long moment, "Aye, aye, sir," before going on.

"The plan is that the *Sunfish* will rendezvous with two Catalinas in the Yellow Sea, a hundred miles northeast of Tientsin, China. She will then refuel these aircraft so they may complete their mission."

"Where are they going?" Buchanan asked without thinking.

"That's . . . right now, Chief, you don't have the need to know," Captain Houser said.

"The Gobi Desert, Chief," Major Dillon said. "They are going to set up a weather station in the Gobi Desert."

"Jesus Christ!"

"My sentiments exactly," Dillon said. "But that's what we're going to do. Some Marines from the Peking Legation, guys retired from the Yangtze River patrol, the 4th Marines, the 15th Infantry stayed in China, roaming around the desert. We're trying to get some people into them now. With radios."

"Jesus Christ!" Buchanan repeated.

"I decided you had the Need To Know, Chief," Dillon said. "We're really not running around in circles. This is damned important."

"I meant no offense, what I said before, Major."

"I know," Dillon said. "I didn't take any. Let me get back to the keeping this a secret business. This operation has to be kept quiet, no matter if this rendezvous/refueling works or not, and not just for the next six months. And it's the sort of thing the men are going to want to talk about. If the Captain gives them a speech, that—no offense, Captain—just makes it a better story. So you're going to have to keep the cork in the bottle, Chief."

"Yeah," Buchanan said thoughtfully, and then remembered to say, "Aye, aye, sir."

The order is understood and will be obeyed.

"How do you plan to refuel the airplanes?" Buchanan asked.

"We haven't figured that out yet," Dillon said. "All suggestions will be gratefully accepted."

"That's going to be a bitch," Buchanan said.

"According to Lieutenant Lewis, you submariners can do anything," Dillon said.

"Captain," Lieutenant Youngman said, "it's 0712."

"Thank you, Mr. Youngman," Captain Houser said. He reached behind him and pressed a lever on a communications box.

"This is the Captain speaking," he announced. "Bring her to periscope depth."

Four men were in the conning tower: Captain Houser, Major Dillon, Lieutenant Lewis, and a sailor serving as lookout and talker. All had large Navy binoculars hanging from their necks. Chambers Lewis had an electrically powered bullhorn in his hand, and Jake Dillon had a clipboard. The clean, fresh, early-morning air was very welcome, although they had been running underwater for only eight hours.

The *Sunfish* was making a slow, wide circle across the calm, deep-blue Pacific.

"This would be as good as it gets, Jake," Captain Houser said. "It's winter in the Yellow Sea. It's not going to be nearly as calm as this."

"Yeah," Dillon said, as much a grunt as a word.

"Captain," the lookout said. "Aircraft dead astern."

Everyone turned to face the stern, binoculars to their eyes. A Catalina, at perhaps 2,000 feet, was making a slow descent toward the water.

"Chief of the boat to the conning tower," Captain Houser ordered.

"Chief of the boat to the conning tower, aye," the talker parroted into the microphone strapped to his chest.

Buchanan appeared through the hatch less than a min-

ute later. He looked dubiously at Lewis's bullhorn, which
he was seeing for the first time.

"The fewer radio transmissions, the better," Lewis said,
answering Buchanan's unspoken question.

"Are they going to be able to hear you? Over the sound
of their engines?" Buchanan asked.

"That's one of the things we're going to find out," Dillon said. "Option Two is running a telephone line out to
the airplane in a rubber boat."

"What rubber boat?"

"Today, the one on the plane. If we do this—"

"When we do this," Lewis corrected him.

"*When* we do this, there will be rubber boats aboard
the *Sunfish*," Dillon finished.

Buchanan had a thought as the Catalina approached the
surface of the sea. "Give me the mike," he said to the
talker. "And go below."

The talker's face showed he didn't like the order, but
he raised the microphone over his head and gave it to
Buchanan, who lowered it in place on his chest.

"What you say when you go below and they ask you
what's going on up here," Buchanan ordered, "is 'I don't
have a clue.' And I want you to keep your guesses to
yourself. Understood?"

The talker nodded his head.

"That's what they call an order, sailor," Buchanan said
firmly, but not unkindly.

"Aye, aye, Chief," the talker said, and started down the
hatch in the conning tower.

The Catalina touched down and then stopped. The pilot
shut down the port engine, then revved the starboard and
taxied toward the *Sunfish*. A sailor—Navy enlisted air-
crewmen were known as "Airedales"—appeared in the
forward gun position of the Catalina with an electric bullhorn.

"Ahoy, the Catalina," Lewis said into his microphone.
Almost immediately the Airedale put his bullhorn to
his lips. "Ahoy, the Sunfish."

"I'll be damned, he heard you," Dillon said.

"Welcome to the Pacific Ocean," Lewis called cheerfully.

"Ahoy, the *Sunfish*," the Airedale called again.

"Wave if you hear me," Lewis called.

"Ahoy, the *Sunfish*," the Airedale called again.

"Shit," Dillon said.

"We can hear him, but he can't hear us," Buchanan said. "We're getting drowned out by the sound of his engine."

The Catalina was now a hundred yards off the *Sunfish*.

Lewis called, "Shut down your engine!" and waited a moment, then made a cutting motion across his throat.

"I don't think I would want to shut down my engines on the high seas off China," Captain Houser observed.

"The wind is going to blow him away from us," Buchanan said.

"Well, then we won't collide with him," Captain Houser said.

The Catalina pilot shut down his starboard engine. Immediately, just perceptibly, the wind began to turn the Catalina's nose, which had been pointed directly at the *Sunfish*'s conning tower.

"Shit!" Jake Dillon said again.

"Welcome to the Pacific Ocean," Lewis called.

"We're going to have to stop meeting like this," the Airedale called back. "People will talk."

"You couldn't hear me before?" Lewis called.

"No, sir," the Airedale called back.

"Not over the sound of that aircraft engine," Buchanan said. "Damn!"

"Put the rubber boat in the water," Lewis called. "When it's in the water, it might be a good idea to start an engine and maintain your position."

"Understood," the Airedale called back.

"What happens now, Chief," Lewis said, "is that the rubber boat is going to bring us two hundred feet of half-inch hose. We'll need two people on deck to take the end of it and tie it to the *Sunfish*. I volunteer. Can you give that talker microphone to somebody else?"

Buchanan replied by speaking into the talker microphone.

"Talker to the bridge," he ordered.

The talker appeared so quickly that it was evident he

had been waiting at the foot of the ladder to the conning tower bridge.

"You and Mr. Lewis are going to climb down, meet that rubber boat," Buchanan ordered, pointing toward the Catalina, "which will have some hose on it, and tie the end of the hose to one of the conning tower ladder steps."

The talker looked at the Catalina, which was parallel to the *Sunfish*. As he did, the Plexiglas bubble on the port-side of the fuselage rolled upward on its tracks. A black package was tossed through it. The package quickly unfolded and expanded into a small rubber boat, held to the airplane with a line.

An officer climbed into the boat, and then the half-inch hose was fed into the boat and coiled on the bottom. Finally, an Airedale joined the officer in the boat and paddles were handed to them from the airplane.

The talker waited until they had started paddling, then started down the ladder. Lewis handed his bullhorn to Buchanan and followed the talker down the steps—steel rods welded to the side of the conning tower.

"We'll have the hose, as well as the boat, *boats*, aboard the *Sunfish*, right?" Captain Houser asked.

"Yes, sir," Jake Dillon replied.

It took what seemed like a very long time for the two men in the small rubber boat to paddle to the side of the *Sunfish*. Once there, it bobbed beside the curved hull of the submarine.

After three tries, a thin line was thrown and caught by the talker, who, with Lieutenant Lewis holding him by his waist belt, leaned as far down toward the rubber boat as he could.

A more substantial line was then hauled aboard, followed by the end of the half-inch hose.

"One of the questions when we actually do this," Jake said, "is whether it will be wiser to load all the hose aboard the rubber boat and then pay it out from the boat as it returns to the plane, or whether just the end should go with the boat, and the hose paid out from the submarine."

Captain Houser grunted.

"Right now, because the hose is already in the boat,

we're going to try paying it out from the boat," Jake
added.

"How are you going to pump the fuel?" Captain Houser
asked.

"That's another of the questions," Dillon said.

The Catalina's pilot started one of the engines and
moved the airplane back to where its nose was again
pointed at the *Sunfish*. He then shut the engine down
again. And the Catalina immediately began to move from
the force of the wind. By the time the rubber boat was
halfway to the Catalina, the Catalina was again parallel to
the *Sunfish*. And the pilot again started an engine, maneu-
vered back into position, and shut down the engine. He
did this a third time when the rubber boat was fifty feet
away.

The rubber boat's return trip to the Catalina took an
even longer time than the trip to the *Sunfish*. And there
was a lever effect. That is to say, the weight of the hose
in the water raised the bow of the rubber boat. By the
time they reached the Catalina, the two men paddling it
were both perched precariously on the bow.

"That's going to be fun in, say, six-foot swells," Captain Houser observed.

"Well, maybe we can do it with just a light line and
pull the hose from the airplane," Jake said, without much
conviction. "This—what do I call it?—dry run is to see
what the problems are."

One of the other problems became immediately apparent: With enormous effort, the end of the half-inch hose
was taken to the wing of the Catalina where the fuel fill
ports were located.

The first Airedale who tried this was dragged off the
wing and into the water, together with the hose, when the
weight of the line and the stress of a small swell stretching
the hose proved too much for him.

Some of the hose was still in the bottom of the rubber
boat. When the Airedale was hauled from the water, he
tried dragging the hose onto the wing again, this time with
an assist from another Airedale. It took their combined
strength to keep the hose from being pulled away again.

"That's not going to work in heavy seas, Dillon," Captain Houser pronounced.

"Like I said, this little exercise was intended to find the problems," Dillon said.

He leaned over the side of the conning tower.

"That hose is about to be lost at sea," he called to Lieutenant Lewis. "Unless you want to try to haul it back aboard."

Lewis cupped his hands around his mouth and shouted, "You sign the Certificate of Loss, right?"

"Cut it loose," Dillon ordered. He turned to the Catalina. "If you can't get that boat back through the hatch," he called over the bullhorn, "slash it with a knife."

"Pilot wants to know: 'Are we through?' " an Airedale called back from the forward gun position.

"We're through," Dillon called. "Tell the guy who took a swim he has his choice of a case of beer or a bottle of booze. See you at Pearl."

The half-inch hose immediately disappeared from the wing of the Catalina. It was partially buoyant. From the bridge of the conning tower, it could be seen snaking four or five feet below the surface. Its weight was so great, however, that it had pulled the simple knot that Lieutenant Lewis had tied to one of the steps on the conning tower too tight to untie. It was necessary to send for a fire ax from the submarine, then carefully lower it to the deck in order to cut the hose free.

By the time that was done, the Catalina had taken off and vanished from sight in the direction of Pearl Harbor.

Lewis and Dillon climbed back onto the bridge.

"I'm at your orders, Major Dillon," Captain Houser said.

"Take us home, please," Dillon said.

"Set course for Pearl Harbor, make turns for fifteen knots," Captain Houser ordered.

"Set course for Pearl Harbor, make turns for fifteen knots, aye," Chief Buchanan ordered, then took the talker's microphone off and gave it back to the talker.

After a moment, the *Sunfish*'s diesels revved and water boiled at her stern.

"I'm sorry, Jake," Houser said, "but I think you're trying the impossible."

"If at first you don't succeed, fuck it, right?" Dillon replied.

"What now, Jake?" Lewis asked.

"I think I know a guy who could solve this problem," Dillon said thoughtfully. "Lewis, how hard would it be (a) to find a guy in the Seabees somewhere in the Pacific, and (b) get him here?"

"It could be done, Jake," Lewis replied. "Who is this guy?"

"A Best Boy I know," Dillon said.

"A what?"

"Did you see *Culligan's Raid*?" Dillon asked.

"The movie?" Lewis asked, obviously confused. "Yeah, sure, didn't everybody?"

"You remember the scene where the train tries to make it across the burning bridge, and doesn't? Where the bridge collapses? The train goes into the gorge?"

"Sure."

"The first time they shot that, something happened to the stock—the film. They had to shoot it again. It took this guy five days to clean the location, rebuild the bridge, and get another train."

"And you think he would know how to refuel a Catalina on the high seas?"

"Yeah, now that I think about it, I think he could figure out a way to do it."

XV

[ONE]
Naval Air Station
Pensacola, Florida
0830 21 March 1943

Without intending to, Major Avery R. Williamson, USMC, watched Mrs. Martha Sayre Culhane enthusiastically kissing Captain James B. Weston, USMC, good-bye. Without really thinking about it, he immediately decided not to bring the subject up to Weston. An officer and a gentleman does not discuss the romantic affairs of a fellow officer and gentleman, especially when the lady involved is the daughter of a senior officer and gentleman and the widow of a fellow Marine and Naval Aviator.

But he approved this particular romantic involvement.

Since he had first met Weston, he had learned from Brigadier General D. G. McInerney much more about Weston's service in the Philippines than Weston himself had provided. The conclusions he had drawn—obviously shared by General McInerney and by Charley Galloway—

was that Jim Weston possessed very desirable characteristics for a Marine officer. He was not at all averse to
sailing in harm's way. And once there, he had proved he
had the balls to do whatever was necessary, despite the
risk posed to his life. And finally, he was extraordinarily
modest about his exploits.

That entitled him to a little extra consideration. The
unfortunate truth was that officers like Jim Weston were
not as common in the Marine Corps as the public-relations
people would have people believe.

With that in mind, and not without difficulty, Major
Williamson had arranged for a Douglas R4–D aircraft to
return Weston to West Virginia, in place of the PBY-5A
Catalina scheduled. Weston had already proved himself to
be a skilled PBY-5A Catalina pilot. It would be a waste
of time for him to shoot any more touch-and-goes in a
Catalina.

Getting the Gooney Bird had required spending several
very large favors that Major Williamson had been saving
for a good cause. This was a good cause. Unless he was
very sorely mistaken, he could return from Asshole, West
Virginia, able to certify in good conscience that Captain
James B. Weston, USMC, was fully qualified to serve as
pilot-in-command of R4-D-Series Aircraft.

Being current in the Cat and the Gooney Bird might
not be important in the immediate future (Weston seemed
determined to go into the cockpit of an F4U Corsair and
General McInerney seemed determined to put him there),
but it would be a consideration, say, six months down the
line when they were selecting captains to be squadron
commanders.

Captain Williamson had not had the privilege of knowing the late Lieutenant Gregory Culhane, USMC, but
everything he had heard about him was favorable. Proof
of that seemed to come from Weston, who had been the
best man at his wedding to Admiral Sayre's daughter,
Martha. Major Williamson believed it to be absolutely
true that birds of a feather flocked together.

In the highest traditions of the Marine Corps, Lieutenant Culhane had died fighting in the valiant—if hopeless—
defense of Wake Island. Likewise in the highest traditions

of the Marine Corps, then Lieutenant Weston had fought in the valiant—if hopeless—defense of Luzon and Corregidor. And when he had not died, he'd gone on fighting as a guerrilla.

It was not surprising to Major Williamson that Admiral Sayre's daughter was strongly attracted to Captain Weston. And, clearly, Admiral Sayre was not at all displeased that Weston had become a suitor of his daughter.

Forty-five minutes after Captain James B. Weston had waved goodbye to Mrs. Martha S. Culhane from the left seat of the R4-D, he had proved to Major Williamson that his previous, though admittedly limited, experience in the Gooney Bird, plus all of his PBY-5A time, plus his natural ability as a pilot, had combined to turn him into a pilot capable of performing any maneuver within the envelope of the R4-D's capabilities.

An hour after that, after eight touch-and-go landings at the U.S. Army Air Corps field near Midland City, Alabama, Major Williamson was convinced that Weston could fly the Gooney Bird at least as well as most Gooney Bird drivers he knew, and far better than a lot of them. He based this professional judgment not only on the fact that all of Weston's touchdowns, including the first one, had been greasers, but also on the fact that both times he had without warning shut down one of the Gooney Bird's engines on takeoff—a maneuver that caused the aircraft to want to turn abruptly in the direction of the shut-down engine—Weston's response had been immediate, calm, and skillful.

And neither was he worried about Weston's ability to navigate. It was more than reasonable to presume that anyone who had acquired 1,200 hours in a PBY-5A, most of it in the left seat flying over the Pacific Ocean, knew how to navigate.

On his eighth landing at the Midland City Army Air Corps field—again a greaser—Weston touched down within ten yards of the end of the runway. When the speed of the landing roll had decreased enough to put the tail wheel on the ground—the end of the "touch"—meaning, he could either slow further and turn off the runway or apply throttle and take off again—"go"—he looked at Major Williamson for orders.

"Ascend again into the heavens, Mr. Weston," Major Williamson ordered, "and set course for Asshole, West By God Virginia."

"Asshole, West Virginia, aye, aye, sir," Weston replied.

With a skilled hand he advanced both throttles. The Gooney Bird accelerated and the tail came off the ground. A few seconds later, the R4-D was airborne again.

"Wheels up," Weston ordered. "Dump the flaps."

And then he remembered he was a student pilot.

"Wheels up, please, sir," he said. "Reduce flap angle to zero, please, sir."

Williamson didn't reply until the green WHEELS UP AND LOCKED light came on, and the arrow on the FLAPS control was pointing to zero.

"Wheels up, flaps dumped," he said.

"Midland, Navy Six Niner Niner," Weston said to the microphone, as he simultaneously set up his rate of climb and turned the Gooney Bird onto a course that would take them just to the east of Atlanta.

"Six Niner Niner."

"Thank you for the use of your facility, Midland. We are now going to try—desperately—to find first Fort Benning and then Atlanta. Would you be so kind as to ask them to keep an eye out for us? ETA Benning thirty-five minutes, ETA Atlanta unknown. I can't count that high on available fingers."

"You're welcome, Navy. We will advise Benning to keep an eye out for you."

"Thank you again, Midland, and a very good day to you."

Major Williamson was not surprised to note how skillfully Weston trimmed up the Gooney Bird. Weston was obviously a skilled and experienced pilot.

Birds of a feather, et cetera.

Twenty minutes later, making 170 knots at 7,000 feet over Eufala, Alabama, Major Williamson spoke again. "She's really a nice girl, Weston," he said.

"Sir?"

"Oh, come on, Jim. I saw you two say good-bye."

"Oh."

"She's a really nice girl," Williamson repeated.

"Yes, sir, she is."

"And a stunning female!"

Weston looked over at him.

"When you get married, you don't take a solemn vow not to look," Williamson said.

"Stunning is an understatement," Weston said.

"In fact, if she wasn't an admiral's daughter and a Marine Aviator's widow, one might go so far as to say she's built like a brick shithouse," Williamson said.

"Oddly enough," Weston said, with a clear mental picture of Martha standing naked in the cabin of her father's sailboat, "a somewhat similar thought passed through my head."

"I probably shouldn't tell you this, Jim—you're not undersupplied with ego—but you're the first guy she's shown any serious interest in as long as I've known her."

"Is that so?"

"Pensacola is a buyer's market for a girl like Martha. One hell of a lot of eligible young officers have taken their best shots at her. And gotten Maggie's Drawers." When a marksman—and every Marine is trained to be a rifleman—completely misses his target on a known-distance range, a red flag, "Maggie's Drawers," is waved in front of the target. "You're the first one to even come close to getting the brass ring."

"With all respect, sir, is your real name John Alden?"

"Not the last time I looked."

"You sound as if you're trying to match me up with the lady."

"It seems to me that Mother Nature has already done that," Williamson said. "I'm just letting you know Mother Nature rarely makes a mistake."

Weston didn't reply.

" 'Lieutenants should not marry; captains may marry; majors should.' You ever hear that, Jim? Or am I putting my nose in where it doesn't belong?"

"As a matter of fact . . ."

"Don't be impertinent, Captain. You are a very young captain; I am a senior major. It therefore behooves me to counsel you on a matter of importance to your career."

"With all due respect, Major, sir, go fuck yourself."

"I was a lieutenant when Margie and I got married," Williamson said. "I didn't want to get married either. October '41. I was on orders to VMF-219. I thought, Christ, we're going to war. The last thing I wanted to do to Margie was make her a widow. But I couldn't tell her no."

Weston looked at him.

"We had a seven-day honeymoon," Williamson went on. "Then I reported to 'Diego, went aboard the *Lexington*—change of orders—and wound up on Midway. I was lucky there. I was determined to go home to Margie. I got six Japs, and that got me railroad tracks, and then I went to VMF-229 on Henderson Field on the 'Canal. Charley Galloway was the skipper. Colonel Dawkins— you know this—was the MAG commander, and he asked Charley which of his pilots should get a squadron, and Charley said me. And I got lucky there, too. I was determined to go home to Margie. And I did, with major's leaves on my collar. I went home to Margie and our brand-new son. Marrying her was the best and smartest thing I have ever done."

"You think you're going to be as lucky the next time?" Weston asked.

"Who knows? On one hand, the statistics suggest that if you live through the first thirty days, you have a good chance of finishing the tour. On the other hand, everybody dies sooner or later. But in the meantime, Jim, I've had Margie and the boy. That's what it's all about."

"Yeah, I guess."

"End of speech," Williamson said. "Except to say, when you're on the merry-go-round and a brass ring like Martha's is within reach, grab it."

Weston shrugged.

Then he pointed ahead, out the window. A flight of perhaps twenty Army Air Corps C-47s—essentially identical to the Navy R4-D they were flying—was 2,000 feet below them, making a wide turn toward Fort Benning.

"What they're going to do," Williamson explained, "is go down to about thirty-five hundred feet and drop their parachutists. There's drop zones all over this area."

"I don't think I'd want to do that," Weston said. "Jump out of an airplane."

"You ever see a drop?"

"No, sir."

"Why don't you drop down to about forty-five hundred feet, and stay behind that formation and watch? It's something you should see."

Weston reached the trim tab to lower the R4-D's nose, then reached for the throttle quadrant to retard power.

With a little bit of luck, he thought, *the "why don't you marry Martha" speech is really over.*

The thing is, he's absolutely right. If it wasn't for one small problem—Janice, who I also really love—I would marry Martha in a minute.

[TWO]
Espíritu Santo Island
New Hebrides, Southern Pacific Ocean
1505 22 March 1943

Chief Boatswain's Mate William Haber, USN, a lithe, muscular, natty thirty-nine-year-old with twenty-two years of Naval service, happened to be standing before the skipper's desk when the telephone rang.

Lieutenant Commander J. K. Sloane, Civil Engineer Corps, USNR, commanding officer of the 3rd Naval Construction Battalion, pointed at the telephone, indicating that Chief Haber should take the call, rather than the clerk in the outer office.

"Third CBs. Chief Haber speaking, sir."

"This is Lieutenant Stevens, Chief, Admiral Henton's aide."

Rear Admiral Jerome J. Henton, USN, commanded U.S. Navy Base (Forward) Espíritu Santo.

"How may I help the Lieutenant, sir?" Chief Haber said, very courteously. He almost came to attention.

Chief petty officers with twenty-two years of service are not normally very impressed with lieutenants. Lieutenants who are aides-de-camp to flag officers—who sit, so to speak, at the foot of the throne of God—are an exception.

Commander Sloane, who looked very much like Chief Haber, lithe, muscular, and natty, picked up on the change of voice. While a mere reservist, he *was* a graduate of the U.S. Naval Academy at Annapolis. He looked up at Chief Haber in interest.

"Yes, sir, we have a Chief McGuire aboard," Chief Haber said.

Now Commander Sloane was really interested.

Chief Carpenter's Mate Peter T. McGuire, USNR, known popularly as "Chief Hollywood"—if he was to be believed, and Commander Sloane was among the dubious, he not only was acquainted with many Hollywood stars, but also had carnal knowledge of many of them—was not only a reservist but had never worn a uniform, much less been to sea aboard a man-of-war, until the day he had raised his hand and been sworn into the Naval Service as a chief petty officer.

In order to form its construction battalions—the Seabees—the Navy had tried to recruit highly skilled civilian construction workers and other civil engineering specialists. Construction foremen, demolition experts, and heavy-equipment operators were not, however, about to swap a job that was high-paying and almost always essential to the war effort, and thus exempt from the draft, in order to become seaman apprentices at twenty-one dollars a month. The solution was threefold: an appeal to patriotism, an assurance that their skills would be utilized by the Navy—that they would not find themselves mopping decks or peeling potatoes—and enlistment in a grade appropriate to their civilian skills and years of experience.

Peter T. McGuire more than met all the requirements for enlistment as a chief petty officer. If his application was to be believed—and again Commander Sloane was among the dubious—he could not only operate just about every piece of heavy construction and road-building equipment known to engineering, but was also licensed by the state of California as an "unlimited explosives technician" *and* as a master electrician. Commander Sloane would be the first to admit that whenever he told McGuire what he wanted done, it had been done—and done well—with astonishing speed. But Chief McGuire did not conduct himself as Commander Sloane—or Chief Haber—thought a chief should. Chiefs are supposed to supervise, not do the necessary manual tasks themselves. Chief McGuire did not seem to understand this. Although he had been told, time and time again, with increasing firmness, that he was to *supervise* his men, Sloane knew that the minute he or Chief Haber turned their backs, Chief McGuire was wielding a sledgehammer, or, more frequently, operating a Caterpillar D-6 bulldozer or a road grader—or some other kind of heavy equipment—most often with his shirt off.

"Aye, aye, sir," Chief Haber said. "I'll have Chief McGuire report to you immediately, sir. Sir, it may take a little while. Chief McGuire is at Auxiliary Field Two, sir."

In addition to other assigned construction tasks, the 3rd Seabees had been ordered to remove the pierced steel planking that "paved" the runway of Auxiliary Field #2 and to extend the length of the runway and then pave it with concrete. Chief McGuire had been charged with removing the pierced steel planking and then with site preparation of the new runway.

Admiral Henton's aide said something else Commander Sloane could not overhear.

"Aye, aye, sir, thank you, sir," Chief Haber said, very courteously, and hung up. He looked at Commander Sloane. "The Admiral wants to see McGuire right now."

"What the hell is that all about?" Commander Sloane wondered aloud.

Chief Haber shrugged.

"Well, you better go out to Auxiliary Two and get him," Commander Sloane ordered, and then changed his mind. "Tell you what, Chief, *I'll* go get him, and *you* get on the horn to your pal in the Admiral's office and see if you can find out what the hell this is all about. What the hell has McGuire done now?"

Although no witnesses could be found to testify against Chief McGuire in a court-martial, it was common knowledge that Chief McGuire, who was six feet three inches tall and weighed 230 pounds, had thrown two fellow chief petty officers through the screen enclosed verandah of the Chiefs' Club after they'd made remarks about the Seabees that he'd considered disparaging.

"Aye, aye, sir," Chief Haber said.

When his aide informed him that Chief McGuire was at Auxiliary #2 and it might take a little while to get him to the Admiral's office, the Admiral also changed his mind about the best place to meet with the Chief:

"Okay," the Admiral said. "The minute he gets here, bring him in."

"Aye, aye, sir."

"Oh, hell, Charley. I've been in the office all day, and I would really like to know how long Auxiliary Two will be down. Find the driver, and we'll take a run out there."

"Aye, aye, sir."

When Commander Sloane's jeep approached Auxiliary Field #2, he was surprised and annoyed to find that the road was blocked by a Caterpillar D-6 bulldozer. He stood up in his jeep, holding on to the windshield. "Get that thing off the road!" he ordered.

The driver of the bulldozer shook his head, "no." He was a stocky, barrel-chested, shirtless Seabee who wore his white cap with the rim turned all the way down and looked like a beach bum. Then, taking his good sweet time about it, he climbed off the 'dozer and walked to Commander Sloane's jeep, remembering at the last minute the quaint Navy custom that you were supposed to salute officers. "Good morning, Commander," he said pleasantly.

"Couldn't you hear me, sailor? Get that 'dozer off the road!"

"It'll be a minute. McGuire's about to blow the pierced steel planking."

"McGuire's about to do what?"

"Blow the runway," the sailor replied.

"You mean dynamite it?"

"Yes, sir. He decided that would be the quickest way to get it up."

Commander Sloane's attention was diverted when he heard the sound of wheels on the dirt road behind him. He turned and saw Admiral Henton's Plymouth staff car, his blue, two-starred flag flapping from a pole mounted to the fender.

Oh, my God!

Admiral Henton and his aide-de-camp got out of the car.

"Good afternoon, sir," Commander Sloane said, and saluted.

"What's going on here?" Admiral Henton said, returning the salute and then shaking Commander Sloane's hand.

When in doubt, tell the truth. When in great doubt, tell the truth, but as little of it as possible.

"We're about to blow the runway, sir," Commander Sloane said. "I was about to walk to the crest of the hill and see how things are going."

"*Blow* the runway?" Admiral Henton asked. "Won't that make salvaging the pierced steel planking a little difficult?"

He had expected to see a crew of Seabees, armed with sledgehammers. They would sledgehammer the interlocking parts of one piece of pierced steel planking free from the adjacent piece of planking. The freed piece would then be loaded onto a truck and carted off for future use.

"Yes, sir, it will," Sloane said.

This maniac McGuire is going to cost me my promotion!

Admiral Henton made a gesture indicating that Commander Sloane should lead the way to a place where they could see what was going on.

"Admiral," the Seabee said, "I wouldn't go too far down the slope, if I was you."

Admiral Henton turned and looked at him. "Thank you very much," he said. "I'll be careful."

"You never can tell how far some of that shit will fly when you do something like this," the Seabee added.

The Admiral nodded, then gestured to Commander Sloane to again lead the way.

From the crest of the hill, the entire three thousand feet of runway could be seen.

Chief McGuire's complement of Seabees were scurrying all up and down the runway, some of them carrying sandbags. Lines of sandbags were laid across the runway at fifty foot intervals.

Neither Admiral Henton nor Commander Sloane could imagine what was going on. When Sloane looked around for Chief McGuire, he was annoyed—but not surprised—to find him standing on the canvas seat of a Caterpillar D-6 bulldozer parked fifty yards off the near end of the runway.

Chief McGuire was naked, except for a pair of khaki trousers cut off above the knees. A disgracefully beat up and dirty chief's brimmed cap on his head was the only symbol of his rank.

"Chief McGuire?" Admiral Henton inquired. "Is he the fellow on the bulldozer?"

"Yes, sir. Sir, in consideration of the heat, and the labor the men are performing, I allow considerable leeway in the way they dress."

"I'm sure it gets hot as hell out here," the Admiral said.

Chief McGuire got off the seat of the bulldozer and crawled up on the hood over the engine. "Clear!" he bellowed.

Faintly, Commander Sloane saw all the Seabees down the length of the runway run off the runway to seek shelter wherever they could find it, most often behind the bulk of eight bulldozers that were parked to the side of the runway.

Chief McGuire then jumped off his own bulldozer and disappeared from sight. He emerged a moment later at the wheel of a jeep that had been parked out of sight beside the 'dozer. He drove down the runway, slowing at each pile of sandbags. When he reached the end of the runway, he drove the jeep into a depression.

Very faintly at first, then more loudly and more clearly as it was repeated by Seabees along the edge of the runway, came the call: "Fire in the hole!"

The first muffled roar came a moment after the last "fire in the hole!" call was shouted, soon followed by a series of roars. Clouds of smoke then appeared at regular intervals down the runway where there had been lines of sandbags.

"My God!" Admiral Henton exclaimed.

Before the smoke cleared, Chief McGuire reappeared in his jeep and started back down the runway toward them. Soon after that, 'dozer engines were revving, and all of the 'dozers started to back up to the side of the runway. Eye hooks were fastened to holes in the pierced steel planking, then to the bulldozers. An engine revved, and a section of runway one hundred feet wide and fifty feet long began to slide off to the side.

"By God, that's clever!" Admiral Henton exclaimed. "You are to be complimented on your initiative, Commander!"

"Thank you, sir."

"I suppose that trucks will now—" the Admiral said, and interrupted himself as trucks appeared. "Very clever," he said. "One crew can salvage the pierced steel, while another starts laying the runway foundation. I'll bet you didn't get that out of a book, did you, Commander?"

"We pride ourselves on innovation, sir," Commander Sloane said.

Admiral Henton started down the hill. Commander Sloane and the Admiral's aide followed him. They arrived just as Chief McGuire reached the end of the runway.

He looked curiously at the Admiral, the Commander, and the Admiral's aide, then drove up to them. He saluted, but did not leave the jeep.

"That was very impressive, Chief," the Admiral said. "How soon can you start preparing the runway?"

"The dump trucks with the gravel will be here any minute," McGuire said. "While they're dumping, we'll start laying the forms. As soon as the 'dozers get the pierced steel out of the way, they'll start scraping. Then we'll get the graders going. With a little bit of luck, we should be able to pour maybe a hundred feet by the time it's dark. It'll be slower at night, of course, and I don't like to pour unless I can really see what I'm doing."

He did not once use the term "sir," Commander Sloane noticed. If the Admiral noticed, he did not take offense.

"Well done, Chief," the Admiral said.

"Commander Sloane said you needed this runway in a hurry," McGuire said.

"Tell me, Chief, do you happen to know a Major Dillon, of the Marine Corps?"

"Sure, we're old buddies. He a friend of yours?"

"I don't have that privilege, I'm afraid," Admiral Henton said. "May I ask where you and the Major know each other?"

"L.A.," Chief McGuire said. "We both used to work for Metro-Magnum."

"The motion picture studio?"

"Yes, sir . . ."

That's the first time he said "sir"! Commander Sloane thought.

". . . I was chief of construction," Chief McGuire went on, "and ol' Jake was the publicity guy."

"Well, Chief, I'm sure you'll be happy to hear that you're soon going to see you friend again."

"Really?"

Admiral Henton handed Chief McGuire a sheet of teletypewriter paper.

```
P R I O R I T Y

S E C R E T

CINCPAC
1005 21 MARTINEZ 1943

FLAG OFFICER COMMANDING US NAVY BASE
(FORWARD) ESPIRITU SANTO

1. CINCPAC RECORDS INDICATE THAT CHIEF
PETTY OFFICER PETER T. MCGUIRE, USNR, IS
ASSIGNED TO 3RD USN CONSTRUCTION
BATTALION ON ESPIRITU SANTO. YOU
PERSONALLY OR A SUITABLY SENIOR OFFICER
IF YOU ARE NOT AVAILABLE WILL ON RECEIPT
OF THIS MESSAGE INTERVIEW CHIEF MCGUIRE
```

AND DETERMINE IF HE IS PERSONALLY
ACQUAINTED WITH MAJOR HOMER C. (NICKNAME)
QUOTE JAKE ENDQUOTE DILLON, USMCR.

3. IF THE ANSWER IS IN THE AFFIRMATIVE,
CHIEF MCGUIRE WILL BE IMMEDIATELY
DETACHED FROM 3RD USN CONSTRUCTION
BATTALION AND TRANSFERRED CINCPAC. AIR
TRAVEL IS DIRECTED PRIORITY AAAAA.

4. CINCPAC WILL BE NOTIFIED BY SEPARATE
PRIORITY MESSAGE CLASSIFICATION SECRET
WHETHER CHIEF MCGUIRE IS OR IS NOT
ACQUAINTED WITH MAJOR DILLON, AND IF HE
IS, THE DATE AND TIME OF HIS DEPARTURE
FROM ESPIRITU SANTO.

5. IF FEASIBLE CHIEF MCGUIRE SHOULD
TRAVEL TO US NAVY BASE PEARL HARBOR
ABOARD A PBY-5A AIRCRAFT. IN THIS CASE,
CREW OF PBY-5A SHOULD FAMILIARIZE CHIEF
MCGUIRE WITH ALL CHARACTERISTICS OF THE
AIRCRAFT, WITH EMPHASIS ON REFUELING,
ENROUTE.

BY DIRECTION NIMITZ, ADMIRAL, USN,
CINCPAC

OFFICIAL: D.J.WAGAM, RADM USN

S E C R E T

"Jesus, I wonder what the hell this is all about," Chief McGuire said.

"I thought perhaps you could tell me."

"I haven't a clue, Admiral. Do I have to go?"

"One of the quaint customs of the Navy, Chief," Admiral Henton said, smiling, "is that when the Commander in Chief, Pacific Fleet, says 'go,' we go."

"I really hate to fly," Chief McGuire said.

"So do I, Chief," Admiral Henton said. "Why don't you give that TWX to Commander Sloane, so he'll know what's going on?"

"Sure," Chief McGuire said. "Here you go, Commander."

[THREE]
Office of the Chief Signal Officer
Headquarters, U.S. Military Mission to China
Chungking, China
25 March 1943

The dusty GM six-by-six truck jerked to a halt before the entrance to a tunnel. Outside was a wooden sign reading, SIGNAL SECTION, USMMCHI. Lieutenant Colonel Edward J. Banning, USMC, holding a Thompson submachine gun in his hand, climbed down from the cab and walked to the rear of the truck. "We're here," he announced, as he began to remove the chain holding the two-foot-high rear "gate" in place.

With a grace surprising for his bulk, Gunnery Sergeant Zimmerman jumped out of the truck. "I'll get that, Colonel," he said.

When the gate was down, Captain Ken McCoy and Master Gunner Harry Rutterman jumped off the truck and started unloading their luggage and the crates marked "Personnel Records, Not To Be Opened Without The Specific Written Permission of the Adjutant General."

Banning entered the tunnel. After his eyes adjusted to the dim light, he could see signs identifying the various offices the tunnel contained. It reminded him of Corregidor, except that on Corregidor the tunnels were lined with concrete; here the tunnel was naked rock. He found a wide area in the tunnel, a place where it looked like someone had decided to carve another lateral and then changed his mind.

He walked back to the mouth.

"Ken," he called, "there's a wide place inside. Put everything there and wait for me. I'll go see what happens next."

McCoy, holding one of the "Personnel Record" crates, nodded and started to carry it into the tunnel.

Banning turned back inside. After proceeding quite a long way, he found what he was looking for, a sign announcing the space off the main tunnel that housed the office of the Signal Officer, USMMCHI. There was a door in a wooden wall; he opened it and walked though, finding himself in a perfectly ordinary military office—except of course, there were no windows. It held four desks, filing cabinets, a safe, and a rack for clothing. At the largest desk sat an Army Signal Corps lieutenant colonel. Banning walked up to the desk, and after a moment the officer raised his eyes from the papers on his desk.

"Good morning," Banning said. "I'm Ed Banning. I'd like to see the Signal Officer, please."

"The General is not available at the moment, Colonel," the army lieutenant colonel said. "Perhaps I can help you?"

"I have to see him, I'm afraid," Lieutenant Colonel Edward J. Banning, USMC, replied. "When could I do that?"

"Why do you want to see the General, Colonel?" the Army lieutenant colonel said. There was a touch of impatience in his voice.

"I'm not at liberty to discuss that," Banning replied.

"The General is a very busy man."

"I'm sure he is," Banning said.

His temper was a little short, too. It had been a very long flight from Newark. The original idea had been to spend only enough time on the ground to take on fuel and perform necessary minor maintenance. That had worked. This meant they had spent long hours trying to sleep on the floor of the Curtis Commando's fuselage, with the roar of the engines as background, three quarters of the way around the world until, after "Flying the Hump," they had arrived in Kunming, China. There the weather had been so bad, they had to spend two days in a flea-infested transient billet until they could make the final leg into Chungking.

No one came to meet them at the airport—which was, of course, to be expected. But the Air Corps personnel running the terminal did not consider it their responsibility to see that incoming passengers got from the airfield to wherever they were going. Gunner Rutterman and Gunny Zimmerman had finally commandeered an Air Corps General Motors six-by-six truck by offering its PFC driver the choice of helping them out or having his arms pulled off at the shoulder.

"My job," the Signal Corps lieutenant colonel said, "is to see that people don't waste the General's time."

Banning was tempted to show his orders to the officer— he quickly came to think of him as "this idiot"—but decided that wouldn't be wise. This idiot was the type who wouldn't be able to wait until he got to the Officers' Club to start telling his pals about the Marines who had just arrived on Top Secret orders issued by the Joint Chiefs of Staff.

The door to the chief signal officer's outer office suddenly opened and a major general marched in. He was a short, stocky man, with a pencil-line mustache. He was wearing a brimmed cap with the crown stiffener removed, à la Air Corps pilots, and an open necked khaki shirt with two silver stars on each collar point. Over that he was wearing a jacket that looked like something Ernest Hemingway would wear while shooting lions in Africa. There were two stars on each epaulet. He had a swagger stick clutched in his hand.

He smiled at Banning. "Colonel Banning, I presume? Welcome to the mysterious East."

How the hell does he know my name?

"Yes, sir," Banning said, and saluted.

The General returned the salute by touching the brim of his cap with his swagger stick. "Well, come on in," the General said, and turned to the lieutenant colonel. "Ask General Newley to come in chop-chop, will you, please?"

"Yes, sir."

"Sir, I had hoped to see the General alone," Banning said.

"I have no secrets from General Newley, Colonel, something you should understand from Step One. He's my deputy."

"Yes, sir."

He motioned with the swagger stick for Banning to

follow him into his office. Inside, he walked behind his desk and sat down. On the ornately carved desk was a nameplate adorned with his name—Frederick T. Dempsey—inlaid in some sort of shell above a painted fire-breathing dragon. On either side of his name were the two silver stars of a major general.

He did not offer Banning a chair. Banning assumed the position of Parade Rest.

"Those were your men I passed in the main lateral?" General Dempsey asked.

"Yes, sir."

"I couldn't help but notice the civilians are wearing beards. They're probably not civilians, are they, but CIC agents? What's that all about?"

Before Banning could reply, another officer entered the office. He was dressed like General Dempsey, except that he had only one silver star on each collar point and epaulet. He took a very good look at Banning.

"Colonel Banning, obviously," he said. "Right?"

"Yes, sir."

And this one knows my name, too! How come? Did General Pickering send them a heads-up? He's pretty casual about classified matters, but I can't believe he would do that.

"I'm General Newley, Colonel. Welcome to USMMCHI." He pronounced the acronym, "U.S. Double M Chi."

"Thank you, sir," Banning said, and shook General Newley's offered hand. Then he turned to General Dempsey. "General, may I show you my orders?"

"You can if you like," General Dempsey said. "But we already know what they are."

"Thank you, sir," Banning said. He took a sealed envelope from his tunic pocket, tore it open, removed a sheet of paper, and handed it to General Dempsey.

TOP SECRET

The Joint Chiefs of Staff

The Pentagon
Washington, D.C.

15 March 1943

SUBJECT: Letter Orders

TO: Lieut. Col. E.J. Banning, USMC
             Capt K.R. McCoy, USMCR
             Second Lt R.F. Easterbrook,
             USMCR
             Master Gunner H.W. Rutterman,
             USMCR
             Gunnery Sergeant E.W. Zimmer-
             man, USMC

1. You will proceed at the earliest possible time by air transportation to Headquarters, U.S. Military Mission to China (USMMCHI), Chungking, China, or such other places as may be deemed necessary in connection with your mission. Priority AAAAAA is assigned.

2. While enroute you will serve as guards of certain classified material which will be entrusted to you at your port of aerial departure.

3. On arrival at USMMCHI, Lt. Col. Banning will explain the nature of his mission to Commanding General, USMMCHI, and Signal Officer, USMMCHI, and ONLY such other senior officers who he, in his sole discretion, believes have the Need To Know in order to facilitate the carrying out of his mission.

4. On arrival at USMMCHI, Lt. Col. Banning will detach, at such time and under such circumstances as he deems appropriate, Captain McCoy and Gunnery Sergeant Zimmerman so they may undertake the execution of their mission as directed by the Joint Chiefs of Staff.

FOR THE JOINT CHIEFS OF STAFF:

Charles M. Adamson

Charles M. Adamson
Major General, USA
Secretary, JCS

TOP SECRET

General Dempsey read the orders.

"As I said, we were expecting you, Colonel. But I was under the impression that the devices would be guarded by CIC agents. Are they on separate orders? Don't tell me those two bearded characters I just saw are Marines?"

He knows about the MAGIC devices. Jesus H. Christ!

"I'm not sure I know how to answer the General's question, sir," Banning said.

"Actually, Colonel, there were two questions. The first was 'where are the CIC agents I expected to be guarding the MAGIC devices?' and the second was 'are those two bearded characters Marines?' "

"I know nothing about CIC agents, sir."

"Then you guarded the MAGIC devices?"

Banning did not reply.

"Something wrong with your hearing, Colonel?" General Dempsey asked, a touch of unpleasantness in his voice.

"Sir, may I speak to the General alone?"

"I thought we'd already been down that path," General Dempsey said. "To answer *your* question, Colonel, when we have finished our business here, yes, I will have a word with you in private if you insist. Now to *my* question . . .

Let's get down to basics. Do you have the MAGIC devices?"

"Sir, as I'm sure the General understands, I am not at liberty to discuss anything of that nature with anyone who does not hold the proper security clearance."

"Frankly, Colonel, I am rapidly moving from appreciation of your concern for security to annoyance. Your own orders direct you to inform me of the nature of your mission. I already know the nature of your mission. You are to serve, as a member of my cryptographic staff, as officer-in-charge of the MAGIC devices."

"Then the General possesses a MAGIC clearance? I was not so informed."

"I'm sure there are many things about which you are not informed, Colonel. Do I have a MAGIC clearance? No. I expect one momentarily. I would have thought you would have brought that with you."

"No, sir."

"Do you, sir?" Banning asked General Newley.

"Not at this moment, Colonel."

"Sir, under these circumstances, I would be in violation of my orders to discuss MAGIC in the presence of General Newley," Banning said.

"Now, listen to me, Colonel, and listen carefully, for I have had just about enough of your word-bandying. I am the person who decides who in this headquarters is cleared for MAGIC. And when I ask you a question about MAGIC, you will answer it. Is that clear enough for you, Colonel?"

"Sir, I respectfully protest you are ordering me to disobey my previous orders."

"I don't give a good goddamn about your previous orders, Colonel. Get that though your head. You are now attached to the Signal Section of Headquarters US-MMChi. You take your orders from me. Got that?"

"Yes, sir."

"Now, for the last goddamned time, do you have the MAGIC machines?"

"Yes, sir."

"How long will it take you to set them up?"

"Once I have a secure area, sir, I can be up and running in about eight hours."

"You will set them up in my crypto area."

"Yes, sir."

"Now, who are those two bearded characters I saw in the main lateral?"

"Captain K. R. McCoy, USMCR, and Gunnery Sergeant Zimmerman, sir."

"And why are they wearing beards and civilian clothing?"

"Sir, it is in connection with their mission."

"Which is?"

"Sir, with respect, Captain McCoy and Sergeant Zimmerman are on an OSS mission that I am not at liberty to discuss."

"You are refusing to answer my question?"

"Sir, with respect, I do not believe the General has the Need To Know."

"We'll see about my Need To Know just as soon as you have MAGIC up and running," General Dempsey said. "In the meantime, I am going to give you two simple orders. One, get MAGIC up and running and tell me the moment we have a link with Washington. Two, have those two characters report to Colonel Platt at the OSS station. I'm sure he'll see that they are shaved and into uniform."

"Sir, with respect, I don't believe you have the authority to issue orders to Captain McCoy or Sergeant Zimmerman."

"Goddamn you! How dare you question my authority? Don't you ever again question any order I give you!"

"Yes, sir."

"You are dismissed, Colonel. Report to me, whatever the hour, when you have established a MAGIC link with Washington."

"Yes, sir."

Banning snapped to attention, saluted, performed a crisp about-face maneuver, and marched out of General Dempsey's office.

Over his shoulder, he heard General Dempsey furiously demand of General Newley, "Jack, can you believe that? Goddamned arrogant Marine!"

He walked back to the wide area in the tunnel and motioned for McCoy to join him.

"Captain," he said, formally, "you may consider yourself and Gunnery Sergeant Zimmerman detached."

"Aye, aye, sir," McCoy said. "What's going on?"

"You've got the gold?" Banning asked.

McCoy tapped his waist. A money belt heavy with U.S. twenty-dollar gold coins was strapped around it.

"There's an OSS station here. Do you know anything about that?"

McCoy shook his head negatively. "First I've heard of it."

"The signal officer here has ordered me to order you to report there, to a Colonel Platt."

"What gives this Army Signal Corps officer the right to give you orders?"

"That's a very interesting question, Captain."

"Is that what you're doing? Ordering me to report to the OSS here?"

"You're detached," Banning said. "I am no longer authorized to give you orders."

"What went on in there?" McCoy asked. "What's going on?"

"I can't go into that, Ken," Banning said. "Sorry."

McCoy looked at him very thoughtfully.

"Correct me if I'm wrong, Captain, but I seem to recall that your last valid order from Brigadier General Pickering was, upon detachment from the team bringing personnel records here, to make preparations to move into the Gobi Desert."

"Yes, sir, that is correct."

"Having been detached, Captain, those orders remain valid unless countermanded by an officer senior to Brigadier General Pickering, such as the major general who is the signal officer here." ·

"I'm getting the message," McCoy said.

"I don't know what's going on around here, Ken, but whatever it is, you shouldn't be involved with it."

"Yes, sir," McCoy said, and put out his hand to Banning.

"Grab your gear, Ernie," he said. "We're leaving."

"Don't go into the desert, Ken, until Pickering tells you to."

"I'll be around," McCoy said, and motioned for Zimmerman to precede him out of the tunnel.

[FOUR]
U.S. Navy Hospital
Philadelphia, Pennsylvania
1615 25 March 1943

"Well, look what's washed up on my beach again," Commander Jerome C. Kister, MC, USNR, greeted Captain James B. Weston, USMC, when he walked into his office and found Weston waiting for him. He touched Weston's shoulder.

"Good afternoon, sir."

"Come on in. Rest your weary bones. It's a long drive from West Virginia, isn't it? Even in your gas guzzler?"

"It's a long ride," Weston agreed.

During which I had a lot of time to think about what I'm going to do about Janice. And did not come up with any answer, except perhaps suicide.

"Sit," Dr. Kister said, indicating an upholstered chair facing his desk.

"Thank you, sir."

"And how was your recuperative leave? Are you appropriately grateful to the grateful taxpayers who picked up the tab for your month in the lap of luxury?"

"I wish they just gave me the money," Weston said.

"But—a little bird told me—you did find the time to work in a little romance. So all was not lost time, was it?"

"I also found time to go to Pensacola," Weston said. "I don't think I'm going to have to learn to fly all over again."

"I heard. Tubby Bolemann has been keeping me up to date."

Weston smiled. Although it made sense, it was the first time he had heard the corpulent psychiatrist called that. "He's a good guy," Weston said.

"Yeah. They offered him retirement—a hundred percent to start, and fifty percent guaranteed for the rest of his life—but he decided to stick around. Now he's trying to go back to sea."

"A good guy," Weston repeated.

"He's also made it official that you are no crazier than any other Marine Aviator. So what happens now is we run you though another quick physical, which I'll schedule for tomorrow morning. And then you can go back to full duty."

"A flight physical, I hope?"

"Since you're not on flight status, I'm not technically supposed to give you a flight physical. But—don't be shocked by this confession—I have made administrative errors before. I don't know if Pensacola will, accept a flight physical from here, but you never know."

"Thank you."

"You can spend the rest of the day tomorrow putting your affairs in order—pay, that sort of thing—and then I'll discharge you from here as of the day after tomorrow. I think you get five days to drive to Pensacola."

"Fine," Weston said.

"It's one hell of a drive from here to Pensacola," Dr. Kister said. "I suppose you have been thinking about that."

"Sir?"

Dr. Kister didn't reply. He reached for his telephone and dialed a number.

"Ah, Lieutenant," he said to whoever answered the phone. "Just the Naval officer with whom I wished to communicate. And how are you this afternoon?"

He's scheduling my physical, Weston decided.

There was a reply, and then Kister said, "Yes, by a wild happenstance, he's sitting right here with me."

He handed the phone to Weston, who took it.

"Captain Weston."

"Hi," Janice said.

His heart jumped. "Hi, yourself."

"How was the drive?"

"Long."

"Listen, I have duty until 2000."

"Damn!"

"Can you meet me in the Benjamin Franklin Hotel at eight-thirty?"

"Sure."

"You can find it all right?"

"I know where it is."

"Eight thirty at the bar," Janice said. "Don't drink too much."

"Yes, ma'am."

Janice hung up.

Weston put the handset in its cradle.

"Thank you," he said to Dr. Kister.

"Nice girl. If I had something like that waiting for me at the end of the long trail, I don't think I'd mind driving all the way up here from Pensacola myself."

"Yeah," Jim said thoughtfully.

"Okay, James," Kister said. "Get out of here. Spruce yourself up. Get a shave and a shower."

"Aye, aye, sir."

"I want to see you before you actually leave, Jim," Kister said.

"Yes, sir. And thanks, Commander."

"I think of myself as Cupid's Little Helper," Kister said.

[FIVE]
The Lobby Bar
The Benjamin Franklin Hotel
Philadelphia, Pennsylvania
0845 25 March 1943

"Hi, honey," Lieutenant (j.g.) Janice Hardison, NNC, USNR, said to Captain James B. Weston, USMC, as she slid onto the barstool beside him. She kissed him, chastely.

"My God, you're beautiful!"

"How many of those have you had?" she asked, nodding at the glass in his hand.

"This is the second," he said.

"Since 1600?" she challenged.

"I took in a movie," he said.

"What did you see?"

"Tyrone Power," he said. "*A Yank in the Royal Air Force*. He doesn't make a very convincing pilot."

She laughed. "But he is," she said. "You don't know?"

"Know what?"

"Tyrone Power is a pilot. He's a *Marine Aviator*."

"No shit?" Weston exclaimed, truly astonished. Then he heard what he had said. "Sorry."

"No shit," she confirmed, then blushed when she realized the approaching bartender had heard her.

God, she's adorable when she blushes.

"Nothing for me, thank you," Janice said to the bartender. "I won't be staying."

"I don't have to finish this," Weston offered. "Where are we going?"

"You're staying. I'm going," Janice said, then waited for the bartender to move down the bar before continuing. "I've got a present for you," she said. "Actually two."

"I didn't get you anything," he said.

She went into her purse and then pressed something into his hand. It was a hotel key.

"Jesus!" Jim said.

Janice blushed again.

"Stay here. Finish your drink slowly. Give me ten minutes."

"Yes, ma'am," he said.

"Nice to see you again, Captain," Janice said, loudly enough so that the bartender could hear her. Then she slid off the stool and walked out of the bar into the lobby.

Weston watched her go, then turned back to the bar. The bartender was there.

"Very nice," the bartender said. "Sorry you struck out."

"The story of my life," Weston said.

"You want another one of those?"

"One more," Weston said. "And then I'll have to go."

"I liked the second present better than the first," Captain Weston said to Lieutenant Hardison. "But of course without the first, I wouldn't have gotten the second, would I?"

They were in one of the two single beds in Room 416. Weston's uniform and the white negligee Janice had been wearing when he came into the room were on the other bed.

"That wasn't a present," Janice said. "Except maybe from God. That's what two people do when they're in love."

"Sorry," he said. "You said 'two presents.' "

"You get the second present in about two weeks," Janice said.

"In two weeks, I will be in Pensacola, Florida," he said.

More than likely in bed with another nice beautiful young girl who thinks she's in love with me. And vice versa.

"And so will I be," Janice said.

"What?"

"Dr. Kister arranged it," she said. "The Navy Hospital at Pensacola had a requirement for a psychiatric nurse, and Dr. Kister got the billet for me."

"Wonderful!" Captain Weston said.

[SIX]
Naval Air Transport Command Terminal
Pearl Harbor, Oahu, Territory of Hawaii
1615 26 March 1943

The PBY-5A Catalina slowly and carefully approached the ramp until the pilot felt the wheels touch. Then, as the engines revved just slightly, the amphibious aircraft rose from the water and taxied onto the concrete parking area.

The area had been famous right after December 7, 1941, when photographs showing it littered with smashed and burning aircraft had been on the front pages of newspapers around the world. Many of the aircraft had been Catalinas.

There was still some evidence of that mess, Major Homer C. Dillon, USMC, had thought, waiting for this PBY-5A to arrive. The hangars were scarred where flames and smoke had reached them, and many of the windows in the hangars were still broken.

What did the Navy do with all the wrecked airplanes? he had wondered idly. *Try to salvage what they could, maybe save the metal to be melted down? Or just load them onto a barge, take them offshore, and push them over the side?*

A team of white hats under the supervision of a chief began to hose down the Catalina's fuselage and landing gear even before the crew climbed out of the airplane.

The first person off it was Chief Carpenter's Mate Peter T. McGuire, USNR, who was wearing a mussed khaki uniform with a white cap cover. Even Major Dillon recognized that that made him out of uniform.

Chief McGuire immediately saw Major Dillon standing alongside a gray Navy Plymouth staff car. Beside him was a tall, good-looking Navy officer in impeccable whites, with some kind of a gold rope hanging from his shoulder. McGuire wondered what the hell that was.

The driver of the staff car started toward him.

"Your gear, Chief?"

"Oh, God, I forgot about it," McGuire said. "It's on that goddamned airplane."

"I'll get it for you, Chief," the white hat said.

"No, I'll get it."

"I don't mind," the white hat said.

"I puked all over it," Chief McGuire said. "I'll get it."

He went back to the Catalina. As he reached it, a fellow chief, this one a chief aviation pilot with the wings of a Naval Aviator on his shirt, appeared in the fuselage bubble gingerly holding a canvas suitcase in his fingers.

"This what you're looking for, Chief?" he inquired with infinite disgust, then dropped it onto the tarmac.

"Hey, buddy, I'm really sorry," McGuire said, sounding as if he meant it. "It wasn't as if I was at the sauce or something. Every time I get in an airplane, I get sick."

"A word of wisdom, Chief," the chief aviation pilot said. "Don't get into airplanes."

McGuire picked up the well-stuffed canvas suitcase and, holding it at arm's length, walked to Dillon and the Navy officer.

"Welcome to beautiful Hawaii, Pete," Dillon said. "What's with the suitcase?"

Chief McGuire finally realized he was supposed to salute, dropped the bag to the tarmac, and saluted.

"I threw up on the airplane," McGuire said. "I threw up a lot on the airplane. A couple of times it didn't make the bucket they gave me." He paused a moment, then added: "Goddamn you, Jake, you know I can't fly!"

"Mr. Lewis, may I introduce Chief Petty Officer McGuire?" Jake said. "Peter, this is Lieutenant Chambers Lewis."

McGuire saluted again and put out his hand. "I used to say, 'any friend of Jake's,' but now I'm not so sure," he said. "I used to think the bastard was a friend of mine."

"The pleasure is all mine, Chief," Lewis said.

"Christ, I can smell the bag from here," Dillon said. "What are we going to do with it?"

"Paul," Lewis said to the driver, "is there a piece of line in the trunk? Or can you get one? Let's tie the chief's luggage to the bumper. Air it out on the way to Muku-Muku."

"I think the Admiral would like that, sir," the driver said, smiling, and went into the trunk.

Jake Dillon leaned forward toward Chief McGuire and sniffed.

"Him, too?" Lieutenant Lewis said. "I'm not sure he'd fit on the bumper."

"You're kidding, right?" Chief McGuire asked.

"Why don't you help him tie your bag to the bumper and then get in the front seat?" Jake ordered.

"Where the hell are we going, anyhow?" Chief McGuire asked.

"Muku-Muku," Jake replied.

"What is that, Hawaiian?" McGuire asked, fascinated.

"Yes it is," Dillon replied, straight-faced. "It means 'Place of Hot Waters.' You need a shower, Pete."

"Goddamn right I do," Chief McGuire agreed.

They drove up to Muku-Muku as Master Gunner Stefan Oblensky, USMC, was walking up the wide stairs to the verandah. He turned and went back down the stairs.

Although Jake was personally glad to see Big Steve, he was sorry he was there right now. Operation Gobi was classified, and Big Steve did not have the Need To Know.

Big Steve saluted, and Jake and Lewis returned the salute.

"What's with the suitcase?" Big Steve asked.

"We had a little airsickness," Jake said.

Chief McGuire stepped out of the front seat. "I threw up all the way from Espíritu Santo," he announced.

"I'm Steve Oblensky," Big Steve announced. "My wife's inside. She probably has something that'll help."

"Help what?" McGuire asked.

"She's a nurse," Big Steve said. "You're sick, right?"

"Not since I got off that fucking airplane I'm not."

As if on cue, Commander Florence Kocharski, NC, USN, attired in a billowing Muumuu, descended the steps from the veranda. "Watch your goddamn mouth around here, Chief!" she said firmly.

Chief McGuire looked at Commander Kocharski in confusion.

"Good afternoon, Commander," Dillon said. "I was just explaining to Mr. Oblensky that Chief McGuire has a little airsickness problem."

"Every time I get in one and they tilt it," McGuire confirmed, and demonstrated with his hand what he meant by tilt, "I get sick."

"They gave him a bucket on the Catalina, Commander," Lieutenant Lewis said. "But he apparently didn't always make the bucket, so to speak."

"I'm really embarrassed about that," McGuire said. "What I really should have done with my clothes was deep them."

"What?" Big Steve asked, confused.

"Deep them," McGuire repeated. "You know, just throw them in the water."

"I think the Chief means 'deep-*six* them,' " Chambers Lewis said, not unkindly, but smiling. "As in 'over the side.' "

"I guess," McGuire said agreeably.

"Chief, why don't you tell Commander Kocharski and Mr. Oblensky how long you have been in the Navy?" Dillon suggested.

McGuire thought carefully before replying: "It will be nine months the first of April."

"Nine *months?* How the hell did you get to be a chief in nine months?" Commander Kocharski asked in disbelief.

"I signed up as a chief," McGuire said. "Why do they call you 'Commander'?"

"Because I happen to be a commander," Flo said.

"I'll be damned!" McGuire said wonderingly.

"How many times in the last eight hours have you been nauseous?" Flo asked.

"Jesus, I don't know," McGuire said. "Eight, ten times. Maybe more. I didn't count."

"You're probably dehydrated," Flo said. "We'll get some liquid into you." She turned to the other men. "You may think this is funny, but it's not. Get those goddamned smirks off your faces."

Chief McGuire looked at Commander Kocharski through eyes filled with gratitude.

Forty-five minutes later, Captain Charles M. Galloway, USMCR, arrived at Muku-Muku. By then Chief Petty Officer Peter McGuire, USNR, was well along on the road to rehydration: At Commander Kocharski's order, he had consumed over a quart of freshly prepared pineapple juice, mixed three-to-one with soda water to prevent further upsetting his stomach, and he was now working on his second bottle of beer. He had also had a shower and was wearing a clean khaki uniform, which Commander Kocharski had provided for him from her husband's closet:

"Charley," Commander Kocharski made the introductions, "Chief Peter McGuire, a friend of Jake's. Pete, Captain Charles Galloway, skipper of VMF-229, and Big Steve's boss man."

Galloway was in his late twenties, slim, deeply tanned, and lanky. His light brown hair was just long enough to part. The two men shook hands, then Charley collapsed into one of the upholstered rattan chairs on the patio and helped himself to a bottle of beer from an ice-filled bucket. "What kind of a chief, Chief?" he inquired politely.

"Carpenter's mate."

"That make you a Seabee?" Galloway asked.

"With nine months in the Navy," Big Steve volunteered, which earned him a dirty look not only from Commander Kocharski but from Galloway himself.

"Yes, sir," Pete replied.

"Well, that's two brownie points," Galloway said. "A Seabee and a friend of Jake's. Welcome to Muku-Muku."

"Thank you."

"Just passing through Pearl?" Galloway asked.

"I don't know what the hell I'm doing here, Captain," McGuire said.

"Really?" Charley replied, chuckling.

"I was minding my own business on Espíritu Santo—"

"You're with the Third Seabees?" Charley interrupted.

"Yes, sir."

"You know anything about Auxiliary Field Two? How long is it going to be out of operation?"

"That's what I was doing, Captain. That's what I still would be doing if this so-called friend of mine hadn't sent for me." McGuire pointed at Jake Dillon.

"Really?" Galloway asked.

"I'd just finished pulling the pierced steel planking," McGuire explained, "when some admiral shows up and asks if I know Jake Dillon. I should have said no."

"But you said yes, right?" Galloway asked, smiling.

"And the next thing I know, I'm on a goddamned airplane here—sick every goddamned mile of the way."

"Pete is unusually sensitive to change of attitude," Commander Kocharski said. "Possibly it has to do with his inner ear, but there are other—"

"Which means what, Flo?" Charley interrupted.

"He gets sick on airplanes," Big Steve said.

"And stays sick," McGuire confirmed.

"I knew a sergeant major at Quantico like that," Galloway said. "He used to get sick before we finished the climb-out. Isn't there anything that can be done?"

Commander Kocharski hesitated, just perceptibly.

"Yes, there is," she said. "There's a pill. A little yellow pill. I'll get some at the hospital tomorrow."

"That's very nice of you, Commander," Chief McGuire said. "But don't bother. I am never ever again going to get on an airplane. Alive."

"So tell me, Jake," Galloway asked, smiling, "Why did the chief have to leave Espíritu Santo, where he was doing something useful, and come here? *Fly* here?"

Major Dillon and Lieutenant Lewis exchanged looks.

"Yeah, Jake, what the hell is going on?" McGuire asked.

"It's classified," Jake said.

"What the hell does that mean? 'Classified'?" McGuire asked.

" 'Classified'?" Galloway parroted.

"We're doing a job for Flem Pickering," Dillon said.

"I don't understand that either," McGuire said.

"A job involving a submarine and a Catalina rendez-vousing at sea?" Galloway asked.

"Where did you hear that, Charley?" Lieutenant Lewis asked.

"At the O Club bar at Ewa," Charley said.

"Tell me exactly, Charley," Lewis said softly.

There was something in Lewis's voice that told Galloway he had touched a nerve. He shrugged and provided the detail. "A Catalina sat down with radio trouble. He couldn't talk to the tower at Pearl, so he landed at Ewa because there's less traffic. And then Big Steve told him we couldn't fix the radios until the next day. So he went to the club, had a couple of drinks, and told everybody, including me, what a lousy day he had had. First he had to take off before zero dark hundred and fly out over the ocean. Then he landed and met a submarine, and after fucking—excuse me, Flo—fiddling around for an hour or so, which included one of his Airedales falling off the wing into the sea, the morons on the submarine—one of them an admiral's aide and the other a Marine major—finally realized what he could have told them all along, that you have a hell of a lot of trouble running a half-inch fuel line across the high seas from a submarine to a Catalina."

"Oh, shit," Jake Dillon said.

"I'll have his ass," Lewis said furiously. "Excuse me, Flo."

Commander Kocharski made a gesture with her hand showing the apology was readily accepted.

"I don't want to get that pilot in trouble," Galloway said.

"He was told what we were doing was secret and to keep his mouth shut. He's in trouble and he deserves to be," Lewis said coldly. "Damn it!"

"I don't know what anybody's talking about," Chief McGuire complained.

"You're not supposed to, Pete," Commander Kocharski said. "That's what 'classified' means. We don't have the Need To Know."

Major Dillon and Lieutenant Lewis exchanged another look, this one a lot longer than the first.

"My decision, Lieutenant Lewis," Jake said formally. "In case anyone asks."

"For the record, I concur in your decision," Lewis said. "And let the record show it came *after* it came to our attention that the *Sunfish*/Catalina operation had already been compromised by a Naval Aviator with a big mouth."

Dillon nodded.

"The following is Top Secret," Jake said, looking first at Charley Galloway and then at Chief McGuire. "Understood?"

Galloway nodded his understanding. After a moment, McGuire said, "Okay, Jake."

"Would you like me to take a walk, Jake?" Commander Kocharski asked.

"As far as I'm concerned, Flo, you're the only one I really trust to keep her mouth shut."

"I don't mind," Flo said.

"Stay," Jake said. "Okay, what we're doing," he began, "what Flem Pickering is doing, with the blessing of CINCPAC—is sending a weather team into the Gobi Desert."

It took him five minutes to explain exactly what they had been doing aboard the *Sunfish* when it met the Catalina at sea. Lewis was impressed. Jake's briefing was just as good a briefing as any given to CINCPAC by senior officers with years of experience.

If not as formal.

"The pilot with the big mouth was right," he said. "Getting fuel aboard a Catalina from a submarine on the high seas is going to be a bitch. It may not be possible at all, which is really going to fu—foul—things up by the numbers. I've seen Pete find answers to problems when nobody else had a clue, so I sent for him."

"Jake, not only do I hate airplanes, but I don't know the first goddamned thing about them," Chief McGuire said. "*Or* submarines. So why send for me?"

"Like I said, Pete, I'm desperate. And I've seen you solve problems when no one else had a clue. I thought it was worth a shot."

"Can I ask a question?" McGuire asked.

"Shoot."

"Let me be sure I've got this straight," McGuire said. "What you want to do is load people and equipment on an airplane—"

"Airplanes. Two airplanes," Dillon interrupted. "Catalinas. The same kind of airplane that you flew on here."

"Thanks to you, you bastard," McGuire said. "Then you're going to land on the ocean, meet a submarine, and refuel the airplanes. Right?"

"Right."

"And the problem is refueling the airplanes from the sub, right?"

"Right."

"Okay. I don't know from zilch about airplanes, so I'll ask what will probably sound like dumb questions."

"Shoot," Jake said.

"How much of a problem would it be to move the people and the equipment from the submarine to the airplanes in rubber boats?" Chief McGuire asked.

"A lot less of a problem," Lewis said, and then understood the implications. "Damn it!"

"I say something wrong?" Chief McGuire said.

"Steve," Dillon said, "tell me about auxiliary fuel tanks carried inside a Catalina."

"It's been a long time since I flew a Cat, or had anything to do with one," Big Steve said. "But the last I heard, there aren't any designed for the Cat."

"Damn," Jake said.

"But you could build them without much trouble," Big Steve said. "BuAir would have a fit. It would be an unauthorized modification; but it could be done."

"You're saying you could build such tanks?"

"If I had the stuff, aluminum, aluminum stringers, something to seal them. Sure."

"And that fuel could be pumped up into the wing tanks?" Lewis asked.

"It could, sure. Or you could add pumps and valves to feed the engines directly."

"*You* could do that, Steve?" Dillon asked softly.

Big Steve nodded.

Lieutenant Lewis pushed himself out of his chair and walked to the low wall that bordered the flagstone patio. He sat on the wall and dialed a number.

"Let me speak to the AAOD, please," he said, referring to the Air (or Aviation) Officer of the Day. After a short delay, Lewis went on. "Sir, this is Lieutenant C. D. Lewis, aide-de-camp to Admiral Wagam, and speaking at his direction. There are two Catalina aircraft at Pearl reserved for a mission of the Admiral's. Both of them are to be at the Ewa Marine Air Station at the earliest possible time tomorrow morning. And please arrange ground transportation to return their crews to Pearl Harbor. And, sir, you may consider this an order from Admiral Wagam: The crews are to be informed that they will not, under penalty of court-martial, tell anyone where they took the Catalinas." There was another pause, and then Lewis said, "Thank you very much, sir," and hung up.

"It would have been nice, Lieutenant Lewis," Galloway said, "if you had *asked* me for the services of Mr. Oblensky."

"I knew in my heart, Captain Galloway, that you would readily volunteer anything you could to this noble purpose of ours."

"Screw you."

"You can fly Catalinas, right?" Dillon asked.

"I can, but I'm hoping nobody remembers that I can," Galloway said.

"Why?"

"You don't know about McInerney's little TWX? Seeking volunteers with Catalina pilot-in-command time for a classified mission involving great personal risk?"

"Oh, yeah," Dillon said.

"Jake, I like what I'm doing. I don't want to fly a Catalina into the Gobi Desert," Galloway said.

"McInerney's asking for volunteers. Don't volunteer."

"If McInerney doesn't get the volunteers he needs, he'll go looking."

"Charley, you're safe. When I saw McInerney, he told me you're the only man in the Corps who could command your squadron of bums."

Galloway looked at Dillon long enough to be assured that he was hearing the truth.

"I'll feel safe when I see the Cats take off for the Gobi with somebody else flying them," he said.

"Chief," Big Steve asked, "you got any experience working with aluminum?"

"Not much," McGuire said. "I've made car bodies out of it. Stuff like that. And once a motorboat. With a V-8 Cadillac in it."

"For Clark Gable, right?" Dillon said, remembering.

"Yeah. I owed him a big one."

"Jake, do I get to use the chief?" Big Steve asked.

"He's yours," Jake said.

"I want one thing understood from right now," Chief McGuire said. "I am not going to get in another goddamned airplane. Not now. Not ever."

"I will take your desires under consideration, Chief McGuire," Major Dillon said.

XVI

[ONE]
The Gentleman's Bar
The Country Club
Memphis, Tennessee
1730 27 March 1943

"I have a matter of some delicacy to discuss with you, Jesse," Braxton V. Lipscomb, President of the Planter's Bank & Trust Company of Memphis, announced to Rear Admiral Jesse R. Ball, USN, Flag Officer Commanding Naval Air Station, Memphis. The two men were in golf clothing, sitting in leather-upholstered captain's chairs at one of the dozen or so tables in the paneled barroom. It had been chilly on the links, and they had decided to have a little taste before taking a shower.

"I didn't think you invited me out here just to give me your money," Admiral Ball replied. At five dollars a point, their scores had been 85 for the Admiral and 97 for the banker, who just couldn't seem to get out of the sand trap on the fourteenth hole. "What's on your mind, Braxton?"

"Let me set the stage," Lipscomb said. "Identify the players, so to speak."

Admiral Ball nodded, took a sip of his Jack Daniel's, and waited for the banker to proceed.

"The first vice president of Planter's Bank and Trust is a fellow named Quincy T. Megham, Jr. They call him 'Quincy Junior.' I don't suppose you know him?"

Admiral Ball shook his head, "no."

"The main reason they call him Quincy Junior is that his father, the president before I took over, was naturally Quincy Senior."

"Makes sense," Admiral Ball said.

"The main reason Quincy Senior was president was that he and his family are the largest stockholders in the bank." He clarified: "Not the majority, but the largest."

"That makes sense, too."

"Now, Quincy Senior was a *banker*," Lipscomb said. "He taught me just about everything I know about banking."

Admiral Ball nodded again, and waited somewhat impatiently for the banker to go on. Admiral Ball was a Yankee. He had been appointed to the Naval Academy from Rhode Island, and his assignment to command the Memphis NAS had been the first time he had ever been stationed in the South. It had taken him two weeks to decide that civilian Rebels were just like the Rebels he had known in the Navy. They never got to the point without looking for at least two bushes to beat around.

"Well, he apparently did a good job," Admiral Ball said.

"Quincy Junior is not really a chip off the old block, unfortunately. He was not prepared to take over the bank when his daddy went to his reward."

"But he still owned a good deal of stock in the bank?"

"So we named him first vice president," Braxton Lipscomb said. "And I stepped into his daddy's shoes. The arrangement works. Quincy Junior is not really all that interested in the bank. But he has a title and an office, and it's something for him to do, somewhere for him to go, when he wakes up in the morning."

"I see."

"He does 'public relations' work, I guess you'd call it. He's a good-looking fellow, and he gives a pretty good speech, and the bank needs something like that."

"I understand."

"About a year ago, when the Tennessee Bankers Association needed someone to head up the Governmental Relations Committee, everybody agreed that Quincy Junior was just the man to head it up. Like I said, he gives a good speech, and he is the first vice president of Planter's Bank and Trust."

"What exactly does this Governmental Relations Committee do?"

"Most of it has to do with helping the war effort. Getting school kids to invest part of their allowances in War Bond Savings Stamps."

"They glue twenty-five-cent stamps in a book, and when they get twenty-five dollars' worth, they turn them in and get a twenty-five-dollar War Bond?"

"Actually, they get a twenty-five-dollar War Bond for eighteen dollars and fifty cents' worth of stamps. In ten years when they cash in the bond, they get the full amount, twenty-five dollars."

"I see."

"Quincy Junior also handles War Bond tours. You know, when Hollywood stars come around, or war heroes? He sets up the tour and handles the details."

"Sounds like valuable work," Admiral Ball said.

"It is. It is valuable, and it's right down Quincy Junior's alley."

"I can see where it would be."

Especially since good ol' Quincy Junior is not, unfortunately, a chip off Quincy Senior's block.

"It gets him out of town a good deal," Lipscomb said.

"I can see where it would."

"That's probably got something to do with the problem we have, him being away from home so much."

"What problem are we talking about?"

"Elizabeth-Sue Megham, Quincy Junior's wife. I can see where she would get lonely. It's natural."

"I don't think I'm following you, Braxton."

"Elizabeth-Sue is considerably younger than Quincy Junior. He's forty-five, she's thirty-three, maybe thirty-two."

"I see."

"To get right to the point, Jesse . . ."

Finally?

". . . Elizabeth-Sue seems to have gotten herself involved with one of your officers from the air station."

"I'm sorry to hear that."

"It's a delicate situation for all concerned."

"Do you have a name?"

"Lieutenant Malcolm S. Pickering. He's a Marine."

"He's a fine young officer, Brax. He served with distinction on Guadalcanal. He's an aviator. An ace, as a matter of fact." *Who is obviously screwing this female, who is at least ten years younger than her husband, who is apparently a jerk.* Admiral Ball thought of something else. "His father is a Marine general," he added.

"I'm sure he's a fine young man," Lipscomb said. "And—I like to think of myself as a man of the world—these things happen between young people. But the potential for real trouble—"

"I'll deal with it, Braxton," Admiral Ball interrupted.

"—is there, and we're going to have to do something about it, you and I."

"I said I'd deal with it," Admiral Ball said.

"I knew I could count on you," Braxton Lipscomb said.

[TWO]
The Marquis de Lafayette Suite
The Foster Lafayette Hotel
Washington, D.C.
1140 28 March 1943

Brigadier General Fleming Pickering, USMCR, was sitting in a red leather armchair in the library, a long thin black cigar in his mouth, his feet up on a matching footstool, and reading the *Washington Star*. Except for his tunic, he was in uniform. Hart had that laid out on a li-

brary table, making sure that all of its insignia, plus the
three-by-five-inch array of ribbons, were precisely in
position.

Hart's own uniform, complete to the cord identifying
him as an aide-de-camp to a general officer, was fresh
from the hotel valet.

Four new, identical canvas suitcases had been placed
in a row by the door to the sitting room. When they returned from lunch, they would immediately leave for Anacostia Naval Air Station. A Naval Air Transport
Command R4-D had been provided to take Pickering to
the West Coast. It would also carry just over two tons of
meteorological equipment and shortwave radios, plus two
Navy meteorologists. They would pick up three more
Navy meteorologists at the Great Lakes Naval Training
Station outside Chicago.

They were all enlisted men. One of those waiting at
Anacostia was a chief weatherman, an old salt with eighteen years in the Navy. With him was a weatherman third
class who had been a meteorologist before being drafted
into the Navy eight months previously. The men they
would pick up en route to San Diego were apprentice
seamen who had been meteorologists before they were
drafted into the Navy. All had volunteered for a "classified
mission outside the continental United States involving
great personal risk." None of them yet knew they were
going into the Gobi Desert to operate a weather station—
more accurately, that it was *hoped* they could be sent
there. Pickering planned to tell them what they had volunteered for on the long flight from San Diego to Pearl
Harbor.

Since their route to Chicago would make a stop at the
Memphis Naval Air Station almost convenient—they had
to refuel someplace en route, and Memphis was a good
choice—Pickering had told Captain David Haughton,
Navy Secretary Frank Knox's administrative assistant, to
schedule an overnight stop at Memphis.

He wanted to have dinner with Pick before departing
again for the Pacific. After wondering whether he was
taking advantage of his position in arranging it, he decided
to hell with it. He wanted to have dinner with Pick. There

was no telling when they would get together again. There was also no telling, in fact, when he'd see his wife again. She was too tied up in San Francisco, she told him, to come to San Diego to see him off.

The chime sounded. Pickering looked up at Second Lieutenant George F. Hart, USMCR. "With a little bit of luck, that will be someone regretting that lunch is off," he said, "and we can get the hell out of here now." He immediately regretted saying that. Hart was really looking forward to the luncheon. He had even told his father and mother about it.

Hart walked quickly out of the library to answer the door.

A moment later, Brigadier General F. L. Rickabee, USMC, entered the library, wearing his customary mussed and somewhat ill-fitting suit. He carried a briefcase chained to his wrist, and there was a bulge in his left armpit Pickering knew was a .45 pistol in a shoulder holster.

"Hello, Fritz," Pickering said cordially. "What's up?"

"I'm glad I caught you," Rickabee said, setting the briefcase on the library table and unlocking the handcuff.

"I was hoping you were a messenger telling me I didn't have to go," Pickering said without thinking.

Rickabee worked the combination lock on the battered briefcase, took from it a single sheet of paper, and handed it to Pickering. "I don't like to think how this came into my hands," Rickabee said.

"What is it?" Pickering asked, as he started to read it.

T O P S E C R E T

SPECIAL CHANNEL

DUPLICATION FORBIDDEN

US MILITARY MISSION TO CHINA
CHUNGKING

1730 25 MARCH 1943

VIA SPECIAL CHANNEL
EYES ONLY
BRIG GEN FLEMING PICKERING USMCR
DEPUTY DIRECTOR PACIFIC OPERATIONS
OSS WASHINGTON DC

1. ALL PERSONNEL AND EQUIPMENT ARRIVED
HERE SAFELY AND WITHOUT INCIDENT 0830
LOCALTIME 25MAR43.

2. MAJGEN F.T. DEMPSEY, USA, CHIEF SIGNAL
OFFICER HQ USMMCHI AND HIS DEPUTY BRIGGEN
J.R. NEWLEY, USA HAD PREVIOUS KNOWLEDGE
OF ARRIVAL PERSONNEL AND EQUIPMENT AND
PURPOSE THEREOF. MAJGEN DEMPSEY HAS
INFORMED THE UNDERSIGNED HIS AND BRIGGEN
NEWLEY'S MAGIC CLEARANCES ARE EXPECTED
SHORTLY.

3. MAJGEN DEMPSEY HAS STATED UNDERSIGNED
IS TO CONSIDER HIMSELF CRYPTOGRAPHIC
OFFICER ATTACHED TO HIS STAFF WITH
RESPONSIBILITY FOR MAGIC AND SPECIAL
CHANNEL. PRESUMABLY SAME APPLIES TO LT
EASTERBROOK, GUNNER RUTTERMAN AND ON HIS
ARRIVAL LT MOORE.

4. MAJGEN DEMPSEY HAS DIRECTED THAT ALL
MAGIC AND SPECIAL TRAFFIC COMMUNICATION
BE ROUTED THROUGH HIM OR HIS DEPUTY.

5. WHEN UNDERSIGNED RESPECTFULLY
DECLINED TO ANSWER MAJGEN DEMPSEY'S
QUESTIONS REGARDING MISSION OF MCCOY AND
ZIMMERMAN, MAJGEN DEMPSEY ORDERED THE
UNDERSIGNED TO ORDER MCCOY AND ZIMMERMAN
TO REPORT TO STATION CHIEF OSS CHUNGKING.

6. COMPLIANCE WITH THIS ORDER WAS NOT
POSSIBLE INASMUCH AS UNDERSIGNED HAD,
PRIOR TO REPORTING TO MAJGEN DEMPSEY,

```
DETACHED MCCOY AND ZIMMERMAN WITH ORDERS
TO PROCEED ON THEIR MISSION. THEIR
PRESENT WHEREABOUTS UNKNOWN, BUT STRONG
POSSIBILITY EXISTS THEY WILL CONTACT
UNDERSIGNED BEFORE LEAVING CHUNGKING
SOMETIME WITHIN NEXT SEVEN TO TEN DAYS.


7. IN COMPLIANCE WITH ORDERS OF MAJGEN
DEMPSEY, ALL FUTURE TRAFFIC UTILIZING
SPECIAL CHANNEL WILL BE BROUGHT TO HIS OR
BRIGGEN NEWLEY'S ATTENTION.


BANNING, LTCOL, USMC

T O P S E C R E T
```

"What the hell is this all about?" Pickering asked. He passed the document to Hart.

"It means MAGIC may damned well be compromised," Rickabee said.

"Yeah," Pickering agreed thoughtfully.

"Who told this General Dempsey?" Pickering asked, then warmed to his anger. "And where did he get the idea he has the authority to tell my people what to do? And what the hell is this 'OSS station Chungking'? *What* OSS station Chungking?"

"The MAGIC compromise, possible compromise, is more important than the Gobi Desert operation," Rickabee said. "This came in two hours ago. To confirm what I suspect, this is the first you've seen of it?"

"Yeah," Pickering said. "Damn!" He looked at Rickabee.

If it came in two hours ago, there was plenty of time to send it over here from the OSS.

"Where did you get it, Fritz?" Pickering asked evenly.

"One of my people was in the crypto room at Navy when it came in," Rickabee said. "A pal of Rutterman's, and an admirer of Banning and McCoy. He thought I would be interested in it, and defying just about every regulation in the book, he brought it to me. I don't know whether I should court-martial the sonofabitch or promote him for his initiative."

"This is the original?" Pickering asked, confused.

"No. That's the JCS file copy. You're supposed to have the original."

"And I damned sure don't!"

"Is Donovan going to be at lunch?" Rickabee asked.

"Oh, yeah. Marshall, Leahy, Donovan, me, and, of course Frank Knox and the President."

"You're in a minefield here, I guess you understand," Rickabee said. "*We're* in a minefield."

"You don't think Donovan is going to blame me for the compromise of MAGIC?"

"I don't know," Rickabee said. "I'm paid to look for the worst that can happen."

"General," Lieutenant Hart said, "the car is supposed to be downstairs right now."

"Okay," Pickering said as he rose to his feet and walked toward Hart, who was holding Pickering's tunic out to him. Pickering put it on and buttoned it, then, examining himself in the mirror, tugged at its skirt. Satisfied, he looked at Rickabee.

"He said his door would always be open to me. Let's see if that was just another campaign promise."

"Keep me posted," Rickabee said.

"Posted hell, General, you're going with me," Pickering said.

Neither the driver of the White House Packard limousine nor the Secret Service agent in the front seat raised any objection when Rickabee climbed into the car with Pickering and Hart. But when they drove across Pennsylvania Avenue to the White House, they were stopped by a determined guard at the gate. He was unimpressed with Rickabee's credentials as a Special Agent of Naval Intelligence, and immune to Pickering's announcement, "He's with me."

"I'm sorry, sir, the gentleman is not on my list, and I can't pass him."

"Get on the phone to either Admiral Leahy or General Marshall and tell him that General Pickering is here with

General Rickabee and we have to see either of them immediately," Pickering ordered. Then he had another thought: "Tell them I am not coming in without General Rickabee."

The guard went into the guardhouse and returned two minutes later.

"Drive to the side entrance, please," he said. "Someone will meet you."

When they were met by an Army colonel wearing the insignia of an aide-de-camp to a four-star general, Pickering concluded that the guard had spoken with either General George C. Marshall or someone empowered to act for him.

The colonel led them into an elevator, and they rode to the corridor outside the presidential apartments.

"I don't suppose any of you gentlemen are armed?" a Secret Service agent standing there asked politely.

"I am," Rickabee and Hart said, almost in unison. Rickabee took his .45 pistol from his shoulder holster and handed it to the Secret Service agent. Hart retrieved a snub-nosed .38 revolver from under his tunic and handed it over.

"I'll have to see what's in the briefcase," the Secret Service agent said.

"Not on your life," Rickabee said.

General George C. Marshall and Admiral William Leahy, trailed by Colonel William J. Donovan, came into the corridor. Donovan was in uniform—surprising Pickering. The top ribbon on his impressive row of brightly colored pieces of cloth was that representing the Medal of Honor he had won in France in the First World War.

"General," Leahy said.

"Admiral," Pickering said, "there's something I think I should bring to your immediate attention."

"A Special Channel from Chungking?"

"Yes, sir," Pickering said.

"May I ask what your aide is doing here, General?" Leahy said. "Before we get into this matter?"

"I asked the President if I might bring him to lunch," Pickering said. "And the President said, 'Absolutely.' "

"My God!" Donovan said in disbelief.

"Lieutenant Hart is cleared for MAGIC, Admiral, and knows all about Operation Gobi."

Leahy looked as if he was about to say something, but General Marshall, perhaps innocently, perhaps intentionally, shut him off before he could speak. "Colonel Donovan was just about to give us his thoughts on the Special Channel when you called from the gate," Marshall said. "You apparently have seen it?"

"Yes, sir," Pickering said, meeting Donovan's eyes. "The Special Channel I'm referring to was addressed to me."

"So I noticed," Marshall said. "I also noticed it was a Duplication Forbidden message."

"What General Pickering has seen, General," Rickabee said, "is the Joint Chiefs' file copy."

Marshall looked at Rickabee closely, even coldly. "Which presumably you have in there?" he asked, indicating Rickabee's briefcase.

"Yes, sir," Rickabee said.

"General Marshall and I," Admiral Leahy said, "are agreed that despite the seriousness of the matter, it is still a matter that can be dealt with administratively. In other words, we shouldn't waste the President's time with it at our luncheon. Does that pose a problem," he asked, looking first at Pickering and then at Donovan, "for either of you?"

"No, sir," Donovan said.

"Sir, I'm scheduled to depart from Anacostia at half past four," Pickering said. "Should I reschedule?"

"Why would you want to do that?" Donovan asked.

"I don't want to leave before this problem is dealt with," Pickering replied, but he looked at Leahy rather than at Donovan as he spoke.

"Once we decide who's responsible for this situation," Admiral Leahy said, "dealing with it won't take long. But to cover all the bases, while we're lunching with the President, General Rickabee, I don't think there will be any trouble setting another place for you at lunch."

"Aye, aye, sir," Rickabee said.

"And now, gentlemen," General Marshall said. "I suggest we join the President."

* * *

The President was in his wheelchair, sitting at the head of a table set for lunch. Secretary of the Navy Frank Knox was sitting beside him, his chair pulled close. Before them on the table was a stack of eight-by-ten-inch photographs that Roosevelt was examining carefully.

"What they have been doing, Frank," Roosevelt said, without taking his cigarette holder from his mouth, "is gathering their courage to face the lion in his den."

"Nothing like that at all, Mr. President," General Marshall said. "An administrative matter."

"I wonder why I have trouble believing that," Roosevelt said, smiling broadly.

" 'Administrative' can cover a lot of territory, Mr. President," Secretary Knox said.

"Good to see you, Fleming," the President said. "You're all prepared, I gather, for your trip to the mysterious East?"

"And all points in between, sir," Pickering said.

"General Rickabee I know," the President said. "It's good to see you, Fritz."

"Good afternoon, Mr. President."

"But I don't know this young fellow," Roosevelt went on.

"Mr. President, may I present Lieutenant George F. Hart?" Pickering said. "He's both my aide-de-camp and my friend."

Roosevelt offered his hand.

"I recognize the name," the President said. "You must be an unusual young man, Lieutenant, if all these old fogies are agreed you can be entrusted to hold a MAGIC clearance."

Hart actually blushed. Leahy and Pickering exchanged looks.

"I'm honored, Mr. President," Hart said.

A white-jacketed steward passed a tray of drinks, indicating with his head which glass the men were to take. Pickering sipped his and recognized the taste. It was Famous Grouse. He wondered if there was a card file kept somewhere with drink preferences listed on it.

"When we're finished," Roosevelt said to the steward,

"ask the photographer to take a picture of me with Lieutenant Hart. Perhaps his parents would like to have one."

"Thank you very much, Mr. President," Hart said.

"I have a soft spot for young Marine officers," Roosevelt said. "Very possibly because my son Jimmy is one of you."

"Yes, sir, I know," Hart said.

"Let me propose a toast," the President said. "To the success of General Pickering's mission."

The others raised their glasses and there were murmured "Hear, hears."

"I feel a good deal better about this," the President said mischievously, "now that Bill and Fleming have kissed and made up."

"I'll agree with the 'made up' part, Franklin," Donovan said, "but I want to go on record as saying we have never kissed."

Pickering laughed politely. None of the others did.

Roosevelt picked up on this and correctly guessed the reason.

"Bill, when you're wearing your uniform, you're supposed to call me 'Sir,' and 'Mr. President,' and bow three times before backing out of my presence."

"No disrespect was intended, sir, if I have to say that."

"What I think it is, Bill, is that you're nervous as the second junior officer present with all these admirals and generals."

"That may be it, sir."

"We're going to have to see if we can't get you a star, Bill, so that you'll feel at home."

There was dutiful laughter.

"Speaking of generals," Frank Knox said, "is someone going to volunteer to tell me why General Rickabee is joining us?"

"An administrative matter, Mr. Secretary," Admiral Leahy said. "We were a little pressed for time. The General met us here, and we'll deal with the matter after lunch."

"What sort of an administrative matter? Important enough to have Pickering bring Fritz here? And look uncomfortable when I asked why?"

"There was a radio from Chungking," Admiral Leahy said. "Something we all felt should be dealt with before General Pickering left for Hawaii."

"Now *my* curiosity is aroused," the President said. "I always get very curious when people are reluctant to talk about anything."

Everyone looked at Admiral Leahy, who took a long moment to collect his thoughts before beginning:

"Mr. President, you are aware that at your direction, and against my recommendation and that of General Marshall, we sent a MAGIC device, together with the personnel to op—"

"Hold it a second, Admiral," the President interrupted. "I just had another one of my inspirations. Correct me if I'm wrong, Frank, but didn't you have Fleming commissioned because you knew he would report back to you what you should know, rather than what people wanted you to hear?"

"That's correct, Mr. President," the Secretary of the Navy said.

"You have the floor, General Pickering," the President said, tempering the order with one of his famous smiles. "Proceed."

"What we know for sure, Mr. President," Pickering began, "is that someone ran off at the mouth about the MAGIC machine going to Chungking."

"Has MAGIC been compromised?" Roosevelt asked, now deadly serious. "Is this what everyone has been working up the courage to tell me?"

"We don't believe, based on the facts available—" Admiral Leahy said.

"Admiral," the President interrupted impatiently, "General Pickering has the floor."

"Sorry, sir," Leahy said, flushing.

"What we do know for sure, Mr. President, is that when Colonel Banning got to Chungking, they knew he was coming and why."

"Banning took a MAGIC machine to Chungking?"

"Two machines, sir."

"Who is 'they' as in 'they knew he was coming'?"

"The signal officer and his deputy, sir."

"And they don't have MAGIC clearances? Then how in the hell did they find out?"

"We don't know that yet, sir."

"How many people knew what was happening?"

"It's a very short list, sir," Pickering said. "Aside from the people in this room, only those people in JCS who were involved."

"Your people were involved, Fleming," Donovan said.

"Plus, of course, two people at OSS, besides Colonel Donovan and me," Pickering said icily. "And I don't think any of my people even know anyone in Chungking—certainly not these signal officers."

"What about the cryptographers in Chungking?" Donovan asked.

"So far as I know, they know *no one* in Chungking," Pickering said.

"Okay," Donovan said. "That narrows it down to people in my shop and people at the JCS."

"Admiral, we can't have things like this," the President said. "It has to be nipped in the bud."

"I agree, sir," Admiral Leahy said.

"I'll leave getting to the bottom of this to you. As well as ensuring that it—or the circumstances that permitted it—never happens again."

"Yes, Mr. President," Admiral Leahy said.

"And I want Bill Donovan and Fleming Pickering involved. Fleming, you might not be able to get away today. I want you here until this is resolved."

"Yes, Mr. President," Pickering said.

"I think General Rickabee should be involved, too," Navy Secretary Knox said. "He's very good about finding snakes under rocks."

It was obvious that neither Admiral Leahy nor General Marshall liked the suggestion. Neither protested, but both looked at the President for his decision.

"That might prove very useful," the President said.

"What about Operation Gobi?" Knox asked. "Is that compromised, too?"

"This signal officer—his name is Dempsey—asked Colonel Banning what McCoy and Zimmerman—"

"McCoy?" Roosevelt interrupted again. "The young

chap who was with Jimmy at Makin Island? Who briefed us on General Fertig?"

"Yes, sir. He's going into the Gobi Desert to try to establish contact with the Americans there."

"What's this signal corps officer got to do with that? I thought it was agreed that you and Bill—the OSS—were going to undertake that mission."

"Apparently, Mr. President, this fellow wanted to know what Captain McCoy's special mission was. On the JCS orders on which Banning and the devices went to Chungking, it was referred to, vaguely, as a JCS mission. When Banning refused to tell him—"

"As well he should have," the President interrupted.

"—this General ordered Banning to have McCoy report to the OSS Station Chief in Chungking," Pickering went on.

"I don't understand," the President said.

"Until I got Colonel Banning's Special Channel, Mr. President, I didn't know there was an OSS station in Chungking."

"You didn't know about an OSS station in Chungking?" the President asked.

"No, sir, I did not," Pickering said, looking at Colonel Donovan.

"That's odd, isn't it, Bill?" the President said to Donovan. "The signal officer in Chungking knows about an OSS station there, and the OSS Deputy Director for Pacific Operations doesn't?"

"Mr. President—" Donovan began.

The President held up his hand to shut him off. Then he kept him waiting while he fished a cigarette from a silver box, stuffed it into his holder, and waited for the steward to produce a light for it. Then he went on, calmly, not smiling: "Do what you have to do, Admiral," the President said, "to straighten out this 'administrative matter.' Just as soon as we finish our lunch."

"Yes, Mr. President."

[THREE]
The White Room
The Office of Strategic Services
The National Institutes of Health Building
Washington, D.C.
1405 28 March 1943

Immediately after lunch, in the corridor outside the presidential apartment, Colonel Donovan suggested that the most suitable place to conduct their business would be at the OSS. "It would attract attention if Pickering, Rickabee, or I appear at the Joint Chiefs of Staff," he argued. "The White Room will provide a secure space, and it's equipped with microphones, in case Admiral Leahy would like a written record of what was said."

Admiral Leahy nodded his agreement.

When Admiral Leahy's Cadillac limousine, the White House Packard limousine that had carried Pickering, Hart, and Rickabee to the White House, and Donovan's Buick Roadmaster rolled up outside the White House, Donovan made a "follow me" gesture to the Buick's driver and climbed into Leahy's Cadillac.

Once they were in the White House Packard, Rickabee gave voice to what Pickering was thinking: "I wonder what that sonofabitch is saying to Leahy?"

"We'll find out soon enough, I suppose," Pickering replied.

As soon as the small convoy arrived at the National Institutes of Health Building, Leahy and Donovan got out and waited for the others to join them. "Colonel Donovan," Leahy began, "has pointed out to me that he is an attorney and has experienced distasteful interrogations. Would either of you object to his conducting the interrogations? We will be able to listen on earphones, he tells me."

"Sir, what if we have questions Colonel Donovan didn't think to ask?" Rickabee asked.

"Colonel Donovan brought that up himself," Leahy said. "When he is finished with the individual, he will join us. If you have any questions, he will either ask them

himself, or you may. Having an experienced man do the
interviews strikes me as the quickest way to get to the
bottom of this."

"I think it's a fine idea, sir," Pickering said.

Rickabee gave him a surprised look.

But first they had to get into the building. In the belief
that he and Hart would not be returning to OSS headquarters before traveling to the Pacific, Pickering had ordered Hart to place their red-striped Any Area Any Time
identification·badges in the safe in his apartment in the
Foster Lafayette. Neither General Rickabee nor Admiral
Leahy had OSS identification badges.

If he were Donovan, Pickering knew, he would have
just marched past the guards, saying something like,
"these people are with me," especially since one of the
people with him was the chief of staff to the President of
the United States.

But Donovan didn't.

"Sorry about the inconvenience, Admiral," he said.
"We didn't plan on having you with us this morning."

Leahy and Rickabee were furnished with Visitor 5th
Floor Only badges, and pinned them to their lapels.

Though Donovan was visibly annoyed when Pickering
told the guard lieutenant, "Lieutenant Hart and I will need
a couple of those, too, please," he said nothing.

They rode the elevator to the fifth floor and walked
down the corridor to Donovan's office.

The Deputy Director (Administration) was behind his
desk. He rose to his feet. "Good morning, Admiral," he
said. "Mr. Director." He nodded at Pickering, Rickabee,
and Hart, but didn't say anything.

"Something's come up, Charley," Donovan said. "Is
anyone using the White Room?"

"No, Mr. Director."

"How long will it take you to get . . . let's say, three
stenographers up and running?"

The DDA didn't respond directly. Instead he picked up
one of the telephones on his desk, pushed a button on it,
and announced, "The Director requires three stenographers in the transcription room immediately." He put the

receiver back in its cradle and went on: "By the time we walk down the corridor, Mr. Director, you'll have your stenographers."

Donovan nodded. "Call JCS," he ordered. "Tell General Adamson that Admiral Leahy wishes to see him and Colonel . . . What's his name, Fleming?"

"Albright," Pickering furnished.

". . . Colonel Albright here as soon as possible. Have badges waiting for them downstairs."

"General Adamson has a badge, sir," the DDA said.

"And locate the Deputy Director (Operations) and tell him I need to see him immediately."

"He's on his way here from the training establishment, Mr. Director."

"Is there a radio in his car?"

"Yes, sir."

"Contact him and make sure he is coming here," Donovan ordered. "And then join us, please, in the White Room."

"Yes, Mr. Director."

"I don't believe you've seen the White Room, have you, Admiral?" Donovan said to Leahy.

Leahy shook his head, "no."

"If you'll follow me, please, Admiral?" Donovan said, and led the group down the corridor to the White Room. By the time they had satisfied the two guards at the door that they were who they represented themselves to be, and Donovan had authorized Rickabee and Leahy to go inside, the DDA had caught up with them.

They entered the White Room.

"Charley, explain to the Admiral and these gentlemen how the transcription system works," General Donovan ordered.

"Yes, sir," the DDA said. "Microphones have been placed in various locations around the room," he began. "They are connected with an amplification system in the room behind that door." He pointed to a door at the rear of the room. "There are provisions for six sets of headphones, although our experience has been that we have never needed more than three stenographers to transcribe even the largest conference. So each of you gentlemen will have earphones."

"I took that precaution, sir. They are either next door, or will be momentarily."

"They will let us know when General Adamson and the others arrive, right?" Donovan asked.

"The Deputy Director (Operations), Mr. Director, said he will be here in no more than ten minutes. General Adamson, who has Colonel Albright with him, has probably left the Pentagon by now." He paused and then added: "Mr. Director, General Adamson was naturally curious about what this is all about."

"I'm sure he was, Charley, and I'm sure you are, too. You find out first. You can be our guinea pig, so to speak. Will you take these gentlemen to the stenographer's room, make sure everything is in place? And then come back in here. We'll start with you. Pure formality, of course."

Well, Pickering thought, *what did I expect Donovan to do? Accuse his Director for Administration of having a big mouth?*

Because of the three stenographers—two middle-aged women and a young man—there were only enough spare headphones for three people. Pickering solved that problem by separating one of the earphones on his headset from the frame and, motioning Hart to stand close to him, handed him the loose earphone.

He saw Leahy looking at him curiously, perhaps disapprovingly. "I like to have George listen in on everything, Admiral," Pickering said. "To refresh my memory."

"I see."

"He used to be a police detective," Pickering went on.

"Perhaps we should have left him in there with Donovan," Admiral Leahy said.

"Okay, Charley, let's have our practice run," Donovan's voice came, very clearly, into Pickering's single earphone.

"Yes, Mr. Director."

"This is pretty serious business," Donovan said. "Someone has been talking too much about MAGIC."

"Yes, sir?"

"We're trying to find out who, and under what circumstances," Donovan said, and then, before the DDA could reply, said, "If you can all hear us in there, let me know."

"George," Pickering ordered.

Hart took his loose earphone from his ear, let it dangle from Pickering's headset, looked at everybody in the room until they nodded, and then walked to the door and announced, "Colonel, we read you five-by-five."

He closed the door and resumed his place next to Pickering.

"Okay, Charley, at least that much works," Donovan's voice came over the system.

"I personally check on the system frequently, Mr. Director," the DDA said.

"Good idea," Donovan said. "Okay. Now . . . I really don't know how to start this . . . The possible compromise occurred in connection with the shipment of MAGIC devices to Chungking."

"When I saw General Pickering, Mr. Director, I thought that might be the case."

"Were you happy with the security arrangements, Charley? You were, of course, familiar with them?"

"Yes, sir. I was familiar with them. And no, sir, I wasn't absolutely satisfied with the security arrangements."

"In what regard, Charley?"

"It's a little embarrassing for me, sir, with General Pickering privy to this."

"That can't be helped, I'm afraid. What is it about General Pickering and the MAGIC movement that made you uncomfortable?"

What is this sonofabitch doing? Pickering wondered. *Asking questions that make me look like a fool? Trying to lay the blame on me?*

"Well, there was the matter of the CIC agents, Mr. Director."

"Tell me about that, Charley."

"General Adamson had arranged for Army CIC agents to accompany the MAGIC devices. General Pickering said that his people could adequately guard the devices and declined the services of the CIC. Is that what's happened, sir? Something has happened to the devices?"

"You and General Adamson worked pretty closely on the whole thing together?"

"Yes, sir."

"And General Adamson told you that General Pickering declined the use of CIC agents?"

"Yes, sir."

"And he wasn't satisfied when you told him that Pickering's people were probably as well-qualified to guard the devices as CIC agents?"

"No, sir, he wasn't. And frankly, neither was I."

"Why was that, Charley? I mean, giving General Pickering the benefit of the doubt here. He has a good deal of faith in Colonel Banning and Captain McCoy . . ."

"They had no real experience in transporting the devices, sir. And General Adamson has."

"Did you discuss this with the Deputy Director (Operations)?"

"Well, I tried to, sir. But he seemed to feel that it was General Pickering's operation, and that we shouldn't interfere."

"But you and General Adamson remained concerned?"

"Yes, sir."

"You were afraid that the movement of the devices wasn't as secure as it could be? That perhaps there was a genuine risk that the operation to move them . . ."

"Operation China Clipper, sir," the DDA furnished.

". . . that Operation China Clipper would be compromised, and perhaps MAGIC itself?"

"Both General Adamson and I felt that was a real possibility, Mr. Director."

"I'm surprised, Charley, that General Adamson didn't do something about it, since both of you were concerned."

"I think he did, sir."

"Really? What?"

"General Adamson and General Dempsey are old friends. Dempsey is the military mission to China signal officer. They were classmates at the Command and General Staff College. He sent him a heads-up."

"So that General . . . Dempsey, you said?"

"Yes, sir. Major General F. T. Dempsey."

"So that General Dempsey would be aware of the potential problem?"

"Exactly, sir. Both the potential problems with Operation China Clipper and with—I don't quite know how to phrase this—the potential problems with Lieutenant Colonel Banning."

"A moment ago you said that you *think* General Adamson sent a heads-up to General Dempsey. Presumably by Top Secret message?"

"He showed me a copy of the heads-up, sir. And, of course, it was a Top Secret, Eyes Only, General Dempsey."

"Does General Dempsey have a MAGIC clearance?" Donovan asked.

"Not at the moment, sir. But I'm sure it's in the works."

"Okay, Charley," Donovan said. "That's enough."

"Sir?"

"What happens now, Charley, is that as of this moment, I have accepted your resignation."

"Sir?"

"As of this moment, your duties will be assumed by your deputy," Donovan said. "His first duty will be to go through your desk, gather up your personal belongings, and have them delivered to your home, where you will have been taken by our security people, and will be waiting, under guard, for my decision about what to do with you. My immediate reaction is to send you over to St. Elizabeth's in a straitjacket and keep you there until the war is over, but I know that reaction is colored by my anger, so I want to think that through." St. Elizabeth's was the Federal government psychiatric hospital in the District of Columbia.

"Sir, I don't understand."

"Most of my anger is directed at myself. I'm the man who put you in a position where you could do all this damage. I should have known that you couldn't take orders."

"Sir, I was simply trying to carry out my responsibilities to the best of my ability."

"Yeah, I know. That's what makes this so sad. I should have known that you weren't equipped to discharge those responsibilities. What you have done, Charley, and I don't think you really understand this, is put hundreds of thousands of lives at risk—and that's what the compromise of MAGIC would mean—by disobeying your orders. If I have to explain it to you: the moment you heard that General Adamson was even thinking of communicating anything about MAGIC to anyone who does not have a MAGIC clearance, you were supposed to bring this to my attention."

"Sir, General Adamson is the Secretary of the Joint Chiefs of Staff. . . ."

"That's my point, Charley, you still don't understand what you both have done," Donovan said calmly, even sadly. "Wait here, Charley, someone will come for you."

Donovan walked into the transcription room.

"Admiral, would you like my resignation?"

"I don't see where that would accomplish anything, Colonel," Admiral Leahy said. "I would recommend to the President that he decline your resignation."

"In that case, sir, what would you like me to do?"

"I think we should next talk to General Adamson, and then to Colonel Albright," Leahy said. "To see how far down this unfortunate business has gone."

" 'We,' sir?"

"On reflection, I will talk to General Adamson, alone," Leahy said. "He is due here any moment. But by the time he gets here, the White Room will be available, will it not?"

"Yes, sir. Give me a moment to find the security duty officer, and to locate Charley's deputy to tell him what he has to do."

One of the White Room guards put his head into the transcription room.

"Colonel Donovan, General Adamson is being checked into the White Room."

"Thank you," Donovan said, and reached for a headset. He sensed Pickering's eyes on him.

"Pickering, I guess I owe you an apology."

"The shoe's on the other foot, Mr. Director," General

Pickering said. "I thought, at first, that you were trying to cover for that sonofabitch. I'm truly sorry."

"So am I," Donovan said, and put the earphones over his head.

"Good afternoon, Admiral," the voice of Major General Charles M. Adamson, USA, came clearly over the transcription system headsets. "I came as quickly as I could."

Admiral William D. Leahy, USN, Chief of Staff to the Commander in Chief of the Armed Forces of the United States, did not respond to the greeting.

"It has been alleged, General," Leahy began, "that you sent a Top Secret message to the signal officer of the U.S. military mission to China which made reference to Operation China Clipper. Is this true?"

There was a perceptible hesitation before General Adamson replied.

"Yes, sir."

"Specifically, to Major General F. T. Dempsey?"

"Yes, sir, the message was addressed, Eyes Only, General Dempsey."

"I'm really sorry to hear that, General," Admiral Leahy said.

"Admiral, may I explain the circumstances?"

Leahy ignored the question.

"General Dempsey apparently believes that both he and his deputy will shortly be granted MAGIC security clearances. Do you have any idea where he got that idea?"

"Yes, sir. Sir, I presumed that it would only be a matter of time before General Dempsey would be granted access to MAGIC. I don't see how he could perform his duties in connection with MAGIC without such clearance."

"And you therefore told him you believed he, and presumably his deputy as well, would shortly have MAGIC clearance?"

"Yes, sir. And I also cautioned him that the MAGIC cryptographic officer who was being sent to military mission China in charge of the devices did not enjoy the full confidence of either myself or the OSS, and that he—"

"Who told you, General, that Colonel Banning does not enjoy the full confidence of the OSS?"

"Sir, that information was given to me in confidence. I'm reluctant—"

"Was it the OSS Deputy Director (Administration)?"

"Yes, sir."

"I regret to inform you, sir, that you stand relieved of your duties at JCS. You will proceed directly from this room to your quarters, where you will hold yourself available for orders from General Marshall. I inform you, sir, that when I speak to General Marshall, I shall recommend to him that you be immediately reduced to whatever permanent grade you hold."

There was a long silence.

"That will be all," Admiral Leahy said. "You are dismissed."

"Yes, sir."

"Donovan," Admiral Leahy said, as he walked into the transcription room, "we have to make sure that nothing like this can ever happen again in the future."

"Yes, sir," Donovan said.

"I think you'd do better talking to Colonel Albright than I would, Colonel."

"Yes, sir," Donovan said, handed his headset to the Admiral, and walked into the White Room.

"I don't like to think, Pickering," Admiral Leahy said, "what would have happened if your Colonel Banning had been cowed by General Dempsey."

"What's going to happen to General Adamson, sir?"

"In any army but ours, he would be handed a pistol and expected to do the right thing. I'm not sure if he's a colonel or a lieutenant colonel in the regular army. I suppose he'll wind up as commanding officer, or executive officer, of a POW camp. Something like that."

"That's sad."

"Yes, it is," Leahy said. "Eisenhower has already reduced six general officers to their permanent grade and sent them home for not being able to keep their mouths shut."

"I didn't know that."

"General, it's not the sort of thing they issue press releases about," Leahy said, and put his headset on.

*   *   *

"To get right to the point, Colonel Albright," Donovan's voice came over the earphones, "it has come to my attention that a back-channel message was sent to the signal officer, Eyes Only, Major General Dempsey, of the military mission to China, which among other things announced the imminent arrival of MAGIC devices and personnel to operate the Special Channel. Did you have anything to do with that message?"

"No, sir," Colonel H. A. Albright said immediately.

"Do you know anything about such a message?"

"No, sir," Albright said immediately.

"Have you any idea who could have sent such a message."

Colonel Albright did not reply.

"Colonel, do you have any idea who could have sent such a message?" Donovan asked, impatience in his voice.

"I don't like to speculate about that sort of thing, Colonel."

"Let me rephrase, Colonel. I am not asking for a name. Do you have any private suspicions about who would have sent such a message?"

Again Albright didn't reply.

"Yes or no, Colonel?" Donovan asked, not unkindly.

After a perceptible hesitation, Albright replied, "Colonel, to repeat myself, I don't like to speculate about such matters."

"Yes or no?"

"If I have your word, Colonel, that you will not ask me for a name?"

"You have my word."

"Yes, sir, I think I could make a good guess who would send such a message."

"But you won't give me the name?"

"That's correct."

"I could get General Adamson in here and have him order you to give a name. For God's sake, Albright, we're talking about the compromise of MAGIC."

Albright didn't reply.

"If you refused a legal order from General Adamson,

you would, as I'm sure you realize, be opening yourself up for disciplinary action?"

"Any accusation—and that's what it would be—I would make without knowledge of the facts would ruin someone's career, even if I was wrong. In that circumstance . . ."

"Wait here, please, Colonel," Donovan said. "I'll be back in a moment."

"If you're going for General Adamson, Colonel," Colonel Albright said, "I can probably save you time. I won't answer the question from him, either."

"Just wait here, please, Colonel," Donovan said.

"I feel like Diogenes," Donovan said when he walked into the transcription room. "I've just found an honest—read, ethical—man."

"In the Navy, they call that loyalty upward. It's commendable," Admiral Leahy said. "But is this the exception that proves the rule?"

"The question is," Pickering said, "did Albright know about the heads-up? If he did and didn't report it, he's wrong. If he didn't, the question is what would he have done if he did know about it."

"Do you think he knew, Pickering?" Leahy asked.

"No, I don't," Pickering said thoughtfully, and only then remembered to add, "Sir."

Leahy pointed at Second Lieutenant Hart.

"I should have asked that question of you first, son," he said. "So your answer would not be colored by hearing what General Pickering said."

"He would have told somebody, sir," Hart replied. "He guards MAGIC like a lioness guards her cubs. And he was almost like one of us, sir. That message could have fucked up McCoy and Zimmerman. Whatever it cost him, he'd have done whatever he had to do to keep that from happening."

"General Rickabee?"

My God, I forgot he's here, Pickering thought, actually surprised to see him, and even more surprised to realize that he had been there all the time.

And he has never opened his mouth.

Does that mean he was cowed by Donovan and Leahy?

Or that he had nothing to say? With the implication he approved of the way Donovan has conducted the questioning?

"Admiral, I'd bet on Albright," Rickabee replied. "He knows when to keep his mouth shut."

So much for my theory that Fritz is cowed by Admiral Leahy.

"Colonel Donovan?" Leahy asked.

"If I had to bet on it, sir—and that's what we're doing, isn't it? Taking a chance with other people's lives?—I don't think Albright knew, and I think if he knew, he would have done whatever had to be done."

"That makes it unanimous, gentlemen," Admiral Leahy said.

"So what do we do now?" Pickering asked. "The way I read Colonel Banning's back channel, anything we send over the Special Channel to Chungking will be read by Dempsey and/or his deputy."

"Can we get something to your station chief in Chungking, Donovan, with any assurance that it won't be read by anyone else?" Leahy asked.

"I know very little about the Chungking Station, or how it operates," Pickering said coldly. "The first time I heard we have—more correctly, that *I* have—an OSS station in Chungking was in Banning's Special Channel."

"You have station chiefs all over the Pacific, General," Donovan said. "Including one in Chungking. You were supposed to be briefed on that. I presumed that you had been."

"Who was supposed to brief me, your Deputy Director (Administration)?" Pickering asked sarcastically.

"As a matter of fact, yes."

"Well, goddamn it, I wasn't," Pickering said. "Now I'm starting to wonder what else I should know that I haven't been told."

"Your position, Colonel Donovan," Leahy asked, "is that General Pickering's—what shall I say, 'inadequate briefing'?—was another failure on the part of your Director for Administration, and that until just now, you knew nothing about it?"

"It's a failure on my part, Admiral," Donovan said sincerely. "It was my responsibility to make sure that *my* DDA did what he was supposed to do. And I just didn't do it."

"What's the damage assessment?" Leahy asked, looking at Pickering.

"Reading between the lines of Colonel Banning's backchannel, Admiral, what he's done is told McCoy and Zimmerman to make themselves scarce while he waits to see what I'm going to be able to do for them."

"There was supposed be a message to the Chungking station chief giving him a heads-up that Banning and the others were coming," Donovan said.

"By *name*?" Admiral Leahy asked softly. But there was enormous menace in his voice.

"No, sir," Donovan said. "The standard phraseology would be 'you will be contacted by an officer whose orders will be self-explanatory,' or words to that effect."

"Was this message sent?" Leahy asked.

"What difference would that make?" Pickering snapped. "Banning wasn't told about an OSS station chief."

Leahy gave him a dirty look.

Donovan picked up a telephone and dialed a three digit number. "I'm in the transcription room," he ordered. "I want a copy of every message sent to Chungking since we became involved with Operation Gobi, and I want them right now."

"Has this officer, whose name I still don't know, been made aware that I was appointed Deputy Director (Pacific)?" Pickering asked sarcastically.

"General, make a very serious attempt to put your anger under control," Admiral Leahy said, almost conversationally, but the enormous menace was again present.

"I beg the Admiral's pardon," Pickering said.

"My original question, which started all this, was 'Can we communicate with the OSS station chief in Chungking without the U.S. MilMission to China signal officer reading it?'"

"If I may answer General Pickering first, sir," Donovan said, and then went on without giving Leahy a chance to stop him: "Of course. He's at your orders."

Pickering said nothing.

"To answer your question, Admiral," Donovan went on. "Sir, since the U.S. MilMissionChi signal officer has ordered Banning to route everything through him, I would say, that we cannot communicate with any degree of security, vis-à-vis the signal officer, with the Chungking station chief."

Pickering thought: *I can raise further hell about Donovan hiding this station chief, and presumably some sort of in-place organization—and goddamn it, it was wrong—and not only look like a petulant child—the sonofabitch is the Director, and can do what he wants—or for once in my life I can keep my mouth shut.*

"I suggest we Special Channel Colonel Waterson in Brisbane," Pickering began.

"Who is he?" Leahy asked.

"The OSS station chief. He works for me," Donovan said, then corrected himself. "He works for Pickering."

"We know the Special Channel there is secure," Pickering went on, "and if Colonel Waterson has not yet been cleared for MAGIC . . ."

"He has been cleared," Leahy said.

And, Christ, I did the same thing Adamson did, Pickering thought. *I told him before the fact.*

"We can Special Channel Waterson with whatever orders you're going to give the commanding general of the military mission to China, plus what orders I'm going to give him, and have him carry them physically to Chungking."

"This is a JCS matter," Leahy said. "I'll be giving the orders, Pickering."

"You'll have to forgive me, Admiral. I don't really know how the system works. But if you're sending orders, sir, I respectfully request that you tell this General Dempsey to keep his hands off my men."

"You may consider that added to the orders I will send to Chungking," Leahy said. "I also consider it important that someone get to Chungking as quickly as possible to see that my orders are carried out. Right now, Pickering, you're the logical choice to do that."

"Am I qualified to do that, sir?"

"If I didn't think so, I wouldn't send you."

"Aye, aye, sir."

"What I'm asking, Pickering, considering the President gave Donovan, me, and you the responsibility to deal with this affair, is whether you are satisfied that Donovan and I can handle it from here on."

Pickering thought that over a moment before replying. Then he looked at Donovan. "I have no doubt whatever, Admiral, that with Colonel Donovan here, I am not needed."

"How soon can you be in Chungking?" Leahy asked.

"I'd planned to stop in Australia on the way, sir," Pickering replied. "But under the circumstances, I could skip that."

"Is there any reason you couldn't go to Chungking the way Banning and the devices went?" Donovan asked. "Via Europe? It would be quicker."

"I'm taking the meteorologists and their equipment with me to Pearl Harbor. I don't want them shunted aside en route because they're enlisted men. And I'd like to see how they're coming with the submarine."

"Do what you think is best," Leahy said, putting out his hand. "But get to Chungking as quickly as you can."

"Aye, aye, sir." Pickering looked around the small room for Hart. "Let's go, George."

"For what it's worth, Fleming," Donovan said, as Pickering reached the door. Pickering turned to face him. "I've changed my mind again. The former Deputy Director (Administration) of the OSS will enter St. Elizabeth's within the hour."

"What good will that do?"

"It'll make me feel better, and it might be educational for others," Donovan said. The two men locked eyes. Finally, Pickering shrugged and followed Lieutenant Hart into the corridor.

XVII

[ONE]
Base Operations
Anacostia Naval Air Station
Washington, D.C.
1730 28 March 1943

One of the petty officers behind the counter at base operations spotted General Pickering as he passed through the door. He came to attention and loudly announced, "General officer on deck!"

Ten people were in the room. All of them popped to attention. Pickering saw that two of them—a chief and a third-class—wore the sleeve insignia of weathermen and presumed they were the meteorologists who had volunteered for the Gobi Desert operation. He smiled at them and waved his hand, ordering them to sit down again.

"As you were," Pickering said, as he walked to the counter. "My name is Pickering. There's supposed to be an airplane—"

"Yes, sir. General McInerney is expecting the general, sir," a chief petty officer said, quickly rising from his desk and walking to the counter. "If the general will please follow me, sir?"

"What did you say about General McInerney, Chief?"

"Sir, General McInerney has been waiting for the general, sir. He asked me to bring you into Flight Planning."

"In a moment," Pickering said, and walked to the two sailors, who rose to their feet.

Pickering put out his hand.

"Chief, I'm General Pickering," he said.

"Chief Spectowski, sir," the chief said. "This is Weatherman Third Damon."

Pickering shook Damon's hand.

"I can tell you this much," Pickering said. "Our ultimate destination, right now, is Pearl Harbor. We're going to spend the night in Memphis, fly on to Chicago in the morning to pick up three more people, and then fly to San Diego. From San Diego, we'll go Naval Air Transport Command to Pearl. I'm sorry, but that's all I can tell you. Except that what you'll be doing will be damned important."

"Yes, sir," Weatherman Third Damon said.

Chief Spectowski nodded but didn't speak.

"When we get to Pearl, I'll probably be able to tell you some more," Pickering said. "But for now, that's it."

"I understand, sir," the chief said.

"I don't know exactly what's happening here, but as soon as I find out, I'll let you know," Pickering said.

"Yes, sir," the two of them said, almost in unison.

Pickering turned, and with Hart on his heels, followed the base operations chief through a door bearing a large sign, AIR CREWS ONLY, into a room whose walls, and a large table in the center, were covered with aerial charts.

McInerney and First Lieutenant Anthony I. Sylvester, his aide-de-camp, were standing in front of one of the aerial charts on the wall.

"Hello, Mac," Pickering said.

McInerney turned to look at him.

"Another ten minutes, General, and you would have

walked to Memphis," McInerney said. "Where the hell have you been?"

"It's a long and painful story," Pickering said, smiling at his old friend. "Not that I'm not glad to see you, but what the hell are you doing here?"

"Before we get into that, General, you don't notice anything different about me?"

Pickering studied him, then shook his head, "no."

"I never thought you were very bright, but I did think you were capable of counting as high as two," McInerney said.

Pickering now understood. There were two stars on each of McInerney's collar points, and on each epaulet. McInerney was now a major general.

"Well, when did that happen? Damn, Mac, it's long overdue!"

"This morning," McInerney said. "Loudly complaining that the Corps is going to hell, the Commandant pinned them on himself."

"Well, congratulations!"

"Thank you, Flem," McInerney said. "Who would have believed, at Château-Thierry?"

"I would have," Pickering joked. "Anyone as ugly as you was sure to get to be a major general, if he stuck around long enough, and didn't get shot by a jealous husband first."

"You can go to hell, General."

"When I come back, we'll have a party," Pickering said.

"That's what we're going to do tonight," McInerney said.

"I'm on my way to Pearl Harbor."

"You're on your way to Memphis," McInerney corrected him. "And I'm driving the pumpkin, Cinderella. Unless, Flem, you wanted to be alone with your boy?"

"Don't be silly," Pickering replied automatically, and then thought it through, and added: "Actually, Mac, I'm delighted. You can keep the grand farewell from getting maudlin."

"You're sure?"

"Absolutely. But let me call ahead and make sure we have a hotel room for you."

"Something wrong with the visiting Flag Officers' Quarters?" McInerney asked.

"Pick's living in a hotel in Memphis. . . ."

"I should have guessed," McInerney said.

"And what was that I heard about wise officers keeping their indiscretions as far from the flagpole as possible?"

"It's 'a hundred miles from the flagpole,' actually," McInerney said. "But you're right. A hotel would be better."

"George," Pickering ordered, "call the Peabody in Memphis and get a suite for General McInerney and me. You and Sylvester can bunk with Pick and Dunn."

"Aye, aye, sir."

"And while Hart's doing that, Tony, you get our passengers loaded."

"Aye, aye, sir."

"You learned how to fly, I seem to recall?"

Pickering nodded. "P & FE has a Staggerwing Beech," he said. "I've got a couple of hundred hours in that."

"You think you could get the wheels up on a Gooney Bird? And then back down again? If so, you can ride up in front with me."

"I think I might be able to do that," Pickering said. "But are you sure it will be all right?"

"What do you mean?"

"I didn't know the Corps let old men like you fly by themselves," Pickering said, straight-faced.

"You sonofabitch," McInerney said. "If memory serves, and mine always does, you're eight months older than I am."

The Douglas R4-D was parked right outside base operations. A ground crew of Navy white-hats was standing by. Several of them manned a fire extinguisher on wheels. One of them had been stationed in the cockpit. The moment he saw General McInerney his responsibility was to stick his arm out the pilot's side window and place a small red flag with the two stars of a major general in a holder.

When McInerney saw Pickering staring at the flag, he

said, "That's the Navy. I have passed the word in the Corps that any Marine AOD found hanging a flag on any airplane I'm flying will have to wash the airplane."

"You've earned the prerogatives, Mac," Pickering said, meaning it. "Enjoy them."

McInerney waved him onto the airplane. A number of packages were strapped to the deck of the cabin. "That's your weather station gear," McInerney said. "No package weighs more than sixty-five pounds, most of them no more than fifty."

"You're not going all the way with us, are you, Mac?"

"No. Sylvester is. We're going to draft a copilot for him at Memphis. I'm taking one of the Memphis MAG's Corsairs back here in the morning."

"You can fly a Corsair?" Pickering asked, genuinely surprised.

"Don't start that crap again, Flem," McInerney said.

"Sorry," Pickering said.

Spectowski and Damon were already strapped into BuAir versions of airline seats. Pickering smiled at them as he followed McInerney into the cockpit. A moment after he sat down in the copilot's seat and strapped himself in, McInerney handed him the major general's flag.

"Stick this in your ear, or some other suitable bodily orifice, General," McInerney said.

"Aye, aye, sir," Pickering said. He took the flag and found a place for it behind his seat.

Lieutenant Sylvester stuck his head in the cockpit door.

"Anytime you're ready, General," he said.

"Okay, Tony. Find yourself a seat," McInerney said, and reached for the plastic-coated checklist. "Ordinarily, the guy in the right seat reads this off for the pilot," he said. "But I realize that the eyes of an old fart like you can't handle the small print."

Three minutes later, Anacostia Departure Control cleared Marine Oh Oh Six for immediate take off on Runway Two Six, and McInerney reached for the throttle quadrant and advanced the throttles to takeoff power.

He was about to reach for his microphone when he heard Pickering's voice in his earphones: "Anacostia, Marine Double Oh Six, rolling."

Thirty seconds later, McInerney eased back on the wheel and the rumble of the wheels stopped.

"Wheels up," he ordered.

"Wheels up," Pickering parroted, and then a few seconds later added, "Wheels up and locked."

McInerney looked at him. "Well, maybe I'm wrong," he said. "Maybe you're not as useless as teats on a boar hog."

When they had reached cruising altitude and McInerney had trimmed the Gooney Bird up, he turned to Pickering. "What do you want first, the good news or the bad?"

"Let's start with the good," Pickering said. "I haven't had much of that lately."

"For once, the phones worked, and I got through to Dawkins at Ewa. You know the Dawk, don't you?"

"He had the MAG on Guadalcanal," Pickering said. "Very good guy."

"Yeah. Well, I had an idea. Big Steve Oblensky has forgotten more about Catalinas than most people ever learn. Before his heart went bad, he picked up a lot of time flying them. And he's one hell of a mechanic, too. Airframe *and* engine. So I asked the Dawk if he would mind lending him to this project of yours. For the first of the bad news, Dawkins seemed to know a lot about it. One of the Navy's pilots involved in the first refueling attempt ran off at the mouth."

"There seems to be an epidemic of that," Pickering said.

McInerney looked at him curiously but didn't pursue it. "Anyway, Dawk told me that Big Steve is already working on the Catalinas with your pal Jake Dillon."

"Thank you," Pickering said. "I should have thought of that."

"Then the Dawk asked me a question, which brings us to Part Two of the bad news. He wanted to know if I was thinking of volunteering Charley Galloway to fly the mission. He obviously hoped I would say no firmly, which I did."

"I didn't even think that Charley would volunteer."

"You know how many volunteers we did get?"

Pickering shook his head, "no."

"Two," McInerney said.

"Two?" Pickering parroted incredulously.

"One of them is up on charges for writing rubber checks all over the West Coast, and the other is facing a Flight Evaluation Board. According to his commanding officer, the Board is almost certain to take his wings for gross incompetence."

"I'm surprised," Pickering confessed. "Only two."

"Almost nobody wants to fly a Catalina in the first place," McInerney said. "And most of the people who are flying them want to get out of Cats. Long-over-water flights are (a) dangerous and (b) boring, and that's what you do when you fly Catalinas, day after day. If I was flying fighters, I damned sure wouldn't volunteer to fly Catalinas. I wasn't all that surprised, but I did think we'd get maybe six, maybe more, volunteers."

"And what do we do now?"

"The night you almost got blown away in France, do you remember volunteering to go take out that machine gun?"

Pickering didn't reply.

"The way I recall it," McInerney said, "Lieutenant Davis said, 'Pickering, go take out that machine gun. And take McInerney and'—what the hell was his name? He got about thirty feet out of the trench."

"Blumenson," Pickering said softly, remembering an entirely different war a long time ago. "Private Aaron Blumenson. He was from Cicero, Illinois. A sniper got him. In the throat."

". . . and *Blumenson* with you.' " McInerney went on. "In other words, realizing (a) that Sergeant Pickering, Corporal McInerney, and Private Blumenson were not about to volunteer to do something dangerous and (b) that unless somebody took that Maxim away from Fritz, a lot of Marines were going to have holes in them, Lieutenant Davis did what he had to do. He volunteered us to do what had to be done."

"Is that what you're going to do?" Pickering asked, and then, before McInerney had a chance to reply, added: "I volunteered McCoy to go into the Gobi and see if he can find those people. It has to be done, and he was the guy to do it."

"You can have Galloway, Flem, if you say so," McInerney said.

Pickering looked at him.

"It has to be done, and Charley's good at this sort of thing," McInerney added.

"I thought you said you told Dawkins you weren't volunteering Galloway?"

"I'm not. I'm really short of fighter pilots, Flem. In my judgment what Charley is doing now, putting some backbone into that collection of misfits in VMF-229, is damned important. I don't know anybody else who could do what he's doing. But it's your call, General. You have the priority. If you want Charley Galloway, you can have him."

Pickering did not reply directly. "Who else is available? Who else were you thinking of volunteering?" he asked.

"One major for sure. He's got a lot of Catalina time, and more important, he's a good officer. That will be important, because the volunteers I volunteer are probably going to show up manifesting a magnificent lack of enthusiasm. I'll get you pilots, Flem. Good ones."

"Let's put Charley Galloway on the Only If Absolutely Necessary List," Pickering said.

"Thank you," McInerney said.

"Where is this major I am going to get? How soon can I have him?"

"He's at Pensacola," McInerney said. "What I think I'll do, Flem, instead of going back to Anacostia tomorrow, is go to Pensacola and tell him that not only has he just volunteered, but he'll see if he can't come up with somebody else, too."

"How soon can I have him? And the somebody else?"

"It'll take a couple of days to get orders cut."

"Plus a week or so for a delay en route leave to see his family," Pickering said.

"He's got his family with him at Pensacola."

"The sooner I can have him, have all the pilots, the better."

"I understand."

[TWO]
Base Operations
Memphis Naval Air Station
Memphis, Tennessee
2245 28 March 1943

Rear Admiral Jesse R. Ball, USN, Flag Officer Commanding Naval Air Station, Memphis, arrived at base operations in his official 1941 Navy gray Plymouth staff car, at almost the same time that First Lieutenant Malcolm S. Pickering, USMCR, drove up in his privately owned motor vehicle, a fire-engine-red 1941 Cadillac convertible coupe. Admiral Ball knew Lieutenant Pickering only by reputation, and to the best of his recollection had never before laid eyes on him, but there was no question in his mind that the driver of the fire-engine-red Cadillac was Lieutenant Pickering.

There had been seven incident reports in the office of the base provost marshal, five of them chronicling off-base speeding-limit violations and two of them on-base speeding-limit violations by a Lieutenant Pickering at the wheel of a Cadillac convertible. Admiral Ball thought it highly unlikely that the driver of the Cadillac was anyone but First Lieutenant Malcolm S. Pickering, USMCR.

Though it had been Admiral Ball's intention to speak with Lieutenant Pickering as this day's first order of business, that did not prove possible. When his aide had called VMF-262 to direct Lieutenant Pickering to present himself forthwith at the Admiral's office, he had been informed that Lieutenant Pickering was leading half a dozen of VMF-262's Corsairs on a cross-country training flight and was not expected back until late that night, or—considering the possibilities of bad weather or some other exigency of the Naval Service—possibly not until the following morning.

Admiral Ball had then directed his aide to ask Captain William C. Dunn, USMCR, Lieutenant Pickering's immediate superior officer, to present himself immediately. Admiral Ball knew Captain Dunn and regarded him as a fine officer. He also knew that Captain Dunn and Lieu-

tenant Pickering had flown together—had indeed become
aces together—flying Wildcats off Henderson Field on
Guadalcanal. It was not surprising, therefore, that Captain
Dunn proved extremely reluctant to discuss his knowledge
of Lieutenant Pickering's amorous activities, or other
strayings from the path of righteousness. In fact, he did a
remarkable job trying to cover his buddy's ass. It became
immediately apparent to Admiral Ball that if he was going
to get a full picture of Lieutenant Pickering, it was not
going to be from Captain Dunn. He sought out other
sources of information.

By noon, it was clear to Admiral Ball that Lieutenant
Pickering was a royal fuckup, even by comparison with
other Marine Corps fighter pilots. His transgressions
ranged from doing barrel rolls at an estimated altitude of
100 feet and a speed of 350 knots over the Memphis Air
Station's control tower to hiding his salami in the banker's
wife. His only surprise was that an officer with such a
history had not previously come to his official attention.

Admiral Ball had left word with VMF-262 late that
afternoon that he expected to see Lieutenant Pickering either at 0800 the next day or immediately upon his return
to Memphis NAS, whichever occurred first.

Then he put from his mind the unfortunate business of
an out-of-control Marine fighter pilot and turned to something pleasant. Memphis NAS had been informed that
Major General D. G. McInerney, the just-promoted Deputy Chief of Marine Corps Aviation, would arrive sometime after 2200 hours and would remain overnight. Jesse
Ball and Mac McInerney went way back. They had done
a tour together aboard the old *Lexington*, when the Admiral had been a j.g. lieutenant and Mac a brand-new
Marine captain. As far as Jesse was concerned, Mac's
promotion was long overdue. They would wet down his
new stars together. Jesse wouldn't have been at all surprised if Mac was coming to Memphis for just that purpose.

And now here was the notorious Lieutenant Pickering,
getting out of his red Cadillac, wearing, the Admiral noticed, his leather flight jacket and not the prescribed uniform, including any sort of uniform headgear. Giving him

the benefit of the doubt, he might just have landed and not yet had time to put on what he was supposed to be wearing. According to record, he'd been cited fourteen times for not being in the properly appointed uniform.

When Lieutenant Pickering saw the Admiral, he saluted. It was more in the nature of a casual wave of his hand in the vicinity of his forehead than a proper salute. "Good evening, Admiral," Lieutenant Pickering said.

Admiral Ball returned the salute. He said nothing about the absence of headgear. That violation of regulation paled in comparison to his other transgressions against good order and discipline.

"Just landed, did you, Lieutenant?" Admiral Ball asked.

There was a slight hesitation before Lieutenant Pickering replied. "More or less, sir."

Which means, of course, that he does not want to lie about it.

"You're going out again, are you, Lieutenant?"

"Actually, sir, I'm meeting someone coming in," Pickering replied.

With a little bit of luck, he'll be standing there, hatless, when Mac gets off his airplane. Once Mac has had a word with him regarding the necessity of Marine officers always being in the proper uniform—all of it, including headgear—he will wear a hat when taking a shower.

Admiral Ball grunted and walked into base operations.

Five minutes later, the R4-D touched down on time (it had filed a Direct Memphis flight plan from Anacostia). Admiral Ball was so informed by the AOD.

Admiral Ball immediately began asking himself questions: Had something happened and Mac wasn't on the Gooney Bird? There had been no word from the aircraft to the tower that a general officer was aboard. And when the plane taxied up to the ramp in front of base ops, there was no general's flag flapping from a short staff next to the pilot's side window.

It wasn't until the Gooney Bird had turned around and its nose was facing base ops that Admiral Ball saw General McInerney's face in the cockpit.

Admiral Ball smiled as he walked toward the airplane.

The smile vanished when he saw that Lieutenant Pickering was doing the same thing.

What the hell is he doing out here?

He waited until Mac had shut down the engines and then called up at him, "Still letting you fly, are they, old buddy?"

"Damn, Jesse," General McInerney called back. "What are you doing out here this late at night? Isn't it long past your bedtime?"

"Well, I was going to buy you a drink, but now I'm not so sure."

"I accept. Let me shut this thing down, and I'll be right with you."

Admiral Ball walked to the fuselage door just as it opened, and the steps dropped down.

The first person off was a Marine brigadier general.

I wonder who that is? Mac's deputy? He's not an aviator.

Lieutenant Pickering addressed the general officer: "What the hell were you doing in the cockpit?"

"I am perfectly able to manipulate the landing gear, as you damned well know, hotshot," the general said, and then he wrapped his arms around Lieutenant Pickering.

My God, it's his father!

General Pickering spotted Admiral Ball and saluted. "I'm Fleming Pickering, Admiral," he said, as Ball returned the salute.

"Welcome to Memphis NAS, General," Admiral Ball said. "We didn't know you were coming, or we'd have had the senior Marine here to greet you."

"No problem at all. This is the Marine I came to see."

Lieutenants Sylvester and Hart deplaned next, followed by Chief Spectowski and Petty Officer Damon. Baggage followed. Finally, Major General McInerney came down the ladder. Lieutenant Pickering saluted him. McInerney returned it.

"How are you, Pick?" General McInerney called cheerfully. "Skating on thin ice as usual, I see?"

God, he knows Mac well enough for Mac to call him by his first name!

"Sir?"

"This aging admiral here is old Navy, Pick," McInerney said, nodding at Admiral Ball. "He likes officers to be in uniform. Where the hell is your cover?"

Lieutenant Pickering snapped his fingers and looked mildly embarrassed. "I must have left it in the car. I'll go get it."

"Don't bother," Admiral Ball heard himself saying. "No one will see you out here."

"Getting soft in your old age, are you, Jesse?" McInerney asked. "There was a time when you would have ordered him keelhauled."

"Now I know a wise officer has to make allowances for Marines," Admiral Ball said. "They're not really human."

I am not going to let this goddamn pup foul up my seeing Mac!

"I'll pretend I didn't hear that, Jesse," McInerney said. "In case you haven't noticed, you're outnumbered by Marines."

"We're going to need more wheels than we have," General Pickering said.

"That means we're really going to have to impose on your hospitality, Jesse," McInerney said.

"What do you need, Mac?"

"We need a guard on this airplane. An armed guard," General Pickering said.

"No problem, General," Admiral Ball said. "And what else?"

"Quarters overnight for the Chief and his friend."

"No problem. What else?"

"In the morning, I'll need a copilot for the Gooney Bird. It's going first to Chicago and then to 'Diego," McInerney said. "And I'm going to have to borrow one of your Corsairs."

"That can be arranged, no problem," Admiral Ball said.

"And then we'll need a ride for the rest of us into Memphis, to the hotel," McInerney said. "We all won't fit in Pick's car."

"You're going to Memphis?"

"To the Peabody," General Pickering confirmed. "And a cordial invitation is extended to you, Admiral, to join us while Mac and I wash down his new stars."

"General McInerney and I go back a long way, General," Admiral Ball said.

"Not as far as Flem and I do, Jesse," McInerney said. "Flem was my sergeant at Château-Thierry."

"Why don't you and your aide ride with me, Mac? And General Pickering and his aide can ride with Lieutenant Pickering?"

Who will as certainly as the sun will rise drive that Cadillac into Memphis wearing his leather jacket and no cover. Probably at twenty miles over the speed limit.

"Sounds fine," General Pickering said. "How about the Chief and his friend? And the guard for the airplane?"

"The AOD can handle that." Admiral Ball nodded at the AOD, who was standing a respectful distance away waiting for his orders. Admiral Ball motioned for him to come over.

"So you and General Pickering are old friends, are you?" Admiral Ball asked General McInerney as they were driving into Memphis.

"I was with him the night he got—and damned well earned—the Navy Cross. All bullshit aside, he saved my life that night."

"I don't think I've ever met him before."

"He got out after the war. He runs—owns—Pacific and Far East Shipping. And his father-in-law owns the Foster hotel chain. Roosevelt commissioned him a brigadier when he came back in the Corps."

"What's the Corps having him do?"

"Keep this under your hat, Jesse. He's the Director for Pacific Operations for the OSS. That's where he's headed now. I can't tell you what for, but my orders from SecNav, personally, were to give him anything he thinks he needs to get his job done."

"Sounds like an interesting man."

"One of the best, Jesse, one of the best," McInerney said. "And the boy, Pick, is a chip off the old block. He could have spent this war running an officers' club. For that matter, he probably could have gotten himself declared essential, exempt from the draft, to run either

P & FE or Foster Hotels. But he didn't. He came into the Corps, went through OCS, then came to me and begged me to get him out of a desk job and into flight school. He flew for Charley Galloway in VMF-229 on Guadalcanal. An ace. Seven Japs, I think."

"I'd heard something about that."

"Turned out to be one hell of an officer," McInerney said.

One hell of a lousy officer, General Ball thought, but did not, of course, say it.

This is not the time to deal with this disgrace to his uniform. Not with his father about to go back to the Pacific, with a lot obviously on his mind. And not when we're all about to wash down Mac's second star.

[THREE]
The Gobi Desert
150 Miles Southeast of Chandmani, Mongolia
1545 28 March 1943

No one had ever come up with a proper name universally accepted for whatever-it-was-they-were. Many of its members thought of it as "The Caravan," for that was the idea, the dream, to get the hell out of China and Mongolia and into either Russia or India, by caravan.

Chief Motor Machinist's Mate Frederick C. Brewer, USN, a large, muscular but tending to fat, florid-faced forty-six-year-old, who had been elected as commanding officer of whatever-it-was-they-were, thought of it, spoke of it, as "The Complement." In the Navy, "ship's complement" meant the enlisted men assigned to a ship. Many—but by no means all—of the other Yangtze sailors followed his lead.

The term "complement" was perfectly satisfactory to Technical Sergeant Moses Abraham, USMC, who had retired from the 4th Marines. But to Staff Sergeant Willis T. Cawber, Jr., U.S. Army, Retired, who was the oldest man in whatever-it-was-they-were, a "compliment" was something you paid: "Nice dress, Hazel." It made absolutely no sense as a term to describe what he privately thought of as a pathetic band of mostly over-the-hill gypsies.

Staff Sergeant Cawber, who had decided in 1933 to take his retirement from the 15th Infantry—after thirty-two years in the Army—described whatever-it-was-they-were collectively as "Us," breaking "Us" down when necessary into the subgroups "The Soldiers," "The Women," and "The Sick, Lame and Lazy."

"The Soldiers" were those who were physically fit and relatively skilled in the use of arms, and could be called upon to fight, if necessary. The Soldiers included some other former members of the 15th Infantry (all of whom, like Cawber, had retired from active duty), many of the Marines, and even a half-dozen Yangtze sailors who had acquired some small-arms proficiency and rudimentary squad tactics while aboard the river patrol boats of the Yangtze River patrol.

"The Women" included the wives (mostly Chinese, but including two White Russian "Nansen" women, a French woman, and a German woman) and the children, twenty-two of them, ranging in age from toddlers to two girls and a boy in their early teens.

"The Sick and the Lame" included those who were really sick or lame, in several cases because of age. But "The Lazy" didn't actually mean that. Rather, it meant those (almost all of them retired Yangtze sailors) who had brought to whatever-it-was-they-were no useful "military" experience. They had been, for example, "ship's writers" (clerks) or some such (one had been a chaplain's assistant) before transferring to the Fleet Reserve and staying in China. But the term "sick, lame and lazy" had been used in the Army, the Navy, and the Marine Corps before the war, primarily to describe those lining up to go on Sick Call. And that term had been adopted by just about everybody.

One major piece of whatever-it-was-they-were was occupied by Sergeant James R. Sweatley, USMC, and seven other enlisted Marines. Sweatley and the others had been assigned to the Marine detachment in Peking and had either "gone off," or "gone over the hill," or deserted, rather than obey orders to surrender and become prisoners of the Japanese.

With twenty-two years of service in the Corps, Sweatley could have retired in early 1941—and now very often thought he should have. If he had been recalled to active duty after retiring, he would now have been with a Marine unit, not wandering around fucking Mongolia with a herd of doggies and swabbies just waiting for the fucking Japs to find them.

But he had shipped over one more time, on the reasonable chance he could make staff sergeant—maybe even gunnery sergeant—in four more years. And on his last hitch, he vowed, he would *really* start saving his money.

Chief Brewer, Technical Sergeant Abraham, Staff Sergeant Cawber, and Sergeant Sweatley were the command structure of whatever-it-was-they-were. They had formally been elected to their positions by all the men. That had been Chief Brewer's idea; it had been the way the volunteer regiments in the Civil War had elected their officers.

They had even chosen by vote the titles of those who would lead whatever-it-was-they-were: Chief Brewer was the "commanding officer"; Technical Sergeant Abraham was the "executive officer"; Staff Sergeant Cawber was the "administrative officer"; and Sergeant Sweatley was the "tactical officer."

In 1937, Chief Brewer had transferred off the USS *Panay* of the Yangtze River patrol into the Fleet Reserve. Soon after that he opened a bar, the Fouled Anchor, installing himself as bartender and bouncer and his Mongolian wife, Doto-Si, as the business manager. Doto-Si handled the cash, the merchants, and the Chinese authorities.

The bar did not prove to be an immediate roaring success. After three months, when there wasn't much left of his savings, he gave in to Doto-Si's suggestion to operate a hotel. There were rooms to let above the Fouled Anchor that could be converted into hotel rooms for not very much money. Fred Brewer knew damned well what kind of hotel Doto-Si wanted to operate. He had met her in one, called the Sailor's Rest.

He was thirty-six when he met her, just off a four-month cruise up and down the Yangtze aboard the *Panay*. He was more than a little drunk, and flush with cash from an unusual run of luck at the vingt-et-un tables in the basement of the Peking Paradise Hotel.

If he hadn't been drunk, he often thought later, he wouldn't have taken her upstairs in the Sailor's Rest. He always thought there was something sick about sailors taking very young girls upstairs.

And Doto-Si was very young. She was new there, fresh from the country. She told him she was sixteen. It was probably more like fourteen. But he took her upstairs, because he was drunk, and because he hadn't been laid in four months. He had been acting chief of the boat on the cruise, and he thought that chiefs of the boat should not set an example for the ship's complement by getting their ashes hauled by whatever slope whore was waiting when the *Panay* tied up.

The truth was, there was something different about Doto-Si. She was small, and she had a pretty face and had a soft voice, and she was shy, and she looked at him funny, as if she really liked him. He almost didn't screw her when they were in the room and she took off her clothes and he saw how young she was. He gave her five bucks and told her to forget it.

She told him that if he did that, she would get in trouble with Kan-Chee. Kan-Chee had told her to treat him right, because he was an important chief aboard the *Panay*.

So he screwed her, and it wasn't at all like getting his ashes hauled usually was. He really liked it, even though he was ashamed of himself for slipping it to a slope whore who was really just a kid.

So he gave her another five and went back down to the bar and had a drink.

A couple of minutes later, she came walking down the stairs and he thought that however the hell old she was, she was too young to be peddling her ass to a bunch of drunken American sailors—and worse—in a joint like the Sailor's Rest.

A bosun's mate second off the *Panay* took one look at

Doto-Si and headed for her like a fucking cat about to play with a mouse.

And Brewer was drunk and he was flush, so he turned off his barstool and told the bosun's mate second he was too late, he wanted that one for himself.

He looked around for Kan-Chee, who wore Western suits and talked pretty good English, even to old hands like Brewer who spoke pretty good Wu, and waved him over.

"You liked that little Mongolian, huh, Chief?"

"Yeah. How much will you take for her?"

"You going in business, Chief? Maybe be my competition?"

"Fuck you. You want to sell her or not?"

"I sell anything for right price. How much you willing to pay?"

"How much, goddamn you!"

"You a friend. A good customer. I treat you right. I paid two hundred American for her. I buy her clothes. Teach her what she has to do. I got at least three hundred American in her, maybe four hundred. I sell her to you for five hundred, and I buy her back in a month, if she still look good, not sick, not pregnant, for four hundred."

Now Brewer was sore, as well as more than a little drunk and flush with cash. Kan-Chee was playing games with him. He didn't think Brewer could come up with five hundred American. Fuck him!

"I'll give you four hundred for her. Take it or leave it."

"After one month, you want me to buy her back, I give you three hundred. American."

Kan-Chee, the bastard, had been more than a little surprised when Brewer reached in his money belt and counted out four hundred dollars American, but a deal was a deal.

So he took Doto-Si back upstairs and told her what the deal was. In the morning, he would give her some more money and she could go back where she came from, to her village in Mongolia, and she didn't have to be a whore anymore; he had taken care of her debt to Kan-Chee.

"If I go back to my village, my uncle just sell me again."

"Your uncle? What about your father?"

"Father dead. Mother dead. Uncle no want to feed me. He just sell me again."

He was really drunk by then, and understood that he wasn't going to make any smart decisions that night, so he said, "Fuck it, we'll talk about it in the morning."

And then he passed out.

When he woke up in the morning, he was naked in the bed, and alone, and remembered what a stupid fucking thing he had done the night before. He saw his jacket and pants hanging on the one hanger in the closet, but no money belt.

He had really fucked up big time, gotten shitfaced, screwed a little girl, and given Kan-Chee a lot of his money. And now what he hadn't given Kan-Chee, the little Mongolian whore had stolen.

Served him fucking right.

And then Doto-Si came into the room, carrying a pot of tea, a plate of egg rolls, and even a little packet of aspirin.

She sat on the bed and poured him a cup of tea and opened the packet of aspirin and handed him two.

He took the aspirin and drank the tea and ate all the egg rolls—he was starving; he hadn't eaten anything yesterday after coming ashore, which explained why he had gotten so shitfaced. And then he looked at her.

"Where's my money belt?"

She unbuttoned her dress and took it off, and stood naked in front of him. She had his money belt hanging from her shoulder. She took it off and handed it to him.

"Lots of money," Doto-Si said. "I afraid to leave it in room with you asleep. Somebody steal."

He took the money belt and unzipped it. There *was* a hell of a lot of money in it. Even if the girl had stolen some, there was a hell of a lot left. He really must have made a killing at the Peking Palace.

And she had the chance to steal all of it, and didn't!

"Thank you," he said, and then had a generous thought. He took out a twenty, and then a second twenty, and then a third, and handed them to her.

"Thank you," he repeated.

"For twenty dollar American, I can get nice room, with real bed, and sink and toilet," Doto-Si said.

"Is that what you want to do? How will you live?"

"I cook for you, and wash clothes, be your woman. You give twenty dollars a month for food?"

"I'm old enough to be your fucking father!"

"My father dead," Doto-Si said.

Brewer said what he was thinking: "I eat aboard the *Panay*. The wash boys do my clothes."

"You can fuck wash boys?"

"Jesus Christ!"

"I like to fuck with you," Doto-Si said. "I be good to you."

"Don't say 'fuck,' " he said.

"What I should say?"

"Just don't say 'fuck.' "

"You sleep. I come back in two hours. Okay?"

He didn't reply.

"You better put money belt and pants on," she said.

"This isn't going to work," he thought aloud. "Christ, I don't want a Chinese woman!"

"I be good to you. We try it, okay?"

When he didn't say no, she picked up her dress and put it on and started to leave.

"Hey!" he said, as she reached the door. She turned to look at him. "What's your name?"

"Doto-Si," she said.

She came back in two hours. He had tried to sleep, but couldn't.

She sat on the bed. "I find two rooms. Living room, bedroom, and toilet. For twenty-five dollar American. Too much money?"

"Let's have a look," he said.

"Okay," Doto-Si said.

They continued to look at each other for a long moment, and then he put his fingers to her cheek. "You're so young," he said.

"I old enough for you," she said firmly, and then she took his hand and pulled him to his feet.

As they walked through the Sailor's Rest bar to the street, Brewer decided it was really a depressing place.

And when he saw Kan-Chee smirking at him and Doto-Si knowingly, he decided he would never come in this fucking joint again, and he never did.

They had one child, a boy, and another was on the way when Chief Brewer transferred off the *Panay* into the Fleet Reserve and opened the Fouled Anchor.

A week after he went ashore from the *Panay* for the last time, Brewer and Doto-Si were married by a minister from the Christian & Missionary Alliance.

Even though Doto-Si thought that was sort of comical, he was uncomfortable about being the proprietor of a whorehouse. The only time he went upstairs was when something—a light fixture, a water pipe, something like that—needed fixing, and he had nothing to do with the girls.

Nobody ever got rolled in the Fouled Anchor, or got the clap or anything worse. A lot of people who came to the bar and restaurant never went upstairs, and the girls didn't come downstairs to the bar looking for customers. Doto-Si handled that side of the business upstairs, where there was a parlor.

The whole thing seemed to be too good to be true. He was making more money than he ever imagined, and Doto-Si was good to him, and he loved the kids. They had a first-class apartment now, and they rode back and forth to work in a 1940 Oldsmobile that had an automatic transmission. Brewer didn't think that would work, or work long, but it did. Didn't even have a clutch pedal.

By then, Brewer didn't tend bar anymore, or serve as the bouncer. Doto-Si hired Chinese to do that. Brewer spent his time in the Fouled Anchor keeping an eye on things, sitting at a rear table in the bar playing poker or acey-deucey, making a few loans, serving as respected intermediary between westerners wanting to do business with Chinese and doing a little business himself.

But war was coming, and when that happened, everything was going to hell. He started making plans. Primarily, he started accumulating gold, which was all anyone was going to take when the war started.

Because he was respected, other old Yangtze sailors and Army and Marine retirees who also knew what was coming sought him out and talked over what they would do when the time came. The Americans could, of course, leave anytime they wanted to and be in San Francisco in a month. But their wives could not get visas to enter the United States. Some Americans went home anyway, just leaving their Chinese wives and children and promising to send money.

But Brewer never even considered leaving Doto-Si and the kids. She was his *wife*, for Christ's sake, the *mother* of his *children*. You don't just up anchor and sail away and leave your wife and kids to make out as best they can to save your own ass.

Soon, several others had decided to band together and get the hell out with their wives and kids. There were nine other retired Yangtze sailors with Chinese wives and kids, and one with a German wife; and there were two retired Marines, one with a White Russian wife, and one, Technical Sergeant Abraham, whose Chinese wife had died, but whose mother-in-law was taking care of his three kids.

And then word of what they were planning also reached some of the soldiers who had retired from the 15th Infantry in Tientsin, and they sent a retired staff sergeant named Willis T. Cawber, Jr., to Peking to see what Brewer had in mind.

From the beginning, Doto-Si had made it clear to the others that the only way they could get out of China was through Mongolia—the Gobi Desert—and into India. That wasn't easy for them to grasp: She was the only one in the band who had ever even been to Mongolia, and most thought the Gobi Desert was miles and miles of shifting sand, like the Sahara. But eventually they came around to her way of thinking. Even though she still looked young as hell, there was something about her eyes that made others realize that she was smart and tough as hell.

Much of the Gobi was rocks and thin vegetation, she told them, not sand. That meant it could be traversed by wagon. In the summer, there was enough grass to feed sheep and goats and horses. On the other hand, water was a problem—you had to know where to find it, but it was there—and it was very, very cold at night.

There was also, Doto-Si told Brewer privately, a genuine threat from Chinese and Mongolian bandits, who robbed caravans whenever they thought they had the caravan outnumbered. That meant they would have to be armed, and prepared to fight.

That was going to be a hell of a problem, Brewer realized. Very few of the Yangtze sailors had any experience in that kind of fighting. And though soldiers from the 15th Infantry could be presumed to know how to handle weapons, he didn't know how many of them would be willing to trust their survival to the Mongolian madam of a Peking whorehouse.

But about that time he began to hear scuttlebutt in the Fouled Anchor that Sergeant James R. Sweatley and some of the other active-duty Marines in the Peking legation detachment had announced they weren't just going to raise the white flag when the war came and turn themselves in as Japanese prisoners.

The very next time—in early November 1941—Sergeant Sweatley came into the Fouled Anchor, Chief Brewer and Technical Sergeant Abraham were waiting for him. They bought him a couple of drinks, then took him into Brewer's office to sound him out.

Brewer didn't think much of Sweatley. He was still only a buck sergeant after twenty years in the Marines, and on several occasions, he had been a troublesome drunk both in the bar and upstairs.

But Abraham argued that he was a Marine sergeant on active duty, and that meant he would be in a position to get weapons, which the others didn't have and damned sure were going to need. On top of that, he and the other Marines he'd bring with him were young. A good thing, under the circumstances—especially considering some of the others who would be going into the Gobi.

"What we say here goes no further," Brewer began.

"What we say about what?"

Technical Sergeant Abraham decided to cut through the bullshit. "The scuttlebutt is that you and some of the other Marines are not going to surrender to the Japanese when this war starts. Is that true, or are you just running your mouth?"

"Who said I said something like that?"

"Two of the Marines who say you're taking them with you," Abraham told him, and furnished their names.

Who else, Sergeant Sweatley wondered, *have those bastards been running their mouth to?*

Then he said the thought aloud.

"As far as I know, nobody else," Abraham replied. "I had a little talk with them. Told them if any of their officers, or even some of their noncoms, heard them, they'd be confined until it was time to surrender."

"What do you want, you and Brewer?"

"The same thing you do, to stay out of a Jap POW enclosure. To get the hell out of China, into India, or maybe even Russia."

"Yeah?"

"And to take our families with us," Brewer added.

Sweatley knew about Brewer's family. And he knew about Abraham. He had three kids with his Chinese woman, and then she'd up and died on him, and he had stayed in China because of the kids, to take care of them.

"If I was planning something like that, and I'm not saying I am, what I would do is head for India," Sweatley said. "On horseback. Traveling fast and light across the Altai Mountains into the Gobi Desert and then across it."

Jesus, Chief Brewer thought, *that makes him the second person—Doto-Si being the first—who understands that the only way to get out of China is through the Gobi Desert.*

"Ride horses across sand dunes?" Brewer countered sarcastically.

"Let me tell you something, Chief. The Gobi is mostly rocks, not sand. If you had a car and enough gas, you could drive across the sonofabitch."

"Then why don't you just drive across it?"

"I thought about it. And did the numbers. For one thing, there's no way I could carry that much gas. For another, trucks would be conspicuous. That's the last thing I can afford."

"You really think a dozen or more Marines on horseback wouldn't be conspicuous?" Abraham asked.

"Meaning what?"

"Meaning you'd be white men in Mongolia."

"I'll worry about that later. If, I mean, I was thinking about something like this."

"I've been thinking along the same lines," Brewer said. "My wife and me, and some other people. My wife is a Mongolian. She knows all about the Gobi Desert."

"No shit?"

"We're thinking of crossing it in horse-drawn, rubber-tired wagons," Abraham said.

They were doing more than thinking about it: Three days before, Brewer had sent Doto-Si to Peking in the Oldsmobile, with the kids and one of the bouncers, to go to Baotou to buy wagons.

"And you don't think you're going to stand out as a white man in Mongolia?"

"I've got a Nansen passport," Brewer said. "It's phony, but I can't tell the difference between it and a real one. I can pass myself off as a White Russian."

"Oh."

Brewer's smarter than I thought, Sweatley thought. *I didn't even think about getting a phony Nansen passport.*

"And I got a Mongolian wife and kids," Brewer went on. "If I stay in the wagon and let her do the talking, I might not even have to show anybody my Nansen passport."

"So what do you want from me?" Sweatley asked.

Brewer looked at Abraham, who nodded. Then Brewer took the chance and told Sweatley. "There's ten Yangtze sailors, including me, who stayed here when we went into the Fleet Reserve. All of us are married. Mostly to Chinese, but there's a German wife, and a White Russian. There's two Marines, Abraham and a guy named Brugemann, who used to be the finance sergeant in the Fourth. And, all told, twenty kids. I have also been talking to some soldiers who took their retirement here. There's maybe six, seven of them in Tientsin."

"Like I said, what do you want from me?"

"We could be useful to each other," Brewer said.

"You tell me, Sergeant Abraham, how are—what did you say, twelve?—twelve wives and twenty kids going to help me get to India."

"You know how to navigate?" Chief Brewer asked.

"I know what a compass is," Sweatley said.

"A compass won't be much help in the middle of the Gobi Desert," Abraham said. "There's only a few roads, and the Japs will be watching them. You're going to have to cross the Gobi Desert the same way you cross an ocean, by celestial navigation, by the stars."

Sweatley understood that he was being told the truth. And navigating across the Gobi Desert was something else he hadn't given much thought to. Brewer and Abraham obviously had.

"For the third time, what do you want from me?"

"You've seen the wagon train movies," Chief Brewer said. "Women and children and farmers, protected by cavalry. That's what you're going to be. The Marines, and maybe some of the 15th Infantry soldiers, would be the cavalry. In exchange for that, we'll feed you, and hide you from the Japs and Chinese bandits."

Sweatley, thinking it over, did not immediately respond.

"The only way to get across the desert is by wagon train," Abraham argued reasonably. "Or camels. You got any money to buy wagons? You think you could ride a camel?"

"I got some horses," Sweatley replied. "Including spares. Pack animals."

"Listen to me. I know what I'm talking about," Abraham said. "There's no way you can cross the Gobi like you're on some cavalry patrol fighting Indians in the movies. It has to be crossed very slowly, maybe five miles a day. When the weather gets really bad, you don't move at all."

Brewer joined in the attack. "We're going to have to take our meat with us, on the hoof. When we find water, we'll fill up our water barrels, because we may not find any more for another hundred miles. You getting the picture?"

Sweatley shrugged. "Your wife's Mongolian?"

"Yeah, and she speaks it, too. Which—correct me if I'm wrong—is something else you don't have, somebody who speaks Khalkha, which is what they call their language. In case you need to ask directions, for example."

"How do you plan to get from here to the Gobi?"

"By car from here to Baotou . . ." Abraham said.

"That's where we have the horses," Sweatley blurted.

". . . and then by wagon from there. Across the mountains into Mongolia and into the desert."

Sweatley grunted, then asked: "How many of the others have Nansen passports? Can you get them for us?"

"Three of us have Nansens," Brewer replied. "And I've got one more. Blank. All it needs is a picture."

He means, Sweatley thought, *that I can have the blank passport. If I join up with him. Him meaning him and the Chink women and half-breed children.*

"How do you know your horses are going to be there when you need them?" Chief Brewer asked.

"Because I got two Marines with Thompson submachine guns up there, living with them in the stable."

"How are you going to get from here to Baotou when the time comes?" Abraham asked.

"We have two trucks, International ton-and-a-halfs."

"Two trucks for how many Marines?"

"Nine, not including me. With the two at Baotou, that makes a dozen of us."

"Supplies?"

"Yeah, we got supplies. That's why we need two trucks."

"And if one truck breaks down between here and Baotou?"

"Then we move our stuff from the one that broke down to the one that didn't."

In turn, Chief Brewer was more favorably impressed with Sergeant Sweatley than he expected to be.

For a Marine, Brewer thought, *Sweatley isn't too slow*.

"What about weapons?" Abraham asked.

"That's a problem," Sweatley confessed. "All we have, in addition to our individual weapons, is the Thompsons and an air-cooled Browning .30. In Baotou."

"You can't get any more from the legation?"

"There aren't any more at the legation. We got the Thompsons and the Browning from the Fourth Marines in Shanghai."

"You heard they've been ordered to the Philippines?" Abraham asked.

Sweatley was surprised. He shook his head, "no."

"And the Yangtze River gunboats," Brewer chimed in. "You know that?"

"One of our guys was a radioman first on the *Panay*," Brewer said. "He was aboard her—'visiting'—when the word came. He's working on getting us a shortwave radio."

A shortwave radio, Sweatley thought, *is something else I didn't think about.*

"Do you know when they're going?"

"It has to be soon," Brewer said.

"Then we don't have much time to get our wagon train on the road, do we?" Sweatley observed, extending his hand to first to Abraham and then to Brewer.

They left Peking, independently, on 7 December 1941, within hours of hearing of the attack on Pearl Harbor.

Taking off was much harder for Sergeant Sweatley than he thought it would be.

It wasn't even going over the hill. Over the hill meant fuck it, I'm going to party until my money runs out or the Shore Patrol finds me, whichever comes first.

What I'm doing is fucking deserting. In time of war, which means they can shoot me if they catch me.

And shoot everybody I'm taking with me.

But the only alternative is not going, which means surrendering, just as soon as the Japs find time to go to the legation. If the Japs don't just line the Marines up and shoot us. Or use us for bayonet practice.

Fuck it, Marines are supposed to fight, not surrender. This way, maybe we can do the fucking Japs some damage, somewhere, somehow, and we sure as hell can't do that if we just put our hands in the air and walk out of the legation and hope they don't shoot us, or bayonet us.

But it was still tough to actually go to the go-down where they had the stolen (and repainted in Marine Green) International trucks, and open the doors and drive away, when everybody knew they were supposed to be in the legation, putting into execution the Plan in the Event of Hostilities.

They had the duty of burning the classified records and smashing the code machine and everything else they didn't want the Japs to get their hands on—including the stock of whisky and wine—and they weren't doing it.

They managed to get out of Peking without trouble, taking back roads to avoid the roadblocks they knew the Japs would set up on the Peking-Changchiak highway. There were roadblocks, of course, but they were manned by Chinese, who were not yet ready to challenge two U.S. Marine Corps trucks guarded by Marines in field gear and steel pots, Springfields at the ready.

It took them a long time, at low speed on dirt or mud back roads, to make it around the Japanese roadblocks and onto the Peking-Changchiak highway beyond them. And it was dark when they reached the Great Wall of China, no more than a hundred miles from Peking. That put them behind schedule, but Sweatley decided it made more sense to stop for the night rather than risk what they might find at the gate in the wall without looking at it first.

At first light, he took a long, good look with a pair of binoculars at the passage through the wall. When he saw only Chinese, no Japs, he decided they could probably bluff their way through this one the same way they'd bluffed their way through the others near Peking.

That worked, too. And by one in the afternoon—five hours after passing through the Great Wall—they were outside Changchiak. There three men stepped into the road to flag them down—scaring Sweatley more than a little. But they turned out to be Chief Brewer, Technical Sergeant Abraham, and Staff Sergeant Willis T. Cawber, Jr., U.S. Army, Retired.

Cawber had brought with him the other retirees from the 15th Infantry, along with their wives and children. One of the wives was a White Russian, and one of them a French woman. They had seven children among them.

Cawber, whom he had not met before, immediately got off on the wrong foot with Sweatley. "You were supposed to be here last night," he complained in a sour voice.

Deciding to let that pass, Sweatley explained why he had spent the night on the other side of the Great Wall.

"You were supposed to be here last night, Sergeant," Cawber repeated.

"You better get this straight," Sweatley snapped. "I don't have to explain a fucking thing to you. So far as I'm concerned, you're just going along for the ride."

And then Cawber made things worse by trying to tell Sweatley how he thought they should organize the convoy of vehicles.

"You don't listen, do you?" Sweatley said. "I've been running convoys around China for six years, and I don't need a retired doggie to tell me how to do it."

Chief Brewer and Technical Sergeant Abraham took Staff Sergeant Cawber aside, and Sweatley proceeded to set up the convoy the way he thought it should be run.

Chief Brewer would head it up in his Oldsmobile, with another car behind him, and a Marine would be in each car. Then would come the first of the Marine trucks, with four Marines in it—including Technical Sergeant Abraham. There were seven other cars. These would follow the first truck, with either a Marine or one of the 15th Infantry retirees carrying a weapon in each. Cawber could ride in any of the cars he wanted to. The second Marine truck, carrying Sweatley and the rest of the armed Marines, would be at the tail of the convoy.

That day they met a pretty fair amount of traffic on the road; and because the Great Wall of China made a U-shaped loop to the west, they had to pass through it again. That meant they didn't reach Chining, 150 miles down the highway, until half past seven that evening. As night began to fall, Sweatley made another decision.

When Brewer stopped to talk things over, Sweatley explained that he thought it would be better to keep going and pass through Chining right now, even if it proved difficult to find someplace to stop on the other side in the dark. By morning, he explained, the Chinese might have gotten word to arrest westerners. Sergeant Abraham agreed with Sweatley, and so did Brewer. Even though Staff Sergeant Cawber didn't say anything, Sweatley sensed he didn't like it when Brewer agreed to the plan without asking him.

They spent the night parked by the side of the road. Sweatley put out a perimeter guard and spent most of the night awake, but there was no trouble.

They started moving again at first light, and made the 175 miles to Huhehot by three in the afternoon. On the other side of Huhehot, Brewer stopped the convoy again. There were problems. Three of the eight automobiles were running low on gas. Though Sweatley's trucks had more than enough gasoline, in five-gallon Texaco tin cans, to refuel them, Sweatley was opposed to doing that.

"We're going to abandon the cars in Baotou anyhow," he said. "Hiding them will be a problem. What we should do is load the people in the trucks and other cars and get rid of the cars here."

"You're making all the decisions, are you, Sweatley?" Staff Sergeant Cawber asked, sarcastically.

"I'll get rid of my Olds," Chief Brewer said, nipping the argument in the bud, "and the Packard and the Buick. The more gas we can take with us, the better. And I don't think we can be sure of finding gas in Baotou."

The supplies the Oldsmobile, Packard, and Buick were carrying were transferred to Sweatley's trucks, while the passengers were distributed among the other cars and trucks. Several miles farther down the road, they came to a narrow trail leading to the left. The cars were abandoned there, out of sight from the road. At Sweatley's suggestion, their ignition keys were left in place, but the Peking license plates were removed.

It began to snow thirty minutes after they resumed their march to Baotou. They reached the city after dark. By then it was covered with snow.

The women and children were put into a go-down Brewer had arranged for, guarded by several of the Marines and soldiers. Meanwhile, the Sick, Lame, and Lazy; the Marines; and the other able-bodied men spent the night at a stable transferring the supplies to the rubber-tired wagons and carts. The cars and trucks were then abandoned—scattered in inconspicuous areas all over Baotou.

Again, the keys were left in the ignition switches. With a little bit of luck, the vehicles would be stolen, and therefore concealed from the authorities.

Chief Brewer and Sergeant Abraham came early the next morning to the stable where Sweatley had spent the night.

"We have a couple of problems," Brewer said. "The snowfall is heavy; under it is ice. We're going to have trouble moving."

"We don't have any choice," Sweatley said. "We have to get out of here before someone turns us in."

"That's just about what I decided," Brewer said. "But as part of that problem, the wagons are pretty heavily loaded. Some of them are likely to get stuck."

"We worry about that when it happens," Sweatley said. "If necessary, we just dump whatever we can't carry. Anything else?"

"You and Sergeant Cawber."

"Fuck him."

"We need him. You're just going to have to get along with him," Abraham argued softly.

"Tell him."

"I have."

"Tell him not to start giving me, or my Marines, orders."

"I did," Chief Brewer said. "He said I should tell you the same thing. From now on, you want him to do something, you don't tell him, you tell either Abraham or me. Understood?"

"You're in charge, right?"

"You don't like that?"

"I'll go along with you two, just as long as Cawber doesn't think he's next in line, and over me."

"Done," Brewer said. "What we have to do, I think, is elect officers."

"Elect officers?"

"We'll talk about that, later. What we have to do now is start to pack essentials on wagons we know won't get stuck."

"*We* start doing that? You and me and my Marines?"

"Everybody," Brewer said.

"Okay."

"The first thing we have to do is decide what has to go and what doesn't."

What had to go with them was food, the bare necessities of clothing, the air-cooled Browning .30-caliber machine gun, and a gasoline generator and twenty gallons of gasoline to run it.

The Yangtze sailor who had been a radioman first on the *Panay* had a shortwave radio. He didn't know how well it worked, but Brewer thought that they should take it with them. Maybe they could establish contact with a radio station someplace.

They left Baotou eighteen hours later.

It took them a month to reach and cross the Altai mountain range, and then to reach the edges of the Gobi Desert.

There Brewer called a meeting; and here they all agreed to a command structure.

With the election of officers came the division of responsibility. Sweatley and his Marines, plus several able-bodied Yangtze sailors and several of the 15th Infantry retirees, provide the armed force to protect everybody. They'd be, so to speak, "the soldiers."

The rest—under Staff Sergeant Cawber—would be responsible for feeding everybody.

The "soldiers," in pairs, mounted on the small Mongolian ponies, went on what amounted to permanent perimeter guard duty. One pair preceded the main body of wagons. One pair moved on each side of the wagon train, left and right. And the fourth pair brought up the rear. Everybody did four hours at a time, but the reliefs were on a staggered schedule. Every two hours, one man was sent out from the caravan to relieve one of the men on each two-man team. No "guard post" was ever unmanned.

Almost as soon as they began their trek, they encountered caravans moving toward China. Most were camel caravans, but a few were like their own with ponies pulling rubber-tired wagons and carts. After the second week, they were overtaken and passed by camel caravans headed toward either India or Russia. On the one hand, they were encouraged that their caravan closely resembled so many others. On the other hand, they were surprised at how quickly the camel caravans overtook and passed them. They seemed to move at least twice as fast as their horse-drawn wagons.

It was three weeks before they risked having dealings with the other caravan people. When one of the perimeter guards caught sight of a caravan coming up on them, Brewer's wife and one of the other Chinese women who spoke Khalkha, would wait on the road, and half a dozen Marines would take the air-cooled Browning .30 and hide away in the rocks where they could come to their aid, if necessary. The gold they had went very far, but they didn't have much gold. They bought sheep, goats, and pigs; food for the animals; firewood; and animal fat for their lamps.

One day was much like any other.

Chief Brewer shot the sun with a sextant whenever the night sky was clear. The chart he kept showed their slow movement across the desert. They were making, on average, about five miles a day.

The radioman first did somehow manage to get his shortwave radio working, or so he thought, but there was never a response to his calls.

The women and some of the children spent most of their days scrounging for wood to feed their fires. Some of the larger wagons kept small fires burning inside on the move. People climbed in and out of these wagons to keep warm.

And there were some bad times: One of the 15th Infantry retirees died of a heart attack. The German woman committed suicide after two of her children succumbed to a sickness no one understood. Some people began to talk of just going back into China and turning themselves over to the Japanese. The Jap prison camps were supposed to be truly awful, but they couldn't be much worse than living the way they were now, at the edge of starvation, in bitter cold, and with no real hope of things ever getting better.

So when the first winter snow of 1942 came, Chief Brewer gave permission to three Yangtze River sailors, the chaplain's assistant, and two of the 15th Infantry retirees to take their families back to China. He gave them horses, wagons, and enough food to make the journey.

And then the caravan moved off again, headed for whatever it was whatever-it-was-they-were would find at the far side of the Gobi Desert.

Corporal Douglas J. Cassidy, USMC, formerly of the Marine Guard, U.S. Legation, Peking, China, rode slowly up to the third rubber-tired wagon of the caravan and swung easily out of his lambskin saddle. His horse looked hardly large or sturdy enough to carry the big Marine. Cassidy was wearing an ankle-length sheepskin coat, fur side out, a lambskin hat, the ear flaps tied under his chin, and lambskin boots. A M1903 Springfield .30-06-caliber rifle hung, muzzle down, from his saddle. A USMC web cartridge belt hung across his chest. He tied the reins of the horse to a rope dangling from the side of the wagon, then climbed up onto it. He pushed aside the double camel skin covering the canvas body of the wagon, ducked his head, and went inside.

It took his eyes a moment to adjust to the dim light. There were no openings in the body of the wagon except for the one around the chimney over the stove. It was May, but it was still bitterly cold. Since the chimney did not adequately exhaust the smoke, the interior was smoky. An oil taper burning in the center of a table with very short legs provided very little light. The "chairs" for the table were pads of sheepskin.

This wagon, one of the four-wheelers, served as the command post of the caravan. Cassidy was not surprised to find the Chief, Sergeant Abraham, Staff Sergeant Cawber, and Sergeant Sweatley there. One of the four was always in here; often all four of them.

He made his way to the stove and used a government-issue mess cup to ladle tea from a large cast-iron pot into a bowl. Then he used a mess-kit spoon to add brown sugar to it. He took several sips of the tea before looking into the face of Sergeant Abraham.

"Something really weird on the road," he announced.

"Like what?" Staff Sergeant Cawber asked, not very pleasantly.

"Two wagons, rubber-tired, each with two camels pulling—both rubber-tired, both two-wheelers. Eight more camels. Three men riding the camels."

"What's strange about that?" Chief Brewer challenged.

"Two women and maybe five, six kids in the wagons," Cassidy went on. "One of the women is white."

"How do you know?"

"They stopped for lunch. One of the women watched the fire and the kids while the other went to take a piss. A piss and a crap. The one who took a crap took off her robe when she did it. She was white."

"Compared to what?" Staff Sergeant Cawber asked.

"Compared to the other one, who was yellow. And shorter. One of them was white."

"They see you?" Chief Brewer said.

"Yeah," Cassidy said. "I rode a little ways ahead and stopped, letting them see me, and one of the guys on the camels rode up and took a good look at me. He had a beard, a white beard, so he's probably white, too."

"And?" Cawber asked impatiently.

"He let me see he had one of them Mauser Broomhandle pistols, the ones with a stock? But he didn't aim it at me or anything. So I just rode off until I was out of sight, and then I come here."

"What do you think, Sergeant Abraham?" Chief Brewer asked.

"If anybody cares what I think," Cawber said before Abraham could reply, "we should just let them go their merry way. If there's only that many of them, they probably don't have anything they'd be willing to sell. If Cassidy made sure they didn't see him turn back this way, they don't know we're here. Leave it that way, is what I say."

"What is a white woman and maybe a white guy with a beard doing out here all alone?" Sergeant Sweatley asked.

"Making a lot better time than we are, Sergeant, I'll tell you that," Corporal Cassidy said. "If we had camels pulling our wagons, we'd be a lot farther down the road."

"I mean, what are they up to?"

"Who the fuck cares?" Cawber said.

"Maybe they have something we can use," Sweatley said.

"And maybe they don't, and maybe they'll just get ahead of us and tell somebody that we're here," Cawber responded.

"Sweatley, you curious enough to ride out there and have a look for yourself?" Chief Brewer asked Sergeant Sweatley.

"Shit," Staff Sergeant Cawber said. "The last fucking thing we need around here is another woman, two women, to feed and worry about. Don't start thinking you're the Good Samaritan, Sweatley."

Sweatley considered the question a minute, then said, "Yeah, I am that curious."

"Shit," Staff Sergeant Cawber repeated.

"Take Doto-Si with you," Chief Brewer said.

"I think I'll have a look myself," Sergeant Abraham said, rising to his feet.

"Cassidy, you're going to have to show us where they are," Sergeant Sweatley said.

"I figured," Corporal Cassidy said.

"Sweatley, you go roll two Marines out of the sack while I go find Doto-Si," Sergeant Abraham ordered.

Father Boris saw the six riders on Mongolian ponies and didn't like it.

Two hours before he had seen the large man with a rifle, and now he was back, with four other men and what looked like a woman—all armed with rifles.

We are in God's palm, Father Boris decided. *Whatever happens will happen.*

Turning the camel, he rode back to the first wagon and told Mae Su what he had seen. Both times.

"I will come with you," she said, and reined in the camels pulling her wagon.

Father Boris brought his camel to its knees and slid off, then went to one of the camels tied behind Mae Su's wagon and tightened its saddle cinch and brought it to its knees.

By then Mae Su was out of the wagon, carrying her Broomhandle Mauser and a blanket. She climbed onto the camel and got it to its feet, then concealed the machine pistol under the blanket.

They rode toward the four horsemen and the woman. Their small Mongolian ponies were standing in a line halfway up a gentle rise.

It took them five minutes to get within shouting distance.

"We come in peace," Father Boris announced, and then he realized that the five men were all white. Their faces were mostly hidden by scarves. But their skin was white, and they had Caucasian features.

"You are the Americans we have been hearing about," Father Boris said.

"Who the fuck are you?" Sergeant Sweatley demanded.

"I am a servant of God, a priest, my son," Father Boris said.

"You are Americans?" Mae Su asked.

"Who are you?" Sergeant Abraham asked courteously.

"I am the wife of Sergeant Ernest Zimmerman, Fourth Marines," Mae Su said.

"You said 'Ernie Zimmerman'?" Sweatley asked, obviously surprised.

"Yes," Mae Su said.

"We talking about the same guy? Used to run the motor convoys out of Shanghai?"

"Sergeant Ernie Zimmerman," Mae Su repeated, nodding her head.

"Shit, I knew him," Corporal Cassidy said.

"I'm Technical Sergeant Abraham, retired from the Fourth Marines," Abraham announced formally. "And these are Marines from the guard detachment, at the U.S. legation in Peking."

"What are you doing out here?" Corporal Cassidy asked.

"Probably, my son, doing the same thing you are," Father Boris said. "Trying to leave China, perhaps go to India."

"How many of you are there?"

"Two of the priest's men, Chinese," Mae Su said. "Another woman. And our children. How many are there of you?"

"Twelve Marines, some soldiers, and some Yangtze River sailors," Sweatley said. "And wives and children."

"In numbers there is strength, my son," Father Boris said.

"The other woman. She's white?"

"She is Russian," Father Boris said.

"She is the wife of Captain Edward J. Banning, of the Fourth Marines," Mae Su said.

"How is it she didn't get out of China with the other officer's dependents?" Abraham asked.

"Because she is a Russian," Mae Su said.

"You mean a Nansen passport Russian," Abraham said.

"Yes," Mae Su said.

"If you're thinking what I think you're thinking, Sergeant, I'm with you. Fuck Cawber," Corporal Cassidy said. "Ernie Zimmerman is one of us."

"Yeah, me, too," another of the Marines said.

Abraham looked at the second Marine.

"Yeah, me, too, Sergeant."

Sergeant Abraham looked at Sweatley, then kicked his little pony and cantered toward the two small wagons below him.

A .45 Colt automatic pistol appeared in an opening of the canvas of the second wagon, aimed at his midsection.

"Mrs. Banning?" Sergeant Abraham asked.

After a pause, in a faint voice, the Countess Maria Catherine Ludmilla Zhivkov replied, "I am Mrs. Edward J. Banning."

Sergeant Sweatley trotted up on his little pony.

Sergeant Abraham turned to look at him, then turned back to Milla.

He saluted. "Technical Sergeant Abraham, ma'am, United States Marine Corps."

Sweatley saluted. "Sergeant Sweatley, ma'am. I know the Captain, ma'am."

The flap opened and Milla was visible. She had the pistol at her side now. She held her baby with her other arm. Tears ran down her cheeks.

I am the daughter of an officer and the wife of an officer. I must not lose control.

"How do you do?" Milla said formally. "I am pleased

to meet you. This is Captain Banning's and my son, Edward Edwardovich."

"Is he all right, ma'am?" Sergeant Abraham asked.

"He's fine, thank you."

"What we're going to do now, ma'am, is take you to the caravan. You'll be better off with us, I think, than out here by yourself."

"Thank you."

Sergeant Sweatley thought of something else. "There's another Russian lady, ma'am," he said, and then reconsidered that. "Well, maybe not a lady, she's married to an old Yangtze River patrol sailor. But at least she's Russian."

"I look forward to meeting her," Mrs. Edward J. Banning said.

XVIII

[ONE]
Base Operations
Memphis Naval Air Station
Memphis, Tennessee
0815 28 March 1943

Admiral Jesse Ball's aide-de-camp arrived at the Peabody Hotel at 0715 with instructions to present both the Admiral's compliments and his regrets to Major General D. G. McInerney, USMC, and Brigadier General Fleming Pickering, USMCR, that he would be unable to join them for breakfast. "The Admiral," the aide said, "will of course be at base operations for your departure, which we have scheduled for 0815."

"You don't suppose ol' Jesse is a little hungover, do you, Flem?" General McInerney inquired of General Pickering.

"If he's not, he should be," Pickering replied. "I feel terrible."

The new stars on General McInerney's shoulders had been well and truly wet down by his old friends.

Admiral Ball's aide then informed the two generals that the Admiral had sent his staff car to transport them and their aides to the air station, and that he further suggested that Captain Dunn and Lieutenant Pickering travel to base operations in their privately owned vehicles. The night before, since Dunn had been in the apartment he shared with Lieutenant Pickering in the Peabody, he had been able to participate in the wetting down of General McInerney's new stars.

"The Admiral, Captain, expressed the desire that you be there to see the Generals off," Admiral Ball's aide said.

"Of course," Captain Billy Dunn said.

In point of fact, Admiral Ball was a little hungover, but that was not the reason he did not take breakfast with his old friends. He had a little ceremony to arrange, and he wanted it to go off without a hitch.

When the Admiral's staff car, followed by Captain Billy Dunn's Oldsmobile and Lieutenant Pickering's Cadillac, pulled up before base operations, a Navy captain in dress uniform, complete to sword, bellowed, "Atten-hut!"

Three squadrons of sailors and three of Marines came from Parade Rest to Attention. The sailors were separated from the Marines by a ten-man Marine flag guard. The national color was in the center, with the flags of the U.S. Navy and the USMC to either side. To the left of the Navy flag was Admiral Ball's two-starred blue flag, and to the right of the Marine Corps flag were the red starred flags to which Generals McInerney and Pickering were entitled.

"Sound off!" the Navy captain bellowed, as General McInerney stepped out of the Admiral's staff car.

The Memphis Naval Air Station band struck up the Navy hymn.

Admiral Ball marched up to Generals McInerney and Pickering, and saluted them with his sword.

"Will the Generals honor me by trooping the line?" he inquired.

"I would be honored," General McInerney said, and

added softly, so that no one but Admiral Ball could hear him, "Goddamn you, Jesse."

With General McInerney in the place of honor, and Admiral Ball and General Pickering trailing after him, the flag officers marched off to troop the line.

After thinking about it a moment, Captain William Dunn trotted quickly to the formation and took up his position as commanding officer before the assembled Marines of VMF-262.

Smiling broadly, Lieutenant Pickering, who was attired in a leather flight jacket but now wearing a fore-and-aft cap, leaned against the fender of his Cadillac and watched the proceedings.

With the trooping of the line completed, Admiral Ball led Generals McInerney and Pickering into base operations.

The band segued into "Stars and Stripes Forever," and the Navy captain and his staff marched to a position at the head of the Navy troops.

"Right face!" the Navy captain bellowed, and when the sailors and Marines had turned, bellowed "For-ward, h-arch!"

The parade moved around the base operations building to the parking ramp.

Lieutenant Pickering went into base operations.

It took just a minute or two for General McInerney to put on a flight suit and to have a quick—but thorough—look at the flight plan for his flight to Pensacola. The Memphis NAS pilot who would be the copilot for the R4-D's flight to Chicago also had a flight plan prepared for the approval of Lieutenant Sylvester, who would be the pilot-in-command.

A Corsair and the R4-D were parked right in front of base operations. There was a red flag with a single white star flapping from a small staff beside the pilot's side window of the R4-D.

"Come see us anytime, General," Admiral Ball said to General McInerney.

"Thanks, Jesse," General McInerney said. He was obviously touched. He shook Admiral Ball's hand and then

General Pickering's. "Take care of yourself, Flem," he said. "And good luck!"

"You, too, Mac," Pickering said.

General McInerney offered his hand to Lieutenant Pickering.

"It was good to see you, Pick," he said. "Keep up the good work."

Good work, my ass, Admiral Ball thought, but he smiled.

"Thank you, sir," Pick said. "It was good to see you, sir."

General McInerney nodded, then walked toward the Corsair.

The band began to play "The Marines' Hymn," and kept playing it until General McInerney climbed into the Corsair and fired up its engine, and until General Pickering—who embraced his son quickly before walking to the R4-D—was aboard. Then the band began playing "Auld Lang Syne."

In the cockpit of the Corsair, General McInerney waited for the needles to move into the green, then looked at Admiral Ball, saluted, and started taxiing. A moment later, the R4-D began moving.

Pick waved at his father.

General McInerney turned onto the active runway and immediately began his takeoff roll. As soon as he had broken ground, the R4-D began to roll. Once airborne, the R4-D took up a course for Chicago. The Corsair, which had made a shallow climbing turn to the left after takeoff, now headed back to the field. It flashed over the field at 250 feet, with its throttles to the firewall, and then pointed its nose skyward. At 5,000 feet, it entered a layer of clouds and disappeared.

Admiral Ball walked over to Lieutenant Pickering.

"I think General McInerney enjoyed all this, don't you, Lieutenant? And your father, too, of course?"

"Yes, sir. I'm sure they did."

"And what about you, Lieutenant. Did you enjoy it?"

"Very much, sir."

"And last night? Did you have a good time last night?"

"Yes, sir."

"Commit it to memory, your disgrace to the uniform you're wearing. It will be the last thing you'll enjoy for a hell of a long time."

"Sir?"

Two Marines with Shore Patrol brassards on their sleeves, one of them a technical sergeant, marched up and saluted Admiral Ball.

"This officer is under arrest," Admiral Ball said. "Escort him to his quarters—his *on-base* quarters—and when he has changed into the prescribed uniform, bring him to my office."

"Aye, aye, sir," the technical sergeant said. "This way, please, Lieutenant."

[TWO]
Office of the Base Commander
Memphis Naval Air Station
Memphis, Tennessee
0910 29 March 1943

Three Marines, two of them wearing shore patrol brassards and armed with .45–caliber pistols, marched in a line into the base commander's office.

"Detail, halt," the Marine technical sergeant ordered, then "Detail, left FACE!" The three were now facing Rear Admiral Jesse Ball, USN. "Sir . . ." the technical sergeant barked as he saluted.

Lieutenant Malcolm S. Pickering, USMCR, started to raise his hand in a reflex action to salute, but catching something in Admiral Ball's eyes—a look of contemptuous surprise—stopped with his arm half up and lowered it.

". . . Technical Sergeant Franz reporting to the Admiral with the prisoner as ordered, sir," the technical sergeant finished.

Admiral Ball returned the salute. "Leave the prisoner and stand by in the outer office," he ordered.

"Aye, aye, sir!" the technical sergeant barked, then went on. "Guard detail, one step backward, ha-arch! Right, FACE! Forward, ha-arch!"

The two Shore Patrolmen marched out of the room.

Lieutenant Pickering remained at attention, facing Admiral Ball.

"Pickering, prisoners are denied the privilege of saluting," Admiral Ball said conversationally. "That's something you might wish to keep in mind."

"Yes, sir," Lieutenant Pickering said.

"Have you any idea why I have placed you under arrest, Mr. Pickering?"

"No, sir."

"I have the odd feeling, perhaps naïvely, that you may possess one—one only—of the characteristics required of an officer in the Naval Service," Admiral Ball said. "You may not be a liar. Are you a liar, Mr. Pickering? Are you capable of answering a question put to you truthfully?"

"Yes, sir."

"Yes, sir, which? Yes, you are a liar? Or yes, you will answer a question bearing on your fitness to be an officer truthfully?"

"Sir, I am not a liar. I will answer any question put to me truthfully."

"Well, then, let's put that to the test. Mr. Pickering, it has been alleged that you have had on several occasions carnal knowledge of a female who is not only not your wife but is married to someone else. Specifically, one Elizabeth-Sue Megham, sometimes known as Mrs. Quincy T. Megham, Jr. Do these allegations have any basis in fact?"

"Sir, I was raised to believe that a gentleman does not discuss—"

"Don't hand me any crap about you being a gentleman, you miserable sonofabitch!" Admiral Ball exploded furiously. "Have you, or have you not, been fucking this banker's wife?"

"Yes, sir," Pick said.

"Knowing that she was a married woman?"

"Yes, sir."

"The basis of all law in what we think of as the Western world, Mr. Pickering, is generally agreed to be the Old Testament. In the Old Testament it is recorded that Moses came down from Mount Sinai carrying in his arms two

stone tablets on which God himself had etched a number
of rules by which God-fearing men were to conduct their
lives. Are you familiar with that story, Mr. Pickering?"

"Yes, sir."

"These ten rules, which came to be called the Ten Commandments, provide for God-fearing people a list of some
things they are supposed to do and some things they are
not supposed to do. Are you familiar with the Ten Commandments, Mr. Pickering?"

"Yes, sir."

"Two of them have a special meaning for us here today.
One of them is 'thou shalt honor thy father and thy
mother, that thy days,' et cetera, et cetera. Are you familiar with that particular commandment, Mr. Pickering?"

"Yes, sir."

"I'm told you are an imaginative young man. I believe
that. When you told the flight safety officer that you
weren't even aware you had barrel-rolled over the control
tower because you had an oil-pressure warning light at
the time, and were devoting all of your attention to that
problem, now, that was imaginative. You were lying
through your goddamned teeth, of course, but it was imaginative."

"Yes, sir."

"You admit that you lied to the flight safety officer?"

"I didn't think of it as a lie at the time, sir."

"Goddamn you!" Admiral Ball exploded again. "Did
you lie to the flight safety officer or not?"

"Yes, sir. I lied about that."

"For your general fund of knowledge, Mr. Pickering,
the Regulations for the Governance of the Naval Service,
to which you are subject, provide that any officer who
knowingly and willfully utters any statement he knows to
be untrue shall be punished as a court-martial may direct."

"Yes, sir."

"We were talking about your imagination, Mr. Pickering. Can you imagine which of the Ten Commandments
in addition to the 'thou shalt honor thy father' one has an
application here today?"

"No, sir."

"You mean you really don't know? Or, sniveling little

smart-ass that you are, you're afraid to say?"

"The one concerned with adultery, sir?"

" 'Thou shalt not commit adultery,' " Admiral Ball said. "Now, that seems a simple enough order to me. 'Thou shalt not commit adultery.' It means you shouldn't screw somebody else's wife. Was that commandment beyond your comprehension, Mr. Pickering?"

"No, sir."

"But you disobeyed it anyway, right?"

"Yes, sir."

"The next real codification of the law as we know it, to the best of my understanding, Mr. Pickering, was the Magna Carta, granted by his Majesty King John of England, Ireland, Scotland, et cetera, et cetera, to his nobles at Runnymede in June in the Year of Our Lord one thousand two hundred and fifteen. Are you familiar with the Magna Carta, Mr. Pickering?"

"Somewhat, sir."

"Goddamn you, you sniveling pup, don't waffle with me! Yes, goddamnit, or no?"

"Yes, sir."

"Then you are doubtless aware, Mr. Pickering, that the Magna Carta is the basis of what we think of as English common law?"

"Yes, sir."

"And that when the Founding Fathers of this great republic of ours got around to writing the laws for it, they incorporated much of English Common law? Except that we pledge our allegiance to the flag of the United States and the country for which it stands, et cetera, et cetera, instead of to the English monarch. You do have that straight in your head, Mr. Pickering?"

"Yes, sir."

"Then possibly you are also aware that the duly elected officials of this great republic of ours, recognizing that the basic law provided for the ordinary citizens of this great republic of ours was not really adequate to govern its navy, came up with what we call the Regulations for the Governance of the Naval Service. You are familiar with that, Mr. Pickering?"

"Yes, sir."

"And you are aware that you, as a Marine, are subject to it?"

"Yes, sir."

"Then perhaps you can tell me what the Regulations for the Governance of the Naval Service has to say about what you can do with the physiological symbol of your gender?"

"Sir?"

"Where you may insert your pecker, Mr. Pickering."

"No, sir."

"Are you trying to plead ignorance of the law, you miserable little prick?"

"No, sir."

"Ignorance of the law is no defense, Mr. Pickering. You might wish to make note of that."

"Yes, sir."

"It says—this is not a direct quote, but it's close enough—that anybody who has carnal knowledge of—sticks his pecker into—any woman to whom he is not lawfully joined in holy matrimony shall be punished as a court-martial may direct."

"Yes, sir."

"Were you aware of that, Mr. Pickering?"

"No, sir, I was not."

"I am not surprised. Now, in addition to providing suitable punishment for someone who can't keep his pecker in his pocket, the Regulations for the Governance of the Naval Service makes special provision for those whom Congress has seen fit to declare officers and gentlemen. Are you aware of any of these provisions, Mr. Pickering?"

"No, sir."

"I am not surprised. Let me enlighten you. The Regulations for the Governance of the Naval Service provide that any officer found guilty of conduct unbecoming an officer and a gentleman shall be punished as a court-martial may direct."

"Yes, sir."

"Did you really believe, Mr. Pickering, that doing a barrel roll over my airfield's control tower, endangering not only the lives of the fine sailors performing their duty therein, but also the valuable aircraft with which you had been entrusted, was conduct *becoming* an officer and a gentleman?"

"Sir, I didn't think about it in quite those terms."

"Did you, for some perverse reason, think that handing the flight safety officer that bullshit about having all your attention on an oil-pressure warning light was conduct *becoming* an officer and a gentleman?"

"No, sir."

"But you did believe that hiding your salami in this banker's lonely and probably sexually unsatisfied wife was in keeping with behavior of a Marine officer and gentleman? That you were, perhaps, performing some sort of public service? Keeping up morale on the home front?"

"No, sir."

"You didn't think it was conduct becoming an officer? And a gentleman?"

"The truth, sir, is that I didn't give it much thought."

"You may have guessed, Mr. Pickering, that I don't like you very much," Admiral Ball said.

"Yes, sir."

"One of the reasons I don't like you is because, in the short time I have been privileged to know him, it is apparent that your father is a fine Marine. Cast from the same mold as my old friend General McInerney. I would have had a fine time last night, celebrating the promotion of my old friend, and in the company of another fine Marine, if you hadn't been there, you miserable pimple on a Marine Corps PFC's ass.

"How, I asked myself, is it possible that a fine man, a fine Marine officer such as General Pickering, holder of the nation's second-highest decoration for valor—a man decorated for valor in both world wars, a Marine who has *shed blood* in both world wars, a man who enjoys the confidence of the Commander in Chief himself, can have spawned such a miserable, irresponsible, amoral, useless sonofabitch like you?"

He glowered at Lieutenant Pickering.

"Any comment, Mr. Pickering? How can this have happened?"

"No comment, sir."

"May I hazard a guess what's running through that

probably diseased mind of yours at this moment?"

"Yes, sir."

"You are thinking, I will bet ten dollars to a doughnut, something along these lines: 'Doesn't this old bastard realize that I myself am something of a hero? I stand before him a veteran of Guadalcanal, a recipient of the Distinguished Flying Cross, a superb fighter pilot who has shot down seven enemy aircraft, and managed to shed a little of my own blood in the process.' Were you thinking something along those lines, Mr. Pickering?"

"Sir, I'm proud of my service with VMF-229," Lieutenant Pickering said uncomfortably. "I like to think I did my duty on Guadalcanal, sir."

"Let me tell you what I think of your service with VMF-229, Mr. Pickering," Admiral Ball said. "First of all, God gave you more hand-eye coordination than he saw fit to give other people. Since you had nothing to do with that, you can't take pride in it. Your hand-eye coordination, from God, gives you the ability to fly airplanes better than most people. But you really shouldn't take pride in that. You are, of course, aware of the study, vis-à-vis pilots, conducted by the University of California?"

"No, sir," Lieutenant Pickering said, confused.

"The behavioral scientists at the University of California, after extensive research, concluded that the best human material to train to be a pilot are classified intellectually as cretins. Do you know what a cretin is, Mr. Pickering?"

"No, sir."

"A cretin is a high level moron," Admiral Ball said. "Judging by your behavior outside the cockpit, it fits you to a T. So you went to Guadalcanal, God having made you a cretin, and the Marine Corps having seen fit to put you in a cockpit, and you got lucky. God, it is said, takes care of fools and drunks, and you obviously qualify for His special concern on both counts. You managed to shoot down seven of the enemy, and—to be fair about this—the enemy pilots were probably divided, say four and three, into the incompetent and the unlucky.

"And then you came home, Mr. Pickering, entrusted by the Marine Corps to train other Marine Aviators in the techniques of aerial combat. To train is to lead. How is the best way to lead, Mr. Pickering?"

"I'm not sure I understand the Admiral's question, sir."

"The best way to train, Mr. Pickering, the best way to lead, is by example. You might make note of that, since it apparently never occurred to you before."

"Yes, sir."

"And what sort of example did you set for the young Marines entrusted to your hands to lead, Mr. Pickering? You made it perfectly clear to the men entrusted to your care that the way to become a splendid Marine fighter pilot like you is to ignore any regulations you find it inconvenient to obey; to spend as much time as possible racing, over the speed limit, out of uniform, between bars; to endanger the lives of enlisted men by barrel-rolling over the base control tower; to lie through your teeth to flight safety officers and other officers; and finally, to hide your salami in the first married woman you could entice to raise her skirt, without one goddamned thought about the trouble this might cause for her, for her husband, for me, and for the United States Marine Corps, which for reasons I don't pretend to understand, thought you had the character of an officer and a gentleman, and gave you a commission."

Admiral Ball met Lieutenant Pickering's eyes for a full sixty seconds, which seemed to be much longer.

"Would you say, Mr. Pickering, that the foregoing was an accurate assessment of the situation?"

"Yes, sir," Lieutenant Pickering said. "Sir—"

Admiral Ball raised his hand to silence him. "I have several options open to me," Admiral Ball said. "One of which, I am sure, you devious sonofabitch, has already occurred to you."

"Sir?"

"The Marine Corps has been sending some of its misfit aviators—fuckups of your ilk, Mr. Pickering—to a squadron based in Hawaii. There is a shortage of fighter pilots in the Pacific, Mr. Pickering, and the reasoning is that it is better to try to salvage these ne'er-do-wells, these disgraces to the uniform, and utilize their flying skills, rather than send them to the Portsmouth Naval Prison. Wiseass that you are, I am confident that you are thinking, 'Fine, let the old bastard send me to VMF-229. Charley Galloway is the skipper, and he appreciates what a fine fellow and all-around splendid aviator I am.' Did that thought occur to you, Mr. Pickering?"

"Sir, if I could be transferred to VMF-229 . . ."

"Transferring you to VMF-229 is not one of the options available to me, you miserable sonofabitch. I know Charley Galloway, too. I have known him for years, I think what the Marine Corps is doing to him is disgraceful, and I am not going to add to his burden by sending him a miserable excuse for a human being like you to baby-sit."

He let that sink in.

"Neither am I going to take you off flight status and send you to Quantico for retraining as an infantry officer. For that matter, as a platoon leader in a mess-kit repair company. You are not fit to command men.

"That leaves me with very few other options. One of them is to offer you the chance to resign for the good of the service, which would make you immediately available for the draft. Unfortunately, you might be drafted back into the Marine Corps as a private, or, God forbid, into the U.S. Navy as an apprentice seaman, and I wouldn't want that on my conscience.

"Similarly, while six months or a year in the Portsmouth Naval Prison—I believe the penalty for unlawful carnal knowledge is five years at hard labor, but I have been told that prisoners are being released early—might give you an opportunity to ruminate on your behavior, I am reluctant to do that, too. The idea of you sitting in a warm cell, eating three hot meals a day while good and decent men are being sent in harm's way, offends my sense of right and wrong.

"Furthermore, if I send you off in irons to Portsmouth, your father would be distressed. And probably General McInerney, too—why he likes you is a deep mystery to me. Your father would be ashamed and humiliated. As I said, I like your father."

Admiral Ball let this sink in a moment.

"Going back to my observation that God takes care of fools and drunks like you, and what I said about there being a shortage of pilots, there is one other option available to me."

"Yes, sir?"

"General McInerney has a requirement for twin-engine, R4-D or PBY-5A, aviators. He was not at liberty to divulge the nature of the operation, except to say that it was somewhere in the Pacific and involves an unusual degree of risk to the participants."

"I have some R4-D time, sir."

"So I understand," Admiral Ball said. "But no PBY-5A time, as I understand it?"

"No, sir."

"My problem in offering you the chance to volunteer for General McInerney's operation—glossing over, for the moment, your manifold character weaknesses—is that if I send you, you might be more trouble to the people involved than you would be worth. This mission does not need fuckups, Mr. Pickering, and you have proved yourself to be a world-class fuckup."

"Sir, am I being offered the chance to volunteer for this mission?"

"I'll have to give that some serious thought," Admiral Ball said. "Right now, on a scale of one to ten, your chances that I will are hovering around two. If you're looking for advice, what I would do in your shoes is get a copy of the Regulations for the Governance of the Naval Service and see what you can learn about defending yourself in a court-martial."

"Sir, I'll do anything to keep flying."

"Marine officers don't beg," Admiral Ball said. "God, you are a disgusting specimen of a human being!"

Admiral Ball pushed the lever on his intercom.

"Send the guard detail in here," he ordered. "And if my aide is out there, send him in, too."

The Marine guards marched into the room.

"Take the prisoner to his quarters," Admiral Ball ordered. "Post a guard outside his door. Arrange for his meals to be brought to him from the enlisted mess. See that he's provided with a copy of the Regulations for the Governance of the Naval Service."

"Aye, aye, sir," Technical Sergeant Kranz barked.

"Prisoner, one step backward, h-arch." Lieutenant Pickering took one ˙step backward. "About-FACE! Forward, h-arch."

Preceded by one Marine Shore Patrolman and trailed by Technical Sergeant Krantz, Lieutenant Pickering marched out of Admiral Ball's office.

Admiral Ball waited until the door was closed before looking at his aide. "God, Marines!" he said. "They're never anything but trouble. If we didn't need them to fight wars, there would be a bounty on them!"

"Yes, sir," his aide said.

"Call flight scheduling," Admiral Ball ordered. "Lay on a PBY-5A, and the best IP on the base for 0730 tomorrow. Tell him I want Pickering qualified in the PBY5-A as fast as possible—I don't care if they fly ten hours a day—and to give me daily reports on his progress. And then send a TWX to General McInerney's office telling him I think, repeat think, I will have a PBY-5A volunteer for him in a week."

"Aye, aye, sir."

Admiral Ball then reached for his telephone and dialed a number. He worked his way through the switchboard of the Planter's Bank & Trust Company of Memphis, and then a secretary, and finally got Braxton V. Lipscomb on the phone.

"Brax, Jesse. That little problem we had? Romeo and Juliet? It's fixed. No further problem, Brax."

[THREE]
Naval Air Transport Command
U.S. Naval Base
Pearl Harbor, Oahu, Territory of Hawaii
1715 2 April 1943

Major Jake Dillon, USMCR, leaned against the fender of a 1941 Ford station wagon, with the logo of Pacific & Far East Shipping painted on its doors, and watched as the huge four-engine NATC Coronado with Brigadier General Fleming Pickering aboard splashed down at Pearl

Harbor. Parked beside the Ford were a General Motors two-and-a-half-ton canvas-bodied truck and the Plymouth staff car assigned to Rear Admiral Daniel J. Wagam, USN, of the CINCPAC staff. A detail of white hats had sought shelter from the brass hats by stationing themselves at the rear of the truck.

Admiral Wagam was in the backseat of his Plymouth, using his briefcase as a desk. His aide, Lieutenant Chambers D. Lewis III, USN, was leaning on the Plymouth's fender.

When the Coronado was safely down, Lewis went to the rear window of the Plymouth and told Admiral Wagam, who nodded, glanced out the window, and returned his attention to his paperwork. He knew it would be a good five minutes before the passengers could be ferried ashore, and five minutes was precious.

Wagam had come to the terminal to see if he could hasten Pickering, whose time was also valuable, and the cargo—which he knew Pickering would insist on seeing through the bureaucratic process—through de-embarkation.

As the first of the barges sent to off-load the Coronado's passengers and cargo reached the wharf, a black 1939 Cadillac pulled in beside the Ford and stopped.

Admiral Wagam saw it out of the corner of his eye and recognized it. It was the staff car assigned to Admiral Chester W. Nimitz, CINCPAC. Wagam hurriedly stuffed his papers into his briefcase and got out of the car.

Nimitz was not in his car. Captain Kurt Groscher heaved himself out of the backseat. In Wagam's view, Groscher was the brightest of the intelligence officers on the CINCPAC staff.

When he saw Wagam, he saluted.

"What brings you here, Groscher?" Wagam asked, as he returned the salute.

"The Boss wants to see General Pickering," Groscher said.

"Am I allowed to ask about what?"

"You're allowed to *ask*, Admiral," Groscher said with a smile.

"Okay, fellas, let's go," Lieutenant Lewis said to the work detail, and led them toward the pier.

Major Jake Dillon walked up to Admiral Wagam and Captain Groscher and saluted.

"Do you know Major Dillon, Captain?" Admiral Wagam asked.

"Only by reputation," Groscher said. "How's the refueling project going?"

Dillon didn't reply.

"Captain Groscher, Major," Admiral Wagam said, "not only knows everything about everything but, more important, is considered to have the Need To Know everything about everything."

Dillon shrugged. "We're just about finished installing some auxiliary fuel tanks in one of the Catalinas," he said. "We'll test that. Them. If that works, we'll put tanks in the other one."

"And if it doesn't?" Groscher asked.

"We'll try something else," Dillon said.

"I don't have to tell you the Boss is personally interested in this project," Groscher said. "Is there anything you need?"

"No, sir," Dillon said.

"There he is," Wagam said, as Brigadier General Pickering and Lieutenant Hart came onto the wharf. The three walked toward them. Salutes were exchanged.

"I trust the General is pleased with the reception he is being given?" Dillon said jokingly.

"Actually, Jake, I'm a little disappointed. When I left Memphis—I stopped in to see Pick—there were troops lined up and a band playing 'The Marines' Hymn.' "

"Really?"

"Mac McInerney flew me up there," Pickering said, more to Wagam than Dillon. "The base commander turned out to be an old pal of his."

"Jesse Ball," Wagam said.

"Right. We wetted down Mac's new stars together."

"I'm surprised you could get on an airplane after a night with those two," Wagam said.

"Admiral Nimitz's compliments, General," Captain Groscher said. "The Admiral would be pleased if you could see him at your earliest convenience."

Pickering looked at Wagam.

"I'll handle things here, Fleming," Wagam said. "The Admiral does not like to be kept waiting."

"I don't want that equipment to disappear somewhere," Pickering said.

"Where do you want it? Ewa?"

"That would mean we'd have to bring it back here when we need it," Pickering said. "But on the other hand, it probably wouldn't disappear at Ewa."

"It will be at Ewa, under guard, in an hour or so."

"Let's go, Captain," Pickering said, then called to Lieutenant Hart. "George, go with the equipment to Ewa. Find Lieutenant Colonel Dawkins, and tell him I would regard it as a personal favor if he put this stuff somewhere safe, and under guard. Then I'll see you—and you, too, Jake— at Muku-Muku."

"Aye, aye, sir," Hart said.

Pickering got into the Cadillac.

The car had barely started to move when Captain Groscher reached into the interior pocket of his tunic and handed Pickering a sealed—but not addressed or otherwise marked—envelope.

"I thought it would be better if you were familiar with these before you saw the Admiral," Groscher said. "The one from Marshall came in two days ago; the one from Donovan this morning."

Pickering tore open the envelope and took off two sheets of paper and read them.

```
T O P S E C R E T

THE JOINT CHIEFS OF STAFF
WASHINGTON
0900 30 MARCH 1943
VIA SPECIAL CHANNEL

CINCPAC HAWAII
EYES ONLY ADMIRAL CHESTER W. NIMITZ
```

FOLLOWING PERSONAL FROM CHIEF OF STAFF US
ARMY TO CINCPAC

DEAR CHESTER:

THE MESSAGES ATTACHED TO THIS ARE FOR
YOUR INFORMATION, BUT OF GREAT
IMPORTANCE AS WELL TO BRIG GEN PICKERING
WHO IS PRESENTLY ENROUTE TO HAWAII.
PLEASE SEE THAT HE SEES THEM AS SOON AS
POSSIBLE ON HIS ARRIVAL. HIS EXPLAINING
THE BACKGROUND TO ALL OF THIS MAKES MORE
SENSE TO ME THAN TRYING TO DO SO IN A
MESSAGE OF THIS TYPE.

BEST PERSONAL REGARDS

GEORGE

END PERSONAL MESSAGE FROM CHIEF OF STAFF
US ARMY TO CINCPAC

ATTACHMENT ONE

COPY OF MESSAGE FROM CHIEF OF STAFF
USARMY TO COMMANDING GENERAL US MILITARY
MISSION TO CHINA.

T O P S E C R E T

OPERATIONAL IMMEDIATE
THE JOINT CHIEFS OF STAFF
WASHINGTON
0900 30 MARCH 1943

COMMMANDING GENERAL
USMILMISSCHINA CHUNGKING
EYES ONLY LTGEN JOSEPH STILLWELL, USA

1. IMMEDIATELY UPON RECEIPT OF THIS
MESSAGE, YOU WILL RELIEVE MAJGEN

FREDERICK T. DEMPSEY AND BRIGGEN J.R. NEWLEY OF THEIR DUTIES. THESE OFFICERS ARE TO BE PLACED IN ARREST IN QUARTERS STATUS PENDING FURTHER ACTION BY THE JCS. THEY ARE TO BE DENIED ACCESS TO ANY COMMUNICATIONS FACILITY UNDER YOUR CONTROL, AND YOU WILL PERSONALLY CENSOR ANY OUTGOING PERSONAL MAIL THESE OFFICERS WISH TO DISPATCH.

2. COLONEL (BRIGGEN DESIGNATE)HULIT A. ALBRIGHT, SIGC, USA, IS PRESENTLY ENROUTE BY AIR FROM WASHINGTON DC TO USMMCHI. BRIGGEN(DES) ALBRIGHT IS CARRYING WITH HIM A LETTER FROM ADMIRAL WILLIAM D. LEAHY, CHIEF OF STAFF TO THE PRESIDENT, TO YOU WHICH WILL EXPLAIN THE NECESSITY OF THE ACTION DIRECTED IN PARA 1 ABOVE. IT IS STRONGLY RECOMMENDED THAT YOU NAME BRIGGEN(DES) ALBRIGHT AS SIGNAL OFFICER, USMMCHI.

3. COLONEL JOHN J. WATERSON, USA, OF THE OFFICE OF STRATEGIC SERVICES IS PRESENTLY ENROUTE BY AIR FROM BRISBANE AUSTRALIA TO CHUNGKING. COL WATERSON HAS BEEN PROVIDED WITH A COPY OF ADMIRAL LEAHY'S LETTER TO YOU (PARA 2 ABOVE) AND DIRECTED TO PRESENT IT TO YOU IMMEDIATELY ON HIS ARRIVAL. THE INTENTION WAS TO GET ADM LEAHY'S LETTER TO YOU INTO YOUR HANDS AT THE EARLIEST POSSIBLE TIME.

4. BRIGEN FLEMING PICKERING, USMCR, DEPUTY DIRECTOR FOR PACIFIC OPERATIONS, THE OFFICE OF STRATEGIC SERVICES, IS PRESENTLY EN ROUTE BY AIR TO USMMCHI VIA PEARL HARBOR. IT IS ANTICIPATED THAT EITHER OR BOTH BRIG GEN(DES) ALBRIGHT AND COL WATERSON WILL REACH CHUNGKING BEFORE BRIGGEN PICKERING, BUT BRIG GEN

PICKERING HAS BEEN ORDERED TO REPORT TO
YOU PERSONALLY ON HIS ARRIVAL IN ORDER TO
EXPLAIN THE NECESSITY OF THE ACTIONS
DESCRIBED IN PARA 1 AND TO ANSWER ANY
QUESTIONS YOU MIGHT HAVE.

5. THE CONTENTS OF THIS MESSAGE ARE TO BE
MADE KNOWN TO LT COL EDWARD J. BANNING,
USMC, PRESENTLY IN CHUNGKING, AS SOON AS
POSSIBLE.

6. EVERY EFFORT SHOULD BE MADE TO RESOLVE
THIS MATTER WITHIN USMMCHI. IF IT IS
NECESSARY TO INVOLVE CINC CHINA THEATER
OF OPERATIONS, JCS WILL BE NOTIFIED BY
SPECIAL CHANNEL.

GEORGE C MARSHALL
GENERAL, US ARMY
CHIEF OF STAFF, USARMY

T O P S E C R E T

T O P S E C R E T

THE OFFICE OF STRATEGIC SERVICES
WASHINGTON
1615 1 APRIL 1943
VIA SPECIAL CHANNEL

CINCPAC HAWAII
EYES ONLY ADMIRAL CHESTER W. NIMITZ

FOLLOWING PERSONAL FROM DIRECTOR OSS TO
CINCPAC

DEAR ADMIRAL NIMITZ:

I WOULD BE GRATEFUL IF YOU WOULD PASS THE
FOLLOWING TO BRIGGEN FLEMING PICKERING

PRESENTLY ENROUTE HAWAII AS SOON AS
POSSIBLE.

BEGIN MESSAGE

DEAR FLEMING:

GENERAL MARSHALL TELEPHONED AT 1345
WASHINGTON TIME TO ASK WHEN I THOUGHT YOU
WOULD BE IN CHUNGKING. I ASSURED HIM YOU
WOULD GET THERE AS QUICKLY AS POSSIBLE
FOLLOWING CONCLUSION OF YOUR BUSINESS IN
PEARL HARBOR.

SENATOR FOWLER TELEPHONED AT 1405
WASHINGTON TIME TO SAY SENATE HAS GIVEN
ITS ADVICE AND CONSENT TO PROMOTION OF
COLONEL ALBRIGHT TO BRIGADIER GENERAL.

BEST REGARDS,

BILL

END MESSAGE

END PERSONAL FROM DIRECTOR OSS TO CINCPAC

T O P S E C R E T

Pickering read both messages twice and then handed
them back to Captain Groscher. He seemed lost in thought
for a moment, then met Groscher's eyes. "Banning works
for me—" he began.

"I know him," Groscher said. Pickering understood that
he had been interrupted in order to save time; an explanation of who Banning was and what he did would not
be necessary.

"When he got to Chungking with the MAGIC devices
the President had sent to China, these two signal officers—
and God only knows who else—knew all about it."

"Who told them?" Groscher asked coldly.

"The Secretary of the JCS and the Deputy Director for Administration of the OSS," Pickering said.

"My God!"

"Yeah," Pickering agreed.

"What happened to them?" Groscher asked. "Admiral Nimitz will want to know."

"The OSS fellow was sent to St. Elizabeth's," Pickering said. "I don't know what's happened to General Adamson."

"Adamson, Charles M.?" Groscher asked. "Major General?"

Pickering nodded.

"They should have been shot," Groscher said.

Pickering looked at him in surprise and realized Groscher was perfectly serious.

"Any explanation why they did what they did?" Groscher asked when Pickering didn't reply.

"None that made any sense to me," Pickering said.

"I know Albright," Groscher said. "I went to Washington when we were going to get MAGIC devices here. He checked me out on them. Good man. He should have been a general long before this."

"I like him," Pickering agreed.

He looked out the window and saw they were pulling up before the two-story white masonry building that housed the Commander in Chief, Pacific, and his senior staff.

Admiral Chester W. Nimitz, CINCPAC, was busy. When one of his aides put his head in the door of his office, a dozen officers were sitting at the conference table. Most of them were admirals and generals, but a few Navy captains and one Marine colonel were sprinkled among them.

"General Pickering and Captain Groscher are here, Admiral."

There were barely concealed looks of annoyance on the faces of the men at the table. They sensed an interruption to their labors and didn't like it. Nimitz understood. He really resented the interruption to his schedule that was about to take place, but it had to be done.

"Gentlemen," he said. "Take a ten-minute coffee break. I'll be as quick as possible."

Everyone began to stuff documents into briefcases. Almost all of the documents were stamped SECRET and TOP SECRET.

For a moment Nimitz considered telling them to belay that. Captain Groscher had already seen everything on the table, or soon would, and Pickering was cleared for anything classified. Time would be saved by telling his staff just to leave the documents where they were. But he immediately realized that that would set a bad precedent. If the Admiral was a little sloppy with classified material, that would constitute a license for the others to be sloppy.

He waited until all the documents had disappeared from sight, then stood at the door of his office until all the officers had filed through it.

"Welcome to beautiful Hawaii, again, Fleming," he called. "Come on in. You, too, Groscher."

"Good afternoon, sir," Pickering said.

Nimitz closed the door himself. He saw the clock on the wall.

"Actually, it's the cocktail hour," he said. "Can I offer you something stronger than coffee?"

"Sir, I think I'd rather wait until I talk to my people," Pickering said.

"Okay, coffee it is," the Admiral said, and walked to a table against the wall that held a coffee machine and a rack of standard Navy, white china cups. He worked the lever, filling a cup, and then handed it to Pickering. He filled another, handed it to Groscher, and finally poured one for himself.

"Would you mind standing?" he asked. "My doctor's been telling me that sitting for long hours with my knees bent is bad for an old man's circulation."

"You're not old, sir," Pickering protested automatically.

"You've read the two messages?" Nimitz asked, getting to the point.

"Yes, sir."

"Fill me in, please," Nimitz said.

Pickering told him what he knew of the events in Chungking and Washington.

"How bad is it? How long can we continue to believe that the Japanese don't know about MAGIC?"

"I just don't know, sir," Pickering said.

"I think that's why George Marshall wants you in Chungking as quickly as possible," Nimitz said. "For the damage evaluation."

"Sir, I think that's why he promoted Colonel Albright," Pickering said. "And is sending him to Chungking. He would be much better at that than me."

"Groscher knows and likes this fellow. He told me he's just the man to keep the barn door closed. The question is, how many cows got out?"

"Let me give you the worst possible scenario, General," Captain Groscher said. "That's my job."

"And he's very good at it," Nimitz said.

"The real harm those two in Washington did was to degrade the secrecy of MAGIC," Groscher began. "Remove the awe for it, if you like. It's obvious—to me, at least— that they regarded access to MAGIC as a prerogative of rank or position, a marshal's baton, so to speak. They didn't really understand the necessity for keeping MAGIC secret."

"Yeah," Pickering agreed thoughtfully.

"I would suppose that of the senior officers around here, ninety percent know something about MAGIC, at least that it exists, and that only a very few, very senior officers— the Admiral and his chief of staff—and a handful of middle-level underlings like me have access to it. Everybody wants to be important, you follow me?"

Pickering shook his head sadly, in agreement, and blurted, "God, in Brisbane, MacArthur's G-2 pouted like a child until he got a MAGIC clearance."

"We have that situation here. It is reasonable to presume it exists in Chungking," Groscher went on. "What was the USMMCHI's signal officer's name? Dempsey?" Groscher asked.

"Right," Pickering said.

"General Dempsey almost certainly knew of the existence of MAGIC and that only important people got access to it. The difference between here, Hawaii, and Brisbane is that the Admiral and General MacArthur knew of the importance of MAGIC, and more important, the absolute necessity of keeping it secret. . . ."

Groscher stopped. "How much do you know of the command structure over there?" he asked.

"Very little."

"There is an overall command," Admiral Nimitz said. "The China-Burma-India theatres of operation. Theatres, plural. Admiral Lord Louis Mountbatten is the Supreme Commander. He's in New Delhi. As of this moment, he does not have MAGIC, although over the objections of Admiral Leahy and General Marshall, he's going to get it.

"There is also, under CBI, the China theatre of operations, with Generalissimo Chiang Kai-shek the theatre commander. He asked for, and got, an American chief of staff. General Joseph Stillwell. Stillwell is also the commanding general of the U.S. military mission to China.

"The President has similarly decided that Chiang Kai-shek will be given MAGIC access. Again over the objections of Admiral Leahy and General Marshall. Probably in the hope that the President can be persuaded to change his mind, neither Chiang Kai-shek nor General Stillwell, so far as I know, has been told either that MAGIC exists or that they are to be given access to it," Nimitz concluded, and then asked, "This is the first time you're hearing this?"

"I knew, sir, of Admiral Leahy's reluctance to give Mountbatten and Chiang Kai-shek MAGIC access."

"Inasmuch as General Stillwell knows nothing of MAGIC—except probably that something with that name exists, classified Top Secret—there has been no reason for him to impress on his staff the absolute necessity to keep MAGIC uncompromised. So far as General Stillwell is concerned, it is just one more Top Secret project, and he has filing cabinets full of those."

"I think I'm beginning to get the picture, sir," Pickering said.

"Go on, Groscher," Nimitz ordered.

"So General Dempsey hears that he is going to get MAGIC and a MAGIC clearance, which means he is now important. He wants to share this proud accomplishment with somebody. So he shares it with his deputy. Why not?

He doesn't know that MAGIC is not just one more military secret. His deputy has a Top Secret clearance. So he tells him. The deputy now feels important. He needs to tell somebody. And since he doesn't know how really important MAGIC is, *he* feels safe in telling a trusted subordinate, one who has a Top Secret clearance. And so on."

"I'm very afraid Groscher may be right," Admiral Nimitz said. "And I think that's why General Marshall wants you to be in Chungking as soon as you can get there, Pickering. You will be the OSS delegate from JCS—for that matter, from the President himself—to General Stillwell. I think you are expected to impress on him the importance of keeping MAGIC really secret, and also to let them know in Washington how far down the chain the breaking of the secret has gone."

"I'm comfortable with the first part, sir," Pickering said. "But I'm not at all sure I'm competent to judge how far MAGIC has been compromised."

"Like an ONI or CIC agent would be?" Groscher asked. "Right."

"To know what they were looking for, an ONI or CIC agent would have to be told about MAGIC," Groscher said. "Too many people already know about MAGIC."

"There is a B-17 laid on for you, Pickering," Admiral Nimitz said. "Whenever you're ready to go, it will take you to Espíritu Santo, where—courtesy of our friend Douglas MacArthur, who also feels it important that you talk with Stillwell in Chungking as soon as possible— another B-17 will be waiting to take you, via India, to Chungking."

"Sir, I really would like to see how my people are coming—"

"They have been told to have the aircraft available as of 0700 tomorrow morning," Nimitz interrupted him. "Will that give you enough time to see what you have to see here?"

"Yes, sir."

"Admiral Wagam is aware of my interest in the Gobi Desert project, and has been asked to make sure that we're doing whatever we can to get that moving," Nimitz said.

Admiral Nimitz put out his hand. "I have every confidence, Pickering, that you are the man who will do what has to be done in Chungking," he said.

"Thank you, sir," Pickering replied, and realized that he was being dismissed.

[FOUR]
U.S. Highway 98
Near Pensacola, Florida
2130 3 April 1943

A billboard was by the side of the road, getting a little seedy, and no longer illuminated, but Captain James B. Weston, USMC, could easily read it when the headlights of his Buick convertible flashed over it.

The San Carlos Hotel

Pensacola's Best

Air Conditioned Rooms and Suites

Swimming Pool

Restaurant-Cocktail Lounge Bar

Free Parking

Downtown Pensacola

The sign triggered a stream of thoughts in Captain Weston's somewhat weary brain:

I can get a room there, and go out to the base first thing in the morning.

What I really need right now is a couple of drinks. I can either go to the bar, or have the bellboy bring me a bottle.

And if I get a room there, I can call Martha. She expects me. But God, I don't want to see her. Not tonight. Not until I can figure out what the hell I'm going to do.

That makes sense, get a room, call Martha, and then get a bottle and have a couple of drinks, and get some sleep. If I don't have a couple of drinks, I'll never get to sleep.

So I'll call Martha and tell her I'm in the San Carlos. . . .

Whereupon she will say, "I'll be right there, darling," or words to that effect.

An image of Mrs. Martha Sayre Culhane in her birthday suit jumped into his brain, accompanied by astonishingly clear and sharp memories of how warm, soft, and exciting the various parts of Martha's anatomy were.

And would be if she came to the San Carlos.

You really are a rotten sonofabitch, Weston. Despicable. Beyond contempt.

You really would do that to her. Exactly as you took advantage of Janice's innocence, her inability to suspect what a conscienceless prick you really are.

An image of Lieutenant (j.g.) Janice Hardison, NC, USNR, in her birthday suit jumped into his brain, accompanied by astonishingly clear and sharp memories of how warm, soft, and exciting the various parts of Janice's anatomy had been in the room in the Benjamin Franklin immediately before he departed Philadelphia for Pensacola.

Though he hadn't actually given his own character much serious consideration until very recently—until Janice Hardison had entered his life, and Martha Sayre Culhane had reentered it—Captain Weston had believed that his character was as good as most, and possibly even a little better than some people's. When he spoke, for example, he told the truth. He was, after all, a Marine officer. Marine officers do not lie.

And he had thought of himself as a gentleman, as well. Perhaps not in the same leagues as Sir Galahad or Cary Grant, but a gentleman nonetheless. A gentleman, he had heard somewhere and believed, never intentionally hurts the feelings of others. A gentleman never takes advantage of the weak, male or female, but with obvious emphasis on the gentle sex.

And of course, when a gentleman does something he knows goddamn well is wrong, he quickly confesses the error of his ways to the individual wronged, tries to make amends, and willingly accepts whatever punishment is involved.

He now knew this to be absolutely untrue.

The facts spoke for themselves.

He was a despicable sonofabitch, period.

He had reached this conclusion while driving from Philadelphia to Pensacola. The long drive had given him plenty of time to think, but the thinking had not produced any solution to his problem.

Suicide had even been considered.

But if he did what probably was the gentlemanly thing to do, and put a bullet through his warped and perverse and frankly disgusting brain, both Janice and Martha would show up at his funeral and each would blame themselves for what he had done to himself. . . . He had had a mental image of them, both dressed in black, wearing little hats with black veils, meeting at his casket.

Neither was capable of understanding what a despicable prick had entered their lives.

Despite the fact that he had been wholly uninterested in getting to Pensacola quickly—in fact, at all—Weston had been twice stopped for violating the wartime speed limit of thirty-five miles per hour while traveling from Philadelphia to Pensacola.

Weston knew why he had been speeding when he was in no hurry whatsoever to get to Pensacola. He had not been paying any but the absolute minimum attention to driving. His mind had been occupied with what was going to happen to him once he got to Pensacola.

The truth of the matter was that he had never been much of a success with the opposite gender. In high school and college, and in the Corps, he'd known several men who were. And indeed, he had been awed by those lady-killers who seemed to have their choice of desirable females—often two or more of them at the same time. Frankly, that had made him more than a little jealous.

What must it be like to have two beautiful women in love with you at the same time? he had asked himself more than once.

Now he knew.

Before the San Carlos Hotel billboard had appeared in the headlights of the Buick, he had resolved to settle the situation once and for all. It was the decent thing to do, and he would do it, whatever the cost.

There was a slight problem with that. He didn't have any idea how to settle the situation once and for all.

And—as if he needed it—the sight of the San Carlos Hotel billboard brought with it further confirmation of what kind of a prick he was. His first thought was getting Martha into a bed in the San Carlos Hotel. And/or getting drunk.

He made a new resolution. He would *not* get a room in the San Carlos Hotel; he would *not* go anywhere *near* the San Carlos Hotel. He would go directly to the Pensacola Naval Air Station, sign in, and get a room in the Bachelor Officers' Quarters.

Ten minutes later, he turned off U.S. Highway 98 in Pensacola and onto Navy Boulevard. Navy Boulevard, as the name suggested, led to the U.S. Naval Air Station, Pensacola. The San Carlos Hotel was on Navy Boulevard. On it was a neon sign, a flashing red arrow above the words COCKTAIL LOUNGE.

In what he recognized as his first victory over temptation in a long, long time, Captain Weston drove past the San Carlos without stopping.

"Captain," the white-hat clerk on duty at Billeting said, looking up from a copy of Weston's orders. "According to your orders, you don't have to sign in until 2359 tomorrow."

"Is that so?"

"Captain, there's a good hotel in town, the San Carlos."

"Will you just give me the key to a BOQ room, please?" Weston said, just a little sharply. He immediately regretted it. "The truth is, I lost more than I could afford playing poker."

The white hat smiled understandingly.

God, I have become an accomplished, automatic liar. I don't even think about whether I'm lying or not. I just automatically say what I think people want to hear, and truth isn't even in the equation.

The frame, two story BOQ building was just what he expected—in fact, hoped for. There was a charge of quarters downstairs, a chubby petty officer. There was a sign on the wall: NO FEMALE GUESTS PAST THIS POINT.

Even if I weaken and telephone Martha, she would not pass that point. She is, after all, the Admiral's daughter.

Tonight, I will be celibate.

I will not even go to the club for a couple of drinks, because I know what an amoral prick I am. I would use alcohol as my excuse for calling Martha.

Christ, I promised Janice I would call her the minute I got here!

But I also promised Janice I would not drive straight through, which I did, breaking my word again. But since she thinks I lived up to my promise and stopped somewhere to get at least eight hours' sleep, she won't expect that call until sometime tomorrow.

And Martha probably doesn't expect me to be here until tomorrow, either. So I have at least ten hours to find a solution.

Which I will try very hard to do, sober, in my celibate bed.

He took his luggage from the Buick, carried it up to the second floor of the BOQ, and then down a long, narrow corridor smelling of new linoleum and disinfectant.

His room was all he thought, and hoped, it would be. Sort of a monastic cell. A single bed, a chest of drawers, one armchair, and a desk with a folding chair before it and a lamp that didn't work sitting on it.

He had just hung his Val-Pak in the closet when a knock came at the door.

It can't be for me. Nobody knows I'm here.

"Captain Weston?" the charge of quarters called.

"Yes?"

My God—she is an admiral's daughter and knows how things work around here—Martha has found me!

"Telephone for you, sir."

"You're sure?"

"Yes, sir."

The telephone was on a small table halfway down the hall. It had no dial. He remembered that from flight school. If you wanted to make an off-base or long-distance call, you had to find a pay station and feed it coins.

Weston picked up the telephone. "Captain Weston."

"You're here, obviously," the voice said. It took a moment for Weston to recognize Major Avery R. Williamson, USMC.

"Yes, sir."

"You drove straight through, apparently?"

"Yes, sir."

"I thought you might. I left word with Billeting they were to call me the minute you got here . . . if you came here. But they didn't. It's a damned good thing I called."

"Yes, sir."

Weston could tell that Major Williamson was upset about something.

"Something has come up. I need to see you right away."

"Yes, sir."

"You know where I live?"

"No, sir."

"Have you a pencil and sheet of paper?"

"No, sir."

"Well, get one, Weston!"

"Aye, aye, sir."

Weston laid the telephone on the table and ran down the corridor and the stairs to the charge of quarters' desk. He took a pencil and a pad, then picked up the telephone on the CQ's desk.

"Ready, sir."

Major Williamson gave him directions from the BOQ to his quarters.

Major Williamson opened the door to his quarters, an attractive, obviously prewar bungalow not far off Pensacola Bay, and motioned Weston inside.

His wife and two kids, a boy and a girl, were sitting on a couch in the living room. All of them looked unhappy. When Weston was introduced to them, they were polite—the wife even offered him a cup of coffee—but Weston sensed that he was somehow intruding. He declined the coffee.

"I'm glad you came in early," Major Williamson said. "I won't be here in the morning, and I wanted to see you before I left."

"Where are you going, sir?" Weston blurted, and immediately sensed he should not have asked the question.

"Hawaii," Williamson said. "You remember that temporary job over there we discussed? I told you it was one of General McInerney's little projects?"

"Yes, sir, I do," Weston said.

Christ, he's talking about that request for volunteers to fly the Catalina. Weston remembered the wording: "a classified mission involving great personal risk in a combat area."

"Well, I was allowed to apply for it," Williamson said. "And apparently, I was the best-qualified applicant."

Applicant, my ass, Weston thought. *You didn't volunteer. General McInerney apparently didn't get the eight volunteers he was looking for, and you were volunteered.*

"How long will you be gone, sir?"

"Not long. Ninety days at the most. Probably a lot less than that."

God, I would kill to get out of here for ninety days, to go someplace where I'd have time to figure out what the hell to do about Martha and Janice!

"You're going first thing in the morning, sir?"

"I'm going in about an hour," Williamson said. "That's what I wanted to see you about. This sort of fouls up the training schedule I was laying on for you."

"Sir, I wonder if I could speak to you privately for a moment?" Weston asked.

"I really don't have the time for your personal problems, Weston," Williamson said, annoyance in his voice.

"I would consider it a great personal favor, sir," Weston said. "It won't take but a minute or two."

Williamson looked at him coldly for a moment, then gestured at the front door.

"With the understanding that I am really out of time, Weston."

"Yes, sir, I fully understand," Weston said.

They walked onto the small porch of the bungalow. Major Williamson closed the door. "Make it quick," he ordered.

"Sir, we're talking about the classified Catalina mission?"

"General McInerney—who got his second star, by the way—flew in here in a Corsair, told me he had gotten zero volunteers, and under the circumstances thought that I might wish to consider the opportunity again."

"You were volunteered?"

"Me and several other people, one of whom doesn't know it yet. I'm out of here in a twin Beech in an hour bound for NAS New Orleans, where I will pick up another, quote, volunteer, unquote, and then head for San Diego. That poor bastard just came back from the Pacific."

"General McInerney must think this project is important," Weston said.

Major Williamson didn't reply.

"What's your personal problem, Weston? Try to explain it in thirty seconds or less."

"Sir, I'd like to volunteer."

"Are you out of your mind, Weston? Christ, you're just out of the hospital."

"Sir, with respect, I have twelve hundred hours as pilot-in-command of a Catalina."

"That's right, isn't it?" Williamson said thoughtfully.

"Sir, I'm a Marine officer. Apparently one with the special qualifications needed for General McInerney's project."

"I thought you wanted to be a fighter pilot?"

"Sir, I am a fighter pilot. Captain Galloway checked me out in the Corsair. I would just be wasting my time, and the Corps' time, to go through the training again here."

"And maybe you're thinking that if you did this job for General McInerney you wouldn't have to do the training again."

"That thought did occur to me, sir, but it's not the reason I am volunteering."

"I know," Williamson said.

"Sir?"

"You're volunteering for the same reason I did," Williamson said emotionally. "Because, goddammit, you're a Marine and you want to serve where you can do the most good for the Corps."

"That's not really it, sir."

"You're sure about this, Weston?"

"I'm sure, sir."

"One more time, I put the question to you. Warning you beforehand that I have orders to appear at San Diego as soon as I can get there, with any qualified Marine Aviator I choose to take with me. As you have pointed out, you have the necessary qualifications."

"Yes, sir."

"You want to go, is that it?"

"Yes, sir."

"How long will it take you to get packed? To say goodbye to Martha?"

"I'm already packed, sir, and as far as Martha goes, I think I would rather call her from San Diego and tell her my orders have been changed. I don't feel up to facing her with this."

"You're chicken, Mr. Weston, but in your shoes, I'd do the same thing. I know how it is. I have lied to my wife about this mission—I don't think she believes me, but that's not the point—and I didn't like having to do that."

"I understand, sir."

"Women just don't seem to be able to understand that a Marine, at least an honorable Marine, has to answer the call of duty even when that involves a certain amount of personal sacrifice."

"I suppose that's true, sir."

"You've got your car?"

"Yes, sir."

"Go get your luggage. Meet me at base operations. I'll arrange for somebody to take care of your car until we get back. And we will come back, Weston. Get that firmly fixed in your mind."

"Yes, sir."

But maybe with a little luck I can stretch the ninety

days a little. Maybe to six months. Maybe for the duration of the war plus six months.

Major Williamson touched Captain Weston's shoulder in a gesture of affection.

"I should have known, since Charley Galloway likes you, that you are really a Marine, Weston. It shouldn't have taken this to prove it."

"Thank you, sir."

XIX

[ONE]
Patrol Torpedo Boat 197
Kaiwi Channel
North Pacific Ocean
0815 6 April 1943

Lieutenant (j.g.) Max Schneider, USNR, into whose twenty-year-old hands the United States Navy had three weeks before placed command of PT-197, had absolutely no idea what he and his vessel were doing floating around the Kaiwi Channel at a point equidistant between the islands of Oahu and Molokai. And he had been specifically ordered to ask no questions.

He had been summoned to the office of the Squadron Commander shortly after lunch the day before. "I have a mission for PT-197, Max," Lieutenant Commander James D. Innis, USN, had announced. "A classified mission."

"Aye, aye, sir. May I inquire into the nature of the mission?"

"The precise nature of the mission will be made known to you in due course, Mr. Schneider," Commander Innis had said.

Lieutenant Commander Innis, in fact, had no idea himself about the nature of the mission. But he was naturally reluctant to admit this to a twenty-year-old newly promoted j.g. who still believed his skipper knew everything.

When Innis picked up his telephone half an hour before, he was somewhat astonished to find himself talking to an admiral.

"This is Admiral Wagam, Commander."

While Commander Innis was not familiar with all the senior officers of CINCPAC, he did know who Admiral Wagam was. Admiral Wagam was not only close to Admiral Nimitz, he had the reputation of relieving, on the spot, officers who did not measure up to his standards. Being in command of a PT boat squadron was infinitely better than being, for example, a morale officer, or a VD control officer, which is usually what happened to officers who incurred Admiral Wagam's displeasure.

What the hell does he want with me?

"Yes, sir?"

"If I told you you were going to lose one of your boats and its crew, for up to a month, which of your boats could you best spare?"

I suspect that no matter how I answer the question, it will be wrong.

When in doubt, tell the truth.

"That would be PT-197, sir."

"Why?"

"It has a new skipper, sir. And some new crewmen. There hasn't been time to bring him and the boat up to speed."

The next question will be, "Why not, Commander? What are you doing all day, lying around on your tail?"

"But the skipper can handle the boat?"

"Yes, sir."

"You sound very sure, Commander."

That's both a statement and a question.

"Sir, Lieutenant Schneider has more experience handling boats than any of my other boat commanders."

Or, for that matter, me. The problem is he doesn't know diddley-shit about anything else in the Navy.

"How is that?"

"Sir, his family operates a fleet of tuna boats out of San Francisco. He was the master of an eighty-footer when he was sixteen."

"He's my man," Admiral Wagam said. "It always pays to ask questions, Commander."

"Yes, sir, I'm sure it does."

"Has this officer got a big mouth? Rephrased: Can he be trusted to keep his mouth shut?"

I have absolutely no idea.

"He's a good young officer, sir."

"Impress upon him, and have him impress upon his crew, that they are not to discuss this mission with anyone."

"Aye, aye, sir. Sir, may I inquire as to the nature of the mission?"

"Not over a nonsecure landline, Commander," Admiral Wagam said. "You will be contacted shortly by either Lieutenant Chambers D. Lewis, who is my aide-de-camp, or Major Homer C. Dillon, a Marine. They will tell you what they feel you should know. From this moment, you will consider PT-197 attached to me until relieved."

"Aye, aye, sir."

The line went dead, and Commander Innis sent for Lieutenant (j.g.) Max Schneider.

Major Homer C. Dillon, USMCR, driving a Ford station wagon bearing the logotype of the Pacific & Far East Shipping Corporation, showed up as darkness was falling. He was followed by a Marine Corps General Motors six-by-six. The truck was driven by a chief carpenter's mate who had apparently lost his cap somewhere.

Lieutenant (j.g.) Schneider quickly descended the ladder from PT-197 to the wharf. "Major Dillon, sir?" he asked, saluting.

"Right," Jake Dillon replied, returning the salute. "Lieutenant Schneider?"

"Yes, sir."

"Where's the captain?" the chief carpenter's mate asked.

"I command PT-197, Chief," Lieutenant (j.g.) Schneider replied coldly.

"No shit? You don't look old enough," the chief carpenter's mate said.

"You'll have to excuse the chief, Mr. Schneider," Major Dillon said. "He's only been in the Navy nine months."

"Before I came in the Navy, Chief, I ran tuna boats out of San Francisco," Lieutenant (j.g.) Schneider said. "What did you do?"

"No shit?" Chief Carpenter's Mate Peter T. McGuire, USNR, replied. "I spent some time on boats like that. Remember *They Go Down to the Sea*, Jake?"

Dillon nodded. "It laid an enormous egg," he said.

"That was a movie," Lieutenant (j.g.) Schneider said. "They rented some boats from my father. I was ten, eleven years old."

"They were your father's boats?" Chief McGuire said. "I'll be damned."

"Can you muster a labor detail, Mr. Schneider?" Major Dillon asked. "The truck is loaded with boxes we need aboard your boat. And two rubber boats."

"It would be best if you could lash this stuff outside," Chief McGuire said. "Rather than put it inside, I mean."

"To the vessel's *superstructure*, you mean, Chief?" Lieutenant (j.g.) Schneider asked. "Rather than *below*?"

"Right," Chief McGuire agreed with a smile.

"Sir," Lieutenant (j.g.) Schneider said, looking at Dillon. "May I ask what the crates contain?"

Jake Dillon smiled at him. "Sand," he said.

"There's twenty-seven of them," Chief McGuire amplified. "Average weight, fifty pounds. Total weight, thirteen hundred and fifty pounds."

"And as soon as Lieutenant Lewis can get here," Major Dillon said, "there will also be two hundred and fifty gallons of avgas, in five-gallon jerry cans. Fifty cans."

"Total weight seventeen hundred fifty pounds, give or take," Chief McGuire added.

"And when we come back in the morning," Dillon said,

"in addition to myself, Lieutenant Lewis, and Chief McGuire, there will be five other men with us."

"Aye, aye, sir," Lieutenant (j.g.) Schneider said. He was nearly consumed with curiosity, but he had been ordered to ask no questions, and didn't. Even when he saw Major Dillon's boxes. They were of various odd sizes and constructed of what looked like aircraft aluminum. Each bore a number, (1) through (27).

The crew of PT-197 had just about finished moving the boxes and rubber boats from the truck to the boat when another GM six-by-six—this one painted Navy gray—drove up.

Lieutenant Chambers D. Lewis III, USN, climbed down from the cab. He was wearing the aiguillette of an aide-de-camp.

He and Major Dillon and Lieutenant (j.g.) Schneider exchanged salutes. Chief McGuire did not.

"I was told the skipper would be here," Lieutenant Lewis said to Lieutenant (j.g.) Schneider.

"You're looking at him," Chief McGuire informed him. "And we lucked out. He used to run a tuna boat out of 'Frisco. He probably knows more about boats than you do."

"I'm sure he does," Lieutenant Lewis said with a strained smile.

Major Dillon coughed into his balled fist. Or laughed.

"My name is Lewis," Lewis said to Schneider, offering his hand.

"Lieutenant (j.g.) Schneider, sir."

"Has the chief explained what we need, Mr. Schneider?"

"Yes, sir."

"Any problems?"

"No, sir. Sir, may I ask where we are going?"

"We'll let you know that in the morning," Lewis said. "I hate to be so secretive, but we've had a bad experience with an aviator who couldn't keep his mouth shut."

"Yes, sir."

"The distance involved will be about seventy-five nautical miles, one way. We may be there a couple of hours. Does that pose any fuel problems?"

"No, sir."

"We will want to put out at first light," Lewis said. "So we'll be here ten minutes before that. Will that give you enough time?"

"Yes, sir."

"Permission to come on the bridge, Captain?" Lieutenant Lewis asked at 0425 the next morning.

"Granted," Lieutenant (j.g.) Schneider replied. "Good morning, sir."

At least one of these people knows how to treat the master of a man-of-war, Lieutenant (j.g.) Schneider thought, pleased.

The good feeling was immediately dissipated when Major Dillon and Chief McGuire came onto the bridge right after Lewis, having apparently decided the permission obviously included them.

Lieutenant Lewis handed Lieutenant (j.g.) Schneider a nautical chart, and Schneider examined it in the light of a flashlight. There was an X approximately equidistant between Oahu and Molokai in the Kaiwi Channel. "Right about there, please," Lewis said.

"Aye, aye, sir."

By the time they had cleared the antisubmarine net guarding Pearl Harbor, it was light. Lieutenant Schneider was thus able to see for the first time where the twenty-seven oddly shaped aluminum boxes and the fifty cans of aviation gasoline in jerry cans had been lashed to his vessel. Patrol torpedo boats are not very large vessels. The packages and jerry cans were lashed all over the deck, fore and aft.

My God, we look like a garbage scow!

The seas in the Kaiwi Channel were moderate. Under ordinary circumstances, Lieutenant Schneider would have been able to push the throttles of PT-197 full forward, and her Packard engines would have sent her sailing magnificently over the water at better than thirty knots. But Lieutenant Schneider, who was in fact very experienced in handling small vessels in the ocean, knew it would be unwise to get her speed up. Sooner or later, her bow would inevitably crash into a swell. She—and the torpedo tubes and gun mounts—had been designed with that in mind. They would take the shock. But not with the added weight of fifty jerry cans and twenty-seven odd-shaped packages weighing an average of fifty pounds strapped to them wherever a line could find a hold.

They had crossed the antisubmarine net at 0450. It was 0750 before Lieutenant (j.g.) Schneider felt secure in informing Lieutenant Lewis that they were at the point he had specified on the chart.

"Captain, please, maintaining headway speed, circle this position," Lieutenant Lewis ordered, then turned to Chief McGuire. "Go get the radio, please, Chief."

"Right," Chief McGuire replied.

The radio equipment came in two pieces: The radio itself sat on a tripod. McGuire handed that up to Lewis on the bridge, and Lewis and Dillon set it up. There was a telescoping antenna on top, like an automobile antenna, but longer, stronger, and colored black. There was also a telegrapher's key, and a microphone was clipped to the side of the case. The second piece looked like a stationary bicycle. McGuire set this on the deck, handed a cable to Lewis, then mounted the bicycle. Lewis connected the cable to the radio, put a headset on his ears, then made a motion to McGuire to start pumping. He did so.

There was a barely perceptible humming noise, and then the dials on the radio illuminated. When he was satisfied with the position of the dials and the switches, Lewis began tapping the telegrapher's key. "This is supposed to have a range of twenty-five miles," he said. "With the telescoping antenna. Let's see." He tapped the key, threw a switch and listened, and then tapped the key again, repeating the process for several minutes.

So far as Lieutenant Schneider could make out—and he had done well in his radio telegrapher's course at the University of California before getting commissioned—Lewis was sending a gibberish of short Morse code letters: A, E, I, N, and so on.

Then, while listening, Lieutenant Lewis smiled.

"They've got us," he said. He threw a switch and resumed tapping the telegrapher's key, tapping it for longer periods, sixty seconds or so at a time, before listening for fifteen seconds.

Lieutenant (j.g.) Schneider wondered whom he had contacted, but he had been ordered not to ask questions, and did not.

Lewis finally picked up the microphone. "Seagull, Seagull," he said into the microphone. "This is Texaco, Texaco. How do you read?"

He listened, but shook his head to Dillon to indicate that he was hearing nothing.

Lieutenant (j.g.) Schneider became aware of the sound of aircraft engines in the distance. He located the source of the sound a second after Jake Dillon did. Jake pointed out the airplane to Lewis. It was several miles away, no more than a thousand feet off the surface of the Kaiwi Channel.

"Seagull, Seagull, we have you in sight. If read, say how. Also wiggle your wings," Lieutenant Lewis ordered.

The airplane lowered first one wing and then the other. By now it was close enough for Lieutenant (j.g.) Schneider to recognize as a Catalina . . . though something wasn't quite right about it.

"Make note, Major Dillon, sir," Lewis said, "that voice communications from the aircraft using the telescopic antenna are somewhat below expectations. They can hear us."

Dillon chuckled. But Lieutenant (j.g.) Schneider saw that Dillon had a clipboard in his hand and was writing something on it.

"Seagull, Seagull, we can't hear you. Set it down, please," Lieutenant Lewis said into his microphone.

The Catalina immediately wiggled its wings again, then began to drop toward the water.

"We need someone to pump the bicycle," Chief McGuire announced. "I'm getting tired."

"You're a chief petty officer, you're not supposed to get tired," Dillon replied.

"Fuck you, Jake," Chief McGuire replied, and got off the generator.

It was evident on the face of Lieutenant (j.g.) Schneider's helmsman that he had never before heard a chief petty officer tell an officer to fuck himself.

"Captain, please make us dead in the water," Lieutenant Lewis said. "We'll let him come to us. And can you get someone to pump the generator, please?"

Lieutenant (j.g.) Schneider retarded PT-197's engines to idle, then took them out of gear. The boat slowed. Then he reached for the speaker switch to order someone up from below, but changed his mind.

He touched the arm of his helmsman and indicated that he should get on the generator bicycle. For one thing, if boat handling was going to be involved, he would do it himself. His helmsman was a nice kid—he was, in fact, six months younger than Lieutenant (j.g.) Schneider—but all he knew about boat handling was what he had been taught in a five-week course. For another, the decks of PT-197 were about to get crowded. The fewer people there, the better.

Chief Peter McGuire came onto the bridge. "I think the first thing to do is get the boats in the water," he said to Lieutenant Schneider. "Your people know how to do that?" he went on without giving Schneider a chance to reply. "First you tie the rope on front to something, and then throw it into the water. Then you jerk on the rope and the boat will blow up."

"I'm sure we can handle that," Lieutenant Schneider said, and reached for the speaker switch. "Chief of the Boat to the bridge," he commanded.

Schneider saw that the Catalina was about to touch down. It created a huge splash, bounced back in the air, and then touched down again, this time staying on the surface of the water.

"I wish the seas were a little rougher," Major Dillon said.

"Yeah," Lieutenant Lewis agreed thoughtfully.

The Chief of the Boat, a first class bosun's mate who was at least five years older than PT-197's captain, came onto the bridge.

"Can you get the rubber boats over the side, Boats?" Lieutenant Schneider asked.

"Aye, aye, sir."

Lieutenant Schneider saw that Major Dillon had a stop-watch in his hand. As he watched, he pushed the button to start it.

The helmsman was now pumping the generator.

"Seagull, how read?" Lieutenant Lewis said into his microphone, and a moment later said, "Five by five now, Jake."

"Got it," Dillon said.

"Bring it alongside," Lewis ordered over the micro-phone.

The Catalina turned toward PT-197.

Lieutenant Schneider now understood the vague feeling he had had when he first saw the airplane. Normal Catal-inas were originally conceived as observation aircraft; they were to be "the eyes of the fleet." That meant they had a large Plexiglas "blister" on each side of their fu-selages to facilitate observation and, secondarily, to be used as a machine-gun position. There was also a machine-gun position on the bow.

The blisters and the forward machine-gun position on the Catalina approaching PT-197 were missing. They had been faired over with aluminum.

"Big Steve reports the main tanks have been topped off," Lewis announced.

"Which should leave the auxiliaries nearly empty," Dillon said. "The first thing we're going to do, Schneider, is move the avgas over there."

"Which we will do with the sub's crew—for now, your guys—paddling the boats over to the plane twice," Chief McGuire amplified. "We figure if they can carry ten jerry cans with them at a time."

"Sub's crew"? What "sub's crew"? Lieutenant (j.g.) Schneider wondered. But having been ordered not to ask questions, he didn't.

"If the seas aren't rough," Lieutenant Lewis said.

"Like I said, I wish they were a little rougher," Major Dillon said. "I think we have to count on something worse than this millpond."

"If the water's too rough for the boats to carry three hundred and fifty pounds," Chief McGuire argued, "it'll be too rough for the airplanes to land, much less take off."

"Airplanes"? Plural? What the hell does going on? Lieutenant Schneider wondered, but kept his mouth shut.

"Don't even think about that," Dillon said.

"Worst case," Lewis said. "They would have to try to land—they wouldn't have enough fuel to get back. I would really hate to have to jump into the Yellow Sea this time of year."

"Jesus!" Chief McGuire said. "Let's see how this works, anyhow. Two trips over there and back, paddled by Schneider's men, and then a fifth trip with the weather guys—who don't come back—paddling."

"Yeah," Dillon said.

"Jake, I think I'm going to go over to the airplane in the first rubber boat," McGuire said.

"I thought you said you were never going to get on another airplane as long as you live," Dillon replied.

"I'm not going *flying* in it, for Christ's sake. I just want to see how topping off the auxiliary tanks works."

Dillon looked at Lewis.

"Go ahead," Lewis said. "Schneider, we need eight boat paddlers."

"Sir, my men aren't experienced in rubber boats."

"Yeah, we thought about that," McGuire said. "We're trying to make this as realistic as possible."

"What are we going to do with the jerry cans?" Lieutenant Lewis said.

"Fuck 'em," Chief McGuire suggested. "Toss them in the water."

"Where they would be spotted as debris by every other airplane flying over here," Lewis said. "We don't want that."

"Empty, they'll float," Dillon said. "Pete, if you're going over there, tie them together, and we'll pick them up."

"Okay," Chief McGuire said. "Why not? No problem."

"For your general fund of nautical knowledge, Chief McGuire," Lewis said, "the correct response should have been, 'Aye, aye, sir.' "

"Aye, aye, sir," Chief McGuire said, smiling broadly. He left the bridge and stood on the deck of PT-197 watching the jerry cans of avgas being loaded into the rubber boats.

Schneider now saw that Major Dillon had not one but three stopwatches, all hanging from cords around his neck, and then, as the ferrying of the avgas to the Catalina was carried out, understood what he was doing with them.

He carefully timed how long it took each rubber boat to move to the Catalina and then return. He timed how long it took both boats to make the trip on a second stopwatch, and used the third to time how long the total operation took.

Finally the four trips paddled by PT-197 crewmen were completed. The weathermen were brought on deck from the tiny mess of PT-197, where they had been waiting, outfitted with Mae Wests, and then helped into one of the rubber boats.

"If they stay on the airplane, how's McGuire going to get back?" Lewis inquired.

"You heard what he said," Dillon said. "Fuck 'em."

"If we didn't need him, Major Dillon," Lewis said. "I would readily concur with your recommendation, sir."

Dillon chuckled.

"I think you better send the other boat back, Schneider, with a couple of extra paddlers," Dillon ordered. "As Lieutenant Lewis points out, Chief McGuire cannot be left to paddle his own boat. We need him."

"Aye, aye, sir."

Ten minutes later, both rubber boats were back alongside PT-197, and Chief McGuire came back aboard.

"I'm not really happy with the topping off of the tanks," he announced.

"What's wrong with it?" Lieutenant Lewis asked.

"Big Steve and I have a couple of ideas," McGuire said. "This will work, but it can be done faster. Safer. With fewer fumes. Big Steve says he wouldn't want to shut down his engines in rough water in the Yellow Sea, and we don't want the airplanes to blow up."

Lewis grunted, then leaned over the bridge and spoke to the helmsman.

"You want to start pumping that thing again, son?"

When the dials on the radio lit up, he picked up the microphone.

"I think that's it," he announced. "You can head back

to Ewa." Then he turned to Lieutenant Schneider. "As soon as we get the boats back aboard, and the jerry cans, we can start for home," he said. "And on the way, Major Dillon will explain to you what this is all about."

[TWO]
Chungking, China
1515 7 April 1943

The first thing Brigadier General Fleming Pickering noticed as the B-17 turned off the active runway onto a taxiway was the contrast between Espíritu Santo and here. Espíritu Santo was a forward base, but it was neat and clean and looked new. This was China, where very little was neat, clean, or new.

When the aircraft had been parked and the engines shut down, he went through the door in the fuselage and stretched his legs.

This smells like China, too, he thought.

If I never have to get on another B-17 as long as I live, it will be too soon.

The pilot came through the door. "The tower says they will *try* to find us a truck, sir," he said. "It looks like a hell of a walk from here to base operations.

"That was an interesting flight," he went on. "It reset my longest flight record by an hour and ten minutes."

"How much fuel did we have left?"

"I don't believe the General really wants to know that, sir. We ran into some really stiff head winds."

"You're right, I don't want to know," Pickering said. "Well, why don't you and I hike to base operations? Maybe I can pull a little rank in person and get us a truck."

They were halfway to base operations when two Studebaker President sedans came down the taxiway. The first, driven by a sergeant, carried the starred plate of a brigadier general, and Pickering saw Brigadier General H. A. Albright and a younger officer riding in the backseat.

Probably his brand-new aide-de-camp to go with his

brand-new star. It didn't take him long to take advantage of a general's perks, did it?

What the hell does that matter to me? Albright is a damned good man, who would have been a general long ago if it hadn't been for that idiot, that Secretary of the Joint Chiefs.

The second car was driven by an Army captain. There were two officers in the backseat. One of them was Colonel John J. Waterson. The other was an Army lieutenant colonel.

That, no doubt, is the Chungking station chief, whose name I still don't know.

Where's Banning? I wonder. And McCoy?

Albright's car stopped beside them, and Albright was out of the backseat before the driver could get out of the front seat to open the door for him. He saluted. "Welcome to Chungking, General," he said.

"It's good to see you," Pickering said, desperately searching his memory for Albright's first name. "Especially with that star on your collar." The name didn't come.

"Being a general is not what I thought it would be," Albright said.

"My experience exactly," Pickering said. "But that was a well-deserved promotion."

The second Studebaker had by then stopped, and Waterson and the two officers got out.

They all saluted.

"How are you, Jack?" Pickering said to Colonel Waterson, offering his hand, pleased that he could remember his first name.

"Did you have a good flight, sir?"

"It was a very long flight," Pickering said. "There is no such thing as a good-very long flight."

Everyone chuckled.

Dutifully, of course. That wasn't very funny. But I am a general.

"Sir, may I introduce Colonel Richard C. Platt?" Waterson said. "The Chungking station chief?"

"Welcome to Chungking, General," Platt said. He was

a rather handsome lieutenant colonel, wearing the crossed cannons of Artillery.

"Thank you," Pickering said.

"And this is my adjutant," Platt said. "Captain Jerry Sampson."

Nice-looking kid, Pickering thought. *About as old as Pick.*

"I believe I have the privilege of the General's acquaintance, sir," Captain Sampson said.

I don't remember ever having seen this fellow before.

"Oh, have we met?"

"I was trying to remember where, sir. Possibly in Shanghai. My father—Harrison Sampson?—was general manager of First National City Bank. And then I was at Harvard with Malcolm."

"Malcolm"? God, he means Pick. But no one's called Pick "Malcolm" since the day he was christened. So they weren't buddies. What is this kid trying to do, charm me?

What was it Drew Pearson said OSS stood for? "Oh So Social"?

"I remember your father, of course," Pickering said, and shook his hand. He turned to Albright. "With that new star on your collar, Hugh," he said—*Thank God! His name came to me*—"I presume you've got some influence around here? We need a truck."

"I think I can get you a truck, General, but to answer your question, do I have any influence around here? Very little. Almost none."

Pickering introduced the OSS officers to the pilot and then to Lieutenant Hart, who had taken their baggage off the plane. "The Captain and his crew need a place to stay. With good beds and decent food," Pickering said.

"I suggest, sir," Albright said, "that you and I need a moment alone, before General Stillwell learns you're here and sends for you."

Pickering saw that neither Waterson nor Platt liked that announcement.

"I want to see him, too, as soon as possible," Pickering said. "But not until I've had a shower and a shave. And a chance to talk to you, Waterson, and Banning. Where is Banning, by the way?"

"General, General Stillwell has left word with the air base commander that he wants to see you immediately after you get off the plane," Colonel Platt said.

"Did you give the tower General Pickering's name, Captain?" Albright said.

"I'm afraid I did, sir."

"Then he will expect to see you immediately, sir," Albright said.

"What's the rush about seeing General Stillwell?" Pickering asked.

"Right now, he hates everybody connected with his having been ordered to relieve Dempsey and Newley," Albright said. "And he thinks you're the man responsible."

"Is there someplace where I can get a quick shower and change my uniform?"

"You'll be staying at the VIP guest house, General," Colonel Platt said.

"Doesn't the OSS have a house here?" Pickering asked.

"Yes, sir, of course, we do," Colonel Platt said. "But I felt you would be more comfortable in the VIP house."

"If General Stillwell has left word here that he wants to see me, I'll bet he left word at the VIP place," Pickering said. "So long as I don't have his invitation to come to see him, I can't be accused of ignoring it, can I? And I have no intention of going to see General Stillwell looking like a bum and smelling like a horse."

"There's a staff car coming this way," George Hart said. "That might be the air base commander."

"Waterson, you have not heard about General Stillwell's kind invitation, and I did not tell you where I was going."

"Yes, sir."

"And you can take care of the Captain and his crew? Get them a truck, whatever they need?"

"Yes, sir."

"I'll want a word with you, too, and you, too, Colonel Platt, before I see General Stillwell. Will you meet me at the OSS house?"

"Yes, sir."

"Let's go, Albright," Pickering said, and quickly got into Albright's Studebaker.

Hart hastily stuffed their luggage in the trunk, then crowded into the front seat beside General Albright's aide-de-camp.

At the last moment, Captain Jerry Sampson jumped into the backseat.

"Colonel Platt suggested I go with you, sir, to take care of things at the house."

"Fine. Thank you," Pickering said, although he was annoyed. He had things to discuss with Albright he could not discuss within the hearing of Sampson.

Or for that matter, in the hearing of either Albright's aide or his driver. So no harm done.

"You never told me where Banning is," he said to Albright.

"He's either in the crypto room—with the Special Channel up; there's a lot of traffic—or out looking for McCoy."

" 'Looking for McCoy'? That sounds as if he's missing."

"Yes, sir," Albright said.

Pickering bit off the impulse to ask for details.

That, too, will have to wait until we're alone.

It was impossible to tell from the cobblestone street what was behind the gray stucco wall surrounding the building on three sides. The compound backed up against a vertical sandstone hill. The wall was topped with broken glass bottles that looked as if they had been there for half a century, and by coiled barbed wire now uniformly covered with rust. On an ornate wrought-iron gate now-rusty corrugated-steel sheets had been affixed, to keep people from seeing what was inside.

A guard shack was occupied by two Chinese soldiers, wearing quilted cold-weather jackets and trousers. Both were armed with Thompson .45-caliber submachine guns. One of them came out of the guard shack when the Studebaker stopped before the gate. He saluted and then pulled the gate open.

Pickering wondered if the guard knew Albright by

sight, which was possible, or if he simply passed any car with a general's star on it, in which case security might just be a little lax.

Inside the wall, Pickering saw a three-story, tile-roofed old building, with its rear wall against the sandstone hill, and four small outbuildings, three against the left wall and one against the street-side wall.

Several vehicles were parked nose-in against the front wall of the house: four jeeps, battered and unwashed; a Dodge three-quarter-ton weapons carrier; a Dodge ambulance, with the usual Red Crosses painted over not quite completely with a brownish paint that did not match the olive drab of the rest of the body; and another Studebaker President sedan.

Heavy closed shutters were on all the windows. Pickering wondered if they were closed for security or as protection against the freezing winds.

Captain Sampson jumped out of the car as soon as it stopped. "I'll get things set up inside," he said.

"All I need, Hugh, is a place to take a shower and to have a word with you," Pickering said to General Albright.

"You make these people nervous, General," Albright said, "in case you haven't noticed."

Pickering got out of the car and walked to its rear, intending to help Hart with their luggage.

Three Chinese in black ankle-length gowns not unlike a priest's vestments came trotting out of the house and snatched the luggage from their hands.

Captain Sampson appeared at the door. "What I've done, General, is put you into our visitor's room," he said. "It's not much—"

"All I want to do, Captain," Pickering said, "is have a quick shower and change my uniform."

"Yes, sir."

They followed him into the house, through an empty foyer furnished with large, dark, and uncomfortable-looking furniture, and up a narrow flight of stairs to the second floor. Halfway down a narrow corridor illuminated with bare bulbs, Sampson pushed a door open and waved Pickering into a large, sparsely furnished room. The house boys scurried into the room after them with the luggage and started to unpack it.

"That can wait," Pickering said. "Where's the shower?"

"Right in here, sir," Sampson said, and showed him a small bathroom. It was equipped with a showerhead on a rubber hose and a hole-in-the floor toilet. A china toilet bowl and seat had been jury rigged over the toilet.

"If you like, sir, I can put you in Colonel Platt's room."

"This will do," Pickering said. "Thank you, Captain. That will be all."

"Would the General like a cup of coffee? Something else, perhaps?"

"That will be all, Captain. Thank you," Pickering said. He waited until Sampson had left.

"Okay, Hugh, first of all, tell me about Captain McCoy. What is this missing business?"

"When Banning got here and Dempsey was being an ass, Banning told McCoy to disappear. To stay in touch, but to disappear. He's disappeared, except for one visit here, when he asked for Banning and disappeared again. He had a run-in with Platt."

"What kind of a run-in?"

"Platt told him to stay here, consider himself part of the station, no matter what his orders from Banning. Frankly, I would have told him the same thing under the circumstances."

"And McCoy elected not to?"

"That's the last time anyone has seen him. Or Zimmerman."

"Do you think something's happened to him?"

"Banning feels that McCoy can take care of himself," Albright said. "I wish I shared his confidence."

"See if you can get word to Banning to come here. Before I go to see General Stillwell, if possible. But come here. I need to talk to him."

"Yes, sir."

"Is there anything I should know before I see Stillwell?"

"He really doesn't like what's happened," Albright said. "He made a point of telling me I was *acting* signal officer, pending his discussion with you."

"I guess I should have asked this first: How badly has MAGIC been compromised?"

"I don't really know. General Dempsey won't talk to me."

"What do you mean, Dempsey won't talk to you?"

"He has the right, under *The Manual for Courts-Martial*, 1928, to refuse to answer any question that might *tend* to incriminate him. And that's what he's doing."

"Christ!"

"The sooner you get over there and see Stillwell, the better," Albright said. "By now, he knows you're here."

"I need a shower, and I'm going to have one," Pickering said.

"I suggest you make it a quick one," Albright said.

"Anything else I should know?"

"To further brighten your day, General, Platt knows all about Operation Gobi, and has his own Opplan—already furnished to Donovan—which he feels is considerably better than yours."

"That wouldn't be hard," Pickering said. "But who told him about Operation Gobi?"

"I don't know," Albright said.

"Okay, Hugh, that's enough bad news for now. Let me have my shower."

Pickering came out of the bathroom wearing only a used towel. It offered little protection against the damp chill, and he was shivering.

He saw with genuine gratitude that Hart had laid out a change of underwear and a clean shirt on the bed for him. He walked quickly to it and pulled a T-shirt over his head. Hart, meanwhile, was trying to get the wrinkles out of their clean uniforms, which were hanging from a light fixture on the wall.

"Thanks, George," he said, as he reached for his shorts.

"We have a shoe problem, General," Hart said.

"What?"

"This is no place to wear low-quarters," Hart said. "Snow, mud, dirt, et cetera. The Army's wearing—did you notice?—boots, like boondockers, except that they have a strap thing on the top, you tuck your trousers in it. General Albright was wearing them." The USMC ankle-high field shoe, constructed with the rough side of the leather out, were known as boondockers.

"I didn't notice," Pickering confessed. "I don't think I would have noticed if Albright's pants were on fire."

"And they shine them."

"They shine boondockers?" Pickering asked incredulously.

"Their version, yes, sir. And what we have is boondockers. I didn't think to pack puttees."

"*Good* thinking. I didn't wear puttees on Guadalcanal, and I'm not going to wear them here. Can you get us, do you think, some of the Army shoes?"

"Aye, aye, sir, I'll get us some."

"In the meantime, we have boondockers?"

"Yes, sir," Hart said, and went to Pickering's luggage. As he bent over it, Pickering saw that he had a Colt Model 1911A1 .45 pistol in the small of his back.

"What happened to your .38, George?" Pickering asked.

"I've got it, sir. But General Rickabee said I was to carry a .45 once we got here."

"And did General Rickabee tell you how he thinks I should arm myself?"

"Not exactly, sir," Hart said. "But he did send this along, and asked me to show you how it works."

Hart stood up with a pair of Marine Corps boondockers in one hand and a Colt 1911A1 .45 pistol in a shiny leather shoulder holster in the other.

"For your information, Lieutenant, I qualified as Expert with the .45 when I was younger than you are now."

"I think he meant the shoulder holster, sir."

"I've never worn one," Pickering said. "I think it would make me feel like a gangster."

"I also have a regular holster and a web pistol belt for you, sir."

"You're not using either," Pickering said.

"You can only do this for a couple of hours," Hart said, patting the .45 in the small of his back. "And even then, sometimes it's uncomfortable. I've got a shoulder holster for it."

"Okay, I'm convinced. Show me about the shoulder holster."

"General Rickabee told me he got these from the Secret Service, sir," Hart said. "The pistol is held by a leather-covered spring. All you have to do is pull on it to get it out." He demonstrated by pulling the pistol from the holster and laying it on the bed.

"And it gets some support from a clip on your belt," he went on, "as well as the strap over your shoulder. The weight is distributed." Hart adjusted the various clips and springs and buckles until the holster fit Pickering's body. Then he picked up the pistol and ejected the magazine. Next he worked the action to make sure the chamber was empty, then reinserted the magazine and handed the pistol to Pickering.

"Seven rounds in the magazine, sir," he said. "The chamber is empty."

"Thank you, George," Pickering said. He put the pistol in the holster, took it out again, then put it back. He waved his arms around to see how the shoulder holster fit, and smiled at Hart. "Very nice," he said.

After that, he started to take the holster off, looking for the snap holding the bottom of the holster to his waist belt.

"Why don't you keep it on, sir?" Hart asked, too politely. "See how it fits after a couple of hours? Get used to it."

A very clear image of the voice of Brigadier General Fritz Rickabee popped into General Pickering's brain. *"And you make goddamn sure Pickering wears it, Hart, I don't care how."*

"If you think I should, George, why not?" Pickering said.

Hart's relief showed on his face.

Pickering sat down on the bed. "Toss me the boondockers, and then we'll go face the lion in his den," Pickering said.

"Aye, aye, sir."

"Did Colonel Banning show up?"

"No, sir."

"Don't take offense, George, but couldn't you use a bath?"

"There's not time, sir. You heard what General Albright said about getting to see General Stillwell as quickly as possible."

"Fuck General Stillwell," Pickering said. "Take a shower, George."

Hart looked at him in surprise.

"I will deny under oath that I said that," Pickering said.

"Said what, sir?" Hart said. "And now, with the General's permission, I think I'll have a shower and change into a clean uniform."

[THREE]
Office of the Commanding General
United States Military Mission to China
Chungking, China
1625 7 April 1943

Brigadier General Fleming Pickering, USMCR, and Second Lieutenant George F. Hart, USMCR, freshly shaved and in clean—if somewhat mussed—uniforms marched into the office of General Joseph Stillwell, USA, and saluted in front of his desk. "Brigadier General Pickering, sir," he said. "Thank you for seeing me."

Another officer was in the room, an Army colonel, dressed like General Stillwell, in a belted olive-drab jacket—which to Pickering looked like something a white hunter in Africa would wear—over a tieless khaki shirt. Both officers wore the insignia of their rank on their collar points, but not on the epaulets of their jackets.

As Pickering entered, the Colonel rose out of the chair beside Stillwell's desk.

Stillwell returned Pickering's salute with a wave in the general direction of his forehead. He was a trim, lean, sharp-featured man in his middle fifties. He examined Pickering coldly and very carefully for a very long moment—long enough to give Pickering cause to worry that the meeting was not going to go well. "I left word at the airfield that I wanted to see you immediately upon your arrival," he said.

"If I have kept the General waiting, I apologize."

"I understand you traveled here by B-17?"

"Yes, sir."

"You must be a very important man, General," Stillwell said finally. "Washington tells me they don't have enough B-17s at the moment to send here. And I know for a fact that General MacArthur has bitterly complained he doesn't have nearly as many as he feels he needs. And yet General MacArthur—who is known for his reluctance to divert assets—seems to have seen fit, in your case, to provide one to fly you here."

Pickering could not think of any reply he could make.

"You may stand at ease, gentlemen," Stillwell said.

"Thank you, sir," Pickering said. He and Hart assumed a position that was closer to Parade Rest than At Ease. "Sir, this is my aide-de-camp, Lieutenant Hart."

Stillwell nodded at Hart.

"This is Colonel Easterbrook," he said. "He's my IG, and my son-in-law."

Easterbrook walked over to Pickering, and they shook hands without speaking. Easterbrook actually smiled at Hart.

To show him, no doubt, that he doesn't believe in guilt by association.

"I'd like to have Colonel Easterbrook sit in on our conversation, General. Is that all right with you?" Stillwell asked, his tone making it clear that he would be surprised by any negative response.

"Sir, with respect, there are some things we have to talk about that I am not at liberty to discuss in Colonel Easterbrook's presence," Pickering said.

Stillwell's pale face colored, and he met Pickering's eyes for a long moment. Finally, he shrugged.

"Ernie, get yourself a cup of coffee," he ordered. "And take the lieutenant with you."

"Yes, sir," Colonel Easterbrook said, and with Hart trailing him, left the room.

"Frankly, General, you're not what I expected," Stillwell said when the door had closed behind Easterbrook and Hart. "When General Marshall informed me you were coming, I got out my Navy Register to look you up. You don't seem to be listed therein, General."

In peacetime, the Navy Register, issued annually, provided a brief biography of every officer in the Naval Service, which of course included the Marine Corps. The biographies included the dates of promotion, assignments, and schooling. Pickering had subscribed to it for years, both to keep track of his World War I friends who had stayed in the Corps, and to identify Navy officers who had some sort of business with Pacific & Far East Shipping.

"I don't believe I am, sir," Pickering said.

"So I went from that—the reputation of the OSS precedes you, unfortunately . . ."

Oh, Jesus, this is really going to be bad.

He doesn't like the OSS any more than Douglas MacArthur or Nimitz does.

". . . to the presumption that I was about to be visited by one of Colonel Donovan's—what is it they call them?—Twelve Disciples? A distinguished member of the business community, perhaps. Or an academic. A *civilian* given a brevet rank as a general officer to better carry out his clandestine intelligence duties . . ."

"I must confess, sir, that's pretty close to the truth," Pickering said.

"Then that Navy Cross on your chest is part of—what shall I say?—your disguise? The Navy Cross and the Purple Heart with how many clusters?"

"I am wearing no decoration to which I am not entitled," Pickering said.

Pickering's quietly cold—even angry—tone of voice penetrated Stillwell's contemptuous rage.

"That's your Navy Cross?" he asked dubiously.

"Yes, sir."

"The Navy Cross isn't passed out with the rations," Stillwell said. "Where'd you get it?"

"In France, sir. At Château-Thierry."

"And you were wounded four times in France?"

"Three times in France, sir. Once in this war."

"Where in this war?"

"I was aboard a destroyer, sir, between Guadalcanal and Espíritu Santo. We were hit by a Japanese bomber."

"You were on Guadalcanal?"

"Yes, sir."

"Doing what?"

"I was filling in as G-2 of the First Marine Division, sir. Until a replacement could be sent in to replace the G-2 who was killed in action."

"And the Silver Star? Where'd you get that?"

"Aboard the destroyer."

"Why?"

"I assumed command when her captain was killed, sir. We got the Jap who bombed us."

"There's more to it than that," Stillwell said. He put what he thought of as two and two together. "You didn't happen to be wounded when you took command?"

"Yes, sir, I'd been hit."

"Where did you learn to command a destroyer?"

"I'm a master mariner, sir. That's what I did before I came back in the Corps."

"That adds up to two things, General," Stillwell said. "First, that I owe you an apology for thinking what I did."

"No apology is necessary, sir."

"And also, as someone used to exercising command, that you should understand how I felt when General Marshall ordered me to place in arrest-to-quarters two general officers in whose professional ability and character I have great confidence. One of whom has been a friend for years."

"I'm sure it was distasteful sir," Pickering said.

"I'm a soldier. I comply with whatever orders I am given. Even orders I consider grossly unjust and stupid. But I don't have to pretend I like it, and I won't."

"The decision to relieve Generals Dempsey and Newley, sir, was made by the chief of staff to the President. I had nothing to do with it, sir, but I must tell you frankly that I wholly agree with it."

"You don't really think, do you, General, that the Japanese are unaware we're reading their messages?"

"I can only hope they are," Pickering said.

"There is really no such thing as a military secret. You should know that."

"I respectfully beg to disagree, sir. MAGIC, so far as anyone knows, has never been compromised."

"Until General Dempsey compromised it, you mean?"

"We have no reason, at this point, to know if it was compromised by General Dempsey or not, sir."

"Then why was I ordered to place him and his deputy—another fine officer—in arrest-to-quarters?"

"I have an opinion, sir. That's all."

"All right, in your opinion."

"He was tainted by those who did act in a manner that made compromise a real possibility. He learned about it, and he should not have. I think it's entirely possible that Admiral Leahy, or General Marshall, wanted to make an example of him. And of General Newley."

"Pour l'encouragement de les autres?" Stillwell quoted sarcastically.

"Oui, mon général," Pickering replied.

"You take my meaning? You remember in France, in the First War, when certain regiments mutinied, the French shot every tenth man in those regiments, innocent men, to 'encourage the others'?"

"Yes, sir. I know that happened."

"Would something like that have 'encouraged' you, Pickering?"

Pickering hesitated.

"Would it have, General?" Stillwell pursued.

"I was about to say, sir, that as far as I know, Marines have never refused to fight. But that wouldn't answer your question, would it?"

"No, it would not have," Stillwell said.

"No, I don't think it would have," Pickering said. "I was a kid at the time. If they had shot innocent Marines, I would have hated the Corps. But that's not the situation here."

"What is the situation here, General? You tell me."

"I am reluctant to do so, sir."

"I don't give a damn if you're reluctant or not."

"General Dempsey behaved in an unacceptable manner, considering the importance of keeping MAGIC uncompromised. He is a general officer. General officers have to be held to a higher standard."

"But he did not, Pickering, compromise MAGIC."

"He took action which might have compromised it."

"Whoever told him about it before he was supposed to know is the man who took such an action. What about him? Who was he? What happened to him? Can you tell me, or is that something else you are 'not at liberty' to discuss?"

"There were two men, General, the Secretary of the Joint Chiefs of Staff and—"

"General Adamson?" Stillwell asked incredulously.

"Yes, sir."

"What happened to General Adamson?"

"When I left Washington, he had been relieved and placed in arrest-to-quarters. I was led to believe he will be reduced to his permanent rank. He may be court-martialed."

"I wasn't aware Adamson was involved in this," Stillwell said, and added: "You said there were two officers?

"The OSS's Deputy Director for Administration, sir. He was also relieved of his duties."

"That's all?"

"Colonel Donovan ordered him placed in St. Elizabeth's Hospital for evaluation."

"He was crazy? I have to ruin the careers of two fine officers because some civilian in the OSS was crazy?"

"Sir, so far as I know, this man was not out of his mind."

Stillwell looked at him curiously for a moment, then took his meaning.

"That's what happens to OSS people who talk too much?"

"It's what Colonel Donovan believed to be the appropriate action to take in the case of someone who jeopardized the security of MAGIC."

Stillwell paused to take a cigarette from a battered case and light it. He did not offer one to Pickering, and it was obvious to Pickering that Stillwell was thinking over their conversation.

"Are you carrying orders for me about what I am to do

with Generals Dempsey and Newley? Or are you relaying
a 'recommendation' like the one I got to name General
Albright as my signal officer, a man I never saw before
in my life?"

"No, sir."

"Isn't that a little odd?"

"I suspect that General Marshall is waiting to hear how
badly—if at all—MAGIC has been compromised. But I
would expect, General, as a minimum, that both officers
will be reduced to their permanent grade and ordered
home."

"To encourage the others?"

"Yes, sir."

"Not court-martialed?"

"A court-martial couldn't be held without getting into
MAGIC," Pickering said. "Something, sir—I feel obliged
to bring this up to you—that has apparently occurred to
General Dempsey."

"Excuse me?"

"Sir, I spoke very briefly with General Albright before
I came here. He met me at the airport. He told me that
when he tried to speak with General Dempsey, to determine how many other people might have been told about
MAGIC, General Dempsey invoked his right to decline to
answer any questions that might tend to incriminate him."

"And General Newley?"

"I don't know, sir," Pickering said. "My suspicion
would be that he would follow General Dempsey's lead."

"Well, I certainly can understand how they feel," Stillwell said. "If I found myself under arrest for nothing more
than having somebody tell me something I wasn't supposed to know, I wouldn't be in much of a mood to cooperate with the people who'd put me there either."

"Sir, the importance of MAGIC—"

"But we can't have that, can we?" Stillwell interrupted.
"I'll speak to both of them. Despite their—wholly justi-
fied—feeling they have been handed the short end of a
very dirty stick, they have the obligation, the duty, to tell
General Albright everything he wants to know. Or you.
Do you want to talk to them?"

"I think General Albright would be better at that than

I am, sir. I was also going to suggest that Colonel Banning talk to them. He is an intelligence officer, and has a MAGIC clearance."

"I'll see that he does," Stillwell said immediately. "Tell them to come see me before they see Generals Dempsey and Newley."

"Thank you, sir."

"Was this little chat of ours the sole reason you came to Chungking, General?"

"I think it has become the primary reason I'm here, sir."

"You want to explain that?"

"I was coming here anyway, sir, in connection with Operation Gobi." Pickering hesitated, and then asked, "General, did either General Albright or Colonel Waterson discuss Operation Gobi with you?"

Stillwell shook his head negatively.

"They both tried," he said. "I wasn't in the mood to listen. Waterson got here first, carrying Admiral Leahy's not very comprehensive letter of explanation. It said, as you probably know, that you were coming to explain everything in person. I told Colonel Waterson that I didn't at all like having a secret operation running in my zone of responsibility that I don't know anything about, and that I would discuss that operation with you when you arrived. General Albright arrived the next day. I told him that in compliance with my orders, I was appointing him *acting* signal officer until such time as I could discuss that appointment, and this secret operation, with you."

"I understand how you felt, sir."

Stillwell looked at him closely again. "Oddly enough, General, I think maybe you do," he said. "You were saying something about the primary reason you're here?"

"I have come to believe, sir, that General Marshall—or perhaps Admiral Leahy—decided I was the only senior officer with a MAGIC clearance available to come here and see how badly—if at all—MAGIC has been compromised. And as the letter said, to answer your questions. I can think of no other reason why I was flown here so quickly from Pearl Harbor."

Stillwell grunted.

"And I think—repeat, think, sir—that is Admiral Nimitz's belief as well."

"And Douglas MacArthur's?"

"That seems to me to be a reasonable presumption, sir."

Stillwell grunted thoughtfully. "It would explain Douglas's parting with one of his precious B-17s, wouldn't it?" he said. "Okay. Tell me about your secret operation."

Pickering took ten minutes to explain Operation Gobi.

Stillwell listened without responding until he was finished. "For what it's worth, Pickering," he said, "I think you're going to have a hell of a time contacting those people in the Gobi. That's bandit country, and so is the country between here and there."

"Sir?"

"Bandits. Warlords, fighting for the Japanese or the Nationalist Chinese or the Communists, depending on who is paying the most money today. Have you heard from these people lately?"

"No, sir."

"That raises the very strong possibility that they encountered the bandits, and the bandits killed everybody," Stillwell said. "That's their standing operating procedure."

"That's not very good news, sir."

"I suppose there is a reason you could not just air-drop a weather station in there? Together with the necessary operating personnel?"

"We wouldn't know where to drop them, sir. And one of the considerations is concealing the weather station from the Japanese."

"Of course," Stillwell said thoughtfully. "Let me ask some questions, Pickering," he added. "Maybe one of my Chinese can come up with something."

"I would very much appreciate that, General."

"I owe you," Stillwell said. "That wasn't much of a welcome you got from me."

Pickering sensed that he was being dismissed. "By your leave, sir?" he asked.

"Granted," Stillwell said.

Pickering came to attention and saluted. Stillwell returned it casually. Pickering did an about-face movement and walked to the door.

XX

[ONE]
OSS Station
Chungking, China
1920 7 April 1943

Brigadier General Fleming Pickering got out of the Studebaker President and walked to the wooden door and tried it. It was locked. He rapped on it with his knuckles. There was still no reply.

"I guess the doorbell doesn't work," Second Lieutenant Hart observed, then politely nudged General Pickering aside and hammered on the door with the butt of his .45 automatic.

A young Army lieutenant whom Pickering did not remember from his first visit to the house opened the door. As he was pulling the door fully open, Lieutenant Colonel Ed Banning appeared in the corridor behind him. The two men shook hands. "I'm glad you're here, Ed," Pickering said.

"I'm sorry I wasn't at the airport, General," Banning

said. "I was in the cryptographic room. They call it 'the dungeon' here, too."

"I understand," Pickering said.

"I came as soon as General Albright told me you were here, sir."

"No time lost," Pickering said. "I was 'received' by General Stillwell."

"General Albright told me. How did that go?"

"I may be kidding myself, but I think I have calmed him down to the point where he no longer wants to cut me in small pieces with a dull saw and will settle for something like crucifixion. He's one tough cookie." And then he added what he was thinking: "But I like him. I understand why he was sore."

"You were the bearer of bad tidings, sir," Banning said. "Didn't that kill-the-messenger business start over here?"

Pickering chuckled, then asked, "Where's McCoy, Ed?"

"I don't know, sir," Banning said.

"How did that happen?" Pickering asked.

"Right after I had my initial run-in with General Dempsey, I told him to make himself scarce. He's good at that."

"I got that much from your Special Channel. McCoy has made no attempt to contact you at all?"

"He was here once . . ."

"Albright told me."

". . . and apparently had words with Colonel Platt."

"He told me that, too," Pickering said. "That doesn't sound like McCoy. What was that all about?"

"Platt felt that as the OSS station chief here, everybody in the OSS belonged to him. McCoy didn't think so—" He cut himself off in midsentence when he noticed Colonel John J. Waterson and Lieutenant Colonel Richard C. Platt walking across the foyer toward them.

"Good evening, General," Waterson said.

"We were about to get into the subject of Captain McCoy," Pickering said. "But I need first to visit the head, and then I want a drink."

"The facility is right over there, General," Platt said, pointing. "And we could talk in the bar, if you'd like."

"I'd hate to run your people out of the bar, Colonel."

"All of my people have Top Secret clearances, General."

"But none of them, so far as I am aware, have the Need To Know about Operation Gobi," Pickering said.

"Sir," Platt said uneasily, "Washington has been keeping us up-to-date on Operation Gobi."

"That was done without my knowledge, Colonel," Pickering said. "From this moment, no one is to hear anything more about Operation Gobi unless it comes from Colonel Banning or myself." He turned and walked across the foyer to the toilet.

"I don't really understand this, sir," Lieutenant Colonel Platt said to Colonel Waterson.

"I'm sure the General is about to explain it all to you, Colonel," Waterson said. "Right now, I suggest that you either clear everybody out of the bar, or find some other place where we can all talk."

When Pickering entered the room Platt was calling the "bar," he found Waterson, Platt, and Banning standing at a bar, but there was no liquor in sight. George Hart, seeing his boss, lifted himself out of the chair in which he had been sitting at a small table. Pickering signaled for him to keep his seat.

He looks about as tired as I feel.

"Is there any scotch?" Pickering asked.

"No Famous Grouse, sir," Banning said. "I guess I should have thought to bring some with me."

"Beggars can't be choosers," Pickering said. "I'd like a weak one, Ed, if you'd—"

"Coming right up, sir."

"And I'd rather not drink alone," Pickering said.

Banning went behind the bar. Hart got out of his chair and joined him. Hart found glasses and put ice in them. Banning rummaged under the bar and came up with two bottles of scotch whiskey, Cutty Sark, and a brand Pickering had never seen before. He held them up to give Pickering his choice.

"The Cutty, please, Ed," Pickering said. "And, if there is any, a little soda."

"There isn't any, sir. Water?"

"Please," Pickering said.

Hart poured water from a pitcher into a glass and then carried it to Pickering.

Pickering waited until the others had drinks. "I feel that a toast is called for," he said. "But all I can think of is somewhat obscene, so I'll have to settle for 'your health, gentlemen.'"

Everybody took a sip.

"Jack, the first thing that comes to mind," he said to Colonel Waterson, "is getting you back to Brisbane. Unless you go back on the B-17 that brought me here, God only knows how long it will take to get you there. So make sure that airplane doesn't leave without you."

"Yes, sir."

"Next question, Jack, how much did you tell Colonel Platt about what brought you here?"

"Almost nothing," Platt answered for him.

"I told Colonel Platt, sir, that I was not at liberty to discuss why I was here, other than that I carried a letter to General Stillwell."

"I should have known that, but I had to ask," Pickering said. "You did the right thing. And what did you tell Colonel Banning?"

"I thought the Colonel should know you were on your way here, sir. And that the relief of Generals Dempsey and Newley had been ordered. And that General Albright was also en route. I told him all of that."

"You spoke with General Albright, Ed. How much did he tell you?"

"Not much, sir, other than that you were en route, that Generals Dempsey and Newley were out of the Special Channel loop, that he had been appointed acting signal officer of USMMCHI, and, until further orders from you, we would be taking our orders from him—we being Easterbrook, Rutterman, and me."

"Okay," Pickering said. "Colonel Platt, there has been a possible breach of security. I'm afraid I can't tell you more than that, except it was of such importance—*potentially* of such importance—that Generals Dempsey and Newley here have been relieved of their duties, and so have the Secretary of the JCS and the OSS's Deputy Director for Administration."

"Jesus Christ!" Colonel Platt said.

"I hope you understand, Colonel," Pickering said, "that the fact that you cannot be given more information about this is in no way a reflection on you. You just don't have the Need To Know."

"I understand, sir."

"You've said you were advised of Operation Gobi?".

"Yes, sir."

"By the Deputy Director Administration?"

"Yes, sir."

"That was something else he shouldn't have done," Pickering said. "Or at least shouldn't have done without my knowledge and permission."

"Sir . . ."

"That wasn't your fault," Pickering said. "And General Albright tells me you have some ideas of your own—a proposed Opplan—on how Operation Gobi should go forward?"

"Yes, sir."

"And that you sent this Opplan to Washington?"

"Yes, sir."

"Addressed to whom?"

"The Director, sir."

"I want to see that. I was about to say tonight, but I wouldn't know what I was reading tonight. First thing in the morning."

"Yes, sir."

"You can give it to Colonel Banning tonight," Pickering said. "I'll want his opinion. Which brings us to Colonel Banning. Colonel Banning, and the people he brought with him, work for me. They are not part of the Chungking OSS station. Having said that, I want them housed here."

"Yes, sir. May I ask why, sir?"

"Because they are engaged in work that can't help but attract the curiosity of their fellow cryptographers. Banning knows how to say none of your goddamn business, but it's a little harder for two junior officers and a warrant officer to say that to senior officers. If they're not in the BOQ, no one can ask them questions."

"I understand, sir."

"Going off at a tangent. Ed. Did John Moore arrive?"

"Yes, sir. Two days after I did. It took him a long time to get here from Brisbane."

"That's probably my fault, General," Colonel Waterson said. "I got him a triple A air priority. I didn't think there was a rush, and I didn't want to call attention to him."

"He's here, that's all that matters," Pickering said, and then asked, "Where's he billeted, Ed?"

"In the company-grade BOQ, sir."

"Among other things Moore does, Colonel Platt," Pickering said, "he's a special kind of intelligence analyst. I can't go further into that. And I want him to do that, rather than what a headquarters company commander—who can't be told what Moore really does—thinks are appropriate duties for a second lieutenant. I want him moved in here right away."

"Yes, sir."

"The next priority is to find McCoy," Pickering said.

There was a knock at the door.

"With a little bit of luck," Banning said. "That will be the Killer."

Hart went to the door and opened it. It was Second Lieutenant Robert F. Easterbrook, USMCR.

"We just got a Special Channel for you, General Pickering," he said. "I thought I'd better get it right to you, sir."

"How are you, Easterbrook?" Pickering said, rising from his chair and walking over to him. "I was just talking to your cousin Slats."

"Sir?"

"Colonel Easterbrook. General Stillwell's son-in-law. Isn't he kin?"

"Not so far as I know, sir," Easterbrook said seriously.

"What have you got for me, Bobby?" Pickering asked.

Damn, I did it again. He's a Marine officer, and you shouldn't call a Marine officer Bobby. Unless he's six feet three, weighs two hundred twenty pounds, and comes from Alabama.

I must be tired. Of course I'm tired.

Easterbrook opened his buttoned-to-the-collar overcoat, reached inside, and produced a manila envelope. He handed it to General Pickering, who tore the envelope open and read it.

```
T O P   S E C R E T

FROM ACTING STACHIEF OSS HAWAII
1210 GREENWICH 7 APRIL 1943
VIA SPECIAL CHANNEL
DUPLICATION FORBIDDEN

TO BRIGGEN FLEMING PICKERING USMCR
OSS DEPUTY DIRECTOR FOR PACIFIC
OPERATIONS
THRU: US MILITARY MISSION TO CHINA
CHUNGKING

SUBJECT: PROGRESS REPORT

1. SIMULATED RENDEZVOUS REFUELING
OPERATION USING PT BOAT AND ONE AIRCRAFT
SUCCESSFULLY COMPLETED 6 APR 43.

2. PROBLEMS REVEALED BELIEVED TO HAVE
BEEN RESOLVED. A SECOND SIMULATION USING
PT BOAT AND BOTH AIRCRAFT WILL TAKE PLACE
10 APR. THE VOLUNTEER PILOTS ARE NOT
REPEAT NOT YET AVAILABLE, BUT IT IS
BELIEVED THEY WILL BE AVAILABLE IN TIME
FOR THE DRY RUN WHICH WILL INVOLVE THE
SUNFISH.

3. POTENTIAL PROBLEMS BEYOND OUR CONTROL
FOLLOW:
(A) THE POSSIBILITY OF INABILITY OF
AIRCRAFT TO EFFECT RENDEZVOUS WITH
SUNFISH BECAUSE OF RADIO NAVIGATION AND
OR WEATHER PROBLEMS.
(B) POSSIBLE ROUGH SEAS AT RENDEZVOUS
POINT WHICH MAY MAKE LANDING AND
```

ESPECIALLY TAKE OFF OF HEAVY LADEN
AIRCRAFT IMPOSSIBLE.
(C) ADMIRAL WAGAM POINTS OUT THAT IF
CONDITION OF SEAS PROHIBITS LANDING,
AIRCRAFT WILL NOT, REPEAT, NOT HAVE
SUFFICIENT FUEL REMAINING TO DIVERT. THE
NECESSARY ABANDONMENT OF AIRCRAFT AT
RENDEZVOUS SITE WILL POSE GREAT HAZARDS
TO AIRCREWS, AS WATER TEMPERATURE WILL
LIKELY CAUSE DEATH BY HYPOTHERMIA WITHIN
MINUTES OF PERSONNEL ENTERING WATER.
(D) AN ABSOLUTE MINIMUM OF FORTY FIVE (45)
MINUTES WILL BE REQUIRED TO TRANSFER
FUEL, PERSONNEL AND CARGO. THIS PRESUMES
SMOOTH SEAS. CONDITION OF SEAS MAY DOUBLE
THE TIME REQUIRED. THERE IS THE
POSSIBILITY OF DETECTION BY ENEMY
VESSELS OR AIRCRAFT. ADMIRAL WAGAM HAS
DIRECTED THE CAPTAIN OF THE SUNFISH, IN
SUCH AN EVENT, TO DESTROY THE AIRCRAFT,
MAKE EVERY REASONABLE EFFORT TO TAKE THE
AIRCREWS ABOARD BEFORE SUBMERGING, THEN
RETURN TO PEARL HARBOR.
(E) A SECOND RENDEZVOUS ATTEMPT WILL NOT
BE POSSIBLE UNTIL TWO REPLACEMENT
CATALINAS CAN BE MODIFIED (MINIMUM
ESTIMATED WORK TIME SIX DAYS),
REPLACEMENT METEOROLOGICAL EQUIPMENT CAN
BE OBTAINED AND TRANSPORTED FROM
MAINLAND US TO PEARL HARBOR, AND SUNFISH
CAN RETURN TO PEARL HARBOR TO TAKE
METEOROLOGICAL EQUIPMENT ABOARD AND
RETURN TO RENDEZVOUS SITE.

HOMER C. DILLON
MAJOR, USMCR

T O P S E C R E T

Pickering handed it to Colonel Waterson.

"Pass it around, please, Jack," he said, "when you've finished."

"To Colonel Platt, too, sir?"

"Uh-huh," Pickering said. "Platt, that message deals with refueling a Catalina at sea, from a submarine. Did Washington get into that with you?"

"Only in a general sense, sir."

"Well, until we come up with a better idea, that's how we're going to go. This was good news. The first dry run they had, with a submarine, was a disaster. They've apparently got it working now. Jake Dillon recruited a Seabee chief petty officer he knew in the movie business to help, and he's apparently fixed the problems."

Colonel Richard C. Platt looked mystified at the reference to a Seabee and the movie business.

Banning chuckled.

"I don't believe, General," he said, "that Colonel Platt knows Major Dillon."

"Of course, he doesn't," Pickering said. "How could he? Well, I'll leave that to you, Ed. I'm too bushed to tell Jake Dillon stories tonight, much less to get into the implications of that Special Channel, or listening to Platt's ideas on Operation Gobi. We can have all of it first thing in the morning. What I need now is some sleep."

He got up and walked to the door. Everyone stood up. Pickering turned.

"Make sure Colonel Platt has a good idea of everything, Ed."

"Aye, aye, sir."

Colonel Platt looked pleased.

As if, Pickering thought, *he was just told he can play with the big boys after all.*

"Good evening, gentlemen," Pickering said and, with Hart trailing him, left the bar.

[TWO]
OSS Station
Chungking, China
0715 8 April 1943

Brigadier General Fleming Pickering, USMCR, lay in his bed and wondered if he was about to become sick. He would not be at all surprised. He was wide awake—had been for fifteen minutes—but did not seem able to muster enough energy to sit up and drag himself out of the bed. Simply being awake was itself surprising. He'd barely been able to keep his eyes open before he went to bed, and would have bet he'd sleep for at least twelve hours.

"There are obviously *some* drawbacks to the miracle of faster-than-a-speeding-bullet transoceanic flights," he said aloud, and then added, "Okay, stop feeling sorry for yourself, you old bastard, haul your ass out of bed and get to work."

"Sir?" Second Lieutenant George F. Hart, USMCR, asked. A moment later, his face appeared from behind a screen in one corner of the room.

I didn't know that he was in there.

"I was talking to myself, George, something that old men tend to do," Pickering said. "Sorry to wake you."

"I thought I'd sleep into next week when I went to bed last night," Hart said. "But I've been wide awake for thirty minutes." He walked into the room, wearing his uniform, except for the tunic.

Pickering pushed himself up and swung his legs out of the bed. Then he pushed himself to his feet and reached for his trousers. "And you are presumably bursting with energy, eager to face the challenges of the new day?" he asked.

"Actually, sir, my ass is really dragging. I really didn't want to get out of bed."

"I'm glad to hear you say that, George," Pickering said. "I feel exactly the same way. I thought maybe I was getting sick."

"We spent a lot of time on those airplanes, General."

"Where did you sleep, George?"

"There's a little alcove behind the screen, General. I had them get me a cot."

"Have we got a phone number for Banning?" Pickering asked. "I want to know if he's located McCoy."

"We do, sir," Hart said. "But he said, last night, that he would be here about seven. He's probably on his way by now."

"I want to talk to Albright, too," Pickering said, as

much to himself as to Hart. "Let's find ourselves some breakfast. I need a cup of coffee. Give me a minute to finish dressing."

"Yes, sir."

Captain Jerry Sampson, the one who'd been at Harvard with "Malcolm," was standing by a double sliding door off the foyer of the house. He was wearing what Pickering thought of as "a white hunter's jacket."

He came to attention. "Good morning, General," he said.

"Good morning," Pickering said, smiling at him.

"Ah-ten-HUT!" Sampson bellowed in Pickering's ear, startling him.

There was the sound of scraping chairs and six officers sitting around a large table got to their feet and came to attention.

"Good morning, gentlemen," Pickering said. "Please take your seats." He turned to Sampson. "That was very nice, Captain, but we'll dispense with that in the future. And we will also dispense with anybody waiting for me to show up to eat."

"Yes, sir," Captain Sampson said.

The table was set for breakfast. There was even a rack of toast before an empty place—where Pickering knew he was expected to sit—at the head of the table. Colonel John J. Waterson remained standing at the position to the right, Lieutenant Colonel Richard C. Platt remained standing to the left.

"May I introduce my officers, sir?" Platt asked.

"Of course," Pickering said.

Platt led him around the table and introduced him to the officers of OSS station Chungking.

They all look like they were stamped from the same mold as Sampson, Pickering thought. *Nice-looking, intelligent-looking, young men.*

"I'll gratefully eat whatever is put before me," Pickering announced when he had taken his seat.

Lieutenant Colonel Platt rang a small silver bell, and a line of houseboys marched into the room and began serving breakfast.

Lieutenant Colonel Ed Banning came through the door, noticing as he did an empty place beside Colonel Waterson. He wondered if it was left empty by coincidence or was reserved for him. He slipped into it. "Good morning, General," he said.

"Any word on McCoy, Ed?" Pickering asked.

Banning, looking uncomfortable, shook his head, "no." "I did talk to the B-17 pilot, sir. He'd like to take off at four, if that fits in with Colonel Waterson's schedule."

"You have any problem with that, Jack?"

"No, sir."

"Okay, Ed, confirm that."

"Aye, aye, sir," Banning said. "And there's been another Special Channel for you." He reached into his tunic pocket and handed Pickering a sealed envelope.

" 'Special Channel'?" Captain Sampson quoted curiously. "May I ask—"

"No, you may not," Colonel Platt said.

Well, at least Platt learns quick, Pickering thought, suppressing a smile at the look on Captain Sampson's face. He tore open the envelope and read the Special Channel.

```
T O P  S E C R E T

CINCPAC HAWAII
VIA SPECIAL CHANNEL
DUPLICATION FORBIDDEN
0905 GREENWICH 8 APRIL 1943

US MILITARY MISSION TO CHINA
EYES ONLY BRIGGEN FLEMING PICKERING,
USMC

BEGIN PERSONAL FROM ADM NIMITZ TO BRIG
GEN PICKERING

DEAR FLEMING:

REFERENCE REPORT FROM YOUR MAJOR DILLON
DATED 7 APR 43:
```

FOR YOUR ADDITIONAL INFORMATION, I HAVE
BEEN ADVISED BY MAJGEN MCINERNEY THAT
FULLY QUALIFIED VOLUNTEER PILOTS WILL BE
ON STATION HERE WITHIN NO MORE THAN FORTY-
EIGHT (48) HOURS.

SUBMARINE SUNFISH WILL BE AVAILABLE TO
OPERATION GOBI AS OF 1600 GREENWICH 8
APRIL AND DRY RUN IN HAWAIIAN WATERS
INVOLVING BOTH AIRCRAFT WILL BE
CONDUCTED AS SOON AS POSSIBLE
THEREAFTER.

INASMUCH AS ESTIMATED BEST POSSIBLE
SAILING TIME TO RENDEZVOUS POINT
FOURTEEN (14) DAYS TWELVE (12) HOURS AND
ACTUAL SAILING TIME WILL LIKELY TAKE AS
MUCH AS FOUR (4) DAYS LONGER, REARADM
WAGAM RECOMMENDS THAT SUNFISH SAIL FOR
RENDEZVOUS POINT IMMEDIATELY AFTER
CONCLUSION OF SUCCESSFUL DRY RUN AND
REMAIN ON STATION UNTIL RENDEZVOUS IS
MADE OR MISSION ABORTED. IN ABSENCE OF
OBJECTION FROM YOU THIS WILL BE ORDERED.

AGAINST THE POSSIBILITY THAT THE FIRST
RENDEZVOUS ATTEMPT MAY FAIL, WITH THE
LOSS OF AIRCRAFT, AND MAY TAKE PLACE
AFTER SUNFISH HAS BEEN ON STATION FOR
SOME TIME WITH RESULTANT EXHAUSTION OF
FUEL AND FOOD, I HAVE DIRECTED REARADM
WAGAM TO HAVE TWO ADDITIONAL PBY-5A
AIRCRAFT MODIFIED AT EWA IMMEDIATELY,
AND TO BE PREPARED IMMEDIATELY UPON
NOTIFICATION THAT THE FIRST RENDEZVOUS
ATTEMPT HAS BEEN UNSUCCESSFUL AND
SUNFISH IS RETURNING TO PEARL HARBOR TO
DISPATCH A SECOND SUBMARINE FROM PEARL
HARBOR TO EFFECT AN AT-SEA RENDEZVOUS
WITH SUNFISH. REARADM WAGAM ESTIMATES
PERSONNEL AND EQUIPMENT ABOARD SUNFISH

```
CAN BE TRANSFERRED TO SECOND SUBMARINE IN
ONE HOUR.

I HAVE EVERY CONFIDENCE YOU HAVE BEEN
ABLE TO EXPLAIN TO GENERAL STILLWELL THE
SERIOUSNESS OF THE SECURITY PROBLEMS
THAT HAVE OCCURRED.

BEST PERSONAL REGARDS

CHESTER W. NIMITZ
ADMIRAL, US NAVY
CINCPAC

END PERSONAL FROM ADM NIMITZ TO BRIGGEN
PICKERING

T O P S E C R E T
```

Pickering handed the message to Colonel Platt. "Give this to Colonel Waterson when you've read it," Pickering ordered. "Then it goes to Hart."

"Yes, sir."

"Ed, several questions. Are you familiar with Platt's proposed Opplan?"

"Yes, sir. General Albright showed it to me."

There was a look of surprise on Platt's face.

"Among Ed's other responsibilities, Colonel," Pickering said, "is keeping me up to speed on whatever's going on. To do that, he gets to read everything."

"Yes, sir, of course," Platt said.

"Same thing applies to Hart," Pickering said.

"Yes, sir."

Pickering turned back to Banning. "Was Moore up all night, Ed?"

"No, sir, the Easterbunny had the duty."

"General Stillwell wants to talk to you before you talk to Generals Dempsey and Newley. What I'm thinking of doing is sending you there with last night's Special Channel and this one—and Lieutenant Moore."

"Yes, sir?"

"I don't want General Stillwell to get the idea we're not showing him everything he has every right to know," Pickering said. "And I want him to meet Moore and to know what Moore's function is. That make sense to you?"

"Yes, sir."

"That 'yes, sir,' Platt," Pickering said, "was not an automatic reflex on Banning's part. If he doesn't agree with me, he says so. I want you to do the same thing."

"Yes, sir."

"It's not hard, Colonel," Banning said. "The boss is usually right."

"Flattery will get you everywhere, Colonel Banning," Pickering said. "And while you're with General Stillwell, Platt will show me his Opplan."

"Makes sense, sir," Banning said.

"And when you have finished with General Stillwell, Ed, you go find McCoy."

"Aye, aye, sir," Banning said. "I'll try, sir."

"I'm really getting concerned, Ed."

"I don't think he would take off without telling me," Banning said.

"The operative words in that sentence, Ed, are 'I don't think.' "

"Yes, sir."

"You have any ideas on that subject, Platt?" Pickering asked.

"Chungking is a large city, General," Platt said. "If someone wants to make himself scarce here, it's not hard."

"Even for two Westerners with beards?" Pickering asked.

"He's right, General," Banning began. "I'll look—"

"If the plane is leaving at four," Pickering interrupted him. "That means Colonel Waterson will have to leave here at three. Be back here by then, Ed. Whatever you learn from Dempsey and Newley I'll want Waterson to know so that he can tell MacArthur the minute he gets to Australia."

"Aye, aye, sir."

[THREE]
OSS Station
Chungking, China
1450 8 April 1943

After breakfast, Pickering and Hart followed Platt to his office, which had been set up for a briefing. On either side of a blackboard, there were two easels, supporting maps covered with a sheet of canvas. Four armchairs faced the easels and blackboard.

"Sir," Lieutenant Colonel Platt said to Pickering a little uneasily, "I'm aware, sir, of what you said about no more information about Operation Gobi being made available to my people without your permission . . ."

"But?"

"Captain Sampson has spent a good deal of time with my proposed Opplan. He knows details about it I don't."

"And you would like him in on this?"

"The truth is, he can give you a better briefing than I can."

"Okay," Pickering said. "Let's get on with it."

The briefing lasted more than an hour, and Captain Sampson did a good job, calling to Pickering's attention facts about the Gobi Desert that he had not learned in Washington. Platt's proposed Opplan—mostly written by Sampson, Pickering quickly concluded—to go into the Gobi and establish a weather station had obviously been given a good deal of thought. With one major exception, Pickering could find nothing wrong with it. The one exception: Despite Platt's obvious ability and experience in China, and Sampson's intelligent attack on the problem, the two of them had no more idea how to find the Americans thought to be in the desert than he did.

Platt's Opplan was essentially based on the premise that the Americans could not be found. It was also obvious that neither of them thought much of the idea of sending the meteorological team into the Gobi on Navy reconnaissance aircraft. The phrasing they used was, of course, polite: *"In the event transport of the meteorological per-*

sonnel and equipment by Naval aircraft proves not to be feasible . . ."

"In the event that it proves impossible to locate the American personnel believed to be somewhere in the Gobi Desert . . ."

The tone of the Opplan made it clear that they regarded "in the event" to be as likely as the sun rising.

Practically, their Opplan called for two companies of Nationalist Chinese infantry, mounted on trucks, accompanied by a six-man team of OSS agents. These would take the meteorologists and their equipment through the desert on known caravan routes until they found the Americans who were supposed to be there.

In the event Americans could not be found, the weather station would be in the desert ready to go to work. Meanwhile, the two companies of Chinese infantry would provide adequate security for the weather station against the possibility that the Japanese would learn they were there, and against the bands of bandits roving the area.

After the briefing, Pickering made no comments, announcing—truthfully—that before he offered his own thoughts he wanted to think it over, and discuss it with both Banning and Captain McCoy, if and when he turned up. At one point, however, he openly disagreed with Platt, when Platt announced that "Chungking agents have more experience in this sort of thing than Captain McCoy does, and that certainly is not intended as a reflection on Captain McCoy."

The implication was clear: he and Sampson didn't think McCoy was necessary, and further that he would get in the way of the local experts. Pickering decided he couldn't let that pass unchallenged. "I don't think there is anyone in the Marine Corps, or the OSS, better equipped for this sort of thing than Captain McCoy," he said. "And no matter what we ultimately decide is the best way to go about doing what we have to do, McCoy will be involved."

Am I doing the right thing? he immediately wondered. *Platt has offered me a perfectly valid reason for not sending McCoy off—again—on a dangerous mission.*

And how much is my ego involved: Bill Donovan will be delighted to report to Leahy and the President that, "once he got over there, Pickering decided that the OSS people on the scene were better able to carry out the mission than that young captain he had originally put in charge."

Pickering spent the rest of the morning reading Platt's after-action reports of the various operations OSS Chungking station had carried out.

After making half a dozen trips to the filing cabinet, taking out one file at a time and then replacing it when he was finished, he finally—with Hart helping—took all the files from the cabinet and stacked them on the floor on the right side of his armchair, and then as he read them, stacked them, none too neatly, on the left.

The files showed that Platt, generously using OSS non-accountable funds, had been running a wide range of generally successful operations intended to harass the Japanese and/or garner information about their troop dispositions. As he read through them, Pickering had a growing feeling that Platt really knew what he was doing here, and that he himself did not.

I'm a mariner, a business executive. What the hell am I doing in the intelligence business, trying to tell—from a position of monumental ignorance—people who know all about this sort of thing how they should do it?

McCoy—the missing McCoy—was never out of his mind for long, and McCoy was the first thing that came to his lips when Brigadier General H. A. Albright, USA, and Lieutenant Colonel Edward J. Banning, USMC, came into Platt's office.

"You find McCoy, Ed?"

"I have no idea where he might be, General," Banning said.

"For the good news, General . . . " Albright said.

"Let's have some of that," Pickering said.

"We talked to Dempsey and Newley. General Stillwell had them come to his office, and we talked in his conference room. Banning and I are agreed that they are telling the truth when they say that, with the exception of Dempsey's sergeant major, they told no one else about MAGIC."

"And the sergeant major?"

"He told us that it went no further," Banning said. "I believe him."

"Maybe because he felt that was what you wanted to hear?"

"I don't think so, sir. I believe him."

"What do we do about him?" General Albright asked.

"That would seem to be up to you, Hugh," Pickering said. "You're going to need a sergeant major."

"I think I'll keep him," Albright said. "He understands the importance of MAGIC now, for sure. Banning really read the riot act to him."

"Your decision, Hugh. But I think you had better apply that 'no duty in which there is any chance at all that he would be captured' restriction to the sergeant major."

"He was a cryptographer at one time," Albright said. "Since he already has his nose under the tent flap, how do you feel about getting him a MAGIC clearance? Banning's going to need more people to handle the Special Channel than he has."

"Up to you."

"No, sir. It's up to you."

"Ed?"

"I'd go along with him," Banning said. "Rutterman likes him."

"Okay, then. I wouldn't even mention his name to Waterson when we tell him he can tell MacArthur we think the genie didn't get out of the bottle."

"You're going to have to let Washington know that, too," Albright said.

"Draft a message for me to Admiral Leahy, copy to Donovan, Ed, please, right here and now. I don't know the jargon."

"Aye, aye, sir."

"There's a typewriter over there," Pickering said, pointing. "Do it now, so I can have a look at it before I take Waterson to the airport."

"Aye, aye, sir."

"And there is more good news," Albright said. "Stillwell seemed pleased with Lieutenant Moore. He apparently fancies himself an analyst of the Japanese mind himself. And he told me I can consider myself his signal officer, not just acting."

"I like him," Pickering said. "In his shoes, I think I would have been just as angry."

There was another knock at the door. Banning opened it. Colonel Waterson was standing there.

"Sir, I'm going to have to leave for the airport right about now," he said.

"I'll see you off," Pickering said. "George, can you find the airport?"

"Yes, sir, I'm sure I can."

"Then get us one of those Studebakers, without a driver. Then I can talk to Colonel Waterson on the way."

"Aye, aye, sir."

General Pickering rode to the airfield with Colonel Waterson in the backseat of the Studebaker. After Waterson was safely aboard the B-17 and the aircraft had taken off, Pickering got in the front seat beside Hart for the trip back into town. Five hundred yards beyond the gate, as they drove down the dirt road paralleling the runway, Pickering became aware of a horn bleating imperiously behind them. He turned and looked out the rear window. "It's an ambulance with the red crosses painted over," he said. "Let him by, George."

"Goddamn Chinamen," Hart said, and steered to the left of the road. He cursed again when the Studebaker leaned precariously with its right wheels in the ditch beside the road. The ambulance pulled parallel but did not move ahead. Hart got a brief glimpse of a Chinese officer in the passenger seat. He was gesturing for Hart to pull over.

"I don't like this, General," Hart said. Hart's hand was inside his overcoat, obviously reaching for his pistol.

Then the ambulance cut them off, and Hart slammed on the brakes.

Pickering took out his pistol and worked the action. He noticed that Hart merely pulled the hammer back on his pistol. "You better charge that piece, George," he said.

"I carry it charged," Hart said matter-of-factly. He was now holding the pistol in a position essentially out of sight from outside, but from which he could easily fire it through his side window.

The passenger door of the ambulance opened and the Chinese officer stepped out and walked back toward the Studebaker. He was wearing a well-tailored Nationalist Chinese army uniform, complete to a shiny Sam Browne belt, from which hung a molded leather pistol holster.

"Oh, shit!" General Pickering said.

The Chinese officer walked to the driver's side of the Studebaker, leaned down to it, and smiled. Hart cranked the window down.

"Do you realize, young man," the Chinese officer said, "that you were going forty-five in a twenty-five mile zone?"

"McCoy, goddamn you," Brigadier General Pickering said. "Where the hell have you been?"

"Good afternoon, sir," McCoy said. "Sir, I didn't know for sure until about half past one that you were here."

"You sonofabitch," Pickering said. "I'm really glad to see you."

"I'm glad to see you, too, sir," McCoy said. "I'm even glad to see your dog-robber. You can put your pistol away now, George."

"He almost shot you," Pickering said. "Goddamn it!"

"He's probably a lousy shot, sir."

"Was this necessary?" Pickering said. "Why didn't you just go to the OSS house?"

"I'm not one of Colonel Platt's favorite people, sir. And I wanted to talk to you before he made good on his promise to have me thrown in the stockade."

"Who's driving the ambulance?" Pickering asked.

"Zimmerman, sir."

"Well, tell him to follow us to the OSS house," Pickering said. "And then get in here."

"Aye, aye, sir," McCoy said. Then he added, to Lieutenant Hart, "You have an honest face, young man. I'm going to let you off with a warning this time."

"Fuck you, McCoy!"

McCoy laughed and walked to the ambulance, which immediately started to move out of the way. He started back to the Studebaker.

"I'll be a sonofabitch if he doesn't look like a Chinese, dressed up that way," Hart said. "I wonder what the hell that's all about?"

"Me, too, George," Pickering said, and waited for Mc-Coy to get in the backseat.

McCoy got in the backseat of the car and closed the door. Pickering turned to look at him, resting his arm on the back of the front seat. "First things first, Ken," he began. "Tell me about your run-in with Colonel Platt."

"Sir, I don't know how much Colonel Banning told you about telling me to make myself scarce?"

"You tell me, Ken."

"First, he told me that Zimmerman and I were detached from the guard detail. Then he told me that he had been ordered—by the army signal officer here, the one that's in arrest-to-quarters now. . . . What's that all about?"

"One thing at a time, Ken."

"Yes, sir. Then he told me he had been ordered by the signal officer here to order me to report to OSS station Chungking. But that since I had been detached, he could no longer give me orders. Can I talk out of school?"

"You can always talk out of school to me, Ken," Pickering said.

"That wasn't hard to figure out. Colonel Banning didn't want me to report to the OSS here. Until that moment, I didn't even know there was an OSS station here."

"Neither did Banning until he got that order from General Dempsey," Pickering said.

"He told me that, sir."

"And neither did I. If it makes you feel any better, Ken, the man responsible for not telling us, your friend the OSS Deputy Director for Administration, is now in St. Elizabeth's."

"For not telling you about an OSS station here?" McCoy asked incredulously, and then, a moment later, added, "Oh."

My God, he knows!

"Explain that 'Oh!', Ken."

"I'm guessing, sir."

"Guess."

"I heard—what, four, five days later—that General Dempsey and the other one?"

"Newley?"

"Yes, sir. That they had been placed in arrest to quarters. That had to be serious; they don't relieve general officers without good reason. And then Colonel Waterson shows up from Brisbane, and right after him, Colonel Albright, now a general himself, and takes General Dempsey's place. And now you tell me that the guy from the OSS has been put in St. Elizabeth's. The only explanation for that is MAGIC."

"What do you know about MAGIC, Ken?"

"It's only another guess, sir," McCoy replied.

"Guess."

"First of all, it's a special cryptographic system, one that regular crypto people don't know anything about. With special crypto devices. Which we brought here."

"Anything else?"

"It has something to do with Japanese cryptography. Pluto and Moore are analysts, as well as crypto people. That looks to me like we've broken Japanese codes, are reading their communications, and damned sure don't want them to even suspect we are."

"I'm not going to comment on your guesses, Captain McCoy," Pickering said. "But I am going to give you a direct order."

"Yes, sir?"

"You are forbidden to discuss with anyone, except Colonel Banning or myself, in any manner whatsoever, anything connected with MAGIC."

"Aye, aye, sir."

All I have done, of course, is let him know his guesses are right on the money.

"How did you hear about General Dempsey being placed in arrest?"

"I sent Zimmerman to the NCO club to find out whatever he could."

"In uniform, presumably, and freshly shaven?"

"Yes, sir, the beards were the first thing to go. They made us stand out like a couple of whores in church."

"And the word was out that General Dempsey had been relieved?"

"Yes, sir. Nobody seems to know why. I sent Zimmerman back another time to see if he could find out, and what the NCO's were saying . . . I'm not sure you want to hear this, General."

"Yes, I do."

"That they were queer," McCoy said.

"MAGIC never came up?"

"No, sir."

"Go on, Ken."

"So I put on my uniform and went to the OSS house to see what I could find out. I was hoping to see Colonel Banning, but he wasn't there. Colonel Platt was."

"And?"

"I showed him my ONI credentials and told him I was Navy Intelligence, and was looking for Colonel Banning. That didn't work too well. He had my name from someplace. Probably this General Dempsey gave it to him. And he told me he knew that I was in the OSS, that he knew all about Operation Gobi, and told me I was now under the orders of the OSS station here. Meaning him. I told him, with respect, that I couldn't put myself or Zimmerman under his orders."

"And what did he say?"

"First, if I 'remained insubordinate' he would court-martial me, and then if I tried to leave the OSS compound, he would have me shot. He was really pissed. He actually took his pistol out when I started to leave."

"You weren't worried that he would actually shoot you?"

"He's not the type to shoot somebody," McCoy said. "And neither was the captain—Sampson, I think—in his office. But if he'd had a couple of MPs around, he *would* have ordered them to throw me in the stockade."

"So then what happened?"

"Well, I started making preparations to go into the Gobi."

"General," Hart said. "We're getting close to the house. Do you want me to drive around the block?"

"Go very slow for a minute, George," Pickering ordered. "How did you know I was here, Ken?"

"I had a couple of Chinese boys watching the airport, sir," McCoy said. "And a couple more watching the OSS compound. When they reported that a tall, American general got off an enormous airplane, and General Albright and Colonel Waterson met him and took him to the OSS house, I thought it would probably be you."

"You've been spying on the OSS?" Pickering asked.

"I thought some 'discreet surveillance' wouldn't hurt anything, sir. I didn't get the reports about you until about an hour and a half ago. I came as soon as I could. When I got to the OSS house, I saw you driving out with Colonel Waterson, so I followed you to the airfield."

"Sir, we're at the gate," Hart said. "What do I do?"

"Go in, George," Pickering ordered. "I want to properly introduce Captain McCoy to Colonel Platt and Captain Sampson."

"Aye, aye, sir."

Hart stopped the car before the OSS compound gate. One of the Chinese guards came out of the guard shack and ambled slowly to the gate in the wall.

McCoy rolled down the window and barked something in Mandarin.

The guard spun around, came to quivering attention, and saluted.

McCoy said something else in Mandarin.

The guard saluted again and hastily opened the gate.

"What was that all about?" Pickering asked.

"Nothing important, sir."

"I'll be the judge of that, thank you very much, Captain McCoy."

"I told him to pass the ambulance, he's with us, sir," McCoy said.

"He didn't pop to attention like that because you told him to pass the ambulance through," Pickering said.

"I also told him that if he ever fails to salute you again, I will send his private parts back to his commanding officer on the point of a bayonet," McCoy said. "In the Chinese army, they take threats like that seriously."

The Chinese sentry saluted crisply when the Studebaker

rolled through the gate, and again when the unmarked ambulance passed.

"Oh, I'm glad you're still here, Ed," General Pickering said to Banning when he pushed open the door to Platt's office and found Banning, Platt, and Sampson standing before a map of northern China on one of the easels. "Look who found me."

"I'll be goddamned," Lieutenant Colonel Banning said.

"Good afternoon, sir," McCoy said, smiling.

"Colonel Platt, I understand you and Captain Sampson have met Captain McCoy," Pickering said. "But I don't think you've met Gunnery Sergeant Zimmerman."

Platt and Sampson were literally wide-eyed at the sight of the two American Marines wearing the uniforms of officers of the Nationalist Chinese Army. "Captain," Colonel Platt said uneasily, "I hope you understand that when we met, I wasn't fully aware of the situation."

"Yes, sir," McCoy said.

"I was about to clear the air between you two, Colonel," Pickering said, "to tell you that Captain McCoy was correct in his decision not to place himself under the authority of OSS Chungking, but just now I had an unpleasant thought."

"Sir?" Platt asked.

"Captain McCoy tells me that when he showed you his ONI credentials that you already knew his name?"

"Yes, sir."

"Where did you get his name?"

"General Dempsey telephoned me about Captain McCoy, sir."

"And what exactly did he say?"

"He said there were two OSS agents, one of them Captain McCoy, whom he had ordered to report to me, and that he hoped that I would quickly order them to shave and get into uniform."

"I thought that might be it," Pickering said. "I have something to say about that. Until just this moment, I was actually very sympathetic about General Dempsey. Maybe, as an individual, I still am. But as an officer, I just lost my sympathy for him. Captain McCoy's orders were issued by the JCS and were classified Top Secret. General Dempsey did not have the authority—and damned sure should have known he did not—to pass on to you any Top Secret information that had come into his hands just because he knew you had a Top Secret clearance and thought you should know what was in Banning's and McCoy's orders."

"Sir, with respect," Platt said, "I'm the Chungking station chief. Are you saying . . . ?"

"I'm saying, Colonel, that you had no right to know anything about Banning's and McCoy's Top Secret orders until it was determined by competent authority that you had the Need To Know. Banning has the authority to show you his orders—or anyone else he deems has the Need To Know. That's spelled out in the orders. General Dempsey did not have that authority, but he assumed it. Presumably because he thought that as a major general he had that authority. It has nothing to do with rank, and everything with the Need To Know."

"Yes, sir."

"I think, Ed," Pickering said, "that General Dempsey's relief came just in time. Before, in other words, he started talking about other things because he thought somebody should know, and that he had the authority to determine Need To Know."

"Yes, sir," Banning said. "That occurred to me, General."

"I want you to have a talk with your people, Colonel Platt, to make sure they understand the importance of Need To Know."

"Yes, sir."

"I dislike delivering lectures," Pickering said. "But it seemed to me that one was necessary." He looked around the room at each man in turn. "The immediate application of what I just said, Captain Sampson, is that from this moment—despite what they know about it already—no further details concerning Operation Gobi will be provided to anyone in OSS Chungking unless I, Colonel Banning, or Captain McCoy determines they have the Need To Know. Do you understand that?"

"Sir, Colonel Platt told me that yesterday."

"Okay, now let's talk about Operation Gobi," Pickering said. "To begin . . ."

"Sir, may I suggest we begin by asking Captain McCoy why he is wearing the uniform of a Nationalist Chinese major?" Banning asked with a smile.

"Why not?" Pickering said. "It was your idea, as I recall, Ken, to pass yourselves off as caravan people. What's with those Nationalist uniforms? Not that you don't look very natty."

"It didn't take me long to figure out that wasn't going to work, sir. But the real reason is that almost as soon as Colonel Banning ordered me and the gunny to make ourselves scarce, I realized that probably the worst way to do that was to wander around Chungking wearing beards and civilian clothing. We really attracted a lot of attention at first."

"Why Chinese uniforms?" Pickering asked.

"Well, so far as I know, the Marines in this room are the only Marines in Chungking," McCoy replied. "And when I came here to see Colonel Platt, it seemed to me my Marine uniform attracted as much attention in Kiangpeh—"

"Kiangpeh?" Pickering interrupted.

"It's a town down the river a little, sir. A suburb, I suppose."

"And that's where you've been?" Banning asked.

"Yes, sir. I rented a house there."

"Before or after you became a Chinese major?" Banning asked.

"After," McCoy said. "When I came back here in my Marine uniform, that attracted as much attention as the beard and civvies. But I had noticed a dozen, maybe more, westerners in Nationalist uniforms. And found out they were White Russians. The only people who ask questions about Nationalist Army majors are lieutenant colonels or better."

"Why a major, Ken?" Pickering asked. "Or is that a dumb question?"

"The Chinese have to make mercenaries they recruit at least majors, sir. They don't pay much in the Nationalist Army."

"Where'd you get the uniforms?" Pickering asked.

"We went to a tailor."

"And did you give some thought to what might happen to you, Captain," Colonel Platt asked, "if you were stopped by the Chinese military police and asked for identification?"

"Yes, sir," McCoy said, and reached in his pocket and came out with an oblong piece of cardboard. It was printed in Chinese and had a photograph stapled to it.

"Major K. R. MeeKoy," he said, handing it to Pickering. "Of the 2035th Liaison Group, Nineteenth Corps."

"That looks legitimate," Pickering said, handing it to Platt.

Platt looked at it, then handed it to Banning.

"That's what it says," Banning said. "It identifies him as Major MeeKoy of the 2035th Liaison Group, whatever the hell that's supposed to be."

"Zimmerman got them from the same printer that does them for the Chinese Army," McCoy said. "And with the Nansen passports we got in Maryland, it works like a charm."

"You hope," Banning said.

"We've been stopped," McCoy said simply, "several times."

"You don't speak Russian," Colonel Platt challenged. "What do you do about that?"

"I speak Cantonese, Wu, and Mandarin," McCoy said. "That seems to be enough."

"Why did you rent a house?" Banning asked.

"Because the houses here come with outside walls, making the building lot into a little compound, an interior court? You know what I mean. I needed someplace behind a wall to hide our ambulance. We also have a weapons carrier and a couple of water trailers."

"Where did you get the ambulance? And why?" Banning pursued.

"Where? From a Chinese merchant who had one to sell. I don't know where he got it."

"He probably stole it from the Nationalist Army," Captain Sampson said, a trifle indignantly.

"Probably," McCoy agreed with a smile.

"What are you going to do with it? Drive it to and across the Gobi?" Banning asked, not unkindly, but sarcastically.

"Yes, sir," McCoy said. "That seems the best way to go, sir."

"You're serious?" Banning asked, surprised.

"Yes, sir."

"You're aware, Captain," Colonel Platt said, "that there is a good deal of bandit activity between here and the Gobi Desert, and all over the desert itself?"

"Yes, sir, I am."

"The bandits don't concern you?"

"I think there's a way to handle that, sir," McCoy said.

"I'd like to hear it," Platt said.

"So would I," Pickering said, his eyes on Captain Sampson. "But what I think we should do right now, before that, is ask Captain Sampson to deliver that Opplan briefing again. I'd like to know what McCoy and Zimmerman think of it."

It took Sampson forty-five minutes this time to lay out again the Chungking station's Opplan. During this time, McCoy didn't ask questions or otherwise interrupt the briefing. Pickering had no idea what he was thinking.

"I'm learning to be a general," Pickering said when Sampson was finished. "What generals do, when asking for opinions, is ask the junior man first. That keeps their answers from being colored by what someone senior to them has said first. So, Gunny Zimmerman—or should I say Major Zimmerman?—what do you think?"

Everyone but Zimmerman chuckled, and it was a long moment before he finally spoke. "With respect, sir, McCoy's idea makes more sense."

Is that his considered opinion, or did he say that because he knows McCoy and doesn't know these people?

"You want to expand on that, please, Gunny?" Pickering said.

"Sir?"

"General Pickering wants to know what you don't like about Captain Sampson's Opplan, Ernie," McCoy said.

"Too many people," Zimmerman said immediately.

"Perhaps you don't fully understand the threat the bandits pose, Sergeant," Captain Sampson said.

Pickering happened to look at McCoy, and saw ice come briefly to his eyes.

"Both Captain McCoy and Gunny Zimmerman, Sampson, have had experience with Chinese bandits," Banning said.

Zimmerman glanced at Banning with gratitude in his eyes.

"You don't think the bandits pose much of a threat, is that it, Zimmerman?" Pickering asked.

"Sir, they only attack when it ain't going to cost them much," Zimmerman said.

"With that in mind, Gunny," Banning said, "let me go off on a tangent. What do you think are the chances that the people we think are in the Gobi have had a run-in with bandits?"

"I think we have to take that as a given, Colonel," Lieutenant Colonel Platt said. "I personally would be very surprised if we'll be able to find them."

"Meaning, you think they've been killed?" Banning asked.

"I think that's a reasonable assumption."

"Zimmerman?" Pickering asked.

"Sir, they only attack when it ain't going to cost them much," Zimmerman repeated doggedly. He turned to McCoy for support. "You know Sweatley, Killer, and he's not dumb enough to go into the Gobi—"

"Who is Sweatley?" Captain Sampson interrupted.

"One of the men whose names we have," McCoy said. "He was a buck sergeant with the Marine guard detachment at the legation in Peking. I think Gunny Zimmerman is saying that we can *reasonably assume* that the people in the desert are armed."

"Yeah," Zimmerman said.

"They may even have machine guns," McCoy went on. "I know there were four air-cooled Browning .30s in the armory there."

"How do you know that?" Captain Sampson asked.

McCoy glared at him icily.

"Tell him, Captain McCoy," Banning said.

"Before I went to work for Colonel Banning, I had the machine-gun section in Baker Company, Fourth Marines in Shanghai," McCoy said. "I used to maintain the Peking legation guard's weapons."

"I see," Sampson said.

"What did the sergeant call you, Captain? 'Killer'?" Colonel Platt asked.

"Gunny Zimmerman is one of two people who can call Captain McCoy 'Killer' without running a great risk of severe bodily harm," Pickering said.

"Oh, really? And who is the other one?" Platt asked.

"I am, Colonel," Pickering said, and turned to Zimmerman. "To get to the bottom of this, what you're saying, Gunny—and presumably McCoy agrees with you—is that you believe these people in the desert are well enough armed to keep the bandits from thinking they would be an easy target?"

"Yes, sir," Zimmerman said.

"In other words, you would bet they're out there somewhere?"

"Sir, with respect, I'd say it's fifty-fifty," Zimmerman said.

"I hope the sergeant is right, of course," Platt said. "But if I may speak freely?"

"Of course," Pickering said.

"I don't think we can mount this operation on a fifty-fifty chance that these people are still out there, and an even slimmer chance that we can find them if they are."

"Colonel," McCoy said, "Marines don't abandon their own because there's a good chance they might be dead."

"That's a very noble sentiment, Captain, but I would suggest this is a question of priorities." He looked at Pickering, obviously seeking support.

"How do you see the priorities here, Colonel?" Pickering asked.

"It seems to me that getting this weather station up and operating is the obvious priority."

"May I speak freely, sir?" McCoy asked.

"That's what this is all about," Pickering said.

"The priority is to have a weather station operating over

a long period of time, not just get it up and running," McCoy said.

"Of course," Platt said. "That's understood."

"This place is crawling with Japanese spies, or maybe more accurately, Chinese selling information to the Japs," McCoy said. "There's no way you could send a convoy carrying two companies of Nationalist infantry into the desert without the Japs learning about it. They would wonder what was going on."

"They have radio intercept capabilities, as I'm sure you know, Captain," Colonel Platt said, his tone making it clear that he felt McCoy did not know. "Once the weather station begins to transmit data, they'll know something is going on."

"The station will be on the air no more than ten minutes a day," McCoy responded. "It will probably take the Japanese some time to figure out what's being transmitted, and even when they do that, they'll have to find the transmitter."

"Finding a transmitter using triangulation isn't at all difficult," Captain Sampson said.

"It's not as easy as it sounds, either," McCoy said. "Have you seen the SOI for the weather station?"

"No," Sampson said.

"A different time every day, a different frequency, a different code. I don't think they'll be able to locate the station by triangulation easily, and if we move the station, it will be even harder for them."

"How are we going to move the station?"

"In the ambulance," McCoy said. "Send it twenty, twenty-five miles from the radio station, in a different direction, every day."

"Where are you going to get the gasoline to do that, Ken?" Pickering asked.

"That's one of the things I haven't figured out yet," McCoy said. "One possibility is to have caches of it, and another is having it flown in by the Catalinas. I figure it would take five gallons of gas a day, a hundred and fifty gallons a month, to send the ambulance twenty-five miles away from the weather station every day."

"Caches of gasoline?" Colonel Platt asked. "Where would you get those?"

"I think it's time," Pickering said, "that we hear Ken's ideas on this operation. Start at the beginning, Ken."

"Aye, aye, sir," McCoy said. He paused, obviously collecting his thoughts. "Well, when we started to ask questions, we heard about the bandits—which was not exactly news—and we heard that the Nationalists are sending patrols into the deserts. Long range patrols, on camels and Mongolian ponies."

"We're aware of those patrols," Sampson said. "In addition to their intelligence-gathering function, they are supposed to suppress the bandit activity."

Pickering looked at McCoy, who was staring at Sampson with a strange look in his eyes.

Is he annoyed at the interruption? Pickering wondered. Or is he amused? Or disgusted? Or maybe all three?

"More likely," McCoy said, "they're holding hands with the bandits."

"I don't think I understand," Pickering said.

"Sir, it's more than likely that, in exchange for letting the bandits operate, the patrols—or at least the patrol's officers—get a cut of what the bandits have stolen, and the bandits provide intelligence about the caravans, and maybe even about the Japanese."

"Or, Ken," Banning said thoughtfully, "maybe about a group of westerners running around out there."

"We are regularly furnished with intelligence reports from the Chinese about what those patrols have turned up," Colonel Platt said. "We have specifically requested information about any Americans. There has been nothing, absolutely nothing."

McCoy ignored him.

"The Nationalist Chinese, on patrol and off," he went on, "have to live a lot off the land. They have to, or starve. Which is one of the reasons Mao Tse-Tung's Communists are so popular; they don't steal from the peasants the way the Nationalists do."

"You sound as if you approve of the Communists, Captain," Colonel Platt said.

"I don't, sir, but if I were a peasant, and the Communists didn't steal my last pig, and the Nationalists did, I probably would."

"What's your point, Ken?" Banning challenged.

"The first thing I thought was that I would get in touch with these Nationalist patrols, to see if they had heard anything about Westerners that they hadn't sent up through channels."

"If they had heard something, why wouldn't they have reported it?" Colonel Platt asked.

"Because, sir, they might get orders to investigate further," McCoy said. "If I was a Nationalist lieutenant, I wouldn't want to get an order like that. Life is tough enough as it is without me almost volunteering to stick my neck out to look for a bunch of Westerners."

"You said that was the first thing you thought of, McCoy?" Pickering asked.

"Yes, sir. Then I realized that there is no way that a long-range patrol can live off the land in the Gobi. There's nothing to steal out there except from caravans. And caravans would not have enough food to feed forty men for long. Which meant that the patrols would have to be resupplied. And I found out they run regular truck convoys out there, to preestablished rendezvous points. Sometimes it's just rations, and sometimes they take troops, even horses, out there to replace lost horses and bring back the sick, lame, and lazy."

He stopped and took a thin cigar from his pocket and lit it. Then he went on.

"That's when I started to think that if Zimmerman and I could hook up with one of these motor supply convoys, we could go as far as they go, then take off on our own. With a little bit of luck, maybe we could get them to tell me what they've heard about a group of Westerners."

"What makes you think they'd tell you something they haven't reported through the appropriate channels?" Captain Sampson asked.

McCoy looked at him coldly, then decided the question was a request for information rather than a challenge.

"I'd pay them," McCoy said. "They aren't getting paid by whoever sends them out there."

"What makes you think they'd tell you truth?" Colonel Platt asked.

"I'd have to take a chance on that, sir," McCoy said. "But my gut feeling is that if I was a Nationalist officer, I'd be a little afraid to lie to a White Russian officer."

"Why?" Captain Sampson asked. Again McCoy gave him the benefit of any doubt that it might be a challenge.

"They all came out of the Imperial Army," he explained. "A lot of them say they were colonels and generals—and maybe they were. The way I understand it, if you lied to an officer in the Czar's army—for that matter, talked back to one—they shot you on the spot, and let the paperwork catch up later."

"You seem to know a good deal about both the Chinese and Czarist armies, Captain McCoy," Colonel Platt said.

He's barely able, Pickering thought, *to control his sarcasm. Well, that's understandable. They not only had a serious run-in the first time they met, but now the man who in essence told him to go fuck himself is making it very clear he thinks very little of an Opplan Platt thinks solves all our problems.*

"I knew some Chinese officers in Shanghai, sir," McCoy said. "And some White Russians."

McCoy's and Banning's eyes met.

"Going along with your line of thinking, Captain," Platt went on. "As I understand you, you're suggesting that you just drive off into the Gobi in your ambulance . . ."

"And the weapons carrier, sir. Both towing five-hundred-gallon water trailers filled with gas."

". . . in the hope that you will be able to establish contact with this group of Americans thought to be somewhere in the desert."

"Yes, sir."

"And what if you run out of gasoline before finding the Americans?"

"Then we fire up the radio, sir, and hope the Catalinas can find us."

"Wouldn't it really make more sense, Captain, to just find some good location for the weather station and establish contact from there? Without running around an immense desert looking for people who might not be there?"

"I'm not prepared to give up on the Marines out there, sir, without trying."

"That may not be your decision to make, Captain," Colonel Platt said.

"No, sir," McCoy said. "As I understand it, that would be General Pickering's decision to make."

"That's pretty close to insolence, Captain!" Platt flared.

"Whoa!" Pickering said sharply. "For one thing, I'm sure Captain McCoy didn't intend to be insolent. For another, he's right. This is my decision, and I just realized that I'm not prepared to make it without further information."

He waited a moment, until he thought Colonel Platt had regained control of his temper.

"What I suggest we do now is have a drink," Pickering went on. "Maybe more than one. And then dinner. Then we'll sleep on this, and have another go at it in the morning. Is there room for Captain McCoy and Gunny Zimmerman to spend the night here, Platt?"

"Sir, we could put a couple of cots in my room," Captain Sampson said.

McCoy looked at him in surprise. Then he turned to Pickering.

"I'd hate to put the Captain out, sir. And our place isn't that far away." He turned to Sampson. "But thanks, anyway."

"Tell me about your place," Pickering said.

"Actually, sir, it's pretty comfortable. It's a nice house, and we have a pretty good cook." He looked at Banning. "I'd almost forgotten how nice it was in Shanghai to have houseboys bring you a cup of tea in the morning, when they deliver your wash and pressed uniform."

"You have houseboys?" Banning asked, smiling.

"And you don't think your house and your houseboys have attracted attention?" Platt asked.

"You really can't hide anything in China, Colonel," McCoy said, on the edge of condescension. "What you *can* do is make something look like something else. What we look like is a couple of White Russian officers living like White Russian officers. In other words, well. Zimmerman got uniforms for the houseboys. Every White Russian officer in the Nationalist Army has at least two orderlies. And orderlies are expected to have rifles."

"How many 'orderlies' do you have?" Pickering asked, smiling.

"Fourteen," McCoy said. "Two of them take care of us, two take care of the vehicles, and the others are our perimeter guard, and run errands."

"Errands like watching this place and the airport?"

"Yes, sir."

Pickering saw that Colonel Platt did not at all like hearing that McCoy had had people watching his compound.

"Your own private army, huh?" Pickering chuckled.

"More like my private squad, sir," McCoy said.

"What had you planned to do with this private army of yours if you followed your original plan and went into the Gobi by yourself?" Platt asked. "Take them all with you?"

There is an implication in that question, Pickering thought, *none too subtly phrased, that he has decided McCoy's plan is dead.*

He looked at McCoy and saw in his eyes that McCoy had come to the same conclusion.

"When I go into the desert, Colonel," McCoy said, "I'm going to take four of the Chinese with me—maybe six; I haven't thought that through yet. The rest I'd planned to turn over to Colonel Banning. The men, and the house."

"What's that all about?" Platt asked.

"Sir," McCoy replied, but looked at Pickering as he did. "I thought Colonel Banning—and the Easterbunny and the others . . ."

"The *'Easterbunny'*?" Colonel Platt asked incredulously.

". . . would need a place to stay besides a BOQ . . ." McCoy went on.

"The *'Easterbunny'*?" Platt repeated.

". . . and I didn't think they'd want to live here," McCoy finished doggedly.

Platt glowered at him.

"Unfortunately, Colonel Platt," Pickering said, "Captain

McCoy can't seem to remember not to call Lieutenant Easterbrook 'The Easterbunny.' Worse, neither can I."

"Sorry, sir," McCoy said.

"There'd be room for all of us in this house of yours?" Banning asked.

"Yes, sir."

"It's got beds, et cetera?"

"Not enough for everybody, sir. But getting what else we need wouldn't be hard."

"From the same place you got the vehicles, right?" Banning chuckled.

"Yes, sir, you can buy anything you want in Chungking, if you have gold."

"You had five thousand dollars' worth of gold twenty-dollar pieces," Banning said. "I'm almost afraid to ask, but how much is left?"

"About eighteen hundred. I got a good deal on the ambulance, the weapons carrier, and the five-hundred-gallon water trailers," McCoy said, smiling. "But I had to pay six months' rent in advance on the house. And good tailors—as Pick taught me—don't come cheap. And then I have rations to buy, and the weekly payroll to meet."

"In other words, you're going to need more money to go into the desert?" Pickering asked.

"Yes, sir, I am."

"I think I want to see this house of yours, McCoy," Pickering said. "Is there any reason we can't go there?"

"Would you mind riding in the back of the ambulance, sir? One of these OSS Studebakers would make people wonder."

"I've no problem with that," Pickering said. "After dinner we'll go there. At least Colonel Banning will know where to find you in the future."

XXI

When Lieutenant Commander Warren T. Houser, commanding officer of the United States Submarine *Sunfish*, was shown onto the patio behind the house, he was wearing a fresh-that-morning khaki uniform that now bore grease and oil stains in several places. Commander Houser had not changed into a fresh uniform before leaving the *Sunfish*, reasoning that he was going directly—in a staff car—from the pier at Pearl Harbor to Muku-Muku, and directly back. He would almost certainly not be seen by anyone who might look askance at an officer attired in an oil-stained uniform. Soiling a uniform could not be avoided on a submarine—even on an extraordinarily shipshape boat, as he believed the *Sunfish* to be. Some Naval officers just didn't seem to be able to understand that. Usually, they were officers who had never been to sea on anything smaller than a battleship, and had spent the preponderance of their Naval careers behind a desk on the beach.

Furthermore, upon returning to the *Sunfish*, Commander Houser intended to inspect his boat from bow to stern planes. He was going to sea at first light, and he wanted to once again personally check the storage aboard of fifty five-gallon jerry cans of avgas; twenty-seven odd-shaped aluminum crates; and two inflatable rubber boats. Commander Houser was understandably nervous about having that much avgas in his boat.

Any uniform he wore when he made his way around the *Sunfish* would become oil-stained. Since the one he was wearing was only lightly stained (compared with what usually happened to his uniforms), it just made sense not to change it.

In the morning, of course, he would put on fresh, crisply starched khakis. He suspected that Rear Admiral Wagam would be on the pier to offer a few words of encouragement before the *Sunfish* sailed off into the Kaiwi Channel to try to move the avgas and the aluminum crates from the boat to a Catalina without drowning anybody and/or blowing up the airplane and/or the *Sunfish*.

Tonight, Major Jake Dillon, USMCR, had invited him out to Muku-Muku to have a couple of drinks and a nice dinner. They'd be joined there by Wagam's aide-de-camp, Lieutenant Chambers D. Lewis III. Lewis was a submariner himself; he knew all about oil-stained uniforms; and Jake Dillon was not unfamiliar with them, either. It was also likely that Charley Galloway would be there, and Big Steve Oblensky; both of them were fliers, so both of them understood oil-stained uniforms. And it was also likely that Peter T. McGuire, the most incredible character he had ever encountered in the uniform of a chief petty officer of the U.S. Navy, would break bread with them. What McGuire thought about Houser's uniform was unimportant.

When Commander Houser walked onto the patio, he found that Rear Admiral Daniel Wagam had also been invited to Muku-Muku. He was standing, with a glass in hand, at the edge of the patio, gazing down at the surf.

Admiral Wagam was wearing a crisp, immaculate, pure white, high-collared dress uniform. Also attired in snow-white dress uniforms were the other Naval persons on the patio: Lieutenant Lewis; Commander Florence Kocharski Oblensky, NC, USN; and even Chief Carpenter's Mate Peter T. McGuire, of the Naval Reserve. When Commander Houser last saw Chief McGuire—two hours before, as the chief left the *Sunfish*—he was naked except for a pair of torn-off-above-the-knees khaki trousers and a pair of rubber-and-canvas sneakers.

The Marine contingent—Major Jake Dillon, Captain Charles Galloway, and Master Gunner Big Steve Oblensky—was also magnificently attired in dress white uniforms.

"Good evening, Admiral," Commander Houser said.

"Came right from the boat, did you, Houser?" Admiral Wagam asked.

"If I have kept the Admiral waiting, sir . . ."

"You didn't know I was coming," Wagam said. "*I* didn't know I was coming myself until Commander Kocharski called at 1500."

"Good evening, Commander," Lieutenant Commander Houser said.

"I thought we all needed a little party," Flo said. "You guys have been working around the clock."

"I apologize for my appearance, sir," Houser said.

"Your appearance? I thought all submariners look that way," Admiral Wagam said, visibly pleased with his sense of humor.

A white-jacketed steward appeared with a tray of drinks. "Bourbon in the red glasses, Commander," he said. "Scotch in the green. Or whatever you want, sir."

"A little bourbon will do just fine, thank you very much," Commander Houser said gratefully.

"The Chief," Admiral Wagam said, "has just been telling me he anticipates no trouble at all in the dry run tomorrow."

"We think, sir, we have everything under control," Houser said. "But it's nice to have Chief McGuire's vote of confidence."

"Don't mention it," Chief McGuire said graciously.

Captain Galloway, in the midst of taking a swallow of
his drink, suddenly found himself coughing.

"What I'm going to do tomorrow," McGuire went on,
"is just get out of the way, and let your boys do the whole
thing themselves."

"You think we can safely take that risk?" Houser asked,
unable to restrain his sarcasm, which sailed six feet over
Chief McGuire's head.

"Well, if they screw up, I'll be there to set them
straight," Chief McGuire said. "I was about to say that I
won't be there when they do it for real, but I've been
thinking about that. I've just about decided I'd better go
along when you go on the real thing."

"You've decided that, have you, Pete?" Big Steve Oblensky asked.

"Just about. I mean, what the hell, this is supposed to
be damned important. Why take a chance?"

"Why indeed?" Admiral Wagam said. "Have you ever
been aboard a submarine, Chief?"

"No, but I'm a deepwater sailor, Admiral."

Captain Galloway had a second fit of coughing.

"Tell me, Chief," Admiral Wagam said, "how do you
define 'deepwater sailor'?"

Chief McGuire looked at the Admiral as if he thought
an admiral should know how to define a deepwater sailor.

"Admiral, Chief McGuire," Major Dillon answered for
him, "was Errol Flynn's relief captain of choice when he
had to leave his yacht someplace."

"Really? You're a real sailor then, Chief?" the Admiral
said. "I've seen pictures of that yacht. A sloop, as I recall?"

Chief McGuire looked at him without the faintest spark
of comprehension.

"How many masts?" Admiral Wagam pursued.

"Two, I think," McGuire said after a moment's thought.
"No, three. Two in front and one in back. Errol had people
who took care of that. I steered and handled the engine."

"Well, let me say, Chief," Admiral Wagam said, "that
I think the Navy is fortunate to have someone like you."
He immediately regretted saying it. There was a strange

look in McGuire's eyes, as if he had finally realized they were making fun of him.

I don't want him to think that, although we were all guilty of it.

"Both Major Dillon and Mr. Oblensky have told me, Chief," Admiral Wagam went on seriously, "that the *Sunfish* wouldn't be going to sea tomorrow had it not been for your solving the fuel-transfer problems on the Catalina."

"I've never seen anybody better at welding aluminum," Big Steve chimed in.

Admiral Wagam was genuinely pleased to see the hurt look disappear from McGuire's eyes. "So actually, Chief," he went on. "You're the reason we can have this party tonight. You've given me genuine cause to celebrate."

"Sir?" McGuire asked.

"Whenever a problem that CINCPAC asks me about twice a day is solved, I feel justified in celebrating."

"Chief," Commander Houser heard himself say, "if you want to come with us when we go into the Yellow Sea, we'll be glad to have you aboard."

I'll be damned, he thought, *I actually mean that.*

"So ordered," Admiral Wagam said. "Chambers, you'll see he gets some Momsen lung training?"

"Aye, aye, sir," Lieutenant Lewis said.

"And this is my contribution, Chief," Commander Kocharski said, picking up her purse and coming out with two six-inch-tall medicine bottles, one filled with small yellow pills, the other with small white pills.

"What is this stuff?" McGuire asked, taking the bottles, which bore "US NAVAL HOSPITAL Pearl Harbor" prescription labels with his name on them.

"They affect the inner ear," Commander Kocharski said very seriously. "Take one of each before boarding the *Sunfish*, one of each every six hours thereafter, and one—or two, if you think it necessary—the moment you start to feel a little queasy."

"Well, gee, Flo, thank you," McGuire said, visibly touched. "But it's really not necessary. I'm not going to get seasick. I have no problem with boats. It's airplanes that get me."

"Really?" Admiral Wagam asked.

"All I have to do is look at one of the sonsofbitches, Admiral," Chief McGuire explained. "And I start getting sick."

"You take those with you, Chief," Commander Kocharski said. "That's an order."

"Okay, Flo," Chief McGuire replied. "Whatever you say."

None of the officers present, all but one of whom were career officers of the Naval Service, felt it necessary to point out to Chief McGuire that the correct response to an order was either "Aye, aye, sir" or "Aye, aye, ma'am."

[TWO]
Kiangpeh, Chungking, China
0915 11 April 1943

"Who's there?" Brigadier General Fleming Pickering called in answer to a knock at the door.

"Bell Telephone," Brigadier General H. A. Albright replied, as he pushed the door open.

He had a battered, French-style telephone in one hand, a leather-cased U.S. Army EE-8 field telephone in the other, and a second EE-8 was hanging around his neck on its strap.

"What the hell are you doing?"

"Dazzling my telephone sergeant," Albright said. "He can now spread the word that the General actually knows how to hook up a field phone, and hasn't forgotten how to strap on climbers and go up a pole."

"You really climbed a pole?"

"Three of them," Albright said. "The one inside your wall, the one just outside your wall, and the one down the street. If the line in here is tapped, they're doing it someplace else. It may not be tapped at all, but I would not regard this magnificent instrument as anything close to a secure telephone line."

He held up the ancient French-style telephone.

"I didn't know generals did this sort of thing," Pickering said.

"Basic rule of leadership, General," Albright said, smiling. "Have your subordinates convinced that you can do anything you tell them to do at least as well as they can."

Pickering sensed that Albright was perfectly serious.

"The second rule of leadership," Albright went on, "is to start out as a prick and get nice later."

Pickering laughed. "My first sergeant told me that when I made corporal in France," he said.

"When I get these hooked up," Albright said, dropping to his knees by the wall, "the magnificent instrument will connect you to the Chungking telephone service. There's an extension downstairs and another in Banning's room. One of the EE-8s—on the case of which I wrote the number one—is tied into the USMMCHI switchboard. Your number is 606, which I also wrote on the case. The other EE-8—marked number two—is connected to the OSS house switchboard. I put one of these in Banning's room, and there's another downstairs."

"Hugh, what's the rule of leadership if a commander comes to believe a subordinate knows more about what he's doing than he does?"

Albright sensed that Pickering was asking the question seriously, and turned from the wall, still holding a telephone wire in needle-nose pliers. "Banning?"

"Oh, no. It's a given that Banning knows more than I do about the intelligence business. I was thinking of Platt."

"Is there a specific problem?"

"I've spent most of the last two days reading Platt's after-action reports, and taking a look at his ongoing operations."

"And?"

"He obviously not only knows what he's doing, but is a fine commander as well."

"Then what's the problem?"

"Banning doesn't like him. McCoy doesn't like him. And neither do I."

"Then get rid of him," Albright said simply.

"I also think he's wrong—which makes McCoy right—about how to get the weather station into the Gobi, even if it means we don't make a real effort to find the Marines—and other escapees—out there."

Albright grunted.

"I'm just not sure whether that is a judgment based on the facts, or because I don't like him—and whether I don't like him because Banning and McCoy don't."

Albright cocked his head to one side and nodded, but didn't speak.

"This is the third operation like this I've run," Pickering said. "The first time, I sent McCoy onto Buka Island, to make sure a Coastwatcher station stayed on the air, and to take a couple of Marines who were there—in very bad shape—out. The second time, I sent McCoy into the Philippines to establish contact with our guerrillas there."

"And you pulled those operations off, as I recall," Albright said.

"In neither case was there someone around who knew more than I did about how to do what had to be done. Or to tell me I was wrong. In this case, I know very little about China, and Platt knows a hell of a lot."

"When do you have to make up your mind?"

"Soon. McCoy and Zimmerman went to Yümen to try to arrange to travel with one of the convoys the Chinese send out with supplies for their patrols in the desert. When they come back—"

"If you go along with Platt, what are you going to do about the meteorologists and their equipment?"

"The equipment, other equipment, could be sent from the States," Pickering said. "And I suppose we could also recruit some more meteorologists." He paused thoughtfully. "And I wonder if my ego isn't somehow involved. Bill Donovan would love to be able to report to the President that when I saw the situation here, I came to the conclusion that his people were better able to do this than I was."

"I have one comment to make," Albright said, "and pay attention, because it's the only comment I am going to make."

"Okay," Pickering said.

"Whatever you decide, you'll decide as a soldier—excuse me, a Marine—because you think it's the right thing to do, not because of your ego, or because you don't like Platt, or some other personal reason."

"You don't think—"

"You weren't paying attention, General. I said one comment, and you have had it."

"Okay, Hugh," Pickering said. "Thank you."

"For what?" Albright said, and turned back to the wall.

A moment later, he reached for one of the EE-8 field telephones and cranked the folding handle of the small generator on its side. "Unless someone has already stolen my brand-new wire, this should work," he said. And then, his voice changing, "Ring niner zero one, please."

"It works?" Pickering asked.

"So far," Albright said, and then spoke into the telephone: "General Albright, Lieutenant," he said. "Checking your boss's new telephone. How do we sound to you?" He paused, listening for a moment. "In that case, you better have somebody bring it over. He's here with me."

He cranked the generator again, said, "Break it down, please," and then turned to Pickering. "You have mail," he said. "You may be sorry you spent so much effort to get the Special Channel up and running."

Second Lieutenant George F. Hart announced the arrival of Master Gunner Harry Rutterman twenty minutes later, five minutes after General Albright had left. Rutterman had a World War I–vintage Winchester pump-action Model 97 12-gauge trench gun cradled in his arm like a bird hunter.

"Where'd you get the trench gun, Harry?" Pickering asked.

"Captain McCoy got it for me, sir," Rutterman said, as he took a sealed envelope from an inside pocket and handed it to Pickering.

Probably from the same Chinese who sold him the ambulance and the truck, Pickering thought.

"Stick around a minute, Harry, 'til I see what this says."

"Aye, aye, sir. There's two of them, sir," Rutterman said.

T O P S E C R E T

FROM ACTING STACHIEF OSS HAWAII
1005 GREENWICH 10 APRIL 1943

VIA SPECIAL CHANNEL
DUPLICATION FORBIDDEN

TO BRIGGEN FLEMING PICKERING USMCR
OSS DEPUTY DIRECTOR FOR PACIFIC
OPERATIONS
THRU: US MILITARY MISSION TO CHINA
CHUNGKING

SUBJECT: PROGRESS REPORT NO. 2

1. RENDEZVOUS AND REFUELING DRY RUN USING
SUNFISH AND TWO PBY-5A AIRCRAFT
SUCCESSFULLY COMPLETED 0900 LOCAL TIME
THIS DATE.

2. SUNFISH WILL DEPART PEARL HARBOR 0600
LOCAL TIME 11 APR 43. LT C.D. LEWIS AND
CHIEF MCGUIRE WILL BE ABOARD.

3. BOTH PILOTS-IN-COMMAND OF DRY RUN PBY-
5A AIRCRAFT HAVE VOLUNTEERED TO FLY
MISSION, AND VOLUNTEER PILOTS FROM
MAINLAND WILL ARRIVE HERE WITHIN TWENTY-
FOUR HOURS AFTER UNEXPLAINED DELAY IN
TRANSIT.

4. FIRST TWO PBY-5A AIRCRAFT ARE PREPARED
TO COMMENCE MISSION ON THREE (3) HOURS
NOTICE, AND CAN PROBABLY DO SO IN LESS
TIME.

5. CONVERSION OF TWO BACKUP PBY-5A
AIRCRAFT AT EWA WILL BE COMPLETED WITHIN
SEVENTY-TWO (72) HOURS.

6. INASMUCH AS UNDERSIGNED CAN MAKE NO
FURTHER CONTRIBUTION TO PREPARATION OF
MISSION HERE, AND BELIEVE MY SKILLS WILL
BE USEFUL DURING REFUELING OPERATION,
UNDERSIGNED WILL BE ABOARD FIRST FLIGHT.

RESPECTFULLY SUBMITTED

HOMER C. DILLON

MAJOR, USMCR

T O P S E C R E T

"Goddamn him!" Brigadier General Pickering said.

"Sir?" Rutterman asked.

"Send Major Dillon a Special Channel, Rutterman," Pickering said. "Quote. Not only no, but hell no."

"Aye, aye, sir," Rutterman smiled. "I saw the Major wants in on this. I was thinking I'd sort of like to go myself."

"Then you're as crazy as Dillon," Pickering said. "Belay the 'hell no,' Harry. Send him . . ." He paused to frame his thoughts. ". . . send him: 'In absence of Lieutenant Lewis, your liaison function between—' "

"I think I'd better write that down, General," Rutterman interrupted him. He took a notebook and a pencil from his pocket. "Go ahead, sir."

"In the absence of Lieutenant Lewis, your liaison function between CINCPAC and the widely scattered elements of this mission is critical to success of mission, and cannot be performed by someone else," Pickering dictated. "And therefore your request, while deeply appreciated, to accompany the flight element is denied."

"Yes, sir."

"And add, Harry, 'in other words, Jake, not only no, but hell no.' "

Rutterman chuckled. "Aye, aye, sir."

Pickering turned to the second Special Channel message.

```
T O P   S E C R E T

OFFICE OF THE DIRECTOR
OFFICE OF STRATEGIC SERVICES
WASHINGTON
VIA SPECIAL CHANNEL
DUPLICATION FORBIDDEN

0905 GREENWICH 10 APRIL 1943

USMILMISSION TO CHINA CHUNGKING
EYES ONLY BRIGGEN FLEMING PICKERING
USMCR
BEGIN PERSONAL MESSAGE FROM DIROSS TO
OSSDEPDIR PACIFIC OPERATIONS

DEAR FLEMING:

IT SHOULD GO WITHOUT SAYING THAT EVERYONE
CONCERNED IS DELIGHTED THAT THE
POTENTIAL SECURITY PROBLEM WAS NIPPED IN
THE BUD BEFORE ANY REAL DAMAGE
TRANSPIRED, AND THAT EVERYONE
APPRECIATES YOUR CONTRIBUTION.

IT SHOULD ALSO GO WITHOUT SAYING THAT I
HAVE NO INTENTION WHATEVER OF SECOND
GUESSING YOU ON THE EXECUTION OF
OPERATION GOBI AND THAT YOU ENJOY THE
COMPLETE CONFIDENCE OF ADMIRAL LEAHY,
GENERAL MARSHALL AND MYSELF TO CARRY IT
OFF SUCCESSFULLY.

HOWEVER, GENERAL MARSHALL AND I SEE IN
THE OPPLAN SUBMITTED BY LTCOL PLATT SOME
VERY INTERESTING POSSIBILITIES FOR THE
EXECUTION OF OPERATION GOBI IN CASE THE
PICKERING OPPLAN PROVES TO BE ULTIMATELY
UNFEASIBLE OR FAILS. GENERAL MARSHALL
AND ADMIRAL LEAHY ARE BOTH CONCERNED WITH
```

THE GREAT POTENTIAL FOR DISASTER THAT AN AIRCRAFT/SUBMARINE RENDEZVOUS ON THE HIGH SEAS AT THIS TIME OF YEAR POSES.

THEREFORE TAKING INTO CONSIDERATION THE NECESSITY TO GET THE WEATHER STATION UP AND RUNNING AS SOON AS POSSIBLE, GENERAL MARSHALL SUGGESTS AND I AGREE THAT YOU CONSIDER PROCEEDING WITH THE PLATT OPPLAN AS A BACKUP OPERATION TO THE ONE YOU PRESENTLY PLAN.

TO THAT END, THE FOLLOWING STEPS HAVE BEEN TAKEN:

(1) TWO COMPLETE SETS OF METEOROLOGICAL EQUIPMENT ARE BEING ACQUIRED AND WILL BE PRIORITY AIRLIFTED TO CHUNGKING AS SOON AS AVAILABLE. THEY SHOULD BE AVAILABLE TO YOU IN CHUNGKING WITHIN THREE WEEKS.

(2) AN URGENT CALL FOR VOLUNTEER METEOROLOGISTS HAS BEEN DISTRIBUTED WITHIN THE NAVY AND ARMY AIR CORPS. ADDITIONALLY, JCS HAS DIRECTED THE ADJUTANT GENERAL AND BUPERS TO IMMEDIATELY PREPARE A LIST OF FULLY QUALIFIED METEOROLOGISTS, FROM WHICH, IN THE EVENT THERE ARE INSUFFICIENT VOLUNTEERS WITHIN THE NEXT SEVEN DAYS, TWO TEAMS OF FULLY QUALIFIED METEOROLOGISTS WILL BE SELECTED AND AIRLIFTED TO CHUNGKING IN TIME TO COINCIDE WITH THE ARRIVAL OF THE METEOROLOGICAL EQUIPMENT.

(3) GENERAL STILLWELL IS BEING REQUESTED IN A PERSONAL FROM GENERAL MARSHALL TO PROVIDE WHATEVER TROOP AND LOGISTICAL SUPPORT YOU CONSIDER NECESSARY.

```
WITH BEST PERSONAL REGARDS,

BILL

END PERSONAL MESSAGE FROM DIROSS TO
OSSDEPDIR PACIFIC OPERATIONS

T O P S E C R E T
```

"In a pig's ass," Brigadier General Fleming Pickering said furiously.

"Sir?" Rutterman asked.

"You decrypt this, Harry?"

"Yes, sir."

"Then you read what Donovan said about 'having no intention whatever of second-guessing' me?"

"If I may speak freely, General, in a pig's ass he doesn't," Rutterman said.

"I'll tell you what he did do," Pickering said. "He made up my mind for me."

"Sir?"

"George, pick up the field phone—the one with number one painted on it. It's connected to the USMMCHI switchboard. Present my compliments to General Stillwell and ask him when he can find time to see me."

"Aye, aye, sir," Hart said and went to the telephones—which were still sitting on the floor—and cranked the one marked "#1."

"General Stillwell's office, please," he said when the operator answered, and then a moment later surprise—maybe shock—became visible on his face. He went on: "General, I'm Lieutenant Hart, aide-de-camp to General Pickering. Sir, the General presents his compliments . . ." He stopped, said, "One moment, sir," and extended the telephone to Pickering.

"General Stillwell, sir," Hart said.

Pickering went quickly to the telephone.

"Good morning, sir."

"I don't know about your aide, Pickering, but mine has

more important things to do than make manners on the telephone."

"So does George, sir," Pickering blurted. "I was trying to play the game by the rules, General."

Stillwell snorted.

"Every time you play the game by the rules, somebody changes the rules," Stillwell said. "I'm surprised you haven't learned that. What's on your mind, Pickering?"

"Sir, could you spare me a few minutes? It's important."

"As a matter of fact, I was about to try to find you. I just got a personal about you I don't like much. You want to come right now?"

"Yes, sir. I can be there in fifteen minutes."

The line went dead in Pickering's ear.

He realized that, having had nothing else to say, General Stillwell had hung up.

[THREE]
Office of the Commanding General
U.S. Military Mission to China
1010 11 April 1943

General Pickering was inside Stillwell's office door just long enough to notice Colonel Easterbrook's presence when Stillwell began the conversation by saying, "Pickering, I feel compelled to tell you I am not, at the moment, in a very good mood."

"Good morning, General," Pickering said, shifted his eyes to Easterbrook and added, "Colonel," and then met Stillwell's eyes again. "I'm sorry to hear that, sir."

"Yesterday afternoon, Ernie and I drove Colonel Dempsey and Lieutenant Colonel Newley—now reduced to their permanent grades—to the airfield, where, in compliance with orders from the JCS, they will proceed by air to Calcutta and from Calcutta by sea to the United States for further assignment."

Pickering said what came to his mind: "That was very gracious of you, sir."

Stillwell gave him a strange look. "They are both fine officers, Pickering," he said finally. "Who will now contribute to this war by commanding a WAC basic training battalion, or perhaps serving in public relations."

This is not the time to tell him I think their relief came just in time to keep them from doing real damage.

"I think I understand how you feel, sir," Pickering said.

This earned him another cold glance.

"And then, just before we spoke, your Lieutenant Moore delivered a Special Channel Personal to me from General Marshall." This was delivered as a challenge. "May I infer from the look on your face, General, that you know of General Marshall's 'request'?"

"I learned about it thirty seconds before I called you, General. I got a Special Channel Personal from Colonel Donovan which told me such a message would be sent. I knew nothing about it before then."

He reached into his pocket and handed General Stillwell Donovan's message.

"Presumably I have the appropriate security clearance to be made privy to a communication from the Director of the OSS marked 'Eyes Only General Pickering'?"

"General, so far as I am concerned, you have every right to read everything that moves over the Special Channel."

Stillwell examined him carefully for a moment and then read the Donovan message. "May I show this to Colonel Easterbrook?"

"Please do, sir."

Stillwell handed the message to Easterbrook, then turned to Pickering. "Okay. Is that what you wanted to see me about?"

"Yes, sir."

"Having established that General Marshall's 'request' was not your idea, you're now going to ask me for troops and other logistical support for this operation of yours, right?"

"No, sir."

"Why not?"

"Sir, are you familiar with the Opplan proposed by Colonel Platt?"

"No."

"I can have a copy of it here in ten minutes, sir."

"Tell me about it," Stillwell said with an impatient wave of his hand.

"The bottom line, sir, is that I don't agree with it."

"The chief of staff of the United States Army, as well as your boss, apparently think it's a better plan than what you've come up with."

"Yes, sir. And I disagree with them."

"Briefly, what don't you like about a plan that has General Marshall's approval?"

"I've decided that sending that large a force into the Gobi—not to mention keeping it there, with the supply operation that would require—would call too much attention to the operation, General."

"*You've* 'decided,' against the recommendation of General Marshall and Colonel Donovan?"

"Yes, sir. As I interpret Colonel Donovan's message, it was a suggestion, not an order."

"You are officially declining my offer to give you what logistical support I have been directed to provide? And 'a force of at least two companies of infantry'?"

"Yes, sir. But I may have to come back if my plan fails."

"And your plan is what? To send a couple of your men into the Gobi in a couple of trucks to see if they can find the people that are supposed to be there? And then supply them by air?"

"Initially by air, sir. It may be possible to get everybody but the essential personnel out, and then supply them from here. The Japanese, so far as we know, have not shown any interest in the people who are already in the desert. I want to make every effort to keep it that way."

"You're presuming that. For all you know, the people who were out there may be in a Japanese POW camp. Or dead. Either from Japanese action, or else because the bandits got to them."

"Yes, sir, that's true. If Captain McCoy cannot make contact with them by the time his fuel runs out, he will call for the Catalinas to bring the equipment and the meteorologists to wherever he is."

"I have two questions about that," Stillwell said. " 'By the time his fuel runs out'?"

"Captain McCoy has an ambulance, a weapon carrier, and two five-hundred-gallon trailers. He plans to accompany a routine Chinese Army resupply convoy into the Gobi, then strike off on his own. He believes, and I concur, that doing so will not attract much attention."

"Question two. If the resupply by aircraft fails?"

"Then we'll have to follow the Platt Opplan, sir. By then, the extra equipment and the meteorological team will be here."

"That suggests your man—just the two of them . . ."

"He plans to take four Chinese with him, sir."

". . . is not concerned with the bandits?"

"I'm sure he's very concerned, sir. But he believes he will be able to avoid them, or be able to run away from them, or, in the worst case, be able with six men to make them decide any attack on them would be too costly."

"I can see why General Marshall and Colonel Donovan don't like your plan," Stillwell said.

Colonel Easterbrook grunted in agreement.

"Ernie, what do you think?" Stillwell asked.

"There is no question that sending two companies of infantry into the desert would attract Japanese attention," Easterbrook said. "And they're tenacious. They would keep looking until their curiosity was satisfied."

"What makes you so sure the Chinese will be willing to let your Captain McCoy accompany them?"

"He plans to compensate them for their effort, sir, and he also believes that the patrol officers have probably heard more about the Americans out there than they have reported to their superiors."

"Why wouldn't they report what they've heard, General?" Colonel Easterbrook asked.

"If they did, they would probably be ordered to investigate further," Pickering replied.

"And your Captain McCoy plans to 'compensate' the Chinese for whatever other information they may have and have neglected to pass upward?"

"Yes, sir."

"There is an implication in what you've said that you

intend to commence this operation in the immediate future?"

"Yes, sir. McCoy is en route to Yümen right now. The Nationalist troops who go into the Gobi on patrol are stationed there."

"That's a thousand miles," Easterbrook said.

"He plans on making twenty-five miles an hour," Pickering said. "That's forty hours on the road. If he can average thirty miles an hour, that's thirty-three hours."

"That's if he gets there at all," Stillwell said. "There's Nationalist roadblocks every fifty miles or so. I've heard some unpleasant reports from Americans sent into the hinterlands. They are stopped at roadblocks and detained until their bona fides are established. By the time that's been done, their vehicles and supplies seem to get stolen by party or parties unknown."

"I don't think Captain McCoy will have any trouble getting past roadblocks, sir."

"Why not?"

"McCoy and Gunnery Sergeant Zimmerman both speak fluent Wu, Cantonese, and Mandarin and are wearing the uniforms of Nationalist Chinese officers, sir, and carry very credible-looking identification documents. They're both old China hands, sir. Fourth Marines."

"Passing themselves off as White Russians?" Easterbrook asked.

"They have Nansen stateless person passports," Pickering said.

General Stillwell looked at Colonel Easterbrook for a long moment, but Pickering could detect no reaction on Easterbrook's face. "Are you thinking what I'm thinking, Ernie?" Stillwell asked.

"I hope so, sir," Easterbrook said.

Stillwell turned to Pickering. "Whether you like it or not, General, I am going to augment your force with a couple of Chinese," Stillwell said.

Easterbrook chuckled.

"There is on my staff an interesting Nationalist officer. Educated at the University of Chicago and Yale Law School. Brigadier General Sun Chi Lon. He's connected with Chiang Kai-shek's family—I think they're second cousins, something like that. I'm going to put him and his aide—an enormous Mongolian major—on a plane to Yümen. I think the two of them can make things considerably easier for this Captain McCoy of yours."

"That's very good of you, sir."

"No, Pickering, actually it's selfish," Stillwell said. "I'm chief of staff to Generalissimo Chiang Kai-shek. No one would question my authority to order two companies of Nationalist infantry—and the necessary logistical tail—into the Gobi. But I would have to pay for it—with interest—sooner or later, by having to replace the troops and their supplies. And I have better things to do with my available troops and supplies than taking them from what they're doing and sending them to Yümen to replace troops and supplies which have disappeared in the Gobi."

"Nevertheless, thank you, General," Pickering said. "Sir, would it be possible for me to accompany General . . . ?"

"Sun Chi Lon," Stillwell furnished. "He lets his friends call him 'Sunny.' Sure, if you want to go."

"Thank you, sir."

"Ernie, will you see if you can find the General? Ask him to come in here for a minute."

"Yes, sir," Colonel Easterbrook said, and left the room.

Pickering realized that Stillwell was smiling at him. "It just occurred to me, Pickering," Stillwell said, "and I have been around the Army a long time, that you are the first person I ever met who is cheerfully ignoring a 'suggestion' from the chief of staff of the U.S. Army."

"With respect, sir, 'cheerfully' is not the appropriate word."

"Well, since you're obviously not a fool, 'cheerfully' may *not* be the appropriate word. You have decided it's the right thing to do. The word for that is 'courageous.' "

"How about 'with great trepidation'?" Pickering said.

"Stop fishing for compliments, General, it's unbecoming," Stillwell said. "Can I offer you a cup of coffee?"

"Thank you, sir."

Two minutes later, a very small and slight Chinese officer entered Stillwell's office, trailed by a heavily built, flat-featured man who Pickering guessed had 250 pounds on his six-foot-four-inch frame.

"Sunny," General Stillwell said, "this is General Pickering. He's a friend of mine, and he needs your good offices."

"Anything I can do, of course," Brigadier General Sun Chi Lon said in accentless English, offering Pickering his hand. "It's a pleasure, General."

[FOUR]
Kiangpeh, Chungking, China
1700 11 April 1943

From the moment Stillwell summoned General Sun to his office, it was obvious to Pickering that the small and natty Chinese officer would have to be brought in on all the details of Operation Gobi. Otherwise, he could not bring to bear his good offices on the Chinese authorities in Yümen to solicit their support.

That was almost a classic definition of Need To Know. But for reasons Pickering did not really understand, he was reluctant—unable—to bring himself to discuss Operation Gobi with Sun, either in Sun's office, where they went after leaving Stillwell, or at lunch in a private room in the General Officers' Mess.

I want to think about this—maybe talk it over with Banning—before I start telling Sun anything.

During their luncheon, Sun almost conspicuously avoided discussing their forthcoming—just-as-soon-as-an-aircraft-could-be-found-and-the-weather-permitted—trip to Yümen. Pickering suspected that the Chinese general did not want to embarrass him by asking questions Pickering would not want to answer. Sun made it subtly clear, however, that since the request for his good offices had come from General Stillwell, that was all he needed to know. He would do whatever he could for Pickering.

Later Pickering had the feeling that by not telling him what was going on, he had, if not insulted General Sun, then at least hurt his feelings.

If I had come recommended by General Stillwell, pre-
pared to help in any way I could, and the guy I'd been
sent to help avoided telling me what he wanted and why,
I'd be hurt. Insulted. Pissed.

It was five o'clock before Banning came through the
door of the house in Kiangpeh. Pickering immediately
told him about General Sun, and the funny feeling he'd
had that he should not divulge to him anything about Operation Gobi.

"Permission to speak freely, sir?"

"Oh, for Christ's sake, Ed!"

"That was a mistake, sir. Probably no lasting harm was
done, but it was a mistake. He came recommended by
Stillwell. If you didn't want this guy's help, you should
have told Stillwell."

"How do I fix the mistake?" Pickering asked once Banning had confirmed what he had already concluded.

"Have George Hart call him and ask him to dinner,"
Banning began. "No, better you call him yourself, and tell
him that you've gathered together all the details of what
you were reluctant to discuss earlier, and would he be
available to go over them with you at dinner?"

"Where do I take him to dinner?"

"Here. The cook McCoy hired is really first class. I'll
make sure you're left alone."

"If he doesn't tell me to go fuck myself," Pickering
said. "Which I would do under the circumstances. I'll
want you at dinner."

"I've got an even better idea," Banning said. "You remember the name of his aide? The Mongolian?"

"Major Kee Lew See," Pickering furnished.

"I'll call Major Kee, identify myself as your deputy,
and ask him to ask his boss to dinner, so that the two of
you can discuss what obviously you couldn't discuss in
the headquarters building earlier. And I'll tell him that you
would be honored if he, too, were free."

"You think that'll do it, Ed?"

"I really hope so. We really need to stay on the right
side of this guy. The last thing we want to do is piss off
the Chinese."

"I have no intention of doing that," Pickering said, adding a little ruefully, "more than I have already."

"I'm talking about McCoy," Banning said.

"I don't think I follow you," Pickering confessed.

"When McCoy gets to Yümen—and he may be there already—I don't think he's going to walk into Headquarters of the Thirty-second Military District, either as Major MeeKoy of the Nationalist Army or Captain McCoy of the U.S. Marine Corps, ask to see the General, and tell him that he wants to sneak into the Gobi with one of their supply convoys."

"I'm still a little confused," Pickering said.

"I know how Ken operates well enough to know what he's going to do. As inconspicuously as possible—which means in his Chinese uniform—he's going to nose around Yümen until he finds the Chinese major or lieutenant colonel who actually runs the convoys. Then he'll bribe him to take him along. That was a good idea until this Chinese general, who is a second cousin once removed or something of the Generalissimo, turned up. He flies into Yümen with you, and says he wants to make sure Captain McCoy gets what he wants, and the General there says, 'Captain who? I have seen no American captain.' Who authorized this American to put on the uniform of a major in the Nationalist Army? Et cetera, et cetera. This could get out of hand in a hurry."

"God, I didn't even think about that."

"Let's just hope we can convince General Sun that what McCoy was doing was necessary," Banning said. "Have you got his telephone number?"

Pickering reached into his pocket and handed Banning the slip of paper with General Sun's number.

Banning picked up the EE-8 field telephone connected to the USMMCHI switchboard and cranked the generator on its side. He gave the extension he wanted to the operator in English, but the moment there was an answer began to speak Chinese, of which Pickering understood not a word.

What the hell am I doing here? Not being able to speak the language is a minor item on a long list of things that make me wholly unqualified to do what I'm doing.

Banning was smiling a good ninety seconds later when

he cranked the phone again and said, "Break it down."

"Don't tell me. The General regrets?" Pickering said.

"The General would be delighted to accept the General's kind offer of dinner at half past seven," Banning said. "Keep your fingers crossed. Maybe all isn't lost."

General Sun arrived at precisely seven-thirty, accompanied by his enormous Mongolian aide-de-camp.

The meeting went well from the beginning.

"General, may I present my deputy, Lieutenant Colonel Banning?"

Sun smiled at him. "Major Kee tells me you speak Wu like a native, Colonel."

Banning replied in Wu.

"And obviously you do," General Sun said, still in English.

Kee, grinning broadly, shook Banning's hand, then handed him a package.

I don't care what Banning's doing around here, he's going to Yümen with me, Pickering thought.

"I thought we might have a little wine with our dinner," General Sun said.

"That's very kind of you, General," Pickering said, taking the package from Banning.

It held two bottles of French wine—good French wine—causing Banning to wonder where Sun had gotten it in wartime Chungking, and then to wonder if there was some significance in a gift of expensive wine.

"This is very nice," Sun said, looking around. "I didn't know about this house."

"Captain McCoy only recently rented it. He's the officer I hope you can help get into the Gobi Desert as inconspicuously as possible."

"I thought this might have something to do with the Gobi Desert," Sun replied. "I couldn't imagine what other interest the OSS would have in that part of China."

"I hope you understand why I was reluctant to talk about the operation earlier, General."

"Completely, General," Sun said. "Unfortunately, China is not in a position to adequately compensate its officers. That too often results in the selling of information, especially information about the actions of someone else. The Japanese would be very interested to hear about your interest in the Gobi, and would pay very well for the information."

"I'm glad you understand," Pickering said.

"I would have been disappointed if the Deputy Director for Pacific Operations of the OSS had been less prudent," Sun said.

Either he's swallowed that whole, or he's decided to be gracious.

"Why don't we try that fine-looking wine?" Pickering asked. "And I'll try to explain Operation Gobi to you."

By the time the second bottle of wine was empty—before dinner—Pickering was able to hope that he had once again skirted a disaster by the skin of his teeth. Sun seemed to understand the necessity of getting McCoy and Zimmerman into the Gobi Desert as quietly as possible.

"It was rather clever of you, I think," General Sun said, "not to mount this operation from within China. There is no way it could have been kept secret."

"The truth of the matter is that wasn't a consideration. We just didn't think it could be done from inside China. Or actually, I didn't think it could. The OSS station chief in Chungking, on the other hand, doesn't think we can do it the way we plan to. He wants to send the station in by truck, guarded by two companies of soldiers."

"That would attract a good deal of attention from the Japanese," General Sun said. "It's probably not my position to say so, but if keeping the weather station secret is a major consideration, I think he's wrong."

Pickering chuckled.

"Did I say something funny?"

"General, did you ever hear that the true test of another man's intelligence is how much he agrees with you?"

"No," General Sun said, smiling. "But now that I have, I'll remember it."

That left only the question of McCoy to deal with, and Pickering decided this was the time to do that. "There is one thing I've done," he began, "or at least didn't stop—this was before I knew you were going to be involved—that you should know about. Captain McCoy felt the best way for him to move around was in the uniform of a Chinese officer."

General Sun's smile faded. "The uniform of a Chinese officer?"

"A major. Both of my men have Chinese Army identification, and Nansen passports identifying them as White Russians."

Sun frowned and shook his head, then spoke, in Chinese, to Major Kee, whose face showed both disbelief and disapproval.

"And we don't think Captain McCoy has made himself known to the Thirty-second Military District Headquarters," Pickering continued. "Or if he's not yet there, will when he gets there," he added.

"That may cause serious problems," Sun said. "Let me think about that. If they are discovered and arrested . . ."

"Captain McCoy is very capable, General," Banning said, "and knows China."

"I respectfully disagree, Colonel," General Sun said. "If he thinks he can successfully masquerade as a Chinese officer, he is *not* capable, and he does *not* know China."

He forced a smile, and went on. "But as I said, let me think about it."

[FIVE]
Headquarters, Marine Air Group 21
Ewa Marine Air Station
Oahu, Territory of Hawaii
1400 13 April 1943

When his attention was distracted by a Navy-gray Plymouth station wagon pulling up before his headquarters building, Lieutenant Colonel Clyde W. Dawkins, USMCR, was sitting in his spartan office, in a flight suit, tilted back in his chair, his feet resting on an open drawer, working his way through the day's supply of directives from higher headquarters—ninety-five percent of them useless, in his judgment. A fleet of such vehicles was assigned to CINCPAC, allowing Navy chair-warmers in the grade of lieutenant commander and above to move about the island, spreading Naval bureaucratic nonsense in their wake.

Christ, that's the last thing I need!

But it was not a Navy officer but a Marine officer whom Dawkins knew personally, who stepped out of the passenger seat, walked to the rear of the station wagon, and withdrew two canvas suitcases. He started up the walk to the building.

The last time I saw him was on the 'Canal, when I pinned the DFC onto his sweat-soaked khaki shirt.

The officer was now wearing a splendidly tailored Marine Green uniform. His gold Naval Aviator's wings sat atop three lines of ribbons.

He's got his weight back. He looks good.

Dawkins looked at the document in his lap. It directed him (and every other commanding officer of Navy and Marine units on Oahu) to personally encourage his officers and men to participate in religious-worship services of their choice on a weekly basis. He tossed the document into his wastebasket, rose from behind his desk, and walked out of his office.

The officer whom he had last seen on Guadalcanal was standing before the desk of Dawkins's sergeant major, who was reading the officer's orders.

"Well, I'll be damned," Colonel Dawkins said. "Look what came in with the tide. How are you, Pickering? What brings you here?"

"Good afternoon, sir," Lieutenant Malcolm S. Pickering, USMCR, said.

Dawkins went to his sergeant major and took the orders from his hand. "A word of warning, Sergeant Major," Dawkins said. "Don't play poker with this officer."

"Yes, sir," the sergeant major said, smiling. He'd liked the looks of this Marine officer from the moment he walked in the door. Not only did he look like a Marine officer was supposed to look, but he had the DFC and the Purple Heart to prove he wasn't a candy-ass. The way he was greeted by Colonel Dawkins confirmed that judgment.

As Dawkins read Lieutenant Pickering's orders, he

shook his head in what could have been either disbelief
or disgust.

S E C R E T

UNITED STATES NAVAL AIR STATION
MEMPHIS, TENNESSEE
30 MARCH 1943

SUBJECT: LETTER ORDERS

TO: 1ST LIEUTENANT MALCOLM S. PICKERING,
USMCR
VMF-262
US NAVAL AIR STATION
MEMPHIS, TENN.

1. REFERENCE IS MADE TO TWX (SECRET) HQ,
USMC, DATED 9 MAR 1943, SUBJECT:
"SOLICITATION OF VOLUNTEERS FOR
HAZARDOUS DUTY."

2. HAVING VOLUNTEERED FOR SUCH
ASSIGNMENT, YOU ARE THIS DATE DETACHED
FROM VMF-262, THIS STATION, AND ATTACHED
TO CINCPAC ON TEMPORARY DUTY FOR AN
INDEFINITE PERIOD. ON COMPLETION OF THIS
TEMPORARY DUTY, YOU WILL BE PERMANENTLY
ASSIGNED BY CINCPAC WITHIN THE PACIFIC
THEATER OF OPERATIONS.

3. YOU WILL PROCEED NO LATER THAN 5 APRIL
1943 TO US NAVAL BASE, SAN DIEGO,
CALIFORNIA, FOR FURTHER SHIPMENT TO
CINCPAC. A FOUR (4) DAY DELAY EN ROUTE
LEAVE TO YOUR HOME OF RECORD (C/O PACIFIC
& FAR EAST SHIPPING CORPORATION, SAN
FRANCISCO, CAL.) IS AUTHORIZED.

4. TRAVEL BY US GOVERNMENT AND/OR
CIVILIAN RAIL AND AIR TRANSPORTATION IS

AUTHORIZED BETWEEN USNAS MEMPHIS AND
USNB SAN DIEGO, AND US GOVERNMENT AND/OR
CIVILIAN AIR TRANSPORTATION PRIORITY
AAAAA IS DIRECTED BETWEEN SAN DIEGO AND
OAHU, T.H.

BY DIRECTION: JESSE R. BALL, REAR
ADMIRAL, USN

OFFICIAL:

Roger H. Walters

CAPTAIN, USN

S E C R E T

When he finished reading the orders, he exhaled audibly before handing them back to his sergeant major. He looked at Lieutenant Pickering and shook his head.

"When I got to Pearl Harbor, Colonel," Pick said. "They sent me here to report to you."

"Come in here, Pickering," Dawkins said, pointing to his open office door. He added to his sergeant major, "Unless it's Admiral Nimitz, I'm unavailable at the moment and will get back to them."

"Aye, aye, sir."

"Or Major Dillon. I'll talk to him. As a matter of fact, see if you can find Major Dillon."

"Aye, aye, sir."

Dawkins followed Pickering into his office and closed the door after them. "You want to tell me what this is all about, Pickering?"

"Sir, I was given the opportunity to volunteer for this mission, and did so."

"Why does your nobility strike me as bullshit, pure and simple? Unless, of course, you've lost your mind," Dawkins said, not unkindly. And then, before Pickering could even begin to frame an answer, he thought of something else.

"Where did you get qualified in a PBY-5A? The last time I looked at your records, you had maybe twenty-five hours in the right seat of a Gooney Bird, all of it when you went off with Charley Galloway on that lunatic mission to Buka. And you had zero hours in a Catalina. Is my memory failing me, Lieutenant Pickering?"

"Just before I came over here, I got a crash course in the Catalina, sir. Thirty hours in four days."

Dawkins looked at Pickering for a long moment. "Up to you, Pick," he said finally. "You can tell me what's going on or not. If you're in some kind of jam, I'll go to bat for you, you know that."

"The truth is, sir, I got in a little trouble in Memphis. I was offered my choice of volunteering for this, or a court-martial. Preceded by grounding."

"What kind of trouble?"

"There was a lady involved, sir."

Dawkins raised his eyebrows.

"And there were some minor things, too, sir, to be truthful. Speeding tickets, out of uniform. Things like that."

"If Billy Dunn offered you the choice between a court-martial and volunteering for this operation, there's more to it than a couple of speeding tickets. Or were you perhaps drunk when they arrested you for speeding?"

"Just once, sir, and I got that downgraded to reckless driving. And it wasn't Billy who gave me the choice, it was the Admiral."

"What you're saying, in other words, is that Billy—out of misguided loyalty—covered for you while you were showing your ass, but you were such an all around fuckup that it got to the Admiral? What admiral?"

"The Memphis NAS admiral, sir. Who is friend of a friend of the lady's husband."

"You were fooling around with a married woman?"

"Yes, sir."

"Did this admiral know who your father is?"

"Yes, sir. Dad—and General McInerney—were at Memphis just before the Admiral . . . sent for me."

"You were about to say something other than 'sent for me'?"

"Placed me under arrest, sir."

"You're a disgrace to your uniform, Pickering. Do you understand that? There's more to being a Marine officer than flying an airplane."

"Yes, sir. I've had time to consider that."

"Worse than that, you let Billy Dunn down. He needed you. The kids you were training needed you."

"Yes, sir. I've had time to consider that, too."

"Let me tell you the situation here. For administrative convenience, all the volunteers for this mission—the legitimately noble volunteers and you—will be attached to MAG-21 for rations, quarters, and administration. I command MAG-21."

"Yes, sir. 'Will be', sir?"

"You're the first one to show up. Don't interrupt me again."

"Yes, sir."

"The mission is being run by Major Jake Dillon—"

"My father's involved in this?" Pick blurted.

"Goddamn it, I told you not to interrupt me!"

"Sorry, sir."

"And the volunteers will be housed at Muku-Muku. Both to give the condemned a hearty meal before they fly off on this idiotic mission, and to keep them from running off at the mouth in the O Club bar about what they're doing. I would really like to order you to draw a pup tent and pitch it behind Hangar Two, but that would draw attention to you. You will proceed to Muku-Muku and there await further orders from Major Dillon."

"Aye, aye, sir."

"While you are at Muku-Muku, you will not confide in anyone—Major Dillon, Captain Galloway, Gunner Oblensky, and especially not the bona fide noble volunteers—what has caused you to be in their midst. Is that clear, Mr. Pickering?"

"Yes, sir."

"You will engage in no activity while you are under my administration that might possibly draw attention to you or the mission. You will not drive a privately owned vehicle. You will not go into Honolulu, and you will not partake of the facilities of any officers' club unless you

are accompanied by Major Dillon or Captain Galloway.
You get one drink of spirits a day. Do you understand
these restrictions, Mr. Pickering?"

"Yes, sir."

"Good, because if you violate any one of them, I will
ground you and I will court-martial you. Your father and
Admiral Wagam—and, I am reliably informed, Admiral
Nimitz himself—regard this operation as very important.
I am not going to run any chance whatever of having it
fouled up by a spoiled child wearing a Marine officer's
uniform who doesn't have enough sense to know when to
put his whisky glass down and his zipper pulled up."

"Yes, sir."

"You are dismissed, Mr. Pickering," Colonel Dawkins
said. "Ask the sergeant major to arrange for a jeep—a
jeep, not a staff car—to transport you to Muku-Muku."

"Aye, aye, sir," Lieutenant Pickering said, did an about-
face movement and marched out of Dawkins's office.

[SIX]
Headquarters, Marine Air Group 21
Ewa Marine Air Station
Oahu, Territory of Hawaii
1530 13 April 1943

Lieutenant Colonel Clyde W. Dawkins's sergeant major
put his head into Dawkins's office. "Captain Galloway
would like a couple of minutes, sir," he announced.

"Send him in," Dawkins ordered.

*He's heard Pickering's at Muku-Muku and wants to
know what's going on.*

Galloway, in an oil-stained flight suit, came through the
door. "Good afternoon, sir."

"Close the door please, Captain," Dawkins said.

Galloway turned and did so.

Dawkins took a bottle of scotch from his desk drawer.
"You flying, Charley, or can you have one of these?"

"I'm through for the day, sir. Thank you."

Dawkins poured stiff drinks in Kraft cheese glasses and
handed one to Galloway.

"To Marine fighter pilots, goddamn them," Dawkins said, raising his glass. "If we didn't need the bastards, I'd put a bounty on them."

"I'll drink to that," Galloway said. "I just came from 'counseling' one of the bastards. And I need this."

He raised his glass, then drank half of it.

"I see no scrapes, bruises, or contusions," Dawkins said. "This was one of your smaller hooligans?"

"I haven't actually had to . . . 'strongly counsel' anybody in some time," Galloway said. "All I have to do now is show my fangs and growl."

Dawkins chuckled. "What's on your mind, Charley, or did you just come in to drink my liquor?"

"Lieutenant Stevenson," Galloway said.

"A problem?"

"Sort of."

"What happened? Did somebody teach him how to box?"

"Actually, he's pretty well been on the straight and narrow," Galloway said. "He wants to fly one of Dillon's Cats."

"Does he, now? And what does he know about Dillon's Catalinas? Are we about to have another problem with somebody's big mouth?"

"He's figured out they're going to make a long, long flight," Galloway said. "And he came to me and said he'd heard the pilots were all volunteers for whatever it was, and he'd like to volunteer."

"Just for the record . . . Belay that: *Off* the record, Charley, are you volunteering this guy?"

"No, I'm not," Galloway said. "This was his idea."

"And what do you think prompted this selfless act on the part of Mr. Stevenson? We are talking about the same Stevenson, right, the one you wiped the hangar floor with when McInerney was here?"

"What I was doing was offering a little extra instruction in the manly art of self-defense. Yeah, same guy. He wants to redeem himself."

"And you believe him?"

"Yeah, I do," Galloway said. He drank the rest of his drink and looked at Dawkins. "I really do. He's come around. He's a regular, you know. I think he wants to see if he can salvage his career by doing something heroic."

"Who told him the pilots were going to be volunteers?"

"Probably the Navy pilots who volunteered. He drinks with them."

"Jesus Christ, what do we have to do to get people to keep their mouths shut?"

"Okay, Skipper," Galloway said, holding up his hand in a mock gesture of self-protection. "I told him I would ask. I asked. I will now leave without even asking for another taste."

"I would be ever so honored, Captain Galloway, if you would join me in another libation," Dawkins said.

"I accept your kind offer with great gratitude, sir," Galloway said, then walked to where the bottle sat and picked it up.

"How much Catalina time does this guy have?" Dawkins asked.

"About six hundred hours pilot-in-command. He flew antisubmarine patrols on the East Coast."

"Before or after he got in trouble?"

"When they kicked him out of a fighter squadron, they sent him to the Cats. When he got in trouble there, they sent him to VMF-229, the Alcatraz of Marine Aviation," Galloway said. "So I guess you could say, while he was getting in trouble."

"*On* the record, Charley. There's no one in the Corps who could have done what you've done with that collection of misfits and ne'er-do-wells."

"And *off* the record?" Galloway asked, trying to make a joke of the compliment.

"*Off* the record, Charley," Dawkins said seriously, "there's no one in the Corps who could have done what you've done with that collection of misfits and ne'er-do-wells."

Galloway was now visibly embarrassed. He tried to change the subject: "Can I tell him I asked and you're thinking about it?"

"You can tell him to come see me," Dawkins said, then plunged on. "I got a back channel from McInerney, on that special communications system that Dillon has somehow managed to latch on to. There have been damned few volunteers. General Mac is down to volunteering people. He said he wants Marines to fly the Cats. By using the term loosely, your pal Stevenson can be considered to be a Marine."

"I wouldn't volunteer for something like this, myself," Galloway said. "I'm not surprised."

"We do have one volunteer," Dawkins said. "He came in right after lunch. I sent him over to Muku-Muku."

"Oh, yeah?"

"Another pretty good fighter pilot who couldn't behave and was offered the choice between a court-martial and volunteering to become a legendary Marine hero, flying a Cat in harm's way."

"I'm surprised they didn't send him to me," Galloway said. "How did he fuck up?"

"The usual things young fighter pilots do. Drunk driving. Speeding. Out of uniform. And he was sleeping with a lady who is joined in holy matrimony to somebody else, and the somebody else happens to be acquainted with the flag officer commanding Naval Air Station, Memphis."

"Hell, that's called upholding the reputation of Marine Aviators," Galloway said.

"This guy was setting a lousy example for the young Marine Aviators he was supposed to be training," Dawkins said flatly.

"Yeah, I suppose," Galloway said, and then thought he was changing the subject again. "Young Pickering is at NAS Memphis. He's Billy Dunn's executive officer."

"Young Pickering is by now at Muku-Muku," Dawkins said. "Under a direct order not to tell you how come he's no longer in Memphis."

Galloway looked at Dawkins as if surprised that he would make such a lousy joke. Dawkins nodded, and Galloway realized he wasn't kidding at all. "Give him to me, Skipper," Galloway said after taking a moment to collect his thoughts. "I can straighten him out."

"Sorry, Charley, forget it. I don't have the authority to do that, and I don't think I would if I did."

"Skipper, he doesn't have much time in a Catalina—if any, come to think of it."

"He's qualified as pilot-in-command," Dawkins said. "That's all it takes."

"I was feeling pretty good when I came in here," Galloway said.

"I was feeling pretty good when I saw Pick get out of the station wagon," Dawkins said. "Would another drink make you feel any better?"

"No, sir," Galloway replied. "Thank you just the same."

"In that case, good afternoon, Captain Galloway."

"Thank you for seeing me, sir."

Captain Charles M. Galloway came to attention, executed an about-face maneuver, and marched out of Dawkins's office.

[SEVEN]
Headquarters, Marine Air Group 21
Ewa Marine Air Station
Oahu, Territory of Hawaii
1915 13 April 1943

The charge of quarters knocked at Dawkins's office door and opened it wide enough to put his head in the crack. "Colonel, there's a Major Williamson out here, says if you're not tied up he'd like to make his manners."

Dawkins had not finished going through the directives he'd started on after lunch and thrown into the wastebasket. His sergeant major had gone through the wastebasket, salvaged the directives that needed Colonel Dawkins's attention, and put them back in his In basket.

"Aviator type?"

"Yes, sir. Captain Weston is with him."

"A Captain Weston, Andy, or *our* Captain Weston?"

"Ours, sir."

Like most everybody else in MAG-21, Sergeant Ward had been impressed with the Marine Aviator who had spent a year as a guerrilla in the Philippines.

"Well, damn, Andy, send them in."

"Aye, aye, sir."

Major Avery R. Williamson and Captain James B.

Weston came through Dawkins's door a moment later.

"What brings you two to this tropical paradise?" Dawkins greeted them, as he came from behind his desk with his hand extended.

"Apparently," Williamson replied, "there's nobody over here who knows how to drive a Cat. We have leapt to fill the breach."

Dawkins's smile faded. "Weston, tell Sergeant Ward to get you a cup of coffee," he said.

"Aye, aye, sir," Weston said, left the room, and, sensing that he was being dismissed, closed the door behind him.

"What the hell's going on, Dick?" Dawkins demanded.

"General Mac came to see me at Pensacola," Williamson said. "He told me that not enough people had volunteered for this Catalina mission of his; that he considered it a damned important operation; and stood there with the Marine Corps flag in one hand and the colors in the other and waved them at me until I finally—a long couple of minutes later—saw it as my duty to sign on the dotted line."

"Jesus Christ!" Dawkins said. "Do you know what it is?"

Williamson shook his head, "no."

"It has been decided that we can't win this war without a weather station in the middle of the Gobi Desert. And apparently the only way we can get one in there is to fly it in—a one-way flight, by the way—on a couple of Catalinas which will be refueled by a submarine a hundred miles off the China Coast in the Yellow Sea."

"Jesus!"

"We have modified two Catalinas—and two others are in the process of being modified—by fairing over the turrets and the bubbles and installing auxiliary fuel tanks. Somebody apparently thinks that refueling a Cat from a sub on the high seas in the Yellow Sea this time of year may not work so well, and spares may be required."

"Jesus!" Williamson repeated.

"If I was running this operation, I would go over to VMF-229 and select the worst four of Charley Galloway's ne'er-do-wells and send them," Dawkins said. "There are better things for you to do, Dick. And Weston, too." He paused, then went on, "General McInerney actually waved the flag at Weston, too? I would have thought he would be entitled to a pass on something like this."

"That's a fine young man, Dawk," Williamson said. "A damned good Marine."

"If not too bright," Dawkins said, "to volunteer for something like this."

"He's a Catalina IP. I rechecked him out myself. He can drive one better than I can. And like I said, he's a damned good Marine. He had everything going for him. But he saw this as his duty, when I told him I had been volunteered."

"He's out of his mind," Dawkins said. "No one can accuse that kid of being a shirker."

"You know Admiral Sayre?" Williamson asked. "His daughter?"

"The one who married Culhane? Who we lost at Wake?"

"Uh-huh."

"Until Weston—he was the best man at their wedding— showed up at P'Cola, they called Martha Culhane 'the Ice Princess.' One look at Weston and she melted. And the Admiral thinks Jim is the answer to his prayers for the Ice Princess, too."

"Really?"

"He told me to give him a Cat check-ride, and since I was already going to do that, why didn't I do it by flying up to the Greenbrier—You know about the Greenbrier?"

Dawkins nodded.

"—and give him the check-ride while flying back and forth to P'Cola?"

"Then he really is a goddamn fool!" Dawkins said angrily.

"No, Dawk," Williamson said. "What he is is a damned good Marine. Duty first."

Dawkins looked at Williamson for a long moment. "Just because you're right, Dick," he said, "doesn't mean I have to like it."

"No, but you have to admire him," Williamson insisted.

"I admired him already," Dawkins said sadly, and then raised his voice: "Captain Weston!"

Weston came back into the office.

"Yes, sir?"

"Captain Weston," Dawkins said, "on behalf of the Commander in Chief, Pacific, permit me to thank you for volunteering for this mission. Your selfless dedication to duty is in keeping with the highest traditions of the officer corps of the Marine Corps. That's official. Off the record, Jim, I think you're a goddamned fool, and if you give me the word, I'll do my damndest to get you out of this."

"With respect, sir, I'd like to fly the operation."

"You don't even know what it is, for Christ's sake!"

"Sir, I know the operation needs experienced Catalina pilots. I have a good deal of experience in the Cat."

"So Major Williamson informs me," Dawkins said. "Okay, Jim. Your decision."

"Thank you, sir."

"I'm going to send you two over to Muku-Muku . . ."

"I think you'll like Muku-Muku, Major," Weston said, smiling.

". . . where you will find another heroic Marine who volunteered to fly this operation, immediately after he was offered his choice of doing so or being court-martialed."

"Really?" Williamson asked, amused. "For what?"

"It's not funny. I know this officer. Seven kills, DFC, flying Wildcats for Charley Galloway on Guadalcanal. Fine pilot. Lousy officer. Did you ever meet General Pickering's son, Jim?"

"No, sir. But I heard about him," Weston said. "That's who you're talking about?"

Dawkins nodded.

"How did he fuck up, sir?"

"As far as I'm concerned, by failing to do his duty. He was at Memphis, where he was supposed to be training Corsair pilots. The best way to train is by example. The example this Marine ace with the DFC set for the people he was supposed to be training was that it's all right to be grossly irresponsible. But the straw that broke the back, that almost got him court-martialed, was his personal life, his love life."

"What did he do?"

"He was having an affair with the wrong female. For

all I know, more than one. But I do know about one. A prima facie case of Conduct Unbecoming An Officer And A Gentleman." Dawkins let that sink in a minute. "I believe in a clean sheet," Dawkins went on. "This is not known to anyone involved with this operation, and I don't want you to let him know I told you about it."

"I understand, sir," Weston said.

"Okay," Major Williamson said.

"The only reason I'm telling you this is because he doesn't have much time in a Catalina—I think thirty hours, something like that. The admiral commanding Memphis got him a quick qualification course just before throwing him off the base. So he's going to need some more Catalina time, as much as we can get him, and you two are the obvious people to give it to him."

"Aye, aye, sir."

"And there may be one more student for you," Dawkins went on. "One of Charley Galloway's fuckups, according to Charley, has decided to salvage his fucked-up career by volunteering for this idiotic operation. That's not for sure; I'll make up my mind in the morning, after he comes to see me. But you might as well plan on it."

"Aye, aye, sir," Williamson and Weston said almost in unison.

"This 'gentleman's' name is Stevenson. First Lieutenant. I had a look at his record again this afternoon. Another sex maniac, apparently, who regards screwing any female—without regard to the consequences—as a sport. This sonofabitch, believe it or not, was screwing two women at the same time, both of whom he promised to marry."

"Well, there are some guys like that," Major Williamson said. "They just don't know when to keep their trousers buttoned. And we joke about it, but it's not funny."

"No, it isn't," Colonel Dawkins said.

Captain Weston did not comment.

XXII

The aircraft provided by the United States 14th Air Force to transport Brigadier General Fleming Pickering, USMCR, Brigadier General Sun Chi Lon, Nationalist Army, and their entourages from Chungking to Yümen was a well-worn Douglas C-47. That morning it had been equipped with four airline-type seats, to accommodate the general officers, Colonel Banning, and Major Kee. They were mounted behind the bulkhead that separated the cockpit from the rest of the cabin. The entourages, General Sun's two orderlies, Second Lieutenant George F. Hart, USMCR, and Captain Jerry Sampson, USA, were obviously expected to make themselves as comfortable as they could on aluminum pipe and canvas seats that folded down from the bare walls of the fuselage.

Captain Sampson had been a last-minute and not entirely welcome addition to the party. When General Pickering had told Lieutenant Colonel Platt that he was headed for Yümen to see if he could assist McCoy, Platt took Pickering by surprise and immediately offered to send Sampson with them. "He might prove helpful."

Pickering was unable to immediately think of a good reason Sampson shouldn't go—he'd already told Platt that Stillwell had arranged for the airplane to take him to Yümen and back—so he smiled and said, "Thank you." Pickering had no doubt that Sampson might indeed "prove helpful," but he was equally certain that the primary reason Platt had so generously offered the Captain's services was to make sure he learned what Pickering was up to in Yümen.

Pickering was not exactly eager at the moment to make that information available. Because McCoy and Zimmerman were running around Yümen in Chinese uniforms, Pickering was very much afraid that the whole mission was likely to go down the toilet.

General Sun, Major Kee, their two orderlies, and a dozen pieces of luggage were waiting for them at the Chungking airfield when they arrived—Pickering, Banning, and Hart had one piece each. Sun greeted Pickering courteously but did not mention the McCoy problem, and Pickering decided this was not the time to bring it up.

It turned out to be a long flight.

Before they took off, the pilot explained to Pickering that while Yümen was within the C-47's range, flying directly there was unwise. If the field was socked in— very possible this time of year—there was no alternative airfield they could reach with the remaining fuel aboard.

So they flew to Lanchou, a six-hundred-mile leg that took them almost four hours, refueled there, and then taken off for Yümen, which was a slightly shorter leg.

Twenty minutes out of Lanchou, General Sun turned to Pickering and offered him a cigarette from a gold case.

"No, thank you," Pickering said. "I'm a cigar smoker."

"I have been giving some thought to our problem with your Captain McCoy," Sun said, tapping a Chesterfield on the case.

Pickering nodded and waited for him to go on.

"The most difficult situation will be if he has been discovered," Sun said. "That's also the most likely. I don't really think he can successfully masquerade as a White Russian officer. And, because of its location, the counterintelligence services in the Thirty-second Military District are very thorough."

"If they have been discovered, what will that mean?"

"That there is no chance they will be allowed to accompany a supply convoy into the desert. Or, in the remote chance that they were, someone would be sent along to report on their activities, and I doubt very much if they would be permitted to leave the convoy."

"Yeah," Pickering agreed.

"I could have arranged all this, had I known about it in time," Sun said. "What we are doing now is reacting, not taking action, and we don't know to what we are reacting."

"I understand," Pickering said.

"It is entirely possible that they will have been subjected to a rather intensive interrogation," Sun said.

I don't even want to think what's behind that euphemism.

"In that case, it seems to me inevitable that they would disclose their purpose. That would make it even more difficult for them to go into the desert—even after their story is verified by me." He caught Pickering's eye. "Still, I don't think the commanding general would conduct an *authorized* execution without making his superiors aware of the situation. He would want them to know his counterintelligence was working. We'll have to wait until we arrive to see what the situation is."

"Yeah," Pickering grunted. "Would they tell you of an incident like this?"

"I think so. They would regard it as a worthy accomplishment," Sun said. "But let's look at the other side. Defying the odds, your men have somehow managed to reach Yümen and have *not* been arrested. I suggest in that case that I immediately inform General Chow that they are in his area, dressed in the uniform of Chinese officers—"

"We have another expression," Pickering interrupted. "Never look a gift horse in the mouth."

"I know that one," General Sun. "But how does it apply here? I'm the gift horse? And you disagree with me?"

"If you tell General—Chow, you said?"

"Major General Chow Song-chek," Sun furnished.

"If you tell General Chow, he will very likely be annoyed that he wasn't previously advised that a pair of American agents are working in his area of responsibility. And even if he's sympathetic, I think we would lose any chance of keeping this operation quiet."

"And if we don't tell General Chow, and fifteen minutes after we arrive he learns that two spurious White Russians have been arrested in the uniforms of Chinese officers?"

"Then you tell him you didn't know. I didn't tell you."

Sun thought that over for a long moment. "On the odd chance that your men are in Yümen, and have managed to avoid General Chow's counterintelligence, have you given any thought about how you are going to find them?"

"A good deal of thought, and come up with no better answer than I'll just have to look for them."

"There is one possibility," Sun said. "And that is this. I will tell General Chow that you have been sent by General Stillwell to have a look at his operation. He will brief you. It's too late to do that today. He would schedule a briefing for tomorrow morning. If we can find your men between the time we land and the time of the briefing— which seems a very long shot indeed . . ."

"If we can't find them when we see General Chow in the morning, you can tell him I just told you about my men."

"He will consider that he has been deceived by you. There would be repercussions."

"I think it's worth the chance," Pickering said.

General Sun thought that over a moment. "Are you familiar, General Pickering, with the phrase 'no good deed goes unpunished'?"

"Yes, I am."

"If we can't find your men by eight o'clock tomorrow morning, I will tell General Chow that I sent your men, in Chinese Army uniform, into his area of responsibility."

"That's putting your neck on the chopping block."

"It isn't exactly what I had in mind when I agreed to use my good offices with General Chow, but I think it is what's called for."

Because of head winds, the flight from Lanchou to Yümen took them just over another four hours. When they landed at sunset, a light snow was just beginning to fall. The commanding General of the 32nd Military District, a tall, stern-looking man in his fifties, was there to meet them. He had with him several senior officers and four vehicles—an ancient Packard touring car, a 1941 Packard Clipper, a 1941 Ford, and a Dodge weapons carrier for the luggage.

As General Sun's orderlies loaded the luggage into the weapons carrier, Sun introduced Pickering as an officer on Stillwell's staff whom Stillwell wanted familiar with the operation of the 32nd Military District.

"If we had only known you were coming, General Pickering," General Chow said in excellent English, "we would have been honored to prepare a more detailed briefing than I can offer you on such short notice."

"I didn't want you to go to any special effort, General," Pickering said. "General Sun has been telling me what a busy man you are."

"I will arrange with my staff to have a briefing prepared for you in the morning. Would ten o'clock be convenient for you?"

"It has been a long flight, General," Pickering said. "But whatever is convenient for you."

"I understand completely," General Chow said. "Perhaps you will take lunch with me tomorrow, with the briefing to follow?"

"That would be splendid," Pickering said. "Thank you very much."

"And now we will take you to your quarters," General Chow said. "Where we will have a drink and then dinner."

"You are very kind, sir."

General Chow gestured toward the ancient Packard touring car. Its canvas roof was already covered with snow, and there were no side curtains. But General Chow obviously regarded it as the most prestigious of his vehicles, and was honoring Pickering and Sun by inviting them to ride in it.

Pickering looked at his watch. It was five minutes to six. Presuming everybody was wrong—including Generals Stillwell and Sun—and McCoy had somehow managed to make it here, that gave him eighteen hours to find him.

That seemed like a very long shot, indeed.

Ten minutes after leaving the airport, they drove past a building with an adjacent parking lot. It was full of military vehicles. One of them was a Dodge ambulance with the normal red crosses not entirely painted over, and another was a Dodge three-quarter-ton weapons carrier. Both had five-hundred-gallon water trailers attached to them. Three Chinese soldiers armed with rifles were guarding them—and keeping themselves warm by standing beside a fire blazing in a cutoff fifty-five-gallon drum.

Pickering nudged General Sun with his elbow, but by the time Sun looked at him curiously, they had passed the opening to the parking area.

And Sun wouldn't know what I was showing him anyway.

And there are probably fifty weapons carriers towing water trailers in Yümen.

"Excuse me," Pickering said.

"Certainly," General Sun said.

Their quarters turned out to be a large and comfortable house. Inside General Chow led them into a room off the foyer that had been turned into a bar. There he began to offer a series of champagne toasts to Generalissimo Chiang Kai-shek, President Roosevelt, General Stillwell, and—Pickering thought with growing impatience—every general officer, Chinese and American, in China.

Though he was fully aware that the ambulance and weapons carrier he had seen en route to the house were almost certainly not the ones McCoy and Zimmerman had driven to Yümen, in the absence of any other alternative, he was perfectly willing to grasp at a straw. The moment General Chow and his officers left the house—or sooner, if he could get General Sun alone for a moment—he was going to tell him he may have seen McCoy's trucks, and wanted to go looking for him.

General Chow failed to leave General Sun's side, and showed no interest in dinner. He did show every sign of too much drink, which meant the cocktail hour could go on forever, with dinner to follow.

"Sir, may I speak to you a moment?" a voice said in Pickering's ear.

"What's on your mind, Sampson?" Pickering asked, not entirely cordially.

"Not in here, sir."

What the hell does he want?

Sampson gestured toward the door to the foyer of the house. Pickering marched out of the room into the foyer.

"Sir, I was hoping that General Chow would leave—"

"What is it, Sampson?"

"Sir, on the way here from the airport, I believe I saw Captain McCoy's vehicles."

"Is that so?"

"Yes, sir. I'm sure it was the ambulance he drove to the OSS house in Chung king. The paint didn't quite obliterate the white of the red cross markings—"

"There's probably fifty ambulances with bad paint jobs in Yümen," Pickering said.

"The door of the ambulance Captain McCoy drove to the OSS house had a longitudinal scar on it, sir. So did the ambulance I saw before. And both vehicles here were towing five-hundred-gallon water trailers. Sir, with respect, I think having a look makes sense."

"So do I," Pickering said. "Go back in there and as discreetly as possible have Colonel Banning come out here."

Banning came into the foyer a moment later, and on his heels was Major Kee Lew See, with a curious, concerned look on his face.

"You wanted to see me, sir?" Banning said.

"Sampson and I both think we know where McCoy is. Or at least was," Pickering said.

"Where?"

"We saw the ambulance and the weapons carrier in the parking lot of a building—"

"How do you know it was McCoy's ambulance and weapons carrier?" Banning interrupted dubiously.

"I don't, obviously," Pickering said sharply. "But in the absence of a better idea where McCoy might be, I think I want to have a look."

Major Kee politely but insistently asked a question.

"Major Kee," Sampson translated, "would like to know if there is any kind of problem, and if so, how he might be able to resolve it."

"Tell him we need a vehicle for about thirty minutes," Pickering ordered.

Sampson translated, and then translated Kee's reply: "Major Kee says that he hopes you will not give General Chow any reason to believe that you are not pleased with the festivities."

"Tell him that I am delighted with the festivities."

Sampson translated again and a moment later, translated Kee's reply: "Major Kee believes that General Chow will misunderstand if the General does not immediately return to the festivities."

"Banning, you and Major Kee go back in there and tell General Sun that I will return in about an hour, and look forward to resuming my role in the festivities."

This time Major Kee did not wait to hear Sampson's translations. He uttered a string of rapid-fire Chinese.

Sampson smiled. "How much English do you speak, sir?" he asked.

"I understand a good bit," Kee said in heavily accented but perfectly understandable English. "Be so good, Captain, as to translate my comment to General."

"Yes, sir," Sampson said. "General, Major Kee said—"

"That it would be better," Banning interrupted him, "if I went back in there and made your apologies. He feels he would be more use going with you when you look for Captain McCoy."

"Thank you, Major Kee," Pickering said. "Can you get us a car?"

"We will take the Packard Clipper, General," Major Kee said. "That has been set aside for General Sun's use."

"Make my apologies, please, Colonel," Pickering ordered.

"Aye, aye, sir."

[TWO]
**The Inn of the Fattened Goose
Yümen, China
2005 13 April 1943**

Captain Kenneth R. McCoy, USMCR, and Gunnery Sergeant Ernest W. Zimmerman—both of them out of uniform in a manner not even dreamed of by the United States Marine Corps—sat at a small table near the center of the dark and smoke-filled room. More than a dozen "other" Chinese officers were in the room, and as many well-dressed civilians, but McCoy and Zimmerman were the only Caucasians.

On McCoy's table were plates; bowls of cooked and raw onions and sweet peppers; glasses; and two liter bottles of beer. A roaring fire, built on bricks, was set in the center of the floor. It was both a source of heat and a stove. Cantilevered from a pole rising from the floor to the ceiling was a fire-blackened cast-iron dome that could be swung over the fire. A very large Chinese woman in a black gown sliced a thin piece of beef six inches by four from a quarter carcass of beef, hung from the same pole, threw a glance at McCoy's table, held up the beef, and asked if that would be enough.

"Two, no, three slices like that for me," McCoy called to her in Cantonese. "And for my fat friend, five."

The large Chinese woman smiled and pushed the fire-blackened dome over the fire. Then she picked up her knife and sliced more thin oblongs of beef from the carcass.

"That thing is like an upside-down wok," McCoy said.

"It's made out of cast iron," Zimmerman protested. "They hammer woks out of sheet steel."

"Well, pardon my ignorance," McCoy said.

"That's the way the Mongolians do their beef," Ernie said. "It ain't Chinese."

"She's going to melt the wok if she leaves it in that fire much longer," McCoy said.

"I told you, it ain't a wok," Zimmerman said.

"Drink your beer, Ernie," McCoy said.

"Shit, I don't like that," Zimmerman said softly.

McCoy followed Zimmerman's eyes.

A very large Chinese officer was standing just inside the door. His hand rested on the molded leather holster hanging from his Sam Browne belt.

"He looks like he was looking for something interesting, and just found us," Zimmerman said.

"I don't like the way he's dressed," McCoy said softly. "Too well."

"Are we going to get fucked up this late?" Zimmerman said.

"Just play it nice and easy, Ernie," McCoy said, and directed his attention to the large Chinese woman.

She swung the inverted cast-iron dome off the fire. Then, moving quickly, she dipped four of the thin slices of beef into a bowl and laid them on the dome. There was a sizzle, a delicious smell, and a cloud of smoke. Using a fork, she turned the slices over, let them cook momentarily, and then placed them on two plates. She handed the plates to a boy who started toward McCoy's table, and then she pushed the cast-iron dome back over the fire.

"It's us he's after. Here he comes," Zimmerman said very softly.

"Easy does it, Ernie," McCoy said softly.

"Sir, you are American?" Major Kee Lew See asked in English.

"What did you say?" McCoy replied nastily in Cantonese. "What do you want?"

"I asked if you are American," Major Kee asked in Cantonese.

"And who are you to ask me what I am?" McCoy said.

"I am Major Kee Lew See, aide-de-camp to General Sun. Your papers, please, Major."

The Chinese boy reached the table and laid the plates of beef on it.

"You don't mind if I have my supper first, do you, Major?" McCoy said, and shifted in his seat.

"Your papers, please, Major," Kee repeated.

McCoy, with a look of patient resignation on his face, took out his fraudulent identification and handed it over.

As Major Kee very carefully examined it, McCoy, hoping he couldn't be observed, opened the top of his holster and put his hand on the butt of the 9mm Luger Parabellum automatic pistol it held.

"This is a very good forgery," Major Kee said, handing the identification document back to McCoy. "Very few people would question it."

"What are you talking about?" McCoy said, easing the Luger from the holster and putting his finger on the trigger.

The only thing I can do is stick the barrel in this guy's belly, march him out of here, put him in the back of the ambulance, get the hell away from here, and worry about what to do with him later.

"Killer," Zimmerman said softly, and nodded toward the door.

Brigadier General Fleming Pickering, USMC, trailed by Captain Jerome Sampson, USA, was making his way across the crowded room to them.

McCoy let the Luger drop back into the molded holster.

"Who the hell are you, Major?" he asked in English.

"I told you, Captain McCoy. I am Major Kee Lew See, aide-de-camp to General Sun."

Major General Chow Song-chek was feeling absolutely no pain when he started to climb up into the rear seat of his ancient Packard touring car. Then some thought stopped him, and he stepped off the running board.

God, now what? Pickering thought.

General Chow's departure from the front door of the VIP villa had taken him almost as long as his departure from the dinner table.

"General Pickering, my friend, may I say something to you man-to-man?"

"Of course, General."

"You tend to underestimate Chinese hospitality," General Chow announced.

"General, I am overwhelmed by your hospitality," Pickering said. "I have difficulty finding the words to express my gratitude."

"Nevertheless, my friend, you did not fully understand that all you had to do was give me a small hint that all that you wished was not being furnished."

What the hell is he talking about?

"That's probably true, sir, but there is, I assure you, nothing that I wish to have that has not already been so graciously provided."

"Not now, of course, at this hour. We are all tired. It was otherwise, may I dare to say, a satisfactory welcome to Yümen and the Thirty-second Military District?"

"It exceeded anything I would have dared to hope for," Pickering said.

"I am pleased that you are satisfied with our poor attempt to welcome such a distinguished visitor as yourself," General Chow said. "And I assure you, my dear General, that tonight there will be nothing . . ." He winked at Pickering and struck his right shoulder in a gesture of masculine friendship. ". . . nothing at all, missing to entertain you."

Pickering saw that Lieutenant Colonel Banning was having a very hard time keeping a straight face.

"That's very kind of you, General," Pickering said.

General Chow—for the fifth time—shook Pickering's hand, came to attention and saluted, and finally climbed again into the backseat of the ancient Packard.

It drove away from the house in a cloud of blue exhaust smoke.

"What was that all about?"

"When he missed you before dinner, General," Banning said, "General Sun told him that you had gone off to seek female companionship."

"Good God!"

"And when you came back," Banning went on, "General Chow asked Kee if you had found what you wanted and were satisfied with it. Kee assured him you had."

"General Chow was a little embarrassed that he hadn't thought of female companionship for you himself," General Sun said, smiling. "He apparently intends to make up for his oversight tonight."

"Jesus Christ!"

"With all respect, sir," Lieutenant Hart said. "I hope the General realizes that the reputation of the Marine Corps rests on the General's performance tonight."

"Oh, for God's sake, George," Pickering said, hoping he sounded properly indignant. He looked around the yard, spotted McCoy's ambulance—which did indeed have a "longitudinal scar" on the driver's door—and made a "come here" wave toward it.

McCoy and Zimmerman got out and walked to the door of the house. They saluted.

"General Sun, may I present Majors MeeKoy and Zimmerman of the 2035th Liaison Group?" Pickering said.

General Sun shook their hands and spoke to both of them in Chinese, asking each a question that required more than a monosyllabic reply.

He's checking their Chinese, Pickering quickly decided. *I would.*

"Please come in the house, gentlemen," General Sun said, switching to English. "We'll get something to drink—not that I need anything more—and then I hope you will tell me how I can be of assistance."

McCoy was prepared for this. There hadn't been much time to talk in the Inn of the Fattened Goose. Pickering had understood the necessity of getting back to General Chow's party as quickly as possible. But there had been time to explain why he and General Sun were in Yümen, and to tell McCoy that he was going to have to brief Sun about how his Gobi Desert plans were going, as well as solicit his advice and help with the other Chinese.

It took McCoy about ten minutes to explain what he planned to do. He went on to report that there was "gossip" about a caravan of "foreigners" making their way across the Gobi, and produced a map from the billows pocket of his Chinese Army tunic to show General Sun where the "gossip" indicated the "foreigners" were.

"I figure it will take, sir," McCoy said, "about five days

for the supply convoy to reach this point"—he punched at the map with a pencil—"where they have scheduled a rendezvous with a camel patrol currently operating in the Gobi. To be on the safe side, I'm planning on seven. And from that point to here"—he indicated again with the pencil—"another five or six days. There's some variables we won't know about until we get out there."

"What kind of variables?" Banning asked.

"I don't know how fast we can move, or how much time we're going to lose getting around arroyos and other obstacles. We're counting on ten hours of light a day. There may be more or less. It may snow. It probably will. There probably will be ice. All of that will slow us down. I don't want to use headlights, so I don't think we'll be able to move much at night, unless we have moonlight. There will be some moonlight, but we don't know how much cloud cover there will be, which means there might not be enough moonlight to drive."

"So what you're saying, Major," General Sun said, "is that it will take you something like two weeks from the time you leave here to reach the point where the Americans *may* be?"

"Yes, sir. That could vary. Downward say two days if we have a smooth desert, no ice or snow, and maybe a little moonlight. And upward for only God knows how long. We're going to go as far as we can on our fuel, and then get on the radio."

"And how soon do you plan to leave?" General Sun asked.

"At 0600, sir."

"Excuse me?"

"Six in the morning, sir."

"Tomorrow morning? More accurately, *this* morning?" General Sun asked incredulously.

"Yes, sir. We're going to rendezvous with the supply convoy about twenty miles out of town."

"I didn't know you were going so soon," Pickering said.

"You were told not to go into the desert without letting anyone know," Banning said.

"It was either go now, Colonel, or wait for ten days or two weeks. I decided to go."

Banning looked at Pickering to get his reaction to that. Seeing none, he correctly concluded that Pickering agreed with McCoy's decision. "What about communication?" Banning said.

"I'll get on the radio to Pearl Harbor when we find the Americans or run out of gas, whichever comes first," McCoy said. "Is that what you're asking, sir?"

"No, it wasn't," Banning said. "What if we have to communicate with you?"

"About what, sir?"

"Maybe we'll hear from the Americans, for one example."

"I don't think that's likely, sir," McCoy said. "We haven't heard from them for some time. Their radio is probably shot."

Or, they have been discovered by the Japanese, or murdered by bandits, or just starved to death out there, Pickering thought.

"We should have some way to communicate with you when you're out there, Ken," he said.

"Sir, neither Zimmerman nor I are very good with radios. Neither one of us takes code very fast, and we can't send any faster than we receive. And I'd really rather not run the risk of taking a radio from its case, setting it up, and then taking it apart again until we really need them to call Pearl Harbor."

"What kind of radios are they?" Captain Sampson asked.

"Special," McCoy said, looking at him as if on the verge of telling him to mind his own business.

"How special?" Sampson pursued.

"We got them from the Collins Radio Company. That's about all I know about them."

"I know about radios," Sampson said. "As a matter of fact, I know a lot about the shortwave radios Collins makes. So far as I'm concerned, they make the best short-wave equipment."

McCoy looked disgusted. "Who cares what you think?" was written all over his face.

"General," Sampson said, "I'd like to go with Captain McCoy, if he'll have me."

"To do what?" McCoy asked.

"Before my commission came through, I was a high-speed radio operator, a corporal, in the Signal Corps," Sampson said. "Before that, before the war, I was a Ham." He looked at McCoy. "I can send Morse at thirty words a minute, and take it that fast."

"You know how they work? Can you fix them if they break?" McCoy asked.

"I made a lot of my own equipment," Sampson said.

"General?" McCoy asked.

I'll be damned, Pickering realized, *McCoy is asking me if he can have Sampson.*

"It's up to you, Ken," Pickering said.

"The Chinese may not like it," Zimmerman said.

"I don't want to find myself in the middle of the god-damned Gobi Desert trying to call in the Catalinas with a radio that's not working," McCoy said.

Zimmerman shrugged. "Okay by me," he said.

"Okay by me, too, Sampson," Pickering said. "Thank you." He looked at his watch. It was quarter to two in the morning. "McCoy, if you're leaving in four hours, you'd better get some sleep," he said. "There's beds here."

"We've got to go back to the Fattened Goose and finish loading, sir," McCoy said. "We'll be able to sleep on the road."

"In that case, gentlemen," General Sun said, "let me wish you Godspeed and good luck."

"Thank you, sir," McCoy said.

Sun offered his hand to Zimmerman, who looked a little embarrassed.

"If you are really going with us, Sampson," McCoy said when General Sun reached him, "and it's not too late to change your mind, go get your gear."

The departure was completely without ceremony. General Pickering, Colonel Banning, and Major Kee, in the Packard Clipper, followed McCoy, Zimmerman, and Sampson in the ambulance back to the Inn of the Fattened Goose.

They stood in the snow while the Chinese "soldiers"

McCoy had hired lashed, under Zimmerman's direction, an astonishing amount of supplies—including ten five-gallon jerry cans, two fifty-five-gallon drums of gasoline, and an assortment of burlap sacks—wherever space could be found on the bumpers, fenders, and running boards of the weapons carrier and ambulance, and onto the roof of the ambulance.

Finally, Zimmerman walked up to the other Americans. "Anytime you say, Killer," he said.

Banning gave his hand to McCoy, and then to Zimmerman.

"You guys be careful," he said.

"We'll try," McCoy said.

"Consider that an order," Pickering said, touching McCoy's shoulder.

"Aye, aye, sir," McCoy said. He and Pickering looked at each other a moment, and then McCoy saluted. "By your leave, sir?"

Pickering nodded, and he, Banning, and Kee returned McCoy's salute, but no one said anything.

McCoy turned and gave an order in Chinese.

"Freely translated, sir," Banning said, "that was, 'Okay, let's get this circus on the road.' "

Major Kee chuckled.

The Chinese "soldiers" squeezed themselves into the back of the ambulance and the weapons carrier. McCoy pointed to Sampson, indicating that he was to ride with Zimmerman in the weapons carrier, and then climbed behind the wheel of the ambulance beside one of the Chinese. He slammed the door, started the engine, and drove off, with the weapons carrier following him.

As he turned into the street, McCoy tapped the horn in the rhythm of "Shave and a Haircut, Two Bits."

And then they were gone.

Though Pickering expected Brigadier General Sun Chi Lon to be in bed soundly asleep, the General was instead wide awake and waiting for him when Pickering, Banning, and Kee returned to the VIP Quarters. When they made their appearance Sun was wearing an ankle-length silk dressing gown and holding a brandy snifter. "Did they get off all right?" he asked.

"You wouldn't believe all the stuff they had lashed to their vehicles," Pickering replied. "To the bumpers, the fenders, on the roof . . ."

"Captain McCoy—or should I say Major MeeKoy?—obviously knows if you need something in the desert, you'd better take it with you," Sun said.

"He's a very clever fellow," Pickering said.

"His Chinese—Mandarin, Wu, and Cantonese—is impeccable," Sun said, his voice showing mingled surprise and admiration. "You don't often encounter Americans with that ability."

"You don't often encounter people like Captain McCoy," Pickering said.

"I have received an encoded message from USMMI-CHI," General Sun said. "I thought I would discuss it with you before we went to bed."

"What did it say?" Pickering asked.

"Actually, it's gibberish," Sun said. "It will say what I tell General Chow it says."

"I don't quite follow you," Pickering said.

"Whenever I make a trip like this, I arrange to receive one message a day," Sun said. "While I don't suggest that General Chow's cryptographic people would even think of attempting to decode a message addressed to me personally, if they did, they would fail. Not because the code is so good, but because the message is a random series of characters, having no meaning whatever."

"General, you're a devious fellow," Pickering said.

"You're surprised? I thought it was a rule of faith among Westerners that all Orientals are devious."

"Aren't you?" Pickering asked innocently.

Pickering was surprised when Major Kee touched his arm and handed him a brandy snifter.

"Thank you," Pickering said.

Kee handed Banning a snifter.

"To the success of Captain McCoy's mission," General Sun said.

"Hear, hear," Banning said.

They raised their glasses.

"I suggest that my message will say, General," Sun said, "that you and I are directed to report to General Stillwell immediately for consultation, even though this will require you to cut short your visit here."

"But the girls are coming tomorrow night," Banning said.

"And I was further going to suggest to General Pickering," Sun went on, "that he leave you here in his stead, so that at least you will be able to receive the briefing General Chow has scheduled."

"Please extend my regrets to the ladies, Colonel," Pickering said.

"If you stay for several days, Colonel, that will alleviate any suspicions General Chow might have about the real purpose of our trip here."

"I understand, sir," Banning said.

"Thank you very much, General," Pickering said.

"I think the time has come, don't you, after all we've been through together, that we can use our personal names?"

"Thank you very much, *Sunny*," Pickering said.

"You're entirely welcome, Fleming."

[THREE]
Headquarters
U.S. Military Mission to China
Chungking, China
1615 14 April 1943

As the C-47 taxied up to the area before base operations, the eyes of Brigadier General Fleming Pickering, USMCR, fell on Second Lieutenant Robert F. Easterbrook, USMCR, leaning on the fender of a Studebaker President staff car, cradling a 12-gauge trench gun in his arms. The sight brought a smile to his lips. *So the Easterbunny has seen Rutterman with one of the "people killers,"* he thought, *and is—the most sincere form of flattery—imitating him.*

What was incongruous, so far as Pickering knew, was

that Master Gunner Rutterman, who looked as if he had been sent over from Central Casting in response to a request for an actor who looked like a seasoned, veteran Marine, had yet to hear a shot fired in anger in this war, and nineteen-year-old Lieutenant Easterbrook had two Purple Hearts and the Silver Star.

It occurred to Pickering that Master Gunner Rutterman never referred to Easterbrook as "The Easterbunny" either. That privilege seemed to be reserved for those who had been with him on Guadalcanal.

After the airplane was parked, Easterbrook waited for Pickering to say good-bye to Brigadier General Sun Chi Lon and Major Kee, and then for their mountain of luggage to be loaded by their orderlies into the two cars sent to meet them, before coming over to Pickering and Hart. He saluted, then started to help Hart carry their suitcases to the car.

"You know how to use that shotgun, Bob?" General Pickering said, beating him to his own suitcase and picking it up.

"Yes, sir, I do," Easterbrook replied. "Did you know, General, that every one of those itty-bitty little balls it shoots—there's a dozen of them in every shell—is like a .32 pistol bullet? Just as powerful?"

"I think I remember hearing that somewhere," Pickering said.

"I have a hell of a time with the Thompson," Easterbrook went on. "I can't keep the muzzle from climbing. But I can handle a trench gun."

So much for my theory that the Easterbunny is aping Rutterman.

"Colonel Banning and that OSS captain still on the plane, sir?"

"Colonel Banning is at the moment learning more about the Thirty-second Military District than he really wants to know," Pickering said. "He won't be back for a couple of days."

"By now, the Colonel is probably working very hard to preserve the reputation of the Marine Corps," Hart said.

"That is quite enough on that subject, Lieutenant," Pickering said.

"Yes, sir," Hart said, unabashed.

"And McCoy took Sampson with him into the Gobi," Pickering said. "To work the radios."

"I'll be damned," Easterbrook said. "Did he want to go or did the Killer volunteer him?"

"He wanted to go," Hart said. "And Captain McCoy— who isn't happy when somebody calls him 'the Killer'— said he could go."

"I'm not too happy when people call me 'Easterbunny' either," Easterbrook said. "When the Killer stops calling me the Easterbunny, I'll stop calling him the Killer."

"The difference, *Lieutenant Easterbrook*," Hart said, smiling broadly as he slammed the trunk closed on their luggage, "is that you're a second lieutenant and he's a captain."

"McCoy wouldn't pull rank about something like that," Easterbrook said with absolute confidence.

Well, he's got McCoy figured correctly, Pickering thought. *There really is more to the Easterbunny than at first meets the eye.*

"There have been no messages for me, Bob?" Pickering asked.

"There's one, sir. I thought I'd wait until we got in the car, out of the wind. Will you drive, George?"

"Sure," Hart said.

That was an order, Pickering thought. *It was phrased as a question, but it wasn't even a request, it was an order.*

"I don't think you're going to like it very much, sir," Easterbrook added.

When they were in the backseat of the Studebaker together, and Pickering had read the two Special Channel messages, Pickering realized that Easterbrook was right. He didn't like what the Special Channel message said.

```
T O P  S E C R E T

FROM ACTING STACHIEF OSS HAWAII
11115 GREENWICH 13 APRIL 1943
VIA SPECIAL CHANNEL
DUPLICATION FORBIDDEN
```

TO BRIGGEN FLEMING PICKERING USMCR
OSS DEPUTY DIRECTOR FOR PACIFIC
OPERATIONS
THRU: US MILITARY MISSION TO CHINA
CHUNGKING

SUBJECT: PROGRESS REPORT NO. 3

1. RECEIPT OF YOUR MESSAGE SUBJECT:
IMPORTANCE OF LIAISON DATED 11 APRIL 1943
RELUCTANTLY ACKNOWLEDGED.

2. SUNFISH WITH METEOROLOGISTS,
EQUIPMENT, PLUS LT C.D. LEWIS AND CHIEF
MCGUIRE ABOARD DEPARTED PEARL HARBOR
0600 LOCAL TIME 11 APR 43. ETA RENDEZVOUS
POINT NOT SOONER THAN 25 APRIL. YOU WILL
BE ADVISED DAILY AS ETA IS REVISED BASED
ON POSITION REPORTS FROM SUNFISH AND
OTHER FACTORS.

3. FOLLOWING VOLUNTEER USMC AVIATORS
HAVE REPORTED ON TEMPORARY DUTY TO MAG-21:

WILLIAMSON, MAJ AVERY R. USMC (PENSACOLA
NAS)

WESTON, CAPT JAMES B USMC (PENSACOLA NAS)

PICKERING, 1/LIEUT MALCOLM S USMCR
(MEMPHIS NAS)

4. ADDITIONALLY, STEVENSON, 1/LIEUT
THEODORE J. USMC (VMF-229, EWA MCAS) HAS
VOLUNTEERED AND REPORTED ON TDY.

5. LT COL DAWKINS REPORTS THAT ALTHOUGH
WILLIAMSON, WESTON AND STEVENSON HAVE
EXTENSIVE CATALINA EXPERIENCE, THEIR
TRAINING AT EWA WILL CONTINUE ON A DAILY

```
BASIS UNTIL EXECUTION OF MISSION IS
ORDERED. THE 6 (SIX) US NAVY AVIATORS WHO
PARTICIPATED IN ONE OR BOTH RENDEZVOUS/
REFUELING DRY RUNS REMAIN ON TDY TO MAG-
21, AND ANY OF THEM WOULD BE AVAILABLE AS
A REPLACEMENT SHOULD ANY OF THE MARINE
AVIATORS REQUIRE REPLACEMENT.


RESPECTFULLY SUBMITTED


HOMER C. DILLON
MAJOR USMCR


T O P  S E C R E T
```

I have not yet recovered from my emotional reaction to watching Ken McCoy and Zimmerman—and Sampson—driving off into the Gobi—with that cheerful "Shave and a Haircut, Two Bits" tooting of the horn—and now this.

What motivates these young men? Don't they want to live?

"Bad news, sir?" Hart asked from the front seat.

"I'm trying to make up my mind," Pickering said. "Dillon sent us the names of the pilots who will fly the Catalinas."

"Something wrong with them?"

Good question. Yeah, there's something wrong with them. They're all crazy, the regulars, the Old Breed, McCoy, Zimmerman, and Weston, and probably this Major Williamson, and the amateurs, my son and his Harvard classmate, Sampson. They are perfectly willing, perhaps because they are Marines, and Marines are supposed to do heroic things, or perhaps because they consider that voluntarily taking enormous chances with their lives—this would apply to Pick and Sampson—is what is expected of them as members of the social elite. Or maybe just to prove to themselves that they are not only men but a special kind of men.

"There's a Major Williamson, from Pensacola, I don't know who he is. . . ."

"General, I don't know how I know this," Hart said. "But I think he's a pal of Captain Galloway," Hart offered. "He's probably all right."

That figures, both that he's a pal of Charley Galloway and "all right."

"And a fellow named Stevenson, who's in Galloway's squadron," Pickering went on.

Which means by definition . . . "One of Galloway's misfits?" Hart asked, surprised.

. . . one of Galloway's misfits.

"I don't think Galloway would volunteer this fellow for this to get rid of him," Pickering thought aloud. "Or that Colonel Dawkins, for that matter, would permit him to do that. So he's probably all right."

"Yes, sir," Hart agreed. "They both know how important this is."

"The other two officers, George, are Captain James B. Weston—"

"Our Captain Weston?" Hart asked incredulously.

"Our Captain Weston," Pickering confirmed. "And the fourth one is Pick."

"My God!" Hart said. "He didn't say anything to me when we were in Memphis."

"Or to me," Pickering said.

"You didn't say anything about Operation Gobi to him in Memphis, did you, George?"

"No, sir."

"Then I guess he just saw General McInerney's request for volunteers," Hart said. "And volunteered."

"What I can't understand is why they took him," Pickering thought aloud again. "I don't think he knows how to fly a Catalina."

He doesn't. That explains that business in Jake Dillon's Special Channel . . . Pickering picked up the Special Channel and read the last paragraph again.

. . . They know Pick does not have the "extensive experience" flying the Catalina that the other three have. What Jake is doing is telling me that Dawkins is doing all he can to give Pick the training he needs.

"They know what a hell of a pilot he is, General," Hart said. "That's why they took him. It won't take him long to learn how to fly a Catalina."

"And the same is presumably true of Jim Weston," Pickering said. "He was selected because he was the best man available for the job."

"Yes, sir."

And the selector was Mac McInerney. Who would base his decision on that alone. With no consideration of fairness, of sending someone who hadn't spent a year as a guerrilla in the Philippines instead of someone who did. Or sending someone who has never been in combat at all—or hasn't already flown an incredibly hazardous mission like Pick did with Galloway to Buka—in place of someone who has.

A general officer cannot permit himself to let his personal feelings interfere with his decisions, even when his decisions may send men to their deaths. Mac really likes Weston, and he showed at Memphis—again—how much he likes Pick. But he's a Marine General, and he can't let anything get in the way of his responsibilities.

So what does that make me?

The Easterbunny is getting next to me in the backseat of this staff car because I arranged it so that he wouldn't get himself killed storming some beach in the Solomons.

It makes me—because I would trade my life for a senior officer somewhere who would make the emotion-based decision to send someone else in place of Pick and Weston—a lousy general officer.

"Pick will be all right, General," Hart said, reading Pickering's mind. "And so will Weston. They walk between raindrops."

"Well, we'll soon find out, won't we, George?" Pickering said.

[FOUR]
The White House
Washington, D.C.
2315 16 April 1943

The President was sitting in his wheelchair in his dressing gown, lighting a fresh cigarette from the butt of another, when Admiral William D. Leahy, General George C. Marshall, and Colonel William J. Donovan were shown in.

He looks tired, Donovan thought.

"Good evening, Mr. President," Admiral Leahy said.

"What do we have here?" Roosevelt said, as he stuffed his fresh cigarette into an ivory holder and flashed his famous smile. "The Army, the Navy, and he who hears all evil, sees all evil, and speaks all evil?"

"Is that how you think of me, Mr. President?" Donovan asked.

"A poor attempt at humor, Bill," the President said. "I tend to tell terrible jokes when I am forced to make decisions I would rather not make."

There was no reply.

"Would anyone like coffee?" he asked. "Or something stronger?"

There was a chorus of "No, thank you, Mr. President."

"Let me see it, please," the President said.

Donovan reached into his interior pocket and handed the President a white, blank, unsealed, letter-size envelope.

Roosevelt took two sheets of typewriter paper from it. He glanced quickly at both of them. "Oh, we've heard from Halsey, too?" he asked.

"I thought we should wait for Admiral Halsey's recommendation before coming to see you, sir," Admiral Leahy said.

Roosevelt carefully read the messages.

```
T O P   S E C R E T - M A G I C

OPERATIONAL IMMEDIATE
1005 GREENWICH 16 APRIL 1943
DUPLICATION FORBIDDEN
```

FROM SUPREME COMMANDER SOUTH WEST
PACIFIC OCEAN AREAS
BRISBANE

TO CHIEF OF STAFF US ARMY
WASHINGTON
EYES ONLY GENERAL GEORGE C. MARSHALL

INFO COMMANDER-IN-CHIEF PACIFIC
PEARL HARBOR
EYES ONLY ADMIRAL CHESTER W. NIMITZ

SUBJECT: OPERATION FLYSWATTER, REQUEST
FOR PERMISSION TO EXECUTE

1. SUPREME HEADQUARTERS SWAPO HAS
INTERCEPTED AND DECRYPTED THREE (3)
MESSAGES FROM JAPANESE IMPERIAL GENERAL
STAFF DEALING WITH VISIT TO BOUGAINVILLE
BY ADMIRAL ISOROKU YAMAMOTO COMMANDER OF
JAPANESE COMBINED FLEET BY AIR ON 18
APRIL 1943, INCLUDING DESCRIPTION OF HIS
ROUTE, AIRCRAFT TYPE, AND ESCORT.

2. SUBJECT MESSAGES WERE CLASSIFIED IN
HIGHEST SECURITY CATEGORY. ANALYSTS
ATTACHED TO THIS HEADQUARTERS BELIEVE
THEM TO BE GENUINE, BUT SUGGEST THE
POSSIBILITY THAT THIS MAY BE A RUSE ON THE
PART OF THE JAPANESE WITH THE PURPOSE OF
DETERMINING WHETHER THE CODE USED HAS
BEEN COMPROMISED BY US. IF IT IS A RUSE,
ANY ACTION OF MINE TO INTERCEPT ADMIRAL
YAMAMOTO WOULD CONFIRM THAT WE HAVE
BROKEN THEIR CODE.

3. IT IS EMPHASIZED THAT MY ANALYSTS DO
NOT REPEAT DO NOT BELIEVE IT IS PROBABLE
THAT THE MESSAGES ARE A RUSE, SOLELY THAT
THIS IS A POSSIBILITY REPEAT POSSIBILITY
WHICH SHOULD BE CONSIDERED.

4. AT MY DIRECTION, A MISSION CODENAME
FLYSWATTER INVOLVING FOUR (4) ARMY AIR
CORPS LOCKHEED P-38 AIRCRAFT BASED IN THE
SOLOMON ISLANDS HAS BEEN PLACED IN
READINESS TO INTERCEPT AND DESTROY THE
YAMAMOTO AIRCRAFT OVER BOUGAINVILLE. I
HAVE BEEN ASSURED THE MISSION WOULD HAVE
A SEVENTY-FIVE (75) PERCENT CHANCE OF
SUCCESS.

5. IN VIEW OF THE RECENT POTENTIAL BREACH
OF MAGIC SECURITY AT US MILITARY MISSION
TO CHINA, IT IS SUGGESTED THAT THERE MAY
BE A TENDENCY TO ERR ON THE SIDE OF
CAUTION IN THIS CASE, BY DENYING ME
PERMISSION TO EXECUTE OPERATION
FLYSWATTER IN THE BELIEF THAT SO DOING
WOULD PROTECT MAGIC.

6. BRIG GEN PICKERING'S REPRESENTATIVE
WHO WAS IN CHUNGKING WITH GENERAL
PICKERING HAS INFORMED ME THAT BOTH HE
AND GENERAL PICKERING BELIEVE MAGIC WAS
NOT REPEAT NOT COMPROMISED BY THE RECENT
EVENTS AT US MILITARY MISSION TO CHINA. I
HAVE COMPLETE CONFIDENCE IN GENERAL
PICKERING'S JUDGMENT IN MATTERS OF THIS
NATURE.

7. NEVER BEFORE IN THE HISTORY OF NAVAL
WARFARE HAS THERE BEEN AN OPPORTUNITY TO
REMOVE A BRILLIANT AND FORMIDABLE
ADVERSARY SUCH AS ADMIRAL YAMAMOTO FROM
THE SCENE OF BATTLE, AND WE SHOULD NOT
FAIL TO TAKE ADVANTAGE OF THE OPPORTUNITY
TO DO SO BY TAKING COUNSEL OF OUR FEARS.

8. PERMISSION TO EXECUTE OPERATION
FLYSWATTER IS REQUESTED IN THE STRONGEST
POSSIBLE TERMS.

DOUGLAS MACARTHUR
GENERAL, US ARMY
SUPREME COMMANDER SOUTH WEST PACIFIC
OCEAN AREAS

T O P S E C R E T – M A G I C

"Douglas does have a way with words, doesn't he?" the President said, and turned to the second message, which was considerably shorter than MacArthur's.

T O P S E C R E T – M A G I C

OPERATIONAL IMMEDIATE
1635 GREENWICH 16 APRIL 1943
DUPLICATION FORBIDDEN

FROM COMMANDER IN CHIEF PACIFIC
PEARL HARBOR

TO CHIEF OF NAVAL OPERATIONS
WASHINGTON
EYES ONLY ADMIRAL WILLIAM D. LEAHY

INFO SUPREME COMMANDER SOUTH WEST
PACIFIC OCEAN AREAS
BRISBANE
EYES ONLY GENERAL DOUGLAS MACARTHUR

1. REFERENCE IS MADE TO TOP SECRET–MAGIC
MESSAGE FROM SUPREME COMMANDER SOUTH
WEST PACIFIC OCEAN AREAS TO EYES ONLY
CHIEF OF STAFF US ARMY SUBJECT OPERATION
FLYSWATTER, REQUEST FOR PERMISSION TO
EXECUTE DATED 16 APRIL 1943.

2. THE REFERENCED MESSAGES CONCERNING
ADMIRAL YAMAMOTO WERE INDEPENDENTLY
INTERCEPTED, DECRYPTED AND ANALYZED
HERE. ANALYSTS HERE CONCUR THAT MESSAGES

ARE GENUINE, AND SHARE CONCERN THAT THEY
MAY BE A RUSE.

3. THE UNDERSIGNED SHARES GENERAL
MACARTHURS CONFIDENCE IN BRIG GENERAL
PICKERING'S DAMAGE ASSESSMENT REGARDING
POTENTIAL BREECH OF MAGIC AT USMMCHI.

4. THE REMOVAL OF ADMIRAL YAMAMOTO FROM
COMMAND OF THE JAPANESE COMBINED FLEET
WOULD BE CATASTROPHIC TO JAPANESE
MILITARY AND NAVAL OPERATIONS, AND HIS
LOSS PER SE TO UNITED STATES ACTION WOULD
SERIOUSLY DAMAGE JAPANESE NAVAL PRESTIGE
AMONG THE JAPANESE PEOPLE.

5. THE UNDERSIGNED STRONGLY URGES THAT
THE CHIEF OF NAVAL OPERATIONS RECOMMEND
TO THE JOINT CHIEFS OF STAFF THAT GENERAL
MACARTHUR BE GIVEN AUTHORITY TO EXECUTE
OPERATION FLYSWATTER.

CHESTER W. NIMITZ
ADMIRAL, US NAVY
COMMANDER-IN-CHIEF, PACIFIC

T O P S E C R E T - M A G I C

"Halsey thinks MacArthur is right," the President said.
"Is that a unanimous feeling here, too?"

He looked at Donovan, who was the junior man present, for an answer.

"Mr. President, I don't think I should second-guess either Douglas MacArthur or Admiral Nimitz," Donovan
said.

"Go ahead, Bill, second-guess them."

"It boils down to a choice between a chance to eliminate Admiral Yamamoto or possibly, I emphasize possibly, compromise MAGIC."

"No, it doesn't," the President said. "The choice is between sharing Fleming Pickering's belief that MAGIC has not been compromised by those people in Chungking, or not believing him. I don't think we're in a position to cavalierly dismiss the possibility that the Japanese at least suspect we're reading their mail. A deception like this would be entirely appropriate if they did."

"We have no reason to believe we have given them any reason to be suspicious, except for the Chungking business," Donovan said.

"Do you think Pickering's right, or don't you?" Roosevelt asked, a tone of impatience in his voice.

"I'll go with Pickering's judgment, Mr. President," Donovan said after a perceptible pause.

Roosevelt nodded and looked at General Marshall.

"If we didn't take advantage of the opportunity, Mr. President—" General Marshall began.

"Even at the risk of confirming to the Japanese that we've broken their codes?" Roosevelt interrupted.

"Yes, Mr. President," General Marshall said.

"Admiral?" Roosevelt asked, turning to Leahy.

"This seems to be one of those very rare instances, Mr. President, where Admiral Nimitz and General MacArthur seem to be in complete agreement. I don't want to challenge their judgment."

"But, truth to tell, out of school, everybody's more than a little nervous with this, right?" Roosevelt said.

There were nods, and Donovan said, "Yes, sir, I am."

"And so am I," Roosevelt said. His cigarette had burned down close to his ivory holder. He snatched it out, dropped it into an ashtray, and stuffed a fresh cigarette into the holder.

"Okay," he said, as Donovan walked up to him with a cigarette lighter. "We'll do it. Admiral Leahy, send Douglas MacArthur the following: Direction of the President. Execute Operation Flyswatter."

"Aye, aye, sir," Admiral Leahy said.

"If that offer of a drink is still open, Mr. President?" Donovan said.

"Of course it is, Bill," the President said. "Now that we each can tell ourselves that when we made this decision we were stone sober."

XXIII

[ONE]
Somewhere in the Gobi Desert
Mongolia
1115 20 April 1943

The 32nd Military District supply column, sent to supply
the patrols it was operating in the Gobi Desert, consisted
of two jeeps (one at the head of the line of vehicles, the
other bringing up the rear); two GMC six-by-six two-and-
a-half-ton trucks, both towing five-hundred-gallon trailers;
three Studebaker open-bodied trucks carrying, four to a
truck, a dozen Mongolian ponies; and two Dodge three-
quarter-ton weapons carriers.

All of the vehicles were grossly overloaded, and there
had been frequent breakdowns during the six-day trip
from Yümen, almost all of them due to blown tires. The
repair technique was simple. The wheel with the blown
tire was removed and replaced with a spare wheel from
the half-dozen or so spares lashed to each vehicle. The
wheel with the blown tire was then moved to one of the

weapons carriers, now converted to a mobile tire-repair station. And the march was resumed. The blown tire was repaired, if possible, while on the march. But tires beyond repair were not without value in wartime China, and bad tires were lashed wherever space could be found.

The convoy stopped at nightfall. The Mongolian ponies were then encouraged—by the point of a bayonet—to jump from the Studebakers, and Chinese soldiers mounted four of them bareback and began a roving perimeter patrol. Other soldiers lit fires, and still others rigged pieces of canvas tarpaulin wherever they could, to provide shelter from the icy winds.

Breakfast in the morning was the same as dinner, rice with sweet peppers and onions and chunks of lamb and pork. After breakfast, bayonet jabs at their ribs—in the case of reluctant animals, at their genitals—encouraged the ponies to climb back on the Studebakers, and the march resumed.

The first day they met a Yümen-bound camel caravan. But after that, the convoy encountered no other travelers. After the second day, McCoy and the others in his party began to notice evidence of what they could expect to find farther into the Gobi. The desert all around them was windswept flat rock, huge sheets of it, with no landmarks at all. In some places large rocks were strewn about. But in most places the flat, indifferent landscape was broken by nothing at all but patches of snow where the wind had blown it.

There was, however—good news—very little ice. Probably, McCoy decided, because the snow would have to melt during the day and then freeze at night. But it was too cold during the day—and the wind was blowing so hard, keeping the snow moving—that the sun could not melt it.

The bad news was that the snow often covered the path they were following—it could not be called a road—making it frequently necessary for the convoy commander, a taciturn captain, riding in the lead jeep, to halt the convoy because he couldn't see the "road." When that happened, the trailing jeep scouted ahead of the convoy, making wider and wider sweeps through the shallow snow, until he found the faint signs marking the "road." Then the march resumed.

As they moved deeper into the desert—and this was also good news—McCoy and Zimmerman had both reached the conclusion that there was absolutely nothing suspicious about their ambulance and weapons carrier, which McCoy had put in the line of vehicles immediately behind the GMC trucks. They looked as if they were a perfectly ordinary part of the convoy.

When the convoy came to a halt on the morning of 20 April, McCoy expected that somebody had once again blown a tire or else that the "road" was again obscured by snow. But then Chinese soldiers started jumping down from the six-by-sixes and moving off to the side. When McCoy looked closer, he saw that they had stopped by fire-blackened rocks and were about to light fires.

That meant they had reached the point where they would rendezvous with the patrols out in the Gobi.

He got out from behind the wheel of the weapons carrier and went back to the ambulance. "I think we're here," he said to Zimmerman. "You go see Captain Whatsisname, and remind him that our deal was full tanks of gas and good tires all around. I'll go see that sergeant who seems to know where we're going and take another look at the so-called map."

"We're moving on now?" Captain Sampson asked.

"We can make five, six hours before dark," McCoy said.

"I can have the radio on the air in forty-five minutes, if I can get help to string the antenna," Sampson said.

"We're not going to do that," McCoy said simply.

"But they'll be expecting to hear from us," Sampson protested.

"Tonight, when we stop, you can set up the receiver," McCoy said. "I gave you the SOI. You can listen when they're scheduled to contact us and see if they have anything for us."

"They'll expect us to respond," Sampson said.

"We don't have anything to say," McCoy said reasonably. "And if we don't go on the air, nobody can hear us and wonder what's going on."

"But you were ordered to maintain communication," Sampson persisted.

"Easy, Killer," Zimmerman said, recognizing the look in McCoy's eyes.

"What you're going to do, Captain," McCoy said, "is wake up two Chinese. Station one in the back of the ambulance and one in the back of the weapons carrier. Tell them if they fall asleep while on duty, you will shoot them. Any questions?"

Sampson looked at him for a moment, then shrugged. "Yes, sir," he said.

"Then help Zimmerman make sure both gas tanks, and all the jerry cans, are full."

"Yes, sir," Sampson said. "Sir, may I ask a question?"

"Shoot."

"Why does Sergeant Zimmerman call you 'Killer'?"

"Because he kills people who give him trouble," Zimmerman replied, very seriously.

"Fuck you, Ernie!" McCoy flared.

Zimmerman growled in his chest. When he saw him smiling broadly, Sampson realized that this was a laugh. And then McCoy laughed.

"It's a long story, Sampson," McCoy said. "Maybe I'll tell you sometime."

McCoy set off in search of the sergeant who was in effect the convoy's navigator.

Fifteen minutes later, the ambulance and the weapons carrier pulled out of the line of vehicles in the convoy and drove alongside it. McCoy stopped to exchange a handshake and a salute with the convoy commander, then got back in the weapons carrier, tapped "Shave and a Haircut, Two Bits" on the horn, and drove farther into the Gobi Desert.

[TWO]
The Oval Office
The White House
Washington, D.C.
1645 24 April 1943

When Colonel William J. Donovan was shown in, the President was sitting in his wheelchair looking out the window into the garden. "Good afternoon, Mr. President," Donovan said.

Roosevelt spun the wheelchair around. "You don't look as if you've just learned the world is about to come to an end," he said. "So what's so important that you asked to see me right away?"

Donovan set his briefcase on a coffee table, unlocked it, took from it an unsealed white business-size envelope, and handed it to him. "Neither Admiral Leahy nor General Marshall was available to bring these to you, Mr. President, and I thought you would like to see them right away."

```
T O P S E C R E T - M A G I C

OPERATIONAL IMMEDIATE
1005 GREENWICH 23 APRIL 1943
DUPLICATION FORBIDDEN

FROM COMMANDER IN CHIEF PACIFIC
PEARL HARBOR

TO CHIEF OF NAVAL OPERATIONS
WASHINGTON
EYES ONLY ADMIRAL WILLIAM D. LEAHY

INFO SUPREME COMMANDER SOUTH WEST
PACIFIC OCEAN AREAS

BRISBANE

1. DURING THE PAST FIVE (5) DAYS, A TOTAL
OF THIRTY-ONE (31) MESSAGES, SEVENTEEN
```

(17) FROM THE JAPANESE HEADQUARTERS AT BOUGAINVILLE TO THE JAPANESE IMPERIAL GENERAL STAFF IN TOKYO, AND FOURTEEN (14) FROM JIGS TO BOUGAINVILLE USING THREE DIFFERENT HIGH LEVEL CODES, HAVE BEEN INTERCEPTED AND DECRYPTED, AND ANALYZED. ALL MESSAGES MADE REFERENCE TO THE SHOOTING DOWN OF ADMIRAL YAMAMOTO AS HIS TRANSPORT AIRCRAFT APPROACHED BOUGAINVILLE, AND TO THE RECOVERY OF HIS REMAINS AND PLANS TO HAVE THE REMAINS SENT TO JAPAN.

2. IN THE OPINION OF THE ANALYSTS, THE MESSAGES REFLECT BOTH THE CHAOS WHICH WOULD BE EXPECTED TO RESULT IF ADMIRAL YAMAMOTO HAD INDEED BEEN KILLED, AND ALSO POSSESS A CERTAIN TONE OF RESPECT FOR THE DECEASED ENTIRELY CONSISTENT WITH WHAT THE ANALYSTS WOULD EXPECT TO FIND IN SUCH CIRCUMSTANCES. THE ANALYSTS DO NOT REPEAT DO NOT BELIEVE THE MESSAGES ARE CONSISTENT WITH AN ATTEMPT TO DISSEMINATE FALSE INFORMATION.

3. FURTHERMORE, THE JAPANESE CONTINUE TO USE THE CODES THEY HAVE BEEN USING, AND HAVE NOT INTRODUCED ANY NEW CODES AS THEY WOULD HAVE HAD THE YAMAMOTO FLIGHT BEEN A RUSE. THIS LEADS THE UNDERSIGNED TO BELIEVE THAT THE MAGIC CAPABILITY IS NOT AT THIS TIME IMPAIRED IN ANY WAY.

CHESTER W. NIMITZ

ADMIRAL, US NAVY
COMMANDER-IN-CHIEF, PACIFIC

T O P S E C R E T - M A G I C

T O P S E C R E T

OPERATIONAL IMMEDIATE
VIA SPECIAL CHANNEL
1005 GREENWICH 23 APRIL 1943
DUPLICATION FORBIDDEN

FROM SUPREME COMMANDER SOUTH WEST
PACIFIC OCEAN AREAS
BRISBANE

TO CHIEF OF STAFF US ARMY
WASHINGTON
EYES ONLY GENERAL GEORGE C. MARSHALL

FOLLOWING PERSONAL FROM SUPREME
COMMANDER SWPOA TO CHIEF OF STAFF US ARMY

MY DEAR GEORGE:

I THOUGHT YOU WOULD BE INTERESTED TO KNOW
THAT I JUST DECORATED A FINE YOUNG ARMY
AIRCORPS OFFICER NAMED LANIER FROM
MONTGOMERY, ALABAMA, WITH THE
DISTINGUISHED FLYING CROSS. WHILE
LEADING A ROUTINE PATROL OF FOUR OF MY P-
38 AIRCRAFT NEAR BOUGAINVILLE HE SHOT
DOWN A JAPANESE TRANSPORT OF THE TYPE
NORMALLY RESERVED FOR THE USE OF SENIOR
JAPANESE OFFICERS. HIS FELLOW PILOTS
SHOT DOWN THREE OF THE TRANSPORT'S
ESCORTS AS WELL.

THE TRANSPORT AIRCRAFT CRASHED IN FLAMES
INTO THE JUNGLE, AND IN THE OPINION OF THE
PILOT WHO SHOT IT DOWN, THERE IS NO CHANCE
OF ANY SURVIVORS. ALL FOUR AIRCRAFT
RETURNED SAFELY TO THEIR AIRFIELD IN THE
SOLOMON ISLANDS.

```
I VERY MUCH APPRECIATE THE PRESIDENT'S
AND YOUR CONFIDENCE IN ME,

WITH BEST REGARDS,

DOUGLAS

END PERSONAL TO CHIEF OF STAFF, US ARMY
FROM SUPREME COMMANDER SOUTH WEST
PACIFIC OCEAN AREAS

T O P  S E C R E T
```

"Well, that is good news," Roosevelt said, "if it can ever be called good news to learn that my orders to have someone assassinated have been carried out successfully."

"You probably saved thousands of American lives, tens of thousands of American lives, more than that, by ordering the elimination of Admiral Yamamoto, Mr. President," Donovan said.

"It's a bit different, isn't it, Bill, when you know the name of the man you're having 'eliminated'? When you know what he looks like? That 'kill or be killed' seems a little remote from this office, doesn't it?"

"You saved lives, Mr. President," Donovan repeated.

"Do you think Fleming Pickering knows about this?"

"I don't think so," Donovan said. "I don't think either Admiral Leahy or General Marshall saw any need to bring Stillwell in on any of the Yamamoto business."

"You don't think Stillwell is going to be told?"

"I think that he'll be informed by a hand-delivered message, sir."

"Pickering's with Stillwell, right?"

"Yes, sir."

"How's his weather station operation coming?"

"It could be going a little better, Mr. President," Donovan said.

"In other words, something went wrong," Roosevelt said. "What went wrong, Bill?"

"I don't mean to suggest, sir, that the mission will fail,"

Donovan said. "But, unfortunately, it's looking more and more like something happened to the two men Pickering sent into the Gobi from Chungking."

"Explain that, please?"

"Captain McCoy and Sergeant Zimmerman left a town called Yümen with a Nationalist Army supply truck convoy headed into the desert to rendezvous with a patrol—a camel patrol—the Chinese operate in the desert."

"A *camel* patrol? Sounds like Lawrence of Arabia," Roosevelt said.

"Yes, sir. Pickering's idea was for McCoy and the other to travel with the supply convoy as far as it was going, then head out by themselves, looking for the Americans Pickering apparently believes are out there somewhere, until, in Pickering's words, they either found them or ran out of gas, whichever comes first. At that point they would attempt to establish contact with Pearl Harbor. Once contact was established, the seaplanes would attempt a rendezvous with a submarine at sea, where they would take on fuel, as well as the meteorologists and their equipment, and then fly into the Gobi. They would then try to put themselves within a hundred miles or so of McCoy and the other Americans, and from there they hoped to find them by homing in on a radio signal."

"Did you disapprove of this plan before Pickering put it into execution, or is this from the position of hindsight?" Roosevelt asked, not very pleasantly.

He knows and likes McCoy, Donovan thought. *McCoy and Jimmy Roosevelt are pals. They made the Makin Island raid together. I can't forget that.*

"I thought, sir, that the plan prepared by the OSS station chief in Chungking had a greater chance of success," Donovan said. "Unfortunately, it looks as if I was right."

"What did Pickering find wrong with the other plan?"

"He thought it would call too much attention to the weather station, sir."

"And what makes you think Pickering's plan has failed?"

"McCoy had orders to maintain communications with Pearl Harbor—his messages to be forwarded Special

Channel to Pickering in Chungking—and he has failed to do so."

"He hasn't been heard from at all?"

"No, Mr. President."

"And what happens now? Plan Two is put into execution?"

"Yes, sir. Before Pickering's men started out, another two sets of meteorological equipment and the personnel to operate it were procured. The people and the equipment are at the moment en route to Chungking—they're due there April thirtieth. When they arrive, we'll put the OSS plan into execution."

"The OSS plan versus the Pickering plan?" the President said. "Odd, Bill, I was under the impression that I had named Fleming Pickering Deputy Director of the OSS for Pacific Operations. Wouldn't that make his plan an OSS plan, too?"

"That was an unfortunate choice of words, Mr. President," Donovan said.

"Yes, it was," Roosevelt agreed. "And I was also under the impression that you and Pickering had put your differences aside for the duration."

"We have, sir. I take no pleasure in the failure of his plan."

"What exactly do you think has happened to young McCoy?"

"I have no idea, sir. There are bandits operating all over that area. That's one possibility. Another is that they had the bad luck to run into a Japanese patrol."

"You have no idea?" Roosevelt said sarcastically. "But, Bill, I count on you to know what I want to know. You're the director of the OSS."

"I'm sure that as soon as General Pickering hears anything, he will advise me."

"What about the supply convoy McCoy was with? Have they been heard from? Do they know anything?"

"The convoy will return to Yümen about the thirtieth, sir."

"Do you think that Fleming Pickering will have someone there to meet them, to see what they might know?"

"I'm sure he will, sir."

"How can you be sure?" Roosevelt asked. "You don't seem to have much faith in his ability to run an operation like this."

"I will recommend to General Pickering, sir, that he have someone on hand."

"Do that," Roosevelt said. "But don't make it a recommendation. He has a tendency, apparently, to ignore your recommendations. Tell him I said to do it."

"Yes, Mr. President."

"Thank you for coming in, Colonel," the President said, and turned his wheelchair back to the window overlooking the garden.

[THREE]

```
OPERATIONAL IMMEDIATE
ALL RECEIVING USNAVAL COMMUNICATIONS
FACILITIES RELAY TO CINCPAC
ATTENTION RADM WAGAM

GASSTATION ON STATION AS OF 0230
GREENWICH 25 APRIL 1943

PROCEEDING ACCORDING TO ORDERS

HOUSER, LTCMDR, USN COMMANDING
```

[FOUR]
Kiangpeh, Chungking, China
1325 26 April 1943

Brigadier General Fleming Pickering, USMCR, was playing chess with Second Lieutenant George F. Hart—not with any interest, but rather because he could think of absolutely nothing else to do—when Lieutenant Colonel

Edward Banning, USMCR, knocked at his open door.

"Ed, I hope you're going to tell me you've heard from McCoy," Pickering said.

"No, sir. Not a peep. But this just came in, and I thought you'd better see it right away.

```
T O P S E C R E T

OFFICE OF THE DIRECTOR
THE OFFICE OF STRATEGIC SERVICES
WASHINGTON
0324 GREENWICH 26 APRIL 1943
VIA SPECIAL CHANNEL

US MILITARY MISSION TO CHINA
EYES ONLY BRIG GEN FLEMING PICKERING,
USMCR

FOLLOWING PERSONAL FROM DIRECTOR OSS TO
BRIG GEN PICKERING

BEGIN MESSAGE

DEAR FLEMING:

THE PRESIDENT IS NEARLY AS HEARTSICK AS I
AM ABOUT THE BAD LUCK CAPTAIN MCCOY
APPARENTLY HAS HAD, AND VERY ANXIOUS FOR
INFORMATION OF ANY KIND REGARDING WHAT
HAS HAPPENED TO HIM.

BY DIRECTION OF THE PRESIDENT, IF YOU
HAVE NOT ALREADY MADE ARRANGEMENTS TO
HAVE SOMEONE WITH THE PROPER
QUALIFICATIONS MEET THE NATIONALIST ARMY
SUPPLY CONVOY ON ITS RETURN TO YÜMEN,
WITH THE EXPRESS PURPOSE OF LEARNING
WHAT, IF ANYTHING, THEY KNOW ABOUT
CAPTAIN MCCOY'S FATE, YOU WILL
IMMEDIATELY DO SO.
```

```
YOU WILL IMMEDIATELY ACKNOWLEDGE BY
SPECIAL CHANNEL RECEIPT OF THIS MESSAGE.
AS SOON AS POSSIBLE YOU WILL FURNISH BY
SPECIAL CHANNEL THE DETAILS OF YOUR
COMPLIANCE WITH THE PRESIDENT'S
DIRECTIVE. ALL REPEAT ALL INFORMATION
OBTAINED IN YÜMEN WILL SIMILARLY BE
DISPATCHED BY THE MOST EXPEDITIOUS
MEANS.


SIMILARLY, YOU WILL ADVISE ARRIVAL IN
CHUNGKING OF WEATHER PERSONNEL AND
EQUIPMENT, AND PROGRESS IN EXECUTING
BACK UP OPPLAN.


BEST REGARDS,
BILL


END MESSAGE

T O P   S E C R E T
```

Pickering looked up at Banning as he handed the Special Channel to Hart.

"I sent the 'we got it', sir," Banning said.

"I'd like to go up there myself," Pickering said. "God knows, I feel as useless as teats on a boar hog around here."

"You can't do that, sir," Hart said.

"I could send Colonel Platt," Pickering said.

"I wouldn't give the sonofabitch the satisfaction, sir," Banning said.

" 'Son of a bitch'?" Pickering quoted.

"You know the expression 'crocodile tears'?" Banning asked. "He calls twice a day to ask if we have any word from McCoy. He is always so very sorry to hear we haven't."

"Sampson is with McCoy," Pickering said.

"Sampson is the price he's perfectly willing to pay for having everybody know he was right in the first place."

"I hope you have been able to keep your distaste for Colonel Platt to yourself, Colonel," Pickering said.

"With great effort, sir."

After a moment, Pickering went on: "Easterbrook doesn't speak Chinese, and neither does George. Moore does, but Stillwell likes to bounce ideas about the Japanese mind off him. Rutterman doesn't speak Chinese. And I don't want to send any of Platt's people up there, unsure as I am about where their loyalties lie. That leaves you, Ed."

"Aye, aye, sir. What about getting there?"

"Send a Special Channel to Donovan over my signature. Tell him that I'm sending you. Take this Special Channel, and the one to Donovan, and show them to General Stillwell. He'll either get you on a plane, or get you your own plane. The Commander in Chief has spoken."

"Aye, aye, sir," Banning said. Something in his tone caught Pickering's attention.

"Say it, Ed," Pickering said.

"You don't want to go see General Stillwell yourself, sir?"

"I don't have the balls," Pickering confessed. "I just about promised him he wouldn't have to come up with two companies of Chinese infantry he can't spare, and now it looks like I'm going to have to ask him to do just that."

[FIVE]

T O P S E C R E T

VIA SPECIAL CHANNEL
1605 LOCAL TIME 30 APRIL 1943
DUPLICATION FORBIDDEN

FROM OSS DEPUTY DIRECTOR FOR PACIFIC
OPERATIONS
TO DIRECTOR OFFICE OF STRATEGIC SERVICES

WASHINGTON
EYES ONLY WILLIAM R DONOVAN

1 METEOROLOGICAL PERSONNEL AND THEIR
EQUIPMENT ARRIVED SAFELY BUT IN NEED OF
REST 1400 LOCAL TIME THIS DATE.

2. IT WILL BE NECESSARY TO MOVE THE
PERSONNEL AND THEIR EQUIPMENT TO YÜMEN BY
AIR. GENERAL STILLWELL HAS ARRANGED FOR A
14TH US AIR FORCE C-47 TO MAKE THE TRIP
DEPARTING CHUNGKING MORNING OF 1 MAY WITH
ETA YÜMEN LATE SAME AFTERNOON, PRESUMING
GOOD WEATHER.

3. LTCOL BANNING, PRESENTLY IN YÜMEN,
ESTIMATES STAGING OF DEPARTURE FROM
YÜMEN WILL TAKE TWENTY-FOUR HOURS AFTER
ARRIVAL OF NATIONALIST CHINESE INFANTRY
ESCORT. GENERAL STILLWELL ADVISES TROOPS
CANNOT BE MADE AVAILABLE BEFORE 0600 4
MAY 1943.

4. LTCOL BANNING FURTHER ADVISES THAT
ORIGINAL ETA OF SUPPLY CONVOY RETURNING
TO YÜMEN HAS BEEN INDEFINITELY EXTENDED
DUE TO WEATHER CONDITIONS AND OTHER
FACTORS, AND FURTHER THAT DESPITE
INTENSIVE EFFORT HE HAS BEEN UNABLE TO
DEVELOP ANY INTELLIGENCE REGARDING
LOCATION OF MCCOY.

FLEMING PICKERING, BRIG GEN USMCR

T O P S E C R E T

[SIX]
Somewhere in the Gobi Desert
Mongolia
0900 1 May 1943

Nothing but snow could be seen in any direction. Three days before, the skies had cleared following two days of intermittent blowing small-flake snow. When the sun came out, it came out brightly, reflecting off the snow. It didn't quite blind them, but it effectively limited their vision to about one thousand yards, less sometimes when the wind blew the snow especially hard.

McCoy's decision was to keep moving day and night, despite the snowfall.

It was very cold. The ambulance—designed to provide as much comfort as possible for the wounded—had a heater mounted on the firewall. The weapons carrier had an open cab and no heater. But those crowded onto the seat—McCoy, Sampson, and two of the Chinese—found a certain amount of warmth from the engine and transmission by draping a blanket over their laps.

They moved on what McCoy hoped was a dead easterly course, determined by a U.S. Army–issue compass. McCoy had no idea how much the metal mass of the weapons carrier was affecting the compass, but at least they were moving in a straight line. They used a kind of stop-and-go technique. That is to say, the ambulance would be stopped and used as a reference point while McCoy drove the weapons carrier ahead, making every effort to keep the tracks through the snow perfectly straight, moving as slowly as he could in third gear to conserve fuel.

In order to keep further control of all this, he also stationed one of the Chinese on top of the mountain of supplies and jerry cans in the back of the truck, with orders to instantly report if the tracks didn't make a straight line, or if he lost sight of the ambulance.

At night, they drove without headlights. Doing that proved to be not so difficult as he feared, after Zimmerman removed the lenses of a "blackout light" mounted on the front of the weapons carrier, from one at the rear, and from the one mounted on the front of the ambulance. The bare bulb on the front of the weapons carrier and the ambulance provided enough light for steering, and the bare bulb on the rear of the weapons carrier was bright enough to guide the driver of the ambulance—even at a thousand yards.

Anytime he had difficulty seeing the ambulance during the day—or its bare bulb at night—McCoy stopped and shut down the engine. The ambulance then caught up with him.

Because Zimmerman maintained—with the certainty of an article of religious faith—that after sixty seconds, more fuel was conserved by shutting an engine down and then starting it again, than by letting it idle, McCoy decreed to do that . . . but only so long as the batteries held up. And under no circumstances would both batteries be shut down at once. That way they could attempt to start a vehicle whose battery was exhausted by pushing it with the other vehicle.

In third gear each truck would go about fifteen miles per hour. That meant it took not quite three minutes for McCoy to drive the weapons carrier as far as he could without losing sight of the ambulance, and then it took the ambulance about that long to catch up. Thus the engines of each vehicle could be shut down for nearly three minutes during each stop-and-go cycle.

So far, the batteries of both vehicles seemed to be holding up, and McCoy was beginning to hope that the fuel-saving technique would work indefinitely. If a battery did become exhausted, he decided, he would get the vehicle started by pushing it. And then he'd try shutting the engines down every other time, or every third time. That way they'd have a running time of six or nine minutes to keep the batteries charged.

The move-stop-wait, move-stop-wait routine quickly became automatic and boring.

McCoy was startled when the Chinese lookout came crawling down from his perch.

He braked to a stop as the lookout began to climb over the passengers and windshield onto the hood, in the process striking with his boot the head of the Chinese soldier sitting next to Sampson. "Your mother is a whore who fucks dogs," the one kicked muttered in Cantonese.

After a glance at the rearview mirror, which proved he could see the ambulance clearly, McCoy turned his full attention to the lookout, who had by now made it onto the hood of the weapons carrier. He was pointing into the distance. McCoy stared hard but could see nothing.

Sampson stood up, awkwardly hanging on to the windshield frame. "There's a guy on a horse out there," he said, and corrected himself: "On a pony."

McCoy finally saw the same thing, as the man and the pony suddenly came to life and trotted off into the distance. They were lost to sight within seconds because of the glare.

"What the hell was that?" Sampson said.

"He was probably as surprised to see us as we were to see him," McCoy said. "What was he, an outrider?"

"If he was, he saw us, that's for sure."

McCoy put the weapons carrier in gear again and resumed moving. As he stopped to let the ambulance catch up, the pony and its rider came into sight again. Not moving, just watching.

The ambulance began to move.

"What do we do now?" Sampson asked.

"Wait," McCoy said.

The ambulance caught up with them two minutes or so later.

The rider on the pony moved toward them.

"He's not afraid of us, obviously," Sampson said. "Is that good or bad?"

"He's got a rifle slung over his shoulder," McCoy said.

He suddenly pushed himself out of the seat and started to climb over the windshield.

"Let them see that we have soldiers with rifles," he ordered. "But for God's sake, don't point a rifle at him. If he unslings his rifle, be prepared to kill him."

McCoy climbed onto the hood, then slid forward and climbed down to the ground over the jerry cans and burlap sacks tied to the bumper.

He held his hands away from his body to show that he wasn't holding a weapon, and walked toward the man on the pony.

The man on the pony started to unsling his rifle, then changed his mind. He waited for McCoy to approach.

The man on the pony had a full beard, and in the moment it occurred to McCoy that few Chinese had luxuriant beards, it occurred to the man on the pony that the Chinese officer approaching him with the flaps of his cap tied under his chin had a white man's skin.

"Major," the man on the pony said in Cantonese, "do you speak English?"

"Who are you?" McCoy replied in Cantonese.

The man didn't reply.

"Do you speak English?" McCoy asked in English.

"Yes."

"Are you American?" McCoy asked.

"Yes. Are those American Army vehicles?" ·

"Actually, they're Marine Corps vehicles," McCoy said. "Does the name Sweatley mean anything to you?"

"Sergeant Sweatley?"

"Sergeant James R. Sweatley," McCoy amplified.

"He's the tactical officer," the man on the pony said.

"What does that mean?" McCoy asked, and then, without giving the man on the pony a chance to reply, "Where is Sweatley?"

The man on the pony gestured over his shoulder. "We're not moving," he said. "Waiting for the snow to blow away."

"Let's go to see Sergeant Sweatley," McCoy said. "How many of there are you?"

"You *are* an American, right?" the man on the pony asked.

"I'm an American," McCoy said. "Get going."

He waved at the weapons carrier to come after him.

The man on the pony turned the animal and started

moving off. The weapons carrier and the ambulance followed him.

Twenty minutes later, they came to a circle of wagons covered with snow. Smoke and steam rose from inside some of the wagons.

If we had passed this five hundred yards to either side, we never would have seen it.

The man on the pony kicked it in the ribs, and it moved a little more quickly toward the circle of wagons.

"Americans!" the man shouted. "Americans!"

Then he rode the pony inside the circled wagons. Several people appeared, some peering out of the tarpaulins covering the wagons, some brave enough to come out of the circled wagons to stare as the two vehicles drove up. Some of these had weapons, but no one brandished them threateningly.

McCoy dropped off the weapons carrier and walked up to them.

"I'm looking for Sergeant James R. Sweatley, formerly of the Marine detachment in Peking," McCoy said to an older man who looked as if he might be in charge.

"Go get Sweatley," the man ordered. "I'm Chief Frederick Brewer. I transferred to the Fleet Reserve off the *Panay.* Who are you?"

"My name is McCoy," McCoy said, and was interrupted by a tall, dark-haired woman.

"Oh, my God!" she said.

McCoy knew who she was.

"Corporal McCoy," she said. "Do you remember me? I was Mrs. Edward J. Banning. My husband was a captain in the Fourth Marines. You once came to our apartment."

"It's Lieutenant Colonel Banning now, Milla," McCoy said. "You're still Mrs. Banning. It's good to see you, Milla."

"Oh, my God! Ed is alive?"

"Yes, ma'am. He's alive. Is Zimmerman's wife here? Their kids?"

Milla nodded, unable to find her voice.

"Ernie," McCoy called, raising his voice. "Mae Su and the kids are here!"

Zimmerman came out of the ambulance and ran toward the circle of wagons.

"I'll be a sonofabitch," Sergeant James R. Sweatley, USMC, said, walking up as he shrugged into an ankle-length sheepskin coat.

"Hello, Sweatley," McCoy said, offering his hand. "Good to see you."

"Killer fucking McCoy in the fucking flesh!" Sweatley said. "What the *fuck* are you doing here, Killer?"

McCoy pulled his hand back. "It's Captain McCoy to you, Sergeant," he said icily. "And my first order to you is to watch your mouth in the presence of a lady. And don't you ever call me Killer again." He stared Sweatley down and turned to Chief Brewer. "Are you in charge here, Chief?"

"Yes, sir."

"Let's go find someplace to talk out of the cold," McCoy said. "We've got a lot to do." He turned to Sergeant Sweatley. "There's an Army officer getting a radio out of the back of the ambulance," he said. "Make yourself useful to him."

"Aye, aye, sir."

[SEVEN]
Naval Communications Facility
U.S. Naval Base, Pearl Harbor
Oahu, Territory of Hawaii
0530 Local Time 1 May 1943

"Flag officer on the deck!" the radioman first class called, as he rose to his feet from behind his desk in the foyer of the building.

"As you were," Rear Admiral Daniel J. Wagam, USN, said quickly, and then asked, "Commander Toner?"

"Right here, Admiral," Commander Lewis B. Toner, USN, said. "Good morning, sir."

Admiral Wagam needed a shave, and when he removed his gold-heavy uniform cap, his short hair was uncombed.

Commander Toner also suspected that Admiral Wagam's white uniform was the one he had worn the day before.

"Good morning," Wagam said. "What have you got?"

"Contact, sir. Not much more than that. If you'll come with me, sir?"

He pointed to a steel door that had a large AUTHORIZED PERSONNEL ONLY BEYOND THIS POINT sign on it.

Wagam looked at the radioman first class. "A Major Dillon of the Marines is on his way here. See that he gets to wherever I'm going."

"Aye, aye, sir."

He followed Commander Toner through the steel door and down a corridor. They came to a Marine PFC armed with a Thompson guarding a second door.

"Open it," Commander Toner ordered.

The Marine pushed the lever of an intercom. "Passing the duty officer and an admiral," he announced.

Bolts were slid open, and then the door was pushed inward. Toner waved Admiral Wagam into a large room. There was the peculiar odor of high voltage. A dozen sailors sat before communications radios, some working telegraph keys, others pounding typewriters. Two radio Teletype machines clattered against the wall.

Toner led Wagam to a glass-walled office with a sign reading DUTY OFFICER. Inside was a desk, two chairs, a chief petty officer, and a seaman first class who looked about seventeen years old and very nervous.

The chief put a china mug quickly on the desk.

"Good morning, Chief," Wagam said. "I'd kill for a cup of coffee."

"Aye, aye, sir," the chief said, stepped to the door, and ordered, "Coffee, now!"

"Good morning, son," Wagam said to the young sailor.

"Epstein, sir," the kid said. "Lester J. Seaman, First Class."

"What have you got for me, Epstein?" Admiral Wagam asked.

Seaman Epstein thrust at Admiral Wagam a sixteen-inch-long sheet of yellow paper, obviously torn from the roll of paper that had been fed into his typewriter.

0426

20 METER MONITOR

KCG TO KNX
KCG TO KNX

GA *GO AHEAD*

KCG TO KNX VERIFIER GYPSY ACK

STAND BY

ACK VERIFIER G A

KCG TO KNX

FIVE THREE FIVE THREE *READING ME SX3*

ONE ONE ONE ONE *SOI 21*

ACK

READING YOU SX5 ACK USING SIG OP ONE

KCG TO KNX

ZERO ONE ZERO ONE

ALL WELL IN CONTACT WITH GYPSIES

ZERO EIGHT FIVE SEVEN ZERO EIGHT FIVE SEVEN

ALL WELL WITH GYPSIES STRENGTH S7

ONE ABLE TWO FOUR ONE ABLE TWO FOUR

MEN 24

ONE BAKER THREE THREE ONE BAKER THREE THREE

WOMEN AND CHILDREN 33

TWO ABLE 1456 X 3401 TWO ABLE 1456 X 3401
NOT RELIABLE

MAP COORDINATES 1456X 3401 NOT RELIABLE

TWO DOG SEVEN TWO DOG SEVEN

WILL RETURN TO NET IN SIX HOURS

ACK

ALL ABOVE ACKNOWLEDGED

KCG OFF

The chief handed Admiral Wagam a cup of coffee. "We
didn't have much time, sir, to clean that up for you, sir,"
he said. "Can you read his handwriting? The material he
took from the Signal Operating Instruction? What he sent
to them?"

"I can read it just fine, Chief," Admiral Wagam said.
He smiled at Seaman Epstein. "Well done, son."

Seaman Epstein flushed. "Can I ask a question, Admiral?" he asked, which earned him a withering glare
from the chief.

"Sure," Admiral Wagam said.

"Who are these gypsies?"

"Mostly, son, they're a group of old sailors and soldiers
and Marines who didn't like the idea of surrendering to
the Japanese. And until they talked to you, I suspect many
of them were beginning to wonder if the Navy had forgotten about them."

Which raises an entirely new question, Admiral Wagam
thought. *How the hell are we going to get thirty-three
women and children—not to mention the men—out of the
Gobi Desert?*

"May I have this?" Admiral Wagam asked, holding up
the sheet of yellow paper.

Commander Toner looked uncomfortable.

"I'll get it back to you," Admiral Wagam said. "I think Admiral Nimitz will want to have a look at it."

"Of course, sir."

"When Major Dillon shows up, send him over to my office."

"Aye, aye, sir," Commander Toner said.

"Keep up the good work, son," Admiral Wagam said to Seaman Epstein. "Thank you for the coffee, Chief."

Jake Dillon drove up in a civilian Ford station wagon as Admiral Wagam was about to get into a staff car.

He looks, damn him, despite the hour, Admiral Wagam thought, *as if he's about to go on parade.*

"Follow me to my quarters, Dillon, and you can read what we have. Admiral Nimitz said to let him know immediately of developments, whatever the hour; but he's going to have to wait until I have a shave and get into a decent uniform."

"Aye, aye, sir," Dillon said. "Good news or bad, Admiral?"

"I suppose that would depend, Major, on whether or not you are a pilot who's about to be ordered to find a submarine in the Yellow Sea and then somebody in the Gobi Desert."

The Commander in Chief, Pacific, in a crisp white uniform, was having a cup of coffee when Admiral Wagam and Major Dillon were shown into his office.

"This is the original, sir, I hope you'll be able to understand the jargon."

"It may come as a shock to you, Dan, but before I got this job, I was actually a seagoing sailor. Let me see what you have."

"Aye, aye, sir."

"Help yourself to some coffee, Dillon," Admiral Nimitz said. "The steward doesn't come on duty until 0630."

"Thank you, sir."

Nimitz read the long sheet of yellow paper. "I don't like that 'unreliable' position report," he said.

"They're going to be in contact again in five hours, sir,"

Wagam said. "Perhaps they'll be able to give us a better one then."

"But this means, as I read it, that neither Pickering's people, nor the people they found, seem to know exactly where they are."

"Yes, sir, it would seem so."

"Is this position, the unreliable one, within range of the Catalinas?"

"Yes, sir."

"Then I suppose you'd better alert Colonel Dawkins, and start this thing rolling."

"Aye, aye, sir."

"As I recall the Opplan, the aircraft will depart at midnight to give them daylight both at the rendezvous site and in the desert?"

"Yes, sir," Wagam said. "The exact time is 2330, sir."

"Then we still have time to get them off today," Nimitz said. "But I'd like an on-site weather report from the *Sunfish* before we send them."

"Aye, aye, sir."

"Tell Colonel Dawkins to prepare for a 2330 departure," Nimitz ordered. "Subject to change. And get off a Special Channel personal to General Pickering. We were expecting contact before this, and he's probably concerned."

"Aye, aye, sir," Admiral Wagam said.

XXIV

[ONE]
Kiangpeh, Chungking, China
1115 2 May 1943

"Good morning, General," Lieutenant Colonel Richard C.
Platt said, saluting as he came through the door of McCoy's
house.

"Thank you for coming so quickly," Pickering said.
"To get right to the point, get word to Yümen immediately
that the expedition is not to move into the desert until
further orders."

"Is that wise, sir?" Platt said.

"The proper reply in the Marine Corps to an order is
'Aye, aye, sir,' which means the order is understood and
will be obeyed. What do they say in the Army, Colonel?"

"Sir, no disrespect was intended. But under the circumstances, sir, I felt obliged—"

"The circumstances? Meaning that Captain McCoy has
not been heard from, and that we must reluctantly conclude that he has been lost in a futile hunt for Americans

who we must also reluctantly conclude are lost?"

"Yes, sir."

"In the Marine Corps, Colonel, if we feel an explanation of an order is necessary, we say, 'Aye, aye, sir. May I ask to be told the reason?' If you had done that, Colonel, I would have shown you this." He handed Colonel Platt the most recent message to have come over the Special Channel.

```
T O P S E C R E T

CINCPAC HAWAII
VIA SPECIAL CHANNEL
DUPLICATION FORBIDDEN
0700 LOCAL TIME 1 MAY 1943

US MILITARY MISSION TO CHINA
EYES ONLY BRIGGEN FLEMING PICKERING,
USMC

BEGIN PERSONAL FROM RADM WAGAM TO BRIG
GEN PICKERING

DEAR FLEMING:

AT 0430 THIS MORNING CINCPAC WAS
CONTACTED BY MCCOY. HE IS IN GOOD SHAPE
AND WITH THE GYPSIES, WHO NUMBER FIFTY-
SEVEN (57) INCLUDING THIRTY-THREE (33)
WOMEN AND CHILDREN WHO ARE ALSO IN GOOD
SHAPE.

REFERENCE OPPLAN GOBI DESERT MAP OVERLAY
NUMBER THREE, HE GIVES HIS COORDINATES AS
1456 × 3401 REPEAT 1456 × 3401 BUT STATES
THEY ARE UNRELIABLE. HOWEVER EVEN
ALLOWING FOR A TWO HUNDRED (200) MILE
ERROR THIS POSITION IS WITHIN CATALINA
RANGE.
```

ANOTHER CONTACT IS SCHEDULED IN SEVERAL
HOURS, AND PERHAPS HE WILL BE ABLE TO
FURNISH A MORE PRECISE LOCATION AT THAT
TIME.

ADMIRAL NIMITZ HAS ORDERED THE CATALINAS
TO BE PREPARED TO DEPART AT 2330 1 MAY BY
WHICH TIME WE SHOULD HAVE AN ON-SITE
WEATHER REPORT FROM *SUNFISH*, WHICH WILL
ALSO BE ADVISED OF CATALINA ETA ON SITE.

I WILL OF COURSE KEEP YOU ADVISED OF ALL
DEVELOPMENTS.

BEST PERSONAL REGARDS,
DAN

END PERSONAL FROM RADM WAGAM TO BRIGGEN
PICKERING

T O P S E C R E T

"This is very good news, General," Colonel Platt said.
"Yes, I thought so. That will be all, Colonel, you are
dismissed."

[TWO]
United States Submarine *Sunfish*
121° 03" East Longitude 39° 58" North Latitude
Yellow Sea
1025 2 May 1943

Since he'd come aboard the *Sunfish*, Chief Carpenter's
Mate Peter T. McGuire, USNR, had to some extent increased his knowledge of the customs of the Naval Service. Thus as he stuck his head through the port leading
to the conning tower, he politely inquired, "Permission to
come up, sir?"

Lieutenant Commander Warren T. Houser, USN, and

Lieutenant Chambers D. Lewis III, USN, looked down at him. Except for his face, Chief McGuire was bundled in cold-weather gear, including a parka with a wolf fur–trimmed hood. All of those on the conning tower were wearing cold-weather gear. "Permission granted," Captain Houser said.

The third man on the conning tower, the chief of the boat, chief bo'sun's mate Patrick J. Buchanan, did not look at Chief McGuire. Chief Buchanan had come to loathe and detest Chief McGuire—who had the bunk immediately above his—virtually from McGuire's first moment aboard. He did not wish to look at him. If he never saw him again in his life, it would be too soon.

These feelings were perhaps not very charitable, and he knew it. He was well aware that some lesser human beings were simply not equipped by their Maker to sail aboard submersible vessels. In fact, he was usually quite sympathetic to their plight. But Buchanan's patience and understanding had been pushed beyond his limits.

Early on, Captain Houser explained to him that Chief McGuire suffered from claustrophobia, a malady that was unsuspected until the first time the *Sunfish* slipped beneath the surface. There was simply nothing to be done about it, Houser elaborated. They were just going to have to deal with it for the duration of the patrol.

Chief McGuire's symptoms went far beyond a feeling of unease at being contained, at feeling that the walls, so to speak, were closing in on him. There were psychosomatic manifestations. He had severe headaches, for one thing.

For another, he suffered psychosomatic gastric problems, including nausea, flatulence, and diarrhea. In Chief Buchanan's many years at sea, during many patrols on submarines, he had never before encountered smells as foul as those he encountered when visiting a head vacated as long as a half hour before by Chief McGuire.

For another, Chief McGuire's sleep was disturbed. He tossed and turned as long as he was in the sack, and he frequently whimpered in his sleep, like a small child having a bad dream. It is not pleasant under any circumstances to take one's rest in a small, confined area with one's nose separated from the man above by not more than twenty inches. When the man above is whimpering or breaking wind, or worse, regurgitating without warning and with astonishing force ninety percent of what he ate at the last meal, it is even less pleasant.

Chief Buchanan often thought that in the old Navy—and maybe even today, on say a destroyer, or other smaller man-of-war—the problem would have solved itself. The chief would have fallen overboard. The skipper would have penned a letter of condolence to his next of kin, authorized the auctioning off of the contents of the chief's sea chest, conducted a brief memorial service, and that would have been the end of the sonofabitch.

"How are you feeling, Chief?" Lieutenant Lewis asked.

Lewis actually showed sympathy to the bastard, as did Captain Houser. And Lewis was even genuinely worried about the state of Chief McGuire's health generally and his mental health specifically. McGuire had lost perhaps twenty-five pounds, and there were deep black rings under his eyes. No one on a submarine has an enviable tan, but McGuire's skin was an unhealthy white.

"I'm all right," McGuire said, not very convincingly. "It's only when I'm downstairs and they close the hole in the roof that I start getting sick."

"Well, if everything goes all right in the next hour or so, Chief," Captain Houser said, "we'll be on our way home."

"I hope," Chief McGuire said, and then broke wind. The sound immediately penetrated his cold-weather gear. By the time the odor inevitably followed, the skipper of the *Sunfish*, her chief of the boat, and Mr. Lewis, her supercargo, all had independently decided to look in the direction of the prevailing wind to see what might be out there.

"Bridge, Radio," the squawk box went off.

To provide Chief McGuire with a space on the bridge, Captain Houser had decided to dispense with the services of the talker who normally would have relayed commands from the bridge.

Captain Houser bent over the squawk box, pressed the switch, and said, "Radio, go."

"Captain, I have a faint signal on the aviation frequency, transmitting G.S."

"Radio, send five G.S. signals at thirty-second intervals," Captain Houser asked.

"Aye, aye, sir," the radio operator replied.

"You don't suppose they've actually found us, and on schedule?" Lieutenant Lewis asked.

"You don't believe in miracles, Mr. Lewis? Shame on you," Captain Houser said.

"Captain, I've been thinking," Chief McGuire said.

"Not now, Chief, please," Captain Houser said.

"That maybe I could go with the airplanes," McGuire plunged ahead.

"I thought you got sick on airplanes, Chief," Lieutenant Lewis asked.

"Not as sick as I am on here," McGuire replied. "And anyway, Flo gave me some inner-ear airsickness pills."

Captain Houser held up his finger before Chief McGuire's pale face and said, "Sssssssh!"

"I believe, Captain," Lieutenant Lewis said, "that Chief McGuire is referring to Commander Florence Kocharski, of the Navy Nurse Corps."

Commander Kocharski had confided in Lieutenant Lewis that the inner-ear seasickness pills she had given Chief McGuire were placebos, usually prescribed for women in the early stages of pregnancy. Sometimes, Flo said, they stopped morning sickness and sometimes they didn't. But they wouldn't do Chief McGuire any harm.

"Thank you, Mr. Lewis, I never would have guessed."

"Bridge, Radio."

"Go."

"Aircraft sent Verifier Sea Gypsy. It checks."

"Continue sending G.S. at thirty-second intervals."

"Aye, aye, sir."

"I hope he's not far away," Houser said, almost to himself. "I don't like sitting out here like this."

"There's supposed to be *two* of them," Chief McGuire said. "*Two* Catalinas."

"What do I have to do to make you shut up, McGuire?" Captain Houser flared, and was immediately sorry.

McGuire's face was that of a kicked child. A *sick* kicked child.

"Sorry, sir."

Chief Buchanan suddenly stopped in his binocular sweep of the skies, moved to the port bulkhead, and rested his elbows on it.

"Got anything, Chief?" Lieutenant Lewis asked.

"I have two objects at estimated two miles."

Captain Houser pressed the lever on the squawk box. "Suit up the deck crew. Notify when ready." This command was necessary because it was too warm in the interior of the *Sunfish* for the deck crew to put on their cold-weather gear until they were needed.

"Two Catalinas at two miles," Chief Buchanan said.

Captain Houser reached inside his hood and came out with a cord for his earphones. He plugged it in, then picked up a microphone. "Sea Gypsy One, this is Gas Station."

"We have you in sight, Gas Station. What are the seas?"

"The seas are three-to-four-foot swells. The wind is from the north at estimated twenty miles," Houser replied.

"We'll turn into the wind and have a shot at it," the pilot replied.

Captain Houser pressed the squawk box switch. "Pass the word, aircraft in sight," he said. Then he looked at Lieutenant Lewis. "Would there be space? Weight-wise?"

"I'd say the chief weighs about thirty-five gallons of avgas," Lewis said, and then added: "He's really sick, I think."

"Yeah," Captain Houser said thoughtfully. "McGuire, make up your mind. Do you really want to go on one of the airplanes? You know where they're going."

"Yes, sir," Chief McGuire said. "I think I could probably make myself useful, sir. Maybe help the weather people. Keep their generator working. I can fix practically anything—"

Houser held up his finger again. "Sssssh!"

"Do you think they could make do with one less meteorologist?" Lieutenant Lewis asked.

"I don't think we could go that far," Houser said. "But that would be your decision, wouldn't it, Mr. Lewis?"

He bent to the squawk box. "As soon as the deck crew goes on deck, suit up the supercargo," he ordered.

"The first one's down, Skipper," Chief Buchanan reported.

Captain Houser looked. The first Catalina had not only landed but had slowed enough for her pilot to start turning toward the *Sunfish*. As Houser watched, the second touched down.

He bent over the squawk box. "Deck crew on deck, break out and prepare to launch rubber boats. Suit up the supercargo. Prepare to pass cargo onto the deck."

He picked up the microphone. "Sea Gypsy One, what would an additional two hundred and fifty pounds do to you?"

"That would depend. Any change in our coordinates?"

"No."

"We can handle another two hundred and fifty pounds."

"Thank you," Houser said. "McGuire, your decision. You want to go?"

"Yes, sir."

"Then go below, and have someone show you how to go on deck."

"Aye, aye, sir," Chief McGuire said. "Thank you, Captain." He saluted, which Captain Houser returned. Then he saluted Lieutenant Lewis, which Lewis returned. "I'm sorry to have been such a mess, Buchanan."

Chief Buchanan turned and looked at him, then put out his hand. "Take care of yourself, Chief," Buchanan said. "Don't take any wooden nickels or anything."

[THREE]

```
OPERATIONAL IMMEDIATE
ALL RECEIVING USNAVAL COMMUNICATIONS
FACILITIES RELAY TO CINCPAC
ATTENTION RADM WAGAM

RENDEZVOUS SUCCESSFULLY COMPLETED IN ALL
ASPECTS. SEA GYPSIES DEPARTED 1105 LOCAL
TIME.
```

> WILL CONDUCT ROUTINE PATROL ACTIVITIES
> EN ROUTE TO PEARL HARBOR.
>
>
> HOUSER, LTCMDR, USN COMMANDING

[FOUR]
Somewhere in the Gobi Desert
Mongolia
1500 2 May 1943

For the past several hours, people had been removing all
the supplies stored inside the ambulance—and lashed all
over its outside—and then distributing them among the
wagons and carts of the caravans. Doing all that had converted the ambulance into the radio room of what, if
everything went well, would be known as Station Nowhere. The single radio in the rear of the ambulance at
the moment was one of the two small portable radios designed and built by Collins Radio to be transported on
camelback. It was connected by a cable to a stationary
bicycle–driven generator set up just outside the rear doors
of the ambulance.

A long wire antenna came out of the passenger window, the other end fastened to the three-quarter-ton weapons carrier. It was a jury rig, but it worked. Proper,
collapsible antenna masts and more powerful radios were
aboard the Catalinas. According to their last contact with
Pearl Harbor, these had left Pearl Harbor just before midnight the day before.

It was now time to find out if they had found the *Sunfish* a hundred miles off the coast of China in the Yellow
Sea, had landed, and more important, had taken off again,
and when.

So far as McCoy was concerned, there were entirely
too many people crowded into the ambulance. He had
considered ordering everybody but Jerry Sampson out, but
decided against it, partly because he understood their interest and partly because he was aware that most of the

gypsies had already decided he was a prick. While he really didn't care what they thought of him, that might get to be a problem.

McCoy was sitting in the driver's seat. Chief Motor Machinist's Mate Frederick C. Brewer, Fleet Reserve, USN, sat in the passenger's seat. As McCoy saw it, the chief had a right to be in the ambulance. He was the ranking man, and the gypsies were accustomed to doing what he told them to do. Captain Jerome Sampson sat on the floor of the rear of the ambulance. He was the radio operator, and obviously had to be there.

The man sitting beside Sampson didn't need to be there. He was the gypsies' radioman, a radioman first who had transferred off the gunboat *Panay* into the Fleet Reserve when McCoy was in the fifth grade. The radio he had somehow managed to cobble together from parts "borrowed" from another Yangtze River patrol gunboat had allowed him to transmit the few messages announcing the very existence of the gypsies. His delight at seeing the Collins radio, and his awe at the tiny little radio's capability to so easily communicate with Pearl Harbor, had been almost pathetic. McCoy didn't have the heart to tell him to get out of the trailer.

Technical Sergeant Moses Abraham, USMC, who had retired from the 4th Marines; and Staff Sergeant Willis T. Cawber, Jr., who had retired from the US Army's 15th Infantry; and Sergeant James R. Sweatley, USMC, were also in the back of the trailer and had no business there, except for the positions of authority they had given themselves.

McCoy had immediately disliked Cawber; and Technical Sergeant Abraham had immediately made it apparent he didn't like taking orders from a youngster who was a corporal in the machine gun section of Baker Company of the Fourth two years before and now thought he was really a captain of Marines. Though McCoy was sure he had put Sweatley in his place, he had no doubt that Sweatley considered it a great injustice to a longtime Marine such as himself to take orders from Zimmerman, who was a corporal when he knew him before, and was now a gunnery sergeant.

The truth was that this was one of those situations where people had to do what they were told, when they were told, and not ask questions. McCoy knew there was going to be a confrontation sooner or later, but decided that provoking one now by ordering Cawber, Abraham, and Sweatley out of the trailer didn't make any sense.

"Okay, McCoy?" Sampson asked.

"Go ahead," McCoy said.

Sampson raised his voice, and one of the Chinese "soldiers" they had brought with them started to pump the generator. Sampson put earphones on and, when the needles on the dials came to life, started to tap his radiotelegrapher's key. "Got 'em," he announced thirty seconds later. And a moment after that, he began to recite numbers, which McCoy wrote on a small pad. There were not many numbers. "That's it. They want an acknowledgment," Sampson said.

McCoy translated the numbers from Signal Operating Instruction Number Three.

Four Able meant that the Catalinas had successfully completed their rendezvous with the *Sunfish* and taken off again with the meteorologists and their equipment aboard. Two Fox gave the time of their departure. Two X-Ray gave the estimated time—six hours and thirty minutes—it would take them to reach the gypsies.

"Acknowledge, Jerry," McCoy ordered. "Tell them to monitor continuously, and sign off."

"Gotcha," Sampson said, and began to tap on his key.

"What do they say, McCoy?" Technical Sergeant Abraham demanded.

I can either tell him to call me Captain, or I can ignore the old sonofabitch.

"Captain Sampson, starting in thirty minutes, send SN for ten seconds once a minute."

McCoy hoped that Sampson would reply, if not "Aye, aye, sir," then "Yes, sir."

"Gotcha," Sampson said.

"Captain," the old radioman said. "I could do that."

"Have you got a watch?" McCoy asked.

"No, sir."

McCoy unstrapped his. "I'll want this back," he said, and handed it to him.

"Yes, sir."

"Captain Sampson, why don't we go check on the fires?" McCoy said.

Sampson finally caught on. "Yes, sir," he said.

"And you, too, Chief," McCoy said to Chief Brewer.

"Aye, aye, sir," Brewer said.

McCoy looked at Technical Sergeant Abraham. "The aircraft are due in here from forty-five minutes to an hour. You are in charge of keeping everybody away from them when they land. I don't care how you do it. I don't want anybody chopped up by a propeller, or the aircraft damaged by excited people."

"What difference does it make if you're going to destroy them anyway?" Abraham replied.

"What did you say?" McCoy said.

"I think you heard me," Abraham said.

"Let me tell you something, Sergeant," McCoy said. "The moment I got here, you were recalled to active duty for the duration of the war plus six months. That means you're back in the Corps. And that means when you get an order, all you say is 'Aye, aye, sir.' You don't question the order. Do you read me, Sergeant?"

After a moment, Sergeant Abraham said, "Aye, aye, sir."

McCoy opened his door and stepped out of the ambulance. Chief Brewer got out on the other side, and a moment later Sampson came out the back door.

Earlier, McCoy and Zimmerman had driven over an area of the desert long enough to serve as a runway. Once they'd determined a suitable place for it, they'd walked all over it, carefully searching for holes or rocks that would damage the Catalina's landing gear. When the "runway" had been marked off, he ordered the building of two fires, to be ignited on order, marking the ends of the runway. When—if—the Catalinas appeared, they would be lit and made as smoky as possible. This would indicate to the Catalina pilots not only the position of the runway but the direction of the wind, which would tell them the direction to land.

Because material for building fires was scarce, there was a good deal of resentment when the gypsies were ordered to part with material to build them.

Furthermore, McCoy suspected (a suspicion Milla confirmed) that he was going to be looking at more resentment as soon as most of the women—and even some of the men—realized that their long ordeal was far from over the minute he showed up.

McCoy had some new ideas about how to get the women, the children, and even some of the men out of the desert, but that wasn't going to happen now. What was going to happen now was that once the Catalinas had off-loaded their cargo and anything on them that might be useful, thermite grenades would be set off on the wing, over the fuel tanks, and the aircraft destroyed.

Then they'd leave the burned aircraft where they were, and take the wagons, the carts, and the two vehicles as far away as they could get as quickly as they could go. The hope was that if reports of two aircraft flying into the desert triggered aerial reconnaissance of the area, the reconnaissance pilots would think both had crashed and burned. If people were then sent in to check on the "crashed and burned" aircraft and no bodies were found, it was hoped that it would be deduced that the aircrews had bailed out. Thus any subsequent search would look for airmen, not a caravan of pony- and camel-drawn wagons.

There was going to be disappointment and resentment when the aircraft were destroyed. According to Milla, as soon as the women were informed that aircraft were coming, some of them immediately decided they'd be able to fly out on them. That wasn't going to happen.

[FIVE]
Aboard Sea Gypsy Two
Somewhere Above the Gobi Desert
Mongolia
1525 2 May 1943

Lieutenant Malcolm S. Pickering, USMCR, climbed into the cockpit of the Catalina with the call sign "Sea Gypsy

Two," slipped into the copilot's seat, and strapped himself in. Moments before, he had been sleeping in the fuselage. Lieutenant Pickering and the pilot-in-command, Captain James B. Weston, USMC, had alternated flying the aircraft and sleeping during the long haul from Pearl Harbor. They didn't actually follow a schedule. Instead, one or the other kipped out when he felt the need to take a nap.

"Anytime, Jim," Pick said.

Weston took his hands off the control wheel in an exaggerated gesture. "You've got it," he said, as Pick put his hand on the wheel. For some time they'd been flying the airplane without the assistance of its autopilot. Though it had worked well on the eleven-hour leg from Pearl Harbor to the rendezvous with the *Sunfish*, it had gone out either during landing at the rendezvous, or while taking off. At near takeoff velocity, they had run into a large swell that had really shaken the bird.

"Where are we?" Pickering asked.

"I would estimate that we are perhaps two hundred feet above and three hundred feet behind that airplane out there," Weston said, indicating the Catalina with "Sea Gypsy One" as its call sign.

"In other words, you have no idea?"

"I just told you where we are," Weston said.

"There's not much down there, is there?"

"If there was something down there, there would probably be fighter strips to protect it," Captain James B. Weston, USMC, replied. "You have to learn to look on the brighter side of things."

"Do you have any idea where we are in relation to where we are supposed to be?"

"We should be where we're going in about an hour, God willing, and if the creek don't rise. I have faith in Major Williamson."

"And if the sainted Major Williamson has fucked up somehow?"

"He's not the sort to fuck up, Pickering," Weston said loyally.

"Excuse me," Pick said sarcastically.

"On the other hand," Weston said, a smile at the edge

of his mouth. "You are a bona fide—capital *F*—fuckup, having been caught in carnal dalliance."

"Fuck you, Captain, sir."

"You know where that word comes from, don't you, Mr. Pickering?"

"I have no fucking idea."

"England. When the cops locked up some guy for what you were doing, they wrote 'F.U.C.K.' in the blotter, standing for: For Unlawful Carnal Knowledge."

"My education is now complete," Pick said. "Thank you so much!"

"Was she worth it, Mr. Pickering?"

"I am under orders, sir," Pick said sarcastically, "as you well-know, not to discuss the reasons I 'volunteered' for this."

"We're no longer at Ewa," Weston said. "And we're friends, right?"

Pick didn't reply.

"I'm curious, that's all," Weston said. "If you're uncomfortable talking about the lady who got you in so much trouble, don't. Your silence will, of course, confirm my worst suspicions."

Pick looked at him. It had been decided from the first day that Major Williamson would train Lieutenant Stevenson as his copilot, and Weston would train Pickering as his. They had spent a lot of time together, both in the cockpit of the Catalina and at Muku-Muku.

During that time, Weston did not join Major Williamson and Lieutenant Stevenson on their frequent tours of the various officers' clubs on Oahu. Soon Pick had come to the conclusion that Weston was depriving himself of that pleasure because he was aware that they were off-limits to him, and didn't want to leave him alone. Even though being left alone at Muku-Muku was not the same thing as being locked in a basement with nothing to eat and drink but bread and water.

Pick had long before decided that Jim Weston was a really nice guy, even if he, like Williamson, was obviously out of his mind for volunteering for an idiot mission like this one.

I don't want this guy to think I did something really

immoral, like getting caught with some sixteen-year-old girl.

"I loved, Captain, sir, not too badly, but rather unwisely," Pick said.

"What does that mean?"

"In hindsight, she wasn't worth getting myself all fucked up like this, but at the time I was thinking with my talley-wacker, not my head," Pick said. "And she did have magnificent teats."

"What was wrong with her? You said you weren't serious about her?"

"I was solely interested in carnal pleasure, the sinful lusts of the flesh, as they are known," Pick said. "The beloved of my life having recently told me that she had no interest at all, thank you, in becoming my blushing bride."

"You got a Dear John?"

"Delivered in person. She went with me to a hotel— you know the San Carlos, in P'Cola?"

"Yeah, sure."

"And no sooner had I closed the door and started to open the champagne than she delivered the Dear John in person. And then walked out the door, leaving me with chilled champagne, an untouched bed, and a badly broken heart."

"You know the other guy?"

"I don't think there was another guy," Pick said. "That's why it hurt. I think she just didn't like me, period."

"So you were on the rebound when you met this other woman?"

"I was, in the best traditions of a Marine officer, looking out for the welfare of my men. She was one of the chaperones at a service club dance for the enlisted men, and I went there to thank her for saving my innocent men from the wild women and other sinful pleasures of Memphis."

Jim Weston chuckled. "And?"

"Out of a sense of duty, I danced with the lady. Whereupon she told me—while rubbing her belly against mine—that, one, her husband was out of town a lot, two, that he was considerably older than she was and, three, that she was lonely. One thing, as they say, led to another."

"So what happened?"

"She was well-known in Memphis. There was talk. The admiral commanding Memphis NAS placed me under arrest, had me hauled before him, and offered me my choice of volunteering for this, or a court-martial."

"That's hard to believe," Weston said.

"Write this down. It is a court-martial offense to have carnal knowledge of any female to whom you are not joined in holy matrimony."

"If they enforced that, three quarters of the pilots I know would be in the Portsmouth Naval Prison."

"Not including you, sir! Please don't tell me that, and shatter my impression of you as the perfect Marine officer."

"That's all you did, diddle this one lady?"

"I diddled her more than once, of course," Pick said. "But, baring my breast, there were a few other little things, like being out of uniform, et cetera, et cetera, but nothing serious. And you miss the point. I embarrassed the Admiral."

"Did the Admiral know your father is a general?"

"He said that was the only reason he was giving me a chance to volunteer."

"Does your father know?"

"By now, I'm sure he does. But he probably thinks I'm doing the noble thing. I'm not sure if I like that or not."

Turnabout is only fair play, Jim Weston decided at that moment. *And I'm more than a little sick of people thinking I'm here because I'm being noble. And I think Pickering is entitled to know the real reason why I'm here.*

"Can I tell you something in confidence?"

"That you have had carnal knowledge of a female to whom you are not joined in holy wedlock? I'm shocked to the core!"

"I'm serious, Pick. I wouldn't want this to go any further."

"Sure. My lips are sealed. Boy Scout's Honor."

"I didn't volunteer to fly this bus to be noble, either,"

Weston said. "But pretending to be noble was the only way I could get Williamson—who really is noble—to take me along."

"I don't follow that at all, sorry," Pick said. "You didn't want to volunteer, but you did anyway? What are you talking about?"

"I needed to leave where I was," Weston said, "and the only way I could get Major Williamson to take me along—he thought I had paid my dues to the Corps with that year in the Philippines; and between you and me, so do I—was to convince him that I was just as noble a Marine officer as he was, eager to sacrifice all for the glory of the Corps. That was pure bullshit, but he swallowed it, hook, line, and sinker."

"You were at P'Cola, right? They were going to teach you how to fly all over again, was the story I got from Charley Galloway. You didn't want to do that?"

"There was a girl," Weston said. "Actually two girls."

"Really? Two at once?" Pick said. There was a tone of admiration in his voice.

"Two. One in Philadelphia, a Navy nurse. I think I'm in love with her."

"And the other?"

"She was already at Pensacola. And I think I'm in love with her, too."

"Well, then, you do have a problem," Pick said. "You were actually dumb enough to propose to both of them at the same time?"

"Actually, they sort of proposed to me," Weston said. "You know."

"You mean, you diddled them, and in the morning they smiled sweetly at you and said, 'When do you think we should be married?'"

"Not exactly like that," Weston said.

"I've been down that road several times. There is a very simple solution. You let them know that you're diddling someone else. Or two or more someone elses. You get a lot of tears, and on occasion, a slapped and/or scratched face; and they invariably take ten minutes to tell you what an unmitigated sonofabitch you are, but you're off the hook."

"I'm not so sure I want off the hook," Weston said. "My problem is that I would like to marry both of them."

"They have laws against marrying more than one at a time," Pick said.

"Yeah, I know," Weston said. "The girl in Philadelphia, the one who got herself transferred to Pensacola to be near me, is really sweet. I'd hate to hurt her feelings."

"But the one in P'Cola is a great piece of ass, right?"

"The best I've ever had," Weston confessed.

"Then dump the nurse and marry the good piece of ass," Pick said. "Sex is what makes the world go around."

"I don't mean to give the impression that the girl in Pensacola is a tramp or anything like that."

"Of course not," Pick said. "But fucking is like golf. The more you do it, the better you get at it."

"The one in Pensacola was married," Jim Weston said. "Maybe that has something to do with that. She really likes to do it. I mean, if you're married, you get to like it, and then if you don't get it anymore you really miss it, right? Once we . . . started—"

"You mean began to screw?"

"Yeah. Once we began to screw, she couldn't seem to get enough. Once we did it in her father's quarters with her parents not fifteen feet away."

"They call that condition 'hot pants.' In my experience it is a condition to be carefully nurtured. You said she was married?"

"Was," Weston said.

"You ever happen to ask her what happened to her husband? What did she do, fuck him to death? That's not a bad way to go—better than getting shot down, for example—but it is something you should think about."

"That's what happened to her husband. He got shot down at Wake Island. He was my best friend. Greg Culhane. I was his best man at their wedding."

Weston looked over at Pickering. There was something very odd in Pick's expression.

"I told you, Pick, she's a nice girl. . . ."

"When we get on the ground, I'm going to kill you!" Pick said.

"Excuse me?"

"When I get you on the ground, you miserable sono-fabitch, you're going to wish the Japs had caught you on Mindanao!"

"What the hell's the matter with you?"

"Get out of here, or I'll kill you right now!"

Captain Weston considered his options and finally decided that the best thing to do under the circumstances was leave Pickering alone until he calmed down. "I'm going to take a leak," he said. "If you need me up here, wiggle the wings." He unstrapped himself and went back into the cabin.

[SIX]
Aboard Sea Gypsy One
Somewhere Above the Gobi Desert
Mongolia
1635 2 May 1943

During preparations for the flight back in Hawaii, it was decided that one of the meteorologists who had some knowledge of radio and navigation would ride with Major Avery Williamson on Sea Gypsy One. While at Ewa, Lieutenant Stevenson had trained him in the use of the radio direction finder, even though he suspected that the instrument wasn't going to work very well when they reached the Gobi.

The radio direction finder, a loop antenna that could be rotated through a 360-degree arc, was mounted on top of the fuselage toward the rear of the aircraft. When a radio signal was detected, the direction of the transmitting station could be determined by a signal-strength meter. When the meter indicated the strongest signal, the position of the antenna showed the direction of the transmitter.

Lieutenant Stevenson's expectation that there'd be problems proved to be correct: First, Station Nowhere was transmitting a signal for only ten seconds in each minute. And second, the signal was so weak that the needle on the signal-strength gauge hardly flickered.

The meteorologist aligned the antenna as best he could

during the ten seconds Station Nowhere transmitted "SN SN SN" over and over again, then made his way forward to the cockpit to give Major Williamson the course toward it.

Williamson nodded his acceptance of the information, saw there was no reason to alter the course he was flying, and said, "Thank you."

A voice came over his earphones: "Column of smoke on the horizon."

There was no need for the person calling to identify himself. There was no other aircraft within hundreds of miles with an English-speaking pilot.

Williamson looked at the horizon. After a moment he was also able to make out what Pickering was seeing from Sea Gypsy Two, two hundred feet above him. It was dead ahead, no more than two degrees off the course they were flying.

Williamson dipped the wings of the Catalina to show Sea Gypsy Two that he had received the message, and decided that Pickering would know he, too, had seen the smoke when he changed course just slightly, but perceptibly, then lowered the nose just a tad and headed toward it.

Three minutes later, he saw two fires sending smoke into the air. A moment after that, he could see that the smoke was blowing directly toward him. He lowered the nose a tad more, retarded the throttles, and a moment later, ordered, "Gear down."

Lieutenant Stevenson put the gear down.

"This will be a very low-and-slow approach," Williamson announced.

"I can't see anything down there but snow," Stevenson said. "Where's the people?"

"I don't know, but there's the wind sock, sort of, I was hoping to find," Williamson said. "The trouble with this kind of snowy area is you can't tell how high off the ground you are."

"Yeah," Stevenson agreed.

Ninety seconds later, Stevenson said, "I can see what looks like snow-covered buildings down there. And there's some horses, and people. Off to the left."

"If we run into a rock, remind me to cut switches," Williamson said.

"Aye, aye, sir," Stevenson said.

Twenty seconds later, the Catalina flew ten feet over the nearest fire. Three seconds after that, Williamson flared it out, and the wheels touched down.

"That was a greaser," Lieutenant Stevenson said.

"It will have been a greaser if I can stop this thing before I run over the other fire," Major Williamson said.

Lieutenant Stevenson was not at all surprised that the Catalina stopped smoothly and in a straight line well short of the second smoky fire.

Williamson turned the aircraft and very carefully taxied off the runway. When he was at right angles to it, he saw Sea Gypsy Two making its approach.

"Jesus, look at that," Stevenson said. "Here comes a Chinese officer on a horse that's not much bigger than he is."

Two minutes later, when he had shut the engines down, Williamson walked through the fuselage and pushed open the fairing that had replaced the Catalina's right bubble.

The Chinese officer on the horse saluted.

It looks like a very large, shaggy dog, Williamson thought.

"Captain McCoy, sir. Welcome to Station Nowhere."

So that is the legendary Killer McCoy, is it?

"Good afternoon, Captain," Williamson said, snappily returning the salute. "It's very nice to be here."

By then Sea Gypsy Two was on the ground and had taxied next to Sea Gypsy One.

The fairing that had replaced the right bubble of Sea Gypsy Two opened and a huge man wearing cold-weather gear and a chief petty officer's cap jumped out. He dropped to his knees and kissed the snowy ground. "Thank you, God!" he announced dramatically.

McCoy laughed.

"What was that all about?"

"That's Chief McGuire," Major Williamson said dryly. "He was thrown over the side, so to speak, of the *Sunfish*."

A second figure came through the opening.

"That's Captain James B. Weston," Major Williamson said. "One hell of a man, one hell of a Marine. He was a guerrilla in the Philippines."

"I know," McCoy said, "What's he doing here?"

"He volunteered. You say you know him?"

"I met him briefly one time," McCoy said. "In the Philippines."

McCoy started to walk toward him.

A third figure came through the fairing and jumped to the ground.

In the instant McCoy recognized him, the third figure shouted furiously: "Don't try to get away from me, you sonofabitch!"

Captain Weston stopped and waited for Lieutenant Pickering to catch up with him. "What the hell is the matter with you, Pick?" he asked, confused, just before Lieutenant Pickering punched him in the mouth. Captain Weston fell over backward.

McCoy rushed to Pick and wrapped his arms around him. "What the hell is the matter with you?"

"That sonofabitch has not only been fucking my Martha," Pick said, "but taking despicable advantage of her!"

"Oh, my God!" Captain Weston said. "You're the one she told me about!"

"Despicable advantage?" McCoy asked incredulously. "What the hell does that mean?"

"He's right," Captain Weston said. "My behavior has been despicable."

"I don't believe what I'm seeing," Major Williamson said. "Pickering, you get your childish temper under control, or, so help me God, I'll have you placed in irons."

"That might be a little difficult here, Major," Captain McCoy said. "But I guess we could spread-eagle the crazy bastard on a wagon wheel."

That was too much for Major Williamson. He could not control his laughter. That triggered the same reaction in Captain McCoy, making it very difficult to hold on to Pick.

"Lieutenant Pickering," Major Williamson said, as sternly as he could, "you will consider yourself under arrest to quarters. And you, Weston, will stop your despicable behavior, whatever it is!"

These words triggered a further outburst of hysterical laughter from Major Williamson and Captain McCoy, and also served to dampen Lieutenant Pickering's fury.

McCoy, feeling him relax, let him go.

Pickering stood where he was, looking embarrassed.

But not before Chief Motor Machinist's Mate Frederick C. Brewer, USN, and Technical Sergeant Moses Abraham, with very confused looks on their faces, rode up to them on two very small ponies.

Only three people were in the ambulance now—Major Williamson, Chief Brewer, and McCoy—all that McCoy felt were needed to talk about what had to be done. This took no more than five minutes, including an explanation to Chief Brewer of the reasons why they had to immediately destroy the aircraft and move out of the area. Though Brewer seemed to accept all this calmly, McCoy wondered how successful Brewer would be in passing it on to the gypsies.

"The only question, as I see it," McCoy said, "is whether we torch the airplanes now or in the morning. If we do it tonight, the light could be seen a long distance. In the morning, ditto for the smoke."

"There is one more option, Captain, that you haven't considered," Major Williamson said.

"Sir?"

"We had a tailwind coming in here," Williamson said. "I think there may be enough fuel remaining between the Catalinas to fly one of them out of here."

"I hadn't even considered that," McCoy said. "From the beginning, this was supposed to be a one-way mission."

"I'd like to try it," Williamson said. "I've got a wife and kids waiting for me in Pensacola."

"Do you have a map?" McCoy asked. "There's an airfield at Yümen. That's where we came from."

"That's where I was thinking we might go," Williamson said. He took a folded map from the side pocket of his leather jacket. "You will notice, Captain, that this is not your standard aeronautical navigation chart," Williamson added. "So this proposed flight plan will not be up to my usual impeccable standards." He took a pencil from the same pocket and used it as an improvised compass to compute the distance from where they were to Yümen. Then, on the back of an envelope bearing the return address of the Pensacola Yacht Club, he made some quick—but careful—calculations.

"Yeah," he said. "I think it can be done. Between the two airplanes, I think we should have enough fuel. Weston is a better Cat driver than I am; he probably has more fuel remaining than I do. And I've got enough for two hundred miles, maybe a little more."

"How many people could you take with you?" McCoy asked.

"The problem there, Captain," Chief Brewer said, "is who would go? We have two really sick men and one sick woman. But who else?"

"I could probably take a ton," Williamson said. "That's seven people at a hundred and fifty pounds per. The old rule of the sea is women and children first."

McCoy did not respond directly. "And torch just the one plane," he said.

"I have a suggestion there, too," Williamson said. "Leave enough fuel in the tanks of the other Catalina for ten, fifteen minutes. Take it off. The pilot trims it up in a shallow climb and jumps. That would take it thirty, fifty miles—maybe more—before it ran out of gas and crashed. Empty, a Cat will glide a long way."

"That way we wouldn't have to move right away," McCoy said.

"Who would you send out?" Chief Brewer asked. "A lot of people will think they have the right to go."

"Gunny Zimmerman is going out," McCoy said, looking at Brewer. "And he's not about to leave his wife and kids again, so they're going."

"That's liable to cause some resentment," Chief Brewer said.

"So is Mrs. Banning and her baby," McCoy said.

"When my people find out that a plane is leaving," Chief Brewer said, "they'll want to decide who goes on it. Either vote on it or maybe pick names out of a hat."

"This is not open for discussion, Chief," McCoy said coldly. "Gunny Zimmerman is going, and so are his wife and kids. And Mrs. Banning and her baby. If there's any more room, then the sick people. And if there's any room after that, you can send whoever you want."

"You're going?" Brewer asked.

"No, I'm not. Major Williamson will pick his copilot. Everybody else stays."

Williamson raised one eyebrow but said nothing.

"If we're going to do this," McCoy said, "we'll have to do it first thing in the morning. So we'd better start getting the fuel transferred."

"Okay. That shouldn't be much of a problem. Chief McGuire, the guy who kissed the ground, built some special fuel-transfer pumps to get fuel to the main from the auxiliary tanks—which he also built."

"And there's one thing more," McCoy said. "Major, I want you to find Lieutenant Colonel Ed Banning—he's probably in Chungking—and personally turn Zimmerman and the women over to him. I'm going to write Banning a letter saying how I think we can get the rest of these people out, and I don't want anybody but Banning to see it."

"Sure," Williamson said after a just barely perceptible hesitation.

I'll be damned. I almost said, "Aye, aye, sir."

"McCoy," Williamson said. "If we can get the Army Air Corps in Yümen to loan us a C-46—or, for that matter, a C-47—we can get these people out of here in a matter of days."

"No," McCoy said simply.

"Just like that, 'no'?" Chief Brewer said. "Why not?"

McCoy turned to look at him. "The priority here, Chief, is to keep this weather station going. The only way to do that is not draw the Japs' attention to it. Every time an airplane leaves Yümen, the Japs know about it. And when it lands wherever it's going, they know about that, too. If a C-46 took off from Yümen and didn't land someplace else, the Japs would start wondering why. And start looking for answers."

"It would only take one flight," Brewer protested.

"I almost told Major Williamson to torch both planes," McCoy said, "because when that Catalina lands at Yümen, the Japs will be wondering where it came from. And start looking for answers."

And, Williamson thought, *if he had told me to torch both planes, I would have.*

"I decided sending Gunny Zimmerman out," McCoy went on, "justified the risk—"

"Your sergeant and his wife and kids, and the Colonel's wife and—" Chief Brewer interrupted.

"Get this straight, Chief," McCoy cut him off, coldly angry. "I don't have to justify a goddamned thing to you."

"McCoy," Williamson said, "I can sort of understand the chief's position—"

"Or to you, either, Major," McCoy snapped, turning to meet Williamson's eyes. "With respect, sir, I'm in command here. My orders regarding you and the other airplane drivers is to get you out of here as soon as I can, without endangering the mission. In other words, you'll go, or not go, when and how I decide."

"No offense."

"If you're uncomfortable flying the one plane out here, fine. I'll have Weston fly it out. The only reason I decided to let you fly it is that you're the only pilot who's married."

"I didn't mean to question your authority, Captain."

"Thank you, sir," McCoy said.

[SEVEN]
Headquarters, 32nd Military District
Yümen, China
1430 3 May 1943

Major Avery Williamson, USMC, estimated that he had had one-point-two-five hours of fuel remaining when he touched down at Yümen, escorted by two Chinese Curtiss P-40 fighters that had intercepted him a hundred miles away.

He felt bad about that. He could have brought out more people, and it didn't help much to tell himself that he had done what he could to bring out as many people as he could, including flying without a copilot.

As he should have expected, Weston refused to fly as copilot. He could not in good conscience do so, he said, if that would mean leaving women and children behind. Weston's selflessness had shamed Lieutenants Stevenson and Pickering into making the same statement. In fact, Pickering was so inspired—or maybe shamed—by Weston that he insisted on flying the other Catalina off into the desert and then parachuting from it.

Williamson waited to hear that Pickering had landed safely—a little bruised, but not seriously hurt—before taking off with Gunny Zimmerman and fifteen women and children aboard, plus two seriously ill male gypsies, a Yangtze River sailor, and a 15th Infantry soldier.

The two P-40s stayed on his wingtips until he actually touched down, then they added throttle and went around to land themselves. Until the very last moment, Williamson suspected, they probably feared he was a Japanese aircraft in American markings. They didn't see many Catalinas in inland China, and, with the bubbles removed and faired over, his Cat did not look like any of the Catalinas in the Aircraft Identification Charts.

Williamson was not surprised when he turned off the runway to find two machine-gun-mounted jeeps waiting for him, in addition to a Follow Me jeep. The fighters had obviously radioed ahead that a very strange aircraft, very possibly a Japanese suicide bomber, was on the way. The machine-gun jeeps followed him to the parking area in front of base operations.

A tall Marine officer came out of base operations. His overcoat collar was turned up against the icy wind.

Well, that's luck. A fellow Marine should know how I can find this fellow Banning.

Williamson shut the Cat's engines down. He wondered if the Air Corps had any people here who had ever even seem a Catalina before, and would be qualified to inspect it before he flew on to Chungking. If something needed to be replaced, whatever it was would have to be flown in, and Christ only knew how long that would take. Presuming that the airplane was OK, was he going to be expected to try to get it from here back to Pearl Harbor? Without a copilot?

Maybe, he thought, as he climbed out of the seat, *I could just leave it parked here and see about getting a ride back to the States. God, I know better than that. I'm stuck in this frozen wonderland until I can fly this airplane out of here.*

"Everybody stay put, please, until I sort things out with the authorities here," he called, and then walked toward the fairing that had replaced the bubble. As he passed Gunnery Sergeant Zimmerman, the tough Old Breed Marine was in the process of changing a diaper. As he passed Mrs. Banning, he saw that she was weeping uncontrollably.

Tough lady, Williamson thought admiringly. *She didn't break down until she knew she and her baby were really out.*

Williamson jumped to the ground. The machine guns in the jeeps swiveled in on him. Only half in jest, he raised both hands above his head.

The Marine lieutenant colonel snapped something furiously in Chinese, waited until the muzzles had been diverted, and then walked toward Williamson.

Williamson saluted. "Major Williamson, sir. Avery R. I've just come, believe it or not—"

"I have a very good idea where you came from," the Lieutenant Colonel said. "Is Captain McCoy all right? And Zimmerman?"

"Everybody is, sir. Zimmerman is aboard the aircraft."

"Zimmerman is? What's that all about? Is he injured?"

"He's carrying a message for a Lieutenant Colonel Banning, sir."

"I'm Banning," Banning said. "What kind of message?"

Before Williamson could begin to reply, Banning spotted Zimmerman getting out of the airplane. "There he is," Banning said, and, raising his voice: "Zimmerman, over here! What have you got for me?"

"Colonel, I think the message can wait a couple of minutes," Williamson said.

Banning turned to him with surprise and disbelief on his face. "I beg your pardon, Major?"

"Mrs. Banning and your baby are on the Cat, sir."

"Excuse me? What did you say?"

"Sir," Williamson began, but he didn't have to repeat any more.

Mrs. Edward J. Banning had appeared in the fairing opening and her husband was rushing to her. And the child she held in her arms.

EPILOGUE

The Oval Office
The White House
Washington, D.C.
1430 5 May 1943

The President's Naval aide opened the door and announced, "Congressman Westminister and Colonel Donovan are here, sir."

"Show them in," President Roosevelt said.

Donovan entered the office first, followed by Representative Westminister, a tall, portly man with long silver hair, wearing a loose-fitting linen suit.

"Thank you for coming so quickly, Congressman," the President said.

"Mr. President," Westminister replied in a thick South Carolina accent.

"You're in distinguished company, Congressman," the President said. "Now that Colonel Donovan has found time to come over to see me, we have two Medal of Honor winners in the room. Do you happen to know Colonel Stecker?"

"No, sir," Westminister said. "I am truly honored to make your acquaintance, Colonel."

Stecker, looking a little uncomfortable, shook the Congressman's hand.

"You know Senator Fowler, of course?" the President said. "And I suppose you met Colonel Donovan coming in?"

"Yes, sir, I did. Always good to see you, Senator," Westminister said.

"Congressman," Fowler said.

"And my son Jim," the President said. "Major Roosevelt, of the Marine Corps, on which I am again smiling with great pride."

"A great privilege, Major," Congressman Westminister said.

"Before we go any further, Congressman," Roosevelt said. "I think you better read this." He handed him a very long sheet of teletypewriter paper, and then added, "I suspect from the look on his face that Colonel Donovan has already seen this."

"Mr. President," Donovan said. "The moment that came across my desk, I called to see when you could find time for me."

"Then I guess my telling Admiral Leahy that I wanted to see anything dealing with the Gobi Desert operation and/or Captain McCoy the moment it came in was a good idea. My copy came into my hands an hour ago."

Donovan smiled. It was obviously an effort.

Congressman Westminister read the long Special Channel message.

T O P S E C R E T

VIA SPECIAL CHANNEL
FROM OSS DEPUTY DIRECTOR FOR PACIFIC
OPERATIONS
OSS STATION CHUNGKING
1845 LOCAL TIME 4 MAY 1943

TO DIRECTOR OSS WASHINGTON
EYES ONLY WILLIAM R. DONOVAN

1. REFERENCE YOUR PERSONAL TO UNDERSIGNED DATED 26 APRIL 1943 IN RE DIRECTIVE FROM COMMANDER IN CHIEF TO IMMEDIATELY PROVIDE BY MOST EXPEDITIOUS MEANS POSSIBLE ALL DETAILS REGARDING ACTIVITIES OF CAPT K.R. MCCOY AND OPERATION GOBI.

2. FORWARDED HEREWITH AS ATTACHMENT 1 IS VERBATIM AFTER ACTION REPORT FROM CAPT MCCOY RECEIVED 1640 LOCAL TIME THIS DATE. THE UNDERSIGNED BELIEVES THE COMMANDER IN CHIEF WILL PREFER TO RECEIVE THIS INFORMATION IMMEDIATELY, RATHER THAN HAVE IT DELAYED FOR HOWEVER LONG IT WOULD TAKE TO PREPARE IT IN A MORE FORMAL FORMAT.

3. FOR YOUR INFORMATION, THE UNDERSIGNED HAS DECIDED TO IMPLEMENT ALL REPEAT ALL OF CAPT MCCOYS RECOMMENDATIONS. COLONEL JACK NMI STECKER, SPECIAL ASSISTANT TO THE COMMANDANT USMC, SHOULD BE MADE AWARE IMMEDIATELY OF CAPT MCCOYS REQUIREMENTS VIS-A-VIS THE MARINE CORPS.

4. ALTHOUGH IT WAS NOT MENTIONED IN CAPT MCCOYS AFTER ACTION REPORT, LT COL EDWARD BANNING'S WIFE, LUDMILLA, AND THEIR INFANT SON EDWARD EDWARDOVITCH AND GUNNERY SERGEANT ERNEST ZIMMERMAN'S WIFE, MAE SU, AND THEIR THREE CHILDREN WERE FLOWN OUT OF THE DESERT AND ARE PRESENTLY IN CHUNGKING.

5. AT THE TIME LT COL BANNING WAS FORCED TO LEAVE HIS WIFE IN SHANGHAI, CONGRESSMAN ZACHARY W. WESTMINISTER III (D.THIRD DISTRICT S.C.) HAD INTRODUCED A PRIVATE BILL AUTHORIZING THE ENTRANCE OF MRS. BANNING TO THE UNITED STATES. THE

STATUS OF THIS LEGISLATION IS NOT KNOWN.
PLEASE INVESTIGATE AND ADVISE AS SOON AS
POSSIBLE, AS COL BANNING IS
UNDERSTANDABLY EXTREMELY ANXIOUS TO SEND
HIS FAMILY TO THE UNITED STATES AS SOON AS
POSSIBLE.

6. PLEASE CONTACT SENATOR FOWLER AS SOON
AS POSSIBLE AND SOLICIT ON MY BEHALF THE
INTRODUCTION OF A SIMILAR PRIVATE BILL
FOR THE ENTRANCE INTO THE UNITED STATES
OF MRS. ZIMMERMAN AND THE CHILDREN.

RESPECTFULLY SUBMITTED
FLEMING PICKERING BRIG GEN USMCR

ATTACHMENT 1
STATION NOWHERE
2 MAY 1943

DEAR COL. BANNING:

IF YOU HAVE TO, SHOW THIS TO GENERAL
PICKERING, BUT WHAT I'D REALLY LIKE YOU
TO DO IS READ IT, PICK OUT THE PARTS YOU
THINK MAKE SENSE, AND THEN GO TO THE
GENERAL WITH THE GENERAL IDEA. I'M NOT
VERY GOOD AT PUTTING THINGS DOWN ON
PAPER.

THE THING IS, ZIMMERMAN WAS RIGHT ALL
ALONG. THE WAY TO DO THIS WEATHER STATION
OPERATION IS BY USING CAMEL CARAVANS.
THAT WOULD HAVE WORKED FROM THE BEGINNING
IF THE GYPSIES HAD A RADIO THAT WORKED,
AND WE COULD HAVE FOUND OUT WHERE THEY
WERE.

WELL, WE NOW KNOW WHERE THEY ARE, AND THE
WEATHER STATION WILL BE MAKING ITS FIRST
REPORT TOMORROW MORNING. THE PROBLEM IS

NOW FIRST HOW TO KEEP IT WORKING, WHICH
MEANS BOTH RESUPPLIED AND WITHOUT THE
JAPS FINDING OUT ABOUT IT, AND SECOND
GETTING OUT THE WOMEN AND CHILDREN,
FIRST, AND THEN THE REST OF THE GYPSIES.

THAT BRINGS US BACK TO ZIMMERMAN'S CAMEL
CARAVANS. I FOUND OUT IN YÜMEN AND ON THE
WAY HERE THAT THE WAY TO DO THAT IS VERY
SIMPLE. GIVE ZIMMERMAN WHAT MONEY HE
NEEDS, AND IT MAY TAKE A LOT, AND LET HIM
HIRE THE CARAVAN PEOPLE AND PAY OFF THE
BANDITS.

THIS IS WHAT I THINK SHOULD BE DONE.

ZIMMERMAN WILL STAY IN YÜMEN AND ONCE A
WEEK OR TEN DAYS SEND A CARAVAN TO
ULAANBAATAR. IT WILL BE A LEGITIMATE
CARAVAN, EXCEPT THAT IT WILL ALSO BE
CARRYING RATIONS AND SUPPLIES FOR THE
WEATHER STATION AND GAS FOR THE TRUCKS.
THEY WON'T EVEN KNOW WHERE WE ARE, JUST
THAT WE'LL MEET THEM ON THEIR WAY, SO THEY
CAN'T SELL US OUT TO THE JAPS.

THE FIRST CARAVANS SHOULD CARRY WITH THEM
SIX MARINES AND SOME BETTER WEAPONS THAN
WE HAVE HERE. AIRCOOLED .30 BROWNINGS AND
BARS AND MAYBE EVEN A MORTAR. WE WILL SEND
OUT AS MANY GYPSIES AS YOU SEND IN
MARINES. THIRTY WELL-ARMED MARINES WILL
GIVE US ALL THE PROTECTION WE NEED. AT
LEAST TWO OF THEM SHOULD BE HIGH SPEED
RADIO OPERATORS.

I KNOW THAT THE MINUTE HE HEARS ABOUT
THIS, THAT OSS LIGHT BIRD IN CHUNGKING IS
GOING TO COME UP WITH ALL SORTS OF REASONS
WHY WE SHOULD HAVE TWO COMPANIES OF
CHINESE INFANTRY OUT HERE PROTECTING US,

AND BE RESUPPLIED BY AIRPLANE. THAT WOULD
BE THE WORST THING THAT COULD HAPPEN. THE
JAPS WOULD BE ALL OVER US, AND IT WOULD BE
OUR FAULT.

DON'T PUT GENERAL PICKERING ON THE SPOT
BY TELLING HIM THIS BEFORE HE MAKES UP HIS
MIND WHAT TO DO, BUT I'M GOING TO SEND
PICK AND LIEUTENANT STEVENSON OUT WITH
THE FIRST CARAVAN, IF THERE IS A FIRST
CARAVAN, BECAUSE THEY'RE OF NO USE TO ME
HERE. WESTON HAS VOLUNTEERED TO STAY, AND
ONE PART OF ME WANTS TO LET HIM, BECAUSE
HE UNDERSTANDS WORKING BEHIND THE LINES,
BUT THE OTHER PART OF ME SAYS THAT YEAR HE
SPENT IN THE PHILIPPINES SHOULD GET HIM
EXCUSED FROM A SHIT DETAIL LIKE THIS ONE.
PARDON THE FRENCH. LET ME KNOW WHAT YOU
WANT ME TO DO WITH HIM.

SO FAR AS THE OTHERS ARE CONCERNED.
ZIMMERMAN IS BRINGING OUT WITH HIM A
ROSTER OF THE GYPSIES, PLUS THE NAMES AND
ADDRESSES OF THEIR NEXT OF KIN. I REALIZE
THAT IT'S A DIRTY TRICK TO PLAY ON THEM,
BUT I AM GOING TO SEND OUT THE MOST USEFUL
PEOPLE LAST, MEANING THE MARINES FROM
PEKING WILL BE THE LAST TO COME OUT, AND
THE RETIRED PEOPLE FIRST, RIGHT AFTER THE
WOMEN AND CHILDREN. DO YOU THINK WE COULD
GET THE MARINES PROMOTED? IT WOULD MAKE
THEM FEEL BETTER, AND AS YOU KNOW, THERE
HAVE BEEN A LOT OF PEOPLE WE KNOW PROMOTED
LATELY WHO PROBABLY SHOULDN'T HAVE BEEN.

WHEN WE ARE DOWN TO THIRTY MARINES AND THE
WEATHER PEOPLE, I'M GOING TO SEND CAPTAIN
SAMPSON OUT. HE'S TURNED OUT TO BE NOT SO
MUCH OF A CANDY-ASS AS I FIRST THOUGHT,
AND I WANT HIM TO TRAIN WHOEVER IS GOING
TO COME IN HERE TO COMMAND THE DETAIL. I

```
GUESS WHAT I'M SAYING IS THAT, IF
POSSIBLE, I'D RATHER NOT SPEND THE REST
OF THE WAR HERE.

FINALLY, I NEED A FAVOR. PLEASE TELL
ERNIE BOTH THAT I'M ALL RIGHT AND LOOKING
FORWARD TO COMING HOME SOMEDAY, AND ALSO
ASK HER TO MAKE SURE, WHEN THIS OPERATION
IS RUNNING SMOOTHLY AND ZIMMERMAN AND HIS
WIFE CAN LEAVE YÜMEN, THAT HE HAS
WHATEVER MONEY HE NEEDS TO GET HIS WIFE
AND KIDS INTO THE STATES AND SET UP THERE.

BEST REGARDS AND RESPECTFULLY,

KEN

K. R. MCCOY, CAPT, USMCR

END ATTACHMENT 1

T O P  S E C R E T
```

Congressman Westminister finished reading the Special Channel and looked at President Roosevelt.

"That's a lot to put on your plate at one time, Congressman," the President said.

"Yes, sir, it is," Westminister said. "But so far as my private bill is concerned, it is the law of the land. But I'm going to have to think a minute about how that applies to the child."

"My understanding of the law, Congressman," Senator Fowler said, "and I just got off the phone with the Attorney General before you came in, is that any child born outside the country to an American officer serving abroad is considered to be a native-born citizen. That clearly applies to Colonel Banning's child, and the Consul General will be directed, today, to issue him a passport."

"The Attorney General wanted to split a hair," the President said, "about whether that applied to Sergeant Zimmerman, who is a noncommissioned officer, not a commissioned officer. I told him that so far as I was concerned, an officer was an officer, noncommissioned or not, and that he was to immediately direct our Consul General in Chungking to issue passports to Sergeant Zimmerman's children, and further to issue Mrs. Zimmerman a nonquota immigration visa, to which she is entitled as the next of kin to an American citizen."

"I believe that is the law, Mr. President," Congressman Westminister said.

"The question then was Mrs. Banning's status, whether she could come here as Mrs. Zimmerman will, or whether your private bill had become law," the President said. "You have answered that question."

"I'll have a copy of my private bill on the Attorney General's desk within the hour, Mr. President," Westminister said. "May I inform Colonel Banning's parents, Mr. President? This—this message, whatever it is, is classified Top Secret."

"I'm glad you mentioned that," the President said. "I don't think the security of the nation would be seriously imperiled if you informed the Colonel's parents that their daughter-in-law will shortly be at their door. But do not get into the circumstances."

"And their grandchild," Congressman Westminister said emotionally. "They don't know about him. Mr. President, Colonel Banning's daddy and I were classmates at The Citadel. I was best man at their wedding. This news will be very welcome in South Carolina."

"Well, then, Congressman," the President said, "why don't you get on the telephone and deliver it? Together with an expression of my gratitude for the splendid service their son is rendering to the country?"

"Yes, sir, Mr. President, that's just what I'll do," Congressman Westminister said. "Thank you, sir."

He handed the Special Channel message to the President and left the Oval Office.

The President waited until the door had closed after him.

"You know what I've always wanted to do?" he asked. "Put someone with a South Carolina accent like that one together with somebody from say, Ogonquit, Maine, and see if either of them could understand a word of what the other was saying."

There was dutiful laughter.

The President turned to Colonel Jack (NMI) Stecker. "Colonel, it should go without saying, but perhaps it would make things easier if you told the Commandant of my great interest in seeing that Captain McCoy gets whatever he wants from the Marine Corps."

"Aye, aye, sir," Colonel Stecker said.

"Sir," Major Roosevelt asked. "Where are you going to get the Marines to send to the Killer?" He paused. "I was thinking about Raiders."

"So was I," Stecker said. "I saw a personnel report a couple of days ago. There's at least that many Raiders in the States, really serious malaria cases sent here to recover. They're all right now, but the medics say it would be best if they weren't sent back to the Tropics. Whatever it is, the Gobi Desert is not the Tropics."

"Wouldn't they have to be volunteers?" the President asked.

"Dad, they're Raiders," Major Roosevelt replied, smiling. "They'll volunteer, especially if they hear the Killer's involved."

"And the promotions Captain McCoy asked for?" the President asked.

"That will be no problem, sir," Stecker said. "I think a two-stripe promotion for all the Marines would be justified."

"I'd like to decorate them," the President said, and then went off at a tangent. "What was behind that crack McCoy made about he and Banning knowing people who shouldn't have been promoted?"

Colonel Stecker looked uncomfortable.

"Let's have it, Colonel," the President said.

"Sir, Captain McCoy questions whether he has the education and experience to be a captain," Stecker said.

"He obviously has the intelligence and experience to carry off an operation that a large number of far senior officers thought couldn't be done," Roosevelt said, looking at Colonel Donovan as he spoke. "So he's wrong.

Please tell the Commandant, Colonel, that the Commander in Chief feels that both Captain McCoy and Sergeant Zimmerman are deserving of promotion."

"Aye, aye, sir."

"And as far as the Killer's—excuse me, *Captain McCoy's*—lack of education is concerned, is there any reason he could not be sent to the Command and General Staff College when he returns?"

"No, sir," Colonel Stecker said.

"See that it happens, Colonel," the President said.

"Aye, aye, sir."

"Finally, will someone translate . . ." The President paused and picked up the Special Channel message and found what he was looking for before going on. "Captain McCoy's reference to Captain Weston's having earned an excuse from this—what a lovely, succinct phrase—'shit detail' because he served a year in the Philippines?"

"Sir," Colonel Stecker replied, "Captain Weston refused to surrender when the Philippines fell. He was serving as General Fertig's intelligence officer on Mindanao until he was ordered out."

"And the minute he was back here he volunteered for this 'shit detail'?" the President asked incredulously.

"That's about it, Mr. President," Colonel Stecker replied. "He's an experienced Catalina pilot, and felt it was his duty to volunteer."

"Is he married?"

"No, sir."

"Where was he stationed?"

"Pensacola, sir."

"Colonel Donovan," the President said, "immediately Special Channel General Pickering that as soon as a replacement for Captain Weston can be sent in, he is to be brought out of the Gobi Desert and returned to Pensacola."

"Yes, Mr. President."

The President put his cigarette holder in his mouth at a rakish angle and smiled mischievously.

"As I recall, the beaches of Pensacola abound with healthy young women clad in bathing costumes Eleanor finds scandalous. Perhaps Captain Weston can, so to speak, cast a line into the water and reel one—or more—of them in."

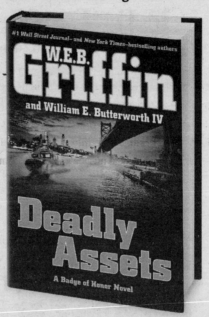

M1584JV1014

THE *NEW YORK TIMES*
BESTSELLING SERIES
THE CORPS
W.E.B. Griffin

Author of the bestselling BROTHERHOOD OF WAR series.

THE CORPS chronicles the most determined branch of the United States armed forces—the Marines. In the same gripping style that has made the BROTHERHOOD OF WAR series so powerful, THE CORPS digs deep into the hearts and souls of the tough-as-nails men who are America's greatest fighting force.

penguin.com